SEVERED WINGS BOOKS 1-4

KELLY CARRERO

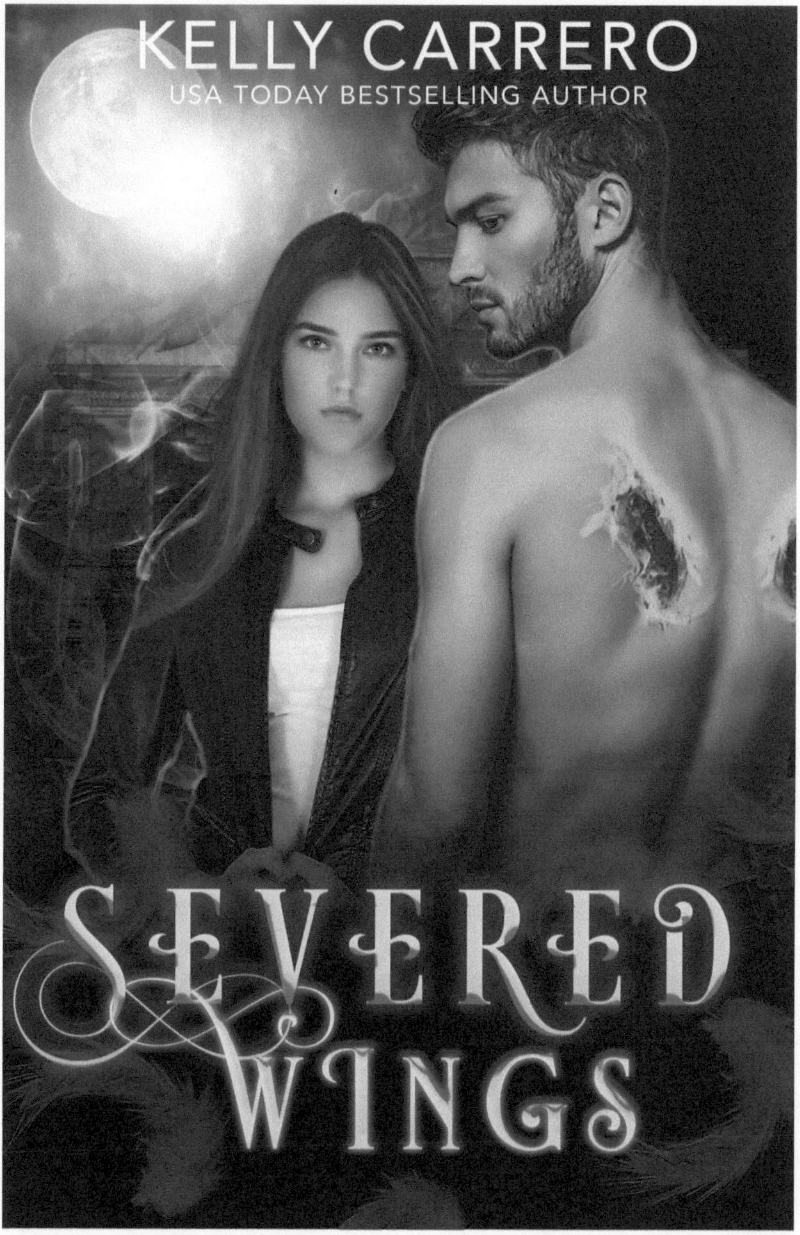
KELLY CARRERO
USA TODAY BESTSELLING AUTHOR
SEVERED
WINGS

CHAPTER 1

*B*lood spilled from the gash as I dragged the blade across my wrist. I prayed it would flow freely and I wouldn't be saved this time.

I repositioned the blade and cut the other way, making sure I hit my artery to increase my chances of a rapid death.

My vision swayed as I lay down on my pillow and stared at the empty container knocked over on the nightstand, every single pill having been consumed to thin my blood. I hoped if I didn't die from blood loss, I'd die from an overdose. A mixture of the two should be a guarantee for success—if I wasn't cursed.

This was the thirty-sixth time I'd tried killing myself this way. Each and every time ended the same. Someone always saved me within the last few moments of my life.

I was cursed, condemned to live a life of suffering. One I couldn't take anymore.

Most people labeled me crazy, others an empath. Only I never took on the good emotions. It was always the pain. My life was an eternal pit of suffering. I was drawn in, consuming what felt like ten times the pain of the person I was taking it from.

My eyelids drifted down, unable to stay open any longer, and my breathing came out in short bursts. I refocused on the blood, letting it be the last thing I saw before my lids closed, and my thoughts became still as darkness took over.

The corner of my lips turned up the slightest, happy it would finally be over.

I was finally free.

Then I heard it. A faint click shattered my hopes just before I passed out.

~

The faint beep I'd grown all too accustomed to sifted into my unconsciousness, bringing me back to the stark reality that I'd once again failed to end my life.

A second later, my eternal suffering came flooding back. I twisted in agony as pain ripped through me. Every single inch of my body screamed for relief. But it wasn't my injury that consumed my mind. It was the pain of the people occupying the beds near me. I knew what was wrong with the other patients without even laying my eyes on them.

The woman on the stretcher closest to me had been brought in with appendicitis, and the guy sitting in the chair closest to me had severed his thumb. The one on the other side had been stabbed through his leg by something that didn't feel like a knife, and the guy with two security guards backing him into a corner was out of his mind on ice, hallucinations of shadowed creatures lurking around the hospital terrorising his thoughts and, in turn, mine.

Slowly opening my eyes, I tilted my head back and saw what I'd feared. The hospital had run out of beds, and the doctors and nurses were using the halls to attend to the patients.

High heels clipped across the floor, the same sound I'd heard every single time I'd been brought in. It was my mother, dressed to impress without anywhere to go. She was a drunken socialite who traveled the country, being the handbag to my father on his business trips. Except when I tried to off myself and she felt the local media would expect her to be here with me. My father hardly ever accompanied her, always having an excuse of a business meeting he couldn't get out of.

She stopped next to my bed, her gaze boring holes in my eyes. "What have you done this time, Zoe?" Mom lifted my arm, briefly inspected the bandage covering my wrist, and dropped it, disgust written all over her face.

I cringed at the sound of the name she'd given me at birth, but I didn't have the strength to correct her.

She leaned down and whispered harshly, "You know, there are millions of people who would give anything to have the life we've given you. But no, you're just an ungrateful, self-centered brat."

Trying to ignore the shadowed creatures, I swallowed hard and licked my lips. "Go."

Her eyes flared with irritation. "Don't you dare suggest I don't care about my daughter."

I winced, curling onto my side as what felt like knives dug into my stomach. "You don't."

Nurse Helen picked up the chart hanging on the end of my trolley as she gave me the same pitiful smile she always wore when I ended up in her emergency room. "What are we in for this time, Lucy?" she asked, perusing the paperwork, knowing full well it wasn't just my wrist that was the problem.

Mom glared at me as Helen addressed me by my chosen name. She grabbed my elbow and lifted it to show my wrist. "She's done it again," she said with a catch in her voice.

I wanted to gag at the falseness of her sincerity, but that would've taken effort I didn't have. "Normal teenage daughter attitude" wasn't something I could muster when I felt as if an alien were trying to claw its way out of my stomach, my brain was telling me my thumb was missing, and evil creatures out of nightmares were chasing me down, lurking around the hospital, waiting for their chance to eat me.

Nurse Helen sighed, her eyes softening as they locked onto mine. "Why do you keep doing this to yourself, baby girl?"

Wasn't it obvious? I wanted to die. And once again, I'd defied death and somehow my injuries were not as bad as I'd first thought. I was sure I had cut deep enough so I couldn't be saved by anyone other than a paramedic who was able to perform miracles. Obviously, I was wrong.

She returned the folder to the end of the bed and rubbed the blanket covering my foot. "I'll get you a room and some painkillers."

"Thanks." I winced as a doctor unwrapped the bandage covering the thumbless guy. "But you better get that woman to the OR." I pointed to the middle-aged lady next to me, writhing in pain. "Her appendix is about to explode," I said through gritted teeth. I'd felt that blinding pain once before, and I never wanted to experience it again.

Nurses weren't supposed to take the advice of an eighteen-year-old patient, or any patient for that matter, but they'd ignored my warning once before and the guy went into cardiac arrest and couldn't be saved.

It seemed as if I knew each and every disease and illness found in medical journals—or on Google for that matter—and could tell them apart. I'd make the perfect doctor if I weren't cursed to actually feel the patients' pain.

Nurse Helen gave me a small nod then turned her attention to the woman.

Just like I'd predicted, within seconds, Helen called for assistance and the woman was raced into surgery.

I sighed with relief when she was far enough away that I was no longer able to feel her pain, but it was only for a moment. Everyone else's injuries and illnesses became all-consuming.

Mom looked down at me, trying her best to cover the mixture of emotions she was going through. I scared the hell out of her sometimes, and even though she wasn't a God-loving church attendee, my mother believed I was an evil spirit she had been cursed to spawn. She was here only for show. My father was a politician, and there was no way she could have the media tarnish his or her reputation.

Her words faded, the delusional ice-head's fears taking over me as the dark shadow creatures swept through the air, closing in on me. I grabbed at her arm, but she pulled it away before I could get ahold. I needed pain relief. I needed to dull my senses. I needed to get away.

I closed my eyes, wishing sleep would take me under and relieve me from the hell I was in. Sleep never came.

I fumbled for the bandage covering my wrist. Finding the edge, I pulled it up and dug my nails into the stitches to reopen the wound.

"Oh my God." My mother clutched her hand over her mouth as blood spilled from my wrist. "She's trying to do it again," she called out. When the nurses got nearer, Mom added for their benefit, "Don't, baby... Please don't do this to yourself."

Darkness came for me sooner this time. I knew I wasn't going to die, and I prayed I'd find myself pumped full of morphine in a private room when I awoke.

Black shadows danced around the room, wisping through the air, then disappeared a moment later, along with my ability to feel others' pain.

Just as my eyes began to close, I saw the all too familiar man, with eyes the color of molten amber, staring at me as if he'd seen a ghost.

A smile formed on my lips as I watched him, unable to look away until the blackness took over.

CHAPTER 2

My eyes shot open as I gasped for air, sheer panic setting in when I realized I could barely draw in a breath.

I pushed myself up onto my elbows, my vision swaying from the movement, which probably had more to do with my blood loss rather than the actual motion.

Knowing full well it wasn't me who couldn't actually breathe, I scanned the room, trying to figure out where this next assault was coming from. There was no one there. I was in a room by myself, and my mother was nowhere to be seen.

Needing to make sure that whoever couldn't breathe was getting the help they needed, I grabbed hold of the nurse call button and pressed it. No one came.

I pressed it again and again as I desperately tried to inhale. Again, no one came.

Rolling out of bed, I ripped the IV out of my good arm then stumbled to the door and yanked it open. The nurse's station was in chaos, with staff running around in a mad panic.

I grabbed the nearest nurse, latching my hands around her wrists, stopping her from going any further.

"You'll have to wait," she said, trying to fob me off.

I shoved her hard, stopping her from leaving me. "I can't breathe," I mouthed, my voice coming out in a gravelly whisper.

Her eyes went wide. "Oh, shit. We've got another one!"

Nurse Helen came over. "It's okay. I'll take it from here." She held my elbow and ushered me back to my room.

"You're okay," Helen said, closing the door behind us. "There's another patient having an anaphylactic reaction to latex."

Relief flooded through me, knowing that whoever's symptoms I was mimicking was being attended to.

Helen guided me over to the bed and helped me back in. She reattached the IV and gave me an extra dose of morphine. "Just breathe, honey."

Yeah, that was easier said than done. I tried to tell myself it wasn't me who couldn't breathe, but my brain didn't get the message. It still felt as if I were suffocating.

Helen pulled the sheets up to my chest and wiped my hair away from my face. "What are we going to do with you?" She sighed when I didn't answer. "It'll kick in soon."

I stared at her as my short gasps eventually turned into even breaths, and soon I was breathing normally again. I wasn't sure if it was because the morphine had kicked in or the patient had either died or gotten their reaction under control. Whatever the reason, I was glad I could breathe.

Helen smiled sadly at me. "I was on my way to tell you we're going to shift you up to the ward in a few." By the ward, she meant the mental ward upstairs, where I'd be locked away, unable to harm myself or anyone else.

I nodded. They had stronger meds there that dulled the pain. They also had a few nutcases, but who was I to talk? I was crazier than most of them.

She tapped my leg. "I'll be back in a few, and I'll take you up there myself."

"Thanks," I said.

The moment she left the room, I rolled onto my side and looked out the window, wondering if the fall would kill me if I jumped. They had never given me a room with a window before, and I assumed it was because they were short of beds.

Slowly, I eased my feet onto the floor and shuffled over to the window in my drug-induced state. I leaned my forehead against the glass and looked down at the street below. People were rushing, wrapped in their coats and scarves, trying to get out of the blizzard-like weather Sydney was experiencing for the first time in almost eighteen years.

I closed my eyes, wishing the pain would go away. I was sick of living like this, consumed with other people's pain. I wanted it to stop. And just like that, it did. Not completely, but enough for me to notice.

Opening my eyes, I caught a reflection in the window of the man I'd seen earlier, once again looking at me as if I were a ghost. His dark locks framed his unnaturally perfect skin as he watched me with sadness in his amber eyes. I quickly spun around to see him, but he was gone.

I shook my head, chastising myself for thinking he was real. I was probably caught up in some drug-addicted hallucination and seeing the man who'd haunted my dreams ever since I could remember. As twisted as it may be, he once again brought a small smile to my lips. Something that rarely occurred.

Shuffling back to the bed, I lay down and looked through the window at the snow falling from the darkening sky as I waited for Helen to return.

CHAPTER 3

$\mathcal{I}$t was customary to have guards escort a psych patient, and Helen had brought three. Two walked on either side of me and the other behind.

We came to the locked set of doors with the added security of yet another guard. A moment later, something buzzed and the guard on the left opened the door, holding it wide for us to enter.

Helen had made sure I had a room of my own and looked at the charts to confirm the dosages of my pain medications were correct.

"Thanks," I said, checking out my new digs. It was much the same as the other rooms I'd stayed in. There was a TV on the wall, bathroom off to the side, and reinforced windows so "us crazies" couldn't escape.

Helen turned to leave but stopped. "I'm not supposed to be telling you this, but I've seen the way your mom looks at you, and well... She's not only agreed but actually suggested you go into rehab straight from here."

I sucked in a sharp breath. Rehab wasn't something I enjoyed. There were always too many people trying to work through the reasons why they did the things they did. No one could help me. I was beyond help. But that didn't mean they wouldn't try to understand my behavior.

"Technically, you're an adult, so you don't have to do anything you don't want to, but..." Her eyes softened. "I really think you should consider it." She took a couple of steps toward me. "This life... There's so much more to live for, and maybe they can work out what's going on in that head of yours."

I wished. However, I doubted they would.

"Just think about it. Okay?"

"Okay," I said to appease her. Helen really was one of the nicest employees in the hospital, and I knew she worried about me. Actually, she was probably one of the only people who did. I didn't have any friends. I didn't have any acquaintances. I didn't have anyone. Which was exactly the way I needed it.

"Good." She smiled then retreated out the door, closing it behind her.

I curled up on the bed and willed myself to sleep. But it didn't come. Instead, I had the pleasure of meeting the new social worker along with my mother.

"Hi, Zoe. I'm Doctor Rebecca Stewart," she said, walking into the room with an iPad in hand. "But you can call me Rebecca."

"It's Luciana or Lucy," I corrected.

Mom rolled her eyes. "Stop being so ridiculous. Your name is Zoe. I should know. After all, I'm the one who named you."

The social worker grabbed my chart from the bed. "It says Zoe here."

"My name is Luciana, not Zoe. I changed it by deed poll a few weeks ago."

"Hmm." Rebecca laid the chart on the overbed table, flicked through the pages, and reconfirmed with the details on the iPad. "Do you have your paperwork?"

I sighed. "No."

"Right. Then I think it's best that we continue to use 'Zoe' so we don't delay your rehabilitation treatment plan while you wait for the paperwork to come in. Those things can take months to arrive."

Mom looked at me nervously, waiting for my refusal to go to rehab. I didn't give her the satisfaction. It really was none of her business anymore.

Rebecca put the file back in its place. "Now, your mother and I have been talking, and after going through your files, I really believe it would be best if you went straight into rehab when you're released from here."

SEVERED WINGS

"It's for the best, honey." Mom placed her hand over mine. "I can't take seeing you do this to yourself anymore. I want my baby back. I want you to be happy and lead a normal life."

I wanted to groan, but I kept up with her show. My mother had kept me at arm's length since I was two and I'd told her my name was Luciana, not Zoe.

Rebecca glanced between my mother and me, sensing something was off. "Lynnette, do you mind if I talk with Lucy on her own?"

Mom stumbled for a few seconds before regaining her composure. "Not at all." She squeezed my hand. "I'll be right outside if you need me."

"Thanks," I said.

As soon as we were alone, Rebecca dragged the chair next to the bed and sat. "I'm sorry if I misread what was going on between your mother and you, but I thought you might want a little time alone to discuss your options."

"Thanks. And you didn't misread us. My mother can be a bit... overbearing."

"Can't they all?" She swiped her finger across the iPad and typed something on the screen. "Now, rehab isn't your only option. There are other kinds of facilities that take a more natural approach."

"By natural you mean no drugs?"

"Yes." She narrowed her eyes at me. "Does that appeal to you?"

"Drugs?" I knew her question was open for my interpretation, but I figured she might as well know what she was dealing with.

"Yes," she replied.

"I need drugs."

"And why is that?"

"Isn't that the age-old question? And probably the first thing you learned at Uni?"

Rebecca frowned. "Is there a reason why you don't want to answer my question? I've already read your file."

I grabbed the remote for the bed and eased it up so I could look at her a little easier. "Then you should already know I'm crazy. I feel other people's pain. All brain scans come back normal. I don't have any reason to feel what I feel. There is no scientific explanation as to what's going on inside my mind."

"There is always a reason," Rebecca said, sounding as if she were reciting what she'd studied in her textbooks.

"I can assure you I feel every friggin' pain and bad emotion you and every other person has within a ten-meter radius of me. I also know that can't be explained unless you believe all the hippy bullshit you read on the net. But even they don't feel what I do. They get the good, not just the bad. And I can tell you, if you had to live feeling other people's loss, pain, and heartache every single day of your existence, you'd want to kill yourself, too. But seeing as though none of you will let me die, I want the next best thing."

"Drugs?"

"Yep."

Rebecca studied me for a moment then said, "Right." She looked down at her iPad. "Then we have two rehabilitation facilities within the city—four on the northern beaches, three south, and two out in the country."

"And they're all okay with administering drugs?"

"If by 'okay' you mean there are qualified doctors to prescribe you medication while they help you learn to work through your issues, then yes. But I can assure you they won't be handing you pills just for the sake of it."

I nodded. "How many patients does each facility take?"

"The ones in the city can accommodate more than the ones in the country, and for someone like you, I'm assuming you would prefer somewhere you can escape the crowd. Somewhere you can be miles away from anyone." She stood and tilted the iPad so I could see it. "After looking at your file, I took the liberty of contacting the one out near Wagga. Now, usually they have a waiting list a mile long, but they also keep a couple of spare spots for those who need it the most."

"Let me guess. I'm one of them?"

She nodded. "They have a great range of facilities. You will be expected to work the farms when you're not in therapy, and you will be expected to give one hundred percent devotion to trying to work through what's making you this way."

"That I can do." I then added under my breath, "I've been trying to do that since I can remember."

"So, do I take that as a yes?"

I looked at the tranquil photos on the iPad screen. The place was miles from anywhere, on acres and acres of farmland with horses and cows in the paddocks. There were also photographs of a serene waterhole surrounded by bush. It actually looked pretty nice. Peaceful. "For how long?"

"Nine months."

"And I can leave if I don't like it?"

"We would hope you'd give it a chance, but yes, you're right; no one can make you stay."

"And when would I go?"

"They can take you tomorrow. Your mother has already offered to drive you there herself."

I bet she did. "And if I decide not to go?"

"Then we're going to keep you here for another month, and your mother will apply to the courts to deem you unable to make your own decisions." She leaned forward. "Something tells me your mother can be very convincing when it suits her."

I sighed. "So, my options are: willingly go to rehab out in the country or stay here and have my mother have a license to rule my life?"

Rebecca didn't answer my question. "What will it be?"

"Looks like I'm going to the country."

She smiled. "I think you're making the right decision." Rebecca patted my arm then headed to the door where my mother was patiently waiting on the other side.

As soon as Rebecca twisted the handle, my mother came bounding in. "What did she decide?"

"I'll let Lucy fill you in."

Mom frowned at the sound of my name then walked over to the bed and sat on the end, careful not to crease her skirt. She smiled at Rebecca as she closed the door behind her then turned her attention to me, her smile no longer on display. "I hope you decided to take the doctor's advice."

"As opposed to you trying to get me deemed unfit to take care of myself—"

"Which, by the way, you have proven on more than fifty occasions. I'm actually surprised the staff here didn't lock you away years ago."

"Well, you should know they can't do that here. It's my choice if I want to cut myself. It's my choice if I forget to look when I'm crossing the road. And it's my choice to have a bit of an addiction to drugs and alcohol."

She snorted. "The only addiction you have is trying to kill yourself. God knows why you'd want to do that. But for some reason, you turned out weak, unlike your father and me. If people knew the truth about you—"

"They'd see you for what you really are instead of the person you portray yourself to be for the media."

Mom slapped my face before I realized she'd even raised her hand. Pain radiated across my cheek, spreading up to my eye. But it was nothing compared to what I'd endured since being admitted to the hospital.

My eyes stung, but I couldn't let her see my tears. "Imagine if they saw that. You really should learn to control yourself—especially in a place where anyone could've been walking by and seen what you'd just done to your poor daughter who tried to kill herself."

Horrified, Mom's gaze darted to the window by the door, relief washing over her when she realized no one was watching.

"Doesn't mean to say they didn't see."

Mom stood and smoothed out her skirt. "I'll pick you up first thing in the morning."

"Or I could take a cab."

"We don't take cabs."

"You mean *you* don't take cabs. I'm more than happy to mix with the slums. Most of them are nicer than the snotty elite you like to call your friends."

Mom turned her back to the door and pointed at me. "You had better watch what you say. If anything unsavory comes out in the papers while you're in that facility, I will air your dirty laundry all over the net. There won't be a soul alive who won't know all your secrets and how screwed up you really are."

I swallowed hard, thinking about all the dirt my mother had collected on me over the years. "I wouldn't dream of it," I said through gritted teeth.

She smirked, satisfaction written all over her plastic face. "Just as I thought." Mom turned on her heels then strutted out of the room, closing the door behind her.

CHAPTER 4

$\mathcal{I}$ leaned my head against the backseat window as one of my father's drivers navigated the streets of Sydney then turned onto the open highway.

Last night's dreams consumed my thoughts. It was a different variation of the same dream I'd had time and time again. It was the night before my nineteenth birthday, and I was in the arms of a man with a haunted look in his molten amber eyes, saying he was sorry before driving a knife into my heart. A few short breaths escaped my lips as he folded himself over me, cradling my head in his arms. The last thing I always remembered were his lips on my forehead and his warm breath against my skin as he whispered, "Please let this be the last."

I had no idea what it all meant, but that wasn't unusual for me. After all, I was crazy.

I was thankful Mom had decided to send her apologies for overlooking an apparent appointment she was unable to get out of and done me the favor of not having to listen to her drone on all the way to rehab.

However, she did call to reiterate her promise she'd threatened me with last night if I didn't behave. Thankfully, I was given my meds before I left the hospital, which made the driver's annoyance of everything that was wrong in his life a little easier to ignore.

Trying to find a distraction from my dream guy, I pulled my phone out of the bag our housekeeper had packed for me and swiped the screen. Settling in for the long haul, I opened my reading app and tried to get back into the story I'd been reading. But no matter how much I tried to rid my thoughts of the man from my dreams, it was useless. He was there, doing what no other could do. Giving me peace.

We stopped a few times on the road to use the restroom and get something to eat and eventually made it to the facility by dusk.

Stepping out of the car, I surveyed my home for the next however many months. The place was exactly like the photos Rebecca had shown me. It was a large homestead with a few cabins dotted around the perimeter of the main area.

Yellow grass stretched as far as the eye could see, and dense bushland was to the left. I figured the waterhole I saw in the photos would be in that direction. A barn was in the next paddock with people milling around, attending to the horses before the last of the light disappeared. I wasn't sure if they were workers or if those were the jobs I had to look forward to.

The driver stood beside me with my bags in hand. "Ready, miss?"

"As I'll ever be." I headed up the path that was really just a dirt track created from heavy foot traffic on the grass.

The wooden stairs creaked softly with each step I took as we walked up to the wraparound porch with comfy lounges spread across the deck.

I stood in front of the door for a few moments, trying to work up the courage to knock, when it swung open to reveal a man in his sixties with leathered skin. His gaze swept over me, and he nodded slowly. He tipped his head back and called, "Jo, there's a new girl here."

The man dipped his head in passing then strolled toward the barn.

"Right," I muttered to myself, hoping the rest of the people here weren't that unfriendly. Then I realized, I didn't feel anything with him. He was one of the very few content people in the world, at peace with himself and those around him—well, at least at this moment in time.

It wasn't long before a woman in her early fifties came into view, her smiling face welcoming, making me feel a little more at ease. "Hi. You must be Zoe. I'm Jo."

"I prefer to be called Lucy. Actually, I've changed my name by deed poll but..." I sighed. "Zoe will be fine."

Her smile grew wider. "Come with me, Lucy."

I smiled back. I could tell right away I was going to like her. And again I hoped she wasn't carrying a hell of a lot of baggage she would let loose later.

Jo gestured for me to follow her into the foyer then down the hall, passing various sitting rooms until we came to a large staircase.

As we reached the top landing, Jo said, "Girls are to the left, and guys are on the right. And there are to be no boys in the girls' rooms and vice versa." She gave me a stern look to let me know just how serious she was.

I nodded. Boys were the last things on my mind. Relationships weren't something I had to worry about, considering the male population seemed to think I was a freak show.

Jo took a deep breath and exhaled loudly. "But you won't be staying down here. For now, you'll get to stay in one of the bedrooms upstairs." I followed her down the hall to the left, which led to another set of stairs.

"Now, these three rooms up here are for those that can afford the extra comfort."

I was about to say I would be happy to stay in one of the other rooms, but thankfully, before I opened my mouth, I realized why my mother would've paid the extra. I was further away from others; therefore, I would have fewer emotions to deal with and less chance of me opening my mouth and spilling family secrets my mother didn't want anyone to know.

Reaching the landing, Jo opened the door to the far left. "This is yours for the next three months. After that, if I can see you've made advances with your recovery and I can deem you trustworthy, you will move out to one of the deluxe cabins away from the house."

Remembering those cabins brought a smile to my face. If I could get through three months in the house, I would be able to spend the next six months far enough away from others to avoid their emotions and pain. That would be a dream come true.

I stepped inside with my driver trailing me. He lowered my bags to the floor. "Is there anything else I can do for you before I leave, miss?"

I shook my head. "No. Thank you."

He gave me a curt nod then retreated down the stairs.

"Now, you've got thirty minutes to settle in before dinner will be served," Jo said. "I expect you to be on time."

"Of course," I replied.

She gave me a warm smile. "Welcome to Millford."

CHAPTER 5

$\mathcal{T}$aking in my room for the first time, I wandered into the attached bathroom with a robe hanging on the sidewall. There was no bath, but I figured we were out in the country and who the hell would want to soak in their own filth after working on the land for the entire day?

Returning to the bedroom, I sat on the double bed. I gave it a couple of bounces then hopped up and went over to the window. The view of the orange and pink sun, setting over the horizon was worthy of a marketing spread trying to entice Australians to holiday in the country instead of heading overseas like so many do.

Winter was almost over, and I was actually looking forward to seeing the change in the landscape as spring came into bloom.

Taking the phone out of my pocket, I took a quick snap of the sunset through the window then grabbed my bags and rolled them to the closet located on the left wall of the bathroom.

Our housekeeper had managed to pack almost everything I needed, but I was lacking a few of the essentials. I hoped Australia Post delivered to this area more than once a month and we had an Internet connection so I could shop online. I looked at my phone, relieved to see there was one bar.

Putting away my belongings took most of the half hour. Actually, it was a little over. The bell had rung a couple of minutes ago, which

I assumed was their way of saying "Get your ass to the dinner table."

Nervous beads of sweat formed on my hairline as I prepared to go downstairs. I had no idea what I was in for and prayed to God—if there even was a God—that I wasn't stuck with a bunch of fruit loops for the next nine months.

I sighed. Who was I kidding? I was at rehab. Of course there were going to be fruit loops. Mentally fit people didn't need to go to rehab. Only ones with things they were running from, trying to block out, or escape.

I swallowed hard then pushed off the bed and walked into the hall, closing the door behind me.

Swiping my arm across my forehead, I descended the stairs and tried to put on a brave face as I headed toward the chatter coming from the other end of the house.

I sucked in a sharp breath as an onslaught of emotions consumed me. There were some seriously messed up people here. I had no idea what was causing their pain, but I felt loss, neglect, betrayal, and the heart-wrenching loss of my innocence, which in reality was one hundred percent intact. No one had ever tried to go there with me. I'd never had a boyfriend or been kissed. I couldn't remember being hugged. Not even by my own mother. She'd touch my shoulder or arm when we were in public, but even she kept her distance while still trying to pretend she cared.

Everyone stopped and stared at me the moment I stepped into the room. My gaze swept over the three tables, taking in the various faces staring back at me.

Doing a quick assessment of everyone's issues, I tried to find the table with the least screwed up people, but I came up empty. They were all screwed in the head. But the sad thing was, I was the worst of them all.

Taking a deep breath, I walked over to the table nearest to me and pulled out the only spare chair.

The woman to the right grabbed hold of the seat and quickly pulled it back under the table. "This seat's taken."

"Okay," I mouthed. Her steely gaze never left me, boring a hole into the side of my head as I walked to the next table over.

Rather than assuming the seat was free, I asked, "Is this seat taken?"

"Does it look like it's taken?" the guy across the table asked.

"Shut up, Aaron," the girl to the right of the spare seat said, and then she looked up at me. "Don't listen to him. He's just pissed because they've restricted his after-dinner activities 'cause he tried to sneak off into town."

"And I wouldn't have been caught if you didn't run off and tell, now would I, Sophia?" Her name slipped from his tongue with repulsion.

"We're here for a reason, and if you're not committed to actually wanting to fix your effed up life, then why should you take a spot from someone who actually wants to be here—and not just because you want to stay out of jail?"

Jail? Shit.

"Oh, and you're here because you want to be I suppose?"

"Maybe not at first, but I do now."

"See that's the problem with these places. I know you're fucking lying because we all know why you're really here."

"Shut your mouth," Sophia snapped.

He sat back in his seat and grinned. "She's going to find out sooner or later, so she may as well know what she's getting into before she falls for your crap."

"Don't listen to him." Sophia pushed the chair back. "Sit."

I looked over my shoulder at the only other table in the room. *Crap.* The spare seat was now taken.

Sighing, I slid into the seat and tried my best not to freak out that I was sitting among criminals. My mind was strangely empty, and I was almost positive everyone's thoughts were on me. Maybe that was what I'd been doing wrong all these years. I'd always tried to go under the radar when I should've drawn attention to myself at all costs to avoid people's minds going where I didn't want them to go. Their underlying issues were still niggling away at me, but it was nothing compared to the endless pit of emotions I usually endured.

Sophia twisted in her chair, holding out her hand. "Hi. I'm Sophia."

I looked at her hand, not wanting to make contact with her but also not wanting to make the wrong first impression. I was stuck with these people for the next nine months, and I needed to make an effort.

Placing my hand in hers, I said, "My name is Luciana or Lucy."

"Luciana? Is that Italian or something?"

"Yep."

Releasing my hand, she twisted back to face the table. "Well, I hope you don't miss your mamma's cooking too much while you're here. Steak and veggies or salad are on the menu almost every night."

I barely held back a snort. I was not Italian. And my mother sure as hell wasn't a good cook. Our housekeeper was a good cook, but we rarely had anything you'd find at an Italian restaurant.

Aaron held up his fork with a piece of steak on it. "Yep, we feed them. Then they feed us."

My stomach lurched as I looked at the meat he was shoving into his mouth.

He grinned. "What? You think this is a dairy farm?"

"No. I thought it was rehab."

Everyone at the table stifled their laughs.

Sophia scowled at him. "It is rehab. But the douchebag is right. We do eat our therapy. Hope you're not a vegetarian."

I wasn't, but the idea of eating something I cared for made me rethink the whole meat thing.

"Anyway," she went on. "This is, Sarah, Amelia, Justin, Hamish, and Jake." Sophia pointed to each person as she said their name. "And you've already had the unfortunate pleasure of meeting Aaron."

"Hi." I gave them a small wave as more emotions swept through me.

"So, what are you in for?" Amelia asked, leaning over Justin, who was sitting on the other side of me.

"Uh…" I had no idea what to say. I didn't want to tell them I really should be in the loony bin.

Sarah whacked Amelia's arm. "Leave her alone."

Amelia sat back in her seat and shrugged. "She's going to have to tell us tomorrow." She cut a chunk of steak off near the bone and popped it into her mouth.

Sophia grabbed my wrist as she stood. "Come on. Let's get you some food. And none of you better do anything to mine while I'm gone." She eyed Aaron as she pushed in her chair. "On second thought…" Sophia grabbed her plate, holding it with two hands. "Come on." She gestured for me to follow her.

I drew in a deep breath and let it out slowly as we left the dining area and made our way into the commercial sized kitchen with a buffet of food spread out on the counter.

I'd been kidding myself thinking I was going to be okay here if I couldn't even leave my food while I ducked off for a couple of minutes.

"Grab one of those plates, and pick what you want." She plucked a pea off her plate and popped it into her mouth.

Picking a plate up from the top of the stack, I looked at the assortment of food. The meat wasn't as enticing as it would've been before I'd associated that the animal once used to live on this farm.

Sophia leaned against the cupboard. "Where are you from?"

"Sydney," I said, scooping enough salad to cover my plate. "How about you?" I moved over to the pumpkin and potatoes.

"Everywhere."

Putting the tongs back onto the tray of veggies, I turned to her, drawing my brows together. "Army brat?" She looked a couple of years older than me, but I guessed kids stayed at home for longer these days.

"Nope. As in, I don't really have a home."

"Oh," I mouthed then quickly looked back to the food, trying to work out what else I could fill up on that hadn't been a living, breathing creature.

"There you are," Jo said, coming into the kitchen. She stopped a few feet from me, putting her hands on her hips. "Sorry I wasn't here when you decided to come down." Jo gave me a stern look to say "Don't do it again." "But I had to take care of something out in the barn."

"That's okay, Jo," Sophia said. "I don't mind showing Lucy the ropes."

Jo's lips pinched together, and there was a worried look in her eyes. "Yes, thanks for that, Sophia. But I think I'll take over from here."

Sophia held up her hand in defence. "Sure thing." Her gaze fell on me, and she smiled. "See you later."

"See you," I replied.

She popped another pea into her mouth as she turned and strutted out of the kitchen.

I grabbed a roll and put it on the plate.

Jo looked me up and down, her brow furrowing. "This is your first time in rehab, isn't it?"

I nodded.

"Right." Jo leaned her hip against the bench and spoke quietly. "I'm going to give you one piece of advice. Don't assume you can trust everyone here. People come here for all kinds of reasons..."

I got what she was saying, or not so much saying, but I really didn't get that vibe with Sophia. And I was usually spot-on. "I'll be careful."

"Good." She went over to the fridge and grabbed a bottle of water. "And please don't think I was referring to Soph. I just meant you should be aware in general."

I nodded again.

She tapped the lid against the palm of her hand. "Okay, well you may as well head back and finish dinner. Normally we have a session straight after and then relaxation time, but I'll let you off for tonight. However, it would be nice to see you down here for some games or a movie after eight."

"I'll be there," I said with a smile that wasn't at all real. I really didn't want to spend time so close to people and their issues.

*H*eading back into the dining room, I was relieved to find my spot was still vacant. As soon as I took my seat, the questions started. The others were finished with their meals and had nothing better to do than stick their noses into my business.

I was tempted to get out of this place, but the constant reminder of what my mother was planning to do if I didn't stay in rehab kept my ass on the chair. There was no way in the world I would be able to handle having my mother rule my life any more than she had done for the last eighteen years.

I tried to answer their questions as politely as I could without actually giving anything away. Basically, they were fishing for details about why I was there and if I was in trouble with the law. I wished. That would be treatable. What I had wasn't.

A man donning a cowboy hat obstructing his eyes walked into the room and clapped his hands together to gain our attention. "Come on. Night sessions begin in two minutes." He spun around and headed toward the hall leading to the front door. His voice sounded young, and his jaw was covered in a light stubble. He looked nothing like the leathery-faced guy I saw when I'd first arrived. He was yet another staff member.

"You coming?" Sophia asked when I made no attempt to get up.

Amelia frowned. "You're not on clean-up duty on your first day, are you?"

"No." By the looks on their faces, I wasn't sure if Jo giving me time off was a normal thing, so I went with an answer I hoped wouldn't make them think I was getting any favoritism. "I'm not supposed to start my sessions until tomorrow, but Jo wants me to come down for relaxation time to get to know everyone a little better."

Amelia grabbed her plate off the table. "I don't know why you'd come here earlier than you were supposed to." An absent look crossed her eyes. "I would give anything for another day on the outside."

I shrugged then took a bite of my buttered roll.

Everyone left with their plates, taking them into the kitchen before walking back through the dining room on their way to their next therapy session. A few moments later, the niggling anguish of their problems sifted out of my body, leaving me in peace.

Only it was short-lived.

Justin, another guy, and a woman came back, heading toward the kitchen. "Bring your plate in when you're done," Justin called to me on his way through.

Finishing up, I took my plate into the kitchen where I found the unknown guy old enough to be my father stacking the dishwasher, Justin wiping down the benches, and the woman washing the pots and pans.

Great! Just another thing to look forward to.

"I'll take that." Justin came over, his hand held out. He wore a warm smile, making me wonder what his story was. I couldn't pick up on any pain, just an underlying current of something he was trying to ignore. The other's emotions were palpable. I hated to think what they were going through when they weren't heavily medicated.

The loss of a wife and child wasn't something anyone should experience. And the woman had major trust issues.

"Thanks." I handed it to Justin.

He walked over to the sink and placed the plate on the bench. "I'll see you in a little while."

I stuck my hands into the pockets of my jeans. "Sure thing." I turned on my heels and scurried back upstairs to my room.

Relief washed over me as I leaned against my closed door. One hour down. Only a million more to go. *Sigh.*

CHAPTER 7

The bell rang, signaling the nightly sessions had finished and relaxation time was beginning. It reminded me of a school bell. Only this one sounded like one of those handheld bells that Santas use as they walked down the streets at Christmastime.

I slipped on my jacket and shoes then looked at myself in the mirror. My long brown hair draped down the sides of my face just the way I liked it, shielding me from others' stares.

"You can do this," I said, trying to stop myself from crawling into bed and sleeping away the night. If Jo wasn't expecting me downstairs, I would've done just that.

The sound of laughter filtered through the closed window. I walked over and peered through the glass. Hat guy was standing next to a fire surrounded by patients sitting on perfectly sculptured sandstone boulders the size of gym balls, only flat on top.

Everyone looked as if they weren't going anywhere soon. I hoped we weren't expected to sit outside on a cold winter's night, talking about feelings and shit. I looked down at my jacket, knowing that even with the fire, it wouldn't keep the chill out of my bones.

I was about to change into a thicker jacket when I was thrust into undeniable cravings for a quick fix of ice. The urge got stronger, making me think someone was coming closer to my room. I prayed I wasn't going to have to share the floor with an addict going through withdrawals.

Subconsciously I'd dug my nails into the skin on my wrist, trying to relieve the cravings by focusing on the pain instead. When I realized what I was doing, I pulled up my sleeve, praying I hadn't ripped my stitches. I breathed a sigh of relief. Then my gaze went to the faint white lines covering my wrist. I pulled down my sleeves and pressed my hands against my thighs as someone knocked on the door.

"I'm coming," I said, hoping visitors weren't going to be a common occurrence.

Opening the door, I stepped back as the onslaught of cravings had me wanting to tear myself apart.

Sarah stood in the hall, scratching at her jaw, neck, and cheek. "Jo sent me to get you."

"Right." I was guessing Jo had done that to get Sarah's mind off her cravings.

Wasn't working.

"How long have you been here?" I asked, trying to get her attention on something else.

"This is my first week. I arrived a couple of days before you." She scratched at her chest then squeezed her hands together, her knuckles going white from the pressure.

"Do you want to stay inside or go out?" Sarah asked.

I realized I hadn't bothered to change my jacket. "Inside."

She raised a brow. "Okay. You can kick it with the oldies. I'm going outside."

I followed Sarah through the house, coming to a stop at the lounge room. Sofas lined three of the walls, and beanbags were dumped in the middle. A home theatre was set up on the fourth wall, and they were watching a movie that was made before I was born.

But that wasn't the worst of it. Hanging with the "oldies" as Sarah put it was okay with me, but one of them, a woman in her early forties was curled up on a beanbag in the corner, reading a book that wasn't doing anything to alleviate her mind from reliving the reason why she was here.

"You sure you don't want to come outside?"

I backed away from the room, until I hit the wall, stopping me

31

from going any further. I didn't know if she'd been in the dining area while I was there, or if I had been fortunate enough to not have to deal with her horrific issues.

Letting her hands fall to her sides, Sarah laughed but stopped as my legs buckled and I slid down the wall.

She rushed over to me, coming to a halt a couple of meters away, her expression marred with confusion. "Are you okay?"

Forcing myself to get up, I nodded then took off toward the front door. I needed air.

"Hey. Wait up," Sarah called out.

Ignoring her, I opened the door and stepped outside. The cool night air hit my lungs, drowning out the woman's pain. I was finally able to breathe again.

Sarah came up beside me. "Do you need me to get Jo?"

Leaning my hands against the rail, I shook my head. "Nope. I'm okay now." I glanced at her and hated that she was looking at me like everyone else in my life did. "It's just my asthma," I lied. "Dust can set it off, and I… I just needed fresh air."

Sarah raised her brows. "Whatever you say."

I pushed off the balustrade. "I'm all good now." Except that she thought I was a freak. I didn't know why I bothered. I should've let everyone know what I was from the beginning, let them jump to the same conclusion everyone else did, and then I wouldn't have to pretend I wasn't a freak. Plus there was also the added bonus that I wouldn't have to deal with people actually wanting to speak to me.

We walked down the steps, Sarah's cravings no longer having the effect they'd had only minutes before. "What are they doing?" I gestured toward the fire.

"Talking, telling stories." She bumped her shoulder against mine. "But don't worry; this isn't a therapy session. You get to avoid telling us anything about yourself for another few hours."

Sarah led us over to the boulders where mostly all of the guys from our dinner table were sitting, along with a few from the other tables.

She tapped Hamish on the shoulder. "Move over." He shuffled to the left, and she sat beside him.

"Sit here." Sophia grabbed my wrist, making me flinch. Her eyes narrowed on my wrist, and she quickly released her grip on me. Her gaze darted up to mine, recognition flashing in her eyes. She knew.

I expected her to turn away and shuffle her ass over so there was no room on the rock, but she tapped the spot beside her and smiled, a friendly smile, unlike everyone else's in my life. "I won't bite."

I returned her smile and sat next to her, tucking my hands into the sleeves of my jacket.

Focusing on the guy in the hat, I was finally able to see his face as he tilted his head back, letting out a laugh. He was handsome, and by the way he captured every single girl's attention, I knew it wasn't just me who thought so. However, I was sure I was the only one who wasn't interested. There wasn't a man alive that made me ever want to go there.

My thoughts instantly went back to the only man who'd ever had that effect on me. He was someone I would go there with—if he weren't just a—

I cut off my thoughts. Going there was never healthy.

Resting my face in my hands, I leaned my elbows on my knees and focused on what Hat Guy was saying.

Sophia leaned closer and subtlety cocked her head in Hat Guy's direction. "Liam's friggin' hot, isn't he? But just so you know, he'd never go there."

It was pointless telling her neither would I, so I just nodded instead.

Liam turned in my direction. "Anyone who doesn't know how to play The Winking Assassin, raise your hand."

Having no idea what he was talking about, I lazily lifted one hand head high.

"Lucy, isn't it?" Liam asked.

I nodded.

"Right, Lucy. The game's pretty simple. Everyone closes their eyes except the godfather AKA me, who'll tap one of you guys on the shoulder. That person will then become the assassin.

"The assassin will try to kill off all the players one by one by secretly winking at them. As soon as someone is winked at, they must fall over and play dead. And if someone witnesses the assassin, they must say who the winker is to win the game. But, if anyone guesses wrong, then they're dead," he explained. "Got it?"

Sounded pretty stupid but I nodded. "I think so."

Liam winked then turned to face the others. "Okay, everyone close your eyes. The godfather is about to choose his assassin."

We all closed our eyes—at least I thought everyone else did. I had mine shut, so I actually had no idea.

Footsteps padded the dirt behind me, and I prayed Liam would just keep walking. I really didn't want to be the assassin on my first go.

Thankfully, he kept walking. Then a few moments later, Liam said, "Okay, everyone open your eyes."

The game was more fun than I'd anticipated thanks to everyone's overly dramatic deaths. Half the people were dead when I finally got winked at. I'd known who it was since the very first wink, but I didn't want to call Sarah on it.

Falling down, my back arched over the boulder, my head facing away from the fire giving me an upside-down view of the house.

And something a little more interesting.

A car had pulled up, and someone was lifting a suitcase out of the trunk. I couldn't see their face, but something was drawing me to them.

The person looked up, their shadowed face staring in my direction. By the look of their clothes, I thought it was a guy, but it very well could've been a woman who liked to dress like a man—and had a body like a man. And walked like a man.

Okay, it was definitely a man. Or a very manly woman pumped up on steroids, giving her broad shoulders, biceps pulling on her shirt, and very noticeable—

Sophia slapped my thigh. "Get up. The game's finished."

Shaking my thoughts away, I took one last look at the person I thought was a man as he/she headed into the house, and then I pulled myself into a sitting position.

We played another couple of rounds before moving on to another game. I was surprised to say I actually had a pretty good time. No one was thinking about their problems. They were all too focused on having a good time. Plus, if Sarah was anything to go by, their meds had already kicked in. She'd stopped digging at her skin almost halfway through the first game.

Justin had joined us after he'd finished clean-up duty and was trying to get everyone to tell ghost stories. I did have a couple of good ones up my sleeve, but my mind was elsewhere. So, I just sat on the boulder, hugging my knees to my chest, absently listening to their stories as I watched the fire crackle in the still winter's night.

CHAPTER 8

The sound of the bell rattling my brain woke me from my sleep. It was still dark, and I was pretty sure there were no midnight sessions we were supposed to attend. I had no idea what was going on.

Rolling out of bed, I realized that for the first time in... ever, I'd had a peaceful sleep, free from nightmares, pain, and even the man who'd been in my dreams for as long as I could remember.

I grabbed my phone off the bedside table and looked at the time: 5:30. "Shit."

After pulling on a pair of jeans, boots, and a jacket, I walked into the hallway, closing the door behind me. The door beside me was cracked open, which it hadn't been last night when I'd gone to bed. I couldn't feel anyone inside, so I assumed the room was being cleaned or something.

Trotting down the stairs, I came to the landing where the rest of the resident's rooms were located. Their emotions were a little clouded, probably because they were all still just waking up.

Amelia ran into me as I rounded the stairs heading down to the ground floor. "A girl with money, huh?" She cocked her head toward the top floor.

"Uh... No," I replied. "More like a parents with money."

"Same thing." She stayed by my side as we descended the stairs.

Actually, it wasn't. But I really didn't want to get into the details of my relationship—or lack thereof—with my parents. Then I'd have to explain why they were willing to put up the money for the private room but were unwilling to give me the little day-to-day stuff I needed.

Justin caught up to us, swinging one arm over Amelia's shoulders and his other over mine. "Are we all ready to scoop some poop and milk the cows?"

I looked up at him, a mixture of feelings racing through my body as I processed the fact that someone was actually touching me and I was expected to shovel poop. "Seriously?"

Justin laughed. "What did you think the pics on the brochure were all about? It's part of our therapy. Which, mind you, is working a treat. I haven't had a craving for..." He paused to look at his watch. "Three minutes and fifty-two seconds." He tapped my shoulder. "Gotta go." He took off, slowing down when he reached Liam.

"So, Money Bags," Amelia started. "I'm guessing this is the first time you've milked a cow or got your hands dirty." She grabbed my bandaged wrist, making me flinch.

I really needed to learn to stand next to someone on the side of my good wrist.

Ignoring my discomfort, she turned my hand over, palm side up. "Yep. No marks on your rich little hands."

Pulling my hand away, I sighed. "I'm not rich. My parents just have good health care, which pays for the room."

She looked at me dubiously.

"Seriously." I grabbed at my hair. "If I had money, do you think I would have this mouse brown hair that looks like a cat threw up all over it?"

She assessed my hair before dropping her gaze to my face and then my nails. "Okay, point taken."

"Thank you." I let go of my hair, letting it fall back into place.

We all gathered outside the barn where Liam was giving directions. I was given the role of cleaning up horse poop in the barn. The cows were located further down the paddock, which was accessible via horseback or four-wheelers. They did have SUVs, but this was a farm, and horses and four-wheelers were the preferred methods of transport.

Walking into the barn, Liam quickly put me to work, handing me a shovel and pointing to a wheelbarrow. Sarah was also on poop duty as were another two oldies.

In the few hours I'd been at Millford, I'd learned the oldies rarely associated with the young ones and vice versa. I wasn't sure why that was, but I wasn't going to rock the boat to figure it out.

Sarah showed me what to do. Apparently, poop duty was for the newbies as well as the one's who'd done something they weren't supposed to, and this was their form of punishment.

It wasn't long before everyone's thoughts went to the reasons why they were there. I couldn't actually hear their thoughts, but I felt their reasons, and that was all I needed.

Doing my best to block their issues out, I threw myself into my work, loading the wheelbarrow before any of the others.

"Where do I take the poop?" I asked Liam.

He drew his brows together then walked to the stall I'd been assigned to clean. "You've finished," he stated more than asked.

I dug the shovel into the thick pile of straw and leaned against it. "Yep."

"Looks like we have an ass kisser," the woman in the next stall said under her breath.

Liam gave me a small shake of his head, telling me to ignore her comment. "Follow me. You'll need your shovel."

Sticking the shovel into the wheelbarrow, I grabbed the handles and lifted, feeling the full weight of the poop as I pushed it, following after Liam.

Pain radiated through my arm from the weight, but there was no way I was going to show any weakness around a group of people who'd spent time in prison. They might not have been able to kill me; however, they could inflict major pain, and there was no way I could defend myself. I wasn't a fighter. I was a runner.

Liam led me to the poop dumping ground. "Empty your wheelbarrow here. Then you can go back to the house and clean up before breakfast."

Liam started to turn but paused. "Oh, and if you keep up the hard work, you'll be out of poop duty before you know it."

"Good to know."

He gave me a wide smile then tipped his hat toward me in that good old country boy way. "See you later, Miss Evergreen."

CHAPTER 9

*D*umping the poop didn't take as long as I'd thought, and I was back up in my room, taking a shower in no time at all.

The sun had started to rise as I headed to my bedroom, ready to get started on the rest of my day.

I groaned. Who was I kidding? I so wasn't ready to ruin my day. I was going to be stuck on poop duty for the rest of my stay because I sure as hell didn't want everyone knowing how screwed up I was.

I sat on the foot of my bed, trying to figure out what I could say in my group sessions that would match my files. The more I thought about it, the more I realized I had only two options. I could lie and end up on poop duty or tell the truth and watch the patients show the same disgust everyone at school had shown me since my very first day. Back then, I wasn't as good at hiding my condition, but I'd learned over the years.

The bell rang, signaling us to get our asses downstairs. I was already getting sick of that damned bell, and I hadn't even been here for twenty-four hours.

Tucking my hands into the pockets of my jacket, I took each step slowly as I tried to figure out what I was going to do.

As I rounded the middle landing, my mind went crazy. Some of the residents were happy to share their stories, while others weren't so keen. Dread churned in their stomaches as they relived what had brought them here and the root of their problems, which they didn't want to admit out loud—or even to themselves.

Rubbing my temples, I jogged down the stairs, taking them two at a time. I had to get away from them. I needed air.

Doubling over, I reached for the door, opened it, and raced onto the porch, not stopping until I was down by the scorched wood and ash from the fire last night.

Hands behind my head, I drew in a deep breath and looked around the farm. I didn't want to go back to the house, but if I stayed out here I was pretty sure I'd get put on poop duty for the next month or more.

It was worth it.

Crossing my legs, I sat on the ground, making sure the boulders hid me from the house. The dirt was damp, sticking to my jeans thanks to the morning dew, which had settled over the land. The smell of ash lingered faintly in the air, reminding me of the time I'd…

I squeezed my eyes shut. I wasn't going to relive all the moments I'd tried to end my life and failed—miserably.

A car pulled up, peeking my interest. I peered around the boulder and saw the car that had arrived last night had changed position.

And someone was getting out.

Last night's shadows were gone. And my heart skipped a beat—or five. I'd stopped breathing, completely captivated by the man wearing the baseball cap.

Lifting his cap, he ran his hand through his dark brown hair then popped his cap back into place. He grabbed a bag out of the trunk and headed toward the house.

I shook my head and refocused on the guy. "It can't be," I whispered.

Breathing out harshly, I turned back to the fire pit and leaned against the boulder.

"You know," a man said, making me jump. "Hiding out here won't work forever."

The leathery-faced man stood to the right of me, worn Akubra on his head and a piece of straw between his fingers. He lowered himself onto the boulder two over from me.

"I'm not…"

He raised a brow.

I rolled my eyes. "Okay, maybe I am."

He chuckled then coughed. "Excuse me." He thumped his hand over his chest. "Look. The way I see it, you stay out here and everyone knows you've got something to hide or you're weak. That might not be true, but in a place like this, you don't want to be seen as weak. Or, you could go back inside, sit through your session, and come work it off after."

When I didn't answer, he sighed. "I don't like to pry into anyone's personal life, but I do read each and every file before I give the okay for anyone to come stay on my farm."

"This is yours?"

He chuckled, ending in a cough once again. "Yeah, this is mine." He looked up, scanning the acres of farmland before returning his gaze to mine.

"You know what was on my file?"

He nodded. "I make no judgements, but I could see how my place might be beneficial to your treatment. And maybe, just maybe, you might find peace in the land."

"I hope you're right." I doubted he was, but that didn't stop me from hoping.

He lifted his hat, wiped his arm across his forehead, and plopped the hat back into place. "I usually am." There was absolutely no smugness in what he'd said. The guy truly believed the land would heal me in some way. Maybe that was what had happened to him. This guy was one of the few people who walked the Earth that didn't have issues. I didn't have to feel it; I could see it in his eyes.

There were a few moments of silence before he said, "I'll make you a deal. If you go back inside, I'll make sure you help me after. We can go for a ride, check the perimeters. And I can promise you there'll be nothing but cows, horses, the two of us, and fresh open air. What's it going to be?"

"Just us?"

"Just us."

Sighing, I got up and shoved my hands into the pockets of my jacket.

He smiled. "I'll see you after breakfast."

I started to walk away but stopped and turned back to him. "Thanks err…"

"John." He tipped his hat to me then strode toward the barn.

Out of all the people here, I think he was my favorite so far. His soul was completely at peace, and I couldn't help but pray he was right—that I, too, would find peace out here. I hadn't seen it the first day I'd arrived, but I could sure see it now. He was one of a kind.

Drawing in a deep breath, I looked at the sun rising over the land and smiled. I could already tell there was something special about this place. Change had come, and I hoped it was for the better.

CHAPTER 10

*C*hange had come—in the agonising, soul-crushing kind of way. Therapy sessions were like being doused in fire and unable to put out the flames, which not only scorched my skin but also burned deep within my soul.

The other guys were all too happy to share their stories and commiserate with each other. But I was the only one unlucky enough to actually feel their pain. Feel every part of their inner torment, multiplied tenfold. Then that pain was multiplied by the number of people in each session, and I was about ready to rip my stitches out and drive a knife through my heart.

Our counselor, Mitch, who I'd not seen before, kept looking at me as if I were going to have a mental breakdown any second, and he'd need to throw me down on the ground and hold me while they waited for the ambulance to arrive to take me to the loony bin.

I bet he didn't read my files. Otherwise, he would've known that yes, I was insane, but dangerous to others? No.

I squeezed my eyes shut, trying to block out the pain. It didn't work.

Slipping my fingers under the cuff of my jacket, I scratched at the stitches, trying to redirect the pain from everyone else's issues to pain that *I* was actually experiencing.

My fingertips became wet, and blood seeped through the fabric of my jacket.

My vision began to sway, not from the loss of blood, but from the other patients' emotions consuming me. The woman who had been curled up with a book in the lounge room last night was in my group, and her thoughts were consumed with her own story.

Unable to control myself, my head tipped back then jerked forward as I tried to steady myself. *I'm not going to pass out. I'm not going to pass out. I'm not going to pass out.*

I ripped the stitches some more. Blood trickled down my hand, forming a small pool in my palm. It wouldn't be long before I couldn't hide what I'd done and I'd be the talk of rehab. But I couldn't stop myself. I needed a release.

Just as I was about to rip out the remaining stitches, a sense of peace washed over me, and within seconds, everything became still.

I could breathe.

"Sorry I'm late," a man said, walking into the room.

My breath caught in my throat as I looked up, my eyes locking onto the man with the baseball cap, who was looking straight at me.

His stride faltered for a second, and his lips parted. An undeniable force that didn't make any sense was drawing me to him.

He was the guy from my dreams. The very same one I'd thought I'd seen at the hospital, and now he was walking into the very room I was in. A living breathing person who looked as captured with me as I was with him. It was as if we were the only two people in the room. No one else mattered.

It was just us.

Mitch cleared his throat, reminding me we weren't alone. "Take a seat." He gestured to the only spare seat all the way across the circle from me.

Not taking his eyes off me, the guy from my dreams sat in the chair and exhaled slowly, as if he too hadn't been able to breathe until this very moment.

A few minutes passed as the session continued. Then his eyes changed, the light disappearing and darkness taking over as he stared unashamedly at me.

His gaze flicked down to my lap, and he closed his eyes, turning his head to the side.

I looked down and sucked in a sharp breath when I saw the

blood soaking my jacket and jeans. He'd seen me. He knew I wasn't normal. And something about that crushed my soul.

Tears pooled in my eyes. I couldn't stay here. I couldn't let *him* see me this way. Clutching my arm against my waist, I jumped to my feet, raced upstairs, and locked myself in my bedroom.

Slumping to the floor, I leaned against the door and let my tears flow. Tears that hadn't shown themselves before this very moment. I couldn't remember a single time in my entire life that I'd cried. Yet this guy, this amazingly beautiful guy, brought the tears out with a single look.

He was my undoing.

CHAPTER 11

$\mathcal{T}$rue to his word, John waited for me in the barn, ready to take me away from this place.

I'd rewrapped my wrist in a bandage I had found in the very basic first aid kit in the bathroom, which really only consisted of a couple of bandages, Band-Aids, and an eye washer. They obviously didn't trust us with scissors. And rightfully so. If they had, I was pretty sure I would've used them to slit every artery in my body to avoid having to see *him* again.

Donning clean jeans and a jacket, I watched as John showed me how to saddle a horse, put the bridle on, and then mount it. I really had to hand it to the guy. His patience was impeccable while I tried my hardest to do something he made look so simple, and yet I failed miserably.

Thirty minutes later, we rode beside the left fence of the first paddock, heading away from the house.

John only spoke when necessary and kept the horses at an easy pace as we rode for what seemed like hours before he pulled up under a tree with a water trough and post underneath it.

He dismounted then helped me off. "Tie the reins on the post. We're going to rest here for a bit."

I held the reins in my hand, not having a clue how to do the simple task that he'd completed with his horse's reins in a blink of the eye just like in an old cowboy movie.

Chuckling, John grabbed the reins from my hands and showed me how to tether Milly to the post. "You'll get the hang of it."

He grabbed his water bottle from the saddle, walked over to an old log lying on the ground, and took a seat.

Figuring we were going to be here for a while, I retrieved my bottle, planted my ass on the other end of the log, and twisted the cap off my bottle. Putting it to my lips, I downed half the contents in one go before wiping the back of my hand across my mouth.

My eyes widened when I realized my sleeve had crept up. I yanked it down, spilling half the remaining water on my thigh. *Shit!*

"Is it okay?" John asked, his gaze remaining on the horses.

It took me a few moments to realize he wasn't talking about the water I'd spilled. He knew. But there was no way I was going to talk about it. "Uh… yeah."

He gave a single nod then tipped his bottle up and took another long sip. "Sometimes I like to come out here to get away from all the noise." A few moments passed before he added, "I can make this your regular job here, but I'll only be able to get you out in the paddocks for a couple of hours a day. Any longer and the others might think I'm playing favorites."

"Really?" I asked, wondering why the hell he was helping me. John wasn't one of the counselors and really didn't have to do anything to make my life easier.

He gave a small nod as his answer.

"Thank you. That would be great."

"I'll expect you to take care of Milly. She'll be yours while you stay here."

My eyes widened again. This guy was full of surprises. "Wow," I mouthed. "Of course."

"There will be rules. For one, you can't take her out by yourself until I know you can handle her on your own. Second, you mistreat her in any way and the deal's off. And last, you treat her with respect and you might just discover that she'll give you so much more in return."

"Absolutely." I ran my hand along Milly's neck as she bent down to eat some grass by my feet. "Just show me what to do and I'll do it."

A smile tugged at the corner of his lips, and he nodded. John wasn't a man of many words, and I liked that. He didn't pass judgement, and he had given me the relief I so desperately needed. He was a good man.

We stayed there for another twenty minutes then hopped back on the horses and followed the fence line until we'd looped around the paddock, back to the barn. Apparently, we hadn't gone around the whole farm. There were many more acres I had yet to discover. But these were the lines John wanted me to learn so he could focus on the rest. Really, I thought he was just giving me something to do, and I honestly couldn't fault him for it. I was glad for the distraction. Hell, I was glad for anything that kept my mind off Baseball Cap Guy.

Except, he was all I thought about as I sat in the saddle, swaying with the movement of Milly's rhythmic steps. But somehow, the smooth motion under me made it somewhat bearable.

Coming to a stop outside the barn, John dismounted his horse and tied its reins to a post under a tree.

I swung my leg over Milly's rump, slid down her side, grabbed her reins, and did my best to tether her to the post. Only it didn't go so well. Neither did the next three attempts. On the fourth go, I finally got it.

John gave me a small nod. "We're just going to leave the girls here for twenty minutes so they don't assume going home means they get to stop working.

"Sometimes you'll need to hop back on, take her for a quick ride, and come back."

"Okay," I said, thinking of all the time this would take up. I was all in for this.

He cocked his head in a "follow me" way, and I did just that.

Leading me to the produce area inside the barn, John opened the lid of a large plastic container and grabbed a carrot. "Here." He passed it to me.

I looked at the carrot, wondering if it was for me or for Milly.

John chuckled, followed by another cough and a thump to his chest. "It's for the horses, Lucy."

"Right."

He selected a carrot for himself, closed the lid, and moved over to

47

a large barrel. Opening the lid, he dipped the carrot inside and lifted it out. A dark, gooey substance covered the carrot.

"What's that?" I asked.

"Molasses. Horses love it."

I dipped my carrot into the barrel, making sure to cover the whole damn thing. Milly was going to love me even if I had to bribe my way into her heart. After all, she was going to be my savior for the next nine months.

John was right. Milly *loved* the carrot. Her gigantic lips opened wide, revealing massive chompers, which crushed the carrots to bits. Then her tongue stuck out, licking the last of the molasses off her lips. She was determined to get every last bit.

Smiling, I rubbed the side of her face. "You like that, huh?"

John leaned against the post, fiddling with a piece of straw. "That was a treat. Make sure you don't give it to her too often. Otherwise, she'll bolt back to the house thinking she's going to get some whenever you head in this direction."

I was sure my face had paled at the word "bolt." I had never ridden a horse before today, and I knew I would fall on my ass if she went any faster than a walk.

With a smile pulling at his lips, John shook his head. "You're going to have to learn to ride her properly. That includes learning how to stay on in the off chance Milly takes off on you."

I drew in a deep breath and nodded. I would fall on my ass a thousand times if it meant getting away from all the other patients.

CHAPTER 12

*W*hen I arrived back at my room, there was a blank piece of paper stuck to the door. Opening the door, I plucked the paper off and turned it over to find a schedule on the other side.

Week 1

04:45 Wake up
05:00 Poop Duty
06:55 Report for medication
06:30 Breakfast
07:30 Session 1A
09:00 ~~Maintaining Vegetable Gardens.~~ Report to John
~~11:00 Counselor~~
12:00 Lunch
13:00 Session 2C
14:00 ~~Mop Common Areas.~~ Counselor
15:00 Afternoon Tea
15:25 Report for Medication
15:30 Wash Dishes
16:00 Report to John

17:30 Dinner
18:00 Session 3B
18:30 Relaxation
21:30 Bed

Wow! They had our whole day planned out. I wondered what I would've been made to do in the gardens if John hadn't come to my rescue. I really didn't have a green thumb.

Glancing at the clock on my nightstand, I saw lunchtime was in five minutes.

Crap! I tossed the schedule onto my bed and went into the bathroom. Turning on the tap, I tried to avoid looking in the mirror while I waited for the water to heat up. I didn't want to see the look in my eyes, but every time I closed my eyes, I saw the disgust in *his* as he turned away. My dream guy was repulsed by me.

Steam rose from the faucet, breaking me out of my thoughts. Turning the cold tap on a bit more, I flicked my fingers under the stream, waiting until it reached a temperature I could handle.

Cupping my hands together, the water pooled in my palms as my thoughts went back to my dream guy. I sighed then closed my eyes and splashed the water over my face, rubbing profusely as if it would take away the shame.

That was it. I felt ashamed.

I turned off the taps just as the bell rang, signaling it was lunchtime.

I patted my face dry with the towel hanging on the rack then headed downstairs, making sure I took my time to avoid the masses I'd run into on the staircase the previous times.

The only problem with that was everyone else got their food and found a seat before me. And as if it couldn't get any worse, the table with the guys I'd sat with last time was full. Cap guy was sitting in my seat, cap removed. I sucked in a sharp breath as my gaze settled on his perfectly tanned skin, framed by dark brown, almost black hair.

He stilled as if he knew I was watching him, but he didn't turn around.

Shaking my head, I strode into the kitchen and filled my plate with sausages and two types of salad. I grabbed a glass of juice then returned to the dining room.

Shit! I almost dropped my plate when I realized the only seat left was next to the one woman I wished wasn't there. The woman who should've been dead but somehow survived to keep reliving the horror of someone she thought she could trust.

My heart was practically beating a hole through my chest as I resigned myself to the fact that I had no other choice but to sit beside her. I kept waiting for her pain to take over my body, but it never did. *Huh.*

With my brow furrowed, I took a seat and dug into the food on my plate. No one tried to talk to me, but that didn't stop them from staring every chance they got.

No matter how much I tried to focus on my food, I couldn't stop my gaze from lifting to *him*. The others at his table seemed to have taken a real liking to him—especially the girls. But that was a no brainer. There was something about him. And it wasn't just his looks. There was a magnetic force drawing me to him, which I was sure the other girls felt as well.

That bugged the hell out of me.

It took me a few seconds to realize he'd turned around and was staring back at me.

I quickly diverted my gaze down and willed myself to eat, but I couldn't. Just the thought of food made me want to hurl.

I grabbed my glass and took a sip before chancing a peep in his direction. He was still looking at me.

Scooping up my plate, I headed into the kitchen, dumped my leftovers in the bin, and deposited my plate in the sink. I had every intention of rinsing it off, but my hands clutched the bench instead, and I hung my head as I relived the look in his eyes.

Someone put a plate down beside me, making me jump. I twisted around to find *him* standing next to me. He opened his mouth to say something, but nothing came out. Worry lines formed across his forehead as he stared into my eyes.

After what seemed like an eternity, he shook his head. "Have we met before?" He shook his head again. "Wow. That sounded like a really bad pickup line, didn't it?"

I smiled, unable to look away, completely captivated by the melodic undertone in his voice. "Yeah, it kind of did." Except no one had ever tried to pick me up before, so I knew it couldn't be possible. He was still the same guy who'd looked at me as if I were a freak. Nothing had changed.

"Let's start again." He held out his hand. "My name is Marcus."

I usually had to force myself to make contact with someone, but my hand was drawn to his like a magnet. I expected sparks to fly, but all I felt was… nothing. Actually, that was a lie. I felt peace. As if I'd found the cure to what I'd been searching for all my life.

"And your name is?" he prompted.

"Lucy."

"Lucy." My name sounded like Angel's wings passing over his lips. "Is that short for something?"

"Uh yeah, Luciana."

Marcus's eyes widened, and I was sure he'd stopped breathing. His grip tightened on mine, and he closed his eyes and exhaled slowly.

I knew I should've pulled away, but I was completely captivated not only with the way he'd said my name but the way his soul called to mine.

I wanted to slap myself. "Soul called to mine?" What the hell kind of crap was that? Yet, I couldn't deny there was something between us. And the way he looked at me in sessions was all but forgotten.

Marcus opened his eyes as he lowered our joined hands in a "definitely not friendly" handshake kind of way.

"Do you guys know each other?" Justin asked, casually walking into the kitchen.

I pulled my hand away from Marcus's. "Uh, no," I said, trying to ignore my aching desire to touch Marcus once more.

Justin placed his empty plate and glass onto the bench then dropped his arm over my shoulder. "Why didn't you sit with us this morning?"

"There was no spare seat."

"That was my fault," Marcus said softly, chastising himself.

"We could've made room for you," Justin said.

That was true, but I hadn't wanted to sit at the same table as Marcus. The look he'd given me when he saw the blood seeping from my wrist had haunted me ever since.

I shrugged and stole a glance back at Marcus. His steely eyes were locked on Justin and the way his arm fit over my shoulders. Marcus looked as if he wanted to rip Justin's arm out of its socket.

I don't know why I felt as if I were doing something I shouldn't. But I couldn't stop myself. Slipping under Justin's arm, I backed toward the door. "I have to go see Jo." It wasn't until I said her name that I realized I hadn't taken my medication this morning.

Turning on my heel, I headed outside where I found Jo sitting on one of the sofas on the deck, eating a sandwich.

"Hi, Lucy," she said. "Is something wrong?"

"Uh, yeah…" I fiddled with my fingers. "I forgot to get my medication this morning."

She raised her brow. "The rules are, if you don't show up for your disbursement at the allocated time, you have to wait until your next assigned time.

"However, since you only received your schedule when you got back from riding with John, I'm going to make an exception just this once." She glanced at her watch. "But, because of the time, if you do take a dose now, you'll have to miss the next one."

I thought back to my schedule. From memory, I had sessions for the next two hours. Then I got to escape with Milly until dinner. I prayed my memory served me correctly. "I understand."

"Good." She lifted her sandwich, stopping just short of her mouth. "Wait for me in the kitchen. I'll meet you there when I'm finished here."

I headed back into the house, my chest constricting when I thought about where I was going, or more so, whom I hoped would still be there. I wasn't sure why Marcus had looked at me as if he wanted to draw me into his arms, when only hours before, the very sight of me and what I'd done had repulsed him.

To my dismay, Marcus was still in the kitchen and so was Justin. They were on dish duty—together.

I didn't have a problem with Justin. He'd been nothing but nice to me since I'd arrived. It was Marcus who had the problem with him, and I couldn't understand why.

Justin looked over his shoulder at me as I walked into the kitchen. "You're back?"

"Obviously," Marcus said under his breath.

I took a seat on a stool on the other side of the bench. "Jo asked me to wait here for her."

"In trouble already?" Justin asked, completely ignoring the way Marcus glared at him.

"Ha-ha." I folded my arms on the bench. "No. I didn't get my schedule until just before lunch, so I missed out on my meds." I quickly looked to Marcus, wanting to see how he reacted to my declaration of my need for pills to cope with the reason why I was here. I didn't know why I cared what he thought. He obviously had issues that brought him to Millford, as well.

My stomach dropped when I saw the way he looked at me. We were back to square one.

CHAPTER 13

I didn't know whom he thought he was to be able to make me feel like the scum scraped off the bottom of his boot, but that was exactly how I felt when he looked at me that way.

I'd almost skipped out on waiting for my pills, but Jo had shown up with impeccable timing and gave me my dosage.

It was time for another session for us to talk about our feelings and shit. Lunch had finished, and I'd found my group sitting in a circle on the back deck. There weren't as many in this group as the last one I'd been part of. There were only five people. And although my motto was usually the fewer people around the better, that didn't apply now. It meant that unless the others took over ten minutes each to discuss their issues, I was going to have to talk.

I didn't want to talk.

Liam was leading the group, which made it all the more awkward. I didn't see him as a guy with a degree. He seemed more like someone who'd worked the land all his life.

I picked at the nail on my thumb while I listened to a guy named Karl talk about how he had gotten into the wrong crowd when he was a teen, started selling drugs to get by, got addicted himself, somehow fell into the prostitution ring, ended up in jail where he became addicted on heavier stuff, and was now trying to see the light at the end of the tunnel, working toward getting visitation to his kid, whom he'd never even met.

I zoned out as he went on about the cravings that still had a hold on him. All I could think about was keeping my ass in the seat and resisting my instinct to run off to find a hit of ice or heroin. Ice was my new addiction that my body craved even though I had never actually used anything other than prescription medication—even when I'd tried overdosing.

Biting my lip for distraction, blood seeped into my mouth, the coppery taste doing nothing to control my cravings as I waited for my meds to kick in.

I could barely sit still. My legs were jittering and sweat was accumulating on my—everywhere. My stomach constricted, doubling me over as my mind screamed for another hit.

Everyone looked at me as I rocked back and forth on my seat, barely able to control the urge to run. I needed to stay put so my time with Milly wasn't taken away.

Karl stopped "sharing," but the cravings didn't stop.

"Who wants to go next?" Liam asked, looking at me.

I shook my head as I continued to rock back and forth.

"I'll go," a woman with sandy blond hair said. She took a deep breath. "For those who don't know me"—she looked pointedly at me—"my name is Cassie, and I'm an alcoholic."

Crap! Not only did I have to deal with drug cravings, but I also had an unrelenting thirst, which seemed to be amplified by another patient in our group.

I needed it to stop. The meds weren't working. It had to have already been twenty minutes. Something had gone wrong.

Curling my legs up in front of me, I wrapped my arms around my calves and buried my head against my knees.

"Lucy," someone said, but I couldn't make out or didn't really care who it was. All I cared about was getting my next fix. It superseded all the pain from losing my son, three daughters, husband, and friends. Except they weren't my son, three daughters, husband, and friends. They were Karl's, Cassie's, and the other guy's.

Someone grabbed my elbow, lifting it. "Shit." They lowered my arm back to my knee. "Someone get Jo."

Forcing myself to look up, I saw Liam standing over me, blood smeared over his hands.

My eyes widened in fear as I saw blood dripping down my pants, coming from the freshly opened wound on my wrist. There were no stitches left. I'd ripped them completely out.

Shifting my gaze, I saw every single person staring at me. They knew… They knew I was a freak.

I jumped up and ran, not stopping as I entered the bush. I needed to get away.

Footsteps pounded after me, but I ran faster, losing them as my years of running to get away from the noise paid off. Branches whipped my face as I raced through the dense scrub until I was finally alone, free from everyone's issues. I could breathe—sort of.

My head spun as a white fog clouded my vision.

I needed to sit down.

I stumbled another ten meters before collapsing on the ground, smacking my head against a tree root.

A smile formed on my lips as everything took on a hazy glow, and I prayed this was going to be it. I was finally going to die, and no one was going to find me in time.

My eyes became heavier and heavier until I was unable to hold them open any longer.

This was it. It would finally be over.

Warmth encased me as soft unintelligible words sifted through my mind. And everything stopped. There were no more cravings. There was no more pain or fear.

I was at peace.

Something soft pressed against my forehead, and warm air followed as strong arms wrapped around me, lifting me off the ground.

I felt weightless.

With every last ounce of strength, I opened my eyes just enough to see it wasn't a heavenly creature whisking me away to the afterlife, or the grim reaper dragging me into the depths of hell. It was Marcus. And he was pressing soft kisses to my face as he whispered words I couldn't understand.

Pulling away, his eyes glistened as he looked down at me. "I'm sorry," he whispered—the same words he'd said every night in my dreams. Only this wasn't the same. This time was different. This time was real.

I tried to keep my eyes open, but they became too heavy as darkness crept over my vision. Then I passed out.

CHAPTER 14

*M*ovement jolted me awake as something tightened over my chest and legs, holding me in place. I opened my eyes, instantly recognizing my surroundings. I was in an ambulance.

"Hi, Lucy," a man with dark hair and graying sideburns said. "My name's Scott, and I'm a paramedic. You've had a serious injury that we're taking you to the hospital to treat."

I nodded then realized someone was holding my hand—and it wasn't the paramedic.

Tilting my head back, I saw Marcus sitting in the seat to the side of my head

He wore no smile as his thumb brushed across the back of my hand, his gaze holding a million secrets but none he was willing to share. He just sat there, silently staring at me.

Eventually I asked, "What are you doing here?"

Marcus cleared his throat. "You kept calling out my name and wouldn't let go of me The paramedics thought it would be best if I came with you to keep you calm."

Realizing he was still holding my hand, I jerked it away and turned my head to the sidewall of the ambulance.

His words were like a knife to my heart. Marcus was only here because of my screwed-up fascination with him. And he didn't look one bit happy about it.

But if that were true, then why did I remember his lips against my forehead and the warmth of his breath as he whispered words I didn't understand?

"Lu..." he said, his voice barely audible.

My eyes stung as I fought back tears that were threatening to spill. I'd never cried over a guy. But there was something different about Marcus. Something was drawing me to him. My heart ached for a man I'd only just met. I felt as if he was the missing piece of my soul I'd been searching for all my life.

He made me want to live.

My heart ripped open, and tears spilled down my cheeks. I was crying for a guy who... who acted as if the very sight of me caused him pain.

The ambulance came to a stop, and the paramedic opened the doors then jumped out. The driver joined him, and together they rolled the stretcher onto the driveway.

To my dismay and happiness, Marcus stayed with me every second as the doctors and nurses cleaned the dirt out of my wound and replaced the five stitches I'd torn out.

I was humiliated when they not only suggested but insisted on putting a cast on my wrist so I wouldn't be tempted to pull the stitches out again.

"I think you should listen to them," Marcus said from a chair he'd pulled up beside my bed.

"Like I've got a choice," I muttered, looking out the window.

He inched the chair closer to my side and grabbed my hand. I pulled it away, clasping my fingers together over my stomach.

Sighing, he put his head in his hands and stayed that way for a couple of minutes.

"You don't have to be here," I said, my voice coming out weaker than I'd wanted.

Marcus looked up at me. "Is that what you think I want?"

I choked on a laugh. "I think it's pretty obvious you don't want to be here. You only came because I wouldn't let go of you."

"Lu..." His eyes took on that pained look they so often did whenever I was around.

I stared up at the ceiling, a lump forming in my throat. I hated seeing the way he looked at me. I knew I was a freak, and everyone else in my life saw me that way but *him*... He was different. "Go," I whispered.

Marcus stood, and I thought he was going to run for the door the second I'd given him permission to leave. Instead, he sat on the edge of the bed. "I'm not going anywhere. And there's no place I'd rather be." He quickly added, "Well, maybe not in the hospital, but with you..." He smoothed the hair away from my face, his fingertips lighting a fire deep within, my soul yearning for his.

I wanted to know the rest of his sentence, but his gaze pierced through the ironclad armor I'd built around my heart, making me incapable of forming a coherent sentence.

Images of Marcus holding me in his arms, kissing me, and me kissing him in return swept through my mind. It wasn't the memory of him carrying me out of the bush. These were different. We were different. We were in love.

Marcus leaned down, stopping inches from my face. "It's always been you." He kissed my forehead, and I slipped into a dream-filled sleep.

I jerked awake, afraid I'd imagined everything that had gone down between us. Marcus was still sitting in the chair reading a book he'd gotten from God knows where.

Realizing I was awake, he lowered the book and placed it on the windowsill, the corners of his lips tipping up into a smile. "How are you feeling?"

I rubbed my eyes, my cast smacking me in my face. "Shit."

He laughed. "Maybe that's not a good idea."

Staring at the lime-green cast on my wrist, I drew my eyebrows together. "When did I get this?"

Marcus stood, moving over to sit on the edge of my bed. His fingers closed around mine, lowing my cast to his lap. "They took you away about two hours ago."

I gaped. "I slept through the whole thing?"

He nodded. "You were out like a light."

The last thing I remembered was the softness of his lips on my forehead. I wasn't sure if I imagined it... My heart squeezed in my chest as I remembered his words, "It's always been you."

I had definitely imagined that. There was no way he would say something like that to someone he'd only just met. Unless... that was his problem. Maybe he was at rehab because his underlying problems were attachment issues. Maybe he was an unloved child, desperate to be loved, and latched on to any girl who showed the slightest bit of interest. Or maybe he was a sex addict, and I was next on his list. Although that didn't seem right considering the way some of the other girls in rehab looked at him. He wouldn't have chosen me to try to get laid.

"What are you thinking about?" he asked.

"About you." I slapped my hand over my mouth. "I can't believe I just said that. It must've been the drugs talking."

Marcus chuckled. "You haven't been given any drugs strong enough to cause you to say something you didn't mean."

Blood rushed to my cheeks.

He brushed his thumb over the back of my hand. "So, what exactly were you thinking about?"

No matter how much I wanted to keep my mouth shut, something compelled me to tell him what I didn't even understand myself. I felt for him, something I'd never experienced before. I wanted him. I needed him. I was in—

A nurse walked into the room, saving me from the verbal assault of my feelings, which I'd been seconds away from spilling.

Marcus clenched his jaw as he looked at the nurse.

"Hi, Zoe," the woman said, paying no attention to Marcus. "I've got your paperwork here for you to fill out. Then you can go."

I rolled my eyes at the sound of my birth name. But I couldn't be bothered telling her my name was Lucy. If I did that, then I was pretty sure they would keep me in for a few hours longer while they checked all the paperwork.

I couldn't wait until my name change certificate came in the mail. Although I was pretty sure I wouldn't be seeing it any time soon. My mother would probably rip it to shreds to keep it from me.

The nurse placed the paperwork on the table and pushed it over to the bed, forcing Marcus to let go of my hand. "I'll leave these with you. Fill them out. Then you can bring them up to the desk, and you'll be free to go home."

"Thanks," I said as she left the room, my mind still on the absence of Marcus's fingers entwined with mine.

Shaking my thoughts away. I picked up the pen, looked over the details on the papers, and signed on the dotted line.

Marcus collected the papers in one hand and pushed the table away from the bed with his other. "Let's get out of here."

Sitting up, I swung my legs over the side then froze as his arm wrapped around my waist, helping me off the bed.

I turned in his arms, staring up into his eyes, which were like nothing I'd ever seen. I was completely captured by him as the world around us faded away. My heart exploded with something I'd never experienced before and desperately wanted to deny.

I loved him.

Then it hit me. I wasn't in love with him. I must've been reciprocating his feelings for me. But that didn't make sense. How could Marcus love someone he'd only just met?

My breath caught in my throat as more visions of us entered my mind. We were lying down in a field of flowers, hands entwined with each other's as we watched the stars twinkle in the sky above. I'd never seen stars that bright before, and come to think of it, my clothes were not something I'd normally wear.

Coming back to the present, my hands slid up his chest, hooked around his neck, and pulled him down until our lips were only separated by a sliver of light. Our breaths came out fast and uneven as we stared into each other's eyes, my heart swelling with a love that seemed to come out of nowhere.

Forcing myself to ignore my desires, I stepped back, breaking his hold on me. These images weren't real. They couldn't be real. And these feelings most definitely couldn't be real either. Swallowing hard, I walked over to the window, putting some distance between us. Then I turned around to face him. "What are you in rehab for?"

He looked away, his expression once again filled with pain I couldn't feel. Was it because of what we'd almost done or because we had come so close and I'd pulled away? "Let's get out of here."

Marcus walked out the door, leaving me wondering what the hell was going on between us.

CHAPTER 15

$\mathcal{I}$n the cab on the way back to Millford, my mind was reliving what had gone down between us. I'd never taken on anyone's good feelings before. It was always the negative. The strange thing was that I didn't feel hate. All I felt was my undeniable love for him.

When we arrived back at the farm, I realized I had nothing to pay the driver with. "Can you wait here? My purse is inside."

"No need." Marcus pulled out his wallet and handed over a credit card.

"I'll pay you back," I said trying to pull down my sleeve to cover my new cast as we walked up to the house.

Marcus shoved his hands into the pockets of his jeans. "No need."

"Well, thanks. But I prefer if I do."

He caught my elbow, stopping me from going up the steps. "I know you don't understand what's going on, but I need you to know it's real—"

"What are you in here for?"

Ignoring me, he said, "I know this is freaking you out, and it's not normal, but nothing about us is normal. You must know that by now."

"Are you schitzo?"

"This connection I feel with you, I'm pretty sure you feel it, too."

"Split personality disorder?"

"I know it must be scary, and you're probably completely freaked out by it, but I need you to not fight it. I need to know what you're remembering. I need to know if this time's different."

I stepped back, breaking his hold on me. "Did you smoke something?"

He took a step toward me. "Please don't fight this."

An aching desire to be with him consumed my entire being. No matter how much I knew I should run, I couldn't refrain from leaning against his chest. Closing my eyes, I exhaled slowly, my lips trembling as more images flooded my mind. The two of us were making love. My heart swelled to capacity as the words "I love you" flowed from my lips, and to my relief, he responded with, "I love you, too."

I scrunched his shirt in my fists as another memory resurfaced.

We were on the beach, walking hand in hand as the water lapped at our feet. He spun me in his arms, pulling me against him. The sun was setting, and the light glowed against my hands, which were cupping his flawless face. I remember noticing something was different about him, but I couldn't say exactly what it was. On reflection, it seemed as if his skin somehow absorbed the light just like it did now.

Standing on the balls of my feet, I pressed a kiss on the corner of his lips then pulled away, biting down on my grin.

He brushed a few wisps of hair behind my ear then traced his fingers over my lips. "I love you," he whispered.

"I love you, too," I said. Then he drew me into a deep searing kiss that exploded my heart into a million pieces for reasons I didn't understand. But the more he kissed me, the faster my heart repaired.

Tears spilled from my eyes as the memories faded. I buried my head against his chest and cried for reasons I didn't understand.

Warm arms encompassed me as he kissed the top of my head. "Don't be afraid."

Problem was, I was terrified because these feelings seemed so real. These memories felt like mine. But that wasn't possible.

Pushing him away, I said, "This isn't me. It's you."

I took another few steps, backing up to the stairs. "Tell me why you're here."

When he didn't answer, I spun around, opened the door, and

raced up the stairs to my room. Slamming the door behind me, all my emotions poured out, combined with the relentless problems of the patients in the rooms beneath me.

I shuffled over to the bed and lay down, the cast on my wrist tucked up beside my face. I blinked in surprise and wiped away my tears. Underneath my middle finger, there was a faint silver infinity symbol drawn on my cast, which I hadn't noticed before.

Furrowing my brows, I wondered why it was on my cast and what it meant. I was pretty sure doctors didn't draw on their patient's casts, and Marcus had been the only other person with the opportunity to put it there without me knowing, but I couldn't understand why he would draw it.

I traced the never-ending line of the symbol with the tip of my finger. The emotions of the other patients began to subside and then were completely gone. I was finally able to breathe again.

CHAPTER 16

$\mathcal{M}$y cast made the next day's poop duty a little harder than the previous day. Jo had said I could skip duties because of my wrist and have an extra counselling session with her instead. That was so not going to happen. I convinced her I was fine and didn't want any special treatment. No matter how much my wrist hurt, the pain was better than spilling my story.

I'd let Milly into the small paddock while I cleaned her stable. It was amazing how much mess horses made. I'd been shovelling for a good five minutes, and I'd barely made a dent in the stall.

"Let me help you," Marcus said, leaning over the rail that was dividing his stable from mine.

Of course he was on poop duty as well. And of course he couldn't keep his eyes off me. Everything I'd put behind me when I went to bed last night was back with full force. "I don't need your help," I said, shovelling another load of straw into the wheelbarrow.

"Well, you don't have a choice." Putting one hand on the rail, he jumped over the fence with such ease and snatched the shovel out of my hands.

I put my hands on my hips. "You have your own poop to scoop."

"I've already finished."

Just to make sure he was telling the truth, I peeked over the fence.

Sure enough, it was perfectly cleaned and new straw was covering the ground.

I sighed. "You don't need to help me."

"I want to." He shoveled another load.

"You can help *me*," Sarah called out.

"You're not injured," Marcus replied.

"I'll be happy to break my arm if it means I don't have to scoop any more poop."

Marcus chuckled then finished off Milly's stable. He even laid the fresh straw, put her food in the bowl hanging over the rail, and pushed my wheelbarrow out before his, leaving me alone with the other two and their issues, which were starting to surface in his absence.

Determined not to look like a helpless girl, I grabbed the handles of the wheelbarrow outside of the stable Marcus had been responsible for cleaning and wheeled it out of the barn. Pain radiated up my arm, but I wasn't stopping.

Marcus saw me as I exited the barn. He was already on his way back. He immediately lowered his wheelbarrow to the ground and jogged over to me. "You shouldn't be doing this."

"I'm fine." I managed to push the wheelbarrow another couple of feet before his hands closed over mine, forcing me to lower it to the ground.

"We can stay out here all day arguing about this, or you could let me take it now."

I was pretty sure we couldn't stay out there all day without one of the staff cracking down on us, but I knew this wasn't an argument I was going to win. Marcus was determined to help me, and if I was being honest with myself, I wanted him to. "Fine."

The corner of his lips tipped up as he pushed the wheelbarrow to the dumping ground.

"What do you think they do with all this poop?" I asked.

"Use it as fertiliser." He dumped the poop.

"Fertiliser for what?"

He cocked his head to the right.

Following his gaze, I saw Sophia, Justin, and a bunch of others ploughing a field lit by floodlights. There was no machinery. They were doing it all by hand.

Marcus stood beside me. "Poop duty's looking pretty good right about now, isn't it?"

I nodded. I wasn't in anyway a spoiled rich kid, but I sure as hell had never done a day of manual labor in my life. I wanted to kiss John for giving me a way out of garden duties.

Marcus looked at his watch. "We've got half an hour before meds are being delivered. Let's get this finished. Then I want to show you something."

I nodded, unable to say no. I'd woken up with the plan to ignore him and what had to be his feelings, but the moment I laid eyes on Marcus, I was back where I'd started last night. I loved him. I was in love with him. And it was scaring the crap out of me. But, and there was a big but, just because I felt that way, didn't mean I had to act on it.

Returning the wheelbarrows to their place, we went over to the taps near the stable and washed our hands.

"Where are you taking me?" I asked as he led me toward the bush.

"It's a surprise." He glanced at his watch.

"You know, a lot of people would say a girl would be stupid to follow a guy she'd only just met into the bush—especially a guy she'd met in rehab *and* refuses to tell her why he's there."

"A lot of people would be right."

I stopped, the blood draining from my face.

He turned to me and smiled. "But they'd be wrong in this instance." When I didn't move he added, "If I wanted to kill you, why would I have saved you yesterday?"

He had a point. But there was also another point he didn't know about; I actually wanted to die. It was my mission in life. Yet, standing there with Marcus, it was the last thing I wanted. I wanted to live. I wanted my life with him.

Where the hell did that come from? Him. It had to have come from him—even if it didn't make any sense.

"Come on," Marcus said, continuing to lead me deeper into the bush.

"How's the cast?" he asked.

Remembering the little drawing, I asked, "Did you draw the infinity symbol on my cast?"

He grabbed my hand, lifting it between us before I even knew I'd been touched.

"Jesus," I said, trying to pull away.

Marcus held on as his gaze settled on my cast. "Yep."

I narrowed my eyes at him. "Why?"

"Why not?"

I raised a brow. "Really?"

He smiled as he continued walking, somehow still holding my hand and making it feel completely normal—natural even.

I knew I should stop him, but… I loved the way my hand fit with his. I loved the way peace settled over my heart. I loved the way he stole glances at me. I loved the way he noticed me noticing him. I loved… him.

Shit!

Coming to a stop on top of a large flat rock, Marcus gestured in front of us.

Stealing my gaze away from him, I turned my head and realized he'd led me onto an elevated rock overlooking the valley below. I could see the house, but that wasn't what captured my attention. It was the sun rising over the trees, bringing life to a brand new day.

Marcus stepped behind me, wrapping his arms around my waist and hanging his head in the crook of my neck. Brushing his cheek against mine, he slowly exhaled.

Pulling his hands tighter around me, I leaned my head against his shoulder, relaxing into his warm embrace as we watched the sun chase away the shadows of the night.

"It's beautiful," I whispered.

"You're beautiful." He placed a kiss on my cheek, lighting a desire within me. Hell, who was I kidding? Desire coursed through me every second I was in his presence.

Even though my heart fluttered, I couldn't ignore the weight of the unknowns between us. "Why are you here?" I asked again.

The seconds ticked by. I thought he was going to pretend I didn't say anything, but then he said, "Why are *you* here?"

"I…"

"Tell me," he encouraged.

I stepped away, breaking his hold on me and breaking my heart in the process. I desperately wanted to feel his arms around me again. Feel his lips against mine, the tender stroke of his fingers brushing over my skin. And most importantly, the obscured love he felt for me.

"I'm not going to judge you," he said. "I'm the last person in the world who would judge you."

"You don't know me."

"I know you better than you think."

I frowned and took another step back. "You see, that's the problem. You don't know me." I took another step back. "We only just met. Yet somehow you've formed this attachment to me. You do things you shouldn't. You say things you shouldn't. You feel things you shouldn't. You don't know me." I took another step back, my eyes widening as I realized there was nothing under my foot and it was too late to stop my fall.

Black wisps swirled around me, taking on a freakishly dark presence, drawing me into the depths of their blackness as I plummeted to the ground. A second later, a blinding light broke through the black wisps and disappeared, taking my sight with it. But I wasn't scared. I was at peace.

I prayed I'd finally managed to do the impossible and I would no longer have to spend another second on this earth.

My head fell back against something soft, which soon turned hard. Light sloshed in the peripheral of my vision until my sight returned. I looked up and saw Marcus kneeling beside me. "I'm sorry," he whispered, sweeping me into his arms.

It took me a few seconds to realize what had happened—and that I wasn't dead. I pushed my legs against his arm, forcing him to let go of me. My legs swung down and my feet hit the ground hard. But he didn't let go of me. His arm remained around my waist.

I jerked away from him and looked up. *Holy hell.* It was at least a ten-meter drop, and I hadn't even cracked my skull open.

"You should sit down." When I didn't listen, he said, "At least let me check you over."

"What? You're a doctor now?" I spun around to face him. "I wouldn't have fallen if you weren't so screwed up." I hated myself the moment the words slipped from my mouth.

"I'm sorry," I said. Not waiting for him to reply, I turned around and jogged back to the house. I could hear him a couple of meters behind me the entire way, and it pained me to ignore him when all I wanted to do was run into his arms and disappear someplace where no one would try to take me away from him. Why anyone would want to was beyond me, but I felt it just the same.

71

CHAPTER 17

*A*rriving back at the house, I pushed the door open and stepped inside. The place was abuzz with patients waiting for their pain suppressors in the form of a pill. In the back of my mind I knew I should be feeling their cravings, pain, and sadness, but I didn't.

Marcus stood behind me in the line as Amelia came trotting into the room; her hair was dripping wet, seeping through the shoulders of her sweater. "Hi, Marcus," she said in a way that made me want to punch her in the face.

He ignored her. At least, I think he did. I wasn't going to turn around and let him see just how jealous I was. Because I was jealous. And I was positive it was written all over my face.

"Lu," Marcus whispered, placing a hand on my hip.

I closed my eyes as my heart swelled at the sound of my name coming from his lips. Only it wasn't my name. No one had ever called me "Lu," yet somehow it was familiar, as if he'd been calling me that my entire life.

The line began moving, and I stepped forward, his hand slipping from my hip.

Marcus didn't try to talk to me again—and it irked me to no end. Amelia had him caught up in a conversation about the movie we were watching tonight. Apparently, the oldies were going outside and it was our turn inside. The rotation wasn't something official. It was just how things worked here.

I could tell Amelia liked Marcus, and he was doing nothing to destroy her hopes. I wanted him to destroy her hopes. I wanted him to want me, which was pretty stupid considering I was doing everything in my power to stop the feelings he displayed toward me.

I got my pills and popped them in my mouth, downing them with a glass of orange juice. Sophia came out of nowhere, grabbing my arm as Marcus strode toward me. She pulled me forward, making me walk next to her, leaving Marcus behind. "What happened to your arm?"

"Uh…"

She gave me a knowing look. "Everyone's been talking about what happened." She quickly added, "Not that I'm judging or anything."

Of course they were. Taking a deep breath, I said, "The doctors thought the cast would help keep my stitches in." I gave her a tight-lipped smile.

"Good idea," she said. "I know you might think there's no hope and ending it all is the only way, but trust me, things do get better." Sophia pulled me to the side, looked around to make sure no one was watching, and lifted the sleeve of her sweater up to her elbow.

Jagged white lines covered her wrist, much like they did mine. "I'm not saying you won't have days that you want to end it all, because there are days when I go back to that way of thinking. I just have to remember it's just one day at a time—or one minute at a time on some days—and it'll pass."

She pulled her sweater back down her arm. "Therapy's really working. Not as fast as I'd like, but it's working. Everyone here has been really helpful, and they have made me see things in a new light. They've given me hope. And I know they can do the same for you if you give them a chance. But you're going to have to admit what it is that's making you do that to yourself. Otherwise, you're just wasting everyone's time—especially yours."

I knew what she was saying was coming from a good place, but the reality was no one could help me. I'd tried. Hell, I'd tried for years.

"Come on." She linked her arm with mine. "What sesh do you have?"

By "sesh" I presumed she meant session. "I'm in A."

"Good. Me, too."

We were one of the first ones to arrive and take our seats. A few moments later, Justin bounded up behind us and sat down next to me. I was partially relieved, yet there was also a burning hole inside my chest, knowing Marcus couldn't sit beside me—if we were even in the same session.

I discovered we weren't.

The session dragged on, and even though Sophia was nudging me to share my story, I remained silent.

"You're going to have to talk sooner or later," she said as we walked out the door onto the front deck.

"I know." I caught sight of Marcus and Amelia disappearing behind the barn together.

I wanted to be sick. Anger, hurt, and rejection pumped through my veins as what felt like a fist closed around my heart, squeezing the crap out of it.

"You like him, don't you?" Sophia asked.

I scrunched up my nose. "Marcus? No."

She chuckled. "I didn't say who."

I gave her a bland look, knowing I'd been caught. "I don't know what to think."

"He's cute," she said. "But not my type. I usually go for the type of guy who actually knows I exist."

"He seems to know Amelia exists."

"Everyone knows Amelia exists. Doesn't mean it's her he wants."

It's always been you. His words replayed in my mind.

"I've seen the way he looks at you," Sophia said.

"Yeah, like I cause him pain."

"I think you know better." She smiled. "Have fun with Milly while I slave away in the gardens." Sophia gave me a small wave before taking off in the direction Amelia and Marcus had gone.

CHAPTER 18

Spending time with Milly was good for my soul. She didn't ask questions and neither did John. He seemed to know something was bothering me and was happy to wait until I was ready to talk.

We didn't follow the fence of the paddock we'd entered last time. John had taken me another way, past the patients working in the gardens and along a trail that lined the bush on the other side of the farm.

Most of the way I could see Marcus. He stood out like an angel among the others. And even more so when he took off his shirt, revealing a body most guys would die for.

I couldn't help but watch as Amelia payed him more attention than I wanted. But for some strange reason, Marcus ignored her. He worked his pickaxe into the ground, digging up the field. Every so often, he looked up, his gaze fixated on me as if he could sense where I was before he'd even looked.

And I felt it. I felt it in every fiber of my being.

"Sometimes, the heart wants what it can't have," John said, breaking the silence, keeping his back to me as he led the way. "And sometimes it can. What we need to work out is whether we should trust our hearts or not."

I wasn't sure what I was supposed to say to that, so I kept quiet.

His words were food for my thoughts. How he even knew what was bothering me was beyond me, but he was right. My heart did want Marcus, and I didn't know if I could trust it or not.

I was also pretty confused as to why he was pointing that out considering one of the rules for Millford was no dating and no relationships of any sort. I took that as no kissing, a rule I'd already broken. I'd kissed Marcus and could still feel the softness of his lips on mine.

Realizing I'd lifted my fingers to my lips, I quickly lowered them so I didn't look like a freak, feeling up my own lips, even though no one was watching.

Or so I'd thought. Looking back to the gardens, I saw Marcus leaning against his pickaxe, watching me. Heat burned in my chest, constricting not just my heart but also my stomach. No matter how much I didn't want him to know how he affected me, I couldn't take my eyes off him. I was completely mesmerised by the way his skin absorbed the light like it had in my memory—or delusion, or whatever it was.

By the time we'd rounded the paddock, tied the horses back up on the post, and given them some fresh water, I was running late for lunch.

"Come back after you've had something to eat. Give Milly a brush down, and then let her into the paddock." John gestured to the small paddock I'd put her in earlier this morning. It still surprised me that a horse would come when called. Then again, most animals were the same. They'd do anything for the possibility of a treat.

I washed my hands in the sink outside the barn and went into the house. As I expected, everyone was already sitting down, eating their meals.

Relief washed over me when I saw Sophia had saved me a seat between her and Justin. Then I saw Amelia was at the same table, sitting next to Marcus, placing her dirty paws all over him.

Jealousy raged within me, all-consuming. I didn't have a right to feel that way. He wasn't mine.

Marcus looked up, seeing me standing there like an utter freak as I watched him and Amelia, who just so happened to lean into him at that very moment, her eyes on me as her hand disappeared under the table—in his direction. Then the worst happened; his hand disappeared under the table, too.

Not being able to watch anymore, I went into the kitchen and stared at the various dishes before me. Someone had cooked a barbeque. I loved barbeques. Just not today.

I wasn't hungry. However, I wasn't going to give Amelia the satisfaction of knowing she'd gotten to me.

I picked up a plate and loaded it with salad and a sausage. I grabbed a roll and took my seat between Sophia and Justin.

"How was the ride?" Sophia asked.

"It was okay," I replied, not wanting to go into how not okay it was to see Marcus working with Amelia.

"Had to be better than digging up a new garden bed. I've got blisters on top of blisters." She held her hands up and inspected her palms. They looked nasty, and I was so grateful I didn't have to endure those things.

Justin dropped his arm over the back of my chair. "How did you manage to get yourself on riding duty? John never takes anyone."

"Uh..." My gaze dropped to my wrist. "Maybe because of this."

Amelia planted her elbows on the table, resting her head in her hands. "So you try to take the easy way out and get rewarded. Sounds fair to me," she said sarcastically.

I gaped at her. Easy way? I wished. Having to go through the torture of actually surviving every single suicide attempt was not easy. However, it did lessen the intensity of other's emotions. Unfortunately it was only short-lived.

"Really?" Sophia gave her a scornful look. "You had to say that to her?"

Amelia shrugged, the corner of her lips pulling up into a smirk. "Just telling it how it is."

"You have no idea how it is. You don't know Lucy. You don't know what she's been through, or what she has to live with every single day of her existence. So why don't you just shut the hell up and mind your own business?"

"You're right." Amelia folded her arms on the table. "I don't know what she's going through because she won't say a word in therapy. Maybe if she did decide to share one of these days, then we'd all know why she's trying to off herself."

"I think that's enough," Marcus warned, his tone low, carrying an authority he'd never displayed before.

Amelia's jaw dropped. "Now you're going to stand up for the freak? You didn't earlier."

"God, you're a bitch," Justin told Amelia, lifting his arm up to my shoulders.

My eyes pooled with tears I was unable to control. I blinked hard, trying to stop them from falling. I'd been called a freak a million times before. That wasn't what bothered me. It was that Marcus had been talking shit behind my back.

His eyes locked onto mine. "Just because I didn't tell you to shut up, doesn't mean I was okay with what you were saying."

"Excuse me." Grabbing my plate, I pushed my chair back as I stood and took off into the kitchen. I put my plate on the bench and wiped away my tears.

Sophia came up beside me and put her plate down next to mine. "Don't let Amelia get to you." Sophia was reliving why she'd tried to take her own life, making my pain so much harder to deal with.

"It's not her," I said before I realized what I was admitting.

"Marcus?"

There was no point denying my feelings when I'd basically blurted out my confession, so I nodded.

Sophia leaned her back against the bench. "Maybe he's not the right guy for you. I mean, what do you really know about him? He's got bad taste if he goes for girls like Amelia. Besides, you're not here to meet a guy. You're here to get better so you can go out there into the normal world and meet someone who doesn't have all these issues everyone in here has."

"Lu?" Marcus said, making me suck in a sharp breath.

I turned around, a lump forming in my throat when I saw him leaning against the doorframe to the kitchen. His eyes were once again filled with pain, tearing a big hole in my chest.

"Can I talk to you for a sec?"

I wanted to say yes. I wanted to hear what he had to say, but I shook my head instead. "I don't think you've got anything to say that I want to hear."

"Please?"

I shook my head again. "After everything you said to me, you just go off and... and... do whatever it is you're doing with Amelia and talking shit behind my back."

"Lu..."

"You kissed me. You said things no one else has ever said to me."

"I think I'll just go," Sophia said, taking a step toward the door.

I grabbed her arm. "No. You stay. Marcus can go."

"If you'll just let me explain," Marcus said.

"Explain what?" I asked. "That you like to play the field? That you like to have options? That you like to make every girl who pays you the slightest bit of attention think she's the one? Like you've got this amazing connection and make it out as if I'm the only girl for you? That you love me even though you've only just met me?" I didn't know why I was no longer making generalised comments and actually telling him the way I felt and the things he made me feel— especially in front of Sophia—but I couldn't stop myself. "You held my hand when I was in the hospital. You kissed me as if I were the love of your life. But it was all bull. The moment someone prettier paid attention to you, you forgot about me and went after her."

"That's not what happened."

"Oh, no?" I raised a brow. "What? You figured out that it wasn't me you wanted? It was always Amelia?"

"I don't want her. I want—"

"Is there a problem?" Justin asked, stepping into the kitchen, stopping when he was halfway between Marcus and me. "Because it sounds like there's a problem."

"Stay out of this," Marcus warned.

"Stay out of this?" Justin said, coming over to me. "You see, it seems like Lu is asking you to go." He dropped his arm over my shoulder, lighting a fire within Marcus's eyes. "You've made your decision."

I settled against Justin's side, not because I felt half the comfort with him as I did with Marcus. It was because I wanted Marcus to feel the way I did when I saw him with Amelia.

Jealousy was a bitch, and I wanted him to feel every bit as jealous as I was.

"I said, stay out of this," Marcus reiterated, his steely gaze locked on Justin as he took a step toward us.

Justin laughed. "Not this time."

Energy pulsed around the room, making it hard to breathe. Sophia could sense it, too. Her eyes were wide with panic. "Why don't you go cool off, Marcus?"

"I'm sure Amelia can help you with that one," Justin said,

making me want to hurl at the thought of Marcus turning to Amelia for anything.

"What can I help with?" Amelia popped her head into the kitchen. She strode over to Marcus and slipped her arm around his waist.

I was done. I couldn't take it anymore. The moment she'd touched him, all the oxygen was expelled from my lungs, and I was left trying to survive on nothing.

My head started to sway as I raced past her and Marcus on my way outside. The fresh air did practically nothing as it entered my lungs. My chest felt as if it were being crushed more and more with every second that ticked by until the pain was all-consuming.

The door swung open behind me. "Lu…" Marcus said.

Not turning around, I walked down the steps and over to Milly.

He followed.

"There is nothing going on between Amelia and me," Marcus said, catching up to me. "Everything you said to me in there… I feel that too."

I had to get away from him. "You're a bullshit artist is what you are." I untied Milly's reins and lifted them over her head.

"I don't even like Amelia in that way," he said as I swung my leg over Milly's back and lowered myself onto the saddle.

"In what way do you like her then?" I asked. "Is it her big boobs? Or her perfect face? Her baby blue eyes? The fullness of her lips?"

"It's none of that."

I raised a brow. "What is it then? Because I can't see that it's her personality that's the draw card. Is she just a good screw for you?"

"I've never—"

"Tell me, Marcus. Why are you here?"

He stared at me blankly, and once again the seconds ticked by.

"Just as I thought." I kicked my heels into Milly's sides and took off faster than I'd ever gone before. I couldn't make out a word of what Marcus was yelling at me over the blood pounding in my ears.

The tears I'd fought off finally spilled down my cheeks as I rode around the back of the house, going a couple of hundred meters past the fire pit before I pulled on the reins, easing her to a stop.

God, I hated the way he affected me. I had never let anyone have that power over me before, and I didn't get why Marcus was different.

He was so, so very different.

The sound of the bell rang softly in the distance. *Shit.*

I struggled for a few moments, actually considering not going back and getting my ass thrown out of rehab. But if I did that, I would be back home with Mom and Dad and all the screwed-up emotions I had to deal with that somehow were quite manageable here. Except that wasn't the biggest reason for staying. If I left, I wouldn't see Marcus, and no matter how much I wanted to deny my feelings, I couldn't bear to lose him from my life when I'd only just found him.

I didn't get where that thought had come from, but it was undeniable. I still wanted Marcus. I would always want Marcus. Somehow, at the tender age of eighteen, I knew that was the biggest truth of them all.

I loved Marcus.

CHAPTER 19

By the time I'd put Milly into the paddock and found my group session, I was late. And to my despair, Amelia was in the group—and so was Marcus.

I took the only spare seat—which happened to be directly opposite Marcus—as one of the guys continued talking about his drug addiction, which for some reason I didn't feel. I didn't give it much thought because my attention was locked on Marcus and the way he looked at me as if he were fighting the very need to continue our conversation right here, right now.

The speaker soon finished, and Liam asked another guy to speak but was cut off by Marcus. "I did something a long time ago that has killed me every day since. I'm responsible for the endless suffering of the one person I've loved more than anyone who's walked this existence or the next. And I have to relive this moment every single day, year after year, for the rest of my life. There is nothing that can undo what I've done. Or make it better. It's the same. It's always the same."

His gaze never wavered from mine. It was as if he were directing his speech at me. The intensity in his stare was all-consuming as his words replayed in my mind.

"Is there anything more you'd like to share?" Liam asked. When Marcus didn't answer, he said, "Okay—"

"I've suffered every single day of my existence," I said, for the first time not caring who was around and what they thought of me. "I feel every single person's pain, heartaches, addictions, and fears. Multiply that by fifty and that's what I have to live with on a daily basis. The doctors don't know what's wrong with me. All my brain scans have come back normal. There is nothing that can explain what I have to live with every single day of my existence. I've tried to kill myself more times and in more ways than anyone can imagine. But I never die. Someone always saves me. I've never been able to find peace until—"

"Me," Marcus said, his voice barely audible, his eyes drawing me into the depths of his pain.

I nodded, tears blurring my vision.

"Well, isn't that nice?" Amelia said. "The freak has just gotten freakier."

"That's enough," Liam snapped. "We are not here to judge or be judged. The circle is about sharing our deepest feelings in order to let us heal. And if you have a problem with that, then you can count your time here at Millford over.

"I..." Amelia crossed her arms over her chest, making her boobs practically pop out of her sweater.

With my breath caught in my throat, I looked back at Marcus. His gaze was still fixed on me, and the intensity of his stare had only increased. Muscles rippled across his neck as his chest rose and fell sharply.

I was unable to look away from him as another person shared and then another. My palms were sweaty, and my stomach was churning. His confession replayed over and over in my thoughts as I tried to convince myself Marcus hadn't been talking about me. And if he had been, what the hell did he mean by "one person I've loved more than anyone who's walked this existence or the next" and "how he was responsible for the endless suffering his loved one has had to endure"?

I couldn't work out how Marcus could possibly be responsible for my suffering, and if it wasn't me he was talking about, then who was this person he loved? And more importantly, how was I going to ever get over him if his heart was already spoken for?

By the time the session finished, I was going out of my mind. My ass was out of the seat before the bell had even finished ringing, and so was Marcus. He strode toward me, meeting me halfway in the center of the circle. "Tell me who you were talking about," I said, my voice cracking with nerves, fearing I was about to get my heart broken.

He reached for my fingers and held them loosely. "You." His voice was barely a whisper, but he may as well have shouted it. The single word radiated in my soul, filling me with a million questions and a million emotions I'd never had the pleasure of feeling before.

Letting go of one of my hands, he cupped my jaw, brushing his thumb across my cheek, the tenderness of his touch bringing tears to my eyes.

He wiped away the first one that fell. "Come with me."

I nodded, unable to form anything coherent on my lips.

Marcus led me through the house, heading toward the back door when Doctor Stein stepped out of the last room on the left. "There you are, Luciana," she said with a smile.

We stopped dead in our tracks. Part of me wanted to pretend she wasn't there, and the other part of me didn't want to get kicked out of Millford.

The latter was winning, only because after what Marcus had just confessed, getting kicked out of rehab meant I wouldn't get to see him every day. And I'd never get to finish the conversation I was so desperate to have.

"Thanks for walking her here, Marcus, but I think I can take over now," she said.

Turning to Marcus, I bit my lip, trying to keep it from trembling. I desperately wanted to know more, to feel his arms around me, to feel his lips on mine, speaking truths that would undoubtedly heal my soul—or so I hoped.

He smiled then leaned down and placed a gentle kiss on my forehead, giving me an unspoken promise that we would pick up where we'd left off as soon as we had a minute to ourselves.

Leaving Marcus standing in the hallway was one of the hardest things I'd ever had to do. As I took my seat on the sofa, I had to remind myself why I was here and what I hoped to gain, which had suddenly changed.

I'd come to Millford with the impossible hope that I'd find the reason why I was the way I was. And it looked as if I was going to get my wish. It just wasn't in the way I'd thought.

CHAPTER 20

I'd hoped to speak with Marcus as soon as I'd finished with good old Doctor Stein, who thought it was her mission in life to understand why I thought others' pains were my own, but the minutes ticked by as I sat at our table, having afternoon tea, and he didn't show. Neither did Justin.

Everyone's issues were palpable. They swirled around the room, taking over my mind.

Dr. Stein would've loved to watch me now. I was fighting the urge to find my next hit thanks to the emotions of betrayal, loss, and hurt others were imprinting on me. It was almost med time, and I was wishing the minutes would tick on by so I could get my next dosage to dull everyone's emotions.

"So." Sophia dragged out the word as she leaned closer, nudging my shoulder with hers. "Is it my imagination or was Marcus directing that 'share' at you?"

"What?" I asked, scrunching up my nose.

"You heard me."

I rolled my eyes. "As if." I fiddled with my napkin, trying to stop myself from ripping it to shreds.

She nodded. "Good. Because if he was talking about you—someone he'd never met before—then I'd recommend you stay as far away from that nutcase as possible."

My eyes widened.

"But he wasn't, so all's good." She patted my forearm, which was leaning on the table.

I sighed. There were so many truths in what Marcus had said, yet I couldn't explain how I knew they were true. Our connection couldn't be explained rationally. There was nothing rational about us.

The bell rang, signaling afternoon tea was over. The empty seat beside me slowly covered my heart in ice. I feared Marcus was having regrets about what he'd said and was avoiding me.

Justin's absence I couldn't explain. However, it wasn't him I wanted to see. I couldn't care less if I never saw him again.

Amelia had moved on to Aaron in Marcus's absence. And unlike Marcus, Aaron was just as caught up with her as she was with him.

I hoped she was over Marcus for good, but I wasn't holding my breath. He had an energy about him that sucked people in—girls especially.

Taking my untouched scone into the kitchen, I put the plate on the bench as Aaron came up beside me. "You think you're too good to put that in the bin yourself?"

"Huh?" I spun around to face him.

"The scone," he said as if I were stupid.

I shook my head. "No. Of course not."

"Good. Then go put it in the bin."

Frowning, I picked up the scone and threw it in the trash can. "Happy?"

"Yes, as a matter of fact I am." Smirking, he folded his arms across his chest as he studied me. "I don't know what Marcus sees in you, but remind me to thank him. I, for one, am happy with sloppy seconds—especially when it's someone as hot as Amelia."

His smirk turned into a grin when I gaped at him. "That is so disgusting."

Aaron shrugged. "Just telling you like it is. Did you seriously think good old lover boy didn't go there with her?" He chuckled and leaned closer to me. "He went there every chance he got. And I should know because my room is next to hers, and I've had a lot of trouble sleeping the last few nights."

I swallowed hard, but it did nothing to ease the soul-crushing heartache within me. I was sure Aaron had just been trying to get a rise from me, and it was working.

"Thanks for being concerned for my welfare," I said. "But I'm a big girl. I can take care of myself. And I don't need you telling me what has or hasn't happened between Amelia and Marcus, or anyone else for that matter."

"A lot's happened," he said with a wicked gleam in his eyes. "The walls are paper thin in this place and—"

"Aaron?" Jo called out. "These dishes aren't going to do themselves. So I suggest you finish your discussion with Lucy later. Otherwise, you'll be on dinner prep and wash-up for the rest of the week."

Aaron grabbed my plate and turned around. "I was just welcoming Lucy to the house."

Jo raised a brow. "This is her third day here."

"One can never be too late." He opened the dishwasher and began stacking the racks.

Jo looked at me. "You better get in line if you don't want to miss out on your meds. Then you can get back to cleaning up."

"Right. Thanks." I was so consumed with what may or may not have happened between Marcus and Amelia that I had completely forgotten about my meds. Then it hit me. She also said I could get back to cleaning up.

Shit! I was stuck on dish duty with Aaron.

Letting a whole heap of profanities loose in my head, I went over and joined the back of the line. Another few late stragglers joined, standing behind me as we slowly began to move forward.

By the time I'd reached the front of the line, Marcus and Justin were still nowhere to be seen. I wanted to ask Jo where they were, but I didn't want to get them in trouble if she didn't know they were missing.

I popped the pills into my mouth and washed them down, then slowly walked over to the sink. "What do you want me to do?" I asked the older guy, whom I thought was named Phil.

"You can help stack the dishwasher then wipe down the tables."

My stomach churned as I went over to the industrial dishwasher where my least favorite person in the world was eyeing me, with that same smirk on his lips that I wanted to rip off his face.

I picked up two glasses and loaded them onto the rack.

"You know what I heard?" Aaron said.

I sighed. "What?"

"That Marcus's mouth had been somewhere else right before he kissed you."

I scrunched up my face in disgust. "You know what I think?"

"What?"

"I think you portray yourself to be this big boy who loves playing the field, sowing his oats or however else you want to say 'screwing every girl he can.' But really, you're just trying to substitute the love you didn't get from Mommy. Because Mommy didn't love you. You were nothing but a parasite to her that included a fortnightly check to pay for her drug addic—"

His hand slammed around my throat, driving me back. I hit the cupboard behind me, knocking the air from my lungs.

I silently pleaded for Phil to help me, but thanks to his years of being a victim of abuse, his fear held him frozen where he stood.

I clutched helplessly at his hand as I gasped for air that never made it to my lungs.

"You fucking little bitch. You read my file," he spat at me, his tone low enough so no one else could hear what he was saying. "Then you should also know I'm capable of killing when I'm pushed too—"

Aaron flew back, hitting the open door of the dishwasher, snapping the door off its hinges. Justin was on top of him, laying his fist into Aaron's face over and over again.

Holding my hand against my throat, I sucked in a sharp breath, relief flooding through me as oxygen finally hit my lungs.

Jo raced over to Justin. "Get off him!"

Someone's hand closed over mine, gently pulling my fingers away from my throat. Their head dipped down, and I finally forced my gaze away from the commotion to see Marcus standing in front of me, inspecting my neck.

He straightened, revealing anger raging in his eyes, which were practically glowing. "Are you okay?"

I nodded. "I think so." My voice deceived me, coming out strained and hoarse.

I swallowed, trying to relieve the pressure in my throat. It did nothing. I could still feel Aaron's fingers gripping my throat.

Marcus wrapped his arms around me, drawing me against his

chest. "I'm sorry. I should've been here." He placed a tender kiss on the top of my head.

My body started trembling. I wasn't sure if it was from the rush of adrenalin or because of the close proximity to him. Either way I held on tightly, burying my face against his chest.

"Marcus," Jo said. "Take Luciana to her bedroom. I'll have Doctor Watts come look at her after she's finished with Aaron."

Keeping one hand around my waist, Marcus guided me past Aaron who was wiping blood from a gash to his cheek, his cold, hard stare directed at me.

Justin was nowhere to be seen.

CHAPTER 21

$\mathcal{M}$arcus helped keep me from falling on my ass as my legs trembled with every step I took toward the stairs. Before I could attempt the first step, he swept me into his arms and carried me up to my bedroom, where he laid me on the bed, my head propped up against the pillows.

Marcus sat beside me and smoothed my hair away from my face. "What happened?"

"I said something I shouldn't have," I replied, my voice still hoarse.

"Nothing excuses what he did to you." Marcus stood, walked into the bathroom, and came back holding a glass.

I pulled myself up into a sitting position, took the glass from him, and put it to my lips. The water relieved the burning sensation as it went down my throat, but as soon as I finished, the burn returned.

"Do you want me to get you another one?"

I shook my head as I placed the glass on the bedside table.

Marcus sat beside me again, his hand finding mine. "What happened?"

"I already told you. I said something to him I shouldn't have."

"Which was?"

I looked at our entwined fingers. I couldn't help but wonder if those same hands had done things to Amelia that would tear my heart apart. My gaze moved up to his lips as I wondered if Aaron had been right.

"What did you say to him?" Marcus prompted again.

Fighting back tears, I said, "I told him the reason why he was here."

"Shit." He ran his hand down his face. "I shouldn't have left you alone."

"I shouldn't have said what I did."

"No. He should never have touched you. Nothing you say gives him the right to lay a finger on you. And if I'd been there…"

Silence enveloped us, crushing me as my mind went everywhere I didn't want it to go. "Where were you?"

"I was with Justin," he eventually said. "We needed to sort out a few things."

I nodded.

"I'm sorry we didn't have that talk."

I nodded again. "It doesn't matter."

"Yes, it does."

I looked away. My chest was heavy with fear. I couldn't help but let what Aaron had said get to me.

Marcus placed his finger under my chin and turned my face until my eyes met his. "Yes, it does. There are things I need to tell you. Things that are going to make no sense at all. Things that are going to make you angry. Things—"

"I already know," I said. "Aaron so kindly filled me in."

He furrowed his brow. "What exactly did Aaron tell you?"

I once again lowered my gaze to our hands. "That you've been sneaking into Amelia's room and screwing her brains out every night since you arrived."

"And you believe him?"

"I don't know what to believe."

"Believe what's in your heart, and know that I will never and have never looked at anyone since the day I met you. You're the girl I was talking about. You captured my heart a long time ago, and I think you know I'm not talking about the day I arrived here at Millford."

"Sophia thinks I should stay away from you if you think I'm that girl."

"What do you think?"

"I think I take on other people's emotions. And the rational part of me thinks you wish I was that girl, and I'm taking on your pain and imagining I'm that girl to ease your suffering."

"And the irrational?" he prompted.

God, I hoped he wasn't just making fun of me to later have a laugh about it with the boys—whoever they might be. "The irrational part of me believes I'm her. I don't know how that's possible, but I feel it within my heart. I know you. I love you even though I've only just met you. The things I feel… These memories I can't explain…"

"What do you remember?"

"I remember being in love with you. I remember you holding my hand as we looked up at the stars. I remember you making love to me and feeling that love at my very core…" I broke off when I saw a fire light up his eyes and a smile form on his lips, which I so desperately wanted to kiss. "But none of that makes any sense."

"You're right. It doesn't. This has never happened before," he said more to himself than me.

My door swung open. "What's never happened before?" Justin asked, waltzing into my room as if it were his.

"Get out," Marcus warned in a low tone.

"I think not." Justin sat on the foot of the bed and curled his hand over my shin.

Marcus's grip on my hand tightened. "Get your hand off her."

Justin was completely unscathed by Marcus's threat. "So what was he telling you, Lucy?"

"Nothing."

"We all know that's not true. I clearly remember Marcus saying this time's different."

I pulled my legs up the bed and crossed them. "It's none of your business."

The air turned cold, sending a shiver down my spine as Justin said, "Oh, I think it's completely my business."

"I think you should get your butt in your own room and pack your bags," Jo said, coming into the room.

The cold air instantly evaporated, but my bones were still chilled from his words.

Getting up, Justin glared at Marcus and strode out of the room.

Jo stood at the end of my bed, her eyes locked on Marcus's fingers entwined with mine. "How are you feeling?"

"I'll be okay."

She nodded. "I'm not sure what provoked Aaron to do that, but I want you to know I've called the police, and they'll be here within the hour to take your statement. Also, Aaron will be leaving us today."

"What?" I asked. "No. You can't. He needs to be here."

"We have a no violence policy at Millford, and both Aaron and Justin broke that rule. There are no exceptions."

Guilt filled me to no end. I knew Aaron was an ass, but he wouldn't have reacted if I hadn't said what I did. He needed help more than I did. I couldn't be helped. He could. And Justin... He didn't deserve to be kicked out for defending me.

"I'm sure you don't mind staying with Lucy for a bit longer, do you, Marcus?"

"Of course not."

"Good." Jo backed away to the door. "Let me know if she gets worse."

"Will do," Marcus said.

Jo left, and to my surprise, she closed the door behind her.

CHAPTER 22

*M*arcus smoothed his thumb over my hand. "We can't stay here."

"What? Why?"

"I don't have time to explain. I need to get you out of here."

"Because of Aaron?" I asked. "Jo said he's leaving."

Marcus edged closer. "No. It's not because of Aaron."

"Then why?"

Marcus lifted my legs at the knees, unfolding them as he shifted my legs over his thighs. "This time's different." He smoothed his hand over my thigh as if he'd done it a million times. The fire burning within me was like nothing I'd ever experienced. Yet, there was a part of me, deep within my soul, that loved the familiarity of his hands on me.

"What's going on? I asked, trying to make sense of the way I was feeling. "Why do I feel as if...? Why am I in love with a guy I've only just met?"

He released his breath slowly, a mixture of pain and relief in his eyes. I inched closer to him, aching to make the pain go away. Before I knew it, I'd climbed onto his lap, straddling him. And God, it felt good. It felt right.

His hands closed around my hips, and he tipped his head down, resting his forehead against mine. All questions were forgotten. All urgency was gone. I wanted to stay in the safe haven of his arms for the rest of eternity.

Tipping my chin up, I brushed my lips over his. He cupped the nape of my neck with his hand, bringing my lips back to his when I went to pull away. The tenderness of his kiss soon deepened into a sweet, searing kiss, further igniting the fire that would forever burn in my soul.

Emotions swirled within me as an unexplainable relief slowly flooded not only from my heart but also my mind. Everything about him seemed familiar but new at the same time. It was as if I'd kissed him a thousand times before—but not like this. This time was different. This time I knew him.

The more I kissed him, the more I remembered. Flashes of us together sharing precious moments in our lives but also the mundane moments like shopping at the markets or cleaning up after a meal. What I didn't understand was how I had these memories in a time when I wasn't alive. I looked the same but different, and so did Marcus.

His love for me was evident in everything he did. I was everything to him. I was also his undoing. Snippets of that haunted look he so often displayed was evident in the eyes of the man in my memories.

Marcus gripped my shoulders as he slowly eased up and placed a soft kiss on the corner of my lips then another on my jaw.

Closing my eyes, I tipped my head back as he trailed a line of tender kisses over the bruises on my neck, stopping when he reached the edge of my sweater.

Pulling me back up, he stared into my eyes. His breaths were coming out just as unevenly as mine, and he looked to be fighting the same desires I was.

In the back of my mind, I knew that should've been a red flag. I felt everything toward him that he felt toward me. Except the sadness.

I never took on his sadness.

That wasn't normal for me. I'd only ever experienced sadness. Marcus was the exception. The only thing I felt when I was around Marcus was his love for me and my love for him. It was an unrelenting love that would last for the rest of my existence.

"I know you have so many questions for me, and believe me, I want to tell you." He licked his lips that I so desperately wanted to reacquaint myself with. "But we need to leave. I don't know if you trust me yet, but I need you to do just that."

"I do trust you," I whispered. "I don't know that I should, but I do." I paused for a moment then said, "And it scares me."

The haunted look in his eyes came back with full vengeance, making me want to take back my confession.

The door swung open. Justin was back. "It *should* scare you."

Marcus went rigid as he glared at him. "This is none of your business. You are not meant to interfere."

Justin waved Marcus off as he strode over to the bed. He flopped down then propped himself up with his elbow, his head resting on his hand. "You two look awfully close. Didn't you guys only just meet?" He raised a brow, a playful grin on his lips. "And you're already sitting on his lap? Who knows what might've happened if I didn't show up when I did?"

I went to get off, but Marcus held me in place, his arms tightening around me. "What do you want, Justin?"

His lips curled up into a smirk. "I think you already know the answer to that question."

"Well, *I* don't," I said. "So why don't you enlighten me?"

Justin narrowed his eyes at me. "Don't you take on the emotions of others?" When I didn't answer, he continued. "You see, you don't take me as the kind of girl who'd climb onto the lap of someone she'd only just met. So, it got me thinking—"

"That I'm going to break every bone in your body if you don't shut the hell up," Marcus warned as thunder cracked in the distance and the room suddenly fell dark from the clouds rolling in.

Ignoring him, Justin continued. "It got me thinking that maybe he's projecting these feelings onto you, and because you take on others' pain, maybe you're feeling the source of his pain and also making yourself the cure. I can tell you firsthand, you do look like the girl who's done this to Marcus."

"I..." I shifted my gaze to Marcus, wishing what Justin had said didn't make sense. But it did.

Marcus swept my hair behind my ear and cupped my jaw in his hand. "You do take on others' pain. But when have you ever taken on their memories?"

"Never," I whispered, knowing that was all I needed to know.

Smiling, Marcus kissed me then stood. He lowered my feet onto the floor and led me into the bathroom.

Justin followed. "Tell me if you've had any memories past—"

Marcus smashed his fist into Justin's jaw, knocking him against the tiled wall. He'd moved so fast I didn't even realize he'd let go of my hand. I could still feel the warm tingles of his skin against mine.

Marcus closed his hand around Justin's neck as another crack of thunder rumbled a little closer to the house. "Don't overstep the boundaries. You know the rules."

Justin laughed then knocked Marcus's hand away. He walked toward the door, the smirk still plastered on his face as he looked at me. "Don't go anywhere."

CHAPTER 23

"Who is he?" I asked as Marcus packed my bag.

"Just an old acquaintance," he replied.

I sat on the toilet lid. "He seems like more than just an old acquaintance."

"We have history." Marcus walked to the sink, grabbed my toiletries, and returned to my bag.

"Is that it?" I asked. "Is that all you're going to give me?"

He knelt down and zipped up my bag. "That's all I can give you until I explain things."

"Which you won't do until we've left here," I said flatly.

Marcus stood and strode over to me. "I know it's a lot to ask, but I need you to trust me."

"I do," I whispered without giving it a moment's thought. I grabbed his hands and stood, wishing the cast wasn't there so there was no obstruction between us.

Leaning down, he kissed me. "You have no idea how long I've waited to hear that." Letting go of one of my hands, he picked up my suitcase and led me downstairs.

"Where are you going?" Sophia asked. She was standing next to Justin and three others whom I was sure should've been anywhere but there. Even with the impending storm, there was no way Jo would've given everyone free time just because of what happened with Aaron.

Justin retreated from the group, disappearing into the dining room.

"We're leaving," Marcus answered for me.

"I was talking to Lucy," Sophia said, coming closer to us. "What's going on, *Lucy*?"

I looked up at Marcus, who smiled back at me. "We're leaving."

"Can I talk to you for a moment?"

Hating myself for doing so, I shook my head. "We don't have time."

"Time for what?" she asked, her frustration growing. "You can't do this. You can't throw your recovery away for some guy you just met who'll probably piss off in a couple of days, leaving you back at square one with the same problems you came here to get help for."

"Sophia's right," Jo said, walking into the room with Justin in tail. "If you leave now, you won't be able to come back. Your spot will be filled and you'll have to wait in line. And it could be months before you get another chance here."

Jo sighed. "Look, I can't tell you what to do. It's your choice and your choice alone to stay here, but I can tell you from experience that you will be back. Whatever you think you feel will only be fleeting. You can't truly move on with your life until you've accepted and worked through what brought you here in the first place."

John's words replayed in my head, "What we need to work out is whether we should trust our heart or not." "I trust my heart," I muttered to myself, knowing I was making the right decision. I knew my mother would try to have me committed, but I didn't care. I drew in a deep breath then said, "I think we both know I'm beyond help." Leaving with Marcus felt right. Maybe I'd live to regret it. Maybe I wouldn't. But the not knowing would kill me.

Jo didn't deny what I'd said. I'd struck the truth, and she knew it. "You'll need to sign out before you leave."

"Okay."

"You, too, Marcus."

"Of course."

She nodded before heading down the hallway toward her office.

Justin walked over to us. "I thought I said you needed to stay here."

"And I thought I told you that you need to stop overstepping your boundaries," Marcus replied. "Follow the rules."

Justin barked out a laugh. "That's a good one coming from you, considering that's why we're in this mess in the first place."

What the hell did that mean?

Marcus led me outside and down the stairs as I tried to figure out what rules he was talking about. And why Justin blamed Marcus for whatever mess they were in.

My mind was telling me I should be wary, but my heart was leading the way, pushing the subtle warnings to the back of my mind and listening to the big piece of my soul that knew without a doubt that Marcus was the only person in the world I could trust.

Justin followed us to Marcus's car as lightning ripped open the sky with flashes of white. "You know I'm right, yet you keep this stupid hope alive in your heart that she will forgive you."

Marcus turned on him with inhuman speed, grabbing Justin's shirt in his fist. He was seething, barely controlling his rage. "It's not up to you to..."

Justin chuckled. "Not wanting to finish that sentence?" He shook his head, and then his gaze fell on me. "Why don't you ask him what he was going to say?"

I swallowed hard, realizing there was a whole crap load of things going on that I wasn't privy to. I looked between the two men, instantly knowing which one I trusted.

Keeping my mouth shut, I hopped into Marcus's car, closed the door, and waited for him to get in. Out of the corner of my eye, I saw black figures hiding among the trees, but when I looked again, they were gone. I shook my head, praying I wasn't seeing things and even more screwed-up than I'd first thought.

Marcus leaned closer to Justin, said something I couldn't hear, and released his grip on Justin's shirt.

Marcus hopped into the car as Justin took a couple of steps back.

"I'll see you soon." Justin grinned then gave us a small wave as we pulled away, heading down the long driveway, leaving the first place I'd ever felt at peace.

I reached over and placed my hand over Marcus's. Peace was leaving with me.

CHAPTER 24

$\mathcal{I}$ rubbed my eyes, the sun's rays hitting my face as it rose in the distance. Fearing my last memories were a dream, I jerked wide-awake and turned to find the most handsome man I'd ever seen sitting beside me.

I smiled when he turned his head toward me. "How long have I been sleeping?"

Marcus reached over and cupped my jaw, brushing his thumb over my lips as if he were giving me a kiss the only way our current circumstance would allow. "All night."

He lowered his hand to mine and squeezed it. "We'll be arriving shortly. We're only a couple of minutes away."

I stretched my neck and looked out the window at the sun rising over the water as we drove along the winding road snaking along the edge of the cliff. "Where are we?"

"Byron Bay."

I raised my brow. I figured we had to be in another state if we were driving half the day and all night. "Shouldn't we have been there by now?"

He turned off the main road onto a narrow street surrounded by lush green trees reaching up into the sky. "I had to make a stop."

"What for?"

"I couldn't drive all night if I wanted to get you here in one piece."

Marcus took a left, pulling onto a long driveway secured by two massive gates that swung open without him pressing any buttons.

Soon, we arrived at a house that looked to be worth more than what I would make in my life. It was a sprawling single-story, ultra-modern home at the far end of a couple of acres of lush green grass surrounded by trees. It was a hidden piece of paradise.

"Welcome home," he said.

I tore my gaze away from the amazing piece of architecture. "You live here?"

Marcus pulled into a garage where another five cars were already parked, then killed the engine. "Yep. This is home." He opened the car door and came around to open mine.

"Your parents aren't going to mind me being here?" I asked, following him around to the trunk.

He chuckled as he grabbed my bags then closed the trunk. "I don't live with my parents."

My eyes widened. "This is all yours?"

Marcus walked over to me and laced his fingers with mine. "It's ours." When he saw the look on my face he said, "I probably shouldn't have said that just yet, huh?"

My pulse was beating erratically as the tiny angel that sounded so much like Justin sat on my shoulder, telling me this guy was seriously deluded and I was nothing more than a replacement.

"Come on." Marcus tugged my hand. "Let's take your things inside. Then we can sit down and talk about why I say such weird things."

Stepping through the oversized garage door into the house, I drew in a sharp breath as I took in my surroundings. Floor to ceiling windows ran the whole way across the lounge room, dining room, and kitchen. It was an open floor plan with a modern fireplace separating the lounge and dining room.

"Follow me." He led the way down a hall, past a few closed doors, and up two steps to another lounge area. "This room is yours." Marcus pointed to the door to the left. "And that's mine." He gestured to the next door about ten meters away.

Opening the door to my room, Marcus stepped inside then waited for me to follow, carefully watching my every move.

"Wow," I said as I looked around what was supposedly my room. It looked more like a suite in a hotel.

Marcus carried my bag into the gigantic closet complete with a round ottoman in the middle for me to sit and look at the vast empty spaces on the racks and shelves. It was almost too much and only reminded me of what little I had.

"I'll leave you to settle in." He cupped my cheek in his hand then kissed me. It started out as a peck but quickly built into something so much more. I hooked my arm with the cast around his neck, and I realized I truly wanted to live. I wanted to see what tomorrow held, where we would be in a year. I could see myself spending the rest of eternity with the man who made me feel alive.

Pulling away, a smile spread across his face as he looked deep into my eyes. "I can't believe I forgot how good you taste." Marcus kissed me again then stepped back. "Come find me when you've finished here." That haunted look reappeared in his eyes.

I smiled and nodded, wondering what would cause that kind of grief to appear during a time when he was supposed to be happy. *Her*. The girl Justin said Marcus was using me to replace. That was who.

CHAPTER 25

I sighed. Watching him walk away was painful, which was pretty stupid. I had so many questions, and he held all the answers. Or so I hoped.

I feared that when we eventually did have that talk, the little angel with Justin's voice would be right. And whatever he was going to tell me would crush my soul. Only it wouldn't be eventually. We were going to have our talk in a few minutes.

Nerves twisted my stomach into knots that seemed impossible to undo. I half wished that my love for him would diminish as he put distance between us, but I think I was too far gone. My heart ached for him in a way that wasn't normal.

I unzipped my bag, grabbed a pile of clothes, and turned to put them on a shelf but stopped. I didn't want to unpack. I wanted answers. But more importantly, I wanted him.

I dumped the clothes back into the bag and strode with purpose through the house. My sense of direction was led by an unexplainable force pulling me toward the kitchen where I found Marcus standing behind the counter, his elbows leaning against the stone bench as he held a glass of ice cubes that were barely covered with what looked to be scotch.

"Hi," I said, wiggling my fingers.

Marcus looked up at me, his jaw clenching as he stared into my eyes.

I bit my lip, fearing what had him so on edge. I could handle just about anything he had to tell me, except that he'd changed his mind and no longer wanted me here. That would be the end of me. Only, it wouldn't because I would continue to live an existence of not only feeling others' pain, but experiencing an all-consuming emptiness in the place where my heart was. Without him I knew my newfound need to live would be gone.

Marcus straightened, finished off his drink, and placed the glass back on the bench. "Did you settle in okay?"

"Not really," I replied. "I figured I can unpack after we have our chat." I bit my lip again, waiting for him to say something.

Marcus walked over and brushed his thumb across my lips. "Don't do that."

I released my lip from my teeth. "Sorry. Nervous habit."

"You have nothing to be nervous about."

"Then why do you look so nervous?"

He curled his hand around my hip. "Because what I'm about to tell you in these next few minutes could have you running as far away from me as possible. Or, if I'm lucky enough, you'll stay."

Oh, shit. The knots in my stomach tightened as Justin's voice in my head became louder. "Am I replacing the girl you lost?"

His lip quivered ever so slightly, making me fear the worst. *"You are the girl I lost."*

My breath caught in my throat as those six words replayed over and over in my mind. Marcus had confessed he'd been talking about me when he'd shared in group therapy, but Justin somehow got under my skin, making me question if I was that lucky.

I was never lucky.

"Say something," he said softly.

There were a million things I should've said, but what came out was the most important one of all. "I'm the girl you love?" To any sane person that reaction would've been stupid. But I wasn't sane. I was certifiably crazy.

Marcus brushed my hair behind my ear. "More than anything." He cupped my jaw in his hands and kissed me. "I've loved you since the very first moment I laid eyes on you. And I've never stopped loving you since." He kissed me tenderly, his sweet, soft lips pulling me into the depths of the unknown, and I was only too willing to dive in. But I had to remind myself there were questions I needed to ask before I completely lost myself in him.

"These memories?" I asked, unable to take my eyes off his lips, which I so desperately wanted to feel against mine again.

"They're all real." He pressed a gentle kiss on the corner of my lips, his fingers grazing my skin as he ran them down my forearm. "I think you should sit down while you hear what I have to say."

I nodded and followed him over to the couch. Just as I was about to sit, he wrapped his arms around me, pulling me into a hug. Lowering his head, Marcus pressed a kiss on the soft spot just below my earlobe. Then he straightened. "Just in case you want to run."

I smiled, stood on the balls of my feet, and gave him a kiss. "Just a taste of what's to come." I wasn't sure where the confidence came from, considering he was my first ever kiss. Hell, he was the first guy to ever touch me, but somehow, I didn't feel as if I were the inexperienced virgin I actually was.

I sat on the couch, and Marcus lowered himself on the seat beside me. He stared at me with that same haunted look in his eyes and eventually said, "What I'm about to tell you is going to sound completely nuts. And you might think I belong in a psych ward—"

I choked on a laugh. "Many people say I do."

He smiled. "No, you don't." Marcus reached over and twirled a piece of my hair around his finger, delaying his confession. "I'm not what you think I am. And there's no easy way of saying this, so I'm just going to come right out and say it and hope you're not going to run." Dropping the strand of my hair, he took a deep breath then breathed out slowly. "I'm not human."

I blinked hard, a laugh bubbling up in my throat at the absurdity of what he'd said. "What do you mean you're not human?"

"I met you a long, long time ago... You're the girl I couldn't collect."

My breath caught in my throat as Justin's words screamed through my mind. I opened my mouth to say something, but no words came out. Marcus was even crazier than I was.

"I'm an angel of death."

"You're what?" I laughed nervously. Adrenalin pumped through my veins as my body kicked into flight mode. Only my soul had me locked where I sat, trusting him and telling me his confession was true. I was pretty sure that just tipped the scale as to who was crazier out of the two of us. I was taking the trophy in that contest.

"I'm an angel of death—a Soul Collector. I met you three hundred and fifty-four years, three hundred and twenty-nine days ago when I was supposed to take your soul to the other side. But when I saw you..." He paused, the unrelenting love in his eyes returning as his gaze swept the length of my body like he was remembering the first moment he saw me. "I couldn't. I couldn't let you die... So, I saved you."

That haunted look quickly consumed him. "It ended up being the biggest mistake of my existence."

"That's definitely something a girl doesn't want to hear," I muttered, focusing on the least important part of his spiel.

"I'm responsible for your endless suffering. As part of my punishment, I have to watch you go through something no one should ever have to go through. Then you'll die, only to be reborn with the exact same curse. It's always the same—except this time. This time's different."

"How so?" I asked, completely captivated by his story.

"This time you remember things you shouldn't. I knew the moment you said your name. You weren't born with the name Luciana, were you?"

I shook my head, trying to absorb what he was saying. "It was Zoe."

"When did you know your name?"

"You mean Luciana?"

He nodded.

"I think I always knew." What he was saying should've had me running as far away from him as possible. I should've feared for my life.

I didn't.

Everything he said felt true. Who was I to say angels didn't exist when my whole life was an unexplainable paranormal curse giving me the unfortunate ability to take on others' emotions?

"Show me," I said, trying to ignore the little angel with Justin's voice on my shoulder telling me I was crazy.

"Show you what?"

"Your wings."

He looked away. "They've been severed."

I raised my brow, Justin's voice telling me how convenient his excuse was and how Marcus was asking me to believe in something that wasn't tangible.

Marcus lifted his shirt over his head, revealing his body, which was sheer perfection, every single muscle screaming at me to touch it. Before I made a complete fool out of myself, he twisted around, his back to me. "Look closely and you can see the scars."

I inched closer and tried to find proof that big old wings had been hacked off his back. "Huh," I said, seeing two lines that reflected the light, unlike the rest of his skin.

I ran my finger down the line on the right, trying to see if it smudged. It didn't. It was real.

Lifting my hand with the cast, I traced the other line. It, too, was real, a stark contrast to the rest of his skin.

Spreading my hands over his back, I was instantly cast into another memory. *Marcus and I were sitting on the steps overlooking the beach, watching the sunrise over the water, the soft morning light dancing over the ripples in the ocean.*

Marcus was on the step below me—shirtless, and I was absently tracing the lines of his scars. I leaned forward, placed a tender kiss on the crook of his neck, and breathed in his intoxicating scent, which was like no other that walked the Earth. It settled the insanity in my soul, allowing me to breathe.

Marcus ran his hands down my calves, grabbed my ankles, and wrapped my legs around his waist. His fingers gently caressed every curve of my legs within his reach.

Hooking my arms under his, I gripped his shoulders as I continued to place a trail of kisses over his collarbone.

My memory vaporized, and I realized I was replaying the scene in this life. My lips were pressed against his back, and my hands were gripping his shoulders in the exact same way.

I knew I should've pulled away, but I couldn't. And no matter how crazy his explanation to what was going on with us was, I was happy to jump head first into crazy-land with him.

Marcus turned around. The intensity in his gaze was all-consuming. Closing the little distance between us, he brushed his lips over mine as if he were testing if I were real.

Taking the opportunity to let him know just how real I was, I ran my hands through his hair as I climbed onto his lap, straddling him.

A soft growl came from deep within him as he melted into the kiss. His fingers trailed over my skin just above the band of my jeans. Then he slipped his hand under my sweater. The sensation of his skin against mine awakened the fire in my soul.

Memories of us making love time and time again burned in my mind. I was in love with him in every single memory of our lives through the ages. However, none of them compared to what I was feeling now. I'd never had these memories in past lives, and now that I did, my love for him in all those lifetimes was somehow compacted into this one.

It didn't matter what Justin or anyone else had said. I knew in my heart that I would follow Marcus down the rabbit hole and never climb out.

CHAPTER 26

$\mathcal{M}$arcus cupped my head in his hands as he eased our kiss into small, tender brushes of our lips against each other's. Pulling back, he smiled and ran his hands down my arms before folding his arms around me. "Thank you."

A small laugh escaped my lips. That was not what I was expecting. "You don't have to thank me."

"Yeah, I do." He pressed a kiss on the tip of my nose. "You have no idea how scared I've been that you would run."

"Never," I said, my voice coming out a little raspier than I would've liked.

He brushed my hair behind my shoulder, placed a tender kiss on the curve of my neck, and pulled back, locking his eyes with mine. "How much do you remember?"

A lump formed in my throat when I thought about him being the guy from my dreams. If they weren't exactly dreams and more like memories, then Marcus was the only one capable of killing me. And he'd done it on more than one occasion.

Looking at the man in front of me, who watched me as if I were the greatest wonder in life, I couldn't fathom how he could ever do that to me. I didn't want him to kill me.

I wanted to live.

I wanted to spend the rest of eternity in his arms, side by side the way we were meant to be.

Looking into his eyes, I could see there was something he was afraid of, and no matter how much I wanted to be honest with him, I couldn't let him know that I knew on the evening before my nineteenth birthday he would drive a knife through my heart and I would take my last breath as he whispered "Sorry" into my ear.

Forcing that thought to the back of my mind, I smiled. "I remember the way you loved me. The way you held me... So many precious moments we've shared." I softly ran my fingers down his back, right where I thought his scars were. "I remember the scars... And how you long to take flight again. I also remember just how much I love you."

I kissed him before he could see there was something else I remembered and neglected to say. The moment our lips touched, I wasn't the girl from my lifetime. I was the girl from my past, filled with a need to have him in every way possible.

But I wasn't that girl. I was an inexperienced eighteen-year-old who somehow knew exactly how to turn him on. How to get under his skin and make sure I was the only woman he ever thought about.

I stopped kissing him momentarily as I wondered where that thought had come from and what the hell it meant.

Marcus gently ran his fingers over the bruising on my neck. "I'm so sorry."

I smiled. "As I keep telling you, it's not your fault." I wrapped my hand around his and lowered it to my lap. "Besides, it hardly hurts at all."

That was a big, fat lie. However, I wasn't going to make him feel any worse for something he had no control over.

"You're lying, but I appreciate the sentiment."

I pursed my lips, annoyed I was so transparent to him. Usually I could hide just about anything, and no one would suspect a thing. I'd spent my whole life pretending I was someone I wasn't. Yet, Marcus could see right through me. It was as if he knew me better than I knew myself.

He stood, pulling me up with him. "I know someone who can help you," he said, leading me toward the back door.

"I'm fine. I don't need any help."

"Yes, you do. She can fix both your neck and your wrist."

I tugged on his hand as he unlatched the lock on the sliding door. "I don't need anyone to fix anything."

He turned to me, pain written all over his face as his gaze settled on my neck. "Yes, you do."

"It's just a couple of bruises—"

Marcus grabbed my hand with the cast on my wrist. "This isn't a couple of bruises."

"No, but it's..." My voice trailed off as I caught sight of a woman climbing over the wall next to the pool and dropping to the ground in a heap.

Marcus whipped his head around to face her. "Shit."

She rolled onto her back and drunken laughter bellowed from her plump, red lips. A moment later, she pulled herself into a sitting position and brushed her bright red hair away from her face, revealing the same color eyes Marcus had.

"What are you doing here?" Marcus asked, stepping in front of me, his muscular shoulders blocking my view of her.

I moved to the side just in time to see the woman push herself to her feet then stagger a few steps before pulling her shit together. And boy was she a sight to see. Her toned, golden-brown legs seemed to go on for miles, and her boobs deserved to be on the cover of a porn magazine. She was absolutely beautiful, which drove me crazy with jealousy. I'd never been the jealous type. Then again I'd never had a completely mesmerizing woman climb over the fence onto the property owned by the man I loved. Actually, I barely remember having a boyfriend to be jealous over, so this feeling was completely new to me. But it was real. And it was eating away at my insides as her all too comfortable gaze fell on Marcus, and a smile formed on her lips.

She brushed her hands down her teeny, tiny shorts. "I heard you were back." A grin pulled at her lips. "And I heard you brought her."

CHAPTER 27

*W*hat. The. Hell?

"You've been drinking," Marcus said as she strode toward us with a small swagger in her step.

She clapped her hands. "Captain Obvious does it again."

Huh?

Her smile dropped. "I guess this means... you and I won't be..." She bit her lip in a way that would've brought any man to his knees.

"No, Abby, we won't."

It felt as if she'd shoved her hand inside my chest and squeezed the crap out of my heart. I looked between her and Marcus, my thoughts going everywhere I didn't want them to go.

Abby drew her brows together as she looked at me. A second later, her eyes went wide. "Oh, no, no, no." Tossing her head back, she laughed. "He and I," Abby pointed to Marcus then herself, "we don't do *that*. We've *never* done *that*. I've done it with almost everyone else here but not him." She poked Marcus's shoulder. "*He* is off-limits." She poked him again. "*He* only has eyes for you." She flicked her tongue out a couple of times then pulled a strand of hair from her mouth and threw it on the ground.

"Come on, Abby." Marcus wrapped his arm around her waist. "Let's go inside and get you sobered up."

He helped Abby to the couch then headed to the kitchen.

Abby pulled herself into a sitting position but immediately slid back down. "So, are the rumors true?"

"What rumors?" I asked, standing in the middle of the lounge room, not knowing what to do with myself.

"That you remember."

I folded my arms across my chest, unsure how to answer that question. I had no idea who the hell she was—

"That is none of your business," Marcus said, coming back into the lounge with a glass of water in his hand.

"The hell it isn't." Abby twisted around to face him. "I've had to listen to you whine about your dearest Lu-Lu for God knows how long—not to mention your constant mood swings—so I think it's completely my business."

He handed her the glass. "I don't whine, and I certainly don't have mood swings."

Abby barked out a laugh. "You have more mood swings than a room full of pubescent teens."

Marcus raised a brow. "You didn't just compare me to a pubescent teen, did you?"

She tipped her head back and downed the water. "I did, and it's true." The glass rolled from her fingers onto the seat.

Marcus snatched the glass just before the last drop of water spilled on the couch. "Don't listen to her, Lucy. Abby's just a drunk nymphomaniac who takes pleasure in other people's suffering."

Nymphomaniac? Jesus. What the hell did I get myself into?

Abby giggled. "You got that right."

Marcus shook his head and smiled. "I'm going to get you some black coffee. Now, play nice while I'm gone." Marcus looked sternly at Abby.

She saluted him. "Yes, sir." Abby watched Marcus as he walked toward the kitchen. As soon as he was out of sight, she whipped her head around to face me as fast as her drunken state allowed. "So, you remember him, huh?" She wiggled her brows, her drunken gaze lighting up.

"Um, yeah," I replied, shifting my feet, trying to figure out who she was and what—if any—relation she was to Marcus. "Don't take this the wrong way, but are you his sister or something?"

Abby barked out another laugh, then quickly shoved her hand over her mouth and glanced in Marcus's direction. Once she'd recovered, she said, "I'm not related to Marcus. I'm just the nymph who lives next door, whose been his drinking buddy on and off for the last few hundred years."

"Oh," I mouthed.

"Abby," Marcus called out in a warning tone. "I hope you're not pressuring Lucy."

"No," she called back, tipping her head in his direction. Rolling her head back to face me, she patted the seat next to her. "Come sit down. I promise I won't bite."

I stood my ground. "I'd rather stand." When she looked at me as if I'd hurt her feelings, I added, "I've been stuck in the car since yesterday. I kinda need to stretch my legs." She may not have been anyone I cared about, but Marcus clearly did, which meant I had to play nice.

She scrunched up her nose. "The feelings are getting worse, huh?"

I stared at her blankly. I had no idea what feelings she was talking about.

Abby rolled her eyes. "Feeling other people's pain and misery."

I don't know why I was surprised she knew that about me. Every single person I'd ever met had always dismissed my issues as being in my head. That was until I met Marcus.

I studied her, wondering how much I should say—if anything at all. Then it hit me; I couldn't feel her emotions either. "Why can't I feel you?"

A smirk played on her lips. "How much has Marcus told you about me?"

Absolutely nothing. The first I knew of her was when she climbed over his garden wall. "He hasn't mentioned you."

She snorted then pulled herself up into a sitting position—and actually stayed. "You don't take on our emotions. We're not human," she said as if it were common knowledge that entities walked among us.

The funny thing was, I could actually feel Justin, yet he was supposed to be otherworldly like Marcus. Justin's emotions may not have been as intense as humans' emotions, but I could still feel him.

"What are you?" I whispered.

"I'm a Succubus. And I can guarantee the myths are incorrect. Men want me, and they're never asleep," she said with a playful gleam in her eyes. "Anyway, that's enough about me. Let's talk about you."

"Let's not," Marcus said, coming back into the room with a coffee in hand.

Abby pulled a face at him as he handed her the mug.

Marcus sat on the couch opposite Abby. I doubted I was hiding my discomfort, but I tried to move past my own issues and give her a chance.

Taking a seat beside Marcus, I tried my best to get comfortable, but it was almost impossible thanks to the goddess with her legs and boobs in the same room. She looked completely at ease in his house, and no matter how much I hated myself for feeling this way, it grated my nerves nonetheless.

Why I had agreed to leave rehab was beyond me. Actually, it wasn't. It was as simple as Marcus asking me to go with him.

That was all I needed.

Marcus put his hand on my knee. I looked up at him and realized he was waiting for me to answer a question I never heard. "Sorry, what did you say?"

"I was just telling Abby how you were wanting to unpack your things."

"Oh, yeah," I said getting up, grateful for a way out of Abby's interrogation. "Nice to meet you." I smiled then quickly headed down the hallway toward the bedrooms.

When I reached my door, I stopped, my hand just inches from the handle. Even though I didn't want to be a part of their conversation, I wanted to know what they were saying. I'd never been the eavesdropping type of girl, but then again I'd never been in a situation like this. The love of my way too many lives was having a conversation with a woman who made me feel like a flat-chested little girl in comparison. They were most likely having a deep conversation about me, divulging things Marcus had been keeping to himself, afraid for whatever reason to divulge to me. I knew it was wrong, but curiosity got the better of me, so I tiptoed back down the hall until I could hear their conversation.

"I'm not going to discuss her with you, Abby."

"What?" she whispered loudly. "After everything—"

"While you're drunk. Sober up, and then yeah, I'll need your help."

"Ohh." She dragged out the word.

There was silence for a few seconds before Abby asked, "So, why do you think this time's different?"

"Not now, Abby."

"Come on," she whined. "You've got to give me something. I mean, this is huge. She remembers. She's *never* remembered. Maybe we can work out what it is about her and why you broke the rules."

Marcus breathed out harshly. "Justin was there."

She barked out a laugh. "Seriously?"

"Yep."

"Holy shit. What the hell for? Wait, he wasn't there for her, was he?"

"No. He was there for someone else."

She giggled. "That would've been pretty ironic if he was after her."

"There would've been nothing ironic about Justin coming for Luciana. She's mine, not his."

"Don't get your panties in a knot. I just meant that after all these years of you having to... you know, now when she remembers and Justin takes it away from you." She paused for a moment. "And I know what you're going to say, but you have to admit something's different about her—"

"Stop with that shit," Marcus said.

I could've slapped him one. I wanted to know what Abby was going to say.

"You and your friggin' pride. What if she's right? What if Luciana is—?"

"She's not. Mava's just an old woman who has lived way too long, believing shit some crazy woman told her. Even her own people think she has a few screws loose."

"What if she's not crazy? What if she's right?"

Marcus didn't answer straight away, but when he did, I could feel the pain in his voice. Not in the same way I normally took on others' pain. This was different. "I can't keep doing this."

"You've got no choice," Abby said. "This might be your one chance to stop it all. So don't be stupid enough to dismiss something that might be the answer to what you've been looking for the last few hundred years. Make this time count."

I would've given anything to know what and whom Abby was talking about. Something was telling me Abby was going to become my new best friend, because she may have been the only one who could help me—crazy woman and all.

CHAPTER 28

$\mathcal{A}$s I put away my measly belongings, my thoughts were consumed with what Abby had said to Marcus. I couldn't help but wonder if I'd ever done this before. If I'd slept in this room. In his room. And if I had, where were all my things from my previous stays?

Stays? I chastised myself. If I was going to believe in Soul Collectors and Succubi, then I was going to have to come to grips with what I was. Luciana was someone who lived many, many years ago, and I was plagued with her memories—my memories. I was Luciana reincarnated, and I needed to find a way to stop the vicious cycle.

I needed to speak with Abby.

Grabbing my toiletries, I went into the bathroom and put them away.

Staring at my reflection in the mirror, I tried to see not what was wrong with me, like I had done every single other time I'd looked in the mirror, but what was different about me that would make Marcus not fulfil his orders.

There was nothing special about me. I didn't look like them. I was the girl next door. I was ordinary. Yet, I couldn't deny my connection with Marcus. I was drawn to him, and I wished I knew if it was because of my past lives with him, or if I was in love with him just as much today as I was the very first moment I saw him. I didn't believe in insta-love, but with Marcus... Something was different. It was as if there was something else at play.

Someone knocked on the door. As much as I wanted it to be Abby so I could press her about the crazy woman, I knew it was Marcus.

"Come in," I called as I made my way into the bedroom.

He opened the door, his eyes lighting up, changing to molten amber the moment he caught sight of me. "Are you finished?"

"Uh, yeah," I replied. "I didn't have much to put away."

He strode over to me and took my hands in his. "We can change that whenever you want to go shopping."

As much as I didn't want to take him up on his offer, I needed to. I had only packed winter clothes for my stay in rehab, and I was in desperate need of summer clothes. Byron Bay was freakishly warm all year round. "Thanks. That'll be good."

He let go of my left hand and ran his fingers over my cast. "But first we need to get rid of this and those bruises on your neck."

I pulled away, fearing he was going to bring me to some healing person who'd heal the wound on my arm, taking away my easy access to slipping into unconsciousness if I ever got too far lost in others' pain again. As much as I wanted to deny my need, I couldn't let go.

"Or not," he said.

"Sorry, I just..." Not wanting to see the disappointment in his eyes, I looked at the cast. "I don't trust myself."

He nodded, letting go of my hand. "Okay, then. Let's go out for a bit."

For someone who wanted to sit back and relax, something told me he wanted out of the house, and I was sure it had everything to do with a certain Succubus. "Has Abby gone home?"

He put his hand on the small of my back and guided me out of the room. "She passed out on the couch not long after you left."

"Oh," I said, not believing a word. They'd had a big old conversation about me, which he didn't seem to want to share. "Does she always drink that much?" I asked, playing along. It didn't take a genius to work out the reason why he didn't want to tell me what Abby had said. I could see it every time I looked into his eyes. It was the same haunted look I found in mine.

"Sometimes," Marcus replied.

"Does that mean you drink just as much?"

"On occasions." He left it at that, but my gut instinct told me the occasions he was referring to were from the times he ended my suffering to the times he walked back into my life. I couldn't do it to him again. Knowing what he had to go through time after time was unbearable. I had to stop it.

True to his word, Abby was passed out on the couch. We made our way into the garage and got in the car. Before long, we were pulling into a parking spot on a street filled with boutique shops.

"Hey," I said, pulling on Marcus's hand as we headed toward the first store.

He stopped and turned to me, the color of his eyes taking my breath away. "What's wrong?"

"Nothing. I just wanted to say thank you."

Marcus brushed his fingers over my cheek then tucked a stray strand of hair behind my ear. "You don't ever need to thank me." There was something about the way he said it that made me believe him. He didn't want to be thanked for something he was to blame for. Guilt was a hard thing to carry around—especially when he'd been carrying it for centuries.

I placed a gentle kiss on the corner of his lips. "Thank you."

We spent the next couple of hours walking from one shop to the next, stocking up on summer essentials and a few nonessentials Marcus had insisted on.

My stomach churned on more than one occasion thanks to the effect Marcus had on women. At least they weren't as blatantly obvious as Amelia had been.

Marcus seemed completely oblivious to the effect he had on the women he came in contact with. Either that or he was just so used to the attention that he didn't react to it anymore.

With the shopping bags in the car, we drove back to his house as the afternoon sun beamed down on us. Somehow the day had slipped away from me, and I couldn't work out where the time had gone.

Abby wasn't anywhere to be seen when we arrived at home. "She's gone," I said, looking at the couch.

"Nope," Marcus replied, carrying my bags down the hall. "She's passed out in one of the rooms."

As much as I'd hoped that room was mine, I wasn't that lucky.

He placed the bags on the ottoman in the middle of the dressing room. "Why don't you get changed into something a little more comfortable and come meet me outside?" He chuckled. "That just sounded like the worst pickup line in the history of pickup lines, didn't it?"

I smiled. "Yeah, it kind of did."

"Sorry. I didn't mean it like that."

"You don't need to say sorry."

The corner of his lips turned up. "You know, I think I'm going to like not having to try to win you over again."

I placed my hand on his chest. "Something tells me you never had to try all that hard." Something told me he didn't have to try at all.

CHAPTER 29

*N*ot having a clue what to wear, I bypassed the dresses Marcus had insisted on buying me and decided on a pair of shorts and a tank.

Making my way through the house, I was relieved to hear snoring coming from the bedroom down the hall. One way or another I was going to talk to Abby, and I was glad she was still here because I wouldn't have to wait too long to get that chance.

Marcus was sitting at the bar beside the pool. There was a bottle of champagne on the black stone bench, two glasses, and an assortment of tapas and dips.

"Wow," I said, taking a seat opposite Marcus. "You didn't have to go to this much trouble."

"This is no trouble at all."

I looked at the assortment of food. "Doesn't look like it."

He gave me a grin that melted my heart. "Champagne?"

"Thanks."

Marcus poured the champagne, handed me a glass, and then raised his own. "Here's to us."

I lifted my glass. "Here's to us—and old beginnings."

He furrowed his brow but clinked his glass against mine without questioning me. "How are you settling in?"

"Good." I took a sip. "You've got an amazing place."

"Thanks." Marcus grabbed something that had prosciutto wrapped around it and took a bite.

I ran my fingers up and down the stem of my glass. "Can I ask you something?"

"Sure."

"How do you know Justin?"

He scratched his forehead. "Justin and I go way back... He's a Soul Collector like I am. Only, he still has his wings."

"There's more than one Soul Collector?"

"Of course," he said with a humorous tone. "It would be impossible for only one Soul Collector to be present for every death around the world."

"Fair enough." I took a sip, delaying my next question, fearing the answer had something to do with me. Even though I wasn't sure I wanted to hear the answer, my curiosity got the better of me. "What was he doing at rehab? I wouldn't think you guys would be able to get addicted to anything."

"That's not true. But you're right. Justin wasn't there because he had an addiction."

"Then why was he there?"

Marcus stared at me for a few moments then said, "For a collection."

A lump formed in my throat as various faces from rehab entered my mind. I tried swallowing the lump, but it refused to budge. "Who?"

"Do you really want to know?"

I didn't, but I couldn't help saying, "Yes."

"Sophia."

My breath caught in my throat. "Oh, God, no." I tried desperately to process the fact that she was about to die and whether there was anything I could do to stop it.

"You can't stop it. It's her time."

"Why? She's so young. I know she had her issues, but she's really trying to make things better."

"I know. Unfortunately that doesn't change anything."

I wanted so badly to race back to rehab to save her. I'd only known her for a couple of days—

"You can't save her," he reiterated. "Look what happened when I saved you."

That lump in my throat grew bigger with the realization that he was right. I never wanted another living soul to become like me. As hard as it was to let go, that was exactly what I had to do.

"If it helps, she's not going to the nether.

I furrowed my brow, but then it dawned on me what he meant. "So there really is a Heaven and a Hell?"

Marcus chuckled. "Where did you think Soul Collectors take the souls?"

"I don't know. To another dimension."

"Yeah, one filled with endless torment with different severities depending on what the person had done wrong, and the other filled with love, happiness, and all things good. Again, there are different levels of Heaven, depending on the purity of the soul. But it's not all it's cracked up to be."

"How so?"

"The powers that be don't always get it right."

I wondered which way he was supposed to take me. However, I couldn't bring myself to ask the question. "So, you just come down to Earth, pick up the soul, and fly away?"

"Pretty much."

"But you don't have wings?"

"I never said I still collect the souls."

I picked up something that looked good, but I had no idea what it was. "So, what do you do now?"

He shrugged. "Exist."

I focused on the piece of food in my hand, which I couldn't bring myself to put in my mouth. "Because of me."

"Because of what I did to you."

I placed the food on the plate in front of me and put on a fake smile, trying to lift his spirits. "Tell me about when we first met."

"I can't," he said, grabbing a smoked salmon wrap.

"Why not?"

"I can't feed your memories. We need to know what you remember on your own."

"Who's we?" I asked, pretending to not have a clue about the conversation he'd had with Abby while I was supposed to be in my room.

Marcus grinned.

My eyes widened in surprise. "You knew I was listening from the hallway?"

He chuckled. "I'm observant."

I slumped in my seat. "And you didn't think to maybe acknowledge I was there?"

Marcus smirked. "What? And call you out for spying on me?"

My eyes widened. "I was not spying on you."

"You weren't?"

"I couldn't see you, so technically, I wasn't spying. Eavesdropping maybe but not spying."

Marcus chuckled. "I've missed you."

I reached across the bar and put my hand over his. "You've got me."

He sighed.

I wasn't a mind reader, yet I could tell he was wondering for how long. Maybe he was even imagining driving the knife into my heart. If my dreams were anything to go by, then it was inevitable.

I didn't want him thinking about that. Standing, I walked around the bar and slid my arm over his shoulder. "I'm here now."

He slipped his arm around my waist and placed a gentle kiss on my cheek. "Want to go for a walk?"

"Where?"

"On the beach?"

I nodded.

We made our way down the steps leading to the sand.

Passing a few people on our way to the water's edge, I said, "Can I ask you something?"

"You can always ask me anything."

"Why don't I feel other people's pain when I'm with you?"

"I don't know, but I can tell you it's been that way each time. I'm the only one who keeps them at bay. At least for a while…"

"Then what happens?"

His jaw clenched. "Then even I can't stop it."

CHAPTER 30

Sleep eluded me that night. I tossed and turned, praying for sleep to take me under. It didn't. My mind was on a loop, replaying every memory I'd had of my past life, every dream of Marcus ending my life, and the conversation I'd overheard between him and Abby.

I rolled over to look at the time on my phone and almost peed myself when I saw Abby standing beside my bed, every inch of her skin illuminated in a soft golden glow. She looked like a goddess. But she wasn't. Abby was a Succubus, and she was standing by *my* bed.

Panic reared its ugly head, fearing what she was about to do. The promise I had made to myself about making her my new best friend seemed like the dumbest thing to ever go through my head.

"Shhh." Abby held her finger against her lips. "We have to go." When I didn't budge, she rolled her eyes. "I'm not going to hurt you. But you heard for yourself, Marcus doesn't want to even consider the witch's ramblings may be true."

I still didn't move.

"Look, I know you don't know me, but I know you. I've known you for the last couple hundred years. And I'll give you that we haven't always gotten along, but most times we have. I like you. And I care about Marcus. I love him, but I'm not in love with him. I never have been, and I never will be. But, I'm the one who's left here to pick up the pieces after you've gone. I don't want him to go through that again if there's a way to stop this cycle."

I didn't know Abby nor if I could trust her. What I did know was I, too, would do anything to stop the cycle. "Okay," I whispered.

She smiled. "That a girl. Now, get your little butt up and let's get out of here."

"Can't this wait until daytime?" I tossed the sheet off me, already knowing the answer to my question.

"There's no way he'd allow me to get my hands on you without him being there to supervise."

"Just give me a sec to change into something." I went into the wardrobe, got dressed into a pair of shorts and tank, and met Abby back in my room."

"Where are we going?"

She cocked her head toward the door leading outside. "Follow me." Abby quietly opened the door, slid outside, and waited for me.

I looked back at my bed, took a deep breath, and joined her.

Abby slid the door back into place then grabbed my hand and led me around the side of the house. I thought there'd be some sort of reaction when her skin touched mine. There wasn't. Her hand felt human, but I was sure she could crush every single bone in my hand without even trying.

Coming to a stop, she turned to me. "Now, you know what I am, don't you?"

I breathed out harshly. "Yep."

"And you know what a Succubus is?"

"Yeah, you screw men."

The corner of her lips tipped up into a grin. "Pretty much. But that's not what I'm talking about now. You see, the quickest way for me to get you to the witch and back isn't by road."

I waited for her to continue, but she didn't. "And?"

"I don't want you to scream when you see wings pop out of my back."

I laughed nervously. "You want to fly there?" I couldn't believe what I was saying. Up until this moment, the whole paranormal thing was just hearsay. Now, I was about to find out if it were real or if I had lost my mind.

The reality of it hit hard. My breaths became short, and I feared I was about to hyperventilate. "Show me."

A smirk crept over her face. "Don't faint on me now."

I swallowed hard. "I can't promise anything."

The next thing I knew, massive black wings emerged out of nowhere. It was one thing to imagine the wings, and it was something else actually seeing them.

I had to remind myself to breathe as I took in the magnitude of what I was seeing. Wings belonged on birds, not on humans... Except she wasn't human. And neither was Marcus.

Me? Not even I knew what I was, and Abby was willing to help me find out.

She tipped her head back as the warm breeze rustled her feathers. When Abby leveled her gaze with mine, her eyes were glowing like an owl's prowling the night sky for its next meal.

Releasing the breath I'd been holding, I stepped closer and ran my fingers over her feathers. "They're real," I whispered to myself, completely mesmerised by the magnitude of what I was seeing. Any doubts Justin had put in my mind about Marcus's sanity were obliterated the moment my fingers touched Abby's wings.

"Of course they're real. What did you think? Marcus was lying?" She scrunched up her face. "And you followed him anyway?"

I chose not to answer that question. Instead, I asked, "Have I ever seen your wings before?"

"Yeah. That's the time when you thought I was a demonic spawn trying to get my claws into you and Marcus, and I was damning you to an eternity in Hell. You thought I was the single reason why you experienced others' pain. You even tried to kill me a couple of times, which didn't go so well." She laughed quietly. "I learned not to bring them out around you after that."

"Until now."

"Now you're starting to remember." She held her hand out to me. "Come on. Let's get going."

I placed my hand in hers. "How does this work—?"

Abby pushed off the ground, taking me with her. She flipped me in front of her and wrapped her arms around my waist as she soared high into the night sky, cutting off the scream that was trying to escape my mouth.

My heart was practically beating a hole through my chest as I looked down at the mountains below. We had to be at least one hundred meters in the air.

A few days ago, I would've relished the idea of falling to my death. Now, I wasn't so sure. There had to be a reason why I never died. There had to be a reason why Marcus saved me. And there had to be an explanation for our connection with each other.

Attempting to stop the wind from stinging my eyes, I tilted my head down and watched the blur of the trees below. What I needed was a pair of goggles.

Abby leaned her head down next to my ear. "You okay?"

I nodded.

"We're almost there."

My stomach dropped as she swooped down and landed softly on the ground, among a group of trees. I collapsed to my knees and fought the bile rising in my throat.

Taking a few deep breaths, I closed my eyes and tried to steady the nausea building inside of me.

Abby put her hand on my shoulder, giving it a little squeeze. "Too fast?"

I nodded then fought another wave of bile that crept up into my mouth.

"Sorry."

The warm breeze evaporated, and the night became still. I looked up, trying to work out what was going on, and found a small-framed woman in her sixties standing at the open doorway to an old shack. A chill ran down my spine as I looked into her eyes, which were void of any irises and glowed pure white.

She shuffled forward, her glowing eyes never leaving mine. "It's time."

CHAPTER 31

*W*hat. The. Hell?

"Stop scaring the poor girl, Mava." Abby put her hand under my arm and lifted me to my feet. "And get rid of the eyes."

The witch gave a curt nod. A second later black irises came out of nowhere. She still looked freaky, but at least I didn't have glowing, white eyes staring back at me.

Abby put her hands on her hips as her wings retracted, miraculously disappearing into her back. "Aren't you going to invite us in?"

Mava gave another curt nod and extended her hand toward the doorway. "Come."

I'd be lying if I said I wasn't freaked out. I was surprised I hadn't peed myself as I followed Abby into the witch's cottage. I just had to remind myself Abby was with me, and she'd stop the witch from harming me—or so I kept telling myself.

Inside, the cottage was even creepier. There were two cauldrons bubbling away with something that made me want to puke. The smell was all-consuming, making me think she wasn't into herbs. It smelled as if she were cooking up rat's eyeballs mixed with lizard's inners and kangaroo paws. Not that I knew what those items smelled like being cooked up in a pot of boiling water.

Mava picked up a strand of my hair and sniffed it.

Abby's hand shot out, knocking my locks from the witch's grasp. "Touch her again and you'll die."

"You don't scare me, young child."

"I'm three thousand years older than you, so watch who you call 'child.'"

"Details." Mava picked a long-handled, wooden spoon up and began to stir the cauldron on the left. "Two lights, become one. The dark will be cast into purgatory. Light will become life.

"You're here for a reason," Mava said, continuing to stir the pot.

"You know what that reason is," Abby said, getting more than a little frustrated.

"Do I?" Mava spun around to face us, scaring the crap out of me. Old women weren't supposed to move that fast.

Abby placed her hands on her hips and sighed. "You're the one who's been spouting cryptic shit for years, and now that I bring her to you, you're going to play as if you don't know?"

"The ears have walls."

"Don't you mean the walls have ears?"

Mava raised a brow. "Do I?"

Abby dropped her hands by her side, balling them into fists. "I can't take this cryptic shit anymore." One second she was standing next to me, and the next she was up in the old witch's face, her fingers curled around Mava's wrist. "Tell me what we need to know."

The witch looked pointedly at Abby's grip on her then returned to her gaze to Abby's eyes.

Abby released her and turned away, giving me an exasperated look.

"This doesn't just involve the girl. There are others at play," Mava said. "When we have unity—and only then—we can face the dark."

I scrunched up my face. "What the hell does that mean?"

Mava whipped her head around to face me so fast I thought her head might roll off. She took a couple of steps closer, making me want to take a couple of steps backward to keep distance between us. But I stood my ground. "It means you are not alone. And if you want this to work, then you need your friend to believe."

She reached for my hair again, but this time I leaned back, avoiding her touch. Mava slowly dropped her arm to her side and stepped closer. I wanted to move back, but I was frozen in place. I wasn't sure if it was because of fear or something else. Either way, her breath sent chills down my spine as she leaned in closer, stopping when her lips were next to my ear. "Come back when you are one. And whatever you do, don't trust anyone. This girl and your other half are the exception. People think I'm crazy but..." She pulled away, a smile playing on her lips.

Mava glanced down at my waist then gave me a knowing look. What the hell the knowing look was for was beyond me.

A second later the craziness returned to her eyes, making me wonder if I had imagined the sane woman out of desperation.

Shaking my thoughts away, I realized Abby was standing two feet to my left, not protecting me like she had done the first time Mava had touched me.

I tugged on Abby's hand. "Come on. Let's get out of here."

CHAPTER 32

$\mathcal{T}$he trip back to Marcus's went by in a blur; black wisps twisted through the camouflage of the trees. My gut instinct warned me they weren't shadows of the night but rather the same creatures I'd seen in the hospital when I thought I was taking on the addict's hallucinations.

Abby leaned down and whispered in my ear, "Don't look at them."

My eyes widened in fear. Up until that moment, there had always been the possibility I was just seeing things. Now, Abby blew that idea to smithereens. I had no idea what they were, and Abby's warning told me they weren't something I wanted to run into. But that wasn't what scared me. It was the fact that no matter how much I knew I should listen to Abby, I had to fight my unrelenting urge to look at them.

Somehow I managed to keep my eyes squeezed shut until we dipped down. Thankfully, Abby took the descent a little slower than she had on our previous flight. My stomach still dropped; however, this time I didn't feel like throwing up.

She landed where we'd taken off and released her grip on me. "What were they?"

"Those black things?"

I let out a shuddered breath. "Yeah."

Abby lifted her wings, stretching them out above her, the soft breeze rustling the tips of her feathers. "They're Soul Scrapers." She smiled. "Don't look so worried. They only take shape if you look at them. They feed on people's fear, so it's simple. Don't look at them, and don't be afraid."

Yeah, as if it were as simple as she made it sound. Creatures of the night could scrape your soul from your body—or so the name suggested—if you so much as looked at them. Real easy.

She folded her wings so they were sitting neatly behind her. "Enough about those parasites. I want to know what Mava said to you when the bitch froze me."

"You were frozen?"

"Do you honestly think I wouldn't have followed through on my threat if I was able to?"

"Right," I said, wondering how powerful Mava was to be able to overpower a demonic creature.

"Well, what did she say?"

"Is it safe to talk here?" I asked, looking at the dense forest behind us. "I mean, Mava said the walls have ears. Maybe someone's following us."

"No, she said 'the ears have walls.' But that's beside the point. It doesn't matter what she said. Marcus has this place locked down so no one other than who he allows can get in. So tell me, what did the witch say?"

"Mava told me not to trust anyone—except for you and my other half." I furrowed my brow. "You know, I don't think she's as crazy as she makes herself out to be."

A big grin took over Abby's face. "I knew it." She lifted her hands to her mouth in prayer fashion and took a few deep breaths, her eyes glowing that unnatural molten amber.

Abby dropped her hands by her side. "All that time… Everyone thinks she's out of her mind, but she's not." A soft laugh bubbled out of her throat. "The old, crazy witch is our answer."

She pointed to my pocket. "What did she put in there?"

I drew my brows together as I shoved my hand inside the pocket of my shorts and felt something that shouldn't have been there. "What the hell?" I pulled out a piece of paper, which was folded over and over again.

When I opened it up, I was staring at what looked to be a poem.

"The moon rises, and
Light and Dark eclipse.
An ancient one will impede,
and memories will forget.
Time stands still until
the light will bloom,
And shines on the key that
unlocks the door to Destiny."

"What does that even mean?" I asked, looking up at Abby.

She carefully snatched the paper from my hands and repeated the words I'd just read.

"I don't get it," I said.

"It's about you. It has to be." Abby retrieved her phone from her pocket and snapped a picture of it. "'Memories will forget.' You forget. But I have no idea who the ancient one is. As for the moon and the eclipse, maybe it's a solar eclipse. We should see if there are any coming up." She shook her head as she stared at the paper. "I have no idea what the rest of it could mean."

I blew out a breath. "Maybe Marcus can shed some light on it."

"Marcus won't believe anything that comes out of that witch's mouth." Abby handed me the paper. "You go back inside, and I'll keep working on it."

Like I was going to sleep. Mava had me spooked. And those Soul Scrapers didn't help either. I had stepped into a world full of creatures of myths, and "Zoe" wasn't ready for it. Luciana, on the other hand, was the only thing keeping me from locking myself in a room and rocking back and forth on the floor in a corner.

Lately, I'd wished on more than one occasion that I was Zoe, the daughter my mother had given birth to. However, every time I thought about Marcus... He was my destiny.

"I'll see you tomorrow," Abby said, bringing me out of my thoughts.

"Sure."

She gestured for me to go inside as if she weren't going anywhere until she knew I was safe—even if Marcus had an impenetrable force around his estate.

"Thanks," I said, a warm smile spreading across my face. The whole "people caring about me" thing was taking me by surprise. I kind of wished I had some sort of memory of Abby, because I wanted to know her on a deeper level. She'd done so much for Marcus—and me.

I hurried to my bedroom. Turning around to shut the door behind me, I saw her take off into the night sky, disappearing in an instant. Apparently, Abby had taken it easy on my first flight.

CHAPTER 33

I couldn't sleep that night. I sat cross-legged on the bed, staring at the riddle for God knows how long, hoping it would all suddenly make sense.

It didn't.

When I finally came to the conclusion I was wasting my time, I rolled to the side of the bed and shoved the note into the top drawer of the bedside table.

The sun was rising to what seemed to be another glorious day in Byron Bay. It was a mockery to what I felt inside. Shit was going on that deserved dark rain clouds drowning out my despair.

God, I was melodramatic. Self-centered as well. The thousands of people living in Byron didn't deserve to suffer for my benefit. They had lives. They were oblivious to what existed around them.

I wished I were oblivious, too. Able to live a normal life with the man I loved. The reality of it was, nothing about my life was normal.

My heart missed a beat when I heard what I thought was Marcus's bedroom door open. I didn't want to be oblivious. I wanted this.

I wanted Marcus.

And I was prepared to go to Hell and back to get what I wanted. So long as it wouldn't be in vain.

I snorted. Who was I kidding? I'd go to Hell and back even if it ended the same as every other life I'd had with Marcus before this one.

I scooted off the bed and raced to the door, opening it just as Marcus was about to knock.

He smiled, taking in my shorts and tank that I hadn't changed out of after I got back from Mava's. "Morning, beautiful."

Suddenly, I wished I'd had the foresight to brush my teeth, because I wanted nothing more than to kiss him. To run my hands through his dark brown hair. To feel the curves of every single muscle in his body—that I was yet to discover in this life.

"You ready for breakfast?" he asked.

If he was on the menu, hell yes. Of course I didn't let that thought out of my head. "I'm starving actually."

We made our way to the kitchen, his hand seeking mine as if he couldn't bear to be in the same vicinity as me without touching me.

The truth was, neither could I.

There was a gigantic clock hovering over us, never letting me forget there was a huge possibility that we were running out of time.

Letting go of my hand, he motioned for me to take a seat on one of the stools at the breakfast bar then opened the fridge. "Croissants?"

"If you're wanting me to put on ten pounds by the time I've finished, then yeah."

He threw the packet onto the bench and pulled out the ham and cheese. "No you won't."

I shrugged. "I thought you knew me."

"I do." He got busy preparing them on a tray and stuck them in the oven. "Coffee?"

I nodded. "Thanks."

Marcus turned on the machine. By the time he'd finished preparing our coffees, the croissants were ready.

With a plate in one hand and coffee in the other, he headed outside. Figuring I wasn't going to get fed if I stayed put, I followed him over to the outdoor couch and took a seat next to him. "You like the outdoors, don't you?"

"Is that a memory or a presumption?"

"Presumption, but I guess I was right." I picked up a croissant and took a bite. God, I loved the taste of those things. My mother had instilled in me not to eat them or any other fatty food, because they'd inevitably cause a heart attack from clogged arteries. Of course that wasn't the real reason she didn't want me eating crap. It was all to do with image. She didn't want to be the mother of an overweight child when she made sure she never put on a pound.

Why I actually listened to her when I didn't care for her opinion on anything was beyond me.

That was a lie. I knew the reason. And it had nothing to do with my mother. It was because I needed to run. It was my escape from the torture of others' pain.

Being out in the bush without anyone around me for miles was soothing for my soul. I doubted I would've gone a full day without trying to kill myself if it weren't for the escape running provided. That was the real reason I liked to watch what I ate.

"What are you thinking about?" Marcus asked.

"Running." Lifting my knee onto the couch, I twisted around to face him. "I like to run."

"Am I keeping you from your daily ritual?"

I shook my head. I didn't need to run when I was with him. Marcus kept all the bad emotions at bay. "Hey, can I ask you something?"

"I thought I told you that you can ask me anything."

"How exactly is it that you're able to keep the pain away?"

Smoothing his hand over my knee, he smiled. "I don't know how. All I know is I'm the only one who can."

I waited for him to continue, but he didn't. "Why do I get the feeling there's more to it than you're telling me?"

He grinned. "Maybe because you're very perceptive."

"You're dodging the question."

Marcus's eyes dropped to my lips, making me suck in a sharp breath, which I was sure hadn't gone unnoticed. He lifted his mug and took a sip. I thought my question would remain unanswered until he eventually said, "There will come a time when not even I can stop your pain." The despair in his eyes was real. "The thought of you hurting and not being able to do anything..." He looked away, focusing on the ocean in the distance.

I shifted the mug to my other hand then inched closer to him, needing to comfort him about something I barely understood.

Marcus lifted his arm, tucked me against his side, and kissed the top of my head, his lips lingering for a few moments before he once again focused on the ocean.

Very few things in this world felt better than being in his arms. Kissing him topped it, and I was sure there was only one other thing that would surpass his kiss.

Actually, spending the rest of eternity with him would take first place. It was an impossible wish.

Marcus took a sip of his coffee then rested the mug on his thigh. "What did you think of the witch?"

CHAPTER 34

I froze. What the hell was I supposed to say to that? He knew I'd snuck out of the house with Abby. I wasn't prepared for this conversation. This wasn't the way it was supposed to go. Abby and I were supposed to figure out the witch's cryptic message before we tried to convince Marcus she was our only hope.

I exhaled slowly. "You knew?"

He chuckled. "I know everything... Well, maybe not everything, but I know what goes on around my house."

I could only guess that the "not everything" he was talking about had everything to do with the merry-go-round we were on.

Rather than trying to justify what Abby and I had done, I figured the best way to approach it was to own it. "I know you have your opinion on Mava, but I think you might be wrong."

"Do you now?" he said with a humorous tone.

I sat up straight and turned to him. "Yeah, I do."

He looked at me sceptically. Marcus naively dismissed Mava, as did most other people.

"I don't think she's as crazy as everyone assumes she is."

"And what makes you think that after one meeting with her?"

"I don't claim to know her as well as you do, but I can tell you there's more to her than she lets on. And yeah, I saw the crazy witch thing you're so hung up on, but I also saw another side to her that wasn't crazy at all."

I looked around. "Your place is safe, right?"

"Of course it's safe."

"I mean, no one can be around here and you not know about it?" Abby had already said it was safe, but I wanted to be certain.

"Not a chance."

"Okay, then…" I jumped off the couch. "Wait here." I ran into the house and raced to my bedroom. I pulled the note Mava had given me out of the bedside table and made my way back to Marcus.

"What have you got there?"

I fumbled with the note. "I know you're going to try to dismiss what I'm going to show you, but can you just think for a second that maybe Abby's right and the witch is our only hope? 'Cause I don't know about you, but I want this to stop. I don't want to feel everyone's emotions. I can't keep living like that."

"Come here." Marcus tugged on my hand, pulling me onto his lap. It was the first time I'd sat on him because he'd initiated it instead of me. Up until now, everything he'd done had been on my terms. Something about that settled my nerves. Marcus was giving this moment to me.

"What's it say?" he asked, taking the piece of paper from me.

"I don't know what it means."

He unfolded the note and began to read. He stared at the riddle, his breathing uneven. "Who else have you shown this to?"

"Apart from Abby, I only showed it to the guy I met down at the beach. Oh, and all those Soul Scraper things? I showed them, too."

"This isn't funny," he said.

"And neither is you thinking I would just show every Tom, Dick, and Harry what could potentially be the only clue to how we can fix whatever this is that's happening to us."

"Nothing can fix it."

I sighed. He'd built walls so tall around the possibility that our cycle could stop that he wouldn't even consider there might be some… I trailed off, remembering something the witch had said. "The ears have walls."

"What?" he asked with a smile.

"It's something Mava said; the ears have walls."

"Isn't it supposed to be the walls have ears?"

"Yeah, that's how the saying goes, but she meant what she said. Your ears have walls. You refuse to take a chance on Mava."

"She's crazy."

"She's also the only lead we have—unless you have something else we can work on?"

"I've got an idea."

"Which is?"

"You know, witches aren't the only ones who have power. We have power. I had power. And there are others who must know why you're suddenly remembering."

"Like Justin?"

"Among others."

"What's the deal with you two?"

I stood up, facing him. "Why are you acting so laid back about all of this? Back at rehab, you were all 'Let's find out what's happening,' and 'We're going to solve this mystery together. I'm going to help you try to put an end to what you're going through so I never have to be the one to drive a knife through your heart,' like you've done over and over again in my dreams, and tell me you're sorry..."

Marcus's jaw popped, and then he was standing in front of me before I even saw him move. "You knew about that and you didn't think it was something I should know?"

"Oh, yeah, it was really something I wanted to bring up. 'Hey, lover-boy, I've dreamed about you killing me every night since I can remember. I've dreamed of finding you so that you can end it.' And then when I finally found you, it feels as if my heart has split right open when I remember what you do to me. And it's not because I know you kill me for whatever reason before my nineteenth birthday. It's because I don't want to die. I don't want to go through another shitty existence just to end up where we always are, with you killing me again.

"I want to live. I want my life with you. I want you to get back your wings. I want to find out if Mava's right. I want to hold onto what could possibly be the stupidest, craziest idea in the hope that it means we might just have a life together. That you might return to what you were meant to be. And just think for a second that maybe that riddle of Mava's has more truth in it than we can possibly imagine. We need to remember. We need to work together. We need to stop harping on about our shitty existences because something tells me that we're running out of time.

"Oh, and if Mava isn't crazy, then why has she pretended she is all these years? What would make her do something like this?"

He raised his brow. "Are you finished?"

"No. I'm not—unless you're finally willing to give her a chance."

Marcus stared at me, then stepped closer and brushed the backs of his fingers over my cheek, stopping at the edge of my lips.

"What is it about you and me?" I asked, my voice choking up just thinking about what he'd done all those years ago. "Why didn't you collect my soul? Out of what I assume would be thousands of souls you've collected over the years, why would you spare me? And how is that even possible? I thought if someone's time is up, then it's up. If my time was up, how were you able to stop it? What made you go against what you are? What did you see in me?"

"I saw you." He caressed my cheek with his hand. "To this day I can't pinpoint exactly what it was about you that stopped me. But letting you die was like letting myself die. I didn't even know you, and yet you were all I could think about. The second I saw you, you somehow became the reason for my existence.

"I wasn't supposed to be there that day. It wasn't supposed to be me who collected your soul. It was supposed to be Justin. But he called in a favor because he was too busy screwing around and wanted me to do his collection for him. If it weren't for Justin, none of this would be happening. I never would have met you. I never would have fallen in love with you. And you wouldn't have been stuck on this never-ending loop I've put you on.

"If Justin had taken you away, you would've served your time in purgatory and you'd now be enjoying the rest of your existence on the other side instead of being stuck down here with me."

I closed my eyes, unable to look at the pain in his eyes any longer.

I could feel Marcus close the distance between us. His warm breath blew against my cheek, and he whispered in my ear, "As much as it makes me a jerk to say this, I don't regret meeting you. I don't regret falling in love with you." His lips brushed over my jaw on his way over to mine. "I regret not being willing to wait for you until time allowed me to find you in the afterlife, instead of giving in to my need to have you the moment I saw you."

He brushed his lips over mine. "I'm so sorry."

"Don't be," I said, my voice barely a whisper against his lips. "If I had to spend the next thousand years on this loop, I'd do it in a heartbeat as long as it meant I got to be with you." I kissed him, softly. No matter how much I wanted to know why he'd ended my life while I was still young, I couldn't bring myself to ask the question.

"I should've waited." He laced his hands with mine.

"Maybe you should've." I kissed him again.

This time he didn't break away to say something else. His hands slid up my arms and cupped my cheeks, deepening our kiss. His need for me was just as great as my need for him.

This body of mine was a virgin, but my mind was far from one. And the heat building inside of me was pulling on my natural instincts and desires.

Slipping my hands under his shirt, I ran my fingers over his taut stomach then back down. I grabbed his shirt and pulled it up, breaking our kiss momentarily to get it over his head.

Marcus wrapped his arms around my waist, his hands seeking out the skin above my shorts. Then they moved higher, leaving a trail of fire in their wake as he tucked his fingers under the band of my bra.

Marcus broke away. "Are you sure about this?"

I nodded. "Yes." My voice came out in a husky whisper.

He unclasped my bra then ran his hands down to my waist and hitched me up, wrapping my legs around his hips.

My soul was alive for the first time in what I knew to be eighteen years as he carried me into his bedroom and laid me on the bed.

Taking his time, he removed every single piece of my clothing as he placed soft kisses against my skin.

Sitting back, he got to his feet and kicked off his jeans.

I stood and strode over to him with the confidence of a Succubus.

He moaned as I placed my hands over his, stopping Marcus from undressing himself. It was my turn. Reacquainting myself with his body, I removed every single piece of his clothing with just as much care as he'd shown me. I was in my element. *He* was what I wanted —what I needed.

It was as if we were two beings that were meant to be. Mixed species meant to be at one with each other... My mind knew there was something to what I'd just thought, but I couldn't stop to think about anything other than the way he held me in his arms, the soft brush of his lips as he explored every inch of my neck, and the unrelenting desire building inside of me.

Capturing my mouth with his, he brought me into a deep, searing kiss that completely undid me.

I stepped forward, pushing him back until his knees hit the bed. Placing my hands on his shoulders, I guided him down and climbed onto his lap. It was as if we'd done this a million times before. There was no awkwardness, only our desires and our need to explore each other's bodies as we were brought over the edge and back, just to relive it over and over again as if we were making up for all the years lost between us.

I was determined to never let us lose another eighteen years together, and I would do whatever it took to make that happen.

Marcus broke away from our kiss just enough to say, "I'll believe in the tooth fairy if it means I won't lose you again."

I smiled as he brought his lips back to mine. He was going to give Mava a chance.

CHAPTER 35

I don't think I'd ever been as content as I was in that moment, but at the same time, something unpleasant that I didn't want to give a name to was churning inside of me as I lay next to Marcus, curled up in his arms.

He gently stroked my hair, picking up a piece and letting it fall through his fingers before starting the process all over again. "Would it be bad of me to say I missed doing that?"

I laughed. "It would make you human."

"But I'm not."

I absently traced the lines of his pecs. "Were you ever human?"

"No. It doesn't work that way."

"Then how does it work?"

"You've read the bible, right?"

"Parts," I said, feeling ashamed I'd dismissed something that was obviously so important to him.

He smiled as he ran the tips of his fingers over my bare shoulder. "Well, forget everything you've ever read. The bible is nothing but a story. Heaven and Hell are everything in between. There are no white, fluffy clouds, nor any loved ones waiting for you at a set of pearly gates. There are no rivers of fire in Hell. And most certainly, evil and good aren't black and white. There are many gray areas and more scary creatures in between this life and the next. God isn't almighty. Satan isn't all bad. There's a balance of good and evil, and the scale has tipped many ways over the years.

"What there is, is life after death. But not in the same way as you experience here. A soul becomes part of something else. A veil is opened up, and eternity becomes what one makes of it."

"Well, that's reassuring," I said, having no real idea what the hell he meant.

Marcus laughed. "Do you think humans would live any differently if they knew the truth?"

"I don't even know the truth. Everything you just said was a cryptic riddle, which sounded much like something Mava would say."

The corner of his lips turned up. He rolled to the side of the bed and retrieved the note Mava had given me.

Pulling himself into a sitting position, Marcus read the words again.

I sat up straight, my eyes lighting up as I remembered something I'd been too distracted earlier to fully consider. "Light and dark will eclipse," I repeated. "I know you tried to explain what you were before, but am I correct in assuming a Soul Collector is dark?"

"Not exactly."

"What about to a witch?"

He tipped his head to the side and gave a one-shoulder shrug. "Maybe."

"Let's just say you were the dark, because let's face it, you were the 'ears having walls' person Mava was spouting on about."

"That's yet to be confirmed."

I raised my brow, trying to hide my smile. "Let's just assume I'm right. What is this light you will eclipse?"

"You," he said as if it weren't half obvious.

I narrowed my eyes at him.

Marcus let out a slow breath, making me wonder if he thought I was a bit slow. "If I were the dark being this riddle is referring to, then maybe you're the light that I eclipsed when I stopped your death from happening."

My heart pounded against my chest as his words sunk in. He continued, "What if my selfishness stopped you from fulfilling your destiny? And if that were true, the second part of the riddle would shunt that theory, because 'an ancient one will impede or hinder and

149

memories will forget.' I think it's safe to say you're the one that sentence is about."

"I think that's fair."

"But if that's the case, why would someone hinder said destiny from being remembered?"

I held my fingertips against my temple, trying to grasp what it all could mean. "This is turning my brain to sludge."

He circled his hands around my wrists then lowered them to his lap. "Okay, let's start again. 'The moon rises and Light and Dark eclipse,' could mean that I eclipsed or stopped you or your destiny when I chose to save you instead of delivering your soul."

"Okay, I got that."

"Well, the next part is 'An ancient one will impede and memories will forget.' Your memories were stolen from you. Maybe this means that some ancient one has done this to you. And if that's true, why would an ancient one want to take away your memories if...? His eyes went wide. "'Time stands still until the light will bloom, and shines upon the key to unlock the door to destiny.'"

"I don't get it." By the look on his face, he'd figured out something major. And it wasn't a happy realization. It was bad.

"It can't be right. It has to be something else." He jumped out of the bed and quickly put on his clothes.

"What is it?" I asked.

"Never mind." He headed toward the door.

Completely naked and not caring the slightest, I climbed out of bed and raced over to him, catching Marcus's wrist as he reached for the door.

He turned to face me, desire consuming his eyes as his gaze swept the length of my body then returned to my eyes. But there was something else in those amber eyes, which were now glowing. There was something he was trying to keep from me, and I wanted to know what it was.

"You can't do that," I said. "You can't just say that and run out on me, especially after what we just did."

His eyes softened, and he pulled me into his arms. "I just need to figure something out." He kissed my temple. "And believe me, the last thing I want to do is leave you in bed after what we just did."

Marcus tried to break away, but I held onto him, his shirt balled in my fists. "Whatever it is, we're in this together."

"Not this…"

"Yes, this. Whatever it is, I have the right to know."

He ran his hand over his face, breathing out a sigh of frustration. "Okay, you're right. This is about you. It's all about you, and I can't handle it. I don't know how I'm supposed to be okay with never seeing you again. This can't mean what I think it means. And if it does, I should be happy for you, but I'm not. I'm a selfish asshole who wants the riddle to mean something else."

"You didn't even believe in Mava's riddle until two minutes ago, and now you're convinced this is the end of you and me?"

"Which is why I have to find out. I have to go see her."

"Mava?"

"Do you know of any other crazy witches?"

I raised a brow.

"Sorry. I'm just…" Marcus sighed again.

I cupped his jaw in my hands. "I get it. You're afraid. I am, too. But… I've got you. And you've got me." I forced a smile that was tearing me up inside. "And maybe Mava's just a crazy witch like everyone thinks she is."

"And maybe you've got it all wrong," Abby called from down the hall.

My eyes went wide when I realized she was probably heading our way and I was completely naked.

Marcus took a step back and leaned against the door. "Go get dressed."

I nodded, collected my clothes off the floor, and put them on. I walked back over to Marcus and placed my hand on his chest. "Maybe you're wrong."

"I hope you're right."

CHAPTER 36

$\mathcal{A}$bby had made herself at home on the couch in the lounge room. She had a bottle of wine on the coffee table and a glass of red in her hand. As soon as Abby saw us, she knew what we'd done. That girl had inbuilt radar for those kinds of things—or so I assumed.

"I think it's safe to assume you've had a very productive day." A smirk played on the edge of her lips.

"Not going to happen," Marcus said, leading me to the couch next to where she was and pulling me down beside him.

Abby shrugged, her smirk remaining in place. "Well," she dragged out. "I've been thinking about that riddle, and it seems you two have as well." She added under her breath, "In among other things."

Blood rushed to my cheeks, but Marcus seemed completely unfazed by her words. He ran his hand up and down my thigh in a relaxing motion. "You might be a whore, but that doesn't mean we are."

I almost snorted.

Abby chuckled. "I beg to differ." She held the glass up to her lips then whispered, "I'm a Succubus. I can feel the sexual energy coming off you both." Her lips parted, and she drew in a slow breath. "It's intoxicating." Abby lifted her glass, downed the contents, and refilled her glass. "Anyway, that's not why I'm here."

"Good," Marcus said. "Because if it were, I'd have to take away your access to the house."

Abby pursed her lips then downed the wine. "Okay, focusing. I overhead what you said to Luciana before, and don't get all shitty about me eavesdropping because we both know you knew I was here."

"I don't deny it."

"Good." Abby reached for the bottle of wine, refilled her glass again, and placed the empty bottle on the table. "Now, I believe you're just thinking the worst because that's where you're mind always goes. You've conditioned yourself to think the worst of every possible ending when it comes to Lucy."

Marcus glared at Abby.

She shrugged. "It's true."

"You better start talking because my patience is wearing thin."

Abby waved him off. "Yeah, whatever, demon boy. As I was saying—or trying to say—maybe Lucy is your destiny, and you're Lucy's destiny. And maybe someone is trying to stop you both from fulfilling some life changing event that will alter the course of history."

"Right," Marcus said. "Say that was true, then why would I be sent to collect her soul?"

"You said you were doing a favor for Justin. You weren't meant to collect her soul. Maybe you weren't supposed to meet Lucy in this lifetime and that's what's stuffed up everything."

Okay, she had a point. "So, what do we do now?" I asked.

"We go see Mava," Marcus replied.

A grin crept over Abby's face. "You're buying into her craziness now, are you?"

Marcus looked at me with longing in his eyes. "Whatever it takes."

CHAPTER 37

*A*bby followed us to Marcus's car and pressed the button to open the garage door. "I'll meet you guys over there."

The look in Marcus's eyes told me how much he missed being able to soar through the sky. Instead, he was stuck, driving around with severed wings.

I didn't want to think about what he must've gone through when his wings were removed. It had to have hurt like hell.

Abby waved to us as we took off down the driveway. I turned in my seat just in time to see her disappear. I didn't even catch a glimpse of her as she pushed into the sky. I hadn't even seen her wings come out. It was as if she'd disappeared into thin air in her human form.

The car trip went by in a blur. My mind was replaying all the moments I could remember from my past lives, trying to find any small piece of information I might have overlooked. The problem was, Marcus was with me in each and every memory, and there was no way he would forget. I knew for a fact that Marcus remembered everything. Nothing got past him. He wasn't human. He had the mind of a… Abby's words came to me, "demon boy."

I wondered if he really was a demon. I was too afraid to ask.

Abby was waiting for us at the entrance to the long, narrow dirt road ahead. She jumped in the backseat and slid into the middle. "I spoke with Justin just before."

"And?" Marcus sounded a little frustrated at the mention of Justin.

"He asked about Lucy and wants to know if she remembers anything else."

"What did you tell him?"

"That he should mind his own business and leave you two alone."

"I thought you and he were friends," I said, looking at Marcus. Why on earth would he have done a favor for someone who wasn't his friend? Then again, there was a ton of animosity between them.

"*Were* friends."

Abby sat forward and put her hand on my shoulder. "Don't ask."

"Right," I said.

We pulled up in front of Mava's shack. I couldn't really call it a house because that would mean there was some sort of structural soundness to the place. It was a wonder the shack hadn't fallen down already.

I looked around as we made our way to the front door. We were out in the middle of nowhere, and thankfully, there was no sign of any Soul Scrapers.

Marcus lifted his hand to knock, but before he connected to the rotting wood, the door swung open and Mava said, "The ears no longer have walls." Her white eyes rolled from side to side as if she were witnessing something none of us could see. A moment later, her iris's appeared, focusing on me then shifting to Marcus.

Raising a brow, Marcus glanced at me. I bit down on my smile, satisfied I had nailed that riddle.

"So, it was about you," Abby said, giving Marcus a small punch on his shoulder.

"Truths aren't always what they appear." Mava stood back and gestured for us to enter. "Come now."

With Marcus's hand tightly entwined with mine, we stepped inside the shack. I half expected to be struck down by some magical force, giving mockery to my stupidity for putting my faith in her. Nothing happened.

The smell of the previous night's cooking still lingered in the air.

Thankfully there were no left over carcasses from whatever she'd been cooking strung up around the place.

Mava disappeared into the corner of the kitchen then returned with a glass vial filled with greenish-black liquid. "Drink this and you will see. The clock's running out. And truths are deceived." She held the vial out to me.

Marcus's hand closed over mine, stopping me from taking the vial out of Mava's hands. "You want Lucy to drink that?"

"Drink it and you will see."

"Me or Marcus?" I asked.

"Neither of us," Marcus said. "We have no idea what is in that thing."

"Doubt will crumble liberty. Faith remains to be given."

Marcus shook his head in frustration. "Can't you say anything without making it into a riddle?"

"You have to have faith," Abby said, stepping forward. "Faith surpasses doubts. And freedoms will be given."

Marcus looked at Abby in disbelief. "Not you, too."

Mava nodded slowly. "Sometimes we must listen to those we choose to negate."

Abby grinned. "See." She whacked Marcus's arm. "I'm good at deciphering all these riddles."

"Take the vial, child." Mava held it toward me.

Ignoring Marcus's stare, I took the vial from her, firmly gripping it as I let my hand drop slowly to my side.

Marcus breathed out harshly then shifted his gaze to Mava. "This riddle of yours about the eclipse and the blooming light, I need to know what it means."

"What do you think it means?" Mava asked.

Marcus looked at me, his eyes practically glowing. "Does it mean I eclipsed Luciana's light when I stopped her from moving on to the other side? And now that this light is blooming, meaning that she's remembering, does it mean this is the last time? That finally, this curse will end and Lucy will be gone from me, forever?"

I wanted to wrap my arms around Marcus and tell him I would never leave his side, but I wasn't so sure he was wrong. And up until a couple of days ago, it was exactly what I'd wanted.

Not anymore.

"Well?" he said, shifting his gaze to Mava.

"Don't get hung up on false truths. There are memories to repair and lies that must be untold. Legacies can be shadowed, and power has its own evils. Trust in what you feel. Not what you know."

"So, what you're saying is I have no fucking idea what's going on and everything I've known to be truths are in fact lies." Marcus wrapped his arm around my shoulder and pulled me against his side. "But trust what I feel?"

"And what you feel is her." Mava tipped her head toward me with a satisfactory smile. She reached for my hand holding the vial and squeezed it. "Drink up and you'll see."

Marcus took a step back, breaking her hold on me as I moved with him. "I think we need time."

"The sand is shifting, and with it goes hope."

Marcus looked at her for a few moments then headed outside with me safely tucked under his arm.

Abby was a few steps behind us. "Well, that was weird."

Marcus opened the passenger door and waited for me to get in. "And I'm even more confused than ever."

"You and me both," Abby said.

I ran my fingers over the vial in my hand. "Whatever it is, I think it's safe to say we don't know shit, and time's running out."

"Yep. That's just about right."

I got into the car and held the vial between my hands, staring at the murky contents. I had a decision to make. I could either trust in the witch and continue down another rabbit hole and possibly wind up dead, or we could try to work it out on our own. Whichever way I went, it was not going to be easy.

CHAPTER 38

"What's the plan?" I asked when we arrived home, the vial secured in my pocket just in case. Marcus hadn't asked me for it, and I couldn't help but wonder if that was because he had faith I wouldn't be stupid enough to swallow some concoction a crazy witch had given me, or if it was because he believed—no matter how much he didn't want to—that it would inevitably come down to me taking the contents. Either way, I wasn't going to broach that subject, because when it came down to it, I knew I'd probably end up doing the latter, and I didn't want to have that conversation with him just yet.

Abby had disappeared for work-related commitments. I didn't even want to know what exactly that meant. Just the idea that her sole existence was to have sex with men kinda unnerved me.

Marcus led me down the hall toward another part of the house I hadn't seen. "The plan, my sweet Lulu, is to figure out if anyone else knows what the witch is talking about."

I smiled at how he called me Lulu. I hadn't heard him call me that for... I couldn't remember a time he'd actually called me that, but it felt right, as if I'd heard it a million times before. No matter how much I wanted to remember all the pet names he had for me, there were more pressing things to worry about. "And I'm hoping you know where to start."

"Nope."

"Well, that's refreshing."

He smiled. "We need to go to the Devil's Playground."

I froze. "You mean playground as in you're taking me down to Hell?" I asked, pointing to the floor.

Marcus laughed. "Hell isn't under the ground. It's only accessible through veils, which we control. But you don't have to worry about that. We're not going through to Hell."

"Then where are we going?"

"We're going to the Devil's Playground, as in the place where we creatures come out to play."

"Oh, God. Please don't tell me you have clubhouses where Demons, Succubi, and Incubi play with humans. Or sacrifice them for some stupid ritual that supposedly gives you more power or keeps your Gods or whatever creatures you worship happy."

Marcus chuckled. "It's not as bad as it sounds."

"Yeah, maybe for you."

He opened the door to a room with what looked like a black liquid-metal dummy standing in the corner. There were no windows or lights, only black padded floors and walls.

Marcus closed the door behind us, turning the room pitch black. "Sorry, it's the only way I can access what I need."

I gulped. "And I'm hoping that what you need isn't going to be used to slice and dice me."

Marcus found my hand with his and gripped my hip with his other. "Don't for a second think I would ever hurt you..."

"Except when it's time," I finished his sentence. I smiled even though I wasn't sure he could see me. "I don't fear you. I fear time."

He brushed my hair behind my shoulder then placed a tender kiss on the curve of my neck. "I'm going to do everything within my power to give time back to you."

"As long as it's with you."

Marcus lifted his head and kissed me. "Always." He stepped back, and I was once again standing by myself in complete darkness.

I heard a few things move, then more noises, followed by some more. "How much longer is this going to take?"

"Why? Does the dark scare you?"

"No," I said. "It's somewhat comforting."

"That's not something humans usually say," Marcus said, his

voice sounding closer. His hand wrapped around mine, and he pulled me toward what I presumed was the direction of the door.

I was right. Light flooded the room, and it took me a couple of seconds to adjust to the brightness. When I did, I saw what Marcus was holding and just about peed myself.

"What the hell are they?"

"Weapons." Marcus turned my hand over and placed an engraved tubular object in my palm.

I breathed a sigh of relief. He hadn't given me the gun or the object that looked as if it would slice through my hand the moment I touched it. "This doesn't seem too bad."

"Don't let the looks deceive you. It will do just as much damage, maybe even more than the gun—so long as you know how to use it." He shoved the gun into the waistband of his jeans.

I gripped the tube. "What am I supposed to do with it? Hit someone over the head?"

He chuckled. "Press that button there and see what happens."

I turned it over to where he was pointing and saw the markings weren't just engravings. There was a part that looked as if it moved.

I looked up at Marcus. "It's not going to hurt me, is it?"

"Do you think I would give you something that was going to hurt you?"

I didn't need to answer him. Placing my finger over the button, I pressed it. Marcus pushed my hand to the side just as a blade appeared with a soft white glow around the edges.

Marcus took the knife from my hands. "This blade is made from materials that aren't found in this world. It has the power to harm but not kill. And when I say harm, I mean you'll incapacitate whoever you use it against long enough for you to get away. It severs the nerves and sends a signal to their brain telling it they're basically paralysed."

"And your weapons?"

"They have the ability to kill some of us but not all."

"Right," I said, adrenaline pumping through my body. I hadn't even used the weapons, and I was already in flight mode. I wasn't sure I could ever be in fight mode. I wasn't sure I had it in me.

Marcus hit the button, and the blade retracted into the handle. Then he handed it back to me. "Keep it on you at all times. You probably won't need it, but I want you to have it as a precaution."

"Mava's potion is looking more and more inviting."

"I don't want you touching that stuff. We don't know if we can trust her."

"Yet you think we can trust the goons you're trying to get information out of tonight even though you need to take weapons in case they try to kill us. Yeah, that sounds real trustworthy."

"The weapons are a precautionary measure." When I looked at him blandly, he added, "If Mava's right, then any one of them could be responsible for what's going on between us. If that person so much as suspects you're remembering, who knows what measures they'll take to keep you from remembering too much?"

I nodded as I shoved the knife into the back pocket of my shorts. "Let's just hope it's none of them."

"Let's just hope we find our answers."

"Agreed."

CHAPTER 39

*T*wo hours later, I was getting into the car, wearing a dress Abby had dropped by for me after she'd finished up her work. Apparently, there was a dress code I had to abide by if we didn't want to draw attention. So here I was, dressed as a tramp with more skin showing than I'd ever shown before. Plus, I had a red wig covering my brown hair. Abby had also taken the time to do my makeup in such a way that I could barely recognize myself when I looked at my reflection in the mirror. Abby really was something. I wished she didn't have to go back to work and could come to the club with us.

"Relax," Marcus said as he pulled onto the road. "You look gorgeous. You'll fit right in."

"Except they're all going to think I'm a tramp."

"Would you rather them know who you really are?"

"That I'm the human you couldn't collect?"

"That you're the only human to ever undo any of our kind."

I smiled. "So, I undid you?"

"As if you don't know."

I bit down on my smile. "Tell me, what else do I do to you?"

His eyes blazed with fire. "I think I better not answer that question if we want to find out what we can tonight."

I bit my lip again and turned to face the window. Shadows

drifting in among the trees caught my attention. "Are they always there?"

"The Soul Scrapers?"

"Yeah."

"Not as much as they have been lately."

"Because of me?"

Marcus didn't answer.

"If they know I'm here, wouldn't the one who did this to me, know I'm here, too?"

"Possibly."

"What do they want from me?"

I thought he wasn't going to answer me, but then he said, "They want what they were denied."

"Me?"

Again, he didn't answer.

"What do they want from me?"

"What do you think happens in purgatory?"

I scrunched up my face. "I have no idea. I've never been there before."

"They're the ones who right the wrongs that aren't bad enough to warrant an eternity of suffering in the person's own Hell.

I shivered at the thought of having those things anywhere near me, let alone touching me. "What did I do to deserve going to purgatory?"

"I don't know."

"What do you mean you don't know?"

"I wasn't the one who was supposed to collect you."

"Then wouldn't Justin know?"

"Yeah."

"Then why won't he tell you?"

His jaw hardened. "Why do you think we're no longer friends?"

"Don't you think that's where we should start?"

"Ideally, yes. But after three hundred odd years of refusing to tell me, I don't think he's about to start talking now."

"Then make him talk," I said. "You've got weapons. Use them."

The corner of his lips turned up briefly. "They don't work on him."

"Why?"

"Because we Soul Collectors are above the level of those that

163

these weapons will affect. We're supposed to be impartial to either side, so there's no way of manipulating the lines."

"The lines?"

"The ones that balance good and evil."

I placed my fingertips on my temples and began rubbing them in soothing circles. Only it did little to help. There was so much I didn't know, and time was running out. "Exactly how much time do we have?"

"Fifty-six days, five hours, thirty-nine minutes, and ten seconds."

I breathed out slowly. It was hard hearing I had such a short time to live. Fifty-six days was not long enough. I wanted an eternity with Marcus, not just over a month. And knowing he knew how long I had left down to the second was something I hadn't considered. He was living on borrowed time, only allowed to enjoy a few moments before I was torn away from him again—possibly forever. The fact that he didn't regret falling in love with me confirmed what I already knew. Marcus loved me more than he ever should, which meant something much bigger than anything he'd ever considered was at play.

CHAPTER 40

$\mathcal{L}$ ights flashed from a neon sign reading "Devil's Playground" as music blasted onto the street. I puffed out a small laugh. "Fitting name," I said under my breath.

"Colton is an original, but he's not the big boss." Marcus draped his arm over my shoulders, tucking me against his side as we headed toward the doors.

People were lined up outside, growing impatient as a group of four left the club and no one was allowed inside. Rather than joining the end of the line, Marcus walked right on through as if he owned the joint. "This club is for my people," he explained. "Only a few lucky humans will get to go inside."

"I guess I'm one of them," I said flatly. I sure as hell didn't feel lucky—especially with the knife tucked away inside my bag.

The light show pulsating around the club was mesmerising, illuminating the faces of those within, only to cast them into darkness the next second before bringing them back into the light.

We caught the attention of almost everyone we passed as Marcus led me toward the back of the club. "Why are they looking at us?"

He leaned down and whispered in my ear. "You're the only human I've been seen with in over three hundred years."

I raised a brow. "So you've only been with humans when no one was watching?" I teased.

Marcus placed his finger under my chin, tipped my head in his direction, and planted a kiss on my lips that almost made me forget where we were. "You know you're the only one."

Of course I was. That was why we were in this predicament in the first place.

We continued on, weaving through the crowds of people, who mostly weren't people at all. To the unknowing they looked the same, and even though I knew most of them were creatures of myth, I couldn't tell who was human and who was not.

Just like in the movies, two men stood in front of a sectioned off area, arms folded in a "Don't mess with me" stance. I wondered if they were there to keep the humans away from what were most likely "the big boys," or if they were keeping away the lesser creatures as well.

Behind them, two men and a woman, who appeared to be deep in conversation, were sitting on a couch large enough to comfortably fit at least ten people—or demons.

"Not her," the burley man on the left said, standing directly in front of me, blocking my view of the trio.

Marcus glared at him. "Move or I'll make sure you never move again."

"If you do that over a human, you know what will happen."

The corner of Marcus's lips turned up. "You should know I don't care for rules." A fire burned in his eyes, as if he wanted to show the guy just how serious he was. I'd never seen that side of him and wondered exactly what I'd gotten myself into all those years ago, and why someone who was implying he was a force to be reckoned with would want to be with someone like me—an ordinary human.

So much didn't make sense, and Mava's riddle was doing a number on my head. I shook my thoughts away. Now was not the time to try to figure it out.

The burly guy raised a brow. "And look where that got you? How are the stumps working for you?" His eyes widened, and a second later, he collapsed on the floor.

I had no idea what the hell Marcus had done to him, but by the look in the other guy's eyes, whatever it was had him scared shitless.

"Want to join him?" Marcus sneered, looking at the blue-eyed guy who'd stayed silent until this point.

Blue Eyes held up his hands as a man dressed in black got up from the couch, strode over to us, and motioned for his henchman to step aside. "You know how long it's going to take for him to regain movement?" He shook his head. "And all of this over a girl." His eyes drifted down the length of my body before eventually returning to my face. "I don't believe we've met." He held his hand out to me.

"My name's Zoe," I said, placing my hand in his. "Is this place yours?" Eyes wide, I looked around, pretending to be in awe of my surroundings. "I can't believe I finally got in. Do you know how many times I've waited in those lines outside and never once stepped foot in this place? So, what's your name?" I asked.

He placed his other hand over mine, gently stroking it. "I find that hard to believe for someone as... alluring as you."

"Oh, no. It's true," I rattled off. "This place is soooo exclusive. None of my friends are going to believe I got in—especially with someone like him." I looked all doe-eyed at Marcus. He stared back at me with a bemused expression. Guess he didn't think I would go all fan-girl on him.

"Well then, I may have to tell the boys out front to keep an eye out for girls like you."

His gaze shifted to Marcus. "So, what do I owe the pleasure of your company?"

"I need to know what you know."

The man rolled his eyes. "How many times have we been through this?"

"How many times have you lied to me? I will continue to ask until you tell me the truth, Colton."

He didn't answer.

"What will it take?"

Colton glanced at me, his eyes eating me up as if I were a delicious candy he wanted to devour. Marcus grabbed my hand and pulled me behind him, hiding me from the predator. "Not her."

"Of course not, because I think we both know she's not just some human you picked out from the line outside."

Damn! Marcus knew the disguise was of no use, but Abby had tried to convince him it would work. I wanted to rip the wig off my head, but I wasn't sure if the others knew or if Colton was the only one perceptive enough to work out the truth.

"You know what I want," Colton said, taking a glass of scotch from the waitress who was serving the threesome their next round.

"But even if I get it, there's no guarantee that what I know will be of any use to you."

Black shadows swept by my right, catching my attention. My heart rate sped up, knowing what they were. Like last time, I had an unrelenting urge to look at them, but Abby's warning stopped me—for ten seconds. Then it became impossible. They were everywhere, and with them came emotions that I hadn't experienced since the moment Marcus walked into my life. He was supposed to keep others' emotions at bay.

He wasn't.

I closed my eyes as my senses overloaded with way too many emotions. Only this time, I felt the good, not just the bad. It was a first.

Ever since I'd realized I was taking on others' feelings, I had wished I could just once have a good emotion, and now that I had not just one but a whole room filled with humans and creatures lusting over one another, I wanted to take the knife in my bag and drive it through my head.

My hand instinctively went to the cast on my wrist, trying to get my finger in just enough to get a hold of one of the stitches and rip it out. I needed the emotions to stop. The love and lust I could handle. It was the fear that was doing my head in. The humans knew exactly what was happening to them, yet they couldn't help but feel an attraction to their monsters as they fed from their souls, making them stay like the little play toys they were.

My finger couldn't reach the stitches, and the emotions were increasing by the second. I needed to get away.

Without telling Marcus where I was going, I raced through the club, making a beeline for where I thought the exit was, only I ended up in front of the women's bathroom. My senses were overloaded and my vision was blurred, but I could still see the black wisps floating throughout the crowd, heading in my direction. The more I looked at them, the more their appearance changed, taking on solid structures.

Backing up, I pushed the door to the restroom open then shoved a woman aside as she was about to enter a stall.

"Hey!" She thumped her fist against the door, the room suddenly becoming colder. "Wait your own turn, you fucking—" She didn't finish her sentence, which I feared had everything to do with the

Soul Scrapers following me. And now, an innocent woman was probably dead because of me.

A chill ran up my spine as my breath came out in an uncontrollable shudder. The air had turned so cold it looked as if I were breathing out smoke.

Panic seized my limbs, locking me where I stood. I knew something was wrong. I knew I needed to run or at least get the knife out of my bag, but I was as frozen as the time Mava had used her magic on me.

I opened my mouth to scream for Marcus, but nothing came out. Not that he would've been able to hear me with all the noise of the club. I'd been so stupid to run. I should've stayed put. The emotions wouldn't have killed—

I stopped mid thought as crystals of ice spread across the door, and the light quickly faded away until all that illuminated the stall was coming from the moonlight shining in from the window.

The window.

I had to move. I had to get…

Black mist spilled like a waterfall over all three walls of the stall, falling to the floor then rising up into the air until they were towering over me, their forms evolving from the shadows and becoming thick like tar. Their smell was all-consuming, spreading through my senses as thick tendrils of black smoke billowed out of a hole in the top of their form, reaching for me.

CHAPTER 41

*A*bby's words screamed at me from my subconscious. *Don't look.*

Slamming my eyelids closed, I backed up, my legs hitting the toilet. I had control over my body again.

Strong wet, slimy fingers wrapped around my jaw and cheek, squeezing as something oozed inside my ears.

I opened my mouth to scream, instantly choked by the cold black smoke slipping over my lips. My eyes snapped open in shock. A mangled inhuman face stared back at me, rotten black flesh falling from the cheekbones, revealing the tar-like substance that swirled underneath. Black holes were in the place the eyes should've been, and the creature's mouth was wide open, allowing black smoke to billow out and into mine.

I choked on the smoke as it entered my lungs, snaking its way through my body like a demon possessing me.

My back slammed against the wall then quickly slid up to the window, my legs dangling limp, unable to move.

With a sudden rush, my head slammed through the window, the safety glass shattering over me as the Soul Scraper dragged my body out the other side, its demented form slick against mine, only parting as we neared the ground.

I braced myself for the impact of the fall, but it never came. I'd stopped, hovering just inches above the ground. I tried to roll over, but my body remained rigid.

A thick tendril of tar wrapped around my neck, quickly spreading out to cradle my head in a spider web-like hold.

Pressure in my chest slowly spread, burning as it made its way up my throat. For a second, I thought I was going to puke, but I quickly realized it wasn't vomit when the same black tar that was wrapped around my head shot out of my mouth.

I gagged as the black sludge snaked its way around the tar on my face, connecting me to it.

A kind of panic I never knew existed completely took over when I saw the slick tar begin to move in time with my own erratic heartbeat. The faster my heart beat, the faster the sludge beat as the sky above began to move. Or more probable, I was moving.

I screamed out to Marcus, but the words never left my mouth, the sludge lapping up every sound I made.

The tar began to shift over my face, blocking my sight, casting me into a complete weightless, soundless, black existence as it dragged my hovering body to the depths of Hell. Or so it seemed.

I needed to get free. I needed to get away from them. But I was completely powerless. They were creatures of nightmares, and I was a human. A human that had somehow captured the heart of a man incapable of loving a human.

The witch's words replayed in my mind. "Drink the vial and you will see..."

If only I'd listened to her and drunk the damn potion—

My body violently spasmed, bringing my captors to a halt. The smell of rotten flesh engulfed my senses as fingers wrapped around the sides of my face, holding me in place.

The sludge shifted to the sides of my eyes, allowing me to see the putrid flesh flapping against the creature's face as a soft wind swirled around us, quickly growing with intensity, turning into a gush of wind, circling us, hiding us in the center of its wrath.

A mixture of slick tar and black smoke billowed out of its mouth and into mine, slithering down my throat, making me gag.

A chill spread from the Soul Scrapers mangled fingers, quickly taking over all my senses and focusing them on the fact that I was going into hyperthermia. Icicles formed on my lashes, spreading down to my eyes. I wanted to shut them, but I remained powerless as the wind whipped around us, howling like a deranged demonic creature about to suck us into the pits of Hell.

Light exploded from above, erasing my vision and casting me into darkness. I was completely blind.

Screams howled around me as the tendrils of tar exploded from my face, the ones stuck down my throat slithering out as if someone had whipped them out of me.

I dropped to the ground, my head hitting something hard, twigs stinging the back of my neck and cheek as they snapped under my weight.

Coughing, I tried to rid the slick feeling that stuck to my throat. But it was useless. The tar was gone, leaving in its place the reminder of the hellish world I'd entered.

I lifted my hand to my cheek, relief rushing through me when I realized I could move on my own accord. The howling continued as I wiped a thick smear of what I presumed was blood off my cheek and held it in front of my eyes, willing my vision to return so I could see.

Warm fingers closed over my hand, and I knew without having to see that I was safe. Marcus had found me. I searched frantically for his arms and clung to him like a child who'd found their lost comforter, never wanting to let it out of their grasp again.

Scrambling to my feet, I clenched his shirt in my fists, his arms wrapping around me as my vision began to return. The smell of sulphur hit me, making me want to gag again.

I buried my face in Marcus's chest and breathed in as he whispered into my ear, "We have to go."

I nodded against his chest then pulled away, squaring my shoulders as I turned to see what I'd been hiding from. The grass surrounding us was smouldered, and black ash floated through the air, which had returned to the soft warm breeze it had been earlier that night.

Marcus put his finger under my chin and tilted my face in his direction, his eyes narrowing on the cut on my face. He ran his thumb over the cut then wiped my blood off on his pants. He must've been satisfied I wasn't going to bleed out because his eyes returned to mine, no longer interested in my scratch. "Are you hurt anywhere else?"

I shook my head. There was no point in telling him about the scratches on the back of my neck. I was hardly going to die from them.

Taking my hand in his, Marcus led me through the trees, glancing backward every so often to make sure I was okay. Shadows moved in the distance, twisting their way through the trees, matching our steps as we headed away from the scene.

"Don't look at them," Marcus warned. "They're defeated for now, but that doesn't mean they can't come back if given the chance."

That was easier said than done. Those creatures had done something to me that made me want to crawl out of my skin. Just the thought of their sludge-like tentacles slithering down my throat made me want to be sick.

Taking a few deep breaths, I focused on the ground moving beneath me as we made our way to God knows where. I didn't even have it in me to find out where we were going. My thoughts were too consumed with the Soul Scrapers who'd tried to scrape my soul away.

Eventually, we reached the clearing where the club and various shops stretched out before us. I could no longer feel the emotions of the people surrounding me—good or bad. Marcus was once again able to keep them at bay.

We hopped into his car and took off down the street, leaving the Soul Scrapers hiding in the shadows. Relief washed through me when I looked in the side mirror and saw they weren't following us.

Turning my attention away from the mirror, I licked my lips, trying to alleviate the dryness in my mouth. "I need a drink. Actually, I need answers. But first I need a drink," I mumbled.

Marcus pulled into the drive-through of the nearest burger joint and ordered a bottle of water. They were out of bottles, so I was given a paper cup they usually reserved for soda. I didn't care. With the way my throat felt as if it were on fire, I would've scooped the water out of a toilet bowl if I were given half the chance.

Taking a long sip, I closed my eyes, overcome with the relief the water provided.

Lowering the cup to my lap, I fiddled with the straw, twisting it around in circles as I tried to work out what exactly happened in the club and how those hellish creatures were able to get their hands on me. I already knew the answer. I'd freaked and run when I should've stayed.

"Why did you run?" Marcus asked, breaking the silence.

"I felt them."

"Felt who? The Soul Scrapers?"

I shook my head. "No. I could feel everyone's emotions in the club, and not just the bad. I could also feel the good." I twisted in my seat to face him. "You're supposed to stop me from feeling them."

Marcus's fingers tightened on the steering wheel, his gaze fixed on the road in front of us. "I'm supposed to. I always have. They're the rules. You shouldn't feel anything until it's time."

I snorted out a laugh. "Rules? And what do you mean by I shouldn't feel anything until it's time? I sure as hell felt something back there."

Marcus pulled the car onto the side of the road, his steely gaze remaining straight ahead. "There comes a time when not even I can stop you from feeling other people's pain. And that day is the day I was supposed to collect your soul all those years ago.

"If I don't kill you, then the emotions get worse, driving you out of your mind. The pain won't stop, medication won't work, and the only relief you get is from slicing yourself. But even that barely works. The suffering you endure gets worse every single day. And as much as it kills me to... I have to—for you."

"That's why you kill me," I said, realizing for the first time that he did it because he wasn't able to keep the emotions at bay.

He looked at me, a million emotions swirling in his eyes. "It's the hardest thing I've ever done. And it's the hardest thing I'll ever have to do. But that's part of my punishment. I'm the only one who can stop your suffering, and I have to do it before the last second you were supposed to die all those years ago. If I don't, then not even I can kill you."

"Shit," I said, taking it all in. I couldn't begin to imagine the soul-crushing agony he must have gone through every single time he'd driven the blade through my heart. To do something like that to someone he loved... The alternative must've been so much worse.

CHAPTER 42

"Why is this time different?" I asked as we pulled onto the driveway.

"I don't know," Marcus replied, his hand closing over my thigh. "Maybe because you remember. Maybe..." He trailed off when the lights from the car hit the front door of his house, or more so, the person standing in front of it.

"Is that Justin?" I asked, trying to make out the man shielding his eyes from the light.

"Yep." Marcus slammed on the brakes, put the car in park, and was out of his seat before he turned the engine off.

I fumbled with my seat belt for a few moments before I got it to unlock. Then I was out the door, racing over to where the two men stood.

The look on Justin's face made me think whatever he was here for wasn't good. He shifted his gaze from Marcus to me then back to Marcus. "I didn't know," Justin said.

Marcus's hands were balled in fists by his sides. "What didn't you know?"

"What's going on?" I asked, coming to a standstill a few feet away from the men. The tension between them was palpable. Whatever Justin was there for wasn't going to end well.

Justin's gaze remained on Marcus. "It was Julius."

"What was Julius?"

Justin ran his hand through his hair as he cast a few glances in my direction. "The order didn't come from Titus. It came from Julius."

Marcus's chest was heaving, his muscles tense with controlled restraint from his obvious dislike of Justin. "Are you saying what I think you're saying?"

Justin stared at him for a moment then nodded.

In one swift movement, Marcus retrieved his weapon from his pants and swung it, connecting with Justin's jaw. A sickening thud echoed around me as Justin's head snapped back, the impact driving him through the closed front door and into the plastered wall behind, where he crumpled to the floor in a pile of white dust.

Before the dust settled, Justin scrambled to his feet as Marcus strode toward him. "I didn't know. I swear to you. I never would've sent you there if I knew."

I grabbed hold of Marcus's shoulder, pulling him back out of fear that he was going to kill Justin before he could explain what the hell he was talking about. "Sent you where?"

Justin pivoted to the side, one hell of a guilty look in his eyes as he stared at me. "It wasn't your time. You weren't meant to die."

CHAPTER 43

W *hat. The. Fuck?*

Now it was *my* turn to lose my shit. I raced toward Justin, my arms swinging, but I never made it close enough to make contact with him. Marcus had wrapped his arm around my waist and lifted me off the ground, holding me tight against him.

"Let me go!" I swung my legs out, hoping I could free myself from his vice-like grip.

Marcus's grip tightened on me as Justin moved to the left and backed away toward the patio door, his hands raised in front of him as if he was declaring he wasn't going to hurt me.

The hell he wasn't.

That bastard was the reason my life was a living hell. I was never meant to die. Marcus didn't have to kill me. We didn't have to...

I stopped struggling, my eyes widening. If he didn't have to kill me, then why were we trapped in this cycle? Marcus didn't disobey a command by not killing me. None of this made any sense. It seemed the more I found out, the more confused I was.

Marcus lowered me to the ground, his arm remaining tight against my waist. "This changes everything."

Justin wiped his finger over the gash on his chin then inspected the blood. I had no idea Soul Collectors could bleed, but then again, I didn't really know much about them. And now wasn't really the time to find out. Justin had just dropped a bomb on us, and we needed to figure out what it meant, not the wonders of the creepy black blood Justin possessed.

"I had no idea any of this was going to happen." Justin wiped the blood off on the front of his navy shirt.

I strained a laugh then lunged toward him again. I wanted him to feel what I'd felt all these years. But once again, Marcus caught me before I'd barely taken a step toward Justin.

Feeling Marcus's weapon against my arm, I grabbed it from his hand and pressed the handle, hoping some big ass sword would come out and I could knock Justin's head off. Alas, nothing happened. He probably had some child-lock thing on it to stop me from doing something stupid.

"Calm down," Marcus said, still holding me a good foot off the ground. "You're not going to get that thing to work. Besides, we need him."

Relief washed over Justin's face.

"But that doesn't mean I'm not going to make you pay for what you've done," Marcus added.

Justin swallowed hard. I had no idea why he was afraid of Marcus if they were the same species, but something told me I would be fearful, too, if I was in his position. There is nothing more dangerous than someone who has had everything taken away from them.

"I have paid," Justin said. "I lost my best friend. I've had to watch you spiral into the pit of hell as you watched Luciana suffer. I have to live knowing I was responsible." All that cockiness he'd displayed at rehab was gone. It was as if it were a different man standing before us.

Marcus's eyes turned golden as he stared at Justin and continued to hold me off the ground as if I were a savage dog he was trying to restrain. "Go."

"Don't you have any questions?" Justin asked. "I can help you figure this out."

Marcus's jaw popped. I could tell he was about two seconds from losing his shit. "Go now while you still can." I had no idea if Soul Collectors could be killed, but by the look on Justin's face, he feared Marcus's threat was real.

Justin gave a curt nod, slipped out the back door, and turned to us. "Let me know when you want to speak. I meant what I said. I want to help."

Neither of us answered.

Justin closed the door and took a few steps back as giant black wings unfurled from his back and stretched out in the strong sea breeze. He took one last look at us then shot up into the air, instantly disappearing from sight.

Marcus lowered my feet onto the floor. "'An ancient one will impede, and memories will forget,'" he muttered to himself. "We've been looking at this all wrong."

He took the weapon out of my hand. "If the order didn't come from Titus, then we need to find out why Julius was giving the orders and why Justin pawned the order off on me. But most importantly, we need to figure out why someone would want you dead if it wasn't your time."

A chill snaked its way up my spine. Someone wanted me dead. And that someone was powerful enough to manipulate time and memories. They were also not only able to make me live a life of feeling others' pain, but also make it so that Marcus was the only one who could end my suffering.

The reason they wanted me dead was anyone's guess, but we were going to find out.

Whoever it was, was going to pay. I had fifty-six days until this life was over, and I was going to do everything within my power to figure out why someone wanted me dead.

SEVERED HEARTS

CHAPTER 1

*S*omeone wanted me dead and no one knew why. And what was worse, I only had fifty-six days to figure it out before Marcus would have to once again drive that dagger through my heart to end my eternal suffering that not even he would be able to stop.

I paced the length of the lounge room unable to sit still as Marcus sat on the sofa with Abby, filling her in on our latest discovery. When Justin admitted that I was never meant to die all those years ago, I'd wanted to kill him for lying to Marcus for so long, but the more I thought about it, the more I realized that I owed my life to him. If Justin hadn't palmed the collection of my soul off on Marcus, then he would've taken me through the veil and left me in Purgatory without giving it a second thought.

What I didn't know was why someone wanted me dead. I wasn't anything special. I was a normal human without any special powers or abilities. Apart from my empath curse, I was ordinary in every possible way. Yet for some reason, I had a target on my head, and Soul Scrapers were watching my every move, trying to get their decrepit hands on me again.

I swallowed hard at the thought of what they'd done to me earlier that night. They had dragged me out of the club and tried to suck my soul out of my mouth, before Marcus came to my rescue. I could still feel the slick, tar-like substance they'd shoved into my throat. It made my skin crawl, and there was nothing I could do to make it go away.

"You're joking, right?" Abby asked, her gaze flicking to me.

I continued to pace the room, too frustrated to speak.

When it became apparent that I wasn't saying shit, Marcus said, "I'm not. And I don't know whether to thank Justin or kill him."

"I say kill him," I said, breaking my vow of silence that lasted all of ten seconds.

"Don't go making any rash decisions." Abby grabbed her glass of red wine off the coffee table. "I mean, what he did was total bullshit, but…" She looked between Marcus and me, and I knew she'd come to the same conclusion as I had. "He didn't have to say anything. And if he didn't ask you to do him a favour, Marcus, then I'm pretty sure we wouldn't be sitting here having this conversation." She slouched back in her seat and twirled the wine in her glass. She peered over the rim as she raised the glass to her lips. "And I think everyone can read between the lines on that statement."

I came to a halt. "I'd be dead."

Unfathomable rage coursed through Marcus's gaze, turning his eyes into the purest shade of amber. I could only imagine what he was thinking. Justin had been keeping a secret for the past few hundred years, letting Marcus continue to blame himself for the pain I'd endured because of Marcus's decision to spare my life.

"Ease up, demon boy," Abby said, placing her hand on Marcus's forearm. "Lucy doesn't need to see…"

See what? I wanted to ask, but something told me that I was better off not knowing. I began pacing again. Adrenaline surged through my veins without any sign of being able to release the pressure of trying to contain myself from completely losing my shit.

I couldn't believe what was going on. I had a hex on me, and I barely had any time to figure out how to stop it. No matter how much I wanted to throttle Justin, it was essential we saw him again. We needed to get all the information out of him in the hope we might come that much closer to figuring everything out. The problem was, I wasn't sure I could trust myself, and by the rage still consuming Marcus's gaze, he couldn't trust himself around Justin either.

We needed another option. We needed to see the witch. Marcus thought she was crazy, as did all the others of her kind, but I had a strong feeling that it was all an act and she knew more than she was letting on.

"We need to pay Mava a visit," I said, coming to an abrupt stop.

Marcus and Abby just looked at me. Anger was still swirling in Marcus's eyes and Abby... Well, Abby was Abby, open to everything that had anything to do with me and Mava. I think she secretly liked all the conspiracies and figuring out all of Mava's cryptic messages. But more so, she probably was enjoying the fact that after all these centuries of feeling completely helpless about my curse and supporting Marcus through his years of pain every time he lost me, she was finally able to help play a part in figuring out how to put an end to it all.

Holding my gaze, Abby sauntered over to me with her arm outstretched. "I think I better take that."

I scrunched my eyebrows together in confusion as I followed her line of sight down to my hands. I was holding Marcus's knife that was capable of destroying most of those within the supernatural world. For a second, I considered keeping it for myself but I snapped to my senses. I couldn't be trusted with such a powerful weapon around Justin. And knowing my luck, I'd probably be the one to wind up dead if I went up against Justin.

Begrudgingly, I handed it over.

"Thanks," she said with a bemused expression.

Turning her back to me, she leaned down to place the knife on the coffee table. Marcus snatched it out of her hands as he stood.

"I'll take that." He tucked the knife into the pocket of his jeans as he strode over to me, then grabbed my hand and pulled me toward the open back door.

Marcus came to a halt midway through the back door then turned around, a mixture of anger and something else I couldn't quite place swirling in his eyes. Maybe he'd momentarily forgotten he no longer had wings and had mistakenly taken me to the quickest route to the outdoors because of his natural instinct to fly, which thanks to me he was no longer able to do.

I waited for Abby to direct one of her smart-ass comments toward Marcus, but her lips were sealed, and the look on her face made me think she pitied him. It must've been truly horrendous to have his wings severed from his body. I couldn't imagine the pain and loss I'd feel if I ever had a limb removed.

I had no idea if Soul Collectors felt pain the same way a human did, but either way, it wasn't something I'd wish on my worst enemy. Scratch that, I wanted to do more than remove a limb from the one who had ordered my kill and put Marcus through a life of living hell ever since he had met me.

Marcus pushed me back a little, then stealing his gaze away from mine, slipped around me and headed toward the front of the house. "Abby, we'll meet you at Mava's."

"The hell you will." Abby pushed past us and led the way. "Bad shit happens when I leave the two of you alone."

I smiled, but Marcus didn't seem to find it half as amusing as I did. The sad thing was, Abby was right. Bad shit did happen when she wasn't around. And the worst of it was when she'd had to go to work instead of coming to the Devil's Playground with us and the Soul Scrapers had gotten their demented hands on me.

A chill ran up my spine. I didn't think I'd ever get over what they did to me.

"Oh," Abby whispered as the front entry came into view. The door was still embedded in the wall from where Marcus had thrown Justin into it when we'd found out that I was never meant to die.

Abby turned to us, eyebrows raised. "I'm not even gonna ask what happened here."

Marcus let go of my hand and yanked the door out of the wall as Abby and I ducked outside, careful not to get in his way. Marcus lined the door up and pushed it back into place. It stood tall for about two seconds before it tilted back then crashed onto the floor.

"Leave it," Abby said, placing her hand on Marcus's shoulder.

Frustration still brimming in his eyes, Marcus gave a slight nod and strode toward the car.

I leaned closer to Abby as we followed him, staying a few steps behind. "He's pretty pissed, isn't he?"

Abby snorted out a laugh. "That's putting it mildly." The smile dropped from her face, as she sighed. "Honestly, I think he's taking it pretty well—all things considered."

Drawing my brows together, I wondered what exactly Marcus was capable of if everything he'd done so far was mild.

As if hearing my thoughts, Abby grabbed my forearm, pulling

me to a stop. She whispered, "He's fighting his natural urges to—"

"Abby," Marcus warned, his tone no longer light-hearted like it had been the other times he'd wanted Abby to keep her mouth shut.

God! He could be infuriating. I didn't understand why there were still things about him he didn't want me to know when I clearly remembered so much. I wasn't afraid of what he was—or Abby, for that matter. What I wanted was the truth, which was exactly what Marcus wanted as well—except when it came to him and his secrets. Those, he was happy to keep to himself.

No matter how much I wanted to pull him up on it, this wasn't the right time.

When we reached the car, I hopped into the front passenger seat as Abby slipped into the back. Marcus started the engine then turned to me, a small smile lifting the corner of his lips. Only, I knew it was forced. His eyes were doing that whole fiery amber, predator thing they'd been doing since Justin's confession. The strange thing was, Marcus wasn't a predator. He was a Soul Collector, not a predatory demon. Soul Collectors were supposed to be impartial, and unable to be manipulated.

I scoffed internally. All of that was a big fat lie. Justin had palmed my "collection" off to Marcus, and Marcus had gone against orders to deliver me to Purgatory.

So far, both Justin and Marcus had proved just how much a Soul Collector could be swayed and go against everything that was supposedly ingrained into their very existence. I wasn't sure if every Soul Collector had similar discrepancies, or if I was the one who broke their mold.

Marcus put the car into gear, and we peeled around the tree-lined driveway then came to a stop at the gates. The thick iron bars inched opened to allow us through. I waited for Marcus to continue, but he didn't move.

I glanced in his direction, the hairs on the back of my neck standing up the moment our eyes locked. His fingers clenched the steering wheel, as he returned his focus to the trees across the road. A moment later he looked up at the rearview mirror. I twisted around just in time to see Abby giving him a barely noticeable nod, urging him to go forward.

"What's wrong?" I asked, knots forming in my stomach.

Marcus slipped the car into first gear. "Soul Scrapers."

CHAPTER 2

*M*y skin crawled at the mention of their name. Just knowing Soul Scrapers were in the same vicinity as me made me want to turn back and lock myself away in Marcus's estate where the Soul Scrapers couldn't get in. But I was done running. We didn't have any substantial evidence, but I knew within my heart that whoever had placed this curse on me, were using them to do their dirty work.

Up until the moment we walked into the Devil's Playground, the Soul Scrapers had remained at a distance. For whatever reason, something had changed at the club, and they were coming closer, instilling perpetual fear into my soul.

Marcus slowly accelerated as I kept my eyes on the woods surrounding his estate. I couldn't see what both Marcus and Abby could, but I wasn't about to look away.

As we merged onto the road, my mind raced with questions I prayed Mava could answer. She was the one person who knew the most, yet no one could get a straight answer from her. All she spouted was riddle after riddle that none of us could figure out.

Then she'd handed me that vial filled with God knows what, expecting us to trust her, when in reality she could've been trying to kill me with some evil potion—if that were even possible. Yet, something about the old witch did make me trust her. It probably had more to do with the fact that nobody else believed her—including her own kind. They all saw her for the loony witch she let everyone believe she was.

Glimmers of the sane person she'd let me see made me realize that maybe it was all just an act. What the act was for was beyond me. Actually, that wasn't true. I had my suspicions and the more I thought about it, the more it made sense.

Abby had once mentioned an old prophecy that none of the other witches believed. Maybe it really did have something to do with us —or me. And Mava was leading everybody to believe that she was just some crazy witch so nobody would take any notice of her. After all, we'd uncovered more truths in that riddle of hers, yet none of us understood what it all meant. It was only after we'd unraveled information from unlikely sources that we were able to put any of it together.

My stomach churning, I squinted at what looked to be black fog heading towards us at an insanely fast speed.

"Step on it." Abby twisted around in her seat to look out the back window.

A moment later, I could make out the mangled faces and hands of the Soul Scrapers as they swirled through the air, heading straight for us.

As we rounded the corner, I caught sight of someone standing in a middle of the road. I expected whoever it was to move, but they remained completely still, their attention focused directly on us.

As we got closer, I realized that the idiot standing in the middle of the road was Justin.

"He's not moving," I muttered.

My heart raced as Marcus shifted down a gear, tearing toward Justin as if he planned on mowing him down.

Darkness folded over the sky, turning the day to night. I knew it had to be the Soul Scrapers but I was too terrified to look.

"Get ready to take her," Marcus said calmly.

Before I could ask what he was talking about, Abby slipped her hand under my arm and gripped me tightly. We were about five seconds from squashing Justin like a toad and Marcus wasn't slowing down. I may not have liked Justin, but I didn't really want him dead—especially when he may have held answers that we desperately needed.

"Stop," I yelled at Marcus.

Marcus ignored me and floored the car.

I opened my mouth to plead with Marcus to stop, but I was too late. We didn't have time to stop. It was inevitable.

Everything went into slow motion as we were about to collide. A split second before impact, Justin pushed off the ground and leaped into the air, one foot coming down on the hood. Then he disappeared over the roof.

A blinding white light shone through the back window, lighting up the inside of the car before darkness took over the sky.

My blood froze as the Soul Scrapers swept through the air, smothering the brilliant white light in the thick of their fold.

"Shit." Marcus lifted the handbrake then swung the car sideways as he clicked my seatbelt free. "Now."

My eyes widened in horror as a car came racing toward us, the headlights shining right on me. The screech of their brakes reverberated in my head, followed by the deafening thud as the metal of my side door crumbled.

CHAPTER 3

*M*y life flashed before me, and I prayed that this wasn't the end again. This was not how I wanted to die. Not in some stupid car accident because Marcus irresponsibly spun the car into the wrong lane. In that split second, I wasn't angry with him. I was sad. If this were it, then he'd once again have himself to blame for my death.

My heart was in my throat as I waited for the impact to crush my body, but it never came. Somehow, I was thrown from the car without smashing through any window.

Strong arms wrapped around my chest but they weren't Marcus's. That much I knew for sure. I wanted to see if it was Abby who had me but I couldn't take my eyes off the scene below as we flew into the sky.

Both cars were a complete write-off. I wasn't sure if whoever was in the other car was still alive, but when I saw Marcus emerge from his vehicle, I barely gave it a second thought.

He glanced up at me, momentarily locking eyes with mine. Then he turned, flicked out the wicked-cool liquid metal blade from his knife, and raced into the thick of the Soul Scrapers. I definitely wanted one of those babies on me twenty-four-seven if they were able to protect me from those monstrous Soul Scrapers.

"Don't worry about him," Abby said, leaning down. "He's just going to help Justin out then meet us at Mava's house."

How she knew all that was beyond me. Those two knew each other better than anyone. It kind of infuriated me, but I knew I had nothing to be worried about. Marcus and I had a much deeper connection—if I only could remember just how deep it actually went.

My chest constricted. Not from being one-hundred meters up in the air without anything more than Abby's arms wrapped around me stopping me from plunging to my death. It was because of Marcus. I was afraid he wouldn't survive.

Abby had said that he would be okay, and I knew that she was more than likely right, but I just couldn't shake the sickening feeling that something was wrong.

The temperature of the air around us had dropped. Icy wind whipped against my face as I shielded my eyes with my hands, blocking my view of wherever we were heading. I needed a pair of damn goggles to see, yet Abby didn't seem the slightest bit fazed by the wind. For all I knew she had an extra set of clear eyelids that closed over her eyes, protecting them during flight. I wanted to laugh at the absurdity of that thought, but all that exited my mouth was a small gurgle.

The cold wind lashing against my face eased into a subtle breeze. Removing my hands covering my eyes, I searched the ground, trying to figure out why we had stopped above a deserted field surrounded by trees. It took me a moment to realize that we'd actually reached our destination. However, Mavas's rundown little shack was nowhere to be seen. What was even stranger, it looked as if her house had never been there in the first place.

"Shouldn't Mava's…" I began.

"Yeah, it should," Abby replied, her tone cold.

Descending a few feet, Abby circled the area slow enough for me to see without the wind stinging my eyes. There was absolutely no sign of Mava's house. All that remained were trees, vines, and overgrown grass where the shack once stood.

Abby tightened her grip on me as black shadows slithered through the trees, matching our pace.

Soul Scrapers.

Coming to a stop, we hovered above a small burned out clearing in the woods with a symbol in the middle of the charred ground that didn't look like anything I'd seen before. I knew Abby had spotted it as well because her grip tightened on me even more. She lifted us higher into the air and then darted straight ahead.

Pulling up, Abby hovered over another symbol surrounded by charred earth. It was similar to the first one, but the markings were slightly different.

She took off again, finding yet another symbol, then another as we continued to circle Mava's property.

Abby pulled up as we spotted the fifth symbol and she drew in a shuddered breath. "We better get you back home."

She didn't mention anything about the symbols, but it didn't take a genius to work out that they had everything to do with the disappearance of Mava's house—or so I assumed.

The flight back to Marcus's remained uneventful. Soul Scrapers slithered through the forest, trailing us. They steered clear of the more populated areas of Byron Bay then came back when there was coverage away from the humans' watchful eyes.

I wondered why they were staying away from the humans now when they'd been more than happy to get amongst people when they'd taken me from the club. They also didn't seem to have a problem when they were in the hospital I'd been brought to after the last time I'd slit my wrist. I hadn't known it at the time, but I wasn't just experiencing the ice-addict's hallucinations. Real Soul Scrapers were watching me then. And for some reason, the addict was the only one who could see them as well. His unbridled terror of the shadowed creatures was far too real for me to ignore.

Abby's arms went rigid, bringing the fear of God into me. We were coming closer to the stretch of road where we'd left Marcus. I couldn't see clearly, but I knew Abby could.

Squinting, I forced myself to look through wind whipping my eyes, as I barely made out the cars below surrounded by flashing lights, which I presumed were police cars and ambulances. At this height, I couldn't tell if anyone was injured, and I prayed Justin hadn't been waiting there, knowing what was going to happen, so he could collect the souls of whoever was in the other car.

Both Marcus and Justin were nowhere to be seen. And apart from the Soul Scrapers that were following Abby and me, the place was deserted.

Abby flew around the perimeter of Marcus's compound without

bothering to tell me why. She didn't have to. I knew what she was looking for. And if I had wings, I'd be doing the same.

My heart stopped as my suspicions were confirmed. The same five symbols that were charred into the ground surrounding Mava's home, were strategically placed around Marcus's land as well.

I still had no idea what the symbols meant, but one thing was clear: the force surrounding Marcus's house remained impenetrable. The Soul Scrapers that had been following us were meticulously looking for a way in, swarming the perimeter and not a single one was able to cross the invisible barrier Marcus had around his place to keep unwanted supernatural species out.

I wasn't sure if all humans could get in, or if Marcus had only made an allowance for me to get through. What I found strange was that Justin was able to get through the barrier last night. After everything that had gone down between Marcus and him, Marcus still let him have access to his home.

I wished that I could remember their relationship, and when exactly it fell apart.

Justin must've been riddled with guilt having to watch his best friend spiral into the pits of hell every time Marcus had to drive the knife through my heart, killing me to prevent eighty odd years of torture.

It sickened me to think that Justin had only just now come out with the truth. If only he'd told Marcus earlier… Maybe things could've been different.

Flying just over the pool, Abby lifted up momentarily before gliding down, landing a few feet from the back door.

I no longer had the urge to kiss the ground when we landed. Flying was the least insane part of everything that was going on. The Soul Scrapers had changed me that night at the Devil's Playground, in more ways than I wanted to acknowledge.

Abby folded her wings behind her body. A moment later, they disappeared as if they'd never been there—just like Mava's home.

"Well, that was unexpected." She flicked her red hair over her shoulder then opened the back door and walked into the kitchen as if that were all that needed to be said.

The hell it was.

CHAPTER 4

ollowing after her, I closed the door behind me in a pathetic attempt to keep another barrier between the Soul Scrapers and me. I tapped my nails against the bench as I watched Abby pull out a bottle of wine, remove the cork, and then pour herself a glass.

"Want one?" she asked, looking up at me as if it were any other ordinary day and she was playing host to her guest.

"That's it?" I asked, completely dumbfounded.

Abby had never appeared to be the type to let anything go. She was into every intricate detail of all the conspiracies surrounding Mava, and all things to do with Marcus and me.

Abby placed the bottle of red on the bench, a fake smile plastered on her face. "Would you like a glass of wine, too, Lucy?"

I raised a brow. I'd done my fair share of trying to block out my senses from going into hyper-drive to get away from other people's problems. But now was so not the time to be drinking. Now was the time we needed to keep level-headed.

Abby sighed. "If Marcus asks, you forced me to have this conversation, okay?"

I nodded, relieved that I didn't have to try to squeeze a demonic creature into talking about something she clearly was trying to avoid. However, Marcus I could handle.

"It's all my fault," I said. "I get it. I made you talk."

"So again, do you want a glass?" Abby gestured to the wine bottle.

I shook my head. "No, thanks."

"Suit yourself." She grabbed the bottle and glass then headed into the lounge room.

Curling her way-too-perfect legs up on the couch, she propped the bottle between her left hip and elbow and held the glass in her right hand.

I sat on the couch opposite of her as she downed the glass of wine then refilled it. Normally I wasn't one to judge, but Abby appeared to have a real drinking problem. And I just hoped it didn't affect the next fifty-six days.

As I stared at her, I once again found myself with a million questions. And the biggest question that had been driving me insane for the last ten minutes wasn't what was going on with the Soul Scrapers, why Justin was standing in the middle of the road, what was the prognosis of the people in the car who'd crashed into us, or what the symbols were. My biggest question was where the hell was Mava's house?

"Please tell me you know where Mava's house has gone," I said, leaning back on the couch.

Abby traced the rim of the glass with her finger. "I have absolutely no idea where that old shack went." She took another sip of her drink, downing half the contents. "That witch has done some crazy stuff in the past, but this eclipses it all." Lost in thought, she shook her head. "I've got nothing."

"She can't just disappear. Houses don't just vanish into thin air," I said, getting a little exasperated. "I mean, you did take us to the right place, didn't you?"

Abby barked out a laugh. "Yeah, that was her place, all right. And last night her decrepit old home was still standing right where it should've been today." She took another sip while holding up her forefinger for me to wait for her to finish the glass. "But, I'd bet my life that one of those other witches has something to do with it. Those symbols weren't there last time we were there."

"So, does that mean one of the other witches can tell us where she has gone?"

"Any witch strong enough to cast a spell like that isn't going to tell us shit. The only way we might find out where Mava's house disappeared to is by going back to Devil's Playground and hope we find someone drunk enough or high enough to talk."

Abby paused as she studied me. "But something tells me you're in no hurry to go back there anytime soon."

I ran my hands down my thighs. I definitely didn't want to step foot in that place ever again. "You got that right. But you can go by yourself, can't you?"

Maybe she couldn't get into the club without Marcus. I had no idea how any of their lives worked and who was welcome where.

"And leave you here?" Abby asked, as if it was the dumbest thing she'd ever heard.

"Well...yeah. Why not?"

"Because Marcus would kill me if he found out that I left you here alone—or anywhere, for that matter."

"But there's that force field thing around his property keeping everyone out. No one can get in that he doesn't want here, right?"

She raised a brow as she poured another glass of wine. "That doesn't matter when it comes to Marcus's obsessive protection he has over you."

As much as I wanted answers, a huge part of me was relieved that Abby wouldn't leave me here by myself. The truth was, I was afraid to be alone. Those Soul Scrapers scared the absolute crap out of me. I was completely powerless against them. I'd never felt so helpless, and I never wanted to experience it again. Abby was like my safeguard against those hellish creatures.

"Fair enough," I muttered, fiddling with a small strand of plaster that had come away from the cast on my wrist. It seemed like a lifetime ago that I'd had the cast put on to stop myself from ripping apart the stitches on my wrist.

"None of those bastards are getting to you on my watch," she murmured over the rim of her glass.

Drawing my brows together, I looked up at her. "If the Soul Scrapers can take on a fog-like form, why don't they come and get us when you're flying?"

"Because they're bottom crawlers. Their range of movement is limited. They can get in through any cracks or crevices as long as it's

197

a couple of meters from the ground. The same goes when they're in purgatory. They don't need to be up with the higher beings."

I scowled, trying to make sense of her words.

"Don't worry about it," she said. "You'll get it all sooner or later."

I seriously doubted I would. The more I found out about this other world, the less I seemed to understand.

"So what was the go with Justin?" I asked. "I mean, what was he doing standing in the middle of the road?"

Abby shrugged as she took a sip. "My guess is he was waiting for us."

"Do you think he knew about the Soul Scrapers?"

Abby nodded. "We can feel them when they're nearby—especially the Soul Collectors. They have an inbuilt detection system for those things. Actually, we know when any one of our kind is around. Some more than others," she muttered then raised her glass and downed the rest of her wine.

I was about to ask her something else about the symbols around the house when my phone rang. Hoping it was Marcus, I shoved my hand into my pocket and retrieved it.

I sighed. It was my mother.

There was no way on earth I wanted to speak to that woman. She'd probably heard that I'd left rehab early, and worse, left with a guy I'd only just met. She was probably calling to threaten me with some legal action, making it out as if I was incompetent and couldn't look after myself. The first thing my mother would do if she ever got the court to agree to deem me unable to care for myself would be to stick me in some psych ward for the rest of my life, so she never had to deal with me again.

I sometimes wondered why she didn't just leave me to my own, but then I remembered just how fanatical she was about keeping up appearances. If she could hide me away in a psychiatric facility where nobody would know where I was, I wouldn't have the chance to ruin what she thought was her perfect reputation. The woman acted as if she was an A-grade celebrity when in fact she was more like D or maybe even a Z.

Nobody cared about her or what she was doing. My father was more in the spotlight, not her—and even he barely made the news. It was only during election times or if he screwed up on some policy that the media covered him. The rest of the time he went unnoticed.

But of course, my mother always did want to feel more important than she was.

After staring at the phone for three rings, I sent the call to voicemail. This was only the start of things to come. My mother wasn't one to give up. She'd hunt me down if it were the last thing she did.

I would deal with her later.

"Should I ask?" Abby said as I dropped my phone on the seat beside me.

I held back a groan. "It was just my mother."

Thankfully, Abby didn't ask any further questions. I really didn't want to go into the complexity of how screwed up my relationship with my mother was. I half wondered if she actually was my mother if I had been reincarnated. Maybe she was just an incubator, cursed to spawn me in this lifetime. That possibility made sense. And for the first time in my life, I kind of pitied her—for about two seconds.

I was still a human who deserved to be loved by the person who'd carried me for nine months.

The next twenty minutes, I watched Abby finish off another three bottles of wine while I listened to her spouting on about humans and their family dramas. How humans weren't happy with their lives, they were all searching for something that would make their lives complete. How they would tread on anyone to get what they wanted and allow the stupidest of things to come between them.

She actually spoke many truths. It must've been weird for their kind to watch us over the years, to see how the human race evolved but no matter how many luxuries we had, everyone was still striving for more.

My tummy groaned loud enough to make Abby stop talking.

"Hungry, hey?" Without waiting for me to answer, she got up and stumbled into the kitchen.

Deciding I should probably help out, I stood and followed, arriving just in time to see Abby grab another bottle of wine. She popped the cork and filled her glass. I was surprised that she bothered to use a glass at all.

Tapping my nails against the counter, I asked, "Shouldn't Marcus be back by now?"

"He's a big boy. He can take care of himself." Abby downed her glass of wine then refilled it.

I suspected she was even more concerned than I was, which only made that nagging feeling in the pit of my stomach grow tenfold.

Abby lowered her glass. "You know, I never used to drink this much." She lifted the glass and finished off the remaining wine.

She twisted around, staggered over to the fridge, yanked it open, and perused the shelves. With her empty glass in one hand, she managed to pull out three containers stacked on top of each other, then kicked the door closed with her heel and placed them on the counter.

"You know," she started as she unstacked the containers, placing them in a perfectly straight line next to each other that anyone with OCD would've been satisfied with. "I started drinking way back in the day just to be supportive of Marcus, which was pretty stupid because I could have supported him without the drinking. But that wasn't as much fun. It started out as just a few glasses of wine to take the edge off his pain."

"Marcus?" I asked.

"Yep." Abby peeled the lids off the containers and placed them into another perfect line to the left. Then, she grabbed two forks out of the drawer and handed one to me. She dug into the first container filled with various cut fruits, moving around the pieces absentmindedly.

"Marcus was able to stop when you came back, but me..." She shrugged.

"I wouldn't have thought you guys could get addicted to anything," I said, pulling the container filled with leftover lasagne toward me while watching her to see if she cared that I messed up her perfect line. She didn't.

"I wish." Abby stabbed a piece of watermelon and put it into her mouth. "It's only because of you that Marcus can switch it off."

I hated to think of what Marcus was like during those times, or how much alcohol he'd consumed from the moment he had ended my life until the time we were reunited in my next life. This life.

It was easy for me. I was the one who died. I was the one who was reborn not knowing anything about my previous lives or the loop that I was on.

Sure, I was cursed with the torture of feeling everyone's bad emotions, addictions, and pain, but that was nothing compared to having to live with yourself, knowing that you were the one who killed the love of your life and you were powerless to stop it—and will inevitably have to do the exact same thing in another eighteen years.

I was determined to never let him go through that again—even if it meant doing things I shouldn't.

CHAPTER 5

$\mathcal{N}$ ight had fallen, and Marcus still wasn't home. Abby had switched the wine for coffee and was lying back on the sofa watching TV as she tried to sober up. Every so often, I caught her looking outside as if she could sense things I could not. Each time I waited for some flash of recognition to register on her face, telling me that Marcus was nearby, but it never happened.

Picking at the cast on my wrist, I tried to ignore the feeling that something was terribly wrong. For all I knew, the Soul Scrapers had dragged Marcus and Justin down into the depths of Hell and were keeping them hostage so we couldn't figure out the answers in time.

"Maybe we should go look for him," I suggested for the third time in the last hour.

"Like I told you last time, he'll know to come back here."

"Maybe he's lying half dead in the bushes, and we're just sitting here waiting, wasting time when we should be out there looking for him. He doesn't even have a car. How will he get home?"

Abby glanced at me sideways.

"Maybe we should take one—" She trailed off, turning her head towards the front door.

I followed her gaze, my heart pounding in anticipation for what I prayed her look meant, that she could sense Marcus coming. I hoped she wasn't just listening to a possum or a koala scurrying up a tree.

My heart skipped a beat when I heard footsteps approach the front door. I felt ridiculous for missing Marcus as much as I did. He'd only been gone for a few hours, and I was acting as if he'd been gone for days. However, the moment he walked into the house all rational thinking disappeared. I wanted to run into his arms and squeeze the hell out of him while telling him never to leave me again. Instead, I forced myself to keep cool and not act like the pathetic girlfriend I was.

Girlfriend. That word didn't sound right. We'd never exactly said what we were to each other, but girlfriend didn't even come close.

Soulmate.

That was what we were. We had a love that lasted through every single one of my lives.

Marcus strode into the room looking beyond frustrated. His hair was dishevelled and he looked as if he'd been to Hell and back. I just hoped it was because of the fight with the Soul Scrapers and he hadn't actually been dragged into the fiery pits.

Abby twisted around in her seat to look at him. "Where the heck have you been?"

Marcus's gaze found mine, then dropped to my arm with the cast resting in my lap. All the frustration on his face vanished. "I'm sorry."

"Yeah, yeah, yeah. We get it," Abby said. "Luciana missed you. I thought Titus nailed your ass. And you're sorry. Now tell us where the hell you've been?"

Titus?

Ignoring Abby, Marcus strode over to me, leaned down, and grabbed my good hand. Pulling me to my feet, he tucked me against his chest and wrapped his strong arms around my shoulders.

I melted into his embrace, the anxiety of the last few hours slowly fading away.

Marcus leaned down and whispered into my ear, "I'm sorry." He kissed the tender spot below my lobe. "And you don't have to worry about Titus nailing my ass. Abby is just being overdramatic as usual."

She scoffed "Yeah, whatever, demon boy. You and I both know what he can do."

Thanks, Abby, for telling me this earlier. It was probably for the best.

My cast wouldn't have copped the damage; instead, I would've gone straight for the stitches.

Marcus ran his hands down my arms and turned to Abby. "Go get me something to eat. I'm starving."

She snorted. "Go get it yourself, demon boy. I'm not your slave."

Marcus shrugged. "Worth a try."

Lacing my fingers with his, Marcus led me into the kitchen, then pulled away to open the fridge and scan the shelves.

I leaned down, folding my arms on the cool stone bench, and waited for him to say something, anything about where he'd been the last few hours.

Empty-handed, he closed the fridge, then opened the door under the bench and pulled out a pile of takeaway menus. He fanned them out then pushed them toward me. "What do you feel like?"

Dumbfounded, I shoved the menus back at him. "Where have you been?"

"See! I'm not the only one who wants answers," Abby called from the sofa. She got up and sauntered over to us. Taking a seat on the stool next to me, she twisted back-and-forth, tapping her fingernails on the bench. "Well?"

Marcus gathered the takeaway menus and flicked through them, stopping on a Chinese restaurant's flyer. Ignoring us, he retrieved his phone from his pocket, dialled the number, and ordered four dishes.

"You could have called," Abby said. "It's not as if you lost your phone or anything."

She looked directly at his phone as Marcus placed it on the bench.

He spread his hands out on the counter. "Julius told Justin that he was just following orders given by Titus, so we went to see Titus."

Abby raised her eyebrows. "And?"

Marcus lifted his gaze to meet Abby's. "We couldn't find him."

"You were gone for all that time, and you're telling me that you didn't find him?" Abby reiterated.

"That's what I'm telling you." Marcus shrugged. "Every time we opened a veil, it took us to the wrong layer. It was as if someone with way too much power and way too much to lose didn't want us talking to Titus."

"How is that even possible?" I asked, still not understanding how the supernatural world worked. Abby had done a terrible job of explaining things so far, and Marcus hadn't done that much better.

Between him, Abby, and Mava, I was going out of my mind trying to understand it all. "I thought these veils took you to whatever area you wanted them to."

Abby twisted around to face me. "It's not possible to alter the veils. Or I should say, it *shouldn't* be possible."

"It's true. I'm not lying," Marcus said, getting a little defensive.

I bit down on my smile.

The corner of Abby's lips tipped up. "Don't get your knickers in a knot, demon boy. I believe you."

Marcus leaned down and reached for my hand. Entwining my fingers with his, he kissed the part of my skin just above where he'd drawn the infinity symbol on my cast. "It got Justin and I thinking. Who would have enough power to manipulate the veils? Maybe Titus."

"If it were possible, maybe one of the higher-ups from my side," Abby said. "Which, let's face it, there are quite a few that would be happy to tip the scales. What they'd get out of doing this to you two is beyond me."

No one had an answer to that one.

Marcus ran his thumb over the back of my hand. "What did Mava have to say for herself? Did she give you another cryptic riddle?"

"She's disappeared," I said. "I mean, her whole house just vanished into thin air."

Marcus narrowed his eyes at me, then turned to Abby for confirmation.

"I don't know what type of magic was used, or if Mava had just decided to relocate her home during what could be the very moment in time that she had been waiting on for the past hundred or so years." She leaned back in her seat and strummed her nails on the counter. "But she was gone. Completely. As if she was never there."

"And the same symbols that were surrounding Mava's land are also surrounding yours," I added.

Marcus's grip on my hand tightened. "What symbols?"

I forgot Marcus wouldn't have seen them because he would've had to come back in a car. Except he'd walked through the front door, not the garage. And his car was totaled.

"How did you get back?"

"Justin brought me home."

Abby glared at him. "You let Justin fly you? You won't even let me fly you anywhere."

"I didn't say he flew me anywhere. He drove me home."

"But Justin doesn't even own a car," Abby said, confusion written all over her face.

"I never said it was *his* car." Letting go of my hands, Marcus stood and stretched his back.

"Justin stole someone's car?" I asked.

Marcus shrugged. "I didn't ask where he got the wheels from."

"So, where is Justin now?" Abby asked, not letting up on her endless line of questions.

Sure, I was also curious about the details, but right now I wanted nothing more than to enjoy the fact Marcus wasn't lying in a ditch somewhere. And he was in one piece—minus his wings.

"He's still trying to get through to Titus," Marcus replied, his gaze remaining fixed on me even though he was answering Abby. Something told me that he wanted to enjoy the moment just as much as I did.

"So, you and Justin are all good now?"

Marcus scoffed. "I wouldn't go that far."

"At least he's trying to redeem himself." Abby pointed out. "I've got to hand it to him. Justin's got guts."

"It'll take a goddamned miracle for him to redeem himself after lying to me for so long."

"Or him figuring out who's doing this to you."

Marcus didn't say anything. Part of me agreed with Marcus. I didn't want to forgive Justin. He deserved everything Marcus was throwing at him, and probably more. Except Justin was also the reason why Marcus and I had crossed paths. And no matter how angry I was with Justin, I still had to give him credit for that.

CHAPTER 6

A loud, drawn-out beep came from somewhere in the house.

"Food's arrived," Abby said, swivelling in her seat again.

"Can you go and get it for us?" Marcus asked.

"Your food, you go get it."

"Please?"

Abby's jaw hung open in surprise. Apparently, that wasn't a word Marcus used often.

"I want to speak to Lucy," he added.

"Fine." Abby slid off the stool, looking pointedly at Marcus. "Just for the record, I'm doing this for Lucy, not for you."

Something told me that Marcus could be a little bit bossy at the best of times, but I was glad Abby had agreed. I desperately wanted to hear what he had to say that he didn't want her hearing. And now I didn't have to wait until she went home to find out.

"Thanks, Abby," he said with sincerity. "I owe you one."

"You owe me a million."

Abby was probably right. She had an addiction that, although it was no one's fault but her own, Marcus's and my situation certainly was a huge contributing factor for getting her started.

When Abby had gone outside, I asked, "What is it you want to talk to me about?"

"You." Marcus walked around the bench and took my hands. He

gently twisted my injured wrist around, revealing the part of my cast that I had picked at while I waited for him to return. "You were worried, weren't you?"

He ran his thumb over my cast.

That was the understatement of the century.

"No," I said, not fooling anyone.

He raised a brow. "Really? Because your cast tells a different story."

I sighed. "Abby started drinking, and I mean really drinking, and I guess I figured it was because she was worried about you and didn't want to say anything."

"I'm sorry." Letting go of my wrist, he raised his hand to my face and caressed my cheek. "I would have called if we weren't stuck in the veils. The phones don't work once we leave this veil. And before you go thinking that I could've just come back through, called you, then continued our search, I wasn't able to. We spent just as much time getting back here as we'd spent trying to find Titus."

I bit my lip.

He brushed his thumb over my mouth. "Stop that."

I released my lip from my teeth. "Sorry. Nervous habit."

"You don't have anything to be nervous about."

"Don't I?"

Curling his fingers around my elbow, he nudged me into a standing position, my body inches from his. "I promise I'll never disappear on you again. This was a one-time only situation. Justin had word where Titus was, and we didn't have long to get to him."

Not trusting my voice to come out even, I nodded instead.

He cupped my head in his hands. "I know how precious our time together is, and believe me when I say that I will never leave again without telling you first."

I bit my lip again. I didn't like it when people made promises that they may not be able to keep. If it happened again, I would go out of my mind thinking that something terrible had happened to him.

"I thought I told you not to do that," he said, his gaze focused on my lips.

Before I could respond, his lips were on mine, slowly prying them apart, making me forget all my worries. Right then, there was no hourglass counting down the seconds we had remaining. It was just us—and an eternity to figure out the other stuff.

"You know..." Abby trailed off. "I'll just leave these here."

Tearing his mouth away from mine, Marcus turned to Abby who was placing the bags of Chinese food on the bench. "You don't have to go."

Jesus, he was a good friend. I was more than happy to see the back of her—at least for an hour.

Abby snorted. "Ahh, yeah I do."

She gave me a wink then slipped out the back door and disappeared over the garden wall with much more grace than she had done the first time I saw her.

A smile spread across Marcus's face. "Now, where were we?"

"You were going to have something to eat."

"I can think of something I'd much rather be doing." He grazed his lips across my jaw, stopping at my ear. "Eating is overrated."

Bringing his lips back to mine, he showed me just how overrated eating was.

CHAPTER 7

*T*he next morning we headed outside in search of the symbols that were surrounding the estate.

"I thought you said the symbols were around here?" Marcus asked as he trudged through the dead foliage covering the ground under the canopy of the trees.

I tilted my head to the side and glared at him. "I was in the air when I saw them, and everything around here looks the same. Besides, if you'd just let Abby take you up, you'd find them in seconds."

Marcus didn't respond. Lowering his head, he ran his fingers across a two-hundred-year-old gum tree as he headed away from me, disappearing amongst the dense bushland.

Obviously, that was a touchy subject, and I could only guess it was because of his wings that had been severed. Plus, Marcus was a little stubborn at the best of times.

I smiled thinking back to the memories I had of him before this lifetime. Previously, he'd never pushed for me to remember him and was happy just to make the most of what little time we had together. This time, he was so different. He was showing me another side of him—raw and vulnerable.

As much as I wanted to go after him, I was stuck hiding inside the safety barrier surrounding his property, in case any Soul Scrapers were still around. Even though I hadn't seen a single one since Abby flew me into the estate, I wasn't about to take any unnecessary chances.

Coming back into view, Marcus said, "It's not here."

I put my hands on my hips and scoured the landscape, searching for anything that looked remotely familiar. It had been night, and all I remembered were those big crop-circle-like symbols burned into the earth. "One of them have to be around here somewhere."

Marcus came through the protection barrier and dropped his arm over my shoulder. "We'll keep searching."

Falling into step with him as we walked along the boundary of the estate, I asked, "And if we still can't find them?"

He smirked. "Then it'll just confirm my suspicion that you and Abby are both going out of your mind."

"Hey." I jabbed my elbow into his side.

Marcus chuckled. "Houses disappearing? Imaginary symbols? Next thing you'll be telling me is that you want to take that crap Mava gave you."

I forced a small laugh even though I hadn't completely ruled out drinking Mava's concoction. If we hadn't worked out what was going on in fifty-six days, then that vial was something I would seriously consider taking. I had nothing to lose by drinking her concoction that would supposedly help me see because Marcus would kill me anyway.

Snuggling into his side, I tried to hide my sorrow. I'd attempted to kill myself so many times, but having Marcus drive the knife through my heart was killing me in ways that death couldn't erase.

Marcus came to an abrupt stop. "I think this is the place." He strode away from me, hopped onto a small boulder, and came to a halt as he looked at the ground in front of him. "Shit."

"Did you find it?"

He drew in a deep breath. "Sure did."

"Let me see," I said, stepping closer.

"No." His hand shot out toward me. A force of wind came out of nowhere, pushing me back then disappeared as if it had never been there to begin with.

My eyes shot open as I steadied myself. "What the hell was that?"

"You need to stay inside the barrier."

Folding my arms across my chest, I slowly rubbed them. "I meant, the wind."

"What about it?"

I glared at him. "It was you, wasn't it?"

He stared at me, jaw clenched.

"I'm not afraid of you, or what you are. You've got to know that, right?"

His features softened. "I keep forgetting you're different this time round." He stepped down from the boulder then strode toward me. "Something like that would've freaked the hell out of you before."

I smiled, remembering the time when I'd apparently thought Abby was trying to possess Marcus with her devilish charms. Her wings had scared the crap out of me. I wished I remembered more of my other lives. I wondered what I'd thought of his scars on his back, and what I'd initially thought of him when he came for his collection. He must've had wings when we first met. Maybe he even flew with me. That was something I wished I could've remembered.

I also desperately wanted to know who I was back when we first met because something was telling me that part of my life was crucial to figuring out how to stop this curse that keeps taking me away from him.

Standing in front of me, Marcus grabbed my hands and tugged me toward him until my chest was flush against his. "As much as this time 'round scares the hell out of me, I'm loving who you are now."

He leaned down and placed a tender kiss on my lips.

"I'm still the same person, aren't I?"

"Of course you are. But that's not what I meant." He gave me one last kiss then headed back to the symbol. "It's like you're becoming more..." He turned back to face me and drew his brows together as he studied me. "Whole." He nodded. "I think that's the best way to describe your changes."

"Whole? As in how?"

"You're more confident and willing to accept what you don't fully understand. In the past, things like me pushing you back would've made you run as far away from me as possible."

I smiled, thinking of how crazy I must've driven him over the years. My thoughts went back to the few times at the rehab where dark clouds had rolled in out of nowhere. "Can you control the weather?"

He shook his head. "Not the weather. But my emotions can control the air around me."

"Is that normal for Soul Collectors?" I couldn't imagine an instant where that would be needed to collect a human's soul.

"Some of us were created with a little extra than others."

"Right," I said, wishing he'd give out a little more information on his own rather than me having to drag it out of him.

I took a few steps closer to him, stopping when he gave me the look, telling me I was close to the boundary. With my palms up, I reached toward the barrier, hoping I would feel some sort of tingle or something when I made contact. I felt nothing. "Did you actually put this barrier around your place?"

"I can't do magic."

"So, only witches can do magic?"

He nodded. "An old friend placed a spell around our estate."

My heart skipped a beat at the mention of *our* estate. I hardly thought of Marcus's home as mine, but he sure did, which only made me love him that much more. After spending my life with parents who most certainly never made me feel at home, it soothed my soul knowing I always had a place with Marcus.

I shook my thoughts away. "Aren't you worried that whoever placed this protection spell may have deliberately hidden a weakness, which is what the symbols were created to activate?"

Marcus chuckled. "No. I trust this witch. She may not know what's going on with us, but I do trust her." He kicked at the dirt surrounding the symbols. "And by the look of it, my trust was placed with the right person. Otherwise, you wouldn't be standing there without a swarm of Soul Scrapers around you."

Something about what he'd said niggled at the back of my thoughts. Why would a witch try to get through the protection layer? And more importantly, what if anything did they have to gain from getting to me?

CHAPTER 8

Sitting on the couch, listening to Marcus fill Abby in on the phone as he paced the length of the lounge room got me thinking about the witches even more. I didn't know anything about them, yet they seemed to be coming up everywhere I looked. Maybe it was a coincidence, or maybe we were onto something. Either way, it would be virtually impossible to find out if I was right.

Marcus hung up and pocketed the phone. "I have to go out for a bit. Abby has to work but should be back here as soon as she can to keep you company."

"Where are you going?" I asked, dread pooling in the pit of my stomach. "You only just got back, and now you're leaving me again?"

He walked over to the hallway table and selected a key from the pile in a bowl. "It's not safe for you out there."

I jumped up from the lounge and strode over to him. I didn't want to be left alone. This was my fight too, and I didn't want to just be sitting around waiting while everyone else tried to save my ass.

"And you think it's safe in here?" I threw my hands in the air. "Because we just spent the last hour walking around outside looking for the spells the witches cast to try to get into your place. Now, does that sound safe to you?"

Marcus ran his hand down his face then let out a slow breath.

He was clearly frustrated, but I wasn't giving up. "You can't expect me to be okay with just sitting around waiting, hoping that you're okay."

He shoved the keys into his back pocket then placed his hand on my hip. "You're right. But I can't let the Soul Scrapers get anywhere near you. Last time, we had Abby to get you away if the situation called for your escape."

A shiver ran up my spine. I wondered if I'd ever get over what they did to me.

I bit my lip as I tried to figure out what to do. I didn't want to let him go without me, but I didn't want to be anywhere near those Soul Scrapers without an exit strategy.

Marcus gave my lip a gentle tap with his finger then cupped the back of my neck in his hand. "I got an idea."

He leaned down and placed a soft kiss on my forehead. Then he reached into his pocket and retrieved his phone, pressed the screen a few times, and put it to his ear.

A few seconds later he said, "Don't suppose you can come here for about thirty minutes before you go to your next job?" He remained silent for a moment then said, "Thanks. I owe you one."

He disconnected the call.

"I'm guessing that was Abby?" I asked.

"Yeah, that was Abby." He put the key back into the bowl then wrapped his arm around my shoulders and ushered me down the hall toward the bedrooms. "She'll be here as soon as she can to watch over you while I pay someone a quick visit."

"By 'pay someone a visit,' I hope you don't mean you're going to be searching for somebody in another veil."

"No. I promise I'll be staying in this dimension, and I'll be back within an hour."

He opened the door to his bedroom and led me over to his bed. For a moment, I thought he planned to spend the next—however long it would take for Abby to get here—in bed with me. Instead, he said, "Wait here."

Then he disappeared into the closet.

Not knowing what to do with myself, I sat on the end of his bed and looked around the room. As much as I liked my own room, it didn't quite compare to the comfort of his. I wondered if I'd ever moved into his room in the past, or if I'd stubbornly remained in my own completely oblivious to how much every second that we had together counted.

I ran my hand over the charcoal cover, memories of our time together flooding my mind. Right now, my thoughts were too consumed with the love that we had for each other and the moments we shared, or the heart crushing moment Marcus ended my life to try to remember any details that could be useful to us. There had to be something in my memories that potentially could hold the key to the mystery that surrounded our curse, but no matter how much I tried to look past my feelings for him, I couldn't. I was completely consumed with every emotion Marcus and I shared as one.

He came back into the room holding something hidden in his closed fist. He sat beside me and unfolded his fingers, revealing a pendant attached to a rose-gold chain. "Do you remember this?"

Taking the pendant from him, I inspected the smooth lines of the quartz as I waited for the moment of recognition to hit. It didn't. "Should I?"

Marcus sighed. "It was yours." I twisted around to face him, resting my knee on the edge of the bed. "When?"

"You mean, when was it yours?"

I nodded.

"It was given to you in your last lifetime. I don't know who gave it to you because you never told me and you refused to take it off."

I drew my eyebrows together. "Why wouldn't I tell you?"

He shrugged. "Honestly, I have no idea. All you said was that someone gave it to you, but you couldn't remember who it was."

"Well, maybe I was telling the truth. After all, someone's been screwing with my mind for the past few hundred years."

Marcus took the pendant from my hands. "Maybe you're right. But it was just strange how you refused to take it off ever since you got it."

Not a single thing about the pendant looked special. I couldn't imagine why I would've been so attached to the rock. It wasn't even pretty, and it didn't look to have any real value.

Marcus slipped it into his pocket.

"So, what are you planning to do with it?" I asked.

"I don't want you to get your hopes up, but I might be able to get a protection spell placed on the pendant that will help ward off the Soul Scrapers from getting their hands on you."

My eyes lit up with hope. Part of me wondered why Marcus was only thinking of this now, but I was grateful all the same.

"As I said, don't get your hopes up. I'm not sure if it's possible."

I nodded. "Are you taking it to the same witch who placed the protection spell around your house?"

"As soon as Abby gets here."

"And then I'll be able to come with you?"

"That's the idea." He spread his hand over my thigh, and rubbed down to my knee. "Unfortunately, we won't know if the spell works until you come into contact with a Soul Scraper."

The thought of being in the same vicinity let alone within arms reach sent chills racing down my spine. This was only the beginning of our quest, though. I needed to push through the fear and do whatever was necessary before we ran out of time.

Marcus shifted back up the bed and leaned against the pillows with his arm raised for me to snuggle under. "Come here."

I crawled over to him and curled up beside him, my head resting against his chest.

Wrapping his arms around me, he planted a kiss on the top of my head and breathed in deeply. "I just want to hold you forever."

I tilted my head back so I could see his eyes and smiled. That haunted look was no longer there. It had been replaced with hope and sheer determination. I prayed to God that he was right and I'd finally be free from the Soul Scrapers clutches.

CHAPTER 9

rue to her word, Abby arrived in no time. She was wearing the tightest dress I'd ever seen, and it was short enough to give any guy over the age of fifty a heart attack. Those long legs of hers instantly made me feel subconscious about mine. She was a goddess.

Once again it got me wondering what Marcus saw in me. And why he was drawn to me to the point that not even someone like Abby could sway him? Not that I knew if she would even go there if he were interested. To me, Abby saw him more like a best friend—and nothing more.

For the first time since I had met her, Abby didn't have a bottle of wine within arm's reach. I hoped the little conversation we'd had earlier had hit home to her. Drinking was never going to solve anything.

Once Marcus had left, Abby made herself comfortable on the couch, switched on the TV and then groaned. "When is this shit ever going to end?"

I turned my attention to what was on the TV. It was yet another broadcast of the war that was going on in the Middle East. Another group of innocents had been kidnapped, demands were being made that would most likely never be met, and all the faces they were showing would one day wind up dead. What I didn't get was why

Abby had a problem with the war when she was a form of demon herself. I thought corruption, pain, and misery was part of her daily life.

"Why do you care? I thought you would be all for the wars?"

Tearing her gaze from the TV, she looked at me with an eyebrow raised. "What? Because I'm a demon?"

It looked like I'd hit a sore spot, but I wasn't backing away. "Well, yeah."

"Just because I'm a Succubus doesn't mean I wouldn't switch sides if I were given half a chance. The scales have been tipped on our side for long enough, and are way overdue to go the other way."

I remembered what Marcus had told me about the scales. He'd said that the scales tipped both ways, evening out the scale between good and evil over the years. There was no heaven and hell like society had depicted, just one big balancing act. I wished to God that there were some sort of good vs evil bible that I could find out all the information about this world of theirs, because, between Abby and Marcus, I was confused as hell.

"Does someone tip the scales?"

Abby scrunched up her face. "Huh?"

"I mean is there a peacemaker—angel or demon—that looks over the scales of good versus evil, and balances the lines between the two?"

"No. There is no one entity that overlooks it all. We each have a job to do, and in the past, that's been enough."

I thought about what she said and how they had all seamlessly worked together over the years. Sure, there had been horrendous moments in time, but none of them had gone on for too long. Something had changed, and the world was going to shit.

"How long overdue are we?"

She thought for a moment then said, "If you're talking about the war in the Middle East, we're about five years overdue. But when you take into account all the other things that have been going wrong in the world, I can't even begin to estimate." She flicked the channel repeatedly, then settled on a light-hearted comedy. Her expression brightened, and she hopped up from the couch. "Want something to eat?"

It seemed she was always either drinking herself silly or shoving food into her mouth. She was lucky that it never showed on her body.

"Well?" Abby asked again, taking a few steps toward the kitchen.

I shook my thoughts away.

"Ah, yeah. Thanks," I said, realizing just how hungry I was. "Want a hand?"

"Nope. You stay here, and I'll go get it." She disappeared into the kitchen then returned a few minutes later with two boxes of the Chinese Marcus had ordered last night and not touched, and two sodas.

She handed me a box and a fork.

"Thanks." I opened the container of steaming hot noodles.

Abby placed the sodas on the coffee table then claimed her position back on the couch. "Did Marcus say who he was going to ask to put a spell on the pendant?"

I shook my head as I twirled the noodles around my fork. "He didn't say the person's name, but he mentioned it was the same witch who'd placed the spell around this place."

Abby barked out a laugh. "Good luck in getting anything from her."

She shoved a forkful of noodles in her mouth.

"What do you mean?"

She held up a finger while she finished chewing. "Astrid stopped practicing years ago."

"How can you stop being a witch?"

"Oh, she is still a witch—and a bit of a bitch, but any witch can stop practicing any time they like. Not that it happens very often because they're so damned power hungry. But for those that do, they just choose not to use their powers. So now Astrid's just running around in a crystal shop, selling shit to tourists."

All my hope that I'd get to leave this house completely vanished. Marcus was wasting time we didn't have and it was all just to appease me and my desire to not sit on the sidelines while he was out searching for answers.

Abby was about to shove more food in her mouth, but paused, staring up at me. "You know, maybe Marcus will be able to convince her."

By the look on her face, not even she believed her words, though.

Settling back in my seat, I moved the noodles around the box with my fork, no longer having an appetite.

It wasn't long before the garage door clattered open and a few moments later, Marcus walked into the room. I couldn't read his expression, which I took as bad news. If he'd been able to convince the witch, he would've been grinning from ear to ear.

Abby stood and handed her box of Chinese with the fork wedged inside to Marcus. "I take it things didn't go as hoped."

Marcus placed the box on the coffee table. He slipped his hand into his pocket and retrieved the pendant. "Actually, it didn't take as much to convince her as I thought it would."

Abby's jaw dropped.

Beaming with happiness, I jumped up from the couch and grabbed the pendant from him.

"Oh, my God," I said with a small squeal in my voice. "After everything that Abby said, I didn't think you had a hope in hell of getting her to do this for you." I wrapped my arms around Marcus's neck and pressed a kiss on his lips. "Thank you so much."

I opened the clasp and secured the chain around my neck.

Then, I lifted the pendant from my chest and rubbed my thumb over it. "Let's just hope it works."

CHAPTER 10

"Well, I'll leave you guys to it." Abby headed for the door, but paused by my side and reached for the pendant. "Ouch."

She recoiled her hand as a fine stream of smoke came from the stone—or Abby's finger. I wasn't entirely sure which one.

Abby put her finger in her mouth then pulled it out to inspect it. Her eyes narrowed then widened in astonishment. "What the fuck?"

She twisted her hand around so we could see her finger. Right on the pads of her thumb and forefinger was a black mark the size of a pinprick.

"Holy hell," I said, guilt sweeping over me. I'd never considered for a second that Abby would be affected by the pendant I'd just assumed it would only work against the Soul Scrapers. "I'm so sorry."

Marcus chuckled. "Guess we know it works."

Abby slapped his chest—hard. "Guess who just lost her wings?"

The smile vanished from Marcus's face. "Shit."

It took me a moment to realize what she meant. Then it dawned on me. If Abby was no longer able to touch me, that meant she could no longer fly me anywhere without being burned. As much as that news would've been a blessing a few days ago, now I was bummed, knowing I'd never be able to get up in the air again while wearing the pendant.

"Touch her," Marcus said. "See if it's just the pendant or if it's her skin, as well."

"I'm not touching her." Abby took a step back, taking with her my hope of flying. "You touch her."

My heart skipped a beat. As horrified as I was that Abby couldn't come in contact with me again, the thought of Marcus never being able to touch me while I wore the pendant was too much. I was ready to rip the damned thing off my neck and take my chances with the Soul Scrapers.

"I'm not a demon. It won't do anything to me," Marcus said with complete confidence.

I held my breath as he snaked his arm around my waist. He must've had complete faith in Astrid because if he were wrong, he was going to have one hell of a burn.

Relief flooded through me when he didn't recoil in pain like Abby had.

Marcus smirked. "See."

Abby scowled at him then pointed to the pendant. "Touch it."

With one arm still around me, he reached for the pendant. Unlike Abby, he was able to hold it without being seared.

"I guess it's only meant to deter demons and Soul Scrapers." Marcus chuckled, letting the pendant fall back against my chest.

"Ha, ha, ha. Very funny." Abby grabbed my forearm. "Shit." She shook her hand as if she'd just stuck it into a fire. She inspected the faint charcoal color of her skin where it had touched mine. "This is not going to be good for business."

Abby held the palm of her hand up for us to see. "How am I going to be able to keep the boss happy when I can't even—"

"Abby," Marcus warned, cutting her off.

"What? I wasn't going to say anything that might offend your precious Lulu." She looked at me apologetically.

I gave her a smile to let her know that I wasn't the slightest bit offended.

"Why did the bitch make it so you can touch it and I can't?" she asked. "And don't give me any of that crap about me being a demon and you're not because we both know that you collected for our side before any of this shit happened."

That was news to me. I thought Soul Collectors weren't aligned to good or evil.

"You know that's not how the rules work."

"Yeah, whatever, demon boy." She waved him off with her good hand. "You probably got Astrid to add me to the spell just to piss me off and give you a good laugh."

Marcus grinned. "As much as I wish I had thought of the idea, I can not take credit for it." When Abby opened her mouth to say something, he held his finger in the air and added, "And, I will be sure to go back to her when we get a chance and see if there's any way we can keep the spell but allow you to still touch Luciana."

Abby pointed at Marcus as she walked backwards toward the front entrance. "You better."

She flicked her hair over her shoulders as she turned her back to us, her hips swinging as she disappeared around the corner.

I twisted around in Marcus's arms, eyebrows drawn together. "You didn't do that on purpose, did you?"

"And get rid of my only way to get you out of immediate danger? Not a chance in hell."

As much as I believed that the two of them had pulled crap on each other over the years, I knew that this wasn't one of those times. There was no way Marcus would risk my safety.

Slipping his hand into mine, he led me toward the garage. I thought he was taking me to the car, but he stopped beside a giant metal cabinet and opened it.

Expecting to see more guns or some other weapon used to kill supernatural beings, I was surprised to find actual tools in the cabinet.

"You don't plan on using that on the Soul Scraper, do you?" I asked as Marcus picked up a hammer.

He chuckled. "Hardly." He grabbed a container of nails and some brackets then closed the door. "I just want to fix the door before we go out."

With the hammer dangling in one hand and supplies in the other, he headed to the front door. I had no idea if he was handy or not but by the look of all the tools he had in the cabinet, I guessed he was, which only made him that much sexier in my books.

I followed him inside to the front door.

"Hold this." He handed me the hammer then lifted the door into place.

Five minutes later, the door was relatively back where it should be. It wasn't operational, but at least there was no gaping hole where bugs, animals, or anyone else could get through.

Remembering how Abby had left the house to meet the Chinese delivery guy at the front gates of Marcus's estate last night, I asked, "Can humans get through the barrier around your estate? Or does it just ward off evil entities?"

"No one, not even humans or animals, can get through the barrier without my permission," he replied, shutting down the bug theory as to why he wanted to repair the door.

"Okay," I dragged. "I get the whole human thing, but what could an animal possibly do to me?"

"Ever heard of a Hellhound?"

I followed him back to the tall cabinet in the garage. "I thought they were just fictional."

"Of course they exist. Just not in this dimension," Marcus said as he put the tools away. Once he'd finished, he turned to me. "Now let's go get you something to protect yourself with just in case that thing doesn't work."

He gently tapped the pendant resting against my chest.

My eyes lit up. "You mean a weapon?"

He laughed. "I really didn't expect you to take such a liking to them."

"What's not to like?" I could barely contain my excitement as we headed down the hall to the room that contained all of his arsenal.

For some reason, I had a huge fascination with anything that could take down Soul Scrapers—or anything else, for that matter. Whether I should be trusted with a weapon that could end the life of someone so easily was another story. But of course, I wasn't going to tell him that.

Once inside the room, Marcus closed the door, plunging us into darkness so he could access the weapons.

He squeezed my shoulder. "Just stay right where you are, and I'll be back in a second."

"How can you see in here?" I asked, holding my hand up in front of my face. I couldn't even make out the outline, and it wasn't even two inches in front of my eyes. It wasn't the first time we'd been in the room, but it still surprised me.

"Just a perk of being a Collector."

I breathed out in frustration. Why was I born with the curse of feeling other people's pain instead of something cool, like being able to see in the dark?

A few minutes later, I heard Marcus's footsteps coming toward me. At least I hoped it was Marcus because really, I had no idea if he'd disappeared and somebody else was coming to off me while I just stood there, waiting for it to happen.

God, I had an overactive imagination. But who could blame me when I had creatures that weren't supposed to exist, clawing their way to get at me?

A sigh of relief escaped my lips as I breathed in Marcus's unique scent.

Placing his hands on my hips, he turned me around then opened the door.

The light in the hall temporarily blinded me. I had to blink a few times before everything went back into focus.

"Are you okay?" he asked.

I nodded, my gaze landing on the items in his hands.

He handed me a five-inch silver knife that looked more like an ice pick.

I screwed up my face. "What am I supposed to do with that? Poke their eyes out?"

Marcus chuckled. "Don't let the size fool you."

I tucked the weapon safely inside my pocket. That sucker wasn't going anywhere. It was going to stay right within arm's reach— exactly where I needed it.

Nervously hopping into another of Marcus's cars I held my breath as I feared that we'd once again have a bunch of Soul Scrapers waiting outside the boundary of the estate. I was immensely relieved when it became apparent that we were on our own, and I let out a slow sigh.

Glancing over to Marcus, I could see he too had relaxed. The hard set of his eyes had softened, and his hands that had been gripping the steering wheel so tight that his knuckles turned white, had now returned to their normal color.

A few minutes later, Marcus pulled over to the side of the road and killed the engine.

I looked around, expecting to see the Devil's Playground. Instead, a bunch of dingy shops lined either side of the street, trying to sell items to tourists that they didn't need.

I glanced at him. "Where are we?"

Marcus cocked his head toward a shop with a big neon tarot sign out the front.

"You're going to get a tarot reading?" I asked, dumbfounded.

Tarot readers never gave any solid information. Their readings were always vague, allowing each person to come to their own conclusion, convincing them that it was true when in reality it was a pile of bull crap.

Marcus looked at me with humor in his eyes. "Just wait and see."

He got out of the car and waited on the footpath for me to join him.

"Why can't I get any straight answers?" I mumbled as I joined him on the sidewalk.

I ignored the strange looks of the few passers-by as we headed into the tarot shop.

The interior was exactly like I imagined it to be. Rich burgundy curtains lined the back wall of the small room. Three chairs stood to the left and on the right were tall burgundy shelves running the length of the wall, holding various sized crystal balls, books, and pentagrams.

Marcus slipped his arm around my shoulder. "Don't look so freaked." Then he turned to face the empty room. "Paege! I know you're in here. I can feel you."

No one replied, and he let out a sigh of frustration.

"Come on." He ushered me toward the back wall.

Gripping the side of the curtain, he yanked it back, revealing a whole new room.

The walls were lined with shelves containing bottles filled with contents that looked straight out of Mava's kitchen.

"Now, this is more like it," I mumbled.

"The tarot shop is just a front for what this place is really about," Marcus explained.

A moment later, a woman with raven black hair, wearing a long flowing black dress, entered the room with her hands clasped together. "What do I owe the unfortunate pleasure of having you in my store today?"

"I think you know exactly why I'm here," Marcus replied.

She raised a brow. "Do I?"

"Cut the crap." Marcus dropped his arm from my shoulder and stalked toward her as if he was a predator and she was his prey. "There's a bunch of symbols surrounding my place, and I want you to tell me what they mean."

Paege stilled before regaining her composure. "I have no idea what you're talking about."

She turned her back to him and started neatening the already perfectly aligned items on the shelves.

"The hell you don't." He grabbed her arm and twisted her around. "Now, I'm going to give you five seconds to start talking, or I'm going to —"

Biting my lip, I shuffled my feet, unsure if his excessive force was warranted or if I should try to stop him or at least calm him down. But I trusted Marcus. He wasn't the type to use unnecessary force— at least I thought he wasn't.

Paege crossed her arms. "Or you're going to what?" she asked with serious attitude.

"Or I'm going to destroy every precious item in this place. It will take years to get some of this stuff back, and you and I both know that there is more here than we see in this room."

She sucked in a sharp breath, her eyes going wide.

Marcus raised his hand and flicked the glass jar that she had just fixed into position off the shelf, sending it smashing on the floor.

Paege's gaze darted from her precious ingredients to Marcus, fear written all over her face. "They were trying to get in!"

"Why?" Marcus knocked another jar off the shelf.

She reached out, trying to catch it, but missed by half a second. It hit the floor, smashing the glass into hundreds of tiny pieces "I don't know why," she sobbed, her hands trembling.

With a swoop of his arm, Marcus sent the rest of the items on the shelf crashing to the floor.

"I don't know why," she cried almost hysterically.

With his back to me, Marcus knelt down, his hand stretched low, hovering a few inches above the floor. I couldn't see what he was doing but whatever it was brought the fear of God into the witch's eyes.

A second later, fire ripped across the floor.

CHAPTER 11

I jumped back, hitting the wall behind me. The witch rushed over to the shelf on the opposite side of the room. She fumbled with the jars until she found one containing what looked to be silvery-black ash then threw it over the fire as she chanted something under her breath. A few seconds later, the fire completely vanished, leaving scorch marks on the floor.

Marcus rose to his feet and stalked towards her, his eyes still doing that whole predatory thing. "We can play this game all day, but we both know who will win."

Oh, shit. Adrenalin pumped through my body with every step he took.

Paege swallowed hard, panic evident in her gaze. "I told you—"

Marcus's arm whipped out in a blur, his hand wrapping around the witch's neck, pinning her against the wall. "Now we can do this the easy way, or..."

A bloodcurdling scream ripped from Paege's mouth. Her hands grabbed Marcus's arm, trying to free herself from his deathly grip.

I couldn't sit still any longer and watch what was going on between them. No matter how much I wanted to figure out who had placed this curse on me, this woman didn't deserve to become collateral damage. For all we knew, she had absolutely no idea what was going on and Marcus was torturing her for nothing.

I raced over to him and desperately tried to pull him back by his shoulders. But Marcus wasn't going anywhere. He was an unstoppable force, hell-bent on breaking the witch.

"Your choice," Marcus said, completely ignoring me.

"Okay, okay." She sobbed. "I'll tell you what I know."

Marcus released his grip on her, revealing a black singe mark in the shape of his hand on her skin around her throat.

What the hell!

Paege swallowed hard as she tried to get herself together again. "All I know is that they want her." She pointed to me.

Marcus's gaze darted to me, fear consuming his eyes. "Why?" He returned his attention to the witch. "What do the witches want with Luciana?"

"I have no idea," she cried. "I'm telling you the truth. It's the Priestesses. They won't discuss it with the rest of us."

Marcus stared at her for the longest moment then gave a curt nod. "I won't let them know what you've told me today." He turned away from her and headed straight to me. "Come on. Let's get out of here."

My feet felt like cement as I followed him out of the shop. I had never seen that side of him and feared what else he was capable of that I wasn't aware of. Abby had warned him not to show whatever side he was about to release when he found out what Justin had done, and I prayed what he had done to the witch wasn't a taste of more scary surprises to come about the one my heart was bound to for all eternity.

No matter what Marcus did to others, I knew within my heart that I would stand by him. I wasn't sure if that made me stupid or if it was beyond my control. What I did know was that I trusted him and would have to learn to control my emotions and what I considered to be right and wrong. The rules of the human world that I grew up in didn't apply to me anymore.

This new world was scary, and something told me that a wolf could be hiding in plain site, disguising himself as a vulnerable puppy that wouldn't hurt a fly. The only thing was, we weren't talking about wolves and puppies. The world I was now living in held demons, angels, and those hellish Soul Scrapers.

I don't know why I was surprised that Marcus didn't bother mentioning what happened back in the store on our way home, because he never seemed to tell me anything about what he could do. Why he was still concerned that I would freak out was beyond me. What I wanted—what I needed—was transparency, which was exactly what I wasn't getting.

"So I guess we're just going to pretend what happened back there never happened," I said when we were about halfway home.

Marcus's grip tightened on the steering wheel. He had no problem displaying transparency when it came to his frustration, and I just wished he was that way with the rest of his life.

"I did what I had to do for us," he eventually said.

"I get it. I really do. But what I don't understand is why you neglected to mention that you're able to set things on fire with your hands when you filled me in on some of the other stuff you could do."

He glanced sideways at me. "Does that scare you?"

I thought about his question. "No. It doesn't."

I was just as surprised by my answer as he was considering how I felt when it happened.

"But I saw the way you reacted."

I strained a laugh. "What did you expect? I had no idea your hands that are so gentle on me can be so deadly to others. You shocked the hell out of me, and I didn't know if Paege deserved your torment or not."

"Do you really think I would hurt an innocent?"

For a moment back at the shop I had, and now I felt guilty for doubting him.

"You did, didn't you?" he said. "That's why you tried to pull me off her, wasn't it?"

"I didn't know what to think. One second you were the sweet, loving man that I know, and the next you turned into this predator that lets fire rip from his fingers."

He folded his hand over mine and squeezed it. "I'm sorry you had to see that. But I want you to know that I would never do anything to harm you and as much as it might make me sound like an asshole, I will do whatever it takes to stop your pain. I will never apologize for that."

"I would never ask you to." The truth was, I knew when it came down to it, I would do the same for him. No regrets.

I relaxed back into the seat and stared out the window at the trees passing by. "So is there anything else I should know about?"

"As far as my abilities go, yes."

His response sounded as if he was still hiding something that had nothing to do with his abilities.

"And things that don't relate to your abilities?" I added.

"There are thousands of years worth of information you know nothing about, some of which may be relevant, and a whole heap that isn't. I've got a large library at home filled with information that you are more than welcome to look through at any time you feel the desire to know more about my history."

I wasn't sure if I was excited or dreaded the prosperity of sifting through countless books pertaining to the workings of his world. After all, just a few snippets of things that he'd told me was already doing my head in.

"I'll keep that in mind," I said.

The corner of his lips tipped up. Something told me he knew exactly how I felt at the prospect of searching through those books.

"Where are we going?" I asked, realizing we weren't heading home.

"I want to go check out Mava's house for myself and see if the symbols match the ones found around our place."

My heart warmed once again as he mentioned that it was *our* place. I still couldn't bring myself to call it mine, but it was good to know that he could. I longed for the day that I could truly feel at home in my own skin because as much as Marcus made me feel whole, there was still something missing.

It wasn't long before I was getting out of the car and staring at the grassy field where Mava's house had stood.

"I don't get it," I said, making my way through the long grass that hadn't been there a couple of days ago.

"Either do I," Marcus said, walking beside me. "All I know is that someone has gone to a lot of trouble to keep Mava away from you." He tilted his head to the side. "Either that, or she's been toying with us this whole time to create some sort of diversion to keep us from finding out the truth."

As much as he didn't trust the witch, I couldn't shake the feeling that someone was keeping us from Mava.

Marcus came to a standstill. "Do you remember which direction the symbols were in?"

I snorted out a laugh. "You're asking me after how long it took us to find the symbols around your estate?"

"True." He slowly turned around in a circle, as if trying to decide which way we should head. "Let's try this way."

Within moments, we came up on a symbol.

"No freaking way." I picked up my pace, heading toward it.

He grabbed my wrist, jerking me back to his side.

I twisted away, then glared up at him. "What the hell was that for?"

He gestured to the ground in front of me.

Following his gaze, I just about pee'd myself when I realized how close I came to stepping on a two-meter Red-bellied Black Snake.

Three more emerged from the scrub, heading toward us. Snakes weren't supposed to slither toward people. They were supposed to be scared and try to get away unless of course, someone was stupid enough to try and attack them, leaving them no other choice than to defend themselves.

These snakes were different.

CHAPTER 12

I backed up against Marcus as the snakes lifted their heads in unison, their beady little eyes completely focused on us. "What are they doing?"

Marcus grabbed my hand, lacing my fingers with his. "Come on. I'll explain in the car."

Not needing to be told twice, I made a dash back to the car, praying I wasn't going to get bitten in the ass. I yanked open the door, ducked inside, and slammed it shut. Marcus slid into the driver seat. The snakes slithered after us, then lifted their heads, as if getting into position to strike. Their eyes remained focused on us as they swayed from side to side.

Marcus started the engine. "Snakes can be used as windows into this world."

A shiver ran down my spine. I not only had Soul Scrapers to worry about, I now had the slithery demonic creatures watching me, as well.

"But at least we can take one positive out of this."

I looked at him in surprise. "Such as?"

"I think it's safe to assume that it's not just the witches that are involved. The only ones who can control the snakes are demons."

Great! That was all I needed to know. I'd thought witches were bad enough, but demons… That was taking it to a whole other level.

When we arrived back at the house, Marcus headed straight to the kitchen. His appetite was crazy similar to Abby's. The two of them could eat all day long and never get full, or put on any weight.

I sat on the stool and watched him search through the fridge, my appetite non-existent thanks to our encounter with the snakes.

Marcus's head jerked to the side, his gaze remaining on the back door. I opened my mouth to ask him what was wrong when I saw through the window massive black wings engulfing the area between the house and the pool.

"Justin." His name rolled off my tongue with distaste.

Marcus looked at me sternly. "Do I need to ask you for your weapon back?"

My hand went to the knife that was still in my pocket. There was no way in hell I was giving it up.

"I won't do anything." When he looked at me dubiously, I added, "I promise."

Justin folded his wings away then entered the house looking more than a little nervous.

"Okay." Marcus walked around the bench and strategically put himself between Justin and me. Yeah, he trusted me—not.

I didn't blame him. I didn't even trust myself.

"Any luck?" Marcus asked, reaching behind him for my hands.

Yeah, he really trusted me.

Moving out of his reach, I twisted on the stool then hopped off and stood beside him. I crossed my arms over my chest to keep me from reaching into my pocket and finding out exactly what the weapon could do.

Maybe Marcus should've taken it from me.

"Justin," Marcus said.

"Do I need to arm myself?" Justin asked with a small laugh as he looked at me.

"You do, and it will be the last thing you do," Marcus warned him. He slung his arm over my shoulders, bringing my back against his chest. That was probably a good idea because I was two seconds from getting the ice pick knife out.

Justin held his hands up in defense. "Okay, I'm sorry. I was just joking. You know, trying to lighten the mood. But I guess we're not ready for that yet."

"Far from it," I said through gritted teeth.

"So, did you find Titus?" Marcus asked.

"Not exactly." Justin pulled out a chair at the dining table and took a seat. "What I did find out, though, is that Colton is planning to meet up with him later tonight."

"When?"

"Well, Colton's got a meeting to attend to first at Devil's playground at about eleven, and then he will be going straight from there."

"Good. We'll make sure we're there before he leaves the Playground. And until then, you might be able to try and help us figure out what's going on with the witches."

Justin narrowed his eyes. "The witches are now giving you trouble?"

I snorted out a laugh. "That's the understatement of the century."

Releasing his deathly grip on me, Marcus slipped his hand into mine and led me to the table. He pulled out the chairs opposite to where Justin was sitting and directed me to sit.

Justin leaned back in his chair, arms by his side as if he didn't have a care in the world. "So, what's been happening?"

"Well, for one, Mava's house is no longer there," Marcus said, taking a seat next to me. "And two, the exact same symbols that are surrounding her house are also surrounding my estate."

"Oh, and don't forget about the snakes that were watching me," I added.

Justin shifted forward in his seat. "What do you mean her house is gone? Houses don't just vanish."

"That's what I thought too," I said. "But sure enough, it has."

Justin looked at Marcus. "When did this happen?"

"Abby took Lu there while I stayed back to take care of the Soul Scrapers with you. Mava's house was gone when they arrived. So, who knows how long it's been gone for."

Justin slowly shook his head. "That can't be possible."

"Oh, but it is," I said getting a little irritated that he still doubted us.

"I'm not calling you a liar," he said. "I just don't get why she would do that."

Marcus breathed out harshly. "That makes two of us."

We spent the next twenty minutes discussing the ins and outs of the symbols. However, we were no closer to figuring it all out. Even though Justin had played a major part in how we got into this mess in the first place and kept a hell of a secret for so long, he had no idea why the witches were involved and what they wanted with me —or so he claimed. With Justin, no one could ever be certain. He was a lying piece of shit whom, for all we knew, was playing us again.

"And there was no note?" Justin asked for the tenth time.

Marcus glared at him. "Like I said, there were no notes and no other evidence of her disappearance. There was no evidence that her home was ever there."

Marcus hadn't brought up the riddles Mava had given us, or the vial she'd insisted on me taking. I didn't feel it was right to bring them up when he was so clearly avoiding them. He obviously didn't fully trust Justin, either.

Justin folded his hands over the back of his head. "Mava has been spouting on about that old legend for as long as I can remember. Why would she all of a sudden disappear?" His hands dropped to the back of his neck. "It just doesn't make sense."

"None of this shit makes any sense," I said. "Especially the reason why you're still here."

The corner of Justin's lips turned up. "Are the symbols still there?"

Marcus nodded. "You want to check them out?"

Justin pushed back his chair as he stood. "Got nothing better to do while we wait until Colton's meeting tonight."

Marcus placed his hand on my thigh. "Do you want to stay here or do you want to come with us?"

That was probably the stupidest question that ever came out of his mouth. There was no way I was going to stay here by myself while there was not only Soul Scrapers out to get me, but also those possessed snakes, which were being used as surveillance cameras for God knows who.

Of course, I wasn't going to say that, though.

"I may as well," I said with a shrug. "I've got nothing else better to do."

We slipped out the back door then headed down the steps toward the beach. Stopping short of hitting the sand, we ducked between the fence and the railing then made our way through the gardens. This time we knew where we were going.

"What's with the pendant?" Justin pointed to the crystal on my chest.

I grabbed hold of my pendant as a thought popped into my head. "It's supposed to protect me from those with evil or bad intentions," I explained. "Want to touch it?"

"Nah, it's okay."

"I wasn't asking. This might just prove how much of an evil snake you really are or it might prove your innocence."

I had no idea if it worked that way. Abby wasn't able to touch me and as far as I knew, she had the best of intentions for me. My main reason for wanting Justin to touch it wasn't because I wanted to see him burn—although that would've been a bonus—I just wanted to know if he was willing to give it a go or if he would try to worm his way out of it.

"Okay," he responded, taking me by surprise. "If it will make you see that I'm not trying to screw you over, I'll do it."

He reached for the pendent and touched it—without getting zapped.

"Shit," I said.

Justin smiled. "You were hoping that I'd get burned, weren't you?"

I shrugged.

Justin chuckled.

"This symbol is the one facing directly east," Marcus said, breaking me from my thoughts of how badly I wanted to smack that smile off Justin's face.

Justin crouched beside the symbol and ran his finger along the markings. "This stuff is heavy shit." He looked up at me. "Someone desperately wants to get their hands on you. We need to move fast."

CHAPTER 13

*J*ustin hung around like a bad smell. No matter how awkward it got, he wouldn't take the hint and leave us alone. We were only just able to convince him to stay outside by the pool while we went inside to gather the ingredients to make a pizza.

"Can't you just ask him to leave?" I bumped the fridge door closed with my hip.

Marcus grabbed two trays out of the drawer and popped them onto the counter. "Believe me I would if it weren't for the fact that we need him tonight."

I groaned as I leaned against the counter, then put one of the pizza bases that Marcus had made onto the tray in front of me.

Marcus scooped the second base up and dropped it onto the other tray.

Turning to me, he tipped my chin up with his fingertips. "Just a few more hours and then we can get him out of our hair."

He leaned down and kissed me.

"And then I'll never have to see him again?" I asked with a hopeful smile.

"Never is a very long time."

He picked up the trays and handed them to me. "Take these outside, and I'll bring out the rest of the stuff."

I wasn't going anywhere near Justin without Marcus. I still didn't trust myself around him. The mere sight of Justin made my skin crawl, and I wouldn't hold myself responsible if I accidentally pulled a knife on him and stabbed him through the heart.

"I'll wait."

The corner of Marcus's lips tipped up but he didn't say anything.

Once he'd gathered the rest of the prepared ingredients for the pizzas, we headed outside to the bar area, which was fully equipped with not only a barbecue, sink, cupboards, and a wine fridge, but also a pizza oven.

Justin stood from his stool. "I'll take them for you." He took the trays from me then got busy putting the dough into the oven.

Apparently, the bases needed to go in there by themselves before we could put the topping on them.

Happy to hand over cooking duties, I sat on the stool farthest from Justin and watched the men prepare dinner.

Justin grabbed the bases out of the oven and placed them on the stone bench. "So, Lucy, how has everything been since you left the rehab? Bet you like not feeling any of our emotions."

I was about bring up the fact that I actually had felt the smallest emotions from him back in the rehab when I remembered why he'd been there in the first place. Justin wasn't there for me. He was on duty, ready to collect the soul of my only friend there.

"How's Sophia?"

Justin looked up at me through hooded lids. "She's dead."

I closed my eyes. Even though I had only known her for a couple of days, she was one of the nicest people I'd ever met. Most people ran for the hills as soon as they found out how crazy I was. Not Sophia. Then again, she didn't know exactly what I was either.

"I meant, how... How did she die?"

Marcus paused halfway through loading the cheese onto the pizza. "Do you really want to know?"

No, but it was eating me up. "Yeah, I do."

"Okay," Marcus said, breathing out harshly.

Justin picked up the container of olives and began placing them one by one on the pizza he was decorating. "They found Sophia in the bathroom. She'd slit her wrist."

"Oh, God," I whispered, putting my hand over my mouth.

Sophia had once confided in me that she used to cut herself and

I'd seen the white scars on her wrist. I really thought Sophia had passed those days. She'd looked so good, so in control.

Looks can be deceiving. I of all people should know that.

"Where did you take her?" I asked, praying she wasn't going to spend eternity in hell—even though Marcus had said there was no such place as the Hell the churches had led the masses to believe in.

Justin put down the olives and picked up a bowl containing mushrooms. "I took her through to Purgatory where she will be cleansed before moving on."

I gulped as my imagination went crazy with what I thought Purgatory would be like. I didn't know much about it except there were Soul Scrapers there. And really, that was all I needed to know. Purgatory wasn't going to be fun.

"On to where?"

"I shouldn't be telling you this, but you already know enough about our world, so I guess it doesn't really matter. Sophia will be safe. She'll be happy."

The tiniest bit of tension lifted from my shoulders, however it was short lived when my thoughts returned to what exactly was in Purgatory. "The Soul Scrapers are going to do to her what they did to me, aren't they?"

Justin drew his brows together. "What did the Soul Scrapers do to you?"

In all the confusion about what had happened to Mava and the symbols surrounding her house and Marcus's estate, we had forgotten to tell Justin about my encounter with the Soul Scrapers.

I was about to explain when Marcus butted in. "They came after her when we were at the Playground. Lucy had run off by herself —"

"I didn't just run off. I was flooded with not only everyone's bad emotions but also their good, and it was all too much for me. I needed to get out of there. I needed to get away from all the people."

"You felt good emotions?" Justin asked, the pizza forgotten.

I wasn't sure if I was supposed to be telling him this but hey, the cat was out of the bag now. "Yeah, and it was pretty intense."

Marcus grabbed the pizzas, not bothering to ask if Justin had finished preparing his, and put them both in the oven.

"And this is the first time you've felt good emotions?" Justin reiterated.

I nodded. "First and last."

"Well, that's interesting." Justin walked over to the sink and washed his hands. "And what did the Soul Scrapers do to you?"

I could still feel the slick tar like substance in my mouth. No matter what I did, and how many times I brushed my teeth, it was there. It was like it was etched into my soul.

"They took me outside, shoved some slick tar-like substance down my throat, wrapped me in their web, and carried me off. Then they put their putrid hands on me, spilled more blackness into my mouth from theirs, and that's when Marcus walked in and saved my ass."

"Shit." Justin grabbed the back of his neck with both hands. "Do you know if they were able to get anything from you?"

"Ah yeah, lets see, they got my dignity, my sense of safety, oh, and let's not forget that they also got a shitload of fear out of me."

Justin glared at Marcus. "I thought you were supposed to take care of her."

"I am. I have." Marcus took a few steps toward Justin. "Why do you care so much?"

Justin held his hands up in defense. "Hey, I'm not accusing you of anything. I was just wondering why they were able to get that far with Luciana."

"I was busy catching up with Colton—I was distracted." Marcus glanced at me. "I've gone over it a thousand times, and I still can't figure out why I couldn't feel Lucy."

Justin leaned down, opened the bar fridge under the bench, and pulled two bottles of beer out. He handed one to Marcus. "At least everything turned out okay."

That I could agree upon. Still, something told me Justin knew much more than he was leading on.

CHAPTER 14

*C*urling his hands around my waist, Marcus lifted me on top of the garden wall near the pool, as I tried not to spill the pizza from the plates I was holding.

Satisfied they weren't going to slide off, I swung my legs over and took in the scenery before me.

From this perspective, I could see the long coastal stretch reaching from one end of Byron Bay to the other. Thick, dense foliage obscured the view of Abby's house next door and I couldn't see any homes on the other side either. His home was a secluded piece of paradise.

Marcus jumped up on the wall then sat beside me.

I handed him his plate then dug into my pizza.

"Thanks." He picked up a slice and took a bite.

I'd hoped Justin was getting the hint and would leave us alone, but like the bad smell he was, he followed—and just my luck, he decided to sit on the other side of me.

"How did you start to feel—" The rest of his sentence was muted by the flapping of wings as Abby landed perfectly on top of the wall, squeezing between Justin and me. I could've kissed her for helping me avoid whatever question Justin was about to fire at me.

She folded her wings behind her, retracting them between her shoulder blades, leaving no evidence that they were ever there. She settled onto the wall.

"Looks good." She grabbed Justin's plate, picked up a slice, and quickly took a bite. "Thanks," Abby said through a mouthful of pizza.

Justin glared at her.

"You're welcome," he said sarcastically. He hopped off the wall and headed to the bar area.

Abby nudged her shoulder against mine. "You owe me one."

Something told me I was soon going to owe her just as much as Marcus did. She'd already proved her weight in gold.

Abby spent the next hour keeping Justin caught up in meaningless conversations, allowing Marcus and me to slip away and finally get some time alone. I guessed that was another one I'd owe her for. I could see why Marcus was already so indebted to her. She was a good friend.

Marcus and I sat in the lounge room near the bedrooms trying to put as much distance as possible between Justin and ourselves without having to leave the house.

"Are you sure you're going to be all right while I'm gone?" he asked.

I was still going with them to the club, but Abby was going to come back to the house with me because we couldn't be sure if the pendant would keep me safe in another dimension.

"I'll be fine." I tucked my legs up onto the couch, my knees resting against his chest. "I'll miss you, but I'll be okay."

He ran his hands down my calves. "We shouldn't be gone for too long. But if we get stuck like we did last time, I want you to promise me that you're not going to do anything stupid."

"Me? Do anything stupid?"

He glanced down at the cast on my wrist.

"I think you're forgetting that only you have the power to kill me."

"That doesn't mean to say that I want to see you try to hurt yourself."

I sighed. "I promise I won't do anything stupid. And I expect the same from you."

"When we're this close to figuring out what is going on, never. I would never be that foolish." He leaned over and placed a gentle kiss on my lips. "I will never do anything to jeopardize you."

"Us."

"Us," he agreed, running his hand down to my ankles. "As much as I'd love to stay here with you, it's time for you to get ready."

"It can't be..." I trailed off as I looked at my watch and saw just how late it was. "How did you know?"

There were no clocks in the room, and he couldn't have seen my watch from his position. It was the first time I'd noticed his uncanny knowledge of the time, something Abby seemed to share as well.

"We have an inbuilt sense for it."

I scowled. Yet another ability I would have preferred. Except I didn't have any abilities. I wasn't special. I was just plain old cursed. I needed to stop thinking of myself as a special entity, even though I felt like one around Marcus.

I didn't bother disguising myself like I had the previous time we'd been to the Devil's Playground. All the paranormal beings knew who I was after the last time I was there, and there was no use pretending I was anything but the girl who Marcus refused to collect.

Abby and Justin had flown off and were going to meet us at the club, while Marcus and I were stuck using good old human transportation. God, I longed to fly.

Something about it woke a part of me that craved to feel the air rustling my wings, which was stupid because I would never have wings. It wasn't possible. All I could do was imagine what it felt like for Abby and Justin. And what it had felt like for Marcus.

My heart felt heavy knowing he had to go through the rest of eternity without his wings all because of me. He had fallen in love with somebody he didn't know and lost everything.

I shook my thoughts away as we pulled into the club's parking lot then into a car space directly in front of Abby and Justin who were sitting on a park bench. They'd obviously been there for a at least ten minutes and were clearly bored out of their brains.

"Finally," Abby said when we got out of the car. "You know there are two of us and two of you." She gestured to Marcus and me. "We could've just flown you guys with—"

"Never going to happen." Marcus grabbed my hand and entwined my fingers with his.

"So you keep saying." Abby stood.

Justin looked away. As much as I wanted to say that it was all his fault, I kept my mouth shut for Marcus's sake. Marcus didn't need another reminder of what he had lost.

"We saw Colton go inside about ten minutes ago," Abby said falling into line as we headed to the club.

"Good," Marcus replied. "Hopefully this will mean we'll get some answers tonight."

"Hopefully it's not another—" A massive force hit my whole body knocking, me back. I stumbled back a few steps, but thankfully Marcus caught my fall, saving me from falling flat on my ass.

"What the hell?" I said, steadying myself.

Abby laughed. "Had a bit too much to drink, hey?"

The look on both Marcus's and Justin's faces was the polar opposite of Abby. They knew exactly what had happened.

CHAPTER 15

"This can't be happening." I stepped forward with my hands up, praying that had been a one-off and this time I'd get through.

My hopes shattered into a million pieces when I felt the push of the invisible barrier banning me from getting any closer to the club.

The smile dropped from Abby's face. "The pendant's stopping you from getting in, isn't it?"

"Shit," Marcus cursed under his breath. "This wasn't supposed to happen." He looked at the club momentarily before returning his gaze to me. "We don't have time to get this fixed."

I could remove the pendant, but that left me vulnerable to Soul Scrapers. Not happening.

I stepped away from the force field. "Don't worry about it. I'll be fine out here."

Marcus gave Abby a look, asking her to stay with me.

"Yes," Abby said with a huff. "I'll stay outside with Lucy while you boys go inside and have all the fun."

"Thanks," Marcus said. "I owe you —"

"Yeah, yeah, yeah. You owe me yet another one," Abby said. "But we aren't going to stand around here waiting for you."

"Good. Just keep a close eye on Lucy. Don't assume that pendant works properly." Marcus lifted the crystal off my chest and studied it as if he could see the magic that was held within. "Take her home."

God, he was bossy.

Marcus let the pendant fall against my chest, then caressed the side of my face with his hand. "I promise I won't be long."

The corner of my lips tipped up. "And I promise not to do anything stupid."

He leaned down and kissed me. All too soon it was over, and I was watching him walk inside the club taking with him his ability to stop me from feeling other people's pain and torment.

I started to turn away, but caught a glimpse from the corner of my eye of a woman staring at me from the entry of the club. The hairs on the back of my neck stood on end. I tried to act nonchalant as I stole glances of her.

She had porcelain skin framed by straight hair the color of a raven, falling perfectly down the length of her back and looked as if she were shooting a hair commercial. But that wasn't what unnerved me. It was the smirk on her face directed at me. There was no mistaking it. She knew me and she was following Marcus inside.

I was cast back into what I presumed was another memory. Unimaginable pain shot through my head as I gasped for air.

I was laying on my stomach amongst the orange and red leaves that had recently fallen from the trees surrounding me. Not more than a few feet in front of me stood the same raven-haired woman, muttering something unintelligible under her breath.

Her devilish smirk was like a knife to my heart, twisting it deeper as all my hopes shattered into a million pieces. She opened her mouth, and the words "forget-me-not" spilled from her lips, followed by a beautiful, haunting laugh that only she seemed capable of.

My arms trembled as I attempted to push myself up from the ground but no matter how hard I tried my body had been too weak to oblige.

The woman with the raven black hair gave me one final look filled with twisted satisfaction then turned on her heels and glided away, leaving me where I lay as if I were garbage.

The blinding pain vanished the moment I was back in the present. With my heart in my throat I scanned the area for any sign of the woman who I'd just seen in my memory. She was gone.

"I have to go inside," I said, panting.

Abby scrunched up her nose. "What?"

Ignoring her, I tried to push my way through the force field, but it was too strong. I wasn't getting through. Marcus was inside and I feared that so too was the woman who had done something to me in one of my previous lifetimes. I was terrified that she was now going after him.

I grabbed my pendant to rip it off so that I could get through and find Marcus. Something in the pit of my stomach screamed at me to get to him now—no matter the cost.

Abby grabbed my arm, stopping me before the chain snapped. "No, you don't. Marcus would kill me if you took that thing off."

I looked at her, wishing she'd instantly understand because I didn't have time to explain. "I need to get to Marcus."

"Don't give me that look." Abby pried my fingers open, letting the pendant fall from my hand. "Whatever you need to say to Marcus can wait until he gets back."

I shook my head fiercely. "No, you don't understand. This can't wait."

"Well, it'll have to wait," Abby said. "They've already left this veil."

I closed my eyes as my whole body filled with an unrelenting anxiety. I was overcome with the fear that Marcus was walking into something he wasn't prepared for.

"You don't understand, Abby. I recognized somebody who I think did something to me in one of my past lives and she just went in after Marcus and Justin. I think she's going to do something to them. Don't ask me how I know. I just know."

All playfulness dropped from her face. "You're serious, aren't you?"

I breathed in deeply, trying to force myself from hyperventilating. I was scared out of my mind for Marcus. I knew in my gut that woman was serious trouble and I was powerless to stop her. All I could do was pray that Marcus would be okay and come back to me before we were out of time.

"Let's get you—" Abby's pupils dilated as her gaze darted to the side.

I didn't need her to tell me what was wrong. I could feel it for myself.

"They're here," I whispered as a chill ran down my spine.

CHAPTER 16

*A*bby's vice-like grip latched around my wrist as she pulled me until I was practically sprinting right toward the Soul Scrapers. I didn't understand why we were running straight at them when my instincts were screaming at me to run the other way.

But Abby was too strong.

"Move," she yelled at me.

I couldn't respond. It was taking everything out of me not to collapse to my knees.

Soul Scrapers twisted through the trees in the distance, heading toward us. Others wound their way through cars parked outside closed shops and café's.

In the split-second, before we were about to collide with the demonic creatures, Abby yanked on my arm, switching directions. My feet slipped out from underneath me. Before I hit the ground, Abby flung me a good twenty feet up into the air.

The Soul Scrapers reached for me, their icy tendrils latching onto my ankle. I screamed as fear ripped through me. This was it. The pendant hadn't worked, and Marcus wasn't here to save me.

Remembering the otherworldly knife in my pocket, I reached inside and grabbed the weapon, ready to fight them myself.

Before I could get it out of my pocket, a force propelled me further up into the air. For a moment, I thought it was the Soul

Scrappers wrapping their slick web around me so they could take me to the underworld. Then I realized it was Abby's arms wrapped around me, lifting me into the air as we flew higher and higher, leaving the Soul Scrapers behind.

Relief flooded through me as I relaxed in her arms and tried to ignore the strange urge I had to break free from her clasp, dive down, and skim the tops of the trees. It wasn't like the other times when I had tried to kill myself by jumping off a cliff; this time I didn't want to die. Instead, I wanted to feel the rush of the wind not only against my face but also through wings that I clearly did not have.

The thing that scared me the most about my new-found desire to fly wasn't that I was going insane. I feared my curse was developing to include supernatural beings' emotions, as well. And if that was the case then I was seriously screwed.

The moment we landed next to the pool in Marcus's backyard, Abby recoiled in pain. "Shit, that hurt."

I whipped my head around to see what she was talking about. "Oh, my God. I'm so sorry." In all the commotion, I'd completely forgotten that she wasn't able to touch me without getting burned.

Angry welts covered Abby's hands and arms. I couldn't see how her torso was from where her body pressed against mine while she carried me home, but if her posture was anything to go by, I could only assume that her clothing had done nothing to protect her from my touch.

Abby reached behind her back and unzipped her dress then peeled it from her body, leaving her wearing nothing but her bra and panties and heels that emphasized her long legs. She looked every bit the goddess she was—if it weren't for the welts that covered her perfect body.

"Holy crap," I said, partly because of the welts, and partly because I was in awe of her and once again wondered how the hell Marcus was so into me when he could've had her.

"You and Marcus owe me big time for this one." She kicked off her heels, then dove into the pool.

Guilt flooded me. I couldn't imagine how much it must've hurt to hold onto me all the way from the club. She must've gone through hell.

"I owe you everything," I said when she resurfaced.

Abby smirked. "Be careful what you say to a demon."

My eyes went wide.

Laughing, she swam to the edge then pulled herself up onto the pavers surrounding the pool. The welts no longer looked as fierce as they had a few moments ago.

"I heal fast," she said. "Plus, the salt of the pool helps speed up the recovery."

Abby leaned down and scooped up her clothes and shoes then headed inside.

CHAPTER 17

Once Abby changed back into her clothes, and was no longer severely damaged from my touch, she yet again stuck her head in the fridge.

While she decided what to eat next, I took the opportunity to ask her about the woman I'd seen at the club. "Please tell me you know who I'm talking about—or at least that you saw her."

Leaning back, Abby peered at me around the open fridge door. "I saw a lot of people go into the Playground. You're going to have to be a bit more specific." She grabbed a tub of yoghurt out of the fridge, closed the door, then went over to the cupboard. "Maybe if you describe her, I can figure out who you're talking about."

"Okay, she was about your height, slim, with almost black eyes, and her hair was the color of a raven, just like it was in my memory.

Abby stilled then grabbed a packet of chips out of the cupboard and put them down next to the yoghurt on the bench. "Are you sure it was the same person?"

I thought about the woman in my memory, and even though she was from a different time, there was no denying it. "I'm positive."

Abby nodded then opened the drawer and pulled out a spoon. "There is no way to be certain, but from what you're saying about seeing her in your memories, I think it's safe to say that you're describing a witch." She opened the yoghurt and dug her spoon in.

SEVERED HEARTS

"Not just any witch either. The raven hair only belongs to one group."

I didn't need her to tell me that the group she was referring to was bad news because I already knew. I could feel it. Everything about that woman chilled me to my core.

"We have to warn Marcus," I said.

"No can do."

"We have to," I begged.

Abby put the tub of yoghurt down, then planted her hands on the bench. "I don't like this any more than you do, but I can't leave you. Marcus would literally kill me if anything happened to you. And before you start freaking yourself out, just remember that Marcus can hold his own. Marcus isn't like the other Collectors. He's faster, stronger, which is lucky for him having no wings."

As much as I hated acknowledging defeat, I had to trust Abby. I couldn't follow Marcus to wherever he'd gone. And for all I knew, we could've been walking into a trap if we went after them, and we'd wind up dead. That was not something I was prepared to lay on Marcus or Abby. My gut told me that the witch was trouble. I just had to trust Abby that she was right and Marcus and Justin could hold their own. After all, they were paranormal beings, and I was pretty sure they were above witches on the hierarchy. Plus, they could defeat Soul Scrapers, and I couldn't imagine that witches could be any more powerful.

Abby picked up the tub and scooped some yoghurt onto her spoon then smiled. "Hey, at least we know the pendant works."

I scrunched up my face in confusion. "No, it didn't. I felt them. They had a hold of my ankle."

"Yeah, for about two seconds before their asses were fried."

I tilted my head. "Huh?"

Abby sighed. "You're seriously telling me that you didn't feel them let go?"

"Well, yeah, of course, I did, but I thought that was because you had taken me out of their reach."

"Nope. They let go first." She shoved another spoonful into her mouth.

I licked my lips. I was so thirsty from everything that happened tonight, or maybe it was just the thought of how close the Soul Scraper had been to sticking their tendrils down my throat again. I shook my thoughts away, grabbed a bottle of water out of the fridge, and downed half the contents, but it did little to quench my thirst. It was as if the Soul Scrapers had ingrained themselves into me and nothing but time would make the feeling go away.

I screwed the bottle cap back on. "I'm going to take a shower."

"Good idea," Abby said. "Might help get rid of stench that the Soul Scrapers got all over you." She waved her hand under her nose.

I gaped at her. "I don't seriously stink, do I?"

She gave me an apologetic smile and nodded.

"Seriously?" I lifted my hands to my nose and sniffed. Apart from the lingering odor that went along with having a cast, I couldn't smell a thing. "I can't smell anything."

She shrugged "You may not be able to, but I can. And I can tell you that you reek of the bottom crawlers."

I furrowed my brow. "Why didn't Marcus tell me last time? I mean, they barely touched me this time, and you're saying I stink. I can't even imagine how bad it would have been after they got their hands all over me and down my throat."

"That's because you're his precious Lulu. You could forever be tainted with their smell, and he'd love you all the same."

Biting down on my smile, I turned around and trotted down the hall. There was nothing like knowing someone loved you even if you smelled like shit.

I closed the bedroom door behind me and switched the light on. Lying on the pillow of my bed was an old, leather bound journal.

I scowled. *Where had that come from?*

I placed the water bottle on the bedside table then crawled onto the bed and picked up the journal.

Leaning against the pillows, I sat cross-legged then opened the book and flicked through it. Page after page of handwritten notes with various drawings of creatures and symbols that I had never seen before stared back at me. I had no idea why Marcus hadn't mentioned leaving this book for me to read before he left but I was grateful for the distraction.

I decided to start at the beginning and work my way through. The first few pages were notes of some of the entities that walked this world and the next, some of whom I'd already heard of and others I was learning about for the first time. The journal then went on to describe a bearer of light who was to be born into this world, right the wrongs, and give back things that had been taken.

My mind went to the poem Mava had given me, and how it mentioned something about light. I put the book face down, so I didn't lose my page, leaned over, and opened the bedside drawer then pulled out Mava's riddle.

> *"The moon rises, and*
> *Light and Dark eclipse.*
> *An ancient one will impede,*
> *and memories will forget.*
> *Time stands still until*
> *the light will bloom,*
> *And shines on the key that*
> *unlocks the door to Destiny."*

No matter how many times I re-read the riddle, I couldn't make any headway with it. Yet, something about it niggled away at me. Mava believed in the prophecy and maybe what was written in the journal about the bearer of light, was it.

I re-read the riddle, focusing on the part pertaining to the light.

"And shines on the key that unlocks the door to destiny," I said under my breath.

I spent the next twenty minutes staring at the pages of both the riddle and what appeared to be a prophecy about light. No matter how much I tried, I still couldn't find anything that tied the two together.

I folded the paper with the riddle and put it back in the drawer, and was about to finally go and have my shower when I was overcome by a not so niggling feeling urging me to continue. It was like a magnet pulling me back to the journal, and the information it contained.

Giving in, I propped myself up against the pillows, bent my knees, and leaned the book against my thighs then continued reading through the journal.

The next few pages contained various notes and symbols that looked interesting but held no power or connection to me. However, the pages that followed appeared to be a spell of some sort that could take someone's memory away.

"Holy shit," I murmured.

With my heart practically beating a hole through my chest, I jumped out of bed and raced into the lounge room where I found Abby sitting on the couch, stuffing chips into her mouth while she watched TV.

I held the journal tightly against my chest. "You are not going to believe what I found!"

CHAPTER 18

$\mathscr{A}$bby rolled her eyes from the TV over to me. As soon as she saw the journal in my hands, she sat up straight. "Where did you get that?"

"It was on my bed. But that's not important," I said in a rush. "What's important is that I found a spell that's able to take someone's memories away."

Abby got up so quickly I barely saw her move.

"Let me see." She grabbed the journal from me before I had a chance to hand it over. "Holy shit."

With her finger bookmarking the page with the spell, she flicked through the rest of the pages then looked up at me. "You said this was just lying on your bed? This couldn't have just appeared on its own. This isn't one of our books. And by 'ours' I mean those of us who are able to walk this world and the others."

"The book belongs to the witches, doesn't it?"

Abby nodded. "That's what I don't understand. There is no way they would let this fall into one of our kinds' hands." She tapped the front of the cover. "This can't be from Marcus's collection."

I shrugged a shoulder. "Maybe it is. I mean, Marcus did tell me that I should do some reading to try to help me catch up on all things about this world I've landed in. He could have easily put the book on my bed. And if you think about it, that's the only plausible explanation, because who else can get access to this place? You said that the only people who can get into Marcus's house are those that he has allowed." I strained a laugh. "Even bugs can't get through the magical barrier surrounding this place." I gestured around me.

"You've got a point, but I don't understand why Marcus would have kept this one from me." She drew her brows together. "Maybe it was Justin. He could have easily put it in your room at any time before you guys left tonight."

"That could be all well and true except for the fact that he never left us alone for a second. From the moment that asshole arrived, he didn't leave our side—not even to go to the bathroom."

I furrowed my brow. "Although he did stay outside with you for a while."

"He didn't leave my side either." Abby frowned then returned her focus to the spell in the book. "This is huge."

"I know," I said, bouncing from one foot to the other. "Which is why I'm hoping you will agree to what I'm about to ask you."

Abby slowly lifted her gaze to meet mine. "Something tells me Marcus isn't going to be happy with whatever it is you're about to say."

I drew in a deep breath. "I'm hoping you'll agree to take me to see Astrid. I know she is not technically practising anymore, but she must know something about this. And, Marcus did say she easily agreed to put the protection spell on this for me." I picked the pendant up off my chest and rubbed it between my fingers.

Abby slowly shook her head. "As much as I'd love to see what Astrid has to say for herself, Marcus would kick my ass if he knew that I took you out without his permission."

I scrunched up my nose. "Who says Marcus has to know?" I felt guilty for going behind his back, but it was his back I was trying to save. "Besides, it's not as if the Soul Scrapers can get to me. We know the pendant works."

"As much as I'd love to see the look on Astrid's face when I thank her for these," Abby said, holding up her palms still covered in red burns, "I promised Marcus I would keep you safe, and he would kill me if he found out that we hadn't waited for him. Besides, it's after two in the morning. Astrid is not going to be in her shop, and the bitch would probably light me on fire if I tried going anywhere near her house at this time of night."

I breathed out harshly. I didn't want to wait, but I could understand Abby's point. "Fine."

"You'll have much better luck seeing her tomorrow with Marcus, when I'm not around."

"Why without you?"

Abby returned to her spot on the couch. "Astrid has always lumped me in the same category as all the other demons."

"What about Marcus?"

Abby smirked. "Marcus is a special boy."

"But you always refer to him as 'demon boy?'"

Abby chuckled. "That's just my little nickname for him. Marcus isn't really a demon. Soul Collectors don't fall into any of the categories. They're immune."

Abby leaned back, making herself comfortable again. "Now, you may as well go to bed. There is nothing we can do tonight—apart from driving yourself even more insane with different theories."

Begrudgingly, I nodded. "I'll see you in the morning."

"Night," she replied.

I returned to my bedroom with no intention of sleeping. I was too wired about the book to even think about going to bed. I was also still worried about the woman who had followed Marcus into the club. Between her and the spell I'd found, I didn't think I was going to get any sleep that night.

After finally taking a shower, I curled up in bed with the journal and continued to read through its pages. There wasn't much in there that made sense to me. One section contained symbols similar to the ones we'd found around Marcus's and Mava's houses, which were labeled as the five elements—earth, air, fire, water, and spirit. It confirmed my suspicions that witches had tried to penetrate Marcus's estate.

CHAPTER 19

*L*ight flooded the room as the sun rose over the water, concealing the shadows of the night and pretending that everything was okay again. Everything was not okay, though. Marcus still hadn't come home, and that unnerving feeling that something was terribly wrong was growing stronger by the minute.

I hadn't slept a wink and fatigue was starting to take over my body. Sometime in the last few hours, I had migrated from my room into Marcus's, hoping that his subtle smell that lingered on his sheets would've been enough to settle me and allow me at least a couple of hours sleep. It didn't.

Leaning against the headboard, I pulled the pillow against my chest, lowered my head, and breathed in deeply.

The leather-bound journal was still open on my lap, and I was once again staring at the pages that mentioned the spell that would wipe someone's memories, praying that it would all just suddenly make sense.

Alas, it did not.

Mava's riddle spoke of light and memories forgetting. She also spoke of the prophecy which I was sure was contained within the first portion of the book. What I needed was something like a big slap in the face telling me exactly what someone had done and why they wanted me dead.

I needed to find out more about the riddle. Everything Mava had said to me was based on me being the one the prophecy spoke of. The problem was, from what I could see, it was a witch's prophecy, therefore, getting my hands on the information just became that much harder.

That damned little voice on my shoulder continued to whisper the words that Mava had spoken to me when she handed me the vial. I had no idea what the vial contained or even if it was safe. And no matter how much Marcus wished I would just forget the vial existed, I couldn't ignore her words that if I drank the contents, I would see.

There were a lot of things I didn't see—Mava's house, for one. However, trusting her came with a monumental risk, with a cost that very likely was too much.

I didn't have long. My time was almost up in this life, and I was afraid that if I did take the chance and trust Mava, then there was a huge possibility that I was going to cut my time short with Marcus. I almost slapped myself. I had no idea what I was worried about when history had proven the only way I was capable of dying was from a knife to the heart at the hands of Marcus and only Marcus.

But that didn't mean to say that I shouldn't be afraid. They may not have been able to kill me, but they sure could screw me over, stealing any chance for Marcus and me to stop the curse in this lifetime. We had limited time, and I wasn't about to do anything that could jeopardize our chances.

Placing Marcus's pillow onto the mattress beside me, I climbed off the bed and went in search of Abby. I found her asleep in the exact spot I had left her in the night before, splayed out on the couch, with her head slightly tipped back.

No matter how much I wanted to go over there and shake her until she woke up, I didn't know her well enough to do something so forceful. For all I knew, she would go all demon on me the moment I touched her. Plus there was also the fact that I'd burn her thanks to my pendant. So, instead, I wandered into the kitchen and got busy making two cups of coffee.

Looking out the window, I prayed I'd see Justin come crashing out of the sky. I never thought I'd pray for such a thing about Justin when all I wanted to do was see the back of him last night. But seeing him meant that Marcus would be nearby—or at least it would confirm my fears that the woman from my memory had done something to him.

When the coffee machine finished doing its thing I carried the mugs into the lounge room and placed one on the table beside Abby.

It wasn't long before its aroma worked. She breathed in deeply, and then lazily opened her eyes, her gaze going straight to the coffee.

"I didn't know if you're a morning coffee drinker, but I thought it would be a bit rude if I just made one for myself," I lied. The truth was, I had hoped that the smell would wake her up, and thankfully it did.

Twisting into a sitting position Abby grabbed the mug. "Thanks." She took a long sip then settled back in her seat. "Marcus isn't back, is he?"

I forced myself to take a seat on the edge of the sofa when all I wanted to do was get our asses out of there. I wanted to take action. I was so sick of sitting around waiting for Marcus to come home.

"No, he isn't," I said, trying to sound calm. "He hasn't called either."

Abby swallowed hard.

"He should be back by now, shouldn't he?"

"Yeah, he should." Abby glanced at my face, then added, "Or they could just be following another lead. Marcus has a tendency to get so focused on something he forgets the time."

I shook my head. "Not after what happened the other night. He promised me he would call before disappearing again."

"Well, maybe he's just stuck between veils like they were last time."

"Maybe," I said, quickly dismissing the idea. I had a feeling in my gut that something was terribly wrong. "Or, maybe that woman from my memory has something to do with it."

Abby studied me for a few moments. "She really got to you, didn't she?"

"Yeah, she did. I don't know what she'd done to me in my memory, but whatever it was, it wasn't good."

Abby breathed out harshly then took a sip of her coffee.

We sat in silence for a few minutes before I finally worked up the courage to ask her about going to see Astrid again. "I know you said that we should wait for Marcus to return but—"

"You still think we should go see Astrid, don't you?"

"Yeah, I do. Maybe she might be able to help me figure out who this woman is that I saw last night."

Abby groaned. "Fine."

"Are you serious?" I figured it was going to take much more effort to convince her to take me to Astrid.

"Yes," she replied. "But I must warn you, Astrid doesn't really like me, so I'm not sure how much we'll get out of her."

I jumped up off the couch, almost spilling my coffee. "That's okay. I'll do most of the talking. I'll go get dressed."

I dashed back to my room and changed into a clean pair of shorts and a tank top. Then, I grabbed the journal and tucked it into my bag.

"I'm ready," I said, practically skipping back into the lounge room. I was full of energy after staying stagnant for so long last night. I hated feeling helpless. I needed to be in control—even if it was just an illusion.

Abby stood from the couch and stretched out her arms. "Excited much?"

Ignoring her comment, I said, "So, how are we doing this?"

"As much as I'd love to fly, there is no way I'm putting myself through that kind of pain again. So, you drive, and I'll direct."

Guilt swept over me. I hated to think about how much pain Abby had been in when she'd rescued me from the Soul Scrapers last night.

"I'm so sorry," I said for what felt like the hundredth time.

"As I keep telling you, it's not your fault. Astrid is the one who did this to me, and I have more than a few words to say to her about it."

"As long as we get all the information we need before you have a go at her."

"Agreed."

It wasn't long before we were standing on the sidewalk, looking through the window of a store packed with customers searching through shelves and stands filled with crystals.

"This is it," Abby said.

I leaned closer to her.

"There are people in there. How can we talk to her about this?" I tapped the spine of the leather bound journal.

"We'll find a way." Abby went to touch the door handle, but the second her hand came in contact with the metal, a spark of electricity shot out toward her. She jumped back in surprise. "What the…"

CHAPTER 20

$\mathscr{I}$ could practically see steam coming out of Abby's ears as she glowered at the door of Astrid's shop.

"Astrid!" Abby inspected the black singe marks on her fingers and palm then dropped her hand by her side. "Astrid! You better get your ass out here."

I grabbed Abby's arm to quiet her down, forgetting I had the exact same effect on her as the door did.

"Shit!" Abby jerked her arm away from my clutch.

"I'm so sorry," I said. "I didn't mean to. I just..." I sighed. "I'm sorry."

"I'm gonna kill that fucking bitch," Abby said through gritted teeth.

"But not before I show her this." I tapped the cover of the book in my bag.

"Fine," she conceded.

"Thank you." I reached for the door, praying that I wouldn't be zapped as well. Relief flooded through me when nothing happened. I pushed open the door, then glanced back at Abby. "I won't be long."

Before she could respond, I slipped inside.

Negative emotions swarmed my senses as the customers

searched for the perfect crystal that was going to make their problems go away.

Yeah, right.

Most of their emotions I could manage, particularly the ones searching for something to bring them good luck with winning the lottery or getting the job they desired. But the couple searching for a cure for the disease that would ultimately take the life of their only child was almost too much to handle. Cancer was a vicious evil that didn't discriminate between wealth, color, creed, age, or gender. This family's pain was one of the worst I had dealt with.

I swiped away the tears that had welled up in my eyes and searched for Astrid. It didn't take long for me to recognize her. She was staring at me with emerald eyes as if I had a glowing sign plastered to my head declaring who I was.

She swept through the crowded store, her wispy tie-dyed dress billowing from her sides. She looked like the definition of the Byron Bay hippie, not at all like Mava. Astrid was beautiful.

Cradling my elbow in her hand, she ushered me to the side.

"What are you doing here?" she asked, her voice barely audible.

"Um, I came here to ask you something. But, I don't think here is the right place." I looked around the room, trying to find somewhere a little more discreet. There was a door behind the register, which I assumed was a storeroom of some sort. "Is there somewhere we can go to discuss something?"

Astrid shook her head. "I'm too busy, as you can see." She gestured toward customers.

"I know. And I'm sorry, but it's really important. And I promise I won't take up much of your time."

She glanced out the window at Abby who looked as if she were about to lose her shit at her. "The demon should've told you that I don't practice any more."

"She did. And I respect your decision. All I'm hoping is that you'll just give me some information about this." I pulled the journal out of my handbag.

Astrid's eyes lit up. "Where did you get that?

"Someone left it for me on my bed."

"You shouldn't have that." She went to grab it, but I moved it out of her reach.

She stared at me with as much frustration as Abby was displaying toward her.

Finally, she said, "Wait for me in the back." She gestured behind the counter. "There is someone in here that I desperately need to help, which I'm sure you know exactly who I'm talking about."

I nodded. "Thank you. And I don't just mean about speaking with me."

The corner of her lips tipped up and she gave me a slight nod. Astrid wasn't nearly as retired as she was making everyone believe. I wasn't sure if it was just for extreme cases like the couple in the store or if it was something she did regularly, which would explain why so many flocked to her crystal shop. Either way, she had my respect.

Making my way through the crowd, I headed for the storeroom door. When I slipped inside, I sighed with relief at being able to distance myself from the emotions.

I stepped around the boxes stacked on the floor that looked as if they'd just been delivered and she hadn't had a chance to put them away yet, then made my way to the shelves on the other side of the room.

I ran my hand along the smooth white counter as I studied the various crystals packaged in clear plastic drawers on top of the bench, until I found the crystal that resembled the one on my pendant.

"Tibetan quartz," I said, reading the label.

My hand instinctively went to my pendant, a sense of security rushing through me, which I hadn't felt before and wondered if it had something to do with being in the shop, surrounded by other crystals.

Curiosity brimming, I opened the drawer and picked up one of the Tibetan quartz. There was no rush of power like when I touched mine. It felt like any other rock.

I returned it to its spot, and pulled out the next drawer.

The door behind me opened, and Astrid walked in. I stifled a yelp, like I was a child caught with my hand in the cookie jar.

"I was... I was just looking," I said, closing the drawer. "I promise I didn't take anything."

Astrid smiled wearily, her eyes no longer vibrant. She looked worn out as she made her way to a chair and collapsed into it. If I had to guess, it had everything to do with what she had done for the couple with the dying child who, I knew without asking, would make a miraculous recovery.

Blinking my tears away, I tried to ignore the emotions of the remainder of the people in the shop and focus on what I came there for.

Retrieving the journal from my bag, I opened the page containing the memory spell.

"As I said before, I respect that you've retired from the witchcraft you were involved in before." I held up the book. "But, I was hoping you could tell me if I'm right in thinking that this spell will wipe away someone's memories?"

Ignoring my question, she asked, "Where's Marcus?"

"That's what I want to know as well."

She furrowed her brow. "What do you mean?"

Lowering the book, I decided to get the whole 'where's Marcus' thing out of the way first because that was clearly where the conversation was heading. I didn't want to be rude to the person who potentially was the only one who could help us.

"Marcus went somewhere last night to try to find out what happened all those years ago when he first met me, and after promising he would keep in contact with me, I haven't seen or heard from him since."

"Oh," she said, tilting her head. "And that worries you?"

God, she sounded like every one of my shrinks. "Yeah, it worries me because he wasn't meant to be gone for this long. And I know this might sound silly, but I saw a woman follow him into the Devil's Playground last night and I don't know who she is but I remember her."

Her steely gaze pierced mine. "What did she look like?"

"She was Abby's height with hair the color of a raven, porcelain skin, and dark brown, almost black eyes. But in my memory, she had an evil presence about her that even a human would feel."

Astrid gripped the arms of the chair as she nearly stopped breathing.

CHAPTER 21

*N*erves rolled through me in waves as I watched the expression on Astrid's face turn from shock to fear.

"Who is she?" I asked.

Astrid looked to the side, as if she were trying to figure out how to respond. Eventually, she raised out of the chair and took two steps toward me then whispered, "If it's who I think it is, I'm going to warn you to stay away from her. Don't do anything foolish. Just stay away."

"Who is she?" I asked again.

"It doesn't matter."

I was about to say "the hell it doesn't" when she continued.

"Mava's disappearance is only a facade. You must look within yourself. You are blind, and you need to trust your instincts in order to *see*."

"That sounds a hell of a lot like something Mava said to me."

"She's not as crazy as everyone believes."

"Yeah, I kind of figured that one out already."

"Good." She nodded. "Well, then you need to trust yourself that you'll make the right decision."

"Decision about what?"

She took my hand in hers then placed her other hand on top. "When the time's right, you'll know."

What was with witches and their riddles? Why would no one give me a straight answer? I was about to pull her up on it when she reached forward and touched my forehead while mumbling something under her breath. A jolt rushed through me, and I gasped.

Astrid swayed on her feet then collapsed to the floor. I wasn't sure if I should touch her or if that was what set her off in the first place. I was cursed beyond anything I could comprehend.

"I'm sorry," I whispered, bending down beside her. "Are you okay?"

"I'll be fine." She waved me off. "And you didn't do anything." She raised her shaky hand and grabbed hold of my pendant. Her lips moved, but I couldn't hear a word. A moment later, she said, "She can touch you again."

I didn't need to be told whom Astrid was referring to. I knew she'd meant Abby, and I was eternally grateful. "Thank you."

Astrid drew in a shallow breath. "Go."

"I can't just leave you here."

"You don't have a choice," she said, pulling herself up into a sitting position then leaned against the box behind her. "I'll be fine in a few minutes. But you... You need to leave. You need to remember what I said, and trust in yourself when the time comes."

I nodded then looked at the journal, realizing I hadn't even spoken to her about what I'd come there for.

Following my gaze, she said, "Everything in there is true. Memories can be taken, and in order for you to find out what was taken from you, you'll need to do as I said, and trust yourself. You need to open your eyes, and I don't mean the pretty brown ones on your face."

She took another shallow breath then closed her eyes. "Don't mention to anyone what I've said. I know you think you can trust Abby, and you're right, but this must stay between us." She opened her eyes and looked at me with a sense of desperation. "It's imperative."

I didn't respond. Nothing she said made sense.

"Promise me," she said.

Not really understanding why it was so important, I nodded, anyway. "Okay. I promise."

"You are much more than you realize." She gave me a weak smile.

"Are you sure you'll be alright?" I asked.

"I'll be fine in a few minutes."

"Okay." I backed up to the door. "Thank you."

I wasn't exactly sure what I was thankful for. Hell, I had no idea what had even happened in the last few minutes. Whatever it was, it took almost all of Astrid's energy out of her and for a supposedly retired witch, that was huge.

"Trust in yourself," she whispered as I closed the door behind me.

As I exited the store, Abby practically jumped on me but pulled short of actually touching me. "What did she say?"

We started walking back to the car.

"Not much," I said keeping my promise to Astrid. "She confirmed there is a spell that has the power to take away my memory, which we already basically knew thanks to Mava."

"Does she know where Mava disappeared to?"

I shook my head as I got into the driver's seat and started the engine. "Astrid really didn't tell me much. She kept going on about how she no longer practices, but she did confirm that this is a book of witch's spells and didn't seem at all happy that I had possession of it."

"I knew that bitch wouldn't give you jack shit."

I pulled out of the parking spot and onto the road. "She may not have told me anything really useful, but she did do something else for us."

"What? Did she tell you where Marcus is?"

"I wish. But no, she didn't know anything about Marcus or where he might be. However, she did do this for us." I placed my hand on her arm.

Abby's eyes widened with a mixture of fear and anticipation, then I could practically feel the relief flooding off her when it became apparent I could once again touch her without zapping her.

"Oh, thank God," Abby said. "If I had to keep driving around in these things I'd go out of my mind." She gestured to the car.

I started to laugh, but stopped when I realized Abby hadn't been able to use her wings for not even a day and she was already going out of her mind; I could only imagine how hard it had been for Marcus when he'd gone without his wings for centuries.

During the remainder of the drive home, I couldn't stop thinking about the conversation I'd had with Astrid. Even though she hadn't come right out and said it, I believed she somehow knew about the vial that Mava had given me and was telling me to trust myself.

Deep down I knew what I had to do. I'd promised Marcus I wouldn't touch the vial and although I'd had every intention of keeping the promise at the time I'd made it to him, things had changed. Marcus was missing and whoever that woman was spelled trouble with a capital T.

"Pull over!" Abby yelled, yanking at the steering wheel.

The car fishtailed as I slammed on the brakes and tried to recover. Thankfully, we didn't end up in the ditch on the side of the road. I opened my mouth to have a go at Abby when she cut me off.

"Get out," she practically screamed me.

I didn't have to be told twice. I could feel *them* myself.

I threw open the car door and climbed out. Four sets of blood-red eyes stared at me through the darkness of the forest as they bounded towards us.

Abby didn't bother to expose her wings before she grabbed me around the waist and pushed off the ground. The red-eyed monsters became more visible, running at us on four legs, yellow teeth bared. They bounded on top of the car and hurled themselves into the air, jaws snapping and claws slashing as they tried to get us.

*A*bby's massive black feathers blocked my view of those hellish creatures as she pounded her wings, taking us higher into the sky.

I wasn't sure if I'd taken a single breath from the time the creatures attacked to the moment we touched down safely inside the dome of Marcus's home.

It took me a few seconds to work up the ability to ask, "What the hell were they?"

"Hellhounds." Abby tucked her wings behind her, and they disappeared into her back. "I'm sure the pendant would've kept them from taking you, but that doesn't mean they wouldn't have done some real damage before they got zapped."

I thought about those rancid sharp teeth. They didn't look like any wild cat or dog teeth I'd ever seen. The Hellhounds teeth were razor-sharp, jagged needles of pain. More like shark teeth.

"Thank you," I said. "Although 'thank you' really isn't enough."

A new round of guilt rushed through me after what she'd just saved me from. I didn't like lying to her about what Astrid had said to me and I just hoped that I wasn't going to regret it.

Abby and I tried calling Marcus again but just like the other times, he didn't answer. Abby even tried to call Justin, but he didn't pick up, either.

With the vial Mava had given me consuming my thoughts, I made an excuse of being tired and headed to my bedroom. I closed the door behind me then opened the drawer beside my bed to get out the vial.

It wasn't there.

Furrowing my brow, I ransacked the drawer. I didn't find it. "Shit."

Hoping I'd got my hiding spot wrong, I opened the drawer above it and sifted through it. The vial wasn't there, either.

I headed over to the closet and spent the next five minutes rifling through every nook and cranny, but still no luck.

Fear ripped through me, and I prayed whoever had put the journal on my pillow hadn't also taken the vial, which potentially was the only thing that could've helped me find Marcus.

"Marcus," I whispered.

I slipped out my room and tiptoed to his, careful to quietly close his door behind me.

I pressed my ear against the door and listened to see if Abby was coming this way. The last thing I wanted was to be caught snooping through Marcus's stuff.

Satisfied that Abby wasn't coming, I went over to the bedside tables in turn, opened the drawers, and sifted through his personal possessions as I searched for the vial.

Coming up empty, I headed into his closet. It was even bigger than mine. I went through the built-in drawers, but again I couldn't find what I was looking for. I then went through the various compartments moving around ties, boxers and socks but still came up empty handed.

The last place left to search was the top shelf, which of course I couldn't reach. So, I dragged the ottoman over from the centre of the closet, climbed on top, and reached up. I was almost convinced that there was nothing to be found when the tips of my fingers brushed against something hard. I tried reaching further, but it was no use. I couldn't get a good grasp on whatever it was to pull it down.

With my hands on my hips, I looked around the closet, trying to figure out how I could make myself that little bit taller so I could get to the mystery item. There were no other chairs, tables, or anything else I could drag over. The only other thing I could do was climb.

"Ah, what the hell," I muttered.

Carefully, I placed my foot on the shelf then pulled myself up just a bit higher, allowing me to get my hand on what appeared to be a box, and dragged it toward the edge. It was heavy, and I needed to use two hands.

Bracing myself for a quick grab, I let go of the shelf I was using to steady myself and grabbed the box then landed back onto the Ottoman, with the big black box in my hands.

Stepping onto the floor, I sat, and rested the box on my lap.

As I lifted the lid, my gaze fell on a photo of Marcus and me. My heart constricted with a deep sense of longing. I didn't remember ever having our picture taken, but I could tell we were happy. By the condition of the photo, I figured it must have been taken sometime in my last lifetime.

I picked it up and traced the lines of Marcus's face, wishing I could feel him once again. My heart ached to touch him, and I hated feeling helpless. I needed to find the vial.

Taking one last look at the photo, I placed it back and did my best to ignore all the other memories Marcus had kept of us as I searched through the contents. A smile broke across my face when I saw the glistening liquid inside the vial.

Relief flooding through me, I wrapped my fingers around the glass and held it tightly in my hand.

Figuring I needed a safe place to hide the vial until I was ready, I tucked it into my cast. It was a snug fit, but it would do. I smiled at the small infinity symbol Marcus had drawn on my cast. So much had happened since the day he'd gone with me to the hospital. I had been clueless to our relationship, and I now knew that the disgust I'd thought I'd seen in his eyes was actually torment. He was consumed with pain and a deep sense of responsibility for what I was putting myself through. It must've been so hard for him to see what I'd done to myself and not be able to say all the things he wanted to tell me.

I sighed. I wished I could've gone back in time and stopped myself from wasting my time with him. I wished I could've trusted my feelings toward him and had known they were mine. It hadn't taken me that long to give in to my connection with him, but I'd still missed out on precious moments. And moments were all we had.

I shook that thought away. I was over moments. Marcus and I were going to have forever.

With the vial safely stored within easy reach, I went to check on

Abby. I desperately wanted to see what else Marcus had in the box, but I knew that once I'd started, I wasn't going to be able to stop until I'd read and looked through everything within it.

With all intentions of pretending I needed a drink, I went back into the main living area where I found Abby with a half-empty bottle of wine in her hand.

"Don't say anything," she warned then took a swig.

As much as I didn't want her drinking, the fact that she was drunk was going to play well for me.

"I wasn't going to say anything." I continued to the kitchen. "I came out here for a drink myself."

"Not alcohol, I hope!" Abby called out to me.

I grabbed a bottle of water out of the fridge then made my way back into the lounge room.

"Nope. Just this." I unscrewed the lid and took a small sip. "But why are you trying to warn me off alcohol?"

Abby took another sip then lowered the bottle to her lap. "I already have one alcoholic on my hands; I don't need another."

I drew my eyebrows together trying to figure out what she meant. Then it dawned on me; she wasn't referring to herself. She was referring to Marcus. Only he seemed to be able to quit cold turkey as soon as I was ready to come back into his life again.

"I'm going to go and lie down for a bit," I said, deciding now was a good time to go through the box. "Is there anything you need?"

"Nope. I got everything I need right here." She patted the neck of the bottle.

Feeling a bit guilty for leaving her there to drink on her own, I turned on my heels and trotted off toward the bedrooms.

Once safely inside Marcus's room, I grabbed the black box and carried it over to the bed, climbed on top, and sat cross-legged in the middle of the mattress.

Carefully, I lifted the lid then removed the photo and placed them both on the end of the bed. I then picked up a piece of paper that had been folded in half. Opening it, I instantly recognized the writing as my own, although the name I'd signed off on was one I'd never heard before. It was a letter from my previous life dated nineteen-nighty-nine.

. . .

Marcus,

You have lifted the darkness that consumed my soul, but I would give it all back if I was able to release you from your demons. I know you tell me it's okay, but I've seen the way you look at me... It's as if you're fighting something you can't control and it's killing me. I wish you'd let me save you as you've saved me.

Please let me in.

Cassie

I bit my lip as I placed the letter back in the box and pulled out what appeared to be a photo album. I set it on my lap, then opened it. There on the first page was a sketch of me from a different time. I looked the same as I did now only I wore clothes from a different era.

I wondered if that was of me in the beginning, when we first met. The look in my eyes told me I was in love and I wished with all my heart that I could remember that moment.

Flipping the page, I was welcomed with more sketches and photos of Marcus and me spanning the years. In most of the pictures we looked happy, although there were a few that made me think I wasn't as in love with him as he was with me. Those photos were my undoing. I was so mad at my previous self for wasting time that we didn't have. And now I was losing time again.

As I removed a photo from my last life, a tear slipped from my eyes as I saw how happy we'd been. We were sitting on the edge of the pool, laughing about something I didn't remember. And even though there was that darkness in Marcus's gaze, I knew it was only because of what was coming.

With a heavy heart and the photo of the two of us in my hand, I dialled Marcus's number again, praying that this time he would answer. But like the other times, he didn't. He didn't even have a message so I could listen to his voice.

I dropped the phone on the bed and curled up with his pillow as I looked once more at the photo of the two of us during happier times.

Tears slipped from my eyes as a new memory came to me. I remembered the day we had the photo taken so clearly. I was so happy that I'd found Marcus. I couldn't believe someone so perfect for me could exist. He'd still had his demons, which of course I hadn't understood what they were at the time. I'd just thought he'd had some bad experience that was going to take years for him to be able to confide in me. The sad thing was, at the time, I thought we had years left. I had no idea that within months, I was going to die at his hands.

I squeezed my eyes shut as more tears slipped out. I wanted to feel him in my arms more than I'd ever wanted anything in my entire life. Fear that it may never happen again in this lifetime choked me.

Opening my eyes, my gaze went straight to the tip of the vial hiding in my cast.

I pulled it out and held it next to the photo. I knew what I had to do. I had no other choice.

Pulling myself into a sitting position, I grabbed my phone and tried Marcus one last time. Again, he did not answer.

With my heart beating erratically, my stomach lurched as I opened the vial and stared at the gooey, glistening contents. I knew I had to do it, but that didn't make it any easier. I was scared out of my mind, but I had to be brave for Marcus.

I couldn't live with myself knowing that he needed my help and I was too afraid to do what was necessary. This was the only way I could help him. Astrid had said that I needed to trust I would make the right decision and that was exactly what I was going to do.

With shaky hands, I lifted the vial to my lips and slowly tipped it up until the bitter contents spilled into my mouth and rolled down my throat.

Within seconds, my vision began to sway and my head felt fuzzy. My heart rate began to lower until I could barely feel a beat and I collapsed on the bed.

I tried to lift my arm, but it wouldn't move. I tried to scream out to Abby, but my mouth wouldn't open. I was completely paralyzed. I couldn't even move my eyes.

Mava had screwed me over.

$\mathcal{I}$ lay on the bed for what seemed like an eternity, my mind trapped in the decision I'd made to trust the crazy woman and break my promise to the man I loved.

Night fell, and the moon no longer hovered directly above. I had never taken notice of how the moon moved through the night sky just like the sun until I had no choice but to stare, unblinking, at the sky through the window of my room.

Abby didn't come to check on me once. She probably didn't want to disturb my sleep.

Everything Mava and Astrid had said to me played like a movie on repeat in my mind. Then there was Marcus pleading for me not to touch the vial. He knew there was a huge possibility that Mava wasn't as trustworthy as she wanted us to believe. He knew that something could've gone wrong. Yet I did it, anyway. And now I was left completely aware, with absolutely no control over my body.

I wanted to scream, I wanted to cry, but mostly I wanted to take back my reckless decision to drink something I knew nothing about. I had trusted the wrong person, and now, it wasn't just me that would pay the price. Marcus was still gone, and there was nothing I could do to find him.

Light started to fill the sky, then the sun began to rise over the water as the waves rolled onto the shoreline. It was another deceptively perfect day. One that would bring—

My thoughts were interrupted by Marcus's voice coming from the other end of the house, followed by another man's muffled voice, which I presumed was Justin.

My chest tightened with a mixture of relief and fear. Marcus was okay. Marcus was safe. But—and there was a big but—Marcus was about to find me. He was going to think I was dead at first, but then he had to see that I was still alive and be able to find help to right the wrong. I knew it would only be moments that he would think the worst, but it would be real for him all the same.

A few seconds later, I heard the pad of footsteps that stopped outside my bedroom door. There was a faint knock, and then another when I didn't answer.

He continued down the hall, then opened the door to his bedroom. I couldn't see him as my head was facing the opposite direction, but it made no difference. I could feel the shift of energy in the room almost instantaneously.

"Lucy?" He hesitated. "Lucy?"

Marcus made his way around the foot of the bed and froze, his eyes wide. Then fear took over.

In a panic, he rushed to my side. "Lucy?" He caressed the side of my face. "Please. No. No. Please, no."

My heart smashed into a million pieces as I watched, completely unable to stop him from spiralling out of control as he dealt with what he thought was my death. I wanted to hug him, and tell him it was okay—I would be okay. But I may as well have been dead because I couldn't do or say a single thing. All I could do was watch him go through something no one should ever have to. And I was powerless to stop his pain.

Shock turned to rage as tears welled in his eyes. "This can't be happening. It's not time. It's not fucking time!"

He climbed onto the bed and cradled me against his heaving chest as his heart ripped in two. "It's not your time. It's not…"

Marcus rolled me with him as he reached for something across the bed then brought it in front of his face. It was the vial.

"I'm going to fuckin' kill her." He threw the vial, smashing it against the wall.

Marcus wrapped me in his embrace and placed tender kisses on my forehead as Justin and Abby practically flew into the room.

"What's wrong?" Abby asked. "What was that—" She rushed over to us and climbed on the bed. "Oh, no, no."

"Shit," Justin said, his gaze falling to the floor.

Abby placed her fingers on my wrist, checking for a pulse. "Come on," she said. But no sign of a heartbeat must have come because all hope dropped from her face. "This can't be happening... I didn't know." She placed her hand on Marcus's forearm and slowly rubbed it. "I swear she was okay last night."

I pleaded with her through my vacant eyes to realize I was alive. She didn't.

Abby turned her attention to Marcus, sorrow filling her gaze.

"She drank the vial Mava gave her," Marcus said through tears.

I wanted to scream out to him that I was still alive. How could he not know? He was a Soul Collector. He was supposed to be able to see souls, and I was pretty sure that my soul was still locked away in my body because I was still alive!

He leaned down and rested his lips against the top of my head and breathed in deeply. "This is all my fault. I never should've gone after Titus. I should've accepted what we have and not try to change it. Because..."

I wanted to know what was after the "because," but he never finished his sentence.

"It's not your fault," Abby said. "This is no one's fault."

Marcus lifted his head, looking toward the closet. "Yeah. It's Justin's fault."

With rage coursing through his expression, Marcus gently laid me on the bed then rushed toward Justin's direction, disappearing from my view. "This is your fault." Something crashed that sounded a lot like when Justin had gone through the front door.

"Marcus!" Abby screamed. "Stop."

As much as I hated Justin, I had to agree with Abby. This was not his fault. It was my fault for trusting Mava and Astrid who I'd only just met. I'd let fear drive me to do something I would forever regret.

Another thump, followed by a grunt then something broke as it crashed to the floor.

"Marcus!" Abby practically flew off the bed toward the boys.

Giving it everything I had, I tried desperately to get up, or at least turn my head so I could see them but once again, I was staring out the window.

"I'm sorry," Justin said. "But I couldn't have known she would listen to Mava. I didn't even know Mava had given her anything."

"So you're saying this is my fault?" Marcus practically screamed at him. "If you hadn't fucked up from the start. If you had told me the truth then maybe this wouldn't have happened. Maybe I would've figured this out by now, and Lucy wouldn't be lying there dead.

"She's dead," Marcus repeated, sounding as if he were breaking down again. "And you're right. It's all my fault. I shouldn't have left her."

"It's not your fault," Abby said, soothingly. "None of us could've known what Luciana was going to do."

Marcus climbed onto the bed and once again pulled me into his arms as he leaned against the headboard.

"I'm so sorry," he whispered. He caressed the side of my face with his hand. "I'm so sorry."

I pleaded with him to see that I was still alive inside my head. I needed him to see me. All this time Mava and even Astrid had gone on about me needing to 'see,' and look where that got me. I could see. That's all I could do.

Abby came into view and placed her hand on Marcus's shoulder. "We'll be in the lounge room if you need anything." She gave him a sad smile then left the room, closing the door behind her.

CHAPTER 24

$\mathcal{M}$arcus cradled me in his arms for what felt like hours before Abby came back into the room with a bottle of scotch in her hand.

Great. She was drinking again.

Instead of lifting it to her lips, she handed the bottle to Marcus. "Here you go."

I wanted to scream at him to stop. I needed him to be sober. To figure this out and save me, not drink himself into a stupor. But that was exactly what he did.

Abby left us alone, coming back every so often to hand Marcus another bottle. On the fourth trip, she brought one for herself and another two refills, as well. She put two bottles on the bedside table then climbed onto the bed and sat beside Marcus.

"Tomorrow we're going to figure this shit out," she said. "But for now…" She lifted her bottle as if she were giving a toast. "Now, we'll drink."

She pressed the opening against her lips then drank until at least half the bottle was gone.

Marcus raised his bottle. "To Lucy."

She clinked her bottle against his. "To Lucy."

They both finished their bottle then Abby replaced them with the ones she'd brought in preparation. This time they took it a bit slower.

"You know," Marcus said, hitting his knee against Abby's, "I thought this time would be different. I mean, I really thought it would be different. And now I don't even know if there will be another life for her. She's only meant to be able to die by my hands."

"This doesn't make any sense." Abby's eyes glistened under the light.

"Hold this." Marcus handed his bottle to her then softly pressed his fingertips against my eyelids and slid them down, taking away my vision.

No, no, no! As much as it hurt to watch Marcus go through this pain, I wanted to see him. I needed to see him. Now all I could rely on was my hearing.

In the darkness, I relished the feeling of his warm embrace. That was what I needed to focus on because I had no idea what was coming, but one thing I knew for sure, Marcus would not hold onto me for the rest of eternity.

As if hearing my thoughts, Abby said, "Justin said he'd take her for you."

Fear ripped through my soul. Marcus couldn't be that foolish. He couldn't let me go. He had to figure out that I was still alive. He just had to.

"Screw that," Marcus replied, relief washing over me. "He's not putting a finger on her."

"You know this really isn't his fault, right?" When Marcus didn't answer, she said, "Right?"

Marcus breathed out harshly. "Doesn't make me want to blame him any less."

"If that's what you need, then blame him all you want, but it doesn't change the fact that you shouldn't be the one to bring her in. You've never done it so far, and now we have even fewer people we can trust."

Marcus strained a laugh. "And you're saying we can trust Justin?"

"I'm saying that maybe Justin should be the one. He's willing— and he's sorry. That guy is sitting out there tearing himself apart. He blames himself for everything that's happened, and no matter how much he has pissed you off, he's still here. He was once your best friend, and the only thing he's guilty of is the fact that he palmed off his collection onto you and didn't tell you that he'd later found out that she wasn't meant to die."

"And I'm now supposed to feel sorry for the guy?"

"That's not what I'm saying. What I'm trying to say is that maybe you should put yourself in his shoes for a second and think about what you would've done if the situation were reversed and you found out that your best friend was stuck in a loop of hell and was never meant to be that way. If he had collected her soul then maybe you and Lucy wouldn't be going through all this."

"I would've told him," Marcus said. "No matter what."

"Well, now he has."

Marcus remained silent, and Abby didn't push any further. All I could hear was the guzzling of the alcohol as they both drank themselves into a stupor.

CHAPTER 25

*M*arcus stayed with me all through the night. I kept hoping that the potion would wear off and I'd at least get my voice back, so I could tell him that I was still alive.

That didn't happen.

I stayed in my paralyzed state, listening to the heart wrenching pain he was experiencing from losing me again, topped with the fear of not knowing if that night at the Devil's Playground was the last time he would ever get to see me again, hold me in his arms, feel my warm lips against his, and hear the sweet sound of my voice.

Marcus told me he would not only make Mava pay for what she'd done, but also that if he was lucky enough to be given the chance of me coming back into his life, he was going to spend the next eighteen years figuring out who'd placed this curse on us, what they had to gain, and make sure that when the time was right for us to be reunited, he would be ready for us to put an end to it all.

I was absolutely heartbroken by the time Justin came knocking on the door.

"Let me know when you're ready," he said, his voice full of sorrow.

Marcus stroked the side of my face. "I'll never be ready." He sighed. "I wish I could see her soul."

"No, you don't," Justin said. "Because if you could, that would mean Lucy is really gone forever."

A few moments had passed before Marcus asked, "Do you think she'll come back?"

"I have no doubt," Justin said with a small smile in his tone that pricked my curiosity. "She'll be back before you know it."

The door closed, leaving Marcus and me once again alone.

He continued to stroke my cheek. "I hope he's right."

Oh, Justin was right. I wasn't dead. I was alive and listening. And what I heard Justin say wasn't what Marcus had heard. Marcus was stuck in the loss of me, and couldn't read between the lines. Me, on the other hand, all I could do was focus on the words. And something told me that Justin knew I was still alive.

The light from the sun had long disappeared before Justin and Abby came back.

"It's time," Abby said, her voice sounding as if she were standing beside the bed.

Marcus tightened his grip on me. "I can't."

"I know," she replied, her tone filled with warmth and understanding.

"This Luciana is gone," Justin said. "And she's already alive, waiting until the time is right for you two to be reunited."

The hell I'm gone!

I wanted to punch him in the face. He knew. I don't know how I knew he knew, I just did.

"I love you," Marcus whispered into my ear then kissed my forehead. "I'll be ready and waiting for you. I promise." He loosened his grip on me.

I wanted to scream at him not to let me go. He couldn't trust Justin. He should never have trusted Justin. I was terrified of where he was going to take me, and I needed Marcus to save me. I needed him. But he thought I was already gone.

My hope surged when I felt Abby take me in her arms. We could trust Abby. She wouldn't hurt me. She'd spent the last few hundred years helping Marcus cope with our vicious cycle.

All my hope shattered as she passed me to Justin.

"I promise I'll take care of her," Justin said as someone opened the sliding door to the back patio.

Please don't let him take me! I tried to yell to Marcus. If we were so connected, then maybe he could hear my thoughts.

Yeah, that didn't work out.

We may have been connected, but that didn't mean either of us were telepathic. Even in a world filled with supernatural creatures, that shit just didn't exist.

The cool night air enveloped me as Justin stepped outside. A moment later my stomach dropped out when he took off into the sky, carrying me to an unknown destination. My nerves were a complete wreck. I was petrified of what lay ahead.

Justin raised me in his arms, brushing his face against mine.

"I know you must be terrified right now," he said. "But I promise you'll soon understand. Everything will be alright."

My blood froze. I was right. Justin had planned this all along.

CHAPTER 26

*I*t wasn't long before I felt the jolt that came along with the landing. Justin rearranged me in his arms.

"Now you can *see*," he said lifting my eyelids.

Before us stood Mava's house, the one that had disappeared only days before. It was right back where it was supposed to be.

Justin chuckled. "It's pretty amazing, huh?"

Pretty amazing was the understatement of the century. And as much as I tried to wrap my head around what I was seeing, the fear of what he was about to do with me consumed my thoughts.

Still carrying me, he walked right up to the front door, gave a little tap with his knuckles, and then entered.

"There she is," Mava said, not sounding the slightest bit insane as she drifted closer to me. She caressed the side of my face with the tips of her fingers. "Don't worry, dear. I will explain everything to you in a few moments." She stepped back and pointed to the side. "Go on through."

Following Mava's direction, Justin carried me into to the lounge room then walked straight through a wall. A freaking wall!

Panic reared its ugly head as I feared that I was no longer in my dimension and Justin had pulled me through one of the veils. If that was true, I had no hope in hell of getting back to Marcus. For all I knew, he was about to hand me over to the Soul Scrapers.

As if sensing my fear, Justin said, "You're safe. No one is going to hurt you."

He already had.

The room was dark. I could barely make the outline of the objects surrounding us. Shadows danced in the corner of my eyes, and I had no idea if it were the Soul Scrapers, or if it was just plain old shadows. Either way, it still set my nerves on edge.

"Let there be light," Mava said.

A soft glow emitted from a mystical ball that hovered just above our heads in the center of the room. A second later it intensified to a warm white light, which flooded the room, chasing away the shadows.

Justin carried me to the end of the room and laid me on a plush couch. He then took a couple of steps backwards, allowing Mava to get closer to me.

She leaned over the top of me so I could see her face. "Justin believes we should leave you in this state while I explain what we have done to you and the reasons why. But, I believe that you are ready for the truth, and even though you are upset, I have complete faith in you. I know you will do the right thing."

Oh, God, I wanted to prove Justin wrong. However, all I wanted to do was scream at the top of my lungs so Marcus could save me from these two crazy people who were holding me captive. Except Marcus wouldn't be able to hear me.

I was on my own, and I had no hope in hell of getting back to my own dimension. I couldn't control the veils. I had no idea how any of the supernatural world worked.

"She'll stay," a familiar voice said from somewhere in the dark shadows of the outskirts of the room.

Astrid.

Coming into view, she said, "Luciana knows what's at stake. And she will do whatever it takes to make sure she and Marcus have their forever that she so desperately wants."

The bitch knew. Everything she'd said was a setup. If I hadn't found the journal, I wouldn't have gone to see her that day, and I wouldn't have drank the vial. I would be at home right now curled up in Marcus's arms. Instead, he was at home mourning the loss of me.

I sighed internally. Who was I kidding? Something deep inside of me was telling me that drinking the vial was exactly what I needed to do.

Mava sat on the edge of the couch and placed her hand over mine.

"Please let us explain." She reached behind me, retrieved a small bowl of water, and sat it on her lap.

She dipped her finger inside then placed it on my forehead, right between the eyebrows. She then murmured something under her breath, and within seconds I had control of my body again.

She jumped back as I jerked myself into a sitting position, gasping and filling my lungs with air.

There were a million questions that had been running through my head, but there was only one that I desperately needed to say.

"You have got to tell Marcus that I'm still alive," I pleaded, glancing between the three of them.

Marcus was beyond devastated, and he didn't need to be. These three people had the ability to make his pain go away. By the look on their faces, not a single one agreed with me.

"We cannot do that, Luciana," Mava said, as if it was set in stone.

"The hell you can't. You drugged me. You lied to us. And now Marcus is at home going out of his mind because he thinks there isn't going to be another chance for us. He thinks this is it and you're telling me that you won't? You're telling me that you think it's okay for him to go through absolute hell while we all know I'm still alive?"

"It's a necessary evil," Justin said.

"Shut up!" I darted over to him. "You of all people should know what he's going through. You were there. You saw him! And you're refusing to tell him that I'm okay? You're supposed to be his best friend! Best friends don't do that to each other."

I turned away from him, unable to look at the asshole any longer.

"Don't take this out on Justin," Astrid said." "This is not his fault. And we're lucky that he was able to help."

"Help?" I couldn't believe what I was hearing. No one was helping. They'd friggin' kidnapped me after putting me in some type of paralyzed state.

I glared at her, anger boiling inside of me as the steps she'd taken to make sure I'd listened to her became clear. "That's why you wouldn't let Abby into the shop, wasn't it?"

Astrid nodded. "I don't hate Abby like she believes I do. In fact, she has been an integral part of this plan—"

My eyes practically popped out of my head. "She knew?"

"No," Justin jumped in. "Abby knows just as much as Marcus, which is zip."

I scowled at him. "Like I'm going to believe anything that comes out of your mouth."

I was seething with rage and I could barely hold back.

"Why don't you come sit down and have some tea? It will help you calm down." Astrid gestured toward the couch.

"I don't want tea. I want answers!" I threw my hands in the air. "More importantly, I want someone to tell Marcus what is going on here!"

Justin shook his head. "I knew we should've left her paralyzed until we had a chance to explain."

I breathed out in frustration, trying to refrain from running over to him and shoving the ball of light down his throat. No matter what I said, not a single one of them planned on helping me. Being angry wasn't getting me anywhere, though. If I wanted to get out of wherever I was, I needed to listen to what they had to say.

I needed to play them just like they'd played me.

"Fine. I'll Listen," I said, barely managing to control my anger as I paced the length of the room. I couldn't sit still. My body was in flight mode, and I had nowhere to go. "Explain to me why you've all lied to us, why you've drugged me and made everyone believe that I'm dead. Why you kidnapped me, and why the hell it is so important that Marcus believes I'm dead."

"I'll go make us some tea," Astrid said.

Mava nodded then turned her attention to me. "I understand this must be hard for you, but I truly believe that once you hear everything we have to say, you will be more than happy to stay here with me. And you'll understand how necessary it is that Marcus continues to believe that you are dead."

"What could be so important for you to go to all this trouble?" I waved my hands around the creeptacular room.

I'd thought Mava's shack was creepy, but this room was taking it to a whole new level. Unlike Mava's, this place was furnished with classic pieces that must've dated back centuries. None of that old and crappy stuff either. Everything in the room had to be worth a fortune. And I didn't even want to get started on that orb hovering just below the ceiling. That was enough for me to lose my mind— especially if I looked at it for more than a second.

I shivered as my eyes darted to the orb and I saw movement within that looked way too much like souls.

Mava glided over to the couch and lowered herself onto the end seat.

Their witchcraft was real. And it was scaring the crap out of me. What hope did I have against a freaking witch who had powers above my comprehension?

"I have been planning this for many years, and I've been waiting for the moment you were ready." Mava chuckled. "It wasn't easy making everyone believe I was crazy for this length of time. But it was necessary."

I came to a standstill and put my hands on my hips. "Necessary for what?"

She tilted her head slightly to the side and smiled. "For you to discover who you really are and what your purpose on Earth is. Far too long you've been living a lie, not knowing who you truly are, and what you were created for."

"Hold up," I said. "I was created?"

Mava smiled again and I wanted to rip it off her face. Now was not the time for smiling. This was serious. I needed answers, and I needed to get back to Marcus.

"Yes, dear. You have made some enemies through no fault of your own," Mava said as Astrid came back into the room carrying a tray with a teapot and four cups. "And it is our duty to help you find what was taken from you."

"My memory?" I asked as Astrid placed the tray on the mahogany side table.

"Yes, dear." Mava smiled again. "An evil has lurked among us for far too long and has done everything within its power to make sure the scale stays where it is for their own selfish reasons."

I slowly shook my head as I tried to make sense of what she just said. Of course, I couldn't.

"You are lucky that Justin was off goofing around when he was supposed to do your collection, otherwise..." She sighed. "Who knows what would've happened."

Mava picked a delicate rose covered cup up and took an elegant sip. She was far from the woman I first met with Abby. It must've been hell to keep up the appearance of such a crazy woman if this was who she really was.

"Did you figure out my clues?" Mava asked.

I scoffed. "You mean that riddle that made absolutely no sense?"

She smiled—again! "There were so many clues in what you read. The biggest of all is that you are the light."

I raised my brows. That was not what I was expecting. "If that were true then who's the dark?"

"Isn't that obvious?"

"If it were obvious I wouldn't be asking."

That smile of hers spread across her face. "Marcus."

I practically snorted. "Marcus is a lot of things, but darkness is not one of them. He's one of the kindest, most caring, honest individuals that I know of."

"Hold up," Justin said, butting his nose in. I was going to punch him if he planned on telling me otherwise. "Mava never said anything about Marcus being evil. There is a big difference between darkness and evil. And we both know that kindness can come from the darkest of places."

"I thought Soul Collectors were neither dark or light?"

"That is true," Mava said. "And Marcus isn't one of them."

CHAPTER 27

I jerked my head back in shock. "What the hell do you mean that Marcus isn't a Soul Collector? He found me because he was there to collect my soul. Justin asked him to collect my soul. This is all because he was supposed to collect my soul and didn't. And now you're trying to tell me that he's not a Soul Collector."

"That's exactly what Mava's saying," Justin said. "I always knew there was something different about him—even Abby could sense it. Just no one thought to question why that was."

"He is not one that walks amongst the dead or the living." Astrid took a seat next to Mava, leaving a wide-open gap on the other end for me to sit.

That so wasn't going to happen.

"I could tell he was different the very first time I met him," Astrid continued. "He is why I went into retirement. I'd always heard about the legend that spoke of you but never fully believed it until I met Marcus. It was instantly obvious that you and he were the ones who would bring order back to the world—and I'm not just talking about your dimension. This goes far deeper than you can ever imagine. There are those that will do whatever it takes to keep the two of you from remembering."

"But only I have the memory problem."

Astrid shook her head and gave me the same smile Mava did. It must've been a witch thing that they'd practice every night in the mirror just to drive me insane.

"Marcus has forgotten as well." Astrid raised a brow. "After all, he still thinks he's a Soul Collector."

"If he's not a Soul Collector, then what is he?"

"Only Marcus truly knows. And until you remember and fulfil your destiny, he will remain in the dark."

"Then how can you be so sure that he's good and that whoever did this to us isn't actually stopping something really bad from happening?"

"Even you can see the light that's buried under all that darkness."

I closed my eyes as tears began to well. Marcus was my light. He was the only one who could make all the pain go away. And if what they were telling me were true, he had a much bigger purpose than keeping my curse at bay.

I opened my eyes and wiped the tears away. "Who's doing this to him? Who's doing this to me?"

"You already suspect one of them," Astrid said.

I drew my brows together as I tried to figure out whom she was talking about, then it dawned on me.

"That woman I saw following Marcus into the club. The same one who I saw in my memory." I let out a shuddered breath. That woman scared me to my very core. "Who is she?"

"Morgana," Mava replied. "She's a high priestess who lost her way a long time ago."

"You mean she's a witch?"

Mava nodded. "The very highest of them all."

"And what does she want with me?"

"Isn't it obvious?" Justin asked. "She wants you dead."

Okay, so that was a stupid question. Of course, she wanted me dead. This was never about me. It was all always about Marcus.

"Don't think this isn't about you, my dear," Mava said.

I jumped. "Did you just read my mind?"

She shook her head. "No, dear. I cannot read minds. What I can do is read your soul."

I didn't even want to think about what that could mean. While I really did want to know what it all meant, there were bigger things at play than my curiosity.

"Okay, so you said that Marcus isn't a Soul Collector and no one but he knows what he is, right? But he doesn't remember who he is, or even know he's missing any memories." When they nodded, I continued, "So how does his severed wings come into play?"

Mava gestured to Justin to answer my question.

"Right," he said. "I know this may sound weird, but for some reason, I can't remember the exact details of his wings. I know he had them, and you've even seen the marks. But everything else is a blur that my brain is telling me that I'm okay with."

"So you're saying you can't remember his wings. What does that even mean?"

"It means that there is a possibility they are not like mine—or even Abby's. He may very well be something entirely different."

I screwed up my face at him, and he sighed.

"Think of it this way: each group of entities has their own unique fingerprint that helps others differentiate them at first glance. Now, you have to wonder why out of every single entity that has a pair of wings and have committed far worse crimes than Marcus, why were Marcus's removed?" He let that sink in then added, "Why is Marcus one of the only entities to have had his wings severed?"

"Because they needed to keep his identity hidden," I said more to myself than Justin.

"Correct," Justin said. "Whoever is Morgana's partner made sure that no one would ever know who Marcus really is, and have tried to do everything within their power to make sure that you and Marcus never met."

"Except they weren't expecting you to palm off your collection." My jaw hung in disbelief. "Holy shit."

"I'd never missed a collection. I was their star player."

"So, does this mean that Titus knows the truth about it all?"

"I believe he knows something, but even after all these years he won't admit it," Justin said.

I rubbed my temples with the tips of my fingers as I tried to let it all sink in.

Then I went over to the couch and melted against the soft fabric. "So what do I need to do?"

Mava and Astrid looked at each other and smiled.

"Now, we need you to remember who you are," Astrid said, her grin like a permanent fixture on her face.

"What do I do?" I asked. "Do I just drink something?"

Justin chuckled. "No, Lucy. You can't just drink something. What you need to do is either going to break you or make you. And only you have the power to decide which it'll be."

"Okay," I dragged, wondering what they had in store for me. "Let's get this over with so I can get back to Marcus, let him discover who he is, then save the day and we can finally have our happily ever after."

Astrid placed her hand on my forearm. "No, dear. It will not be that simple."

"Have you ever heard of astral traveling?" Justin asked with a serious expression.

I blinked at him. "Um, no."

"Well, believe me when I say the tunnel isn't a place you'll ever forget—no matter how much you'll want to."

I stood, prepared to run to hell and back if it meant being able to break this curse we were trapped in. "Where's the tunnel?"

Justin chuckled. "There's no physical tunnel." He strode closer to me and pointed his finger between my eyebrows. "It's through there."

"Good one." I batted his hand away then turned to Mava and Astrid. "Now can someone please show me to the tunnel?"

They both smiled—again.

"I'm afraid Justin is right," Mava said. "There is no physical tunnel. The vortex is only accessible through your mind."

I breathed out harshly. "How the hell am I supposed to go through some magical tunnel when I can't even see it?"

"We will guide you," Mava replied.

Astrid stood. "But first you need to be ready."

"I'm ready."

"Not yet," she said. "You must gather your strength and prepare for what is to come."

I was about to object when Justin jumped in, "If you think Soul Scrapers are the only things you need to fear then you've got a lot to learn. What you experience in the tunnel will probably make what happened to you at the club look like child's play."

A shiver ran down my spine. That night was the most terrifying experience I had ever gone through.

Knots formed in my stomach as I thought about what creatures lay ahead of me and what some entities had already done to me. My instincts were to rush in and get it over and done with, but my brain was telling me I needed to listen to the three of them and prepare myself for what was to come.

I had to do this right. I may not ever get a second chance, and I owed it to Marcus and me to do this right the first time.

I snorted internally. I couldn't believe they had changed my mind in just a few minutes. I came out of my paralyzed state prepared to go back to Marcus the second a chance arose, and now that I had the opportunity, I was going to stay.

Marcus would understand once he found out the truth. No matter how much my death was killing him now, it would be worth it in the end.

"Okay. I'll do it." I walked over to Justin and pointed my finger at him. "But I want you to promise me one thing."

"Sure."

"I want you to promise me that you'll go back to Marcus and make sure he doesn't do anything stupid while I'm gone."

"That I can do."

I smiled for the first time, and it was an actual genuine smile filled with a warmth for Justin I had never felt before.

"Thank you," I said quietly. "I really mean it, thank you."

"You may not believe me still, but please know that I do care about both you and Marcus, and I will do whatever it takes to see this through," he said.

Something told me he would. Call it gut instinct, or something entirely different. Whatever it was, I was ready to not only forgive Justin, but I was also thankful for everything he'd done. Because if what they were saying were true, someone very powerful would stop at nothing to make sure I remained in the dark.

I bit down on a smile. There I was spouting Mava's riddles.

Justin put his arm around my shoulders and ushered me toward the archway Astrid had come from when she'd brought in the tea. "Let's get you fed, then we can discuss how we'll approach the tunnel."

On the other side of the archway stood a rich mahogany table. It was already filled with various meats and vegetables roasted to perfection, fresh bread, salad, and glasses filled with red wine.

"Wow," I said, taking it all in.

"Nice, huh?" Justin gestured for me to take a seat at the round table.

I slid onto a chair. "Can I ask you something?"

"Of course." He sat on the chair beside me.

"Back at the rehab?"

"Yeah?"

I picked my napkin up and ran my finger along the sharp edge. "Why did you try to keep Marcus and me apart if you knew we were part of something much larger that you were apparently in on and are trying to help me discover who I am?"

After the words came out, I realized they barely made sense.

"I had to make sure you remembered," he answered without giving it a second thought. "There were rumors that you were different this time around. And I needed to make sure that we didn't waste any time."

"But you tried to pull us apart."

He chuckled. "Ever heard of wanting what you can't have? Or how if a parental figure forbids their teenager from doing something, you can be sure that teenager is going to try to do exactly what their parents told them not to?"

I whacked his arm. "Are you saying that I'm like a rebellious teenager and you're my father?"

The corner of his lips turned up into a smirk. "That's exactly what I'm saying—except for the father part."

Mava and Astrid joined us, and we all dug in. It wasn't until we neared the end of the meal that Mava brought up my mission.

"In order to prepare you for the tunnel, we'll need to make sure that your mind is ready. What you'll see in there will be those things you fear the most. Demons will stop at nothing to make sure you don't make it through to the other end."

I swallowed hard. "What's at the other end?"

"You spiritual guardians will be waiting for you to help open your eyes and enable you to discover your true purpose on Earth."

"Why do I have to go through the tunnel? Can't you just open a veil or something?"

The three of them gave me that smile as if I were an ignorant child.

"No," Astrid said. "There is no veil to the guardians. Only those with strong minds and souls can make it through. And that's why we need you to prepare. Most humans aren't able to reach their guardians because they can't ignore those who are trying to stop them. Fear takes over their souls, and traps them in their state until they're pulled back to this plane."

Planes? Veils? Dimensions? These guys were doing my head in. I rubbed my temples.

"Okay, so what you're saying is that I'm going to encounter my worst fears, and I have to block them out and keep moving until I reach the end of this metaphoric tunnel? Easy." I groaned.

I'd spent my whole life running from everything that made me feel anything, and now the only way I could make it all stop was to ignore and run. The running part seemed like something I was good at, but the ignoring part... I imagined that was going to be hard.

If what they were saying was correct, I was in for a world of unimaginable pain and suffering because that was what I feared most. Actually, it wasn't. I feared life, I feared death, and most importantly I feared losing Marcus to this curse—and Soul Scrapers. Those things potentially could be the death of my mission.

I looked up at Mava. "There's going to be Soul Scrapers, aren't there?"

She set her fork down. "If that is what you fear, then most likely, yes."

"Oh, she fears them," Justin said.

"Then that is what you must work on." She dabbed the napkin against her lips then placed it next to her plate. "What you must remember while you are in there is that they can not hurt your physical state. You must remain strong. You must ignore them and keep going."

"We will do what we can to help." Astrid picked her glass of wine up and swirled it around. "But ultimately, it will come down to you."

"There is only so much we can prepare you for," Justin added. "And I know you don't like the sound of that, but it's the truth."

"I will help cleanse your soul. But unfortunately, I can only do so much." Astrid glanced at Mava. "Even with our powers combined, we are no match for Morgana and the spell she cast on you all those years ago."

"Do you have any idea who she is working with?" I asked.

"No," Justin answered. "That's why it's imperative we keep this all between the four of us."

"Will I know after I see the guardians?" There was no way I was going to say "if" because I'd already made up my mind. I was not going to fail. I was going to meet these so called guardians, and I was going to get the answers I needed.

"You may, you may not," Mava said. "We do not know what they will say. All we know for sure is that they will give you the direction you need to complete the journey and unlock whatever mysteries lie bound within your mind."

"So, when do we start?" I asked.

"Now."

CHAPTER 28

"Is all this really necessary?" I waved the smoke away from my face as the smell of sage assaulted my nose. We had retreated back into the lounge room and I was once again stretched out on the sofa as Astrid performed one of her rituals.

"Keep your hands down by your side," Astrid instructed as she moved the burning sticks from my head to my torso and then back up. "And yes, it is necessary. We have limited time to prepare you, which means you have to do your part and do what we tell you to do—even if it does seem ridiculous to you."

She continued waving the sticks around. "What I'm doing now will help ward off the negative energy that is surrounding you, keeping you locked in this curse. We'll also need to start the process of cleansing your soul from all the pain that you've endured over the years."

I frowned as Mava placed five lemons on the couch beside where I was laying. "What are those for?"

"To confirm you are cursed."

I choked on a laugh. "I thought that was already obvious."

"We have no doubt that you are cursed. The question is how badly this curse is affecting you now." Almost as soon as she finished speaking the lemons started to rot, and within seconds they looked as if they'd been sitting there for years.

"I'm guessing that's a bad thing?"

"I'm afraid so." Mava gathered the lemons then disappeared toward the kitchen area.

I looked up at Astrid. "How bad is it?"

"Let's just say that they were the worst rotted lemon's I've ever seen."

"I wish I could say that surprises me, but honestly, what did you expect?"

She shook her head. "We expected that outcome, but it doesn't mean to say we didn't hope that the curse had worn off a little by now."

Justin stretched his legs out as he sat on the armchair to the side of the couch. "I would've loved to have seen how quickly the lemons rotted before Lucy started remembering."

Astrid laughed. "This is the first time we've been able to do it correctly. In every other lifetime, we couldn't get close enough to Luciana to perform the ritual the right way."

"So how did you do it?"

"Mainly lemons in your water," Mava said entering the room. "As soon as you came within a ten meter radius of the lemons they rotted and the water turned black and murky. And the smell was something I've been trying to forget ever since."

I sighed. "I'm still cursed."

"But not as much," Justin reminded me.

Once Astrid was done making me smell like a giant sage stick, she instructed me to take a break while they prepared for the next cleansing ritual. I groaned internally as I stood and headed to the kitchen to grab a drink.

"That bad, huh?" Justin said, coming up behind me.

I turned around to face him and leaned my hip against the counter. "Am I that obvious?"

He nodded. "I think they're just happy that you're allowing them to do this—and that you even believe them."

Justin grabbed an apple out of the fruit bowl and took a bite.

I wondered if the apples were supposed to be used in some concoction on me but I figured if Justin was eating one, they were okay and grabbed one for myself.

All that lying around was making me tired and being tired probably wasn't something I should be when I had so much at stake.

I needed to get my head together but it was pretty hard when thoughts of Marcus kept pushing to the front of my mind.

"When are you going back?" I took a bite of my apple.

"To Marcus?"

I nodded as I chewed.

"I have to time it right, otherwise he'll know something is up. In saying that, I'll be leaving in about fifteen minutes." He took another bite.

Suddenly, I didn't feel like eating any more. All I could think about was what Marcus was going to say when Justin arrived back. I hoped he wasn't going to rip into him and blame him for what he thought had happened. Although, theoretically, it was Justin's fault —and Mava's and Astrid's.

"Don't look so worried." Justin threw the apple core into the trashcan. "What Marcus is feeling is only temporary. And you and I both know that he'll be completely okay with our deception once he knows why we had to deceive him." He tilted his head to the side, a small smile playing on his lips. "He may try to kill me for it, but he'll get over it."

I laughed. "I can so see him trying to kill you." The smile dropped from my face as guilt swept over me. How could I be laughing while he was at home trying to mend his heart? "Promise me that you'll make sure he's okay."

Justin's face softened. "I promise I'll do whatever I can to make sure he doesn't do anything stupid. He's probably sitting at home, drinking his sorrows away with Abby. That's what they usually do."

I looked to the floor. "Now I feel like an ass."

He moved beside me and wrapped his arm around my shoulders. "None of this is your fault."

"That you know of." I looked up at him, eyebrows raised. "For all we know I've done something that instigated all this mess to begin with."

"I highly doubt it."

"Do you?" I asked. "Because there is a very real possibility I might find out exactly that. I may have made a deal with the Devil for some reason that we're yet to find out."

"Not a chance," he said then quickly added, "And before you think of something else to make this all your fault, remember that Morgana doesn't make any deals that don't benefit her—"

"Exactly. For all we know I was stupid enough to make a deal with her and whoever else is helping her keep us this way, and there was a gaping loophole in our agreement that I was too dumb to see."

"You wouldn't be cursed to the extent you are if that were true," Mava said, coming into the kitchen. "For this type of curse, the soul must be pure. And I don't mean like a child. I mean that the pureness of your soul is beyond that of a newborn baby." She looked at me pointedly. "You are not like other humans. You are something so much more."

I sighed. "Yeah, I'm cursed to feel the pain of others."

"That might only be the beginning. Something Morgana has used to cloud the truth of your true identity.

"Have you ever wondered about the meaning of your name?"

I frowned. "Luciana?"

She smiled. "Luciana is the Latin meaning of light."

"And you think I'm the light that will unlock the door to destiny."

"I do not think, Lucy. I know," she said. "And I think deep down you know it, too."

I bit my lip as I thought about what she said. As much as I had to agree with her that yes, I was Marcus's light, I couldn't get past the darkness I brought him as well.

Justin dropped his arm from my shoulders to my waist. "As much as I'd love to stay here and chat, I have to get back now."

I turned to him. "I want you to tell Marcus that I love him and miss him but I know that's not possible, so can you give this to him instead?" I removed the chain from my neck.

"Of course." Justin held out his hand.

I looked to Mava before I handed it over. "I don't need this in the tunnel, do I?"

Mava shook her head. "Material possessions can't help you."

"I didn't think so." I placed the pendant on Justin's palm.

He folded his fingers over it. "I'm not going to lie, this will probably break him a little more, but maybe this will make it easier for him to remain at home, drinking it up while you're trying to save yourself."

"You couldn't have kept that one to yourself?" Mava frowned at him. "Luciana doesn't need to know all the details. She has enough to worry about without you going and telling her how her gift will hurt him that much more."

I frowned. "I thought it might bring Marcus comfort, not break him. And if you're saying it will, then maybe I should take it back."

"I think you know Marcus better than me," Justin said, and I couldn't help but think he was just telling me what I wanted to hear. "Good luck. And I'll be rooting for you."

He waved his hand, the air in front of him rippling as he opened what I could only assume was a veil.

"Wow!" I shook my head in disbelief as he stepped through, disappearing from sight.

With my eyes wide open I turned to Mava. "Can you guys do that?"

"Open veils?" she asked as the air in front of us returned to normal.

"Yeah."

"Only the one from here to my home in your dimension." She grabbed my hand. "Come now. We have lots to prepare for."

She led me back into the lounge room and gestured toward the crystals lined in the shape of a rectangle on the ground.

I narrowed my eyes at her. "What's that for?"

"It's a grid," she answered. "It's used to perform a protection spell."

"Protection from what?"

"From what lies ahead."

CHAPTER 29

I stepped inside the rectangle. "Okay. What do I do now?"

"You do nothing. We are the casters," Mava said.

Putting my hands on my hips, I sighed. I felt so stupid just standing there surrounded by crystals. However, I knew both Mava and Astrid held powers I didn't fully understand and I had to lay my trust in them to do their thing, which would allow me to do mine.

Astrid came into the room carrying a tray filled with more crystals. "If you could lie down, that would be great."

"Right." Feeling even more stupid, I lay down on the cold wooden floor.

Astrid knelt beside me, holding a cushion in her hand.

"Here." She lifted my head and placed the cushion under it. "That should be a little more comfortable."

"Thanks."

Mava began chanting unintelligible words while Astrid held various crystals above different parts of my body, moving them in strange patterns as she spoke phrases that made absolutely no sense to me. I was sure she was speaking another language, which I was left trying to decipher.

Of course, I couldn't.

Eventually, I gave up and closed my eyes. A few moments later, I jolted awake. I blinked a few times, realizing I was filled with a newfound energy that I wasn't sure if it was because I had caught a few minutes shut-eye, or if it was thanks to Mava and Astrid. Either way, I was grateful I had the energy to carry on.

Getting to my feet, I surveyed the room. The crystals were gone, and the room once again looked like a rich old person's home, rather than a witches' coven.

Raising my hands above my head, I stretched out my muscles. "How long was I out for?"

"Fifteen hours," Astrid replied, her gaze remaining on the open book sitting on her lap.

"What?" I practically spat the word from my mouth.

She closed the book and placed it on the side table. "The rituals were completed hours before... We just thought you needed the extra time to catch up on sleep."

"Except now I won't be able to go to sleep so I can get to this tunnel."

"You needn't worry about that." She uncrossed her legs. "We will help you get through." She stood. "Now you must eat and then you can be on your way."

My eyes practically popped out of my head. "So soon?"

"Don't look so afraid," she said. "Fear will not help you where you're going."

"Easier said than done."

Astrid gestured for me to head into the dining room. "That is true. But it is the truth none the less."

Taking a seat at the table filled with a generous spread of roast meats and vegetables, I grabbed a bread roll and began to pick at it. "How am I supposed to ignore my fear?"

"That is something only you can work out."

I raised a brow. So much for any coaching.

Astrid took her seat and started loading her plate up with items from the spread of meats and vegetables.

"Fear not. We all have faith in you." She smiled. "There is a reason why this curse was placed on you, and you must remember that the answers you are seeking are at the end of the tunnel. If you don't make it, then you'll never find them."

I nodded slowly. "I will make it."

Astrid smiled again. "You will."

I tore a small piece off the roll and popped it into my mouth. "Where's Mava?"

"She's preparing for your delivery."

I scrunched up my face in confusion. "What?"

"When we deliver you to the tunnel."

"I thought it was in my head?"

"It is, but we need to make sure that you get there the first time round. The moons will be in your corner later tonight, and we must use that time wisely."

Moons… Righty-O.

Mava arrived just after we'd finished lunch. I didn't eat much, mostly because my stomach was churning from the unknown.

Mava placed the canvas bags she was carrying on the kitchen bench then pulled out the contents, most of the items I'd never seen before. Even though I was intrigued, I didn't think my stomach could handle if there were spider eyes or lizard tongues in whatever she was going to concoct and most likely make me consume.

"How are you feeling, Luciana?" Mava asked, wiping her hands on the tea towel.

I leaned back in my seat. "Nervous, but ready."

"Good. Because this shouldn't take me long to prepare." She leaned down, opened the cupboard door, and pulled out a rather impressive mixing bowl that looked more like the top of a giant medieval goblet complete with rubies and sapphires encased in the rim.

"Why don't you go relax for a bit, and I'll let you know when we're ready to proceed," Astrid said.

"Relax," I whispered under my breath. "Yeah, I don't think that's really possible."

I stood then picked up my plate, brought it into the kitchen, and placed it in the sink.

Returning to the table, I went to collect Astrid's plate when she placed her hand over mine, stopping me. "Leave it, dear. I'll clear up here."

"Are you sure? I don't mind."

Actually, I really wanted a distraction so I could focus on anything besides the tunnel.

"I'm sure," she said. "Just go into the lounge room and find something to do."

"Okay," I agreed, even though I was more than a little disappointed.

Making my way back into the lounge room, I looked around for something to occupy my time. There was no TV, the only books seemed to be spell books, and I really didn't want to do my head in any more than it already had been. There wasn't even a window for me to look out.

Frustrated, I sat on the lounge, tilted my head back against the headrest, and looked at the ornate ceiling. Not even that was interesting. And there was no way I was going to focus on the orb and whatever was trapped inside.

I leaned forward, put my elbows on my knees, and rested my head on my hands. Of course, that didn't help keep my mind away from the tunnel. Neither did it stop me thinking about Marcus. I wondered what he was doing now—probably drinking—and if the pendant had torn him apart that little bit more just as Justin thought it would. Or if it had helped him like I hoped it would.

With my luck, it was the former.

Before I knew it, both Mava and Astrid walked into the room.

"Are you ready?" Mava asked.

My heart practically smashed a hole through my chest. "As ready as I'll ever be."

"Good," she replied. "Just remember that the sooner you make it through that tunnel, the sooner you get to return to Marcus and make all his pain go away."

I smiled. "That's what I keep telling myself." I ran my hands down my thighs. "Has anyone heard from Justin?"

"Are you asking how Marcus is?" Astrid asked.

"Maybe."

"Do you really want to know?"

"I think she already knows," Mava jumped in as she carried the goblet bowl closer to me. "But what I will tell you is that he is still at home and has no plans of leaving."

She placed the bowl on the side table. "Justin will keep his promise to you. He knows what is at stake and the last thing we all want is for you to get through the tunnel only to find Marcus has gone and done something stupid."

Mava reached toward the table and retrieved something that made my blood go cold.

CHAPTER 30

"*I* hope you're not planning on using that on me?" I asked, staring at the blade that looked as if it was made sometime in the sixteenth century. Any other time, I would've been captivated by the exquisite details of the double-edged knife, but not today. Today I was freaked out.

Mava laid the knife across her palm. "I am afraid I need a drop of your blood to finish the spell."

"Only a drop?" I asked, knowing how completely ironic I sounded after all the times I tried to kill myself.

"Only a drop."

I held out my finger. "Okay, then."

Taking hold of my hand, Mava placed the tip of the jewel-encrusted knife against my skin. Slowly, she pushed it in until a drop of blood formed around the blade.

Withdrawing the knife, she let go of my hand, then quickly but carefully moved the blade over to the goblet and waited for the drop of blood to fall. It rolled free like a single teardrop.

"It's done." She stood and picked the goblet up. "We must be fast." She turned to Astrid. "Are you ready?"

"Yes, everything is in place."

"Good." She walked toward the door near the bookcase. "Follow me."

315

"Me?" I asked, making sure I didn't make a fool out of myself by presuming she was talking to me. In reality, I made an ass out of myself, anyway. Of course, she was talking to me. No one else was going in the tunnel.

"Yes, dear." With a flick of her hand, the door opened.

I stood and headed through the doorway with Astrid following close behind. We entered a dark room, the only light coming from a blue orb floating in each corner—except there were five, not four like most rooms. There was nothing else in there except for crystals forming a rectangle on the floor again.

"Wow," I said, taking it all in. "This looks like something you'd see in movies about witches." I pointed at the crystal formation. "Is that for protection?"

"You're learning," Astrid said with a smile. "Now, we'll need you to lay down in the center of the crystals."

I did as I was told. "Now what?"

"Now, you must lie still while I open your third eye."

"My what?" I asked with a nervous laugh.

"Each of us are born with a third eye, right between our brows. And we need to awaken yours to enable you to enter the tunnel."

"I hope you're not planning on cutting my head open to let it out." I'd seen those movies, and there was no way I wanted to go through that.

Hell, who was I kidding? Of course, I'd do it, if that meant being with Marcus again. I'd do anything.

"No, child," Mava said with that smile of hers as she kneeled down beside me. "Be still, and I will show you the way."

She dipped the knife into the goblet then held it above my forehead.

"It's not going to burn a hole through my skin, is it?"

"Lie still," she instructed.

Breathing out harshly, I did as I was told as I watched the blood-red liquid slowly drop from the blade. I waited for the pain to explode as it hit my skin but... Nothing.

Mava set the knife beside her on the floor then placed her finger over the droplet on my forehead. She began to chant something that sounded Latin or something else that wasn't English as she drew lines over my forehead.

I kept waiting, expecting to feel some divine awakening but time progressed and nothing changed. "It's not working, is it?"

"Shhh," Astrid said in a soothing voice. "It's working."

Mava sat back and placed her hands on her knees. "Luciana is right. It's not working."

"How is that possible?" Astrid asked.

Mava wiped her finger on her skirt. "Maybe it's already open." She shook her head. "Or maybe she doesn't have one."

"But all humans have one."

Mava tilted her head to the side. "Maybe she is not human."

"Say what?" I asked, jolting myself into a sitting position.

"Relax." Mava closed her hand over my shoulder and gave it a comforting squeeze. "We still do not know everything about you. And this could just be another anomaly. Maybe your third eye exists, but it can't be opened without the help of your guardians."

"Then how am I supposed to reach them if I can't enter the tunnel without a third eye?"

"You can still enter." Mava gently pushed me down, so I was once again lying in the center of the crystals.

Something burning awoke my senses. Astrid was burning sticks that smelled... I wasn't sure what the smell was, and at that point, I didn't care. I was seconds from entering the tunnel, and those things weren't important anymore.

Astrid waved her hand over the sticks, directing the smoke in my direction. Tendrils of smoke billowed from the sticks, reaching toward me the same way the Soul Scrapers had done.

Fear gripped my heart as my consciousness was pulled into the unknown. My eyelids snapped shut, and the witches' voices faded until there was nothing. My body became heavy as if I was falling or being dragged down into the tunnel.

Then, my feet touched the ground and I was looking at a soft grey light in the distance. It was drawing me toward it.

"This doesn't seem—" I started to say.

Something grabbed my ankle and tripped me over. Spreading my hands on the ground, I looked behind me.

A deformed hand with skin peeling off the bones clutched my ankle, its fingers digging into my skin as it reached up out of the damp Earth.

I screamed.

CHAPTER 31

$\mathcal{I}$ tugged my leg free, preparing to sprint my way through the tunnel. As I turned my head sheer terror surged through my body when I saw a gruesome face emerging from the ground. The eyes began to bulge then black bugs broke through and swarmed toward my face.

I let out a blood-curdling scream as I pushed myself to my feet and batted the bugs away. But they were relentless. Thousands of bugs surrounded me, covering every inch of my skin as they tried to get into my eyes, mouth, ears, and nose.

I swatted them away as I ran for dear life, only I never got anywhere, and they didn't stop. The walls started to move, then arms reached for me. A moment later, more heads popped out of the dirt, their faces void of any eyes, and their screams echoed mine.

Something latched onto my foot and brought me down with a thud as my face smacked against the dirt. Pain ripped through me. The ground shifted and the earth swallowed me into its depths.

I'd failed.

I was coming to and could hear the voices of Astrid, Mava, and Justin.

"She wasn't ready," Astrid said.

Mava sighed. "I could've sworn she was ready this time, but it seems you're right. She failed, and we're going to have to wait until her next life to try again."

"Send me back," I said, but my voice was mute.

"We'll be ready next time," Justin said. "But for there to be a next time, I must take her back to Marcus."

Yes. Yes. Take me back to Marcus.

"This is going to break him," Astrid said.

What's going to break him?

"I know," Justin said, sombrely. "But it's a necessary evil if we want there to be a next time."

What's a necessary evil? I wanted to stand up and shake them until they started making sense, but I was as paralyzed as when I'd drank Mava's concoction.

Hands pushed their way under my neck and knees, then I was lifted into someone's arms. It was Justin. I could smell a small tang of deception. I could feel the betrayal as if it were my own.

Something wasn't right. Something most definitely wasn't right.

"Tell him we tried," Mava said. "Luciana just was not ready this time round."

Failure flowed through me. She was right. I'd not only failed myself; I'd failed Marcus.

Strong wind lashed me from all sides, and I could only guess that I was in the air, flying back to Marcus. Why, I didn't know.

The wind stopped, and all that was left was a subtle breeze as the sound of his flapping wings resounded through the air.

"You were right not to trust me. And now you're going to pay the price poor, dear, Luciana." Justin let out a sadistic laugh that sent chills down my spine. "Maybe next time you should trust your first instincts about a person."

My stomach dropped as wind once again thrashed my face. My eyelids opened, and for a second I thought I had control of my body again, but I was wrong. I was free-falling through the sky as Justin's laugh echoed above me.

He caught me in his arms just before I smacked against the ground in Marcus's backyard.

"Not going to let you go that way." He leaned down and brushed his lips over my cheek, on his way to my ear, then whispered, "I couldn't let Marcus miss out on all the fun."

I wanted to punch him in the face, but I couldn't move an inch.

"That's right." Justin snickered. "You just stay there and enjoy the show."

His wicked smirk was replaced by a sombre expression, filled with distraught and sorrow as he landed then headed toward the house.

He opened the door and called out, "Marcus."

"What's wrong?" Abby asked, coming around the corner wearing nothing but her panties and bra.

They weren't any old panties and bra, either. She looked as if she was about to strut down a catwalk displaying the latest lingerie for the sexiest woman in the world competition. What the hell she was doing wearing that was beyond me, but a mixture of fear and jealousy had rooted itself in my mind, and it wasn't letting go.

"He needs to finish her if he wants any chance at there being another lifetime with Luciana."

"Oh, no," she said. "He's not going to like this."

"I know. But—"

"What aren't I going to like?" Marcus asked, sauntering into the lounge room wearing nothing but a pair of shorts hanging from his hips. He faltered when he saw me. "What's Lucy doing here?"

"They said that if I left her there in this state, then there won't be another chance for you. It will be the end."

Marcus's eyes went wide. He strode over to Justin and snatched me from his arms.

He's lying! I tried to scream, but my voice never came out. *I'm still here!*

Turning away from Justin and Abby, Marcus lifted me closer to his face. He brushed his lips over mine as a tear fell from his eyes. He was still gutted.

"What do I need to do?" Marcus asked.

There were a couple of seconds of silence before Justin said, "You need to be the one to drive the knife through her heart to send her onto the correct course she is destined to be on."

Marcus went rigid as I screamed every obscenity I could think of but of course not a sound came from my mouth. I was as good as dead.

Marcus released a heavy sigh then slowly carried me to his room. He sat on the bed and cradled me in his arms. A shudder erupted through him as he stared at my face. He was completely broken, and now Justin was telling him that he had to put the knife through my heart even though I was supposedly already dead.

I prayed that he would see how absurd the idea was and conclude Justin was screwing us both over. He wasn't a friend. He was the enemy. Justin was the sheep in wolves clothing. He was evil.

Marcus kissed my forehead then eased me onto the bed. He climbed off and disappeared into his closet. A few moments later, he returned with a knife that looked almost exactly like the one Mava had used. I'd seen it a million times in my dreams, but it was nothing compared to reality.

I cried internally and screamed for him to hear me as he climbed onto the bed, lifted my head, and cradled me against his side.

His breaths came out loud and fast as he gripped the knife in his trembling hand and raised it above my chest. He then rested the tip of the blade over my heart and closed his eyes as more tears slipped down his cheeks.

"I'm so sorry," he whispered.

Marcus opened his eyes, leaned down, and kissed me. I desperately wanted to kiss him back, but no matter how hard I tried my efforts were futile. I was as good as dead. I was just a soul trapped in my body and Marcus was about to set me free.

He released a shuddered breath then whispered the words I'd heard every night since I could remember. "Please let this be the last."

He drove the knife straight through my heart.

CHAPTER 32

*P*ain ripped through me as the blood spilled from my body. However, it wasn't from having a knife plunged into my body. The pain I was experiencing was Marcus's.

Something had gone wrong. For some reason, I could feel his pain. I wasn't supposed to feel his pain. Yet it was tearing through my soul, severing our hearts as he feared that he would never see me again.

He yanked the blade from my chest, then broke down as he held me in his arms and buried his head in the crook of my neck. There was no rage, there was only heartbreak and fear, and it was completely taking over me.

Every time I'd experienced such loss, I'd always tried to get away. Not this time. Marcus needed me—even if I was nothing but a soul.

I barely gave a moments thought as to why I was still trapped inside my body and still able to think logically as if I were still alive before my mind was once again overtaken by grief and helplessness.

I wished I was able to tell him I was okay and that I was determined to find my way back to him. I wasn't going to forget him. I would never forget him. We were destined to be together, and the next life was going to be different. Next time, we were going to figure it out and kill whoever was responsible for this curse.

Slowly but surely his breathing became more even, and he was able to look at me without tearing up again.

He swiped my hair away from my face and smiled.

"You are so beautiful." He traced the lines of my lips with his finger. "Next time will be different. I will be ready—I promise."

A knock rapped on the door.

"Are you ready?" Justin asked through the door, sounding as if he cared.

"Yes," Marcus replied.

It was useless trying to speak. He'd driven the knife through my heart. It was the only way I was able to die. I was dead. And yet...

Justin opened the door and entered the room. He placed his hand on Marcus's shoulder and gave it a comforting squeeze. "Can I take her now?"

Marcus breathed out harshly then leaned down and kissed me one last time before handing me over.

Justin grasped in his arms as he carried me over to the sliding door, opened it, then stepped outside. "I'll be back soon."

He shifted me so that I was able to see inside the room. I was sure it was on purpose, because there standing beside Marcus was Abby dressed in her lingerie, massaging Marcus's shoulders.

She leaned down and whispered loud enough for me to hear, "Don't worry. I'll help you forget the pain—just like all the other times."

She placed a tender kiss on his cheek as Justin turned me away.

He opened his wings and pushed up into the sky. Once we were a fair distance from Marcus's compound, Justin leaned down and said, "That's something you'll never forget while your ass is in Purgatory. And I'm not talking about how Marcus stuck a knife into your heart; I'm talking about how Abby plans to make Marcus forget about you."

He chuckled.

I wanted to puke. Partially because of what my mind was having Abby do to Marcus, and partially because I was terrified of going to Purgatory and what the Soul Scrapers were going to do to me.

Justin waved his hand, and a ripple appeared in the air in front of us. He flew through the ripple, taking us through a veil into a world filled with sorrow and pain.

323

He landed then let go of my knees, letting my feet fall to the ground covered in thick black ash.

Justin held his hand in front of my face. "Awaken."

I gasped, taking in gulps of oxygen. Only it wasn't oxygen. Coughing, I brought up black slime and wiped it off with my hand.

I turned to Justin. "What the hell have you done?" I slammed my hands into his chest. "What the hell have you done?"

Justin threw his head back and laughed. "All this time you thought I was a fraud and when you had the chance to get away and call me out on it, you actually believed me." He laughed again. "And look where you are now." When I didn't do as he asked, he said, "Look."

I slowly turned my head to the side. My breath was knocked out of me.

I'd feared it was just Soul Scrapers I'd have to contend with, but I was wrong. I was standing at the back of masses of humans being herded by giant Hellhounds.

An elderly man fell out of line, stumbling to the ground.

A Hellhound lunged at him, its jaws ripping into his torso as it picked him up and tossed him back into the heard of humans.

Screams echoed throughout the crowd as they moved forward, away from the ash and through the black sludge that got deeper the further they went, each step draining their energy until they fell to their knees then disappeared as they sank into the sludge.

"No, no, no, no," I said, backing away. "You can't do this to me."

A sadistic grin spread across his face. "I've already done it."

He pushed me forward.

My legs buckled and I fell to my knees, splitting them open on the jagged rocks just under the surface of the dirt.

Justin put his foot on my back and shoved me down, my face landing in the sludge.

Lifting my head, I gasped for air as I wiped the sludge from my eyes. I twisted around to face Justin then pushed myself to my feet.

"This is not happening," I said, taking a few steps back. "Marcus needs me. I need him, and there is no—"

I screamed as I lost my footing and tumbled over the edge of something.

Justin whipped his hand out and caught me by the arm, stopping my fall. He pulled me up and held on as he laughed. "This is so happening. And frankly, I can't believe how easily you fell for it all."

I twisted around to look at what he'd saved me from falling into. All air escaped from my lungs as I saw what had been waiting for me. Decomposing humans and demonic looking creatures littered the walls of what appeared to be a never-ending pit.

The creatures screamed at me to come to them, help them, and release them.

"You don't want to go down there," Justin said, leaning over the edge of the pit. "Those things will kill you." He gripped my shoulder and shoved me forward toward the line of humans. "Get going. You don't want the Hellhounds to get a hold of you."

Just as he said it, a Hellhound about ten metres away turned in our direction, its teeth bared and ready to attack.

"It's watching you. You might want to fall into line."

"No." I spun on my heel to face Justin. "Take me back."

"Never," he said with a wicked laugh. "Now, you can either go forward with everyone else in the line, or you can take your chances with the Hellhound."

I gulped as the pleas of the creatures in the pit next to us called out to me. "What about the pit?"

He smirked. "If you go down there, don't expect to leave anytime soon. You'll be stuck in the walls, crying out to be saved only no one will save you. Eventually, you'll fall through the sludge and end up where you would've gone had you entered the line."

I looked at the line then back at the pit. One was an easy road into Purgatory, and the other would take who knew how long to pass through. The sane thing would be to fall into line, but I wasn't sane. And I definitely remembered what Marcus had said about me going to Purgatory. If I did that, then there would be no next time. I was supposed to die then be reborn, not cross over.

I slowly nodded and pretended to move toward the line. Then I darted to the side and dove into the pit.

CHAPTER 33

$\mathcal{T}$he creatures in the pit clawed at me with bony fingers, their jaws hanging unnaturally open as they cried out to me.

Every conceivable emotion consumed me as their pain and suffering became mine. There were thousands of souls embedded in the wall, their hands clamouring for me, trying to drag me to them. The harder I fought to free myself from their grasps, the further their fleshless fingers dug into my skin.

The pain and suffering they were enduring and passing onto me were too much for me to handle. I thought it had been the right decision to jump. But I was wrong. So very, very wrong.

I should have fallen into line. I should have taken the easy way out.

Closing my eyes, I shook my thoughts away. No. I made the right decision. I needed to buy time for Marcus to figure out what Justin was up to. I needed there to be a next time. And if that meant having to go through the torture of feeling the heart-wrenching agony of everyone's death then that was what I had to do.

"Help me," the creatures screeched, their voices echoing.

"I can't," I cried, trying to yank myself free from their grasp. "I can't help you."

Excruciating pain exploded throughout my body as their fingers clawed their way through my flesh, digging their way into my bones. They pulled me closer and closer to the wall as if enslaving me would free themselves. I highly doubted that was how it worked.

Resigned to my fate, I let go of all urge to fight and let my mind succumb to their pain and suffering. It was worse than anything I'd ever experienced when I was alive. The way these souls had been slaughtered was enough to consume my every thought until I no longer saw it as their pain, fear, and sorrow. Their emotions had become my own.

Exhaling deeply, I closed my eyes and let it all in, allowing their suffering to completely consume my soul. This was my fate. This was where I was destined to remain until I was rescued—if I was rescued at all.

Slowly, the pain of bones ripping into my flesh started to disappear. I opened my eyes expecting to be locked in the wall with all the other souls. Instead, I was gradually being lowered down. Each soul gently passed me on to the next as the ones above me backed away and disappeared into the wall, no longer screaming for my help. Those below still let out a scream every now and then, but by the time I reached them, they were calm.

I had no idea what was going on, and there was no one to ask. The suffering of the souls surrounding me still consumed my every thought but then there was also a calmness that spread amongst the souls that helped me through their despair.

Fear surged through me when I saw the bottom of the pit. There were only a few more feet and then I'd hit the bottom. I couldn't hit the bottom. I couldn't go to Purgatory.

I reached up and tried to hang on to the hands that were passing me to the ones below but their bones were slippery from the black sludge that encased the walls of the pit and it appeared that none of them had any intention of hanging onto me.

"Please help me," I yelled at the decomposing body directly in front of me. "Don't let go. I can't go to Purgatory."

My pleas for help rang unanswered. The creatures continued to hand me down to the next. Then I was dropped into the sludge at the bottom of the pit.

I tried desperately to swim to the side of the pit, hoping that I would be able to climb back up and lodge myself into the wall but the sludge was sucking me under, and I was too weak to fight against it. The soul who'd dropped me into the pit had already receded into the wall, and there was nothing but sludge surrounding me.

I gasped for air as I kicked my legs, trying to stop the sludge from sucking me into its depths.

It was useless. The more I kicked, the faster I went under until I was completely submerged.

I held my breath, waiting to come out the other side.

There was no other side.

I was drowning in the same tar-like substance the Soul Scrapers had shoved down my throat that night they'd abducted me.

My lungs felt as if they were about to explode. I kept telling myself that was stupid. I was theoretically dead therefore I didn't need to breathe. Unfortunately, my body didn't have the same beliefs that my brain did. It was desperate for oxygen, and there was none around.

My lungs and throat started to burn, growing with intensity until I couldn't help but open my mouth and suck in a lung full of sludge.

I coughed and spluttered as more sludge entered my body. My head went groggy, and I no longer had the urge to breathe. I was done.

Then, the sludge around me began to move. I was sucked down, further and further until I was free-falling. My body smacked against a hard surface.

I pushed myself to my knees and wiped the sludge off my face so I could open my eyes. When I did, I was surprised to find the sludge was gone and I was in an almost clinically clean room, where the walls were covered in drawings for kids.

My surprise was short lived when an onslaught of pain, fear, and helplessness ripped through my soul.

I steadily got to my feet and turned around to see a small child with no hair lying in a hospital bed. A doctor was speaking to a couple that was standing by her side, the woman holding the child's hand. The man had his arm wrapped around the woman who was crying silent tears.

"I'm afraid it's time to say goodbye," the doctor said.

"No," the woman cried, her voice breaking as the doctor delivered the final blow to her heart, smashing it into tiny pieces that would never mend.

Tears welled in my eyes as the heartache ripped through my soul. I backed away to the wall, trying to distance myself as much as I could from them. I didn't want to feel their pain. I couldn't help them.

My back hit the wall, and I turned around, relief flooding through me when I came face to face with a door. I grabbed the handle and tried to yank it open, but it was stuck. I jiggled it then tried finding the lock that wasn't there as the couple's pain became all too consuming.

However, that wasn't the only thing I had to deal with. My muscles and bones ached, and there were no drugs that would relieve my pain. It was all too much for me, and I wanted to die. I couldn't keep fighting. I felt selfish when I heard my parent's cries, but I couldn't help it. I wasn't strong enough. I was too tired.

I inched over to the bed and placed my hand over the child. As soon as my skin touched the girl, I was brought to my knees, no longer able to stand the pain.

I tried to let go, but it was as if my hand was glued to hers. Fear erupted inside of me as my skin pressed against hers turned darker and darker until it was virtually black.

CHAPTER 34

*P*ain exploded throughout my body, crippling me as I collapsed on the bed. I couldn't move. I was completely succumbed to the girl's suffering. Then I heard the faint beep of the girl's heart becoming stronger.

I forced my eyes open and looked at the machine by her bed. Sure enough, her heart rate had picked up and was getting stronger and stronger by the second.

"What's going on?" the mother asked, a mixture of panic and impossible hope flooding her mind.

"I don't know," the doctor said as he fiddled with the machine. "This isn't right."

"Don't tell me this isn't right," the mother cried. "I want to know what's going on."

"So do we, Kathleen," the doctor said "But now I need you to go stand over there so I can work out what's going on."

Kathleen didn't look as if she were going to move until her husband said, "Come on. We better let him do his job."

The girl's small hand squeezed mine.

Her eyes flutter opened, and my heart skipped a beat. I tried to scream out to the parents to look, but no sound came out of my mouth. I was a ghost. Except to the girl.

"Thank you," she whispered.

Tears welled in my eyes.

"She's awake," the mother said, her voice breaking with happiness that she wasn't sure was warranted. She was terrified that she was imagining her little girl getting better, only to lose all hope again.

Overcome by joy, I accepted the pain from the girl without giving it a second thought. She was going to be okay. This family wasn't going to be ripped apart.

The unknown force connecting me to the little girl disappeared, but the black smudges on my skin were still coming from her skin and crossing over to mine. She was still sick. She still needed help, and there was no way I was going to let her down—even if I didn't know what I was doing. For all I knew this was part of Purgatory, and I was a willing participant and was about to pass with flying colors. But I didn't care. She needed me, and I wasn't going to let her down.

I gripped my hand over hers and sucked in her pain. A blood-curdling scream erupted from my throat as I let her sickness consume my entire being until there were no dark shadows floating just below the surface of her skin. It was only on mine. And they weren't shadows. My hand looked as if it'd died.

The light came back into the little girl's eyes, and she sat up. "She took it away, Mummy."

"Who took what away?" the mother asked, wiping tears from her eyes.

"The woman right there," she said, gesturing to me. Only the adults couldn't see me. "She took my sickness away, and now I'm better."

The parents broke down as they released sobs of happiness. They didn't need any doctor to tell them that she was better. They could see it for themselves. And they truly believed that an angel had saved their daughter as she was taking her final breaths.

I closed my eyes and fell to my knees, completely consumed with happiness. When I opened them, I found myself kneeling in a field of snapdragons, a warm breeze blowing the sweet scent under my nose.

In the distance stood a small group of people watching me. It was as if they were waiting for me. Their long flowing white attire brought fear to my heart. They looked like angels. And If I was seeing angels, then that meant I'd passed through the veil.

Everything that had just happened to me was part of Purgatory, and now I was free.

A tear slipped from my eye as peace once again swept over my soul. I didn't want to feel peace. I wanted to feel pain because peace meant no Marcus and I couldn't fathom a life without Marcus.

I sat amongst the flowers staring at the unwavering angels not wanting to move forward because that meant I was walking away from Marcus. I couldn't do that. I tried to figure out how I could get back to him but it was useless. I couldn't get back. I was destined to move forward.

I wasn't sure exactly how long I'd been there because the sun never moved. It was as if I were frozen in time while I got myself together enough to greet the angels.

Slowly, I got to my feet and ran my fingers across the various colored petals as I made my way to the group of angels. There were two males and one female. They were dressed in white sashes, just like I'd seen in so many religious paintings.

I waited for one of them to say something, but they remained silent.

"I guess this is it then," I said, fiddling with my fingers. "I'm dead. It's over. No more Marcus." I couldn't stop the verbal garbage spewing from my mouth.

The woman smiled in the same way that Mava and Astrid did. "You are not dead. In fact, you are far from dead."

I narrowed my eyes at her. "But... Justin delivered me to Purgatory."

"No, Luciana. You, my dear, are unable to die without being reborn."

"But I'm cursed. That's my destiny."

"Ah, but it isn't," she said. "Your memories have been bound, but you are not cursed to die." She slowly walked toward me. "Ever wondered why whoever has been messing with you, didn't just kill you and be done with you? Why it always had to be Marcus?"

"Ah... yeah." I'd thought about it a million times and always came to the same conclusion. "They just want to mess with us because it brings a form of sadistic enjoyment to them."

"No, my dear." She placed her hand on my lower back. "Come sit down. We have much to discuss."

She ushered me toward a group of logs that reminded me of the ones I'd sat on with John back at the rehab. My eyes widened as I snapped my head to the side and realized that one of the angels was, in fact, John from the rehab. "What are you…"

John smiled. "I think the question is, why was I at Millford."

"I think they're both questions that I would love to hear the answer to. Unless…"

"No, Luciana. I haven't died. You can't die if you were never alive."

I collapsed on the log and put my head in my hands, trying to make sense of what they were saying.

"Okay. So, if I'm not in Heaven or whatever it is you guys call it, then where am I? And why are you here, or back at the rehab, or whatever?" I looked at the other man. "And who's this?"

"My name is Thomas," the man said. "I'm your creator."

CHAPTER 35

"*M*y what?" I spat.

"Your creator," he repeated as if I hadn't heard him the first time.

Oh, I'd heard him. It just didn't make any sense.

"Why is it that no one can ever just tell me what's going on?" I whispered under my breath.

"Because this is something you need to remember on your own," John said.

The woman sat beside me. "My name is Alissya, and I'll be happy to fill you in on the things I can. But some truths you have to discover on your own."

"Right," I said. "So where am I and why is John here?"

"You've reached the end of the tunnel."

"You're my guardians?"

Alissya smiled. "Yes, dear. That is what we are."

I looked at John. "Why were you at the rehab?"

"I was there to guide you," John replied, taking a seat on the log opposite where I was sitting. "We've known for a long time that this lifetime of yours was different. The spell is weakening, and your memories are returning. And I needed to give you that little push in Marcus's direction."

I thought about everything that had happened when Justin

returned me to Marcus to drive the knife through my heart. "Please tell me that Marcus didn't kill me."

"That's correct," Alissya said with a warm smile. "Everything you experienced since entering the tunnel was part of the test designed to keep you from us."

"So, Justin didn't backstab us?"

"No," Thomas said. "Justin has remained loyal to both you and Marcus since he found out the truth."

"What's the truth?" I asked.

"There are many truths, but the truth you seek is hidden inside of you."

I groaned. "Why can't you just tell me?"

"Because that's not how it works," Alissya said. "Your truth lies within you. And we are here to help you find your way."

Thomas, my creator, took a seat a few feet from where John was sitting. "Have you ever wondered why a mere human would capture the heart of a Soul Collector?"

"And why a Soul Collector would be part of an ancient legend?" John added.

"Justin told me that Marcus wasn't just a Soul Collector," I said. "Is that true?"

Alissya tilted her head to the side as if she were looking at an innocent child trying to understand the meaning of life. "I think you already know the answer to that."

"Then what is he?"

"That is what I created you for," Thomas said.

"To find out what Marcus is?"

He nodded. "You are the key to unlocking his destiny."

"That sounds a hell of a lot like Mava's riddle."

The corner of his lips tipped up. "Where do you think she got it from?"

Wow! "How am I supposed to unlock his destiny? And how am I a key?"

"Isn't that obvious yet?" Alissya asked.

"No," I said. "If it was, then I wouldn't be asking."

She raised a brow.

"Sorry. It's just all doing my head in."

"We are here to guide you. No one said the journey would be easy. But you will find the answers you seek."

"Okay," I said. "Help me find them, then. How am I a key?"

"First you must acknowledge your true power."

"What power?" I asked. "I'm human. I have no powers."

"That is where you are wrong," she said. "Did you not learn anything from the tunnel?"

"Yeah, that creatures out of my nightmares are real."

"Anything else?"

"Think about it," John added.

Every moment of my journey since I entered the tunnel played through my mind. I shuddered at the memories of the creatures I'd encountered. Absentmindedly, I ran my hand over where I'd thought the creatures had ripped through my skin. There wasn't even a scratch. It hadn't been real. And if those parts weren't real, then what was it that I was supposed to remember?

What was I supposed to get?

The little girl seemed completely out of character. She wasn't scary. She did, however, break my heart.

"I helped her get better." I looked each of them in the eye. "How is that possible?"

They remained silent.

Alissya gave me a barely noticeable nod, urging me to continue.

I didn't do anything to the girl. I hadn't given her some magic potion, or a miracle drug that cured her illness. All I'd done is hold on to her and feel her pain. "Does it have anything to do with feeling others emotions and pains?"

They all smiled.

"Think about how you passed through each stage, or test if you want to call it that," Thomas said.

With Marcus, I had done nothing. Although I did feel his pain for the first time ever. The bodies in the pit asked me for help and only let me pass when I gave in to them, and the girl…

My eyes widened as snippets of new memories flashed through my mind.

"I'm not an empath," I said in disbelief. "And I'm not crazy."

"No, my dear, you are not." Her eyes went wide then I felt a pull as if I were being sucked out of their existence. Alissya grabbed my arm and reached for my forehead with her other hand. "You must remember."

The scenery turned grainy, and everything became distorted as the colors washed together. I couldn't see my guardians anymore. I tried desperately to hold on, but her hand slipped away as if it were made out of water.

I felt something swipe up my forehead then everything exploded into balls of color surrounded by darkness until eventually all I could see was darkness.

"Take her," a familiar voice screamed through the explosive noise that made my ears ring.

A hand closed over mine, and I felt my body slip away as I opened my eyes. All I could see was a flash of red before everything turned white. A second later, the colors returned, and I was back in my world being shoved into Justin's arms.

I didn't get a chance to see who handed me over to him before Justin whipped out his wings and held onto me tightly as he soared into the air. Adjusting his wings, he glided through the sky. "I'm going to take you back to Marcus's where you'll be safe."

I looked down and saw pieces of Mava's house scattered in the distance.

"What happened?" I asked, my voice muffled by the wind.

"They found you," he whispered. "They—"

Something slammed into us, knocking me from Justin's grasp, sending me free-falling to the ground.

I screamed as the force of gravity took over, sucking me into its clutches.

Twisting my head around, I tried desperately to find Justin, but all I could see was a bundle of white and black feathers tumbling toward the earth. A white pulse that looked like one of those plasma balls exploded from the middle of the feathers, sending Abby flying thirty feet back.

It had been her. Abby had knocked me out of Justin's arms for reasons I didn't understand.

From one hundred feet above me, Justin locked his gaze on me, folded his wings back, and darted toward me, with Abby close behind. Only I was going too fast. The ground was getting nearer, and Justin was still so far away.

CHAPTER 36

*W*ind thrashed against my face as I plummeted to the earth. My back began to itch, growing stronger and stronger by the second until pain tore through my shoulder blades. White plasma danced around my vision, wrapping me in its folds.

Terror surged through my veins, as I feared I'd been entrapped in a witch's magical spell. I didn't know why Abby had ploughed into Justin, all I knew was that I was going to pay the ultimate price for her actions.

I jerked upwards as arms closed around me, trapping me in their embrace. I still couldn't see, but I knew it was Justin. He'd caught me.

"What the hell have you been hiding from us?" Justin asked, confirming my suspicion that it was indeed he who saved me.

"Huh?"

"Never mind," he whispered.

A pulse of electricity surged through my body then disappeared as quickly as it had started. A few moments later, the wind evaporated, and my feet were set on the ground.

I felt something tingle a part of my body that I couldn't place where exactly it was, then the layers of plasma peeled back, revealing Justin's face. We were back at Marcus's.

"Since when did you get wings?" he asked.

My eyes widened as the word *wings* replayed on a loop in my mind.

He lifted his other hand and peeled back the wing, and sure enough, I felt every bit of his touch.

"Who the hell is that?" Abby asked from behind him, with a drunken slur. "And how did they get through the boundary?"

Justin stepped back, allowing Abby to see me.

"Holy shit," she said, her eyes practically popping out of her head. "Is that..." She stepped closer and ran her fingers over the plasma. "Are those...wings?"

"Looks like it," Justin replied.

"On Lucy?" She shook her head, then locked eyes with me. "You're supposed to be dead." She backed away until she hit the table that was covered in empty bottles of wine and a few that hadn't been opened yet. "I saw you." She grabbed a bottle and twisted the top off. "I saw you up in the sky, and I thought..." She narrowed her eyes at me. "I thought it was you but..." She threw her head back in laughter then turned to Justin. "You're a fucking traitor." Abby sauntered over to him as she took another sip. "We trusted you." She poked him in the chest. "You told us she was dead." She poked him again. "But you've been lying."

Justin pushed her hand away. "You need to sober up. What you did up there could've killed Lucy." He looked at her sternly.

According to my guardians, that wasn't possible, but I wasn't going to bring that up.

Abby rolled her head to look at me. "She didn't have wings before."

"No, she did not," Justin agreed. "But I'm not going to discuss this with you while you're in this state."

Abby grabbed a bottle of wine off the table, took a swish, then wiped the back of her hand over her mouth. "What state?"

"Drunk." He snatched the bottle from her hand and sent it flying into the distance.

"Hey," Abby whined.

"Where's Marcus?" Justin asked.

That probably should've been the first thing that came out of my mouth. Instead, I was left speechless. I had freakin' wings. I wasn't supposed to have wings. I was human...

No, I was not, after all.

"Inside." She gestured toward the house. "He passed out a few hours ago."

Finally finding my voice, I asked, "How do I put these things away?"

"You just do," Abby said, being her usual unhelpful self that she was when she was drunk.

Justin strode over to me. "Just think about them going away, and they should disappear." He tilted his head to the side. "Although I haven't seen anyone with wings like yours before."

"They're fucking awesome," Abby added, her pitch going up a notch or two. Then her face slumped. "Why can't mine be like that?"

"Just ignore her," Justin said. "Think about making them disappear."

Doing as instructed, I tried my hardest to get them to disappear. But no matter how much I tried, the suckers stayed exactly where they were.

"This isn't working," I said with frustration.

Justin put his hands on my shoulders. "Don't worry about it. We'll figure it out."

I nodded, not believing a word he said. With my luck, we were not going to figure it out. It was just another thing to add to the list of freakish things that are Luciana.

"How about you go see Marcus, and we can work on this after?" he said.

My heart skipped a few beats. "Marcus."

Without a second thought, I pushed past Justin and rushed through the door. I was jerked back by the stupid wings I didn't know how to use.

"Come here," Justin said as Abby cracked up laughing.

Ignoring Abby, I stomped over to Justin.

"Let me help you with that." He stepped around me and forced my wings behind my back, making sure they stayed in place. He patted them a few times. "There you go."

"Thanks," I said over my shoulder then darted inside.

Marcus wasn't in the lounge room, so I made my way down the hall, stopping at my bedroom. He wasn't there, either.

Continuing, I opened his door and found him passed out, lying face down on the bed. He looked so sad and helpless. The empty bottles of wine that littered the floor and bed wouldn't have helped his cause.

I guess I had Justin to thank for that. He'd promised he'd make sure Marcus wasn't able to go and do something stupid. Well, he sure kept that promise.

I climbed onto the bed and crawled over to him.

"Marcus?" I wiped a lock of his hair to the side, my fingertips brushing against his skin.

He stirred then opened his eyes, drowsily. "Hey," he murmured, reaching up to cradle my jaw in his hands. "You've come to visit me." He ran his hand over my shoulder. "And you got your wings."

"Yeah, I've got wings," I said, a few tears slipping out.

"And you can speak."

I laughed as more tears welled in my eyes. "Yeah, I can talk."

He sighed. "I killed you." He lifted himself up onto his elbows then let his head fall on my lap and looked up at me starry eyed. "Please don't tell me it's time to kill you again?"

I brushed his hair away from his face. "No, you don't have to kill me. You didn't kill me—this time."

"Yes, I did," he slurred. "It was my fault. I shouldn't have left you. I should've destroyed the vial."

God, he was drunk. He didn't even realize I was real.

He sighed. "I'm going to kill Mava." His tone was void of any menace. He was broken.

"Marcus," I said. "I'm not dead."

"Yes, you are." He rolled so that he was curled around me, his face buried against my tummy.

He muffled something else that I couldn't make out.

I nudged him back then slid down so that I was lying next to him. "How about you sleep now and we can talk when you wake up?"

"You'll still be here?" he asked.

"I'll still be here." I pressed a gentle kiss on his lips. "I'll always be here."

"Like my own personal angel?" He groaned. "You're an angel... I'll never see you or touch you again."

"You're seeing and touching me right now."

Marcus smiled. "I am, aren't I?" He snaked his arm around my waist and pulled me closer, then buried his head against the curve of my neck. "My own little angel—with wings." He brushed his lips over my neck. "I love you."

Nestling down beside him, I slung my arm over his shoulders, wishing that he were no longer drunk. I'd pictured the moment I walked back into his life would've panned out a little different but I wasn't going to complain. I was with him and that was all that mattered. "I love you, too."

I held onto him then noticed my skin, which was touching him was turning a darker shade as if a shadow had fallen over that part of my body. I lifted my arm, and sure enough, there were grey smudges beneath the surface of my skin.

Lowering my arm, I watched in astonishment as black spider veins not only appeared on my skin as it neared Marcus's, but they appeared on him as well. The closer I got to his skin, the darker they turned. It was just like what happened with the girl in the hospital bed. Only with Marcus, it didn't cause me pain. It made me feel a little light-headed, but no pain.

I lowered my arm and watched Marcus carefully to ensure whatever was happening wasn't hurting him either. His breathing remained even, and there was no sign that my touch was affecting him. He was safe.

I must've dozed off at some point because I woke to Marcus sitting with his back against the headboard, staring at me as if he was seeing a ghost.

CHAPTER 37

"Hey, you," I said running my hand up his calf, his eyes locked on my hand the entire time.

His gaze shifted to mine. "You're real? I wasn't just dreaming?"

Smiling, I lifted myself into a sitting position. "I'm real. And you were sloshed. Good to see you're back with us now."

"You have wings?" He still hadn't moved an inch.

I reached behind my back, a strange sensation flowing through me when I touched the plasma-like feathers. "Yeah, and I don't know how to get rid of them."

Marcus sat there staring at me for a couple of minutes before he spoke again. "You're really here?"

I crawled onto his lap, straddling his hips as I ran my hands up his biceps. "I'm really here."

Gingerly, he brushed the tips of his fingers across my cheek, stopping at the edge of my lips. It was as if he still couldn't trust himself that he was actually seeing the real me and I wasn't just a figment of his imagination.

"I'm here," I repeated then kissed him, forcing him to acknowledge my existence.

It didn't take long. One second it was just me in the kiss then the next he was all there, savoring every second of our reunion until one of my wings got free and whacked him in the head as it curled in front of me.

"Sorry," I said, pulling away.

He laughed.

"How did you get wings?" He ran his fingers across the feathers, sending that weird sensation through my body. "And more importantly, how the hell did you come back from the dead?"

I looked over my shoulder at the door. "Is Justin still here?"

"Yeah."

God, I wished I could tell who was around. Instead, I just had wings—which I'd been wanting since the second time Abby had taken me up into the air. What was I complaining about? I had what I wanted. I just needed to learn how to use them.

"Why do you want to know if Justin is here?" he prompted.

I chewed on my bottom lip as I thought about how I could answer that without Marcus losing his cool at Justin. Even though Justin had been an integral part of the witches plan to unlock my memories, there wasn't a possible scenario I could imagine that wouldn't end in Justin going through a wall.

"Don't do that." Marcus tapped my lip with his finger.

"Sorry, nervous—"

"Habit. Yeah, I know. Which has me wondering why you're nervous about Justin being here when all I want to know is how you're still alive. I would've thought I'd owe him somehow."

I rested my hand on his bare chest. "Believe me, we owe him everything. But that doesn't mean I'm going to tell you what's happened while he's still around."

He studied me for a moment then slipped his hands under my butt as he got up and carried me over to the door.

"Justin!" He moved his hands up to my waist and placed my feet on the ground, then opened the door. "Justin!"

I slammed the door closed. "Not now."

His eyes filled with anger but I knew it wasn't directed at me. "What did he do?"

"Saved our lives."

"What did he do?" he asked again.

"What's going on?" Justin asked as the door handle turned from the other side.

I threw my back against the door. "Go away, Justin. And I mean, leave Marcus's estate."

"Why?"

Marcus glared at me. "Because I get a feeling that I'm going to want to kill you if you don't."

"You haven't told him yet?"

"No," I yelled. "I'm about to, and I really think you should stop asking questions and get the hell out of here."

Marcus's jaw popped. "I think you should do as she says."

"I'm not leaving you to deal with the fallout, Lucy," Justin said.

"For God's sake, Justin," I yelled in frustration. "Would you just get out of here?"

"Fine," he said. "Call me when you're ready."

"Will do," I replied.

"What did he do?" Abby asked, her voice coming from Justin's side of the door.

"Oh, God," I said.

"Marcus, do you want me to pin his ass to the wall?" Abby called out.

I banged the back of my head against the door, the impact cushioned by my wings. "Do not pin his ass to the wall."

"I didn't ask you," Abby replied.

I looked up at Marcus. "Please tell her to let him go."

"I'm already leaving," Justin said, his voice sounding a little distant.

"The hell you are," Abby said.

I pleaded for Marcus to do the right thing and call off his demon.

"Fine," he said. "I'm doing this for you, not Justin."

"Thank you." I stood on the balls of my feet and planted a kiss on his cheek.

"Let him go," Marcus ordered.

"Are you sure?" Abby replied. "Because I could take him down."

The corner of his lips tipped up. "Yes, Abby. I'm sure you can."

"No fair," she mumbled, bringing a smile to my face, instantly feeling guilty because the last thing I wanted was for Justin to feel a demons wrath.

Marcus's gaze followed a steady line across the room then lifted up as if he could actually see Justin leaving.

Returning his gaze to mine, he asked, "Now, what was so bad that Justin had to go?"

CHAPTER 38

*M*arcus closed his hands around my hips, as he stepped away from the door, bringing me with him.

"Yeah, what was so bad?" Abby flung the door open. "And why the hell are you alive? Don't get me wrong. I'm ecstatic that you're back with us, but I saw you dead. Justin wouldn't tell me shit while you guys were in here. The bastard kept promising me that he'd tell me when I sobered up. And you can guess how that went."

I looked between Abby and Marcus, trying to find my words.

"So what was it?" She planted her ass on the end of the bed as if she'd done it a million times before.

I couldn't help but think of the way she touched Marcus in my tunnel test.

"Did he do a deal with the boss?" she offered.

I scratched the side of my neck. "Ahh... No, it was nothing like that."

"Then what was it?" Marcus asked.

I breathed out harshly as I tried to figure out where I should start. The usual place to start was the beginning, however, I wasn't sure that would be for the best.

"There's a lot I've learned over the last..." I scrunched up my face as I tried to work out how much time had passed since they thought I'd died. I came up empty. "How long have I been gone for?"

"Three days," Marcus said.

My eyes widened in surprise. "Seriously?"

He tilted his head to the side. "Well, if you want to be technical, it was three days, fourteen hours and fifty-three seconds. At least it was that long before I saw you in my drunken state when I thought I was just dreaming."

"Back to the story," Abby said. "What's been going on?"

Marcus ran his hand along the spine of my wings. He was completely mesmerized as he studied the flow of the glowing, transparent feathers. "What kind of wings are these?"

"The kind that just appeared when Abby decided to take Justin out while we were mid-air, making Justin drop me as they tumbled in the sky."

Marcus raised his eyebrows as he turned to Abby.

"What?" she snapped, screwing her nose up. "I was drunk, and I thought he was messing around with us when I saw a very alive Lucy in his arms."

Marcus clenched his jaw. "You could've killed her."

"Okay, so technically it may have been a bad idea to go after him while he was carrying Lucy, and while I was drunk, but it looks like I was right about something."

"Which is?" he prodded.

"That Justin screwed us over. I mean why else would Lucy tell him to go?"

"Because I didn't want you to do anything you'll regret," I said, then added, "Oh, and technically you wouldn't have killed me. Remember, I can't die by anyone's hand beside Marcus's. And even that isn't exactly death for me. I'm just reborn until I complete the task I was born to do."

"What are you talking about?" Marcus asked.

"Maybe you should sit down for this," I suggested.

"I'm fine standing."

"Okay. Suit yourself." I took a deep breath. "First, I'm going to tell you the end. Then I'll go back and tell you how it all came to be."

I hated seeing Marcus stubbornly standing there. As uncomfortable as it made me, I couldn't make him sit.

"I met my creator," I started. "I don't know all the details because something happened. All I was able to find out is that I was created as the key to unlocking your destiny."

Marcus ran his hand down his face. "More of Mava's shitty riddles."

"No. I know it sounds like hers, and that's only because my creator fed her the riddle. He isn't able to tell me anything more than the reason why I was created. And even that is something I have to figure out on my own to enable me to unlock your destiny."

"This doesn't make any sense." Marcus paced the length of the room.

"I'm not human, and I'm not cursed. My memories have been bound thanks to someone with a lot of power who cast a spell on me. Before I could find out any more, I was ripped from my guardians and—"

Marcus whipped his head around. "You went into the tunnel?"

I nodded.

"Shit." He walked over to the bed and sat next to Abby. "And your creator was waiting for you at the end?"

I nodded. "Along with two others, one of which was John from rehab."

"Who?"

"You know, John. The guy who owned the place?"

He slowly shook his head.

"Are you serious?" I asked in disbelief. "The guy I used to go riding with every day?"

"You always went by yourself."

I couldn't believe what I was hearing. Then again, I had wings.

"No, I didn't. You may not have seen him, but he was there—and he was nudging me in your direction, telling me to follow my heart, not what my brain was telling me was logical."

Marcus stared at me, no recognition in his eyes.

I continued. "Anyway, he was there along with my creator and a woman. They told me that you are not what you think you are."

"Marcus isn't a Soul Collector?" Abby asked in disbelief.

"Apparently not."

"Then what am I supposed to be?" Marcus asked, sounding as if he didn't fully believe what I was saying.

"Hey, buddy," I said. "I've got wings when you thought I was a human and now you doubt that you might not be what you thought you were—even when you're different to other Soul Collectors?"

Marcus gave a slight nod. "Fair point."

"More than a fair point," Abby interjected. "We all knew you were different, demon boy." She whacked her elbow into his side. "Maybe you're one of us. A real demon."

"Something tells me he's not," I said. "Whatever Marcus is, there is someone very powerful that Morgana was able to do a deal with to bind your true identity."

"Morgana?" Abby spat.

"Yeah, turns out that the woman I saw enter the club after Marcus the other night was Morgana."

"Holy shit," Abby said, throwing her head back, a strained laugh escaping her mouth. "You were right to be worried. That witch is something else."

"Morgana followed me into the club the night I went with Justin to see Titus?" Marcus asked.

"Yeah." I had completely forgotten I hadn't told him about my memory of her, and the fact that I'd seen her follow him into the club and I doubted Abby would have passed it on while they were in such a drunken state. "I remember her from a time long ago." God, I sounded as if I were retelling a fairytale, only this was real. "All I remember was lying amongst the fallen leaves as I watched her walk away, and I was unable to get up."

"Morgana's responsible," Marcus said to himself. "That means, this goes way higher than we ever thought."

"I think you're missing the point," I said. "You are more valuable than anyone has ever considered. And I think the question is: why would someone go to all this trouble of binding your true identity? And then have a need for me to be created to bring back order?"

"This stuff is deep." Abby shook her head, lost in her thoughts.

Marcus grabbed my hand. "What about you?"

"What about me?"

He tugged my hand, pulling me down beside him and in turn, knocking them both with my wings.

"Sorry," I said as they righted themselves. It was funny how my wings seemed to flow like silk over the bed, yet still had the power to knock both Marcus and Abby over.

"It's okay." He adjusted them behind my back for me. "You need to learn how to retract them, but first I want to know what you meant by you're not human?"

"Don't the wings give that one away?" Abby joked.

"Not the time for it, Abby," Marcus warned.

"Geez, don't get your panties in a knot."

"This is where I need to go back to the beginning. I'm still trying to figure it all out, and I think I need your help. All I know is that I'm not an empath, I'm not crazy, and me feeling others emotions are not a curse. You need to keep that in mind while I tell you what happened."

I waited for them to agree before continuing. "When you didn't come back, I asked Abby to take me to see Astrid—who by the way, doesn't hate you at all, Abby."

"Yes, she does."

Marcus glared at her. "You took her away from here."

"Back off, demon boy. We thought something had happened to you and when Lucy found that book we thought Astrid might know something."

"What book?" Marcus asked warily.

"The book that someone left for me on my bed the night you went to find Titus at the club."

He raised a brow. "Justin?"

"Actually, I'm not sure, but I guess it was him. Anyway, the point is, Astrid needed to see me by herself, which is why she blocked you from entering her shop."

Marcus glared at Abby. "You let her go in there on her own?"

"She didn't *let* me," I said, getting a little exasperated. "I decided to go in there on my own, and there was nothing Abby could do short of kidnapping me that was going to stop me."

"Then she should've kidnapped you. Anything could've happened."

"It didn't," I said. "And if I hadn't have gone in there then I wouldn't have drank Mava's potion, and I wouldn't be sitting here knowing what I now know."

"Astrid made you drink the potion?"

I closed my eyes and leaned against his shoulder. "Please stop being so defensive. Everything worked out for the best. And no matter how horrible things got, I'm glad everyone played their part in helping me—helping us."

Marcus leaned his head against mine. "I'm sorry."

I curled my arm around his and laced our fingers together. "Between my visit with Astrid, Mava's riddle, and the spell book that was left for me, I somehow knew that I needed to drink the vial so that I could see. I had no idea what I needed to see, all I knew was that we weren't going to find out what was going on unless I trusted my gut and drank Mava's concoction. Which by the way, didn't kill me as everyone thought."

Marcus's head jerked up.

"Say what?" Abby asked.

"It put me in a paralyzed state that allowed Justin to get me out of this dimension without anyone suspecting what they had planned. And before you throw a hissy fit about Justin deceiving you both, it was imperative to the plan. They needed you to believe I'd died so they could help me enter the tunnel without anyone becoming suspicious and stopping me. Only they did stop me, but not before I found out a few truths.

"Anyway, Mava and Astrid helped me into the tunnel where I was met with more than a few creatures I'd rather not know exist. And a few other scenarios that cut me to my core. What I did find out though was that I was only able to get through each stage when I gave in to the emotions that were crippling me, which somehow gave peace to those who were surrounding me.

"I even somehow managed to heal a girl who was about to die— and all I did was touch her."

Marcus narrowed his eyes at me. "Your skin was black. I mean the parts that were touching me when I woke up, fully alert with absolutely no hangover. That's why I was sitting away from you. I thought I was hurting you somehow. When I stopped touching you, your skin eventually returned to its usual color."

So, that explained his unusual behavior.

"It hurt like crazy with the girl... with you, there was no pain. And you seemed okay so I just went with it." I gave him a small smile. "I'm sorry I scared you."

"So, let me get this right," Abby said, breaking up our little moment. "You can take away other people's illnesses?"

"Seems that way," I said.

"Holy crap." She smacked her hand against her lap. "That just confused the hell out of me. I mean why would you be created to remove sicknesses if you were created for Marcus? Which by the way, I just have to say, is really cool. And it explains why Marcus wasn't able to deliver your soul the day he met you—and why he fell in love with you so quickly."

"He was never able to deliver my soul. I was created in a way that I can't be killed. All Marcus has the ability to do is keep my suffering at bay and send me into my next lifetime."

"So, all this time I've been…" He didn't need to say it. We all knew what he meant. "I didn't have to?"

His expression was torn, realising he never needed to drive the knife into my heart.

I twisted to the side, my knee resting on his thigh. "It was the right thing to do at the time. The spell was still too strong for me to fulfil my destiny. We had to wait until it was weakened."

He let out a strained laugh. "Now I know why you sent Justin away." He shook his head. "All this time he knew?"

"Yep."

Marcus ran his hand over my knee. "When did you find out what was going on?"

"As soon as Justin took me to Mava's. I'd been awake, trapped inside my body, since I drank the vial."

"You were aware of what was going on around you?" Marcus asked in disbelief.

I nodded. "And it killed me to see you that way."

He cupped my face in his hand and ran his thumb over the side of my lip. "It doesn't matter now."

"No, it doesn't," Abby agreed. "What matters now is figuring out what exactly Lucy was created to do to you, and who you are." She stood and came over to me. "And to teach Lucy how to retract her wings."

I groaned. "I'm open for any tips."

She ran her fingers across the plasma looking feathers. "These babies aren't like ours. These are special."

"What do you mean?"

"I mean these wings aren't seen on the lower-class angels. These are reserved for the upper-class." She poked her head around my wings so she could see me. "Did your creator have wings like these?"

I shook my head. "They were like yours but white."

"So your creator was a lower ranked being. That doesn't make any sense," Marcus said. "How can a lower-class create an upper-class?"

He directed his question at Abby.

"I don't know," she replied. "I didn't think it was possible."

Marcus shifted his gaze to me. "What was his name?"

"Thomas. Do you know him?"

He gave me a blank look, which was all the answer I needed. "Never heard of him."

"Either that or he's given you a different name to throw us off," Abby offered.

"You're probably right," I agreed.

"Hopefully Justin can enlighten us on that one when he comes back." Abby shifted my wings, so they were folded nicely behind my back. "And in the meantime, let's get these wings of yours away."

I stood. "Sounds good."

"All you need to do is think about pulling them inside your back in the same way you think about scratching an itch. Your mind should know how to do it."

I twisted around and glared at her. "Does it look like I know how to do it?"

"Point taken."

Marcus laughed.

"Okay, demon boy. You teach her."

Marcus quickly shut his mouth.

"That's what I thought." Abby shifted her gaze to me. "There's no special command to make them go back in. You just need to concentrate and try your hardest."

Thirty-minutes later, my wings were still out, Abby had gone to get something to eat, and Marcus was watching me, trying to hide his grin as I tried endlessly to do the impossible.

I threw myself back onto the bed and stared at the ceiling, my glowing feathers wrapping around me as if I needed protection from the cold. I wasn't cold. I was hot and bothered.

"Why is this so hard?" I sat up on my elbows and looked at Marcus sternly. "And don't laugh at me."

Marcus sauntered over to me, making me forget all about my wings. He nudged my knees apart and stood between them. "You know, your wings are kind of sexy," he said, crawling on top of me.

I ran the tips of my fingers down his bare chest, all the way to his abs.

"I'm so glad they do it for you because it looks like they're not going anywhere," I said sarcastically.

Marcus lowered himself on top of me, bearing his weight on his hand tucked beside my chest. "Well, I may as well enjoy them while I can."

He grazed his lips across my shoulder then—

I screamed as he bit down hard on the bone of my wing.

I pushed him off me. "What the hell did you do that for?"

With a smirk, he gestured toward my wings—only they weren't there.

"What the hell?"

He swung his leg off me and collapsed by my side. "It's a natural reaction to pull back your wings when they get injured."

"And if it didn't work?"

"Then I would've apologized profusely."

"You are so evil." I whacked his chest.

He caught my hand. "That's yet to be decided."

I rolled on my side to face him, our hands joined between us. "You're not evil."

"How can you be sure?"

"Because good always triumphs evil in the end, and that's what we're going to do."

He brought our joined hands up to his lips and kissed the back of my hand. "No more cast."

"Huh," I said, my gaze falling to my wrist. "I hadn't even noticed. Mava or Astrid must've fixed it."

"It would've been Astrid." When I narrowed my eyes at him, he added, "That's who I was taking you to see when you first met Abby."

"Oh," I dragged.

"So, you think I'm good," he asked, a smile playing on his lips.

"I do," I said, wholeheartedly.

"Then that would mean that you're the darkness that your creator is referring to in Mava's riddle."

My eyes widened, and I whacked him again.

"I'm kidding," he said, laughing. "You could never be anything but light. Even your wings are made out of light."

"Well, at least now we know that we have more than a month left to figure this out."

He drew his brows together as sadness folded over his features. "You don't want me to end your pain before it's too late for me to stop it, do you?"

I shook my head then kissed his knuckles. "I'm not afraid anymore. What I have is a gift, not a curse, and I'm not going to let anything stop me from figuring out how I'm supposed to save you."

And that was the truth. I was no longer scared. And I certainly wasn't going to let anyone tear our world apart again. We were going to take control and find out what I was created for.

KELLY CARRERO

USA TODAY BESTSELLING AUTHOR

SEVERED
MINDS

CHAPTER 1

I never thought flying would come so naturally.

All those times I'd imagined what it would be like to have wings and soar across the tips of the trees was nothing compared to how it actually felt. The breeze tickled my feathers, sending a tingling sensation through the membranes and awakening a part of me I never knew existed.

Lifting up, I came to a halt midair and twisted around to find Abby. She was much higher than I was, happily floating amongst the clouds in the predawn sky.

Marcus was watching me from below, and even though he was so far away, I could still see the torment in his eyes. He wanted me to learn to use my wings in the very likely chance that I'd need them to save my ass from the Soul Scrapers, but I could tell it was hard on him.

Marcus remembered his wings. He remembered the euphoric sensation that lit up our souls as we did one of the biggest things that separated us from humans—fly.

Only Marcus couldn't fly, and no matter how much he didn't blame me, I think we both knew if it weren't for me, he'd still have his wings.

No longer feeling the urge to soar through the sky, I flew up to Abby to let her know I was done for the morning.

The sun peaked over the horizon, its golden rays illuminating the edges of Abby's black wings. "What's up?" she asked, slowly turning her attention away from the scorched symbols down below to me.

"I think I might call it quits for the day."

She raised her brows. "Wow."

I scowled. "I don't think I need to stay up here any longer than necessary. I mean, I clearly know how to fly, and I really don't want to rub Marcus's nose in it any more than I have to."

The corners of her lips tipped up. "I was referring to your wings."

"What about my...?" I trailed off as I looked to the left and saw what had mesmerized her. I'd thought Abby's wings glistened under the sun's rays, but they were nothing compared to the light that glowed from within each and every feather of mine.

Returning my gaze to Abby, I asked, "These are special, aren't they?"

She nodded slowly. "Which has me going out of my mind trying to figure out why you would have those babies."

"You and I both."

Her gaze darted below. "Something tells me Morgana and whoever she is working with will do everything within their power to stop us from finding out."

Following her line of sight, an icy shiver ran down my spine when I saw the demented creatures below. Dark shadows slunk alongside the Hellhounds as they swarmed the perimeter of Marcus's estate, trying to find a weak spot to break through. They'd been stalking us since Justin brought me home, occasionally disappearing to God knows where only to return with more determination and numbers.

"Why don't Morgana and her witches come here themselves?"

She scratched her forehead. "I think they know they're not going to get through, so they're trying to scare us."

Hugging myself, I ran my hands up and down my arms. "Well, it's working."

She smiled sadly at me then cocked her head toward the house. "I think we should call it a day."

Taking one last look at the hellish creatures below, I glided down, preparing to ease into my landing like Abby and Justin had done. Only, it wasn't that simple.

The ground came up faster than I'd anticipated. I pulled up but was too late, missing my mark and ending up in the pool.

Cringing with embarrassment, I pushed up from the bottom of the pool and surfaced momentarily before my wings got in the way of my hands as I tried to keep myself afloat and pulled me under the water.

I barely had time to register just how bad my situation was and how much more landing practice I would need before strong arms wrapped around me, lifting me out of the water.

I gasped for air as I swatted my glowing feathers away from my mouth. They may not have looked like real feathers, but they sure stuck to my face like them.

Marcus twisted me around in his arms then lifted me into a sitting position on the edge of the pool, my legs dangling on either side of him in the water.

"Are you okay?" He smoothed my slick, dark brown hair away from my face.

Gripping the capping around the edge of the pool, I nodded. "I think I need to work on my landings."

Marcus chuckled. "Might be a good idea if you don't want to drown."

I raised a brow. "Except I can't die by anything but your hand, remember?" I regretted my words as soon as they left my mouth. The haunted look in his eyes had returned with a vengeance. He was having a hard time coming to terms with the fact that he'd never needed to kill me.

Leaning forward, I rested my hands on his shoulders. "You'll never have to do it again."

He tipped his head back and kissed me. I wasn't sure if it was a deflection as to his true fears or because he agreed with me. Either way, I was using the opportunity to make him forget what I'd said.

Slipping back into the pool, I hooked my arms around his neck, deepening our kiss.

A soft growl that was anything but angelic came from deep within Marcus's chest. He may have been the light, but I was pretty sure his thoughts were far from good.

Marcus stepped forward, pinning my back against the side of the pool, and ran his hands down the sides of my hips before hooking them under my ass.

"You know how I feel about sex, but you might want to put a lid on it around visitors," Abby said, breaking our moment.

Pulling away, I gaped at her. "We were not about to have sex."

Abby smirked.

Horrified by the implication of giving in to our urges while in the presence of someone else, I said, "I'm not sure if you're aware, but kissing doesn't always lead to sex."

She raised a brow, the smirk still playing on her lips. "Doesn't it?"

I rolled my eyes as I pushed Marcus back, letting my feet float down to the bottom of the pool. "No, Abby, for us mere mortals, it doesn't."

"Only you're not a mortal now, are you?"

I looked at Marcus, wondering why he wasn't jumping in, but he wore an amused expression on his face that told me he had no intention of contributing to this conversation. "Great help you are."

I twisted around, trudged through the water in my soaking wet runners, and climbed out.

Marcus followed me out of the pool and caught my hand. "Sorry, I just love seeing you get all flustered."

He turned to Abby. "Just so you know, for us non-sex demons or angels or whatever we are, kissing doesn't automatically mean we're about to strip down and make love, not caring if there's anyone else around." He smirked. "Some of us have a little more dignity than that."

Abby shrugged. "Your loss." She strode over to the outdoor lounge and slid into the seat. "So, who wants to talk about the elephant in the room?"

"I'd hardly call them an elephant," I said, twisting the water out of my hair. "Those things out there can either suck the life out of an elephant or rip its throat out with a single bite." I cocked my thumb in the direction of the Soul Scrapers and Hellhounds.

Marcus grabbed a towel. "She was talking about me not answering Justin's calls."

"Or messages," Abby added.

I made an "O" shape with my mouth. "I thought you were talking about those monsters trying to get in."

"I don't think we need to worry about them for now," Marcus said. "They'd be stupid to try something during daylight."

Abby crossed her long legs. "But that doesn't mean we should be complacent. You never know what Morgana is prepared to do. She can hide in plain sight without drawing any attention from the humans."

"But any human who comes anywhere near here can see the Soul Scrapers, and they're going to wonder what is up with those freakishly huge dogs that look as if they've crawled their way up from Hell. Yeah, real discreet."

Abby furrowed her brow. "You do realize most humans can't see them, don't you?"

I tilted my head to the side as I remembered the Soul Scrapers I'd seen in the hospital after I'd slit my wrist. The only person that had seen it was the guy high on meth. I was pretty sure none of the nurses, doctors, or patients had seen them. If they had, I was positive they would've been screaming and running for their lives. No amount of dedication to their jobs would've had them staying put and attending to patients with those otherworldly creatures around.

"Hey, Marcus?" I said.

"Yeah?"

"Remember that day when you came back into my life?"

He smiled as his gaze drifted down the length of my body. "Kind of hard to forget."

I bit down on my smile. That day hadn't been anything special by any normal person's standards. We hadn't even spoken, but that was the day I finally saw the man who could end my suffering. Little had I known the road that laid ahead would have me wanting to live instead of praying for Marcus to drive that dagger through my heart like he had every night in my dreams.

Marcus sauntered over to me, his shirt clinging to his body in all the right places. "You were saying?" He ran the tips of his fingers across my left wing.

I shook my thoughts away, bringing a smile to Marcus's face. "Ah, yeah," I said, trying to refocus. "I was going to ask you about the Soul Scrapers I saw at the hospital. They were Soul Scrapers, weren't they?"

Marcus gave a curt nod. "You thought you were seeing something someone else was hallucinating, didn't you?"

"Yep. Because demonic creatures could only be a figment of someone's imagination—or so I naively thought."

"So, they were real," Abby said, sounding impatient. "Back to the elephant."

Marcus breathed out in frustration and leaned against the garden wall. "I'm not ready."

Abby uncrossed her legs and twisted around to face him. "Do I really need to be the one to point out that we don't have time for you to be ready?"

I peeled my shorts away from my thighs, but it was useless. As soon as I let go, the shorts once again clung to me. "Ready for what?"

Abby looked to Marcus, waiting for him to answer. When it became obviously apparent he wasn't talking, she said, "Justin has been calling Marcus for the past five minutes—and here he goes again."

I scrunched up my face in confusion. "I can't hear any calls."

"That's because Marcus has his phone on silent."

Right, she could hear things I couldn't. Another supernatural perk I didn't have. I stepped closer to him and grabbed his hand. "You know it wasn't Justin's fault, don't you?"

"Doesn't mean I'm not still pissed at him."

I bit my lip as I tried to think of what to say next. "Well, I think you're going to have to get over it. We need Justin."

"That's something I never thought I'd hear you say."

"You and me both." It wasn't until a couple of days ago that I realized the truth of what Justin had done. He'd betrayed Marcus, but it had been necessary. If Marcus had known the truth and hadn't played his part just right, then those who were watching might have figured it out. I wondered if Justin had intended for their friendship to dissolve for that very purpose. It was easier for Justin to keep the secret if everyone thought they were no longer friends.

"Speak of the devil," Abby said, her gaze drifting up to the sky.

Ten seconds later, Justin came into view—and he didn't look happy. He landed a few yards in front of us, jaw set, pupils dilated, and looking as if he were ready to fight. "Why didn't you answer?"

Marcus stepped forward, balling his hands at his sides. "Because I didn't want to."

Ignoring his not so subtle frustration, Justin said, "Jesus, you can be a stubborn ass at times."

Abby barked out a laugh. "Only at times?"

Marcus glared at her.

I stepped around Marcus. "Is everything okay?"

Justin's gaze flicked to the direction the faint growling of the Hellhounds was coming from. "No, it's not." He looked back at Marcus. "And you need to get over whatever issues you have with me, or everything I did will have been for nothing."

"Get over it?" Marcus gently pushed me to the side as he stalked over to Justin. "You lied to me. I thought she was dead," he said, pointing to me. "You let me think she was dead!"

I grabbed his arm, lowering it by his side as I entwined my fingers with his. "It was a necessary evil."

Marcus's gaze remained on Justin. "A necessary evil? Do you have any idea what it's like to lose someone you care about? And that's not the half of it. All those times I killed Lucy were for nothing!"

"It wasn't for nothing," Justin said. "It was necessary at the time. Luciana wasn't ready, and you and I both know she couldn't live the remainder of her life feeling other people's pain while you couldn't do anything to stop it." Justin ran his hand through his hair. "I'm sorry. I'm fucking sorry. But I'd do it all over again if it means I can help break this spell Morgana has cast on the two of you."

He gripped the back of his neck with both hands as his wings retreated into his back. "They have Mava and Astrid."

CHAPTER 2

*M*arcus's entire body tensed, Justin's words transforming him in a blink of an eye. He was no longer angry with Justin. He was afraid, and that wasn't something I normally saw on Marcus. "They're going to get in?"

Justin nodded. "That's why I was calling. I was trying to warn you."

"Only Marcus was too friggin' stubborn to answer your calls," Abby said, her wings unfolding as she stood.

Marcus unclenched his fists, all frustration with Justin forgotten the minute he heard they had the witches. "Shit."

"And 'oh fuck' and every other profanity you can think of," Abby said. "Those things are going to get in here as soon as they break the spell Astrid cast around this place."

Fear ran it's icy tendrils down every inch of my body, latching onto my soul as I not only feared for Mava and Astrid's safety, but also for Marcus, Justin, Abby, and me.

If we didn't have the sanctuary of Marcus's home, then we had nothing. We were going to be sitting ducks, waiting for them to attack, and I barely knew how to defend myself. I'd only just learned how to fly, and I sure as hell didn't know how I was supposed to be the key to unlocking Marcus's destiny.

"I'm going to check on them." Abby didn't wait for anyone to respond before she took off into the air faster than I'd ever seen her go before.

Marcus pulled me in front of him, his arms protectively wrapped around me as if he were getting ready to fly me off to a safer destination—only, he couldn't. "We have to get Lucy out of here."

"I agree," Justin said. "We need to keep Lucy safe."

"Um, Lucy is right here, and she thinks we need to be figuring out how to rescue Mava and Astrid," I said, trying to wiggle free from Marcus's grasp. Of course, I couldn't. He was too strong for me.

"That's not happening," Marcus said.

I turned around in his arms and scowled at him. "The hell it isn't. You can't just leave them to rot away in some witches prison where Morgana will probably torture them or worse, kill them when all they were trying to do was help us." I pushed hard against Marcus, breaking his hold on me. "The hell we're not rescuing them." I looked at Justin. "Right?"

"Actually, I agree with Marcus."

"What?" I practically spat.

"You're not ready to go up against Morgana. Besides, Mava and Astrid would kill me if I let you come after them."

I raised my brows. *"Let me?* You don't *let me* do anything. I decide. You got that?"

"It's not only about you now, is it? You're just the key," Justin said, and then he gestured to Marcus. "Marcus is what this is all about."

"She is not just a key," Marcus said in a stern voice.

Justin breathed out harshly. "Okay. That came out wrong. You're more than just a key, Lucy. I get that. But that doesn't change the fact that both Mava and Astrid wouldn't want you coming after them."

"I can't let them die."

"I'm not asking you to let them die," Justin said.

"Then what are you asking?"

"I'm asking you to go back and find out who you are."

Marcus's arms curled around me. "No way. She's not going back in there."

"Back in where?" I asked.

"It's the only way," Justin said. "Lucy needs to find out what she is. She needs to figure out how she is supposed to fulfill her destiny."

"Her destiny is with me."

"And what is your destiny?" Justin asked, brimming with frustration. "Who are you?"

When Marcus didn't answer, Justin said, "That's right. You don't know. And unlike Lucy, you don't have any Guardians to help you figure it out. And that's what makes this situation so screwed-up. We need to figure out who you are, who Morgana's working with, and how to stop them."

"And save Mava and Astrid," I reminded him.

"And save Mava and Astrid," Justin agreed.

Abby landed a few yards away from us. "They're still behind the boundary, but the numbers are increasing." She retracted her wings. "I don't think we've got much time."

"Which means we need to get Lucy back to the tunnel as soon as possible," Justin said.

"Are you serious?" Marcus asked as if it were the stupidest thing he'd ever heard. "There is no way Lucy's going back into the tunnel, especially when they're moments away from getting through."

"This is still the safest place."

"For now," Marcus said. "But as soon as they've broken Astrid's spell. Those things are going to rip this place apart, and in case you haven't noticed, I don't have wings. Lucy will be stuck in the tunnel, completely unaware of what's going on here, and don't you even suggest you'll be able to take her because that is never going to happen."

"I can take her if things go to shit before she's out," Abby offered. "You know I wouldn't betray you."

Justin rolled his eyes. "I didn't betray Marcus."

"The hell you didn't." Marcus's grip on me tightened as if he were trying to refrain from punching Justin in the face—again.

"I'm not going to get into this again."

"Don't I get a say in any of this?" I asked.

"No," Marcus said at the same time as Justin said, "Yes."

"Justin, can you give us a moment?" I asked.

He sighed. "I'll be inside."

It wasn't until Justin had entered the house that Marcus released his grip on me. "You're not going in."

I spun around to face him. "You can't just say no because you're pissed at Justin."

"This has nothing to do with Justin."

Abby barked out a laugh. "The hell it doesn't."

Marcus glared at her.

She scrunched up her nose. "I'll go wait inside with Justin."

When it was just the two of us outside, Marcus took my hand. "This has nothing to do with me being angry with Justin."

"Then what is it? Why don't you want me to find out what I am?"

He tugged me toward him. "I know what you are. You are the light of my soul. I can't risk losing you to the tunnel."

"You won't lose me."

He stared at me for a few moments then said, "Do you even know the risks of entering the tunnel?"

"Yeah, I get the shit scared out of me, and I get trapped in my own nightmares if I allow myself to get consumed by fear."

He slowly shook his head. "I could lose you to the tunnel. If you can't get through, you can't come back. You'll be trapped in your own living hell that won't end until you reach the guardians, whom you may never reach."

CHAPTER 3

$\mathcal{M}$y heart stopped as I realized how risky it was. "They didn't explain it to me like that."

"I bet they didn't."

I had no idea if I would've still entered the tunnel if I'd known the risks. Who was I kidding? "I still would've done it."

"And that's what scares me the most." Marcus sighed. "You're always so gung ho, wanting to rush into a world you know nothing about."

"I was created for this world." I gripped his shirt in my hand. "Do you get that? I was created for this world of yours. I'm not human. I'm not like any of you."

"That's right. You're not. And that scares me so much more."

"Which is exactly why I need to find out who I am." I gently hit his stomach with my fist. "I need to know what I am. I need to regain my memories."

"And you think the guardians will just come out and tell you?" he asked. "Because you and I both know it doesn't work like that."

"I know. But I also know they can help me figure it out. Up until I reached them, I had no idea that feeling other people's bad emotions wasn't a curse. I healed people. Maybe that's what I'm supposed to be able to do for you."

Marcus swept my hair behind my ear. "But I'm not broken."

"I've never said you're broken. But you can't remember who you are. Doesn't that worry you? I mean, there's something about who you are that has driven someone to such lengths to keep you from finding out."

I nudged his stomach with my hand. "Who are you, Marcus?"

"I'm just a guy who doesn't want to lose the woman he's in love with."

I sighed. "And I'm just a girl who wants to save the man she's in love with."

"Then, we want the same thing, don't we?"

"Except I'm willing to do whatever it takes."

"You're not the one who'll lose if things don't go as planned."

Leaning forward, I rested my head against his chest. "We can't keep doing this."

"I know."

"Nothing changes if nothing changes." I tilted my head back. "I can do this. I'm not afraid."

Marcus curled his arms around my neck and pulled me against his chest. "Then, it looks like we better find somewhere safe for you while you're in the astral plane."

"Seriously?" I asked, tipping my head back again.

He nodded. "If you believe you can make it through, then I have complete faith in you."

Standing on the balls of my feet, I kissed him. "You won't regret this."

Marcus tucked me under his arm as we headed toward the house.

No matter how much I tried to retract my wings into my back, they didn't oblige. Flying was one thing, but it seemed that getting them to do anything else was another story completely.

"Want help with those?" Marcus asked as we neared the doorway.

"No," I said a little too quickly.

He chuckled. "I wasn't going to bite you if that's what you were thinking."

My heart rate went down a notch or three. "Thanks, but I think I've got this." I didn't have this, but I certainly didn't want to be bitten again.

The corner of his lips tipped up, and he ran his hands along the spine of my wings, maneuvering them neatly behind my back.

"Thanks," I said.

"You're welcome," he replied as we headed inside where we found Justin and Abby leaning against the kitchen counter, stuffing their mouths with pasta.

"What have we decided?"

"Umm…" I narrowed my eyes at the arsenal laid out on the bench.

"I thought you'd be excited to see these babies after the trouble you had handing over the knife the other day," Abby said with a mouthful of pasta.

I frowned. "That was when I wanted to kill Justin." I looked at him. "No offense."

He chuckled. "None taken."

I ran my fingers across the largest cylinder. "Hope this one's mine."

"Sure is." Marcus picked up the silver cylinder and twisted off the top. "These are the scrolls of the so-called prophecy that speaks of you." He tilted the cylinder, letting the worn paper fall to the palm of his hand. "How we got our hands on this when it was supposed to be just a myth, I do not know, but I'm not complaining."

"You can thank Mava for them."

Marcus's gaze darted to Justin. "She had them all this time?"

I nudged his side. "Told you Mava wasn't crazy."

Abby licked the sauce off her lips, put down her fork, and wiped her hands on her shorts as she rounded the bench, her gaze trained on the scrolls. "I beg to differ. Anyone who has been hiding these scrolls has a death wish. That prophecy has always been thought of as a myth, but these could very well prove them true."

Justin cocked his head toward me. "I think Luciana is enough proof they're true. Mava was so sure of it she gave up everything to make everyone discredit the scrolls, all the while believing them herself."

He tilted his head to the side. "Mava hasn't always looked that way. It's only because the power she's used keeping the truth hidden has drained her. Everyone, including me at one point, thought she let herself go as part of her sickness."

"Is she sick?" I asked.

He chuckled. "I meant the whole 'everyone thinking she was delusional' sickness."

"Oh," I mouthed, realising why she didn't look youthful the way Astrid and especially Morgana did. I was riddled with guilt over what she'd given up for me. I wasn't sure how old Mava was, but now I knew it was my fault she looked so old.

No. It was Morgana's fault—and whomever she was working with.

Marcus cleared the bench and unravelled the scrolls, stretching them out for us all to see.

CHAPTER 4

"What's it say?" I asked, peering over Marcus's shoulder at the unintelligible words written on the scroll.

He shook his head. "Unbelievable."

"You've got to be kidding," Abby said, her gaze darting to meet Marcus's.

I slapped his bicep. "What's it say?" I repeated.

He shook his head slowly. "It's the riddle."

"What riddle?"

"Mava's," Abby said. "You know, the one about you being the key that will unlock Marcus's destiny."

"This can't be right," Justin said. "There's supposed to be more." He grabbed the cylinder and smacked it against the bench, trying to get something out, then looked through the hole. "Shit."

Justin slapped the cylinder onto the bench, frustration swirling in his eyes. "I've seen the other papers." He shook his head. "They're supposed to be in there."

"What did they say?" I asked.

"Shit." He pushed off the bench and ran his hands through his hair. "If we don't have them, then someone else does, and I'm betting everything it's neither Mava nor Astrid."

"Morgana," Marcus said, her name rolling off his tongue with distaste.

"What did they say?" I asked again.

"They spoke of the one who would act as a peacekeeper of some sort. Someone who would balance the scales and bring order back into the world."

"And if that is true, then Marcus must be the peacekeeper," I said matter-of-factly.

"That's not possible." Marcus tapped his finger on the paper. "I'm not of that league."

"How do you know?" I asked. "Because I'm sure as hell not the peacekeeper if I'm the key."

"Because of my wings." He strained a laugh. "They'd be like yours if I was the peacekeeper. Maybe I'm the one who finds this peacekeeper."

Or maybe this peacekeeper is born from the two of you," Abby added, making me almost choke. "I'm serious," she said when she saw the expressions both Marcus and I wore. "If Lucy is the key to unlocking your destiny, maybe your destiny is to spawn a new entity that has the power to bring order back into the worlds. Maybe key is another term for vessel, where Lucy's womb acts like a vessel to nurture and provide life to the one who'll bring order to the worlds."

"Holy. Fucking. Shit. Balls," I whispered. I was so not a vessel. I was a... I didn't even know what I was, but there was no way the sole purpose of my existence was to carry Marcus's offspring to change the world.

"Does everything have to revolve around sex with you?" Marcus asked, his eyebrows raised.

She waived him off. "Think about it. I mean, really think about it."

"Abby has a point," Justin said.

"You, too?" Marcus asked.

"Well, it's not an entirely impossible notion when you think about it. I mean, you said you were drawn to Luciana the moment you saw her. And Lucy's guardians told her she was created for Marcus. So, if you think about it, it's not that hard to draw the conclusion Abby has."

The color drained from my face. I was so not ready for kids. The thought of children had never crossed my mind. I was too screwed up to ever want to go down the path of being responsible for a child who would throw tantrum after tantrum, and I would have the unfortunate ability to feel every single one of their hissy fits or whatever else kids threw.

Marcus was watching me, but I couldn't keep myself from hyperventilating. Kids were not on my bucket list or any other list for that matter.

"Lucy wouldn't react like this if that was her purpose," Marcus said.

"How do you know?" Abby asked. "I mean, I'm not saying you need to go make a baby now, but maybe that's something that's supposed to happen in a couple of years down the road."

"Except you're forgetting one very important piece of information."

"Which is?"

"We can't have babies."

I breathed a sigh of relief, which didn't go unnoticed. "Sorry," I said to Marcus.

Abby wasn't giving up. "Exactly. Which is why there's this prophecy and why Luciana was created as a key to unlock your destiny. Maybe you're the exception."

"I am not the exception." Marcus turned his back to her and sauntered over to me.

Abby shrugged. "Not now you're not, but maybe one day."

Marcus wrapped his arms around me from behind and whispered in my ear, "As much as I love you, we are not having a baby, so stop stressing."

I pulled his arms tighter around me and rested the back of my head against his chest. "I wasn't stressing," I lied.

Abby barked out a laugh. "You're still stressing because you know there's a huge possibility I'm right, and you're worried you won't be able to handle it, but maybe that's the point. Maybe you're the one who can heal the imperfection in Marcus and give new possibilities to our kind. Maybe this whole process will heal you, while you heal Marcus and your baby."

I think I stopped breathing. I did stop breathing. Abby was making way too much sense, and it was scaring the hell out of me.

"And what if you're wrong?" Marcus said. "Say we're not having a baby and you're so caught up with the idea that you miss the obvious. Because I'm pretty sure if that was the truth, then Lucy would be this baby-loving momma, ready to conceive this magical child, not standing here unable to breathe at the idea."

I forced myself to take a breath, released it, and took another. I went over those steps numerous times before breathing once again felt natural—barely.

"Fine," Abby said, raising a brow. "But I'm pretty sure that when you get back from seeing your guardians, I'll be saying I told you so."

"If that happens, then I'll deal with it," I said. "But I highly doubt that is my purpose."

She grinned. "We'll see."

Justin walked back around the bench and picked up his bowl of pasta. "So you've accepted that Luciana will be going back into the tunnel?"

Marcus hung his head against the crook of my neck. "I've accepted that Lu believes she'll make it through."

"She'll make it." Justin dug his fork into the pesto-covered pasta, making sure to stab a piece of chicken, then popped it into his mouth.

"Thank you." I twisted around to face Marcus. "See, you should have…" I trailed off as Marcus's eyes dilated, turning that molten lava color that sent fear through my soul. He didn't have to say anything. I knew what was wrong. "They're in."

CHAPTER 5

*F*or once I wanted to thank my lucky stars that I already had my wings out because under the circumstances, I wasn't sure they'd oblige to my request. It was as if they had a mind of their own.

And I needed them to save my ass.

I barely finished my thought before darkness covered the sky and the Hellhounds' snarls resounded through the air.

Marcus, Abby, and Justin already had their weapons in hand and had me surrounded, ready to protect me from the beasts that were coming for me from the depths of Hell.

I was pretty sure we could confirm that whoever was working with Morgana had control over the demons. That scared me so much more. We were definitely dealing with a demon who wanted me dead, not an angelic being that was turning to the other side.

The glass smashed, splinters flying toward us as a beast pounced through the window, its giant, razor sharp teeth bared, ready to strike given a chance as it prowled across the bench top.

The Soul Scrapers spilled through the windows, their mouths open, spewing the tar-like substance at me.

I barely had time to register the details of what was going on before I was almost blinded by the light that was coming from the swords my three keepers were holding.

Marcus brought down his sword, slicing through the tar before it had a chance to latch onto me. Then, he lunged forward and severed the head of the Soul Scraper that had tried to take me as Justin and Abby swung into action.

Blood splattered across the white stone bench as Justin plunged the sword into the Hellhound, narrowly missing being ripped apart by the creature's razor sharp teeth.

Justin didn't have a second to spare before the next hound was descending upon us, followed by another and another. The back patio was a sea of supernatural creatures hell-bent on getting their hands on me.

"Get her out of here, Marcus," Justin said, striking his blade through another Soul Scraper's torso and ripping it up through the creature.

A shriek erupted from its mouth, and then it disappeared into thin air. I wasn't sure if it was dead or if they even could be killed, but it had disappeared, and that's what was important.

"Take her." Marcus shoved me against Abby.

She grabbed my arm and yanked me toward the lounge room. As soon as we rounded the corner, she came to a halt. "Shit."

Abby pushed me behind her and drew her weapon out as her wings extended from her back, blocking my view of the creatures prowling through the house. "Marcus!"

A hellhound pounced on Abby as she drove her sword into the beast's chest. She slammed into me, pinning us both under the monstrous creature that was still very alive and determined to sink its teeth into my flesh.

Only Abby wasn't having a bar of it. She plunged another blade into the side of its neck then tore through the creature's throat as blackness surrounded us.

Black goo slithered its way over my face toward my mouth. I tried to fight it off, but it slipped through my fingers as if it were air. I was unable to grab hold of its matter.

Fear ripped through me as my body began to burn. A second later an unattached, decomposing head landed on my face, black tar splattering all over me as the heat became all-consuming.

Screaming, I batted the head off me and tried to sweep away the sludge covering my eyes. I needed to get out of there. I needed to get away.

I was powerless to do so.

I may not have been human, but my ability to remove other people's sicknesses was of no use in a fight. I was a sitting duck, completely reliant on other people to save me. And I didn't like it. I wanted to feel power. I wanted to be in control.

Suddenly, I was weightless, or more so, I didn't have a one-hundred-pound woman with a five-hundred-pound beast on top of her pinning me to the ground.

For a second, I thought it was a new ability of mine coming to surface, but I quickly realized it wasn't me. It was the woman standing before me, fire swirling under her skin as she ripped through the creatures descending on us like a torrential flood wreaking havoc on everything in its path.

What. The. Fuck?

It was Abby. The fire-laden woman was Abby in all her demon glory.

Marcus wrapped his hands under my arms and lifted me off the floor. "You're coming with me."

I didn't need to be told twice.

Gripping Marcus's hand as if my life depended on it—which it did—I followed him down the hallway.

Something grabbed hold of my ankle, tripping me as a wet, slimy substance snaked its way up my leg and disappeared under my shorts.

It barely reached my stomach before Marcus sliced the tendrils from my ankle, severing the sludge from the Soul Scraper coming after us.

The ceiling bowed, and a second later, Marcus shoved me out of the way as a five-hundred-pound monster fell through the roof.

"Go." Marcus sliced the blade through the chest region of the beast then grabbed me with his other hand and threw me through the hole the Hellhound had come from.

Landing on the roof, I screamed out in pain as something sliced through my waist. I twisted around to find Marcus leaping into the air, ripping his blade through the stomach of another Hellhound that was a second away from making me its dinner.

Marcus stood tall then stretched his arms up to the heavens, dark clouds swirling above where he stood.

Gripping my waist, I clambered to my feet and watched with a mixture of wonder and fear as his skin changed. His eyes lit up, turning from the molten lava into a brilliant light, as he threw his hands to the side, expelling a force of air that knocked the creatures from where they stood, sending them tumbling into each other as if they'd been hit by a cyclone. Yet, I was somehow still standing within the light that exuded from his skin, which appeared to be seconds away from exploding into a fiery, electrical mess.

Marcus lowered his head as his arms dropped to his sides. Then, he turned to me, his eyes glowing like the sun. "Let's go."

I nodded, unable to bring together a coherent sentence.

He wrapped his arms around me, pulling my chest against his. "Fly."

My eyes widened as I realized what he was saying. The man who hadn't flown since his wings had been severed was now asking me to take him up into the sky.

When it became apparent I had no idea how to get off the ground —or roof if we were being specific, he said, "I'll push. You flap."

Marcus leaped into the air, carrying me with him, careful not to touch my wound. My wings extended, and it was as if I'd been flying all my life. I flew up into the dark clouds with Marcus hanging onto me for dear life because I sure as hell couldn't hold his weight, yet my plasma wings were strong enough to carry us both through the sky.

"Where are we going?" I asked, trying to ignore the pain radiating down the left side of my body and the stinging of my eyes as the wind thrashed my face.

He stared at me, a mixture of sadness, wonder, and love consuming his eyes. "Can you keep going?"

Gritting my teeth, I nodded.

"Go straight."

A few minutes later, he shifted his hands up to my shoulders, pulling me closer to him. "Take us down there." He turned his head to the right and gestured to the base of a mountain covered in trees.

Crap! So much could go wrong with this landing.

CHAPTER 6

"*P*ull up, and glide down," Marcus instructed.

Yeah, that was easier said than done. I was probably going too fast and was going to add a few more cuts and bruises to my already battered body.

"Pull up," Marcus said again. "Come on. You can do this."

I'm glad he had faith in me because I sure as hell had none in myself. Taking a deep breath, I did as Marcus instructed and pulled up, hovering above the treetops. Now, I had to figure out how to get us through the branches and safely on the ground—without getting impaled.

"Slow it down." His soothing voice did little to calm my nerves.

It was now or never. Easing up, we descended through the canopy of the trees and landed not so gracefully amongst the shrubbery below.

Marcus was quick to give me the once-over. He stepped back, his gaze drifting over my body, stopping when he saw the blood oozing through my tank top. Carefully, he lifted my shirt, revealing four angry slices above my hip. They started a few inches behind my back and stretched over my hip, ending before the top of my shorts.

I winced as he tucked his fingers under the hem of my shorts and he undid the button—something I thought I could do by myself but Marcus wasn't having any part of it.

"We better get this cleaned up." He rolled the hem of my shorts over so they no longer rubbed against the wound. "Come on. We better get inside before they catch wind of us."

Tying a knot in the front of my tank so it sat just below my bra, away from the wound, I looked around. We were in the middle of nowhere. There was no "inside" for us to go.

As if sensing my confusion, Marcus said, "We have to get below the crystals. They'll help cover your signal from the witches."

"What about the demons and whoever else the witches are working with?" I asked as he led me through the trees, being careful to make way for my wings that wouldn't disappear no matter how much I tried. "It'll distort your signal for a while, and then we'll have to keep moving."

We stopped outside a dark cave dripping with water. Only, there wasn't any water source I could see.

"Through here." Marcus placed his hand on the small of my back and guided me into the cave.

"Now I know you can't see, but trust that I've got you and I won't let you fall or bump into anything, okay?"

"Of course I trust you."

Marcus threaded his fingers through my hair and pulled me in for a quick kiss. "I shouldn't have let it get that far." He entwined his fingers with mine and led me further into the cave, guiding me through the pitch-black tunnels within.

"You mean the whole glowing thing you've got going on?"

I knew he'd heard me, but he didn't answer right away. Eventually, he said, "Does that scare you?"

"Of course it doesn't scare me. We already know you're the light, but now it just makes a little more sense."

"How so?"

"Really?" I hugged his arm tightly, my wings magically disappearing into my back as my senses went into hyperawareness of the fact that I couldn't see a damn thing, and if Marcus disappeared I wouldn't be able to find my way out of the tunnels and caves this mountain contained. "You emit light from your eyes. Light dances beneath your skin. You are light."

"I also hold a darkness that... If I let go of my control, you'll think differently."

I pulled him back, stopping him from going any further. I wished

I could've seen his face because I was sure he was hurting. He had something inside of him he was afraid to let out, and somehow I was responsible for releasing that side of him. "You're forgetting I know the truth. I know you are the light and I'm just the key."

He wrapped his hand around the nape of my neck. "You are so much more than a key."

I choked on a laugh. "Yeah, I could also be a vessel to spawn your baby."

"I highly doubt that's what it is." Marcus continued to lead me through the darkness.

Eventually, we came to a stop. "This is far enough," he said.

"I don't suppose you have a light or something?"

"Unfortunately not." Marcus placed his hands on my hips and guided me down until my ass hit what I figured was a flat rock. "The only light I have comes from either the sword or from within me, and both will act as a beacon for my kind."

"Great."

"Now, I'm going to take another look at your wound, okay?"

I nodded.

Marcus's fingers grazed the surrounding area.

"How bad is it?"

He ran his hand down my thigh, stopping on my knee. "It's not good, but you'll survive."

"Geez, way to make me feel better."

"Do you want all warm and fuzzies or the truth?"

I sighed. "The truth."

"Now, I'm going to leave you here for a second while I gather some mud to cover the wound to stop any infections until we can get it cleaned properly."

"Mud?"

"Not mud as in dirt mixed with water. This one's made from the crystals surrounding us. It has protective properties," he said, his voice sounding farther away.

My heart rate picked up as silence enveloped me in its darkness. "Marcus?"

"Yeah."

"Please don't leave me." I didn't know where the fear was coming from, but I was scared. I didn't want to be alone, powerless against whatever creature decided to creep up on me. I wouldn't even know I was in danger until it was too late, and even then I wouldn't have a hope in hell of fighting something I couldn't see.

"I'm right here," he said, his voice still distant. "And I'm not going to leave you."

I bit my lip as I tried desperately to make out his outline—or anything surrounding me. But it was useless. I was as good as blind. And it terrified me.

A few moments later, Marcus was back. "This might sting a little."

"I'll be fine." I was used to pain. I'd inflicted it enough on myself over the years.

I sucked in a sharp breath as Marcus smeared a wet, gooey substance over the wound.

"You okay?" he asked, pausing for a moment.

"I'm good. Keep going."

Marcus finished covering the wound then said, "That should keep it clean until we can find somewhere safer."

"What do we do now?"

He eased himself down beside me and tucked me under his arm, my good side nestled against him. "Now we wait."

"For what?"

"Justin and Abby to find us." He kissed the top of my head. "You should get some rest."

I barked out a laugh. "Like you expect me to fall asleep after what I saw back there. I don't think I'm ever going to close my eyes again." I quickly added, "And before you go thinking I'm referring to you, you know damn well I'm talking about the Hellhounds and Soul Scrapers."

"I know." He kissed the top of my head again.

"And Abby's pretty scary, too."

He laughed. "She is a demon."

"Yeah, but I can't believe she has fire burning under her skin."

He ran the tips of his fingers over my forearm in a soothing motion. "Abby doesn't like to acknowledge what she is—the demon part, not the succubus. She's completely okay with being a succubus if you haven't already figured that one out."

"Oh, I figured it out."

"But she's unlike most of the others. Abby doesn't want to be that scary monster everyone fears. She's got a heart of gold, but when push comes to shove, and one of us is in danger, you better watch out because her claws will come out and she takes no prisoners."

He nudged his knee against mine. "Why do you think I trust her with you?"

"Because she'll go all demon girl on anyone who jeopardizes my safety."

He laughed. "She'll protect you as if her life depended on it."

I snaked my arm around his back and curled up against his side. "Thank you."

"For what?"

"For loving me."

"How could I not?"

Closing my eyes, I listened to the silence of the cave. If it weren't for Marcus's steady breaths, I would've gone insane, feeling trapped with my own senses. It reminded me too much of when Mava had drugged me, and I was powerless.

Nothing in the world could've prepared me for the sensation of losing the ability to control my own body. Sure, I could still hear everything that went on and feel every brush against my skin, but that wasn't an experience I ever wanted to go through again.

"So, do you think we're safe enough for me to enter the tunnel again?"

CHAPTER 7

I was met with deafening silence. "I'm going to take that as a yes, we are safe and yes, Lulu you can enter the tunnel so we can learn to save each other's asses."

"Ahh, no, Lulu, it is not safe. We are not safe."

I lifted my head off his shoulder and twisted around to look at him, which was pretty pointless because I couldn't see shit. "I thought you said this mountain would protect us."

"Yeah, but not for too long. We're going to have to leave shortly after Abby and Justin get here."

As much as I wanted to fight him on it, my side was hurting badly and I needed to rest, so I gave him this one, prepared to bring it up again the next time we had some safety. I leaned my head against his shoulder again. "Then where will we go?"

He breathed out harshly. "I have no idea. I've never had to hide you somewhere other than my house."

"Don't suppose you have another witch you can summon to put another protective barrier around your place, do you?"

He chuckled. "Nope. I'm all out of them."

I bit my lip as I thought about how I was going to get back to the tunnel safely. Marcus didn't even know where we were going after we left this place. For all I knew, nowhere would be safe. He would get his wish, and I'd never get back to the tunnel.

Marcus tapped my lip. "Don't do that."

"God, you're a freak being able to see in the dark."

"I thought you wanted that gift for yourself."

"I never said being a freak is bad, especially when you get all these cool abilities. God, if my mother could only see me now with my wings and all." I barked out a laugh. "She thought I was a freak before. Imagine what she'd say if she saw plasma wings protruding from my back."

"Abby mentioned your mom tried calling you while I was gone."

"Yep, probably to bitch at me and make sure I don't make any problems for them." I laughed again. "She'd definitely have me locked away in a mental hospital if I told her my truth."

"It is the truth."

"Not to her it wouldn't be—unless she had the pleasure of meeting a Soul Scraper or one of those Hellhounds."

"Except she wouldn't be able to see them."

"When she dies she would."

"That won't be for a while."

"Do you know when everyone's life is up? Like, do you see a clock ticking above everyone's head, counting down the hours or however long they have left?"

He chuckled. "There's no clock ticking down how much time someone has remaining. But I can see how much life force someone has left. Fate will take a person when it's their time. If it's not one way, it'll be another."

"What does mine say?"

"You've never had one."

I furrowed my brow. "I have no life force?"

"Nope."

I knew I was different, but I expected to have an indicator of some sort saying I was alive. "Is that normal?"

"When is anything about you normal?"

"Point taken," I said. "What about you guys?"

"We have energy." When I looked at him blankly, he added, "We can feel someone's energy, and each species has its own unique markings. That's how we know who or what is coming."

"Except you didn't get much warning back at your house."

"It's your house, too."

"Actually, I don't think it's anyone's house now that those monsters have taken control of it."

"We'll get control back again."

I snorted out a laugh. "Yeah, only if we manage to rescue Mava and Astrid before the bitch kills them or strips their powers or any other psychotic idea she may have to screw with their lives. Which is why I need to get back to the tunnel."

"I told you it's not safe yet."

"Do you even know where Morgana has them?"

"I have an idea."

"Which is code for 'I have absolutely no friggin' idea,' isn't it?"

"You have such little faith in me."

I shut my mouth. He was right. I didn't have faith that he'd be able to make everything all right because he still lived in fear of making sure I was okay. "What would you be doing right now if I wasn't here?"

"Why do you ask?"

"Just answer me."

"I'd probably be sitting at home, with a bottle in my hand, waiting for time to hurry up so you can come back to me."

I raised a brow. "I meant if it was me they had captured."

He didn't answer me.

"You'd be wherever you think Morgana was holding me, wouldn't you?"

"But she doesn't have you. You and I both know Mava and Astrid would be pissed if they found out I was planning to allow you to go after them."

The corner of my lips tipped up. "Are you saying you're still planning on a rescue mission?"

"I'm saying that nothing has changed. We need them, and I know you need to get back to your guardians. It's the timing that we need to work out."

I breathed a sigh of relief. "And here I was working out how I was going to get back to the tunnel while you thought I was sleeping."

He stilled beside me. "Don't you dare go back without me knowing first, okay?"

I scratched my head. "That's the plan."

"What? That you're going to sneak your way back into the tunnel? Or you're going to wait until I say it's safe to do so?"

God, he knew me too well. "I'm going to be a good girl and wait until you give me the A-OK." I saluted him.

He chuckled.

Guilt flooded me as I nestled back into his side. I wanted to keep my word to him, but I wasn't sure it was the right decision. Every second we waited was giving Morgana and her accomplice another second to get stronger, to discover our secrets and destroy our chances of being free.

Freedom was something I craved. And I knew Marcus was unable to make the hard decisions that needed to be made.

Our fate was trapped somewhere deep inside of me, and it was up to me to set it free.

He was going to kill me for what I had planned—if I survived long enough to make it back to him.

CHAPTER 8

*T*ilting my head to the left, I stretched out the cramps in my neck. I'd planned on entering the tunnel, but I quickly realized I had no idea how to get back. I didn't have a bucket full of crystals or sticks of sage to blow smoke around the cave, and the crystals that surrounded us were of no help.

Every time I closed my eyes, my mind raced with the events that led us to being stuck in a hole in the middle of a mountain.

"Shouldn't Abby and Justin be here by now?" I asked Marcus.

He adjusted himself beside me, his arm remaining over my shoulders, avoiding the gashes above my hip. "They'll be fine."

"That's not what I asked."

"Okay. Yes, they should've been here by now if they were only dealing with the lot we saw when we left, but if more came, it would take them longer to get away."

"But they've both got wings. Can't they fly away?"

"Technically yes. However, they can't leave without clearing out a few things first. So, they're stuck there until they're the only ones left standing."

"Right." I needed to stretch my legs. Go for a walk. Do something —anything other than sitting there waiting, completely at the mercy of Morgana and her crew.

Trying to get to my feet, I stumbled back.

Marcus caught me in his arms and lowered me onto his lap. "You okay?"

I breathed out harshly. "No." And that was the truth. The pain from the gashes was screaming, and I felt at a total loss. "I can't keep sitting here doing nothing."

"Sometimes doing nothing is the right thing to do. We need to bide our time and make sure we look at this from a tactical point of view rather than storming in and winding up dead or getting Mava or Astrid killed.

"We have a better chance at rescuing them if we have Abby and Justin by our sides."

My shoulders slumped. "Wouldn't it be ironic if we found out I have the ability to protect myself and we didn't have to waste all this time?"

"Ironic but necessary."

There was no getting through to him when it came to him thinking I was risking my life. Then again, I would've been the same if the situation were reversed.

I slumped back against him. "Patience is a virtue I don't have."

He folded his arms around me then kissed my cheek. "You need to get some rest. I'll keep a lookout."

I nodded. Closing my eyes, I tried to ignore the thoughts running through my head. As positive as Marcus was that Abby and Justin were okay, I had doubts. Add Mava and Astrid to the equation, and I couldn't help but fear Morgana was doing something horrendous to them. I mean, she must've done something to convince Astrid to break the spell around Marcus's estate, or she gave Astrid no choice. It was the only way those hellish creatures would've gotten in. I hoped Morgana hadn't killed Astrid in the process.

My thoughts kept me awake for what felt like hours before I drifted off for a second before jerking awake again. Only I was alone, smothered by the darkness, unable to hear a sound.

"Marcus?" My voice echoing around me went unanswered.

Panic reared its ugly head as I rose to my feet. "Marcus?"

Again, he didn't answer.

A deep growl I was all too familiar with echoed off the walls of the cave, sending chills down my spine.

Hellhounds.

CHAPTER 9

*T*hey'd found me, and Marcus was gone.

I stumbled backward, hitting the rock I'd been sitting on, and fell, smacking my back against the jagged crystal wall behind me.

My back felt as if it were on fire as I clambered to my feet. I wanted to scream out for Marcus to save me, but that would've only given away my location.

I was trapped deep inside the walls of the mountain, unable to see anything, and I prayed the Hellhounds wouldn't find me before Marcus came back.

I shook my head. Something wasn't right. Marcus wouldn't leave me. After everything we'd been through and how protective he was of me, there would be nothing on Earth that would make him leave me alone.

But maybe it wasn't something on Earth. For all I knew, the one Morgana was working with had taken him when I nodded off, and Marcus was powerless to stop them.

A million things went through my mind as I tried to figure out if what I was experiencing was reality or a dream. I was pretty sure you couldn't feel pain in a dream, and my back and side were screaming with every move I made.

The low, rumbling growls continued getting closer, as if they knew exactly where I was. I needed to move.

I needed a weapon.

Kneeling down, I swiped my hands across the ground, hoping against hope that Marcus had left a weapon for me before he'd disappeared. The chances were slim, and I was holding onto a sliver of hope that was quickly slipping through my fingers.

I scrambled on all fours across the ground, trying to figure out where I had been sitting when I'd woken up. The darkness was terrifying. I had no idea what this cave was like. I didn't even know what type of crystals it contained.

All I knew was they had hurt like hell when I fell against them, cutting deep into my shoulder.

Cut deep.

Still on my knees, I scooted over to where I thought the wall was, but it seemed further away than I remembered. There was nothing there.

Beads of sweat dripped down my forehead. My hands were clammy, and the dirt was sticking to my hands like mud. Only it was thicker, more like goo.

My eyes widened as I realized where I'd felt the substance before.

Jumping to my feet, I darted back the way I'd come, hands in front of me, praying I wasn't going to run off a cliff, or into a wall, or worse, into the Soul Scrapers I was trying to avoid.

Before I could get two yards, I was struck from behind, pinning me face-first to the ground by a force strong enough to be only one thing: a Hellhound.

A deep growl erupted from beside my ear as something wet dripped onto my cheek.

I tried desperately to get free, but the beast's giant paws kept holding me down. The stench of its breath reminded me of the death that followed them everywhere they went.

An ear-piercing scream erupted from my throat as the creature sunk it's claws into my back, but my voice was quickly cut off when sludge slithered into my mouth, forcing its way down my throat and blocking any sound I tried to make.

Absolute fear engulfed me as the slime continued down, filling my lungs and taking control of the inside of my body, taking what it wanted. It was taking my soul.

The slick tar spread across my face and made its way into my ears, taking away my ability to hear. I was completely powerless.

I couldn't be powerless.

I was created for a purpose, and I wasn't going to go down without a fight. I needed to survive. I needed to see. I needed the sight like the monsters that had hunted me down.

My eyes began to burn as if they'd been set on fire, bringing with it light. Light amongst the darkness in which I was entombed.

Not believing what I was seeing, I blinked hard, expecting to be returned to darkness. I wasn't. I could see.

It was a sight unlike what I was normally used to. This was different. It was almost as if I were seeing infrared but with more clarity.

My eyes stung, and I expected them to spontaneously combust under the pressure.

But I could see.

I could see where I was and what had been within my reach all this time.

In one swift movement, I grabbed a long crystal shard off the ground, twisted around as best I could, and drove it into the beast's neck with the last bit of strength I had.

I screamed internally as my shoulder dislocated under the force, then screamed again as the Hellhound collapsed onto my back, searing every inch of my skin that came in contact with the beast.

My lungs ached as I desperately tried to breathe under the creature's weight. It must've weighed at least five hundred pounds.

Tilting my head back, I looked up at the Soul Scraper lurking over me, its slick tendrils billowing from its mouth into mine, sucking the life out of me.

I couldn't let it win. No matter how much it hurt, I had to keep fighting.

With my good arm, I yanked the thick crystal shard out of the Hellhound's neck and plunged it into the Soul Scraper.

It didn't work.

The crystal went through the creature as if it were made of fog. I struck again and again and again. But nothing happened.

The Soul Scraper could morph, allowing the weapon to pass through it.

I was screwed.

The Soul Scraper tilted its head to the side, its empty eye sockets watching me, mocking my futile efforts to save myself.

Tears slipped from my eyes as I realized I was going to die by a force I was unable to fight.

Will. All I had was my will.

I couldn't give up.

I needed to think.

Thinking was impossible when fear gripped my soul, starving my brain of any ideas.

I squeezed my eyes shut, trying to free the part of my mind that held the answers we sought. There was something about me. Something they were willing to kill for. Something that could free Marcus and allow him to become who he was meant to be.

I needed to free that part of me. And I needed to do it quickly. The sludge was choking me, the beast was crushing me, and I needed to get free. I needed more time. I needed to stop the Soul Scraper from sucking the life out of me. I needed to end its life. Suck the life out of it. Then maybe I could fight. Maybe I'd stand a chance.

I coughed, my reflexes convulsing my body as the tar began to move, slithering its way out of me. I was done.

Death was on my doorstep, and I had been too powerless to stop it.

With a heavy heart, I waited for my pain to end, taking me into the afterlife.

It didn't happen.

Tar spewed from my mouth, latching onto the Soul Scraper, engulfing and burning the creature until it was nothing but ashes slowly drifting to the ground, no longer a threat.

I was free—almost. There was still a Hellhound pinning me to the ground.

I'd barely processed that thought when the Earth began to rumble, and then water poured from the walls. I sucked in a lungful of air as the water lapped at my lips, quickly filling the cave and turning the ground to mud.

I was out of air, pinned to the ground by the lifeless Hellhound on top of me.

It was kind of ironic that I'd somehow managed to survive the Hellhound and the Soul Scraper only to drown in a pool of water that magically sprouted from the walls of a mountain that was definitely not below sea level.

Magic. Someone was playing with me, tormenting my soul, hell-bent on stopping my destiny.

Just as I was about to suck in a breath of water, the ground swallowed me into its depths, leaving behind the heavy weight of the dead monster, then dropped me into another cavern in the mountain.

My blood went cold when I saw the smirk on the face of what looked like an angel, because I knew better. I knew who she was.

Morgana.

CHAPTER 10

*A*drenalin pumped through my body as I stared at the woman responsible for everything that was wrong in my life.

A wicked laugh resounded off the walls of the cave as she strode toward me, her feet never once touching the ground. "All this hope you have contained in your little heart seems to be in vain, does it not?"

I rolled onto my back then scrambled backward, trying to get as much distance as I could between her and me.

"Because it is going to end the same. It's always the same. You might have thought for a few brief moments that this time is different. But let me tell you about time. I've got all the time in the world, and nothing brings me as great a pleasure as seeing you squirm beneath my power, thinking you've got a chance, when in reality, I could squash you like a fly."

"You can't kill me," I said, my voice coming out pathetic and wimpy—powerless.

"I may not be able to end your never-ending existence, but believe me when I say I can end you. I've done it on more than one occasion."

My back hit the wall behind me. "Why are you doing this to me?"

She cackled—actually cackled. "Isn't it obvious?"

"No, that's why I'm asking."

Rage lit up her eyes as she glared at me, rendering me frozen to the wall behind me.

I feared her.

More than I ever wanted to admit.

"You will never be. You will never remember. And you most certainly will never believe."

I wanted to know what I was supposed to believe, but I couldn't open my mouth. Every single time I'd imagined the moment I came face-to-face with her, I saw myself as the person who was able to destroy her. And now that I was in her presence, I was terrified. She was the power. I was only the key. And Marcus was the light. Marcus.

"Wh-where's... Marcus?"

"Wh-wh-wh-where's... where's M-m-m-m-marcus?" she stuttered mockingly.

Morgana threw her head back and cackled again. Her beauty was destroyed by the darkness in her heart and soul. She was pure and unadulterated evil.

Snapping her head forward, she whipped her hand out in front of her, and an invisible hand clenched its fingers around my neck, lifting me off the ground, suspending me in midair.

I gasped for air as her grip tightened around my neck.

Morgana strode forward, stopping inches in front of me. "Light will become dark, returning to the earth where it once stood. Time will—"

Her eyes went wide, her mouth opening in a contorted gasp. She collapsed to the ground, releasing her invisible hold on me.

My heart soared with relief when I saw Marcus standing behind her, the glowing blade in his hand, covered in her thick red blood.

I collapsed into his arms and sobs rippled through me. The light from the sword was playing tricks on my eyes as I stared at the changing color of my fist gripping his shirt.

Panic soared through me, and I struggled to draw in a breath, then another, and another until I was gasping for air.

I tried to thump my fist against Marcus's chest, but my hand began to slowly crumble into dust on impact.

I stepped back and stared at my hand. It was literally falling apart.

"What's wrong?" Marcus's panicked voice rang through my head.

He gripped the top of my shoulders and shook me. "No," he whispered in despair, his gaze fixated on his right hand.

I followed his line of sight, and the little air I had left expelled from my lungs as I saw the dust in his hands and the charred part of my body that was once attached to my shoulder.

Collapsing to the ground, I desperately tried to make sense of what was going on. I was disappearing. Morgana had won.

Marcus fell to his knees beside me. He went to touch me but pulled away, his amber eyes glistening under the light from the sword that was long forgotten on the ground. "What did she do to you?"

I reached out and touched his arm with the stump of my wrist. I needed Marcus. I needed him to save me. After everything that had happened, this could not be the way it ended. I could not go like this. I could not leave him.

I yanked my arm back when Marcus's own hand and arm started turning black. It was as if my curse was transferring to him.

His eyes lit up with realisation, and then he wrapped his hand around the stump of my wrist. "Not you," he said, shaking his head. "Not you."

I watched in horror as the darkness swirling under my skin crawled up my arm, somehow jumped over to his hand, and traveled up his arm, charring everything it touched. His hand began to crumble as the last of the darkness left my body.

"No." I tried to grab his forearm, but he swatted me away and stumbled back.

"Not you," he said, his voice coming out in short, breathless bursts.

"No," I cried as his face began to crumble. He couldn't die. I would be reborn. He wouldn't. And even if this was the end of him and me, I was not going to let him die. I was his key, and there was nothing on Earth that was going to stop me from saving him.

I was created to save him, and that was exactly what I was going to do. But I had no idea how. I was clueless, and I was running out of time.

With determination running through my heart, I crawled across the ground, trying desperately to get to him, but I only had one hand and shoulder that weren't crumbling away.

My eyes widened as I realized my body was repairing itself. And if it were repairing, then so would Marcus. All I needed to do was take back Morgana's spell. But I wasn't healing quickly enough. I needed time that I didn't have.

Every inch I moved closer to him, Marcus moved away. He was determined to die for me—save me.

Collapsing, I screamed at him to stop and willed myself to heal him without touching him.

"No," he murmured. "No, no, no," he said, his voice becoming clearer with each word he spoke.

Relief flooded my soul when I realized I'd done it.

I'd saved him.

Marcus darted over to me, his body healing faster than I ever thought possible.

He wrapped his hand around my arm. "No." Pure fear ravaged his soul as he realized my curse wasn't transferring to him. I was keeping it to myself.

"Let me take it," he begged, lying down beside me, his face inches from mine. "Please let me be the one."

"It's always been me," I whispered.

Tears spilled from his eyes as he watched me disappear.

I'd failed Marcus. Yet, somehow I felt as if I'd done what I was meant to do—save him.

"I love you," I tried to whisper, but all that came out was a puff of air.

"I love you, too."

It was the last thing I heard before my world became no more.

CHAPTER 11

I was dead. Only I wasn't. As I opened my eyes, a sense of peace washed over me. Tears slipped down my cheeks as I ran my finger across the snapdragon petals surrounding me.

I'd made it.

Everything that had happened suddenly made sense. I hadn't slain a Hellhound, spewed tar from my mouth, or almost drowned. Morgana wasn't dead. I wasn't dead. And most importantly, Marcus wasn't mourning my death because everything that had happened in the tunnel was all in my head.

Getting to my feet, I smiled as I saw my guardian waiting for me in the distance.

Somehow I'd slipped into the tunnel when I'd fallen asleep. I prayed Marcus thought I was resting. Otherwise, he would've been going out of his mind in fear, afraid that I didn't make it through to my guardians.

I did. And I was moments from speaking with the angelic beings that could help me understand, and time wasn't on my side. Breaking into a jog, I quickly made my way to Alissya.

"You've returned." Her warm smile lit up my soul.

I nodded. "I don't know how I got back into the tunnel, but I'm glad I did."

"The tunnel isn't only accessible through witchcraft. You have the

402

ability to enter when you're at rest." She turned her back to me. "Come, Luciana. We have much to discuss."

I followed her to the same set of logs placed in the shape of a square that we'd sat on during my last visit. "Where are the others?"

"They do not need to be here this time. Unfortunately, your creator is of no further use to you. He does not know why you are here, or what your purpose is. So, he has chosen to stay away this time, so we don't get distracted. We don't want what happened last time to happen again."

I furrowed my brow.

She smiled that same smile she'd had the last time I was there. "You were taken back before I was able to open your mind."

I narrowed my eyes at her.

"Come. Sit." She gestured to the log.

Doing as asked, I returned to the same spot I'd sat on the last time I was here.

Alissya sat beside me. "If you remember, I attempted to open your third eye as you were leaving us."

I remembered her touching my forehead and thinking it was strange. It was the same thing Astrid had done to me before she'd collapsed in her shop. "Is that what you were trying to do? Mava and Astrid already tried to open it and said I mustn't have one."

"Oh, believe me, you have one. It's just not that easy to open."

"Right." I frowned. "And what exactly is a third eye?"

"It is your awareness. The part of you Morgana had bound all those years ago. We do not know what your purpose is, but we do know the information you seek is buried deep inside of you. Who you are has always been there." She pointed to my forehead. "What we need to do is unlock that part of you. Free you from the limitations Morgana has cast on you."

"Will I know who she's working with?"

"That I do not know. I am here to merely guide you, help you find your way."

"See, that doesn't really make sense."

"Why is that, my dear?"

"Because Marcus said his kind doesn't have guardians. And you've said I'm not human, yet I have you and a third eye."

She smiled again as if I were missing the obvious. "You are not of his kind. And although you are not human, you have been created with human qualities. You were created to be human-like, and you are the first of your kind."

"Okay," I said, not really understanding. I could've probably sat there for hours trying to figure out why I was the way I was, when in reality it made no difference. I needed to concentrate on my purpose —what I was created to do.

I ran my hands down my thighs, realizing I no longer had any aches or pains. Not even my side hurt from where the Hellhound had ripped its claws into me. But none of that was important. All the wondering only delayed finding out what my true purpose in life was. "So, how do we do this?"

"First, you need to figure out what you've learned in the tunnel."

I frowned as I recalled what had happened since waking in the tunnel. "I almost got ripped apart by a Hellhound, had my soul sucked out by a Soul Scraper, almost drowned, and was nearly killed by Morgana, but Marcus saved me just in time, only to watch me disintegrate right before his eyes." I closed my eyes as images of him disintegrating flooded my mind. He'd come so close to dying, only for me to take it back. "I took it back…"

"You took what back, Luciana?"

I stared at my hands, which were one hundred percent in tact. "Marcus was dying. I almost killed him when he somehow took it from me, but then I took it back." I jerked my head up to face Alissya. I knew there was a lesson to learn, and it was a big one. Maybe even *the* one.

"Go on," she encouraged. "How did you make it through the other test?"

Staring off into nothingness, my thoughts went over what happened with the Hellhound and the Soul Scraper. "One minute I couldn't see, and the next I could. That was how I survived. Somehow I was able to see, which allowed me to find that long shard of crystal and kill the Hellhound."

"Keep going."

"The next thing that happened was with the Soul Scraper. It had me. I was pinned under the Hellhound, unable to get away. Then for some reason, the tar that the Soul Scraper put inside of me flew out of my mouth and back at it, smothering it until it was no more."

I looked up at Alissya, hoping she'd worked out what I hadn't.

She raised a brow. "I think you already know the answer you seek."

Butterflies were swarming inside my stomach as so many ideas came to mind. The one sticking out the most was the one that scared me. It wasn't because I was afraid of the ability. I was afraid of what it would mean. And most of all, I was afraid for what was to come, because if I was correct, I held a power like no other—an ability Morgana should fear. And, what exactly was Marcus if I was merely the key?

"You know what you are," Alissya said.

My chest restricted with a mixture of fear and happiness. "I've got the ability to take and give, don't I?"

She smiled. "That you do, my dear."

Tears pooled in my eyes, blurring my vision as I finally let myself appreciate what this meant. I no longer had to fear. I was in control. I was the one to be feared.

"You are ready, Luciana. You are ready to know the truth."

Alissya placed her finger on my forehead and closed her eyes. "Sever the ties that bound her soul. Open her eyes to the truth. Let light overcome the darkness, and bring forth her ability to see."

CHAPTER 12

*P*ain soared through my head as a white light stole my vision, pulling me into the depths of the unknown—my unknown.

When my vision cleared I was in a different time. A time I'd forgotten. A memory that had been stolen.

I was walking along the side of a dirt road, my bare feet hurting from the stones. I didn't know where I was going, but I knew I had to find Marcus and return to him what was stolen.

Until moments before, I didn't exist. That was a lie. I did exist, but I wasn't aware. I had grown up thinking I was the same as everyone else. Except, I was different. I wasn't a ward of the state as I'd thought. I was born from the magic of an angelic being taking from himself and giving life to me.

I had a picture in my mind of the one I sought. Tall, dark, handsome. He was the makings of a fairytale. Only, my story wouldn't end happily ever after. I wasn't created for that.

A part of me was from another. I held a light inside my soul that wasn't mine to keep. I was merely a vessel with a mission to return what I'd been entrusted to protect.

I was the key, and he was my destiny.

My heart fluttered when I felt him nearby. He'd found me as I knew he would, but I'd feared others would've intervened before I could return to him what had been stolen.

Taking a deep breath, I turned around, prepared to take my last steps when I saw him—really saw him.

All air was expelled from my lungs as I looked at the entity before me, who had no idea who he was. He'd been stripped of his powers, severed from his true place in this world.

Marcus.

My lips parted, and I drew in a sharp breath. Nothing could've prepared me for this moment. I knew what I had to do, yet I was drawn to him in ways I shouldn't have been.

Marcus strode toward me, a look of wonder in his eyes. He stopped barely an inch from where I stood and let out a shuddered breath.

Slowly, he turned his head to the side and focused on the rocky mountain beside us. Returning his gaze to me, his eyes dilated, and his breathing became uneven as a low rumble emitted through the air and the ground began to shake.

Fear gripped my heart as I looked up and saw the first of the rocks break away from the mountain, followed by another and another. It was a landslide, and we were caught in its path.

Marcus protectively wrapped his arm around me and turned back to the mountain, holding his other hand out toward it.

Seconds later, a force of air expelled from his hand, flying toward the rocks, stopping them in their tracks as if they were cemented to the very spot where they stood.

My vision swayed, changing to another moment in time. One that I'd already remembered. I was walking side by side with the woman who'd promised me the world.

Hope of a happily ever after filled my heart as I listened to her tell me there was a way to have it all. "So, I can still fulfill my destiny and live to see another day?" I'd asked her.

Morgana's kind smile shone through her eyes. "That is exactly what I am saying." She turned to me and held my hands between hers. "You, my dear Luciana, will have your happily ever after with Marcus. You will never grow old. You will forever, have the life you seek with the man you love."

"But what about—?"

"Yes, my dear, you will still fulfill your purpose and Marcus will return to his rightful place with you standing there beside him while he cleans up this world and others."

I smiled, sheer joy overtaking my soul as I entrusted myself to Morgana. It had been three weeks since the day I'd laid eyes on Marcus. I'd come clean to him about who I was and what my true purpose had been, and like the man he was, Marcus didn't want any part of it. He couldn't live to fight for a world that could be so cruel. A world where his perfect other had been created just to die.

Even supreme entities had their selfish ways. And Marcus was like any other.

I couldn't let him throw away everything he was destined for. If there was a way to sever Marcus's light from me without ending my life in the process, then I was going to take that chance.

I would not allow myself to become the woman that, in time, would destroy the world.

And I was ashamed of myself for not giving his light to him the moment we first met. If I hadn't wanted a few moments in time with him, he would never have fallen in love with me. It was a mistake I would forever regret.

His rightful place was much bigger than our love, and I knew deep down there was a massive probability it wasn't me he was drawn to. It was his light buried deep inside my soul.

My hands slipped free from hers as Morgana raised her finger and placed it on my forehead. I closed my eyes, overjoyed with the possibilities that awaited me. I was going to be free. We were going to be free.

I snapped my eyes open. My feet were no longer touching the ground as I was lifted into the air by an invisible force that was choking me.

Gasping for air, I watched in horror as the kind smile she'd worn turned into an evil smirk. "Forget."

She snapped her head back and let out a wicked laugh to match her smile and the gleam in her eyes. Morgana was wicked in every sense of the word. She was pure, unadulterated evil.

She let go of her hold on me, and I collapsed to the ground among the autumn leaves.

I tried to get to my feet, but it was useless. My head ached, and I had no idea why. I tried to remember what she had done to me—or why I was even with her to begin with.

I remembered nothing.

Fear surged through my soul as I watched her turn her back to me and walk away.

CHAPTER 13

Snapping back to reality, I tried to slow my breathing.

"Tell me what you saw," Alissya said, her eyes filled with hope.

"I remember everything."

She closed her eyes as a smile broke across her angelic face. Opening her eyes, she said, "You're ready to go back."

"Hang on." I grabbed her arm. "Don't you want to know?"

"If you wish to tell."

"Oh, I wish to tell. Because who knows what Morgana will do to me if she finds out I know. And I don't want to waste the next four hundred years trying to figure it out again if she makes me forget."

"Okay, then what is it you remember?"

My shoulders slumped as I thought about what I'd seen. The truth was, I still didn't know what Marcus was truly destined for, but I knew a few new truths. "As you already know, I was created for Marcus. But what you don't know is that I hold Marcus's light, which was stolen from him. I have the ability to take and give, and now it's time to return to him what was stolen."

She smiled again. "You're ready."

I breathed in deeply. "To complete what I was created to do."

Alissya placed her hand on my forehead. "You are free."

I sucked in a sharp breath as I jerked my head forward, awakening from my sleep.

"What's wrong?" Marcus asked, fully alert, ready to fight if needed.

I sucked in another sharp breath as I twisted around to face him, but I could no longer see in the dark. The side of my body stung from where the Hellhound had ripped its claws into me, but that wasn't going to stop me. I was pumped. "I remember."

He furrowed his brow. "Remember what?"

"Everything."

There were a few minutes of silence before he said, "What exactly does that mean?" He spoke each word slowly and precisely as if he didn't want to get his hopes up only to be disappointed as to what "everything" meant.

I bit my lip as I tried to get my thoughts together enough to say something coherent. "Before you get upset, I want you to know I had no idea what I was doing. I had absolutely no intentions of going back to the tunnel and—"

"You went back to the tunnel?"

"Calm down," I said, trying to find his hand in the dark. I hated being in the dark, unable to see what was around. "Hmm."

"What?"

"I think I know how to change this," I said under my breath.

Taking a deep breath, I thought about how much I wanted to see the way Marcus could.

A smile spread across my face as light flooded my senses.

Marcus's muscles tensed, and his hand tightened around mine. He quickly stood, bringing me up with him, and then pushed me behind him.

"What are you doing?" I asked.

He turned his head to the left and whispered over his shoulder, "Shhh. Someone's here, and I can't feel who it is."

I frowned as I looked around the cave. "I can't see anyone," I said, my voice low enough for only Marcus to hear.

"You can't see at all—and neither can I. So, I need you to stay behind me and trust that I'll get us out of here."

I dragged in a shuddered breath as I realized what I'd done. "I'm so sorry. I had no idea—"

"Shhh."

Leaning forward, I buried my face against his back and breathed in deeply. In trying to obtain my own sight, I had stripped Marcus of his.

I'd never given back except for those times in the tunnel, which weren't exactly real, but I knew I couldn't keep his sight for my own. I had to try.

Not knowing exactly how it worked, I closed my eyes and willed myself the lack of sight so I could give back to Marcus what I had taken.

I opened my eyes, unable to see as Marcus's muscles relaxed under my touch. I knew I had succeeded. "You can see again, can't you?"

"Yeah," he replied. "I'm not sure what's going on, but we need to leave—now."

I grabbed Marcus's hand and pulled him back. "I took your sight. It wasn't one of the witches or any of your kind. That's what I'm trying to tell you. I know who I am. I know what I am."

"This doesn't make any sense."

"Maybe we should sit down for this." I then added under my breath, "Not that I know where I can sit now that I've given you back your sight."

"You did this to me?"

I nodded. "That's what I'm trying to tell you. I know who I am and what I'm capable of. And being able to take away your sight is only the beginning. I know what I was created to do."

Marcus swept my hair away from my face. "What happened?"

"I need to start from the beginning." I bit my lip as a sharp pain tore up the side of my body.

"You're hurting."

I nodded. "But it doesn't matter. After I tell you what happened, you'll understand what I must do."

I let out a shuddered breath as I stared in his direction, wishing I could see his face again. I hated myself for being so selfish because it didn't matter if I could see him. All I needed to do was give him back what was rightfully his to begin with.

"Abby was right. I'm just a vessel."

CHAPTER 14

*M*arcus curled his hands around my hips. "Don't ever say that."

"I know it's the truth because I remember." Tears slipped from my eyes as I came to terms with the fact that this might be the last few moments I had with him before I fulfilled my destiny.

"Don't cry." He wiped my tears away with his thumb then caressed the side of my face. "Something tells me I'm not going to like what I'm about to hear."

I leaned into the palm of his hand. "I need to tell you the truth."

"You look pale. I think you should sit down."

I wasn't sure if I was pale from loss of blood, an infection from the beast's claws, or if it was because I didn't want to say goodbye. I'd thought we'd have our forever, but that was a lie.

Except it wasn't.

Morgana had given us our forever like she'd promised. Yeah, a forever filled with pain and suffering, giving her time to keep Marcus's true identity bound.

Marcus guided me a couple of steps backward. "There's a rock you can sit on just behind you."

Carefully, I lowered myself down until I felt the rock beneath me. I sighed with relief as the pain shooting up my side began to subside.

Marcus shuffled, the sound of his breathing making me think he was either sitting or kneeling before me. "What happened?"

I swallowed hard, but it did nothing to alleviate the dryness choking me. Saliva didn't alleviate fear. And that was the truth. I was scared of letting go—of saying goodbye. But it was my destiny, and I had to fulfill it. "Okay, it all started when I thought I'd gone to sleep. I jerked awake and found myself sitting here in the cave all alone. You were gone. You didn't answer when I called out to you. Then this Hellhound came after me, and a Soul Scraper was there..." I trailed off as my voice broke. I couldn't do this, but I had no choice. I had to keep going.

I drew in another deep breath and let it out slowly, trying to calm my nerves. It didn't work.

Tears pooled in my eyes as I stared in his direction, trying to make out his outline, his eyes, his mouth—anything that was him. I needed him.

"This isn't going to work," I said. "I just need to tell you who I am and what I'm supposed to do."

"That's okay. Take your time."

I nodded. "I was created as the vessel to hold the light that was stolen from you. I have the ability to take and give. And that's what happened before with your sight. I couldn't see, so I took it from you. But I didn't realize taking from you meant that you could no longer have what was rightfully yours."

Marcus grabbed my hands and held them in my lap. "You need to tell me what's going on. Whatever it is, we can get through it together."

Tears spilled from my eyes. "See, that's the thing. We can't get through this together. It's not the way it's meant to be."

"What are you talking about?"

"I was created to give back what was stolen from you, and once I fulfill my purpose, that's it. There is no more me."

Marcus wrapped his arms around me, burying my head in the crook of his neck. "Then we've got nothing to worry about."

I blinked hard, trying to clear the tears from my eyes. "How can you say that?"

"Easily. You won't give me back whatever was taken, and our lives go on."

I pulled back, a few tears escaping my eyes. "No. I have to do it. I have to give it back."

"No, you don't. If giving back whatever was stolen from me means that I lose you, I don't want it. You hear me? I. Don't. Want. It."

He wiped the tears away from my cheeks then cupped my face in his hands. "You need to listen to me. We're going to find another way. And if we can't, then it isn't going to matter because I am not giving you up. I will never give you up, you hear me? I am never giving you up." He kissed me. "We're going to find Mava and Astrid, kill Morgana, and destroy whoever is behind her. We are not going to let them win. And I am most certainly not losing you."

Marcus drew me into a deep, searing kiss that was filled with promises words couldn't possibly describe. And it was breaking me. I knew what I had to do, but how was I supposed to give him something he didn't want.

"How can you do this?"

"Easy." He ran his thumb across my lips. "I don't want anything that will destroy you. It's as simple as that." He cupped the back of my neck with his hand and leaned his forehead against mine. "And you better not get any ideas about giving it back without me knowing, because that will break me. That will fucking break me."

I didn't have to see to know how serious he was. I could hear it in his voice and feel it in his soul.

"Promise me," he said. "Promise me you'll never give it to me. You'll never put yourself in danger."

I wiped the tears from my eyes. "I promise."

"I'm serious, Lulu. I can't lose you."

"I know." I folded my arms around his neck. "I promise I'll never betray you. You've got me, and you always will."

I leaned forward, praying I was going to find his lips and not end up kissing his eye or nose.

Thanking the Lord or whoever else was responsible for my luck, I was met with a tender kiss that quickly built with a mixture of passion and desperation as our truths collided into something ugly that was destined to tear us apart. I knew it then, and I knew it now. There would come a point where I would be stripped of the naivety we both wanted to succumb to, and I would have no choice but to return his light.

CHAPTER 15

"Hope you two are decent," a familiar voice echoed through the cave. "I've just had the workout of the century, and the last thing I need is a reminder of what I'm missing out on."

"Abby," I whispered.

"Our pants are on, and they were never coming off," Marcus said, moving so he was sitting beside me. He tucked me under his arm and kissed the top of my head.

Abby laughed. "I think we all know that's a lie. If we arrived two minutes later, things would've gone down very differently."

"Not everyone is like you," Justin said from close by. "So, how is everything going?"

"Lucy's hurt," Marcus said, rather than telling them our epic news.

"Where?" Abby and Justin asked in unison.

I leaned back and showed them my exposed stomach and hip.

"Wow, that's a bad one," Abby said, once again making me envy the fact that they could all see in the dark.

"We need to get that cleaned up before it gets infected." Justin sighed. "There goes that idea then."

"What idea?" I asked.

"Abby and I were thinking this would be the perfect place and time for you to try reaching out to your guardians. We're surrounded by these crystals that will amplify the magic inside of you, which should enable you to reach your guardians a little easier. And let's face it, time's not something we have much of."

"I've already been," I said.

"And there's no new information," Marcus added.

I whipped my head around to face him, my brows drawn together as I tried to work out why he was lying to them.

Abby turned on a torch and pointed it at Marcus and me. "Yeah, something tells me that's not entirely true."

I lifted my hand to shield the light from my eyes. "Can you point that somewhere else?"

"Oops. Sorry." She flicked the light so it shone against the ceiling, illuminating the crystals and turning the cavern into a magical display of colored lights.

"Think what you want," Marcus said.

Abby sighed as she shifted her weight onto one leg. "You and I both know you're a shitty liar."

Justin folded his arms across his chest. "What's going on? What don't you want us to know? Or is it that you don't want to tell *me*? Because I thought we were past all that not trusting me bullshit."

As much as I trusted Marcus, this was one of those times he was being a stubborn ass. "It's not that we don't trust you. It's that Marcus doesn't like what we found out and wants to pretend I'm not what I am."

Abby drew her brows together. "Let me guess. We're going to have a baby soon, and Marcus doesn't like it because you were so freaked out about it and—"

"It's not a baby," I said, cutting her off before we lost track of the conversation.

Abby pouted. "Then what is it?"

Marcus's jaw popped. He really wasn't happy I was about to divulge the truth.

I turned my attention back to Abby and Justin. "You were right about me being created as a vessel. Only, it's not to spawn a magical baby. I'm a vessel containing the light that was stolen from Marcus. I have the ability to take and give. That's what I was created to do."

Abby scrunched up her nose in confusion. "I don't get it. That sounds like a good thing."

Marcus looked at me, heartache once again stealing the light from his eyes. "That's because Lucy is forgetting to mention the part about her dying once she's fulfilled her destiny."

"Oh, shit," Abby said.

Justin's gaze dropped to the ground. "I had no idea."

"I know," Marcus said, surprising me. I thought he would've been happy to try and ping this one on Justin for the sake of taking it out on someone, but something had changed. Marcus was no longer angry with him. He was angry with me—with what I was created to do and what he feared would be the inevitable. He didn't have to say it. I could tell. I could feel it in his soul.

And it was crushing me.

CHAPTER 16

*A*bby leaned against the wall. "What are you going to do?"

"She's not giving it back to me if that's what you're thinking," Marcus said.

She raised a brow. "I think you know me better than that."

I looped my arm around Marcus's and leaned my head against his shoulder. "We've decided we're going to find Mava and Astrid and see if they know anything about this."

"And if they don't, then I'm going to find out who did this to us and I'm going to destroy them," Marcus added.

Abby pushed off the wall. "You can count me in. 'Til death do us part and all that bullshit."

I couldn't help but laugh. "That's wedding vows."

She waved me off. "Or the vow of a best friend who will stand by her friends 'til the end."

Justin let his arms fall to his sides. "Then, 'til death do us part."

"'Til death do us part," I said with a smile.

Marcus turned to me. "You are not dying. That's the whole point."

"Then maybe we should get her wound cleaned up," Justin suggested. "It looks pretty nasty."

Nasty was the understatement of the century. I was surprised I hadn't already bled out.

I furrowed my brow as pieces of the puzzle fell into place.

"What is it?" Marcus asked.

"I realized something. I can only die by your hand or when I reach a certain age and am reborn to fulfill my destiny. And if you never take what is yours, then I will never cease to exist."

Marcus's face softened, the pain in his gaze fading away. "Then you will always be, because I will never destroy you."

I blinked away the tears that were pooling in my eyes. "I know."

Marcus wiped a tear away as it fell from my eyes. "Let's get you out of here."

He stood and helped me to my feet.

"Where are we going?" I slipped my arm around his waist.

Marcus wrapped his arm around my back, as he led me through the cavern. "I have absolutely no idea."

"I know somewhere," Justin said, a few steps behind us. "A while ago, Mava told me about a place we could go if anything happened to her. Apparently, no witch will visit there because the creatures that hide in the shadows feed off their souls or something. It's probably not safe for us to remain there, but it should do at least until we clean Lucy's wounds."

"We have a lot to thank her for," Marcus said, jumping on board the Mava fan club. "And I'm hoping we'll have a lot more to add to the list when we find her."

"Any ideas where she is?" I asked, my words coming out through clenched teeth as I tried my best to deal with the pain.

"I think Morgana's home would be a safe bet."

"That sounds easy enough. At least we won't have to go to another dimension and have to deal with someone screwing with the veils."

Abby barked out a laugh. "Yeah, somehow I don't think it'll be that easy. Morgana is way more powerful than both Mava and Astrid combined, and you can bet your ass she's got her home locked up like Fort Knox."

"But you're forgetting something major," I said. "I have the ability to take and give, which means I should be able to manipulate anything she throws at us."

Abby spun and shone the light on my face. "Do you know how to use that ability on command?"

I held up my hand, blocking the light from going into my eyes. "Do you have to do that?"

"Sorry." She flicked the light down to my feet. "Well?"

I shrugged, regretting it as soon as the skin on my stomach pulled tighter from the movement. "I don't know."

She twirled the torch around. "Then I guess we better hope for the best and prepare for the worst. It's probably a good thing Justin and I raided your arsenal before we left."

Marcus helped me forward then hooked his arm around Abby's neck. "You're a good girl."

"Shh. Don't tell anyone. The boss would hate it if word got out." She chuckled.

"Oh, I think you're already in enough shit with your boss after what you did back at my house."

She sighed then looked at me. "Don't suppose you have the ability to take away my demonic side and swap it with an angel?"

I smiled. "And what use would an angel be to us? I saw what you could do back there, and there's no one else I want on my side— other than you two boys."

The corner of her lips turned up. "'Til death do us part."

My smile grew wider. "'Til death do us part."

CHAPTER 17

*E*xiting the cave, I breathed in the fresh salty air while trying
to pretend I was strong enough to keep going. Wherever we
were going, I needed to suck up my pain and fly because I knew
how hard it would be for Marcus to allow either Abby or Justin to
take him while the other one carried me. I couldn't do that to him.

"How far do we need to fly?" I asked, ready to whip my wings
out. I'd finally gotten a handle on getting them out with ease.
Getting them in again was still a little hard, but at least Marcus no
longer had to bite me.

Marcus curved his hands around my hips, being careful not to
touch the wound. "You can't fly."

"She won't have to," Justin said. "We're going through to the
Shadowlands, where we should be safe for a while."

"And you." Marcus twisted around to face him while his hands
remained supporting me. "We can trust you, right?"

Justin narrowed his eyes at him. "Right."

I grabbed hold of Marcus's chin and guided his gaze back to
mine. "I think we've already established that one."

"I can never be too careful when it comes to you."

I rolled my eyes and smiled.

"Don't worry about it, Lucy," Justin said. "I knew it wasn't going to be easy to regain his trust—even if I've technically had his back all along."

"Enough, demon boy," Abby said, flicking the light on and off, while directing the beam into Marcus's eyes. "You two can bicker as much as you want when we're safe. Or are we forgetting why we're here?"

Abby never ceased to surprise me. After all, she was the one usually mucking around, never seeming to take anything seriously. But I guess that was her nature, the playful succubus who had a kickass dark side I envied.

"So, where do we go?" Marcus asked, getting back on track.

"Just follow me." Justin turned away from us and stared off into the bush. A moment later, the air rippled in front of him, starting off small and quickly growing large enough to allow us to walk through without having to bend over.

He turned to us. "Ready?"

"Ready," I said, even though I had no idea if he was talking to me or not.

Justin gave me a curt nod then stepped into the ripple, disappearing from sight.

I'd gone through two veils before, but that didn't make the fundamentals of it any less magical and awe-inspiring.

"After you." Marcus gestured for Abby to enter first.

She tilted her head to the side as she raised a brow. "Scared he's going to pull some kind of trick on you so you're going to offer me up to make sure your precious Lulu doesn't get hurt?" She winked at me.

"You know me too well." Marcus didn't try to deny his intentions.

Abby knew better. She knew the inner workings of his mind. And the thing that surprised me the most was that I was no longer jealous of their relationship. In fact, I was glad he had friends who would stand with us against the world.

I loved that about her. But I also wanted her to know I was there for her in return.

So, I did what any good friend would do—even if my soul mate was going to kill me for it later. I broke away from his grasp and rushed through the veil.

CHAPTER 18

a nanosecond later, Marcus followed. I hadn't even had the chance to take in my surroundings before he was in my face, cursing me for being so silly while making sure I was okay.

Even though it hurt like crazy, all I could do was laugh.

"This is not a laughing matter," Marcus said as Abby came through the veil. "Anything could've been waiting for us on this side."

"Yeah—Justin."

"That's beside the point." He breathed out harshly. "Don't do it again."

Biting down on my smile, I saluted him.

The corner of his lips tipped up as he shook his head. "You are going to be the death of me."

"Nope. Technically, I'm the life of you."

"There is no "technically" about it. You are my life, and that is why I want you to take what I say seriously."

"Fine. I promise not to put myself in harm's way again."

Marcus seemed to be content with my promise because he left it at that. "Let's clean you up." He moved to my side, finally allowing me to see where we were.

I scrunched up my face in confusion. We were in the exact spot we'd been in before walking through the veil, only it was a little darker, the air was thicker and colder, and the sun—if there was a sun—was hiding behind thick clouds that covered the sky. "So, am I right in assuming each veil is a reflection of the others?"

"Basically." Marcus gestured to the cave, which we'd come from in my dimension. "But things are a little different. The environment is different, and it changes the land, which is one of the reasons why we had to leave the cave before entering the veil."

"Why?"

"Because the caverns in this cave will be different than the ones we were in before."

"Oh," I dragged. I folded my arms over my chest and ran my hands up and down them, trying to warm myself up.

"Let's get you inside where the crystals can hide us a little better." Marcus wrapped his arm around my waist, supporting me as we headed back into the cave, which was softly illuminated by the surrounding crystals, unlike the one back home.

When we were safely inside and found somewhere large enough for us to hide out for a while, I sat on the ground, trying to ignore the crushed crystals that were sticking into my skin. The others didn't seem to be bothered by it, and I figured it had something to do with their skin being a little tougher than mine. I didn't want to bring it up. I didn't want to give Marcus any more reason to worry about me.

He already had enough worry for the both of us. I really wished I was confident in my abilities so I was no longer the weak one in the group. I didn't want to be weak. I wanted to be able to hold my own and be there for Marcus and the others like they were for me.

Dumping his backpack next to me, Justin kneeled and rummaged through it. He pulled out a medical kit and opened it.

Marcus snatched the kit from his hands. "I'll do that."

I rolled my eyes. Okay, so we still weren't back to being all good with Justin.

"Fine." Justin stood and backed away. "I was only trying to help."

"You have." Marcus kneeled in front of me and opened the kit. "There are some things I prefer to do myself, and taking care of Lucy is on top of that list."

Justin held up his hands. "Whatever makes you happy."

Abby sat against the wall opposite me and leaned back as she twirled the torch around in her hands, further illuminating the cave.

I adjusted myself so Marcus could access my wound easier.

"This might sting a bit," he said.

"Just do it."

Marcus was right. It stung like hell as he cleaned out the wound. I gritted my teeth, refusing to let him know how much it hurt, and tried to focus on him instead. A few moments later, the pain in my side had subsided. Now, I was calm, but guilt had my stomach in knots because of the pain I was inflicting—on *me*.

I was taking Marcus's emotions.

My eyes widened as I tried to work out what I'd done. I wasn't supposed to feel Marcus's emotions. At least that was how I thought I worked. But I was wrong.

"I can feel you," I said softly.

"I'm sorry. It'll be over soon."

It took me a second to realize what he meant. "I mean I can feel your emotions." I looked up at Justin. "Kind of like how I felt you back at the rehab, except it's stronger with Marcus."

"You were able to feel me thanks to Mava," Justin said. "We haven't done anything to Marcus."

"I can take and give," I reminded them.

Abby smirked. "And let me guess. You can't control it yet, can you?"

My shoulders slumped. "Nope. But it seems to work when I want it to."

"Kind of like how your wings are supposed to work."

"Yeah, they're still not working so great."

Marcus pulled a bunch of gauze pads out of Justin's bag and applied them to my wound. "Can you hold these for me?"

I held the pads against my side, knowing my wound was going to seep, crust over, and rip when it was time to change the bandaging. That was going to hurt like a bitch.

The Hellhound's claw marks were larger than any tiger's. I was unbelievably lucky they hadn't gone deeper, or I surely would've needed to go to a hospital, which would've left us open to Morgana finding us in no time.

Marcus pulled a bandage out of the bag then carefully wrapped it around my waist until the gauze was fully covered and secured. "This should do until we rescue Astrid and Mava."

"That's right. They can heal me, can't they?" I gripped my wrist, remembering how I'd woken up from my trip through the tunnel without my cast or my scars from where I'd slit my wrist.

"They can do a lot of things that we can not," Justin said.

Abby grinned. "And we can do a whole shit load of things they can't."

"Then I guess it's a good thing we're going to rescue them," I said. "Because something tells me we're going to need all the help we can get to work out who's pulling the strings."

CHAPTER 19

$\mathcal{M}$arcus slumped down beside me, leaned back against the wall as he dug through the bag, and pulled out a bunch of packaged food. "Want something to eat?"

"Thanks." I grabbed a granola bar, opened it, and took a bite as he divided the rest of the snacks between the three of them. There wasn't enough food to keep them going for long.

"So, what's the plan?" I took another bite.

Abby unwrapped her granola bar. "We're going to rescue the witches, kill the bitch, and bring hell to whoever else gets in our way."

"Right," I said with a smile. "And how are we going to get to Morgana?"

"Well, dearest Lulu," she said. "We have these things called wings, and I plan on using them to get us to her coven."

I bit down on my smile. Abby sure had a way with words.

"And you think we'll be able to fly right on up to her home or wherever she's holding them captive, grab them, and go."

She tilted her head to the side—again. "Of course not, Lulu. We're going to find the potions Mava left for us, which will help block our print so we can sneak in—"

"What potions? And how did I not know about this?" Marcus asked.

Abby grinned. "Because you decided to leave us in the middle of an epic battle."

Justin sighed. "I told her about them after we finished up at your place. Mava has been planning this for years and has prepared for so many variables."

"Mava knew she was going to get kidnapped?" I asked.

"No. But she thought she may die and wanted to make sure it wouldn't be in vein so you'd still have a chance at stopping Morgana."

"Right." My ass was falling asleep, so I got up to stretch out, but the pain riding up my side made me wish I hadn't.

"We're not going now," Justin said. "You need to get some rest."

"I need to stretch my legs." There was no way I was going to let them know I had pins and needles in my butt.

"Can't you guys go by yourselves then bring it back here?" Marcus suggested.

"We could, I guess," Abby said.

I paced the length of the cave as I watched the light from Abby's torch reflecting off the crystals in the cavern. "Wouldn't it be safer if we all stuck together?"

"Where did she hide them?" Marcus asked.

Justin grabbed an apple from his pile of snacks. "It's in a safety deposit box in the city."

"Which city?"

"Sydney."

I came to a standstill. "All the way down in Sydney? You're joking, right?"

He shook his head. "I'm afraid not. Mava thought it would be better to spread things out a bit. They know our approximate location now, but they're not expecting us to head to Sydney when our lives are here."

Wow! Mava thought of everything. If only she would've predicted that the witches would come after her while I was stuck in the tunnel.

Maybe she had.

"Which is exactly why we don't have time to rest," I said.

Marcus got to his feet and came over to me. He curled his hand around my good hip. "You need time to heal if you want to make it all the way to Sydney."

I placed my hand on his chest. "It's not going to heal anymore by tomorrow. All we're doing is wasting time—time that we don't have."

"Marcus is right," Abby said, surprising me. "You need to rest."

"I'll be fine."

"What happens if you're flying three hundred meters in the air and pass out from the pain?"

I was about to say I'd survive when I realized she wasn't only talking about me. Marcus would go down with me. "I'd never let that happen to you."

Turning to her, I added, "Besides, you guys can catch us if we fall."

"True. But then that goes against Marcus's rule of not letting anyone else carry him." Abby pulled the remainder of the granola bar out of the wrapper and popped it into her mouth.

Marcus glared at her. "We'll drive."

She scrunched up her face. "We're not driving ten friggin' hours so that you don't have to worry about one of us carrying you."

"Actually, Marcus is right," Justin jumped in. "We should probably make the first leg of the journey by car to throw them off. Then, we can dump the car and fly the rest of the way."

"And where are we going to get this car from?" Abby asked.

"I'm pretty sure we know how to sort that one out. Or are you forgetting how we got back after we disappeared?"

Abby stared at him for a few moments too long. "Fine." She was clearly not okay with her decision but was doing what was best for the group.

I grabbed hold of Marcus's shirt. "See, we can get started on our journey now. I can rest for the first length of the trip, and then I'll be good to go."

Abby peeled open the wrapper of a chocolate bar. "You know, we could leave you two here while Justin and I fly down and back."

"That is not happening," Marcus said. "This place won't remain safe long enough for you to fly to Sydney and back. We need to get as far south as quickly as we can without drawing attention to ourselves. From there, we can work out where the witches are."

Justin stood and brushed the crumbs off his pants. "Which means we need to do a location spell."

Abby climbed to her feet. "And how do you suppose we do that?"

Justin grinned. "Witchcraft."

CHAPTER 20

The idea of learning spells excited me in ways I never knew. I had a newfound yearning to learn everything I could.

Making our way out of the cave, I breathed in deeply, the strange air filling my lungs.

"How do you think we should do this?" Justin asked.

Marcus pointed to the left. "If we go up that way, there should be a few houses where I'm sure we can easily get our hands on a car."

We made our way through the dense bushland, Marcus helping me over any obstacle in our path. This world seemed so similar yet so different, and I wished we had more time so I could've explored it.

"Do people live in this dimension like they do in ours?" I asked, breaking the silence.

"Not exactly," Marcus said. "This veil is a forgotten land. Actually, that's not exactly right. The ones that reside in this world are shadow creatures. They're very predictable and highly territorial."

When he saw the look on my face, he said, "You don't need to worry about them. As I said, they're very predictable and territorial. This isn't an area they gravitate toward. They don't like the energy the crystals produce, and we all know this part of the world is a stronghold."

"We do?" I asked.

"Okay, maybe you don't. But the rest of our kind knows of this. And I can assure you we are safe—so long as no one guesses where we've gone."

Abby snapped a twig off a tree she passed. "The land Byron Bay is established on is a stronghold that ties our worlds together, making it easier for us to travel between the veils because of the energy the crystals produce. They also help to enhance and disguise the powers of those within its vicinity. Which is why so many witches reside in Byron."

"There are other strongholds around the world," Justin added. "We have to hope Morgana hasn't taken Mava and Astrid to one of them."

The idea of having to fly across the ocean kind of scared the crap out of me. There would be no land to rest on and nowhere to hide. We would be open for the slaughter, and I wasn't sure I had the ability to draw on my powers so I could be an asset and not the liability I always seemed to be.

I prayed we would remain in Australia.

We made our way out of the bush and were met with a vast expanse of what I could only describe as a wasteland. I could see why no one would choose to live in this veil. It was not pretty. In fact, it looked kind of like what I would think our world would be if we went through an apocalypse.

Trudging through the swampy wasteland, I got a strong sense of what was to become of my world if we didn't destroy Morgana soon.

I don't know how I knew it. I just knew.

Abby reached her arm out in front of her, and the air a few yards ahead began to ripple. "I'll go first." She strode through the opening in the veil without giving the men a chance to object. Not that they needed to be concerned about her safety. She was a lethal killing machine.

I wanted to be a lethal killing machine.

I wanted to be able to protect those I cared about the most.

And I wanted to be able to wake up and discover that all of this was a bad dream.

Only two of those things were possible. The other was purely a dream. And dreams never came true.

Justin disappeared through the veil then Marcus and I followed —together.

Coming out the other side, I breathed in deeply, and let myself pretend for a second that the world was good again—because it felt good. It smelled good. It looked good.

Looks were deceiving.

I scanned the neighborhood as we walked down the street, trying to find ourselves a car. The homes were filled with humans who were none the wiser to the impending war. I hoped they would remain as naive to the world they lived in as they were this very moment.

The world didn't need another thing to worry about. Then again, if they knew the truth, it would put most of their worries into perspective.

Marcus squeezed my hand. "You okay?"

I nodded. "Just thinking about things."

He hooked his arm around my neck and kissed my temple. "We can do this."

"I know we can." That was the truth. I prayed the world wouldn't be different when we finished.

Justin fell back into line with us and cocked his head to the right. "There's one."

Following his gaze, I saw what was going to become our ride for the next few hours. It was a perfectly inconspicuous white SUV that would blend in with all the other soccer moms and dads driving the streets.

CHAPTER 21

*M*y stomach twisted in knots as Abby and I waited behind a hedge for Marcus and Justin to steal the car from in front of a house. It took seconds for Marcus to open the door —without any alarm going off.

He'd obviously done this on more than one occasion over the years since he'd lost his usual mode of transport.

Biting my lip, I glanced at the house the car was parked in front of, hoping no one had noticed them. I hated the idea of stealing someone's car, but we didn't have the luxury of finding transport the legitimate way.

Marcus rolled the car down the road then hotwired the engine. "Get in."

Taking one last glance around the street, I made a dash for the car. Well, it was more like an elongated hobble thanks to the pain tearing up my side.

To my surprise, both Justin and Abby had taken the back seat, leaving the front passenger seat for me. I'd figured they would've wanted to stash me somewhere safe—probably sandwiching me between them. Then again, nowhere was truly safe.

Slipping into my seat, I closed the door and went to put on my seat belt, but the pain was too much. Letting go of the belt, I tried getting into a comfortable position and closed my eyes as we headed for the highway.

Marcus put his hand on my thigh. "You okay?"

Opening my eyes, I nodded. "I'm good." The truth was anything but that. However, I didn't want him to worry. Pain was still radiating through my body, and I would've done anything to get my hands on some painkillers.

Relief wasn't an option.

And so, I sucked it up and concentrated on what was important. Pain would have to wait.

I placed my hand over his. "How far are we traveling in the car?"

"We should probably get to at least Port Macquarie before we head to the air."

"That's about halfway, isn't it?"

"It's roughly a four-hour drive." He squeezed my thigh. "You should get some rest."

Readjusting myself in my seat, I leaned my head against the window and closed my eyes.

All too soon I awoke to Marcus caressing the side of my face. "We've arrived."

I blinked a few times before everything came into focus. It was still night, and we were parked in a burger joint's parking lot. The others were standing outside, leaning against the trunk, once again stuffing their faces. "Okay. I'm ready."

I was so not ready, but nothing was going to stop me from getting us to our destination.

Gritting my teeth, I climbed out of the car then made my way around to Abby and Justin.

Marcus joined me then grabbed the paper bag off the car and opened it. "Want a burger, Lu?"

"Yeah," I replied.

He handed me a burger then grabbed two drinks out of the cardboard cup holder. "Orange or lemonade?"

"Lemonade." I took the paper cup from him and sucked through the straw, the lemonade soothing my throat on its way down. I absentmindedly wondered how much longer I'd be affected by what the Soul Scrapers had done to me that night at the club.

Biting into my burger, I listened to Justin give directions on where the bank was located and how it would be best if we waited until they opened in the morning so we wouldn't trigger any alarms.

"Shouldn't you guys be able to come and go from wherever without leaving a trace?" I asked.

They all looked at me. "We always leave a trace. Most of the time, humans are just too self-absorbed to notice," Abby explained.

"Right." I took another sip of my drink.

"It's best if we wait until opening just to be sure." Justin grabbed a packet of chips out of the paper bag. "We want to eliminate the chances of being discovered prematurely."

I totally agreed.

We finished our meals then disposed of the rubbish in the trash can.

Marcus strode over to me. "You sure you can do this?"

I forced a smile. "I'll be fine." I wrapped my hands around his waist. "And if the pain gets too bad, I could always give it to you," I joked.

"Actually, that's not a bad idea."

I slapped his chest softly. "I was kidding."

"I'm not."

"There is no way I'm putting this on you."

He breathed out harshly. "You're hurting, aren't you?"

"I'm fine," I lied again.

"If you were, you'd be happy to hand it over. But you're not, and that's brave and all, but you don't need to suffer when I can take care of it for you. Besides, we don't feel pain the way you do."

I narrowed my eyes at him, trying to figure out if that was the truth or if he was only saying that so I'd give my pain to him.

Abby strode over to us. "He's right." She slung her arm around his shoulder. "We don't feel pain like humans do. We can handle so much more."

I glanced between the two of them, trying to work out what to do. "It's okay. I can handle this. Besides, I'm not exactly human."

Marcus raised his brows. "We're in this together, and there's no point in keeping it to yourself." He looked up at Justin. "If you're really worried about hurting me, then why don't you give it to Justin?"

Justin whipped his head up. "What?"

"I was telling Lucy you'd be happy to take her pain for her after all the lies you've told."

"Ah, yeah. Okay." He strolled over to us. "Give me what you've got."

A couple of days ago, I would've jumped at the chance. But now… things had changed. I knew the truth, and I felt guilty for even considering what they were asking me to do.

"Come on, Luciana," Justin said. "I deserve it. Remember all those times I deceived you. This can be your payback. Because you know, I really could've let you know the truth, but I didn't. I chose to lie to you, and I put Marcus through all that unnecessary pain. I mean, do you know what state he was in when I headed back from dropping you off with Mava and Astrid? He was a mess. Drinking himself senseless as he cried like a baby.

"Oh, and you should've seen how it tore him up when I gave him that pendant of yours. I'd been right. It cut him to his core. It didn't give him the peace you'd hoped it would. And all that time, I could've told him the truth, but I didn't. I enjoyed watching him—"

"You're an asshole." I barely gave it a moment's thought before seamlessly sending my pain into him. "You deserve this and more."

Justin winced momentarily then stretched his side. "You must've been in so much pain if this is what you've been dealing with."

I breathed a sigh of relief, no longer feeling as if my insides were going to spill out.

He turned his back as his wings emerged, spreading out before me. Then, with a leap, he took off into the sky.

Abby placed her hand on my shoulder. "You do realize Justin was only saying all those things to get you angry enough to hand it over to him."

"I know. And I feel like an ass."

She smiled. "Well, I still think he deserves it the most out of the three of us." Abby took off into the sky after Justin.

"I'm so sorry about what happened," I said. "I should've told you the truth—"

Marcus cupped my cheek in his hand. "No, you shouldn't have. Everything played out how it had to."

He kissed me then opened the trunk and pulled out a couple of bags. "Before we go, Abby got you a change of clothes so that you won't stick out amongst the crowd."

I looked down at my bloodstained clothing. "Yet another thing I owe Abby for."

I took the bags from him and changed in the back seat, thanking God I'd given my pain to Justin because getting changed inside the car would've been impossible if I hadn't.

Dressed in clean pants and a top, I got out of the car. "I'm ready."

Marcus lifted my shirt and looked at the gauze. "It's oozing."

I knocked his hand away and readjusted my top. "It'll be fine for now. We can clean it up properly after we get Mava's package."

I wrapped my arms around him and spread my wings out, the cool night air rustling my plasma-like feathers. "You ready?"

Marcus snaked his arms around my waist and held on tightly as I flapped my wings, taking us up into the sky. I couldn't push off the ground the way Abby and Justin could. Even though I had wings, I simply didn't have the strength in my legs to move us an inch. Marcus was heavy, and I constantly feared I would drop him as we soared through the sky, trying to catch up to Justin and Abby.

The muscles in my arms stung, but I wasn't letting go. What I needed was strength, and it was something I clearly didn't have.

But Marcus did.

And even though he was probably doing the biggest share of holding onto me, I was still hurting. My back ached, and I knew there was a better way. I felt guilty for even considering it.

"Do it," Marcus said, his voice coming out as a whisper thanks to the wind muffling his words.

CHAPTER 22

I looked down at him. "Do what?" I asked, trying my best to hide the pain in my voice. But it was useless. He'd heard it.

"We're in this together, so take what you need and stop worrying. Stop trying to do this on your own."

I was so used to doing things on my own. I'd spent my whole life dealing with all my pain and suffering on my own. No one could help me. And now that I could finally free myself from my pain, I had a hard time letting go.

I was created to take and let go, and that was exactly what I had to do. The trouble was, it was easier said than done—especially when I was taking from the man I loved when all I wanted to do was give to him. I was designed that way. To make sure Marcus was whole. But I had no idea how to do that. I had no idea what he needed fixed, and taking from him was like going against everything that was ingrained in my DNA.

But that didn't mean I couldn't draw from other sources.

Tilting my head back, I looked at Abby and Justin in the distance. *Sorry guys.* Slowly but surely, I stole just enough strength from them to allow me to hold onto Marcus for the remainder of the trip without my muscles aching.

The strange thing was neither of them noticed. Or maybe they did and they just didn't say anything, happy to play their part in keeping their friend from falling to his death because he was too stubborn to allow one of them to carry him for the final leg of the journey.

Only it wasn't the final leg. It was the interim. Or maybe even the beginning. Morgana wasn't going to be an easy kill, finding the witches wasn't going to be easy, and working out who Morgana's partner was and destroying them was going to be the hardest of all.

Drawing on my newfound strength, I tightened my grip on Marcus and caught up to Abby and Justin.

It was early morning. The sky was dark, and it was still hard for me to see. My eyes stung, and I couldn't do anything about it. I couldn't "borrow" any of their invisible eyelids or whatever they had that protected their eyes from the wind.

Trying to ignore the discomfort, I turned my attention to Marcus and the way he felt in my arms now that my strength wasn't an issue. We were finally doing something, and even though we had nowhere safe to call home, we were together. That was all that mattered. That, plus saving Mava and Astrid, and destroying the supernatural world that was hell-bent on keeping us in the dark.

After flying for what felt like forever, Marcus gave me a little nudge. "We're here."

Following Abby and Justin's lead, I brought us down a few feet, getting ready to land on the roof of a building in the city.

Knowing how crappy I was at landing had my nerves on edge. If I missed the mark, there was a good chance we'd either tumble off the roof and plummet to the ground, or smack into the side of a nearby building.

That was probably why Abby did a last minute detour and landed on the top of the tallest building in the city. The problem with that building was it had a smaller rooftop than the other ones in the area.

"You did it in the forest, and you can do it now," Marcus said. "Just have faith in yourself."

Yeah, that was easier said than done. But he was right. I had to have a little faith in him or at least the guts to try. For our own safety, I needed to get this right, or a human might catch sight of us if we fell to the ground.

I was not going to let that happen.

Taking a deep breath, I lined up for the landing and forced my eyes to remain open when all I wanted to do was close them and pray for the best.

What made it worse was that both Abby and Justin had already landed and were watching me like a hawk.

The roof was coming closer, and I had no idea if I was going too fast.

"Pull up," Marcus said. "You don't need to land the way they did. Lift up, hover over your mark, and then slowly glide down."

That sounded easier. I did as Marcus suggested, and before I knew it, our feet were firmly planted on the roof of the highest building in Sydney.

Marcus lifted me in his arms and kissed me. "See. You've got it all in here." He pointed to my temple. "You may not remember it, but that's what I'm here for."

Setting me back on the ground, Marcus slipped his hand into mine and led me over to the others, who were standing on the edge of the building, looking down at the streets below.

"What's the plan?" Marcus asked.

"We've got another hour to wait until the bank opens. We can either stay up here or go get something to eat," Justin said.

"I vote to eat," I said. I was amazed by how hungry I was after having eaten only a couple of hours ago. I finally understood why they all ate so much.

Abby twisted around to face us. "Sounds good to me."

She stepped off the edge of the building and dropped onto a discreet part of the balcony of the restaurant below.

Marcus swept me up in his arms, jumped off the roof, and landed with the grace of a cat beside Abby. Then he set me on my feet.

Justin followed, landing on the other side of Marcus.

We made our way to the main area of the restaurant, which surprisingly was already filled with diners either wanting to take in the sights of the city over breakfast or attending an early morning meeting.

Once we were shown to our seats, the waiter took our order.

I settled back in my chair as I watched the three of them carry on as if it were any other day and they were just enjoying each other's company.

Marcus rested his arm across the back of my seat and ran his fingers over my shoulder. "You okay?"

I smiled. "Perfect."

The truth was anything but perfect. In that moment, ignoring everything that was wrong with our lives, I could see how this was going to end.

We were going to rescue the witches and destroy everyone who stood in our way—who stood in the way of fulfilling my destiny. I had no choice but to complete what I was born to do.

Looking up into his eyes, which were filled with unconditional love for me, made me doubt my words. I'd already experienced his pain when he thought he'd lost me—and there was a massive possibility that I would be reborn. I couldn't imagine how he'd be if I never came back.

How could I possibly fulfill my destiny? How could I do that to him?

There was an unrelenting struggle going on in my mind as I tried to figure out if doing what was right really was the right thing to do.

Who was I to tell Marcus what was right for him? If he didn't want to become who he was meant to be, how could I destroy not only his wishes but also his faith in love?

Marcus leaned closer to me. "It's going to be fine. We're going to be fine. We'll get what we came for. Then we'll be free to complete our mission."

I forced a smile then turned my gaze to Justin. "Am I right in assuming you'll go into the bank?"

He nodded. "Abby can come with me."

I was relieved to know I didn't have to play any part in deceiving the bank staff into letting me get my hands on Mava's security deposit box. Not that I knew if they would have to talk their way in. The details weren't something I cared to know. I already had enough going through my mind. They could deal with the trivial stuff.

Our meals were soon delivered, and the four of us fell silent as we hungrily devoured our food.

Abby was the first to finish. She leaned back in her chair and asked, "So, is anyone going to fill Lucy and me in on what happened the last time you tried finding Titus?"

CHAPTER 23

*I*n all the drama that had happened with Mava drugging me, finding my guardians, and discovering who I was, I'd completely forgotten neither Marcus nor Justin had told us what happen when they'd left Abby and me outside the Devil's Playground and had followed Colton, hoping he'd lead them to Titus.

I'd feared the worst when I saw Morgana following them into the club, but it mustn't have been anything too bad considering both Marcus and Justin were sitting at the same table as us and were in one piece.

Marcus leaned back in his seat, his eyes turning a fiery shade of amber. He remained silent. I wasn't sure if it had to do with the failed attempt or if thinking about that night brought up too many bad memories.

"We never made it to Colton's meeting with Titus," Justin said. "And now that we know Morgana is involved, we probably have her to thank for the distraction."

Abby drew her brows together. "What distraction?"

Justin sighed. "I ended up doing a collection I wasn't listed to make."

I furrowed my brow. "Why couldn't you just leave whoever died for someone else to collect?"

"Because if I did, a demon could've tampered with the soul and the human would've ended up somewhere he didn't deserve to be. Doing what is right outweighs doing what we want."

As much as I didn't like that they still hadn't found Titus, I couldn't blame them for choosing to save a soul. After what I'd seen in the tunnel, I wouldn't wish the wrong fate upon anyone.

"I think it's safe to say our priority after rescuing Mava and Astrid is to find Titus," Justin said. "He must be hiding something if he's doing this much to keep us away."

I shrugged. "Either that or someone is using him as a deflection."

Marcus looked at me. "You could be right, but we won't know for sure until we talk to him."

"And finding Titus doesn't seem to be easy. It might get easier after we dispose of Morgana, though."

Abby raised her brows. "Dispose of?"

"Would you prefer 'kill the evil bitch?'"

Abby chuckled. "I can't wait to see the look on her face when she realizes you remember—and know your true power."

I momentarily glanced at Marcus, and it didn't go unnoticed by Abby. "What was that look for?" she asked.

"What look?" I tried to play nonchalant.

"Drop it, Abby," Marcus warned.

"Fine." She slouched back in her seat. "So, what are you two going to do while Justin and I go inside? We'll probably be gone for a good half hour." Abby wiggled her eyebrows.

I frowned. "Not what you're thinking."

Abby shrugged a shoulder. "Your loss." She looked out the window then whacked Justin's arm. "We better get going. They'll be open in a few minutes."

Again with their freakish ability to tell time. I stuck my hand into my pocket to fetch my phone and see how accurate she was, but it wasn't there. "My phone."

Justin wiped his mouth with a napkin then threw it onto the table. "What about your phone?"

"I must've left it behind."

"Does it really matter?" Abby asked. "At least your mom won't be bothering you anymore."

"True." When I thought about it, I probably should've ditched my phone a long time ago. Mom would've known I'd thrown away her only form of contact with me. But that was the point. I was finally free of her. There was no way she would find me now.

That realization was a huge weight off my shoulders. It was bad enough we were going up against a powerful witch and paranormal being, but my mom… she was a right pain in my ass.

"We'll have to get you another one so we can keep in touch if we get separated," Marcus said.

I raised a brow. "You plan on separating from me?"

"I don't plan on letting you out of my sight, but that doesn't mean we shouldn't be ready in case something goes wrong."

"Fair enough—as long as I get a new number so I don't have to worry about my mom calling."

"Done."

Abby nudged Justin again then stood. "Come on. We better get moving."

Justin grabbed his glass of juice and took a sip as he rose to his feet. "We won't be long." He grabbed his backpack off the floor and rummaged inside for a moment. Then he pulled out a chunk of cash, folded it in half, and threw it to Marcus. "This should cover breakfast and a phone for Lucy."

I stared at the pile of one hundred dollar bills in Marcus's hands. "And a whole heap more." I whipped my head around to ask Justin where he'd gotten that kind of money, but he and Abby had already gone.

Marcus unfolded the cash, removed three notes, and dropped them on the table. "Are you ready to go?" He pocketed the rest of the money.

I grabbed another croissant and stood. "I am now."

He smiled. "Good to see you're no longer worried about what you eat."

Smiling, I took a bite then followed him to the lifts. We weren't the only ones riding the elevators down, and somehow the humans brought comfort to my soul. Humans were predictable—safe. Sure there were psychotic ones, but they could be stopped much easier than a pile of black, misty smoke that could literally slip between my fingers and suck the life out of me. Just thinking about them sent shivers down my spine. I really needed to get over my fear of those damn Soul Scrapers.

Once we were on the ground floor, Marcus and I made our way outside.

"There's a phone shop down the block and to the left," Marcus said.

Even though I'd grown up in Sydney, he seemed to know the streets better than I did. I guess that came with being an immortal—and he'd probably spent the better parts of my life searching the streets for me. Or so I assumed.

Ten minutes later, we walked out of the shop with my new phone. I fiddled with the settings as Marcus guided the way, making sure I didn't bump into anyone because my gaze wasn't where it should've been.

"Can't that wait?" Marcus asked.

I raised my gaze to him and was about to tell him how much it couldn't wait when I saw the look in his eyes. "What's wrong?"

He was scanning our surroundings, and his jaw was set tight. "Nothing."

"A bit of honesty wouldn't go astray."

Marcus scratched his head. "Ah, yeah. Sorry." He momentarily looked at me before returning his gaze to our surroundings. "I'm pretty sure they know where we are."

My eyes widened as I scanned the street, fear clutching its demented fingers around my heart and squeezing the crap out of it. "What? Where?"

"I'm not sure, which is why we need to keep moving and keep our eyes peeled for them."

Shoving my phone in my pocket, I nodded. "Them" referred to a whole range of different species that I wanted to remain as far away from as possible. "Let's get out of here. Where are we meeting Abby and Justin?"

"We're waiting for a call."

We moved through the streets, taking turn after turn, distancing ourselves from our last known location as quickly as possible without drawing unnecessary attention.

Humans crowded the streets, providing a false sense of security. I wasn't sure if Soul Scrapers would come after me in such a public place, but I didn't want to take any chances.

Marcus's phone rang. He retrieved it from the pocket of his jeans, swiped the screen, and put it to his ear. "You got it?"

"We'll be there in two." He disconnected the call then returned the phone to his pocket.

Marcus looked over his shoulder. "We have a problem."

My blood froze. I may not have been able to sense the demonic creatures, but he could. I was positive that was what our problem was. "What is it?"

"We're close to the meeting point, but we're not alone. Soul Scrapers are already scouring the streets, and we also have the pleasure of being hunted by the Hellhounds and Possessions."

"What are Possessions?"

He puffed out a laugh. "You don't want to know."

Marcus may not have thought I needed to know what they were, but I sure wanted to know. "What do they look like?"

"They look like anyone and everyone. They use humans as a vessel to carry out acts that would otherwise cause hysteria amongst the humans if they knew demonic creatures existed."

CHAPTER 24

$\mathcal{M}$y breath caught in my throat as I looked at the people around me. Any one of them could've been a Possession, and I'd be none the wiser. "I don't see them."

"Doesn't mean they're not there."

Marcus led me quickly through the streets, ducking through department stores on our way to our rendezvous point. "We're almost there."

Relief washed over me when we rounded the street corner and Abby and Justin came into view. We still had another hundred meters or so until we were safely in their reach, but we were on the homestretch and—

Marcus shoved me behind him as he smacked someone in the face. Then he dragged the man into a nearby boutique clothing store.

The staff scattered to the rear of the shop then disappeared into the back room as a couple of customers made a dash for the exit.

Adrenalin pumped through my veins. Marcus wasn't a violent man—apart from when it came to Justin and when he'd almost burned down Paege's shop—which only meant one thing: a Possession must've taken hold of the human.

Still gripping the man around the neck, Marcus shoved him against a large mirror hanging on the wall and tipped his head back into an unnatural position as he forced the man's mouth open. I was

449

sure Marcus was millimeters away from breaking the human's neck, but I had to trust he knew what he was doing.

Marcus shoved his hand into his pocket, retrieved a small black capsule about half an inch long, and shoved it down the man's throat, forcing him to swallow it.

The man's face contorted unnaturally as he clawed at Marcus's hands, trying to free himself.

A woman come out of the storeroom with her hands behind her back. At first, I thought she was crazy for potentially putting herself in harm's way. Then I noticed the absent look in her eyes. Something wasn't right.

Without warning, she lifted her hand and propelled a knife toward Marcus.

"No," I screamed, raising my hand in a pathetic attempt to stop the knife.

With his back still to the woman, Marcus dodged the blade, leaving the human straight in the path of the knife. Only it never connected.

My eyes widened in disbelief as I watched the knife hover in midair for two seconds then drop to the floor.

The woman didn't miss a beat. She grabbed a pair of scissors from behind the counter and charged at us, a cold, calculating look in her eyes, which were trained on me.

I'd prepared myself to fight against demonic creatures, but how was I supposed to fight a possessed human without any knowledge or warning?

Marcus threw his hand out toward her, a gush of air propelling the woman and slamming her into the counter. "Run!"

I didn't need to be told twice. Making a dash for the door, I sprinted through the store and onto the street, almost taking out a mother pushing her baby in a stroller.

Pulling up short, I sidestepped the woman and headed up the street. "Abby," I whispered loudly, trying not to draw unnecessary attention to me but hoping her hearing was sharp enough to be able to pick up sounds a human could not.

No such luck. She stood in the distance, chatting with Justin who seemed equally as oblivious to what was going down with us.

Marcus caught up, grabbed my hand, and pulled me until we

were jogging down the sidewalk. We crossed the road, dodging the traffic as we tried to further distance ourselves from the Possessions.

Abby twisted around toward us, and a carefree smile spread across her face. "Took your time."

Marcus grabbed her elbow, forcing her to start walking with us. "We've got company."

Justin caught up. "Where? I can't feel anything."

"Which explains why you didn't bother coming to help out when we had two Possessions a few shops down the road."

Abby's eyes widened as she glanced over her shoulder. "That shouldn't be possible."

I followed her gaze and saw four humans trailing us, careful not to get too close but probably ready to pounce, given the chance.

We weren't going to give them a chance.

I racked my brain trying to figure out a way I could use their abilities, but the only thing I could come up with was either extracting them from the humans they were using and drawing them into me or sending them into another unsuspecting innocent person. Neither were viable options.

Dark clouds swept across the sky, bringing with them rolling thunder, reminding me of the day Marcus and I had left the rehab. That seemed like a lifetime ago. I'd thought the worst I had to deal with was feeling other people's pain, and now I was running from demonic creatures who were hell-bent on killing me.

"What are you doing?" I asked Marcus.

"Deflecting."

A crack of thunder shook the ground beneath us, and the wind suddenly picked up.

People scattered like ants, running for the safety of nearby buildings as the clouds cracked open and rain pelted down, swallowing the light of the day and turning the atmosphere into something that hadn't been seen in years.

Shadows danced in my peripheral vision, sending shivers down my spine. My nerves were on edge waiting for the next creature to make its appearance. I absently brushed my hand over the gauze pads on my stomach, praying I wasn't going to get another injury to add to my collection.

Justin grabbed hold of my wrist and tugged me toward a small alleyway between a restaurant and an office building. "We need to get up to the roof."

For a second, I thought he was expecting me to fly up or scale the wall and was relieved when he forcefully opened a fire escape door, cracking the locks as if they were made of paper. "In here," he said.

Abby and Justin entered first. I followed with Marcus close behind.

Adrenalin pumped through my veins as I raced up the stairs, grateful I still had some of the strength I'd stolen from Abby and Justin. Otherwise, I was pretty sure Marcus would've had to scrape me off the floor and carry me the whole way up.

My lungs felt as if they were on fire by the time I'd made it to the top. I may have had strength, but my cardio had taken a beating since I'd given up running. I'd let myself grow complacent ever since I met Marcus. I no longer needed to run as my escape. He was my escape. And it could potentially be my downfall. I couldn't have weaknesses. Demons thrived on weakness.

I raced out onto the rooftop and quickly took in my surroundings. I was relieved to find it was only the four of us up here.

Marcus slammed the door shut behind him and leaned against it. A few seconds later, the possessed humans thumped against the other side of the door, their screeches reverberating through my mind as they desperately tried to get through.

I folded my hands over the back of my head and breathed in deeply as I tried to ignore their cries and settle the mixture of nerves and adrenalin raging inside of me.

CHAPTER 25

*J*ustin strode over and handed me a small vial filled with murky green liquid. "Drink this. It'll stop them from being able to follow us."

I curled my fingers over the glass, trying to avoid looking at the contents in case I saw something inside that would make me want to be sick. You never knew what the ingredients were when it came to witchcraft. "Where to from here?"

"Drink up, and then we'll fly out of the city."

"Won't the humans see us?"

"That's where I come in." Marcus opened his vial and downed the contents, screwing up his face in the process. "The clouds can cover our departure."

I opened my vial, and no matter how much I tried, I couldn't stop myself from looking at the murky liquid inside. Thankfully, I couldn't see any eyes staring back at me, but fear still ate away inside my stomach because the last time I drank something of Mava's, I ended up almost dead and left Marcus in a world of pain. I prayed this wasn't going to be another one of her tricks.

I shook my head. Of course it wasn't. Mava had done everything for Marcus and me, and I couldn't let a little thing like fear get in the way of our mission.

Resting the vial against my lips, I tilted it up and drank the potion. I almost gagged as the mixture slipped over my tongue. It was so much worse than the previous potion she'd given me, and I tried my hardest not to think about the ingredients that had probably gone into the concoction.

Holding the empty vial I looked around the rooftop. "Where's Abby?"

"Over here," she yelled.

I twisted around in Marcus's direction but couldn't see her.

A few moments later, she came around the side of the stairwell entry, carrying a massive air conditioning unit as if it were a giant balloon. That girl was a force to be reckoned with.

She dropped it beside Marcus then pushed it across the door, blocking it so that Marcus no longer had to.

Abby dusted off her hands. "You ready?"

"Don't you and Justin have to take your potions?" I asked.

"We already took ours while we were waiting for you."

"Right," I said.

Marcus peered up at the dark clouds rolling in. It looked as if the storm of the century was about to let loose, but the storm was us, not Mother Nature.

Justin adjusted the strap on his backpack, which was sitting flush against his chest. "We better get going. We need to put as much distance between us and Sydney before the spell runs out."

I raised a brow. "It runs out?" I wanted to slap myself for being so naïve. Nothing lasted forever. If it did, I certainly wouldn't remember who I was, and I was thankful the spell placed on me had started to wane when it had.

"It should give us about a day or two, and then we'll need to make our own unless we manage to rescue Mava and Astrid before the spell runs out." Justin then added, "There are still another two vials, so you'll remain safe for a few days."

Marcus wrapped his hand around my hip from behind. "We'll find them before we need to worry about that."

I loved his optimism and prayed he was right.

"Plus, Mava's given us the recipe to make some more, so you really don't need to worry," Justin said.

Abby spread her wings. "The ingredients might be a little hard to come by."

I swallowed hard at the thought of trying to get our hands on spider eyes or whatever else went into the concoction.

The air conditioning unit in front of the door scraped a few millimeters across the ground, reminding us that we needed to get moving.

"Follow us," Abby said then took off into the sky, disappearing into the folds of the clouds.

Yeah, following them would be easy—if I could actually see where they were.

"It's clear above the clouds," Marcus said as if he could read my thoughts. I wondered if he also had the ability to read people's souls like Mava could. Now was not the time to find out.

Justin put his hand on my shoulder and gave it a gentle squeeze. "Will you be okay?"

"I'll be fine." I glanced at Marcus, hoping to get a reading on him and how he was dealing with Justin being so personal with me.

His steely gaze remained on Justin, and he looked two seconds from reacquainting his fist with Justin's face.

Even though we owed Justin so much for helping me discover who I really was, we still had a long way to go before their relationship was back on track.

The Possessions slammed against the door again, forcing it another couple of millimeters open. Those buggers were strong, and it wouldn't be too long before they broke through. I had no idea if they could follow us through the air, and it wasn't something I wanted to find out.

I wrapped my arms around Marcus's chest and unfurled my wings, grateful that I could now use them on command.

Marcus held on to me tightly and pushed off the rooftop, propelling us into the dark clouds and hiding us from the humans below.

I pumped my wings, taking us higher until we broke through the clouds into the bright blue sky above.

Abby was hovering in midair, waiting for us to appear. She smiled then took off south. I followed her through the sky with Justin trailing behind me. I wasn't sure if he was behind us due to my pain I'd inflicted on him or if he was keeping an eye on me. Either way, I was glad to be in the middle should anything go wrong.

We'd been in the air for about three hours when Abby pulled up and waited for us to get closer. "There's a motel and a café down there." She pointed to a small town in the middle of nowhere. "We can stop to regroup and figure out where to go next."

"Sounds good," Marcus said.

I had no idea where we were—or even what state we were in. All I knew was that I was hungry, tired, and would do just about anything to wash the stench of blood from my wound off me.

We landed amongst the trees then walked the short distance into town. The motel didn't need any ID, and we were able to grab a couple of rooms without any worries.

Marcus and I were in one room, and at first Abby refused to sleep in the same room as Justin. Then she had a sudden change of heart and not only agreed but insisted. I wondered if she didn't fully trust him either and wanted to make sure he didn't double-cross us.

As soon as we were alone, I headed into the bathroom, peeled off my clothes, and looked at the reflection of my torso in the mirror.

Blood seeped through the gauze pads, and I knew that whatever was beneath wasn't going to be pretty.

Still, I had to see.

I unraveled the bandage then lifted the corner of the pad. I peeled it back and winced at the sight of the wound. It was grotesque.

I grabbed a face cloth from the shelf then turned the faucet on. Once the water warmed up, I ran the face cloth under the water then wiped the smears of blood off my skin, being careful not to actually touch the wound. That proved almost impossible. And of course I scratched the cloth over my open flesh, sending a new bout of pain soaring through my body. "Shit."

Marcus tapped on the half-closed door then opened it. "Let me see."

Blinking away the tears pooling in my eyes, I turned to face him.

His pupils dilated, and his jaw dropped as his gaze drifted over me. "You need to get that checked out."

I'd watched nurses and doctors sew me back together countless times, and I was positive I could do it myself—if only I had the materials. "I know."

He narrowed his eyes as he studied the wound. "Unless…"

"Unless what?"

Marcus lifted his gaze to meet mine. "Unless you take from me."

CHAPTER 26

*H*orrified by his suggestion, I took a step back. "I'm not taking anything from you." When he was about to protest, I added, "Besides, I've already given Justin my pain. What more can I do?"

"You can take my self-healing ability."

I held the cloth under the water and rinsed the blood off. "I can't take from you."

Marcus leaned against the counter. "You can, and then you can give it back as soon as you've healed."

I squeezed out the face cloth and continued to wipe the blood off my skin.

He grabbed my hand, stopping me. "You can't even take a shower because it's so bad. And before you go on about how you can deal with this, the thing is, you don't have to."

Closing my eyes, I leaned my hands on the counter. "I can't."

"I heal fast. You take what you need, and give it back to me when you're finished."

"I can't," I said again. And that was the truth. I was created to fix him, not take from him, and I didn't know how I could go against what was ingrained in my soul.

He lifted his gaze to meet mine. The pain in his eyes was back with full vengeance. "I can't see you like this."

"Then don't look." I turned away from him and took a step toward the shower.

Marcus caught me by the arm and spun me around. "Please take it."

My chest tightened as I tried to ignore his pleas and stay strong to my belief.

He swept my hair away from my face then cupped my jaw in his hand. "I know you think you're doing the right thing, but you're not."

I bit my lip as I fought the urge to put distance between us, and I listened to what he had to say. "I'm not created to take from you."

He smiled. "And I'm not created to spend the next few hours with Justin while I wait for you to get better using his healing abilities instead of mine." Marcus raised his other hand and cupped the back of my neck. "And before you say anything about using Abby, considering what she is, that might not be such a good idea."

My furrowed my brow. "Why?"

"Because she's a demon and there's only so much you can take from her before her inner demons cross over. Justin, on the other hand, is middle ground. But under the circumstances, I think you'd understand why I don't want to be too close to him for longer than necessary."

"You still don't trust him, do you?"

"I trust that he wants to do what's necessary to protect us, but that doesn't mean I trust that he won't do something we don't agree on just to guarantee the end result we all desire."

The sad thing was, I agreed. Doubt played in the back of my mind whenever Justin was involved. Although he'd proven he was there for us, I still couldn't rule out him doing something he deemed necessary and breaking our hearts in the process.

He dropped his hands to mine and entwined my fingers with his. "At least take half, and then we can share."

I forced a smile. "You're not going to let up on this, are you?"

"Not when you're as hurt as you are."

I stared at him, my conscience telling me I shouldn't, and my brain telling me I should. My heart was the deciding factor. I could deal with pain and injuries, but I couldn't handle seeing him look at me that way. "Fine. But I'm only taking enough for it to crust over. Then I'm giving it back to you."

He pulled me forward and planted a kiss on my lips. "Or you could keep it. I'm happy to share with you."

I shook my head. "Never in a million years."

He let go of my hand and caressed my cheek. "All that matters is you're okay."

"We're okay," I corrected him.

He nodded and took a step back. "Take it from me."

Biting my lip, I looked at the ceiling and forced myself to go against what I was born to do. I shifted closer to him, leaned my head against his chest, and closed my eyes. I still had no idea how my ability worked exactly, so I went with my gut instinct and tried to mentally envision myself drawing from him, capturing his healing ability inside of me, and using it to heal myself.

Marcus leaned down and kissed the top of my head. "Thank you," he whispered.

I lifted my head and let out a shuddered breath. I didn't know what to say, so I avoided the subject altogether. "Abby and Justin will be waiting for us."

"Let them wait," he said. "My priority is you, not them."

I smiled. "As much as I love that about you, the fact is they're our priority because they're trying to help save my ass and they're the ones with the location spell."

The corner of his lips turned up. "Technically, we don't need to find Mava and Astrid so quickly now that you've taken from me."

My eyes widened in shock.

"I'm kidding," he said with a small laugh. "We're still rescuing them. It's just not as urgent now."

I gently whacked his chest. "You are incorrigible."

He shrugged. "Honest, in love, and desperate is more like it."

What could I say to that? Nothing. When it came down to it, two of Marcus's mantras were mine as well. I was desperate, and would do anything to protect the man I loved.

Deciding I would shower after I healed a little more, I found a first aid kit and applied another gauze pad.

Once I was dressed, we headed to a small café where we found Abby and Justin sitting next to each other at a booth, digging into their meals.

To anyone else, they looked like a couple wanting to be as close to each other as possible, but the truth was they would never be more than acquaintances that had Marcus and my best interests at heart.

We slipped into the seat opposite them and each grabbed a menu.

Peering over the laminated menu, I looked at what they'd ordered. Justin had a chicken schnitzel with mashed potatoes and roast veggies, and Abby had what I assumed was once lamb shanks served with mashed potatoes and gravy but was now just two bones sitting in sloppy brown mashed potato.

It looked disgusting but delicious at the same time. "I think I'm going to have what Abby had," I said to no one in particular.

She lifted her gaze to meet mine. "Grab me another one while you're at it."

"Seriously?"

She rolled her eyes. "Fine, precious Lulu. You stay here, and I'll order your food."

My mouth dropped open. "I wasn't—"

A grin played on her lips. "I'm kidding." She stood and moved to the end of the table. "What do you want, Marcus?"

"I'll have the shanks as well."

"Justin?" she asked.

"Ahh, could you grab me a strawberry milkshake?"

The corner of her lips tipped up. "Sure."

Justin put down his knife and fork then grabbed his bag as Abby strutted over to the counter. "I want to show you this before we get started."

I refrained from pointing out that he'd already started his meal.

He pulled out a journal similar to the one that was left on my bed when Marcus went missing, except this one was smaller in size and was about a quarter of the thickness.

"What's that?" Marcus asked.

Justin placed the leather bound journal on the table and pushed it toward Marcus. "Mava left this inside the safety deposit box along with the vials."

Marcus opened the book and flipped through the pages. "What am I supposed to be looking for?"

Justin stopped him from turning another page. "That right there." He pointed to a section that spoke of seeking one's desire.

"Shit," Marcus said. "We need a lock of her hair."

Justin pulled a small black felt bag out of his backpack. "We already have that."

"Then what's the problem?" I asked.

"The problem is, we also need to be within a certain radius of Mava for it to work, or it'll just point to a region on the map."

Abby came back to the table and slipped into her seat. "And we only have enough hair for one try."

Frowning, I pointed to the felt bag. "Are you sure that's even Mava's hair in there?"

Justin leaned back in his seat. "I have no idea. Mava didn't leave any instructions. All I know is she stowed away some necessary items in the safety deposit box should anything happen to her."

"So you're assuming she stored her own hair just in case?" Marcus asked.

The waiter came over carrying a tray with four strawberry milkshakes on top. "Here you go." She placed one in front of each of us.

"Thanks," I said with a warm smile. I hadn't had a milkshake in forever.

"You're welcome. Your meals will be ready shortly." She turned on her heels and headed back to the kitchen.

"Thought we could all use some kiddie food to make us feel better." Abby winked at Justin.

He picked up his glass. "Milkshakes are not kiddie food."

She patted his forearm. "Keep telling yourself that."

"Anyway," Justin said, turning his attention to Marcus and me. "We're going to have to try and figure out where would be the most likely place Morgana would keep Mava and Astrid."

Abby twirled her straw between her fingers. "I still think she'd take them back to her place where they'd have the most protection from her priestesses and the greatest chance of keeping us out."

Remembering how Astrid had so easily kept Abby out of her shop and how I wasn't able to get close to the Devil's Playground, I asked, "How are we going to get past their security? I mean, we couldn't even get through the one's around the club or the one at Mava's store."

Marcus nudged his shoulder against mine. "That's where you come in."

I frowned, having no idea how I could possibly play a part in getting through their spells. I didn't know witchcraft, and I certainly wasn't a witch. "How so?"

"Well, I've been thinking about your gift."

"And?"

"If it's as strong as I think it is, then you've got the ability to manipulate everything around you."

"Like you took Justin's and my muscle power on our way down to Sydney," Abby said.

"You noticed?"

She barked out a laugh. "Of course we noticed. We just didn't say anything. And you're welcome by the way."

"Thanks," I said, feeling crappy for stealing from them. "I figured you'd prefer to lose a little than have me drop Marcus."

"I never would've let go," he said as the waitress delivered our meals.

"By the way, where is Morgana's place?" I asked when the waitress left us alone.

Abby scooped some gravy-soaked mashed potato onto her fork. "Near Wellington."

CHAPTER 27

*M*y jaw hung open. "As in New Zealand?"

Marcus cut a piece of lamb off the bone. "Yeah."

I rested my knife and fork on the plate. "How are we going to get over there to cast the spell."

Abby raised a brow. "Fly. How else do you think we'd travel?"

"And I'm guessing you're referring to the good old fashioned way." Flying to Sydney was one thing, but flying to New Zealand was taking it to a whole other level. I'd freeze my ass off on the way over.

"You do know it only takes three hours via plane."

Marcus leaned closer to me. "And about half the time for us."

I grabbed my milkshake and took a sip. "So, do we all fly over, do the spell, and hope it works?"

Justin nodded. "If it doesn't, we have to fly back to see what we can salvage from Mava's place so we can try again."

"Jesus Christ." I leaned back in my seat. "I was hoping you guys were going to tell me Morgana lived about a half-hour flight from here, and we could spend the night in the motel before setting off in the morning." Even though I loved flying, my injury was testing me. I didn't know how long it was going to take for me to heal, and I didn't want to ask because then Marcus would know how bad it was.

Marcus twisted around to face me. "We still can. It'll take less time than the flight from Byron to Sydney." He leaned in closer and whispered, "And you won't be in any pain by the morning."

"Of course she won't," Abby said. "She's already given it to Justin."

I glanced between Abby and Justin. "Actually, that's not what he was referring to. Marcus is helping me heal."

Abby leaned forward and rubbed my hand that was resting on the table. "Good for you. You're finally owning what you are."

I frowned. "I've only known about my abilities for less than a day."

She let go of my hand and sat back in her seat. "I would've been taking and giving the second I found out. I mean, how awesome is that?"

No matter how great it sounded, it was still a form of a curse. To be given the power to control everything around you and not know how to use it was a very dangerous thing. So far, nothing bad had happened, but I had a gut feeling that would change. It was inevitable.

Marcus slipped his hand across the arch of my back. "Not everyone is like you, Abby."

I picked up my knife and fork then carved up my lamb shanks. "What do we do now?"

Justin stared at me for a few seconds. "Abby and I could fly over as soon as we've gathered the rest of the ingredients and do the spell while you two stay here and recover. We don't all need to be there."

"Maybe that's not such a bad idea," Marcus said. "That way if you can't find Mava, we can head back to Byron to see if we can find anything of hers or Astrid's so we can try again."

"It'll cut out more than a few hours," Abby agreed. "We could be over and back by morning."

Marcus grabbed his milkshake then took a sip. "And while you're gone, we can gather the ingredients for another hiding potion."

I mixed a chunk of lamb into the mashed potato then stabbed my fork into it. "Sounds good to me."

"Then it's settled." Abby put down her fork but held onto her knife. "We'll gather what we need and leave as soon as possible." She looked between me and my food. "Eat up. You're going to need your energy."

My stomach churned with anticipation of what we were going to find out. I was glad I didn't have to fly to another country, yet it left Marcus and me slightly more vulnerable. But I trusted Marcus, and he didn't appear to be concerned at all.

Once we finished our meals, we headed outside. The cool air was a huge change from that of Byron Bay's.

It wasn't long ago that I would've been freezing in my jeans and long sleeve top, but whatever had awoken within me was changing my genetic makeup. Either that or it was my brain accepting who I really was and no longer telling me I was human and should feel the cold. The latter was more likely. Then again, when it came to me, nothing was off-limits.

"Show me the list again," Marcus said.

Justin pulled the book out of his backpack, flipped through the pages until he found the one he was after, and handed it to Marcus. "We can either split up or go together."

Abby peered over Marcus's shoulder. "It would be quicker if we split up."

Justin looked at Abby. "I'm guessing that means I'm with you."

"You betcha," she said. "Someone has to keep an eye on you and make sure you're not going to screw us over again."

Justin sighed. "How many times do I have to tell you I did what was necessary, and I've always had Marcus and Luciana's best interest at heart?"

She tapped his forearm. "Keep telling yourself that, but we all know the truth."

Justin rolled his eyes. "I'm not going to win this one, am I?"

With a grin on her face, she winked at me. "Never."

Getting back to the important stuff, I gazed over the list of ingredients. Some I'd heard of but most I hadn't. "Where are we going to get these items from?"

"From a witch," Abby said as if it weren't obvious.

Marcus looked at me apologetically. "Most of the ingredients are easy to come by, but there are others that take time. Most witches carry these in their homes, and others can be found in a store."

"As in a witch's shop?" I asked.

"Exactly," he said.

"So, I guess we'll take the ones in a shop, and you guys can get the easy shit." Abby pulled her phone out of her pocket and took a photo of the ingredients. "We'll see you guys soon."

"You guys keep the book," Justin said. "That way you can get a head start on the other one."

Remembering Mava's caldron, I asked, "Won't we need something to make it in?"

Marcus closed the book and held it by his side. "A normal pot or bowl is all that's needed. Witches like to use old-fashioned caldron's because they believe it connects them to their ancestors."

"When in reality, their ancestors are more than likely serving the rest of their existences paying for their sins." Justin lowered his voice and said, "But don't tell Mava I said that."

I smiled. "My lips are sealed."

"We'll catch up with you guys later." Abby hooked her arm around Justin's neck and dragged him away.

I turned to Marcus. "Where to now?"

"Shopping."

To my surprise, we ended up going to an herbal shop to gather the first of our ingredients. From there, we headed to the chemist to pickup a few different types of oils and essences from the in-store naturopath.

It wasn't long before we had gathered everything on our list and we'd arrived back at the motel the good old human way—without wheels. Luckily, the town wasn't large, and we only had a one-mile round trip to make.

Justin and Abby weren't back and probably wouldn't be for another couple of hours, which left Marcus and me alone with nothing to do.

I lived for nothing to do.

In all the commotion of him thinking I had died, me finding out who I really am, and us being on the run, we hadn't spent any real time together, and I missed him horribly.

While Marcus was on the phone, filling Abby in on our progress, I ducked into the bathroom and took a quick look at my wound.

I was pleasantly surprised it had already improved. The wound had crusted over, and the angry red marks surrounding it had disappeared. By the rate it was healing, I would be almost better by the time Abby and Justin got back.

I stripped, turned on the shower taps, and waited until the water warmed up before hopping in. The water ran over my head, washing away all confusion of the last few days, and brought clarity to my soul that hadn't been there before.

Abby had been right. I should've used my abilities earlier and taken what I needed when I needed it. I had to overcome my doubts because doubt played no part in our mission. We had to think quickly and precisely and be able to live with whatever consequences came from our decisions. I needed to learn to take and give as if it were as easy as blinking.

I needed to own who I was and not apologize or let guilt sweep my ambitions away.

Like the water that was rolling over my body, I had to let whatever came my way glide off me, never changing who I was beneath or the purpose I was created for.

I may not have been giving Marcus back his light, but I could still be that light, ready to give when needed. We were like two sides of the same coin, and together we could be unstoppable. If only we believed in ourselves.

Marcus tapped on the door then entered the bathroom. "How are you feeling?"

"Never been better." I knew he was referring to the wound, but my state of mind was my answer.

I opened the shower door, grabbed his shirt, and pulled him inside.

Marcus laughed. "Couldn't this have waited until I at least got undressed?"

I slipped my fingers under his shirt, grabbed hold of the hem, and lifted it halfway over his chest. "It could've. But then it wouldn't have been as fun." I pulled the shirt over his head then threw it over the shower screen as I kissed him.

Marcus broke away. "Are you sure you're up for this?" He leaned back and looked at my wound. "It should be healed in another few hours."

He was right. But who knew where we would be in another few hours, or if we were even guaranteed another few hours. I was done waiting and doing things the right way. I wanted him. I needed him, and I wasn't going to apologize.

I trailed my fingers down his abs, stopping on the buckle of his jeans. "I'm sure."

That was all he needed to hear. Time stood still as we collided with a sense of desperation, longing, and the fear that we might not live to see another day.

We were playing a game neither of us knew if we were truly prepared for. But we wouldn't stop until I was no longer being hunted. And the fear of what was to come was like a rush of pure adrenalin running through my body. I poured it into Marcus and drew from his need to have me in ways he never understood until now.

I held a piece of his soul inside of me, and I would protect it no matter the cost.

CHAPTER 28

The moon was shining eerily down on us by the time Abby and Justin returned. It was as if the planets knew something was coming. But what I didn't know was if we were being naïve and were walking into a trap.

I had to push those thoughts to the back of my mind and focus on what needed to be done.

Justin unpacked the various ingredients from the shopping bag they'd brought back with them and placed the items on the small table in our room. "We've got everything we need here, and it shouldn't take too long to put it all together."

Eagerly, I watched Marcus, Abby, and Justin work together with an unwavering focus as they crushed, boiled, and burned various ingredients until they all stood back with Justin holding a small jar filled with chunky liquid Mava would be proud of.

"Hope no one needs to drink that," I said.

Justin opened his backpack and slid the jar inside. "Not everything needs to be consumed." He zipped it up and slung it over his shoulder. "We'll call you when we arrive."

"Sure thing." Marcus cupped the back of Abby's neck. "Don't do anything stupid, okay?"

She barked out a laugh. "Me? Do anything stupid?"

"I'm serious, Abby."

The playful look in her eyes vanished in one of the rare moments that she took things seriously. "I know. And I promise I'll wait for you before I do something stupid."

Marcus smiled. "Good." He kissed the top of her head then came over to me and tucked me under his arm. "Take care of her, Justin."

Justin glanced at Abby. "I think she's the one who'll need to take care of me."

Abby whacked Justin's chest. "You bet your ass I'm the force to be reckoned with on this team."

"After what I saw back at the house, I'd have to agree." I slipped my arm around Marcus's waist. "Good luck."

Justin hooked his arm around Abby's neck. "We don't need luck. We have Abby."

She slipped under his arm and headed to the door. "We'll call you in a few."

Justin paused by the door. "Hopefully, we'll find Mava first go and we won't need to worry about trying again."

"Let's hope," I said.

Justin smiled then closed the door behind him.

I looked up at Marcus. "Do you think they'll find Mava and Astrid?"

"I honestly don't know." He twisted me around in his arms so I was facing him. "Which means we have to hope for the best and prepare for the worst."

I sighed. "I'm guessing that means we're not going to be spending a peaceful night in this room like you told Abby and Justin we were going to."

"Are you up for it?"

I didn't need to ask what "it" was. I was ready for anything. "Absolutely."

"Good." He grabbed the room key and slipped it into the pocket of his damp jeans. "Because I was thinking we need to prepare for when we go into Morgana's estate. She's going to have it on lockdown and will no doubt have a few spells surrounding the place to keep us out. We need to prepare for whatever she throws at us and try to find a weak spot."

"Exactly how are we supposed to prepare for that?"

"As I said earlier, that's where you come in. But I've been

thinking a bit more since then, and I've got a hunch we might be able to pull this off a little easier than we first thought."

"How's that?"

"What if we didn't need to hide? What if we were able to walk straight in, avoid all confrontation, get Mava and Astrid, and then get out of there before anyone knows they're missing?"

"Sounds good in theory, but how the hell are we supposed to pull that one off? They're witches. They seem to know everything going on around them."

A smile spread across his face. "Only if you let them."

I furrowed my brow. "I'm assuming you're not talking about going in there all ninja-like, are you?"

"Nope."

"Then how?"

He ran his hands down my arms. "That's where you come in. I've got a theory that I want to test out."

"And that theory is?"

"That you can make people see what you want them to see, hear what you want them to hear, and smell what you want them to smell."

The excitement in his voice was too contagious for me to ignore. "Go on."

"If I'm right, we can either do this without anyone knowing, or we could cause one major diversion that will leave Morgana and her priestesses too focused on something else to worry about Mava and Astrid."

Wow. That was a theory and a half. "How do you suppose we test it out?"

"We'll try something little at first, and then we can work our way up."

He grabbed my hand and led me to the door. "I think we could try seeing if you can hide yourself from others. Then maybe see if it extends to me."

We headed to the local pub, a short stroll from our room. It was filled with countrymen and women either shooting pool, having a family dinner with their kids in the dining area, or just plain old getting drunk.

Marcus leaned in closer. "Now, I'm going to go up to the bar and place an order, and I want you to try to make the bartender not see you."

I pulled Marcus back, stopping him from walking any further. "How do you suppose I'm going to do that?" I figured he had to have a better plan than hoping for the best.

"Like you've done everything else," he said. "Just try."

"That may have been all good and well previously, but this is different. I can't just will him not to see me. I have to be able to take something away from him or give something to him."

Marcus thought about it for a moment then said, "Then pass onto him what you see."

I scrunched up my face. "I'd have to stand by the bar for the view to be the same."

"Fair point."

Marcus tugged me toward an empty table near the front door and took a seat. "Okay, so maybe we need to give this a little more thought."

I rested my elbows on the table. "I can't manipulate people's thoughts or minds or whatever, so I don't know how we can do this."

"Then we need to figure out a way that doesn't entail you manipulating their thoughts."

"I guess I can take away his ability to see," I said, thinking out loud.

"That would cause too much attention here, but it might work for the witches."

"Except the witches would know something was up if I did something that drastic and obvious."

Marcus looked toward the bar area. "Can't you take away his ability to see you without taking away his whole sight?"

"You mean make his vision go blurry?"

He shook his head. "No. I mean just you."

"Maybe I could give him a belief that I don't exist. I don't know how I would do that, but I think it's our best chance unless I suddenly develop magical powers that allow me to manipulate the air and objects around me. And I don't see that happening anytime soon. I may have one hell of a gift, but it's not witchcraft. I can't manipulate time and space."

"What about taking a piece of his memory of the area in front of him and feeding it back to him when he looks at you?"

I turned slightly in my seat and watched the pudgy bartender as he wiped the bar down with a wet cloth. I knew how much easier it would be if I could control what he saw, but maybe I didn't have to. Maybe I needed to control the part of his brain that interpreted what he saw.

"Let me try something." I stood and grabbed Marcus's hand, tugging him off his stool.

CHAPTER 29

"Are you going to fill me in on how you plan to do this?" Marcus asked as we headed to the bar.

"Nope. Just go with the flow, and if it works, then I'll tell you."

"You're the boss."

I grinned as we walked up to the bar. "Order a drink for the two of us in case he can see me."

He glanced at me, the corner of his lips tipped up, and a curious gleam shone brightly in his eyes. "You got it."

Focusing on trying to take from the part of the bartender's brain that processed what he saw, I desperately prayed it would work, and our plan to rescue the witches would become that much easier.

We stood in front of the bar, and it wasn't long before the bartender came over. "What can I get for you?"

"Can I get a beer? And, she'll have a glass of red." Marcus gestured to me.

The bartender looked my way and blinked a few times. He furrowed his brow and glanced back at Marcus. "Whatever you say," he said, his tone telling me he thought Marcus was a nutjob with an imaginary girlfriend.

The bartender filled a glass of beer, put it in front of Marcus, and then poured a glass of wine and put it right next to the beer.

I had to stop myself from laughing. The bartender really thought Marcus was delusional.

Marcus handed him a twenty. "Thanks. And you can keep the change." He grabbed both glasses and followed me back to the table.

I slipped into my seat. "That guy totally thought you had an imaginary girlfriend."

He chuckled. "I don't think it worked properly because he kept blinking whenever he looked in your direction."

"I know." I grabbed my glass and shifted it in front of me. "And I may have another idea for how this could work better."

"I'm listening."

"Well, it may be easier to remove the memory of me from their brain than it is to actually make him not see me. I know what I just did will work well enough for those we can see, but not so well for those we can't."

He nodded slowly. "Okay. We can try that next."

I ran my fingers up and down the stem of my glass. "You plan on ordering another drink for your imaginary girlfriend?"

We spent the next hour ordering various drinks while I tried to perfect making myself invisible to those around me. Most of the time it worked, but every so often I faltered, and the bartender saw me for a split second before I disappeared again.

Before the end of our night, I made sure I took his memory of me being there at all because I didn't want the poor guy to think he was going crazy.

Marcus's phone rang as we walked down the main street of the town. He pulled his phone out of the pocket of his jeans. "It's Abby."

He answered the call. "Did it work?" He paused while Abby filled him in on what was going on, and then he said, "Okay, call me when you know more." He ended the call then pocketed his phone.

I hooked my arm around his. "What did she say?"

"They've arrived but haven't had a chance to do the spell yet."

"Can't they do it wherever they are?"

"They want to get closer to her coven and are going by foot so they'll be less conspicuous. It's going to take a little longer, but they want to make sure it works the first time around."

Sounded logical. And I guessed that was Justin's idea, not Abby's. She was a "charge in first and ask questions later" kind of girl.

I'd thought we were heading home, but Marcus had other ideas. We stopped outside the diner where we'd eaten lunch.

"Hungry?" I asked him.

"Always. But that's not the only reason we're here." He opened the door to the café and held it wide for me to enter.

I stepped inside, and Marcus followed. We slipped into the same booth we'd been in previously then grabbed the menus.

I settled on a steak burger with fries, and Marcus chose chicken alfredo.

When the waitress had finished taking our orders and headed back to the kitchen, Marcus leaned over the table and said, "When she comes back out here, I want you to try to make her believe there's a fire in the kitchen."

I scrunched up my face. "How do you suppose I do that? You're the one who can control fire, not me."

He sat there for a few minutes, pondering what I'd said. "You're right. I could light a fire and burn down the place."

"That would sure get the witches out of their estate."

"But it also might burn Mava and Astrid alive."

"How about a tornado? You could rip the roof off her house, making it easier to figure out where she is."

He smiled. "You're really getting into this, aren't you?"

"What's not to love? You can control fire and air and have this amazing light that burns from within you."

"Yet I can't control witchcraft. But you should be able to."

I breathed out harshly. I got that Marcus wanted to find a way to get in and out undetected, but I had no idea how I was able to do that. The force that had blocked me from entering the Devil's Playground was impenetrable then, and it still would be now. "I can't see how."

He reached over and covered my hand with his. "You can possess anything from anyone around you. You can fly, take someone's sight, manipulate what they see, remove their memories. And now we're about to see if you can make someone believe there's a fire that doesn't exist."

I glanced at the waitress and apologized internally for whatever we were going to put her through over the next hour. Of course, I would remove all her and her co-worker's memories of her strange actions so it wouldn't have a lasting impact on her life.

"Fire," I said under my breath as I tried to think of a time I'd smelled something burning. Okay, that was easy. I'd watched fire rip across the floor by Marcus's hand, and I'd also been amongst the commotion when Mava and Astrid had been taken. That memory wasn't very clear, but the smell that assaulted my nose—

My eyes widened as I remembered the perfect smell to give to the waitress. Burning sage.

I pulled the memory to the forefront of my mind then looked at the waitress and hoped for the best as I focused on giving it to her as if she were experiencing it now.

At first, I didn't think it worked. Then her nose twitched, and she sniffed the air as she looked around her.

"It worked," I said, barely able to contain my excitement.

Marcus squeezed my hand. "Give her something more."

As bad as I felt for admitting it, I ended up having the time of my life. I never knew it would be so much fun to make people believe things that weren't true.

But no matter how much fun it was, I knew going up against the priestesses was going to be anything but fun.

CHAPTER 30

*H*alfway through dinner, Abby called Marcus. "Tell me you have good news," he said, answering his phone.

Marcus looked up at me as he listened. And of course, he didn't give me any hints as to whether she was giving him good or bad news.

"See you soon." Marcus ended the call and pocketed his phone.

"Well?" I asked, my food long forgotten.

He picked up his fork and twirled some spaghetti around it. "They didn't find Mava."

My stomach sunk.

We not only had no idea how long it would take to find Mava and Astrid, but we also had to find something of theirs to use in another location spell. Who knew how long that was going to take?

Marcus gestured to my food. "Eat up. You're going to need your energy."

"Are we flying out tonight?"

Marcus shook his head. "No. I still think you should rest—"

I softly slammed my fist against the table so as not to gain any unnecessary attention but let Marcus know how serious I was. "I will not be a liability."

Marcus raised a brow.

"I'm sorry. I can't stop thinking about what Morgana could be doing to them. And if Mava and Astrid aren't at her coven, there's a huge possibility we may never find them."

Marcus's face softened. "We will find them."

"But it might be too late by the time you deem me ready." I looked at my watch. "It's only 9:00 p.m. We could make it back up to Byron by midnight, and I can still get some rest while you guys work on the next potion."

Marcus studied me for a few moments then said, "How's your wound healing? I mean, do you think you can handle the flight?"

I quickly looked around to make sure no one was watching then lifted my shirt just enough to see the wound then peeled back the gauze. My eyes widened in surprise when I saw the crust had started to fall off.

"I can't believe it," I said under my breath, and I raised my gaze to meet Marcus's. "It's better."

"Told you I heal fast."

"I'll say."

"Abby didn't even heal this fast after the burns she got flying me back to your house when the Soul Scrapers turned up at the club."

Marcus's muscles tensed. "What Soul Scrapers?"

I rolled my eyes. "There's no need to worry. I'm obviously fine, thanks to Abby."

"What happened?"

Resigning to the fact that I was going to have to tell him the full story because he wasn't going to let up, I explained what happened after he left that night.

Marcus leaned forward and squeezed my forearms. "I guess I've got another thing to thank Abby for."

"She really cares about you." Abby would do anything for Marcus, and I was pretty sure he'd do the same for her. Except when it came to me. I was his exception.

"Yeah, she does," Marcus agreed. "And she cares about you, too."

I couldn't help but feel that Abby would do anything for me only because of Marcus.

In my past lives, we hadn't gotten along at the best of times, and now, we were only just getting to know each other on another level. So far she'd proven that her heart was filled with light, even if she was the very definition of darkness.

Leaning back in my seat, I said, "Does this mean we're heading back to Byron now?"

Marcus pulled his phone out of his pocket, swiped the screen, and put it to his ear. "We'll meet you there."

A smile spread across my face. "Thank you," I mouthed.

CHAPTER 31

e called it a night then headed back to the motel to pack our things before setting off for Byron Bay. Actually, Marcus did the packing. I sat on the end of the bed and watched him shove various potion ingredients inside a makeshift bag, which was really one of the motel's pillowcases.

He was silent, which was unusual for him, and I got the feeling he was avoiding talking about something—yet again. "What are you thinking about?"

He continued to pack the pillowcase. "I know this isn't what you want to hear, but we need to think about Titus and figure out how we're going to get him alone."

"Please don't tell me you want to see him before we find Mava and Astrid?"

Marcus came over to me, put his hand on my shoulder, and gave it a squeeze. "He can wait until after we rescue the witches. It's just something we need to keep in mind."

He sat beside me and spread his hand across the small of my back. "I know you're going to have a lot on your mind while we're rescuing the witches, but I was thinking maybe we should poke around and see what else we can find out while we're there."

Our war didn't end with Morgana. Marcus was right. We needed to find out everything we could about who she was working with.

How exactly we were going to do that was beyond me, but I was willing to try. "We'd be stupid not to."

Marcus tapped my thigh then got up and continued to pack the few remaining items.

"What's the plan when we get there?" I asked.

Marcus twisted the pillowcase around and tied it in a knot. "We're going to meet them at the cave. Then we'll head on over to Astrid's together. Justin and Abby figured—and I tend to agree with them—there would be more security around what's left of Mava's home now, and since Astrid's store is in town, the demons will be less likely to cause a scene."

"They didn't seem to care about causing a scene in the middle of Sydney when there were thousands of people around us."

"Humans taken over by the Possessions are still easier to deal with than Hellhounds and Soul Scrapers. There's just a chance for more innocent casualties."

"And you'd rather take out innocent people than demons?"

"I never said that." Marcus passed the pillowcase from one hand to his other. "That was Abby and Justin's idea."

"But you're happy to go along with it."

"Only because I believe we have a better chance there than trying to sort through the rubble that used to be Mava's home." He sauntered over to me. "That's not to say any of us are going in there with complete disregard for human life. Because that's not us." He held his hand out to me.

I placed my hand in his, and he pulled me to my feet. "I know you wouldn't go in there with any intentions of killing an innocent. But it might happen."

"As much as you don't want to hear it, there are always casualties in war. However, that doesn't mean I won't do everything within my power to make sure that doesn't happen to an innocent."

Taking the life of someone who happened to be in the wrong place at the wrong time sat heavily in my stomach. But Marcus was right. There were always casualties in war. And war was brewing.

It was inevitable.

Marcus dropped the pillowcase on the bed then lifted my shirt and peeled off the gauze. "It looks good."

"Amazing, actually," I said, inspecting my stomach. The majority of the crust had fallen off, and all that was left was pinkish skin where the gashes once were.

I lowered my shirt. "Guess it's time to give your healing back to you."

"Or you can keep it." Marcus gave me a hopeful smile.

"Not a chance." Before he could argue the point, I gave his ability back to him.

His face slumped. "You've already done it, haven't you?"

I patted his chest then headed to the door. "The agreement was that I would keep it until I'd healed. And I've healed."

Marcus picked up the pillowcase and slung it over his shoulder as he joined me outside. "You're infuriating, you know that?"

I grinned. "I could say the same thing about you." I slipped my arm around his waist. "That's why we're so perfect for each other."

We headed down the road until we were completely out of sight of any humans, then took off into the air. I still had a small portion of Abby and Justin's strength, which made the flight back so much easier.

Abby and Justin were already waiting for us when we arrived at the rock cave. Thankfully, we hadn't come across anyone who wanted to kill us, and we had Mava to thank for that.

Justin adjusted his backpack, which was slung over his shoulder. "How are you feeling, Lucy?"

Abby shone her torch at me.

I shielded my eyes. "Great." I lifted my shirt enough to show my non-existent wound. The last of the crust had come away during the flight back.

"Good," Abby said, pointing the torch at my stomach. "Because you're going to need to be at your best for what we're about to do."

I swallowed hard as I let my shirt fall back into place. "Do you think they'll be waiting for us?"

Abby shone the light back on my face. "I think they'd be stupid not to."

Marcus snatched the torch off Abby and pointed it at her eyes. "And that's why we need to get in and out of there as quickly as possible."

She knocked his arm. "Get that thing out of my eyes."

"Really?" He flicked the light back into her eyes. "Because you have no problem shining it in Lucy's."

Abby snatched the torch back from Marcus and glared at him for about two seconds before her eyes once again lit up with the excitement of what was to come.

Abby may not have liked war, but she sure as hell liked stopping it.

"How about you guys stay here while we head over to Astrid's?" Justin suggested.

Narrowing my eyes, I took two steps toward him. "I don't plan on hiding in the shadows while everyone else risks their lives for us."

Abby pointed that damn light at me again. "You won't be hiding in the shadows. You'll be hiding in a cave."

I raised a brow at her then turned my attention to Marcus. "I don't want to sit around waiting all the time. Plus, it'll give me another chance to practice."

"Practice what?" Abby and Justin said in unison.

Ignoring their question, Marcus said to me, "As much as I hate to admit it, I think you're right."

I grinned. "Glad you're seeing it my way."

Abby flashed the torch in Marcus's face. "Practice what?"

"Get that out of my eyes."

I grabbed the torch from her. "You can see in the dark. I can't."

"Fine." She held up her hands. "Now, is someone going to fill us in on what you guys have been up to since we've been gone?"

"Marcus came up with a theory where I might be able to make people believe things that aren't real, or not see me when I'm standing in front of them." I laughed thinking about the way the bartender had looked at Marcus when he'd ordered a drink for me.

"What's so funny?" Abby asked.

"Nothing," I replied. As humorous as Abby would've found Marcus's imaginary girlfriend, we didn't have time for laughs. We were on a mission, and we didn't need any distractions.

"How did it work out for you?" Justin asked.

I looked at Marcus. According to him, I was doing really well, but I still thought I could improve. "Pretty well with humans. But I haven't tested it out on any demons or witches, so we have no idea how helpful my new skill will be against Morgana."

Marcus lowered the pillowcase sack onto the ground beside the wall of the cave. "Justin and Abby will go into Astrid's store, and we'll stay in the shadows, watching their backs."

I opened my mouth to remind him I didn't want to stay in the shadows when he quickly added, "So that we can see what's coming and catch them by surprise instead of them catching us by surprise."

Fair point. "Sounds like a plan."

Justin dropped his shoulder, letting his backpack fall off. He caught it before it hit the ground then retrieved the shiny ice pick.

"I guess that one's mine," I said.

He handed me the ice pick. "It's more powerful than you think."

"That's what I keep telling her," Marcus said.

I pocketed the ice pick as Justin handed Marcus and Abby their weapons. Why he hadn't thought to give us something to arm ourselves with earlier was beyond me. Whatever the reason, I was happy I had something to protect myself from the creatures stalking me on the very real chance that I couldn't hide myself in plain sight.

We headed out of the cave, and Justin and Abby took off into the sky, leaving Marcus and me behind.

"We'll leave in two minutes," he said.

I nodded. Adrenaline was already pumping through my veins as I anticipated what was to come. A great deal was riding on me, and I wasn't taking it lightly.

Marcus curled his hand around my hip. "I want you to promise you'll stay with me."

I smiled. "Like I'm brave enough to be anywhere else." The guy could shoot fire from his body and wind from his hands. I'd be stupid to go off on my own.

I stood on the balls of my feet and planted a kiss on his lips. Before I could pull away, Marcus swept me into his arms and gave me a deep, searing kiss to remember.

"You ready?" he asked.

"As I'll ever be," I lied.

CHAPTER 32

*F*lying through the night sky, I looked down at the lights below and wished I were as oblivious as the humans were to the world I was now trapped inside of. But if I were, I wouldn't have the man I loved. I would give everything up for him.

Doing as Marcus had shown me on my last descent, I pulled up then glided down, making sure I landed amongst the coverage of the trees so as to avoid not only human eyes but also those of the supernatural kind.

Marcus's muscles were tensed, and his gaze was not on me. That was a surefire way to tell we weren't alone. We had company, and I had no idea if they knew we'd arrived and we were walking into an ambush, or if we had successfully flown in under the cover of Mava's spell.

Hellhounds and Soul Scrapers weren't already on our asses, so I presumed the latter.

I retracted my wings and followed Marcus to a large bush that had a clear view of Astrid's store. We lay on the ground and army-crawled into a position that allowed us to see clearly but also remain hidden.

Astrid's place was dark, so I couldn't see what was going on inside, but that didn't mean Marcus couldn't. "Are they safe?" I whispered.

"For now." He pointed to an area to the left where there were a couple of cars parked in a neighboring driveway. "A couple of Hellhounds are pacing in the shadows over there. And a group of Soul Scrapers are amongst the trees about one hundred meters in that direction. He pointed to the right.

"It's odd, isn't it?"

He nodded. "Even if they can't feel us, they should've seen Abby and Justin come in. They should've seen us fly in."

"Then why aren't they doing anything?"

"I wish I could say it was you that hid us from them, but the truth is, I don't know."

That made me nervous. So far they'd been predictable. Now, something was different, and it made the hairs on the back of my neck stand up.

Marcus reached into his pocket and retrieved his phone. The screen was dimly lit, and a message from Abby was waiting for him.

Got it.

Marcus typed his reply: **Wait 'til I give the order.**

There he was again, ordering her around. I knew deep in my heart that it was his nature and he didn't mean anything by it. It was who he was, who he'd forgotten he was.

"Can you try to take the memories of the Hellhounds from here?"

I squinted my eyes as I tried to focus on where they were and connect with them.

I shook my head. "I can't. I need to see them."

Disappointment crossed his features, and it killed a small piece of me. If I gave him back what was his, none of this would be necessary. Abby and Justin wouldn't be in danger, and Marcus would be free.

He twisted his head to face me. The disappointment instantly dropped from his eyes the moment his gaze met mine. "Whatever you're thinking, stop it right now."

"I'm not..."

He raised his brow.

I stared into his amber eyes, not knowing what to say. I couldn't very well tell him what was on my mind. To him, me giving back the piece of him that was buried deep inside of me wasn't an option. As much as I wanted to believe it would stay that way forever, I was terrified I would one day break his heart, and I prayed he would forgive me.

The promise Morgana made to me that led us to this never-ending curse wasn't real. But our happily ever after rested in my hands, and being able to take from those without being able to see them would've almost guaranteed our success. Now, we were in limbo.

I didn't like limbo.

Stealing his gaze away from mine, he typed a message to Abby as he said, "Things are going to get ugly when they walk out the door. Are you ready?"

I nodded. I was ready to fight for what I wanted because nothing ever came on a silver platter. That shit just wasn't real.

Marcus pressed send.

CHAPTER 33

*T*he door to Astrid's shop flung open, and Abby and Justin ran outside, armed and ready to take on their enemies lying in the shadows, waiting for them to surface. Everything went into slow motion as the Hellhounds sprinted toward them, their giant paws ripping into the earth, sending puffs of grass and dirt into the air. Their teeth were bared, ready to sink into flesh and bone, and their eyes were filled with bloodlust.

My mind exploded with a mixture of guilt, fear, and pressure as I focused on hiding both Abby and Justin from the creatures. Taking away their memories wasn't as easy as it was with humans. The supernatural creatures were different. They were stronger, faster, and deadlier.

As soon as I managed to remove one memory, they'd already caught up on the situation unfolding before them. They were fast, and I couldn't take the memories quickly enough to keep Abby and Justin safe.

In a last ditch effort, I took the two monsters' entire memories. My eyes widened in surprise as they crumpled to the ground. A split-second later, my mind exploded with bloodthirst and an unrelenting urge to rip Abby and Justin apart, sink my fangs into their flesh, and drink from their souls.

Soul Scrapers swept through the street, no longer remaining hidden, but they weren't what was on my mind.

I leaped up off the ground and raced toward Abby and Justin, ready to feed my newfound desire.

Only I never made it past the bush.

No matter how quick I was, Marcus was faster. He latched his arm around my waist and lifted me off the ground as he brought me back against his chest. "What are you doing?"

I desperately fought my demonic need for our friends, focused my unwanted desire on the Soul Scrapers, and threw that desire back to the Hellhounds.

Fire burned under Abby's skin, causing Justin to take a few steps to the right as she prepared to fight for her life and ours.

Only it wasn't needed.

I relaxed in Marcus's arms as the Hellhounds got to their feet and turned their attention on the Soul Scrapers.

"What did you do?" Marcus whispered in my ear.

"Watch and see."

The Hellhounds stalked toward Abby and Justin then broke into a sprint, tearing straight past them. They leaped into the air and came crashing down on two Soul Scrapers as they sunk their teeth into their demented bodies.

I could only assume the Soul Scrapers hadn't vaporized because they never considered their own kind would turn against them.

Marcus released his grip on me then stood by my side. "I don't believe it."

A grin spread across my face. "Believe it, baby. Because it just happened." I was beyond excited by my accomplishment. But I couldn't bask in my small victory for long. There were only two Hellhounds, and there were many more Soul Scrapers heading in our direction.

We needed to get our asses out of there.

Black shadows broke off from the pack that had been heading toward Abby and Justin and rushed in our direction. They may not have been able to feel us, but they sure could see us.

Marcus grabbed my hand. "Let's get out of here."

I didn't need to be told twice.

He pulled me into a one-armed embrace then pushed off the

ground, taking me a good ten meters into the air with him as Abby and Justin quickly followed.

Wrapping my arms around Marcus, my wings exploded from my back, and I flew us higher into the sky, away from the commotion below.

Once we were a safe distance, I hovered in midair and looked down at the demonic creatures below.

The Soul Scrapers had disappeared back into the shadows of the night, and the Hellhounds were circling the area beneath us, their heads tilted up, their gaze focused on me.

Justin and Abby pulled up in front of us, a look of wonder in their eyes.

"What happened down there?" Abby gestured to the Hellhounds.

"That's what I'd like to know," Marcus said.

I glanced down at the demonic monsters. Their behavior was troubling me. I'd turned their focus on the Soul Scrapers, but now they were once again watching me. I wondered if what I'd done was only temporary.

It was something I'd have to figure out before we tried anything at the coven. The last thing we needed was to assume my abilities were permanent and then have everything go to shit because they were only temporary. We couldn't afford to be caught. We had to do things right—the first time.

I returned my attention to Abby and Justin. "I couldn't keep up with removing the Hellhounds' memories of you guys. They're not like human minds. They're much more efficient and recovered quicker than I could handle. So, I decided to take their whole memories—"

"And that's when they collapsed," Marcus said.

"Yeah. And I had the unfortunate pleasure of experiencing their bloodthirst for you two." I cocked my head toward Abby and Justin. "I wanted to sink my fangs, that I clearly don't have, into your flesh."

"That's when you took off toward Abby and Justin, wasn't it?" Marcus asked.

I nodded. "But you were too quick. And it gave me a moment to consider what I was doing and how I could turn it around. So, I turned my bloodthirst to the Soul Scrapers and gave the Hellhounds back their memories."

"Holy shit," Abby said with a laugh. "That is freakin' awesome."

Marcus wore the proudest smile, which sent my heart soaring. I'd done something none of us ever considered a possibility, and if I could keep it up, I was going to save his ass while keeping mine.

However, life had proven time and time again that nothing was ever that easy. But I could and would hold onto hope. Sometimes, hope was all we had.

"Where to now?" I asked.

"Follow us," Justin said. "We've got a plan."

I took off after them.

A minute later they descended in the backyard of a small timber home, closely surrounded by other houses.

I followed them down and landed almost perfectly, narrowly missing the laundry cart sitting next to the clothesline. I was finally getting used to these wings.

I released Marcus from my grip. "Where are we?"

He glanced back at the house. "This is Paege's house. And I'm guessing we're here to get her to help us with the location spell."

"You got it, demon boy," Abby said.

Justin ducked under the low hanging clothesline as he came over to us. "We figured it would be better if we got Paege to perform the spell so we don't waste any more time. And after what we saw you can do back there, it looks as if we can get her to help us without tipping off the other witches."

"You want me to remove her memory of us being here, don't you?"

He nodded.

"Sounds easy enough."

We headed up the garden path to the back door. Thanks to Marcus, we were inside within seconds.

Justin entered first, followed by Abby, Marcus, and me. Of course I was at the back. I was always at the back with the trio in front, ready to save my butt. Only I didn't need saving.

Old habits were hard to break.

The light flicked on. We'd been busted.

CHAPTER 34

*P*aege stood not more than two yards away from us with a cell phone in her hand, and finger poised above the screen. "Give me one good reason why I shouldn't press this button and alert Morgana that you're here."

"Cut the bullshit," Abby said. "If you were going to call Morgana or one of her little minions, you would've done it by now." Abby pulled out a stool from under the kitchen bench and took a seat as if she were a welcome guest in Paege's home. "But you want to know what we want and what's in it for you."

Paege pressed the home button on her phone. "Start talking."

"Well for one, you'll get to live another day."

"And two?"

"Who says there's a two?"

Paege glared at her then cast a glance at Marcus. "What do you want to know?"

Something told me she didn't want another repeat of what happened back in her shop. She was clearly no match for Marcus, and now we were adding a Soul Collector and a Succubus to the pot. Paege didn't stand a chance. And she knew it.

Justin dumped his backpack on the bench. "We need you to locate someone for us."

Marcus carefully placed the pillowcase beside Justin's bag. "And we need you to do it now."

She studied the three of them. Then her eyes fell on me. "What you're asking could get me into a lot of trouble. There's a price on her head and—"

Leaning his hand on the bench, Marcus positioned himself between Paege and me. "If you value your head, I wouldn't finish that sentence."

I shuffled to the side just in time to see the fear in her eyes. She was terrified of Marcus and rightfully so.

Paege gathered her composure. "Now it is then."

"Glad you see it my way." Marcus pushed off the bench and walked over to me. "Don't let what she said worry you."

"It should worry you," Paege said. "You'd be foolish to think there isn't a bounty on her. Foolishness leads to complacency."

"She doesn't worry me." I stepped around Marcus. "And I can assure you, Paege, there is no complacency here. I'm aware everyone wants me dead."

"And yet you're here."

I pulled out the stool beside Abby and sat. "Being aware doesn't mean I'm going to hide."

Marcus rested his hands on my shoulders. "Get started."

Justin spilled the contents from his bag. The only new things I hadn't seen before were a hairbrush and a toothbrush.

Paege spread the items apart. "May I ask who I am locating?"

"No," Marcus and Abby said in unison.

"Fine."

Justin helped Paege prepare the ingredients then combine them in a small cauldron that fit perfectly on her bench top. When the potion was ready, he spread a world map across the bench.

Paege's eyes widened as she looked at the map.

"What's wrong?" I asked. "Can't you search that far?"

Marcus wrapped his arms around me from behind. "She can, but she's not happy about it."

"Why not?"

"Because it will drain her."

Abby strummed her fingers on the stone bench. "We're waiting."

Paege glared at her momentarily then grabbed the crystal dangling on a gold chain and dunked it into the cauldron. She dipped her index finger into the mixture, raised her finger to her forehead, and placed one dot over her third eye.

She focused her attention on the crystal as she lifted the chain, so it hung over the middle of the map. When the crystal stopped moving, Paege began chanting something under her breath in Latin.

The crystal started to move as if it were a life force of its own. Then, it hovered, deadly straight, over the part of New Zealand where Morgana's home was.

"That can't be right," Abby said, getting frustrated. "We were just there, and the location spell we performed from right outside her estate didn't work."

Paege raised her tired gaze to meet Abby's. "I can assure you it's correct."

Abby rose from her seat, her hands spread across the bench. "I said, we were just there, and they weren't there."

Paege lowered the crystal onto the map. "Who wasn't there?"

Returning to her seat, Abby said, "I don't think so."

"Maybe if you told me, I could help you. But either way, the person you are looking for is in New Zealand."

"Shit," Marcus let go of me then moved to take a closer look at the map. "They must've split them up."

"Impossible," Abby said. "I went closer than I should've, and I didn't feel either one of them."

Paege raised an eyebrow. "Ah. You're looking for Mava."

Realizing how easily I could remove her knowledge about what we were doing, I figured we had no issues divulging information if it might help us in our quest. "Yes. We're looking for Mava and Astrid. Justin and Abby have already done the location spell near Morgana's coven in New Zealand, and neither Mava nor Astrid were there. And now you're saying that Astrid *is* there."

"That's exactly what I'm saying if it were Astrid's hair that we used just now. And I'm assuming you had used something of Mava's previously."

"Well, we think it was Mava's, but we don't really know."

She tilted her head to the side. "How can you not be sure?"

I glanced at Justin. "Well, Mava had put something aside for us in case anything should happen to her, and there was also a lock of hair."

Paege bit down on a laugh. "And you think it was Mava's hair?"

She shook her head. "You foolish child. Mava wouldn't have given you her own hair to find. It would've been yours."

She was looking right at me. Me.

"It was Luciana's," Justin said. "Of course, it was—"

A low, rumbling growl coming from outside sent chills down my spine.

The men were by the window before I realized they'd moved, and Abby had her hand on my arm, ready to rescue me if the situation arose.

We had to be quick and find another way out of the house before we could get away, up into the air, out of the monsters' reach. Either that or we were going to have to fight our way out.

I absently ran my fingers over the area where the last Hellhound that had gotten too close had ripped its claws through my flesh. The memory was still vivid. I could feel it as if it were happening now.

With furrowed brows, Marcus turned to me. "They're acting strangely. What did you do to them?"

Marcus's question didn't go unnoticed by Paege, and I made a mental note to remove that memory as well. "I don't know."

He flicked out his knife and headed to the back door. "Stay here." He looked pointedly at me.

"Fine," I lied. As soon as he'd gone outside, I was out of my seat and yanking the door open, ready to help Marcus. All I needed to do was take their vision and…

My eyes widened in astonishment. Marcus was standing to the side of the garden path, but the beasts took no interest in him.

"What the…?" Abby looked at the scene before her, mouth wide open and disbelief written all over her face.

The moment the beasts spotted me, they trotted over to Abby and me. Their jaws were closed, and their eyes were no longer consumed with bloodlust as they had been every single other time I'd encountered a Hellhound.

Marcus was by my side in the blink of an eye. He positioned himself slightly in front of me but still allowed me to see the black monsters. "Something's different," he said over his shoulder.

I stepped around him. "I know."

The Hellhounds came to a standstill not more than a yard in front of me then dropped to the ground, their giant eyes trained on me.

"What are they doing?" I asked.

496

Marcus spread his hand over the small of my back. "They're submitting."

"Why are they submitting?"

He kneeled down in front of them, his glowing blade resting by his knees. "You tell me."

I dropped to my knees on the dewy grass beside Marcus. "I did this to them, didn't I?"

Marcus nodded. "Their allegiance now lies with you."

CHAPTER 35

Their allegiance now lies with you. Those were six words I never thought I would hear, but sure enough, not more than two feet away were two giant Hellhounds lying down before me.

I had no idea what I had done to change their allegiance from the demonic world over to me, and from the looks of things, it seemed I was stuck with them. I wasn't sure if that was a good or bad thing.

The last time I'd encountered those hellish creatures, I'd almost had my stomach ripped open by one, and I didn't want to go through that again.

Abby cautiously walked up beside us. "Can someone tell us what is going on here?"

Paege came out the back door with Justin following closely. She sucked in a sharp breath as she looked at the beasts lying down before me. Her gaze darted to me, a mixture of panic and awe filling her eyes. "You've been marked," she whispered.

I glanced back at the Hellhounds on the off chance they were going to suddenly switch their allegiance and make me their dinner. "What do you mean I've been marked?"

Studying me, Paege took a couple of steps closer. "Who are you?"

"That's not important," Marcus said.

The Hellhound on the right, which had a large scar across its cheek, crawled a couple of inches forward and jutted its nose out to me a couple of times as if it were trying to get my attention.

"What does he want?" I asked.

"You tell us," Abby said. "You're the one who has this connection with them, not us."

I scowled at her. "You're a Succubus, and they're Hellhounds. Doesn't that mean you guys are family or something?"

She stuck her hands on her hips and raised a brow. "What? Because we're both demons?"

"Well, yeah."

"That's not how it works," Marcus said, jumping to Abby's defense. "Just because they're from the same side doesn't mean they're connected to each other."

"Right," I mouthed.

Justin shoved his hands into the pockets of his jeans and rocked back and forth on his heels. "As interesting as all this is, we need to keep moving."

He was right. As amazing as this situation with the Hellhounds was, we had to keep focused. I stood and backed away from the Hellhounds.

Marcus studied the creatures for a couple more seconds then rose to his feet. "We've done all we need to do here." He turned his back to the monsters. "Lu, it's time for you to clean up." He gestured to Paege.

Paege stood to the side of the open back door. "And here I thought I was the one who'd be left behind to clean up all the mess."

I was about to wipe her memory of the event when I realized leaving everything for Paege to clean up would tip her off that someone had come to her place and her memory had been tampered with.

We needed to be invisible, which meant we needed to clean up.

Smiling, I headed to the house. "After everything you've done for us, the least we could do is help tidy up."

Paege returned my smile. "I may have been wrong about you."

I stepped inside, strode over to the kitchen, and began gathering the dishes we'd used. "What did you think about me?"

"That you were just a myth." She put the plug in the sink, then turned the tap on and squirted detergent into the steaming hot water. "But if Morgana wants you as badly as I've heard she does, there must be some truth to it."

Paege peeked out the window in the direction of the Hellhounds in her backyard. "Plus, the Hellhounds have marked you." She turned around to face me and leaned her hands against the bench behind her. "They're yours to command, but I hope you know what you're doing."

Even though I had absolutely no idea what I was doing, I nodded. I didn't want her to think I could be easily challenged.

It didn't take long to clean up the mess, wash and dry the dishes, then return them to their rightful place in the kitchen cupboards.

"Thanks again, Paege," I said as we headed out the back door.

"I hope you'll find what you're looking for." She closed the door.

I quickly moved so I could see through the kitchen window and waited for Paege to come into view as the others stood to the side, waiting for me to do my thing.

She walked past the window a moment later, heading toward the hallway. I only had a second or three at most to get it right.

Focusing on removing her memory from the moment we'd arrived to the moment we left, I willed myself to take the memory from her.

Within seconds, my mind was filled with new memories of the last hour, most of which I already knew because I was there, but there were also a few new pieces of information I hadn't been privy to before I'd taken her thoughts.

Morgana really was evil, and I knew now more than ever that I would have to watch our backs because there was nothing Morgana wouldn't do to get what she wanted.

The bonus I got from Paege was that I now knew how to cast the location spell. I had no clue if I would still need to be near the person I was trying to find, or if I could search the world the way a witch could, but it was still something.

I hurried back to the others. "What are we going to do about these two?" I gestured to the Hellhounds.

Marcus gripped the back of his neck. "Shit."

Justin leaned against the house. "We can't exactly leave them here. Paege and any other witch or demon will know something is up."

"Then what do you suppose we do with them, genius?" Abby asked.

"I don't know."

"Of course not."

"We'll take them back to the cave," Marcus said. "They can stay there until we get back—if they're even still there when we return."

With Marcus in my embrace, we took off into the air with Justin and Abby close by.

It was strange to watch the Hellhounds rise to their feet then race through the streets and bushes as they chased after us. I could've easily disappeared from their sight, but somehow they still knew where to find me. And as amazing as it was, it was also a very dangerous thing.

They were connected to me in ways I didn't understand, and I prayed it would wear off, because if it didn't, that meant I had to watch what I gave to a person or creature. I couldn't handle having an army of demons by my side—or could I?

I quickly dismissed the idea. Marcus had said I should be careful what I take from a demon, and I refused to do anything that would put Marcus's light in jeopardy.

I would have to take things slowly. Do whatever was necessary and no more.

CHAPTER 36

$\mathcal{W}$e landed near the entrance to the cave and waited for the Hellhounds to catch up—if they were still tracking me.

Abby nudged Justin. "Got any food in that bag of yours?" She gestured to his backpack.

He twisted around to face her. "Did it look like I did when I dumped the contents on Paege's kitchen bench?"

Abby shrugged. "For all I know, you could've taken some of her food without me seeing."

I leaned closer to Marcus. "Those two are like siblings. They bicker about anything and everything."

Both Justin and Abby snapped their heads in my direction. "We do not," they said in unison.

Marcus chuckled. "Abby always gets crabby when she's hungry, and Justin isn't much better."

She scowled at him. "Like you're any better."

"You don't see me trying to pick a fight, do you?"

My ears pricked as the sound of footsteps—or giant paws—thudded against the damp earth in the distance. "They're here."

As they neared, Marcus and Justin whipped out their weapons. I assumed they weren't sure if the Hellhounds' allegiance still lay with me either.

The black beasts came into view as they leaped over a group of rocks that were taller than I was and darted amongst the trees, heading straight for us.

Marcus took two steps forward and positioned himself in front of me.

I appreciated his chivalry, but I could've easily taken the monsters ability to move if they showed the slightest change in their temperament toward us. Although, Marcus had said I had to be careful not to take too much from a demon, which was probably why he was putting himself on the line.

After what I'd felt when I'd taken the Hellhounds' minds, I certainly didn't need to find out why I had to be careful. I sure as hell didn't want to be stuck with their rage—if that were even possible.

My thoughts went back to what Paege had said about me being marked. After taking part of her memory tonight, I knew it wasn't just that the Hellhounds bowed to me. She was also referring to a small piece of my soul that would forever be marked with their prints. And she wasn't talking about the ones on their feet.

The Hellhounds eased up their pace and slowly trotted toward me, every curve of their muscles glistening under the moonlight.

I grabbed hold of the back of Marcus's shirt and gave it a tug. "I think they're still okay with me."

Marcus retracted his blade. "I think you're right."

Abby and Justin walked up beside me, weapons nowhere to be seen.

Abby shook her head in wonder. "This shit just doesn't get old, does it?"

The Hellhounds had only taken a liking to me about an hour ago. Of course, it wasn't old, but I couldn't be bothered pointing that out to her.

She turned her back to the beasts as they pulled up in front of us. "Marcus, you better tell me you plan on grabbing something to eat before we leave. Otherwise, you can go to Morgana's on your own."

He chuckled. "And risk having to deal with a rabid little demon? I wouldn't dream of it."

"I do not get rabid," she snapped.

I raised my brows.

Abby glared at me. "I am not crabby, or rabid, or whatever you want to call it. I'm hungry."

Justin patted her back. "Keep telling yourself that." He walked over to the Hellhounds, reached his hand up to Scar-face's neck, and stopped short of making contact.

Scar-face turned his head toward Justin's hand and sniffed it.

"I can't believe he's letting you do that," I said in disbelief.

Abby cleared her throat. "It's a she."

"Oh," I said as Justin gave the Hellhound a rub along its neck. "And what's the other one?" I leaned down to have a look.

Justin, Abby, and even Marcus laughed.

I stood tall. "What? How else am I supposed to tell?"

"Because all Hellhounds are female," Marcus said.

I put my hands on my hips and scowled at him. "Like I'm supposed to know that."

Marcus grabbed my shoulder and pulled me toward him. "I'm sorry." He wrapped his arms around me and kissed the side of my neck. "I shouldn't laugh."

I gently punched his stomach. "No. You shouldn't." I pulled away. "I'm still new to all this."

The smile dropped from his eyes, and I couldn't help but think his thoughts were going back to how long I'd lived in this world of theirs yet still remained oblivious to so much.

I loosely held Marcus's hand and led him over to the Hellhound without the scar. "I can't believe I'm about to do this."

"I can't believe most of what you're doing," Marcus said.

Taking a deep breath, I gingerly placed my hand on the Hellhound's shoulder and ran my fingers over the curves of its muscles. The beast was warm, not burning like the one that had fallen on top of me back at Marcus's house. I wondered how their body temperature worked and if it had anything to do with their emotions. Or if they only burned while they were in a fight.

She turned her head toward me and nudged her face against mine, forcing me to adjust my stance so it didn't push me over with its sheer strength.

Marcus ran his hand down the length of her back. "This is unbelievable. I never thought I'd see the day when a Hellhound would allow us to touch it this way."

Abby walked up to the one with a scar and patted the creature's chest. "Imagine what we can do with these two."

I peered around the Hellhound at Abby. "Such as?"

"Well, think about it. We now have two more protectors for you."

The Hellhound I was petting rubbed her head against the back of mine.

I lost my footing and stumbled forward.

Justin caught me by my arm before I made a fool of myself. "Watch your step around them."

I nodded then reached up toward Scar-face.

She nudged her head against my hand as a low rumble came from deep within her.

I jumped back, fearing she was about to bite my hand off.

Abby pulled Scar-face back. "You're okay. That noise is her purring."

I screwed up my face. "These things purr?"

She laughed. "Not like a normal cat, but something like it."

There didn't seem to be that much of a difference between their growl and what Abby considered a purr. "I'll take your word for it."

Marcus rubbed the scarless Hellhound behind the ear. "We better find somewhere to put these two while we get some rest."

"We're not flying over there now?" I asked in surprise.

He took a few steps closer to me. "The agreement was that we would fly up here, prepare for our rescue mission, and then you were going to rest until the morning when we would set off for New Zealand."

I folded my arms across my body. That was the agreement, but I was energized and ready to take on the world. I didn't want to waste the next five or six hours being unconscious. "I'll be fine."

"Will you? Because there's nowhere to land when we're out at sea."

I was about to object when I realized exactly what that meant. If I got tired or fell asleep during the flight, we'd be screwed. Marcus would be screwed.

"Okay. You're right."

He hooked his arm around my neck, pulled me into his embrace, and kissed the top of my head. "Of course, I'm right."

"Good," Abby said. "Now we can eat while you get your rest."

I twisted around in Marcus's arms so he was standing behind me. "You know, I'm hungry, too."

She shrugged. "Let's eat then."

Marcus leaned in from behind and kissed my cheek. "We better get these two inside. The crystals in the cave should hide them for a while."

We headed into the cave with the Hellhounds following closely.

"How are we going to make them stay?" I shone the torch around the cavern.

"Tell them to," Abby said as if it was the dumbest question to ever leave my mouth.

Ignoring her, I looked at Marcus.

"I don't know. Maybe give them a command to stay, like Abby said."

I scratched my head as the Hellhounds circled the cavern. "Let's see if this works."

I walked up to the monsters, and they both greeted me as if they were my pets. They weren't my pets. They were evil, demonic creatures that were... my pets. "Guess I should name you girls."

"How about one and two?" Abby offered the moment I'd finished my sentence.

"Really?"

She shrugged. "That would make it quick and easy."

"So that you could get some food," Marcus pointed out.

Abby shrugged again.

Scar-face lay in front of me then rolled onto her back as if she were a dog that wanted its belly scratched. That was so not going to happen.

"This one can be... Scarlett, because of her scar." I turned to the other one. "And this one can be..." I stuck my hands on my hips. "I have no idea."

"One? Two?" Abby suggested again. "Or Hell and Hound?"

I bit down on my smile. "So not happening."

Abby groaned. "Does it really matter?"

Not really, but I wasn't going to tell her that.

"Immensely," Justin said, studying the nameless hound.

"I agree," Marcus said with a serious expression. "This decision can't be rushed."

Abby threw her head back and looked up at the cave ceiling. "You have got to be kidding me."

Both Marcus and Justin smiled at me then quickly returned to pretending to be serious when Abby glared at the three of us.

"Fine," she said. "How about Ruth? Mary? Josephine? Tabatha?" She continued to list at least thirty more names.

I shook my head. "Nah. None of those names really fit her."

Abby groaned again as she strolled aimlessly around the cavern. "You guys are killing me!"

Keeping a straight face, I said, "Well, I'm sorry, but these things can't be rushed. She deserves a good name."

"What? Like Scarlett?"

"Yes, like Scarlett."

"Fine." She strolled over to the nameless Hellhound, kneeled beside it, and studied the creature. "It's eyes glow red in here; how about Red?"

I pretended to consider it for a moment then shook my head. "Nah, that doesn't sound like the right fit."

She twisted around to face me. "Do you realize what happens when a demon get's hungry?"

Marcus chuckled. "Yeah, they get crabby."

"I do not get crabby. Evil, maybe, but not crabby."

Justin stepped closer to the nameless Hellhound. "How about Ruby because of her ruby red eyes?"

My eyes widened, and I clapped my hands together, pretending to be excited by his suggestion when in reality, I didn't care what we named her. "That's perfect!"

"Are you kidding me?" Abby said.

With a smirk spread across my face, I shrugged. "Ruby it is."

I turned my attention back to Scarlett and Ruby. "Stay here, Scarlett and Ruby. That's an order." I had no idea if that was going to work, but I figured Abby knew best.

Abby rose to her feet. "Now, can we finally get some food?"

Justin opened the zipper to a small compartment on the inside of his bag and drew out two granola bars. "Here you go." He threw them to her.

She caught them. "You've had these all this time, and you're only offering them now?"

He shrugged a shoulder. "I only just remembered I'd put a couple away there."

I had no idea if he was telling the truth or if he'd known they were there all this time and happily watched her get more upset the hungrier she got. Part of me thought it was funny, and another part made me wonder if he was still hiding things from us. Then again, I'd acted just as bad.

I chastised myself for even considering his loyalty. Justin had helped us. He was still helping us, and I needed to get over the distrust because they were my issues, not his.

We backed away out of the cavern, and I was pleasantly surprised Scarlett and Ruby actually stayed.

"It worked," I said when we were outside.

"Told you," Abby said, crumpling the last wrapper of the granola bar. "Now can we get something to eat?"

"And somewhere to sleep," Marcus added.

With Marcus in my arms, we took off into the sky, making sure we stayed above the cloud coverage Marcus conveniently brought to us. We headed down the coast, stopping when we reached Coffs Harbour.

CHAPTER 37

$\mathcal{O}$nce again I was glad I'd listened to Marcus and accepted I needed to rest. By the time we'd reached Coffs Harbour, I was ready to crawl into bed and sleep for the next ten hours.

Marcus and I headed to a motel while Justin went with Abby into town to grab some food.

I leaned my head against Marcus's side, his arm protectively around me as we made our way up the driveway of yet another seedy motel that didn't have very well placed security cameras, which was the reason he'd chosen it.

Luxury came at a cost, and I wasn't talking about money. Someone could easily hack into security cameras, and if they were lucky, they would find us while we slept.

Besides, a bed was a bed, and right now, I didn't care if it was a mattress that we'd found under a bridge. I was ready to crash.

The manager, or whoever he was, barely looked our way as he handed Marcus two sets of keys and settled back in his seat to watch the soccer game on TV.

We made our way through the poorly maintained gardens to our room. Most of the lights in the other rooms were off, but there were still a few that were lit, and drunken slurs came from within them.

Marcus opened the door to our room and flicked on the light. He scanned the room to make sure no one was hiding inside, ready to attack. Satisfied we weren't walking into a trap, he held the door wide open for me to enter.

I stepped inside and was welcomed by the bed calling out to me.

As hungry as I was, exhaustion had taken over. I slipped out of my pants and shirt then climbed under the sheets.

Fully dressed, Marcus propped the pillows up beside me. He climbed onto the bed and sat, leaning against the pillows.

"You're not sleeping?"

He shook his head. "No. I need to wait up for the other two, and I want to keep an eye on you."

A warm smile curled up the sides of his lips as he brushed my hair away from my face. "Get some sleep."

Closing my eyes, I snuggled into his side. I slept, a deep sleep filled with absolutely no dreams or disturbances.

The next morning I awoke to Marcus sleeping beside me.

I smiled as I watched him sleep peacefully, his arm wrapped around me.

I didn't mind being locked in his embrace. Actually, I loved it. For a second, I could pretend this was how our life would be once we'd saved the world. Then, reality hit, and I knew there was a very real possibility I wouldn't live to see that day.

"You're awake," he said, his eyes still closed.

"So are you."

He dragged the tips of his fingers down the length of my back, stopping just above my panties. "I never went to sleep."

"Could've fooled me."

Marcus opened his eyes. "And risk your safety? Never."

He rolled onto his back, pulling me with him.

Placing my hands on his chest, I pushed up into a sitting position, my legs straddling his hips.

Marcus ran his hands down my hips, further lighting the fire burning deep within my soul. I knew we should be preparing for our flight, but I was only half-human, and I was alone in bed with the man I loved.

I glanced at the clock on the bedside table. 5:08. We still had some time before the sun rose, and I planned on using our time the best way I knew how.

Reaching behind my back, I undid my bra and let it slide off.

Marcus groaned. "God, you're beautiful." He trailed the tips of his fingers over my breasts and down to my panties. "I could get used to this every morning."

I bit down on a grin. "You better because once this is all over, it's just you and me and nothing but time."

Maybe that wasn't entirely true because we had yet to find out who Marcus truly was, but this, what we were doing now, was worth fighting for. And we both knew it.

All too soon it was time to leave. Abby and Justin arrived, bearing gifts of various breakfast scrolls, muffins, and pastries.

Abby slumped into the tub chair, a big-ass grin on her face. "I see you're feeling better."

I couldn't help thinking she knew what we'd done, and it was driving me insane. A little bit of privacy between a couple wasn't so much to ask for.

Trying to avoid answering her question, I shoved a pastry into my mouth and pretended she hadn't said a word.

Marcus grabbed a croissant and took a bite. "Are you guys ready to go?"

Justin leaned against the narrow desk. "All packed and ready to go."

The corner of Abby's lips tipped up. "We've just been waiting for you two."

Closing my eyes, I turned my back to her then opened my eyes and focused on the food in my hand.

It wasn't long before Marcus and I had finished off the goodies, and we were heading out the door. Like all the other times, we made our way to a discreet area before we took flight. And lucky me, I got to spend the next three hours or so in the arms of the man I loved. Well, that was what I focused on because the trip across the sea was dead boring.

Endless water stretched before us, and if it weren't for Abby and Justin leading the way, I was sure I would've gotten lost and ended up on the other side of the world.

My heart skipped a beat when land came into view. We were getting closer, which was exciting and daunting at the same time. So much was riding on what we were about to do, and I prayed every single one of us, including Mava and Astrid, walked out of Morgana's estate alive.

We touched down in a small beach in Wellington. It was the first time I'd been to New Zealand, and I hoped it wouldn't be the last. The land was amazing, filled with picturesque natural beauty as the snowcapped mountains met the sea.

It was a fairytale setting. Only this wasn't a fairytale. We were about to walk into a nightmare we might never wake up from.

Letting go of Marcus, I stretched my wings and the kinks in my back, then folded my wings behind me and retracted them once more into my back. "Where to now?"

Abby sat on the sand, knees up and arms wrapped loosely around them as she stared out at the sea. "I'm hungry."

"No surprises there." Back when we were in the safety of Marcus's estate, Abby was always stuffing herself with food, but I didn't realize the full extent of how much that girl needed to eat. She was way worse than Justin or Marcus, and I wondered if it had something to do with her being a demon. If that were true, who knew what shape Scarlett and Ruby were going to be in when we went back for them.

I didn't give it too much thought because my mind went back to the situation at hand. We needed to feed Abby, and if I was honest, me as well, then get on our way to rescuing Mava and Astrid.

We'd already wasted so much time, and I didn't want to delay their rescue any longer than was absolutely necessary. "How about we get something to go?"

"Sounds good to me," Marcus said.

Abby climbed to her feet. "I'm up for anything as long as I get some food."

"I'll arrange a car for us and meet you back here in fifteen minutes," Justin said.

Marcus nodded. "I'll get you something to eat as well."

"Thanks." Justin turned his back to us and trudged through the sand, heading up to the road.

Twenty minutes later, we were on our way with a car filled with takeout.

I peeled the wrapper off my second burger. "How long until we arrive?"

"We should be there in five minutes," Justin said, glancing at me from the driver's seat. "And then we'll need to go the rest of the way on foot."

"Sounds easy enough."

I couldn't have been more wrong.

CHAPTER 38

I stared down at the entrance to the old sewerage system that supposedly led up to Morgana's home. "You have got to be kidding me."

Marcus kneeled on the grass and lifted the iron grate that had been concealed by a small bush. "They'll expect us to come from above, not below."

"It's the safest way," Justin agreed. "See you down there." He climbed down the rusty old ladder that looked as if it were about to crumble into dust the moment he touched it.

I scrunched my nose up in repulsion. "What kind of place has a sewerage system leading up to their house?"

"The kind of place that is home to at least ten witches and their servants." Abby jumped down the hole, not bothering with the rickety old ladder.

Marcus looked at me apologetically. "Morgana lives in somewhat of a castle."

I raised my brows. "In New Zealand?"

He nodded. "It's only a few hundred years old. It was built around the time New Zealand was discovered, and her estate has always remained hidden from human eyes."

"What? Because of the location or how far it's set back from the front gates?"

"Partly the location, but mostly thanks to magic. Kind of like the way Soul Scrapers can go unnoticed amongst the human population."

"Are you guys coming?" Abby yelled from below. "Or should we tell Mava and Astrid you were too busy chatting to help with their rescue?"

I rolled my eyes. "On our way." I peered down into the almost pitch-black hole and prayed I wasn't about to step into a river of poop and pee.

"You'll be fine," Marcus said. "The tunnels haven't been in operation for years."

Drawing in what could be my last breath of clean air, I positioned myself at the top of the ladder and climbed down.

My heart rate picked up with each step I took. The dark, stagnant air reminding me of the first time I went into the tunnel, or more so, my trip to Purgatory. Not that I really knew what Purgatory was like. My journey had taken place in my mind, but it had felt real nonetheless.

Hoping I wasn't about to get my feet wet, I took my final step onto the ground. Relief flooded through me when I remained dry and poop-free.

I grabbed the torch out of my jeans pocket and turned it on. Light flooded the tunnel, allowing me to see I had nothing to worry about. The sewer tunnels weren't in use and looked as if they hadn't been for many years.

Marcus joined us, and then we set off down the tunnel. I was positioned behind Abby and Justin, and Marcus's hand was laced with mine in case the need arose for a quick getaway. To tell the truth, I was more than happy to be connected to the love of my life, who could literally set someone on fire.

I leaned closer to him and whispered, "You know how you said I shouldn't take too much from a demon?"

"Yeah."

"Why not?"

He took a moment to respond. "Gut feeling, I guess. And I may have proven myself right considering we have two new friends waiting for us back in Oz."

"Do you think I might also give a part of me when I give something to someone?"

He looked at me for a few seconds before saying, "It's a possibility. Although the bartender didn't seem to be affected."

"That you know of," Justin said, butting in.

I frowned as I tried to work out if I had felt any different when I'd taken either of the human's memories. "Maybe it's only the supernatural world that leaves an imprint, because I didn't feel any different when I took from the humans."

"Could be," Marcus said. "I mean, you're not exactly human yourself. You were only created with human qualities."

Coming to a fork in the tunnel, Justin swung his bag off his shoulder and placed it on the stone floor. "Do you want to stick together, or should we split up?"

"I vote stick together," I said.

Abby tucked her hands into the back pockets of her jeans. "Four are easier to spot than two."

The thought of splitting up made me feel ill. Partly because there was strength in numbers, and partly because I feared something would go wrong and I wouldn't be there to save them. "Two are easier to spot than one, but that doesn't mean we should each go our own way."

"There are only two ways," Abby pointed out.

Ignoring her, Marcus put his hand on my hip. "They can take care of themselves against the witches, and I'm not saying it to protect you, because we both know you can take care of yourself if it comes down to it."

Accepting this was the way it was going to be, I nodded. "Fine. We'll go in pairs."

Justin smiled then opened his bag and pulled a folded piece of paper out of a secret compartment sewn into the inside of his backpack. He opened it. It was a blueprint of what I assumed was Morgana's home.

My eyes widened as I realized they weren't kidding about it being a castle complete with dungeons, wings, and a crap load of space in between. The rescue mission suddenly got so much harder. Astrid and Mava could've been in at least one hundred different hiding spots around the castle, and we'd have to check each and every one of them. "No wonder you wanted to split up," I said under my breath.

"You guys take the left wing, and we'll take the right," Marcus said. "We'll start in the dungeons, and then we can work our way up."

Justin and Abby nodded.

"Let us know if you find anything, and we'll do the same."

Abby traced the lines of the tunnel heading to the left on the map. "Will do."

Marcus put his hand on the small of my back. "You better study the map, just in case..." He didn't have to finish his sentence. I knew he meant on the off chance we were split from each other. That was so not going to happen, but I did what he asked.

The problem was, the map was ridiculously detailed and large, and no matter how much I tried to remember all the different hallways and rooms, my mind was elsewhere.

"Have you got it?"

I shook my head. "There's too much to remember."

Marcus exhaled loudly. "Okay. Take my memory of the layout."

"But then you won't remember."

He smirked. "I can remember again. The map's right there."

Of course, it was—and of course, he could.

"Okay."

Focusing on subtracting that memory from him, I was almost instantly rewarded with the knowledge of every inch of the castle.

The corner of Marcus's lips tipped up when he no longer held the memory of Morgana's estate. He went down on one knee and studied the blueprint. I'd thought he would need a few minutes to recreate the detailed memory I'd taken from him, but he stood within seconds. "Let's go."

Justin packed away the blueprint then stood and swung his bag over his shoulder. "We'll keep in touch."

Marcus and I made our way through the tunnel's twists and turns as we headed deeper into the unknown. Something was grating on my nerves, setting them on edge, yet there didn't seem to be anything tangible to set them off.

"You okay?" Marcus asked.

"This all seems too easy," I replied. "I mean, they must know we're here."

"Witches can't feel us the way we can feel them. But I agree with you. This is too easy."

Marcus barely finished his sentence when I heard the sound that sent chills down my spine. A low, menacing growl echoed through the tunnel, coming from somewhere close. Too close.

Hellhounds.

CHAPTER 39

*M*arcus flicked his weapon out, the glow further lighting up the tunnel. "Stay behind me," he said, his voice barely a whisper.

I reached into my pocket and retrieved the ice pick, ready to see what it could do.

Adrenalin pumped through my veins as we waited for them to show themselves. The light from my torch bounced around the tunnel as I failed to control my nerves.

I'd thought I'd be prepared for this moment, but now that it was actually happening and there was nowhere for me to run and hide, I was terrified.

I felt as if I were going to be sick, and I wished the Hellhounds would hurry up and show themselves.

My wish came all too soon. The beasts tore through the tunnel, their ruby red eyes blazing with bloodlust, reminding me of the time I'd felt that lust myself. It was all-consuming, and I knew these Hellhounds would stop at nothing for a chance to drink from our souls and deliver us to Purgatory.

Shit was about to get real, and I only had an ice pick to defend myself with.

Wrong. I had a man who could shoot fire from his hands and

cause a storm to brew. I had all the power in the world. Except I had to choose carefully what I could live with.

The ground shook as the beasts tore toward us. I whipped my head around when I heard the pounding of feet behind me.

Shit. They were coming at us from both directions.

Marcus's eyes lit up with fear. I had nowhere to go, nowhere to hide, and he couldn't take them all on his own with me caught up in the middle.

His fear brought a sense of calmness to my soul. I couldn't hide, and I most certainly wasn't going to let him lose focus and regret his decision to come here and rescue Mava and Astrid.

"I've got this," I whispered. I turned my back to him, squared my shoulders, and prepared to do whatever was necessary.

Within seconds, the light from my torch found my prey, and I knew the light wasn't going to help me for long. There was no way I could fight and hold onto it so I could see what I was doing.

I had to do what was necessary.

Steadying my ice pick, I waited until the last second then stole the beast's vision and plunged the ice pick into its chest. I stepped to the side, narrowly missing being pinned under the creature as it crashed to the ground.

But the monster wasn't done. Its screeches echoed through the tunnel, igniting the other Hellhounds into a symphonic melody that turned my blood cold.

I chanced a glance behind me and saw the way Marcus tore through the Hellhounds, severing the heads of beast after beast as if they were incapable of landing a blow.

Turning back to prepare myself for the next Hellhound, I was slammed to the ground by a five-hundred-pound beast, its razor sharp teeth inches from my face.

With one swift movement, I stabbed the ice pick into its torso with all the force I could muster.

Absolute fury blazed in the Hellhound's ruby eyes as its body began to glow, growing brighter and brighter by the second until it exploded from within, ripping it into pieces.

My body shook uncontrollably as blood and chunks of the monster splattered all over me.

A second. A single second of fear. That was all it took for me to become the prey of yet another.

The first Hellhound I'd stabbed stretched its front paw toward me and sank its claws into my arm, ripping through my skin as it dragged me closer to her.

I rolled toward it and thrust the ice pick into its throat.

Blood gurgled out of its mouth as the glowing light began to build, and within seconds, I was covered with the insides of that Hellhound as well.

I jerked to a sitting position and wiped the blood and guts away from my eyes just in time to see another five-hundred-pound beast leap into the air, its fangs bared, ready to take a chunk out of me on impact.

I didn't have time to get out of the way, so I lifted the ice pick, ready to stick it into the Hellhound when it connected with me. I prayed I wouldn't lose any part of my body in the process.

Marcus slid past me in a blur, his blade raised toward the monster. A split second later, he reached up and tore the blade through the Hellhound's chest, all the way down to its stomach.

Blood and guts spilled from the creature's body, pouring onto both Marcus and the floor. But Marcus didn't stop. He was on his feet, battling the next one while I was still trying to come to terms with what I'd seen.

The tunnels may have trapped us, but they also stopped more than one Hellhound from coming at us at a time. They were too large to fit two across.

I sat with my arms falling between my legs, staring at Marcus in awe. One after another after another, he slaughtered the Hellhounds. They were no match for him.

It wasn't long before the last head rolled and Marcus turned back to me, blood covering his heaving chest. He looked like a war god in all his glory. I was paralyzed by his beauty.

Marcus sauntered toward me as he put his blade away, and then he kneeled down in front of me. "Are you okay?" He scanned every inch of my body and sucked in a sharp breath when he saw the elongated puncture wounds in my arm.

"It's fine." I tried wiping the sticky, black blood off my face, but it was no use. There was too much. "I can barely feel it." I was pretty sure the adrenaline still pumping through my body was the only reason I felt no pain. But I knew I was going to be in a world of pain when we finally hit safety.

Marcus glanced behind him. "Can you keep going?"

I nodded.

He helped me to my feet then scanned my body once more for any injuries he'd missed when I was sitting.

"I told you I'm fine."

"Can't blame me for worrying." He took the ice pick from my shaking hands. "Told you not to judge a weapon by its size." He wiped the blade on the back of his jeans then handed it back to me.

"Yeah," I said, pocketing the ice pick. "I didn't expect it to explode whatever I stuck it into." The blood and guts splattering all over me was not something I was going to forget in a hurry.

Marcus gently put his hand on my arm. "Are you sure you're okay?"

I breathed in deeply then exhaled slowly, trying to calm my nerves. "I'll be fine."

Stepping around the remains of the Hellhound's I'd killed, I said, "Correct me if I'm wrong, but do you find it strange that a witch would have Hellhounds protecting her coven?"

Marcus fell in step with me. "You're right. It's one thing to have them surrounding us, and it's another to have them as guards."

"Watch your step." Marcus gestured to a pothole in the floor that looked about the same size as a Hellhound's head.

"I can see. I took a Hellhound's sight." I hopped over the hole then continued to dodge the body parts at the same time as I tried to ignore them, which didn't turn out to be that easy.

"Good thinking." As if sensing my unease, he grabbed my hand and guided me through the bodies. "We always knew a demon was helping Morgana try to stop you from fulfilling my destiny, but it seems whoever it is, is also trying to protect her, which makes me think Morgana might have something over them."

"That's one theory," I said.

"And you've got another?"

"I think it's safe to say there are a million theories and any one of them could be correct." That was the truth of it. "Only weeks ago we thought we were trapped inside this curse because you refused to collect my soul, and now we know we couldn't have been further from the truth. I can only imagine what secrets will be revealed when we get ahold of Titus."

"We?"

"You're dead right," I said. "There's no you or me. There's only we."

A warm smile spread across his face, a stark contrast to the blood surrounding it. "We."

I smiled. "'Til death do us part and all that shit."

He pulled me back as we came to another fork in the tunnel. "That doesn't apply to us because you and I will forever be."

I wiped my thumb across his lips. "I am your light. I am your key, but I will never set you free." I knew how it sounded to Marcus, but what he heard and what I meant were two different things. I was still fully aware there may come a day when I would have to give him back his light, but he would never be free. The memory of me would forever haunt him, and I prayed he would never have to feel that way.

Marcus chuckled. "You sound way too much like Mava."

"I know." I turned back to the tunnel. "Which way do you think?"

He gestured to the left. "We should search the dungeons first, then move onto the tower."

"Agreed." Plus, according to the blueprint, the dungeons were closer.

Of course, the tunnels didn't actually lead to the dungeons, but it was close enough.

We carried on for another one hundred yards then stopped under a manhole with a rickety old ladder missing two of its bars.

Marcus climbed a couple of steps then reached up to the blackened iron grate. "Ready?" he mouthed.

If there was someone on the other side, then no, but I wasn't going to say that. I needed to be prepared even when I wasn't. That was the nature of this game. And we were playing to win. "Yep."

CHAPTER 40

*D*irt particles rained on top of me, coating my blood-soaked clothing in dust as Marcus lifted the iron grate and slid it to the side.

I expected an onslaught of witchcraft or at least Soul Scrapers to bear down on us, but nothing.

Taking two more steps, Marcus was through, disappearing from my sight.

My heart contracted with fear as I waited for him to give me the all clear, and as the seconds ticked on, I thought I was going to have a heart attack.

I raced up the ladder, prepared to fight for his life when he came back into view, kneeling down beside the hole.

A shuddered breath escaped my lips as my body trembled with adrenaline. I wanted to hug him and smack him at the same time. "Where did you go?" I shouted in a whisper.

He reached down for me to take hold.

Placing my hand in his, he pulled me up through the hole then set me onto the floor, which was caked in old blood. Eyes wide, I scanned the room, sheer horror taking over my soul as I feared for Mava and Astrid's safety.

"I had to make sure it was safe," he said.

I barely heard him. My mind was consumed by the multitude of barbaric torture contraptions surrounding us. They were old and very much used.

Dried up blood and who knows what else were soaked into the old stone pavers throughout the room. Unimaginable pain and suffering echoed off the walls. I was sick to my stomach, fearing both Mava and Astrid had been subjected to these contraptions while we had been biding our time, waiting for me to heal instead of busting down the doors and walls like we would have if any one of us had been taken.

Marcus cupped my face in his hands and guided my head until I had no choice but to look into his eyes. "Focus on me, not what is in this room."

With eyes wide I nodded, unable to take my gaze off him for fear that I was going to fall apart if I looked at those torture contraptions again.

I was tempted to ask Marcus to burn the room to the ground, but that would've alerted Morgana to our presence. Saving Mava and Astrid was our priority. But that didn't mean I would forget what I'd seen. Morgana and everyone who followed her would fall to their knees. I was going to make damn sure of that.

Swallowing hard, I focused on calming my nerves then followed Marcus through the rickety old reinforced wooden door.

I wondered why they hadn't upgraded the fittings, but if the torture contraptions were anything to go by, I assumed whomever they'd kept in these dungeons wasn't in any shape to make a break for it.

We vigilantly made our way through the dungeon, checking each and every cell, but Mava and Astrid were nowhere to be seen.

Marcus raised his finger to his lips then pointed to a pile of soiled blankets at the end of the corridor.

If I weren't with Marcus, I would've missed it. I would've walked right past and never known there was somewhere else they could've been hiding them.

My heart skipped a few beats as he lifted the edge of the blankets with his foot, revealing a trap door.

"They're down there," he mouthed, pointing to the floor.

I expected him to lift the door and rescue the witches, but he quickly scanned the room and carefully returned the blankets to their position.

I opened my mouth to ask him what the hell he was doing when he placed his finger to his lips again, shushing me.

I hated to be shushed, but I trusted Marcus knew what he was doing. He knew how important this rescue mission was, and I was positive we hadn't come all this way just to leave them behind. But I would've given anything to know what was going on inside that head of his.

Marcus grabbed my hand and led me back into the torture room. I did my best not to look at those barbaric devices again as he scanned the room once more. He stuck his head into the manhole and then lifted himself back out. "You first," he mouthed.

He helped me down the manhole, only letting go when I was firmly on the ladder.

I jumped off the last step as he climbed onto the ladder and repositioned the manhole cover in place. He then jumped onto the stone floor, barely making a sound.

Grabbing hold of his arm, I leaned closer and whispered, "What are you doing? They were right there."

He curled his hand around my hips. "I know. But going down through the trapdoor wasn't the best option."

"Why not?" I asked, trying to control my anger. After what I'd seen in the room above us, it was tearing me apart. The thought of Mava and Astrid strapped into the machines was too much.

"Because they had the door bugged," he explained. "They would've known we were there."

"They already know we're here. If the Hellhounds coming after us wasn't warning enough, I don't know what is."

"Calm down," he said. "I agree with you. Something isn't right here, but that doesn't mean to say we should make a stupid move. For all we know, there could've been a tripwire attached to the door, and we all would've blown up."

As much as he made sense, I couldn't stop thinking about the torture machines. "We can't leave them there."

"We're not," he said, pulling his phone out of his pocket. "We're going in a different way."

I screwed up my face in confusion. From what I could see, there was only one way into the pit, and that was the whole point.

Marcus typed a message to Abby: **We've found them. Head back to the entrance. We'll need to leave ASAP.**

So much for poking around to see what else we could find. Something told me there was more going on that I wasn't aware of, and I wished we had more time for him to explain. But right now, Mava and Astrid were our priority. We would figure everything else out later.

Abby's reply flashed on the screen: **Heading there now. Something's off.**

Marcus punched another message into his phone: **I know. Be careful.**

Always.

Pocketing his phone, he grabbed my hand and led me further into the tunnel. Then he stopped. "They're through there," he whispered, gesturing to the wall.

Everything suddenly clicked into place. We weren't leaving Mava and Astrid behind. We were going to literally break them out of their prison.

CHAPTER 41

$\mathcal{I}$ don't know why I was expecting Marcus to pull an explosive or something equally damaging out of his pocket to break through the wall, but I was surprised to see him raise his fist. "Ready?" he asked.

"Wait. What?"

He lowered his hand. "When I get through, we need to grab the witches and go. We don't have time for anything else, okay?"

In other words, we didn't have time for me to freak out if we found them with puncture wounds covering their bodies from being tortured in the death room barely six feet from our heads.

I gave him a small, curt nod. "Got it." I really didn't have it, but there was no time for me to get my shit together.

Marcus turned his gaze away from mine and pounded his fist into the wall. The stone bricks exploded around his fist as the wall crumbled to the ground.

He wasn't kidding about not having time. Before the last of the bricks fell, Marcus had disappeared through the hole. A second later, another blast came from within.

Forgetting all my fears, I sprinted through the hole then skidded to a stop. My heart pounded with a mixture of fear and relief when I saw both Mava and Astrid, sitting on the wet stone floor, slumped against the wall with metal cuffs around their hands and necks.

Marcus ripped the first chain connected to Astrid out of the wall, then the other. Astrid crumpled to the floor, too weak to stand on her own.

I waited for Marcus to move over to Mava and help free her, but he didn't. He wrapped his arm under Astrid's shoulders, tucked his other arm under her legs, and lifted her to his chest.

It was only when he moved out of the way that I saw it.

My eyes widened, and all air expelled from my lungs when I realized Mava wasn't moving. Her head hung unnaturally to the side, and the color had drained from her skin in a way that could only mean one thing.

Mava was dead.

I didn't have time to fully process the ramifications of that statement before Marcus was in my face, ordering me to move.

The next few minutes went by in a haze as we climbed back through the wall and ran down the tunnel faster than I'd ever run before. My brain barely registered my feet touching the ground as my thoughts were consumed with Mava's death.

She had died for me, and that wasn't something I'd wish upon anyone. The guilt that smothered me was all-consuming, and I didn't know how to let go. But I had to keep going.

The entrance to the tunnel came into sight, silhouetting both Justin and Abby, who were already there waiting for us.

Marcus skidded to a stop and handed Astrid to Justin. "Take her."

"Where's Mava?" Justin asked, adjusting Astrid in his arms.

"Dead."

Astrid, who'd stayed silent up until now, let out a strangled groan. Her eyes remained closed, and she didn't make any effort to move. My heart was heavy knowing the passionate woman who'd done so much for me was too weak to remain conscious.

Justin paused for a second then clicked back into rescue mode. He'd been close to Mava, and I couldn't imagine what he was going through at that moment. Even though he was a Soul Collector and had witnessed countless deaths, nothing could prepare someone for the death of a friend.

Abby practically flew up the ladder and smashed through the grate, sending it flying from my view. Then she climbed through the hole.

Justin slung Astrid over his shoulder then ascended the ladder. Once at the top, he passed her effortlessly to Abby.

"Your turn." Marcus grabbed me by the hips and lifted me onto the ladder.

I don't know how I made it out of the tunnel, but somehow I was standing out in the field, the warm sun shining down on my skin, mocking the memory of Mava. She was gone.

Something latched onto my waist and yanked me back, twisting me around in time to see Marcus emerge from the tunnel.

I had no idea what had hold of me, but whatever it was, Marcus's expression brought the fear of God into me.

"Lucy!" he screamed.

Black tar exploded around my head as I lost all control of my body. The absolute fear in Marcus's eyes burned into my memory as the air around me warped. Then he was gone.

CHAPTER 42

Fear ripped through me as the black tar wrapped further around my face, stealing my sight. The slick substance spilled into my mouth and slipped down my throat, choking me.

I didn't have to see to know what was going on. I was on a slippery slope, spiraling out of control.

I needed control.

I needed to fight.

I had to free myself by any means necessary.

My whole body was still paralyzed. The ice pick in my pocket wasn't an option. The only thing I still had control of was my mind. And lucky for me, that was my most powerful asset.

Remembering what I had done in the tunnel when I'd last encountered a Soul Scraper, I fought the urge to gag and, instead, welcomed the tar as it slowly made its way through my body, devouring my soul. Peace spread throughout my body as I gained control of the tar, tipped my head back, and spewed it back out of my mouth, aiming for where I thought the Soul Scraper was standing.

The tar covering my eyes stretched, parting just enough for me to see my attacker. That split second was all I needed.

Anger, determination, and something I couldn't quite place were pumping through my veins as I looked at the Soul Scraper now covered in its own tar.

It reared its demented face back as it started to convulse, the black tar eating away at its features until it was nothing but smoke.

I fell to the ground, the scorched earth burning my skin, reminding me I was far from home.

Before I could get my bearings, a strong arm wrapped around my neck, choking me as whoever it was attached to lifted me off the ground.

Black wisps shot through the air, slamming into me and reminding me of the Possession that haunted the humans back in Sydney. With each attempt to enter me, they left smudges on my soul, staining the part of me that somehow protected my very essence.

Wrapping my hands around the arm, I desperately tried to free myself. I needed to be able to see my captor. But it was useless. No matter how much I tried, I was fighting blindly. I couldn't latch onto the minds of the Possessions. There simply wasn't anything there to grasp. My only other alternative was to pull the demonic spirits into me, but if that was what they were trying to do, then I wasn't going to help them with their cause. There had to be another way.

My heart stopped when I heard the laugh that would forever haunt my dreams. The same one I'd heard the day when all this started.

Morgana.

Whoever was holding me turned around so I was facing the raven-haired witch that looked like an angel but was as evil as the devil.

Heat rose from the arm of the man holding me until my skin was roasting under its touch. I needed to free myself, but I couldn't take my eyes of Morgana.

"You foolish child," she said with an air of arrogance that only came from power. She reeked of power, and it was smothering me. "Did you really think I would be so incompetent as to leave the bait unattended for you to simply take?"

Morgana let out a wicked laugh that sent chills down my spine. I'd thought Soul Scrapers and Hellhounds were my worst fear, but I was wrong. Morgana was.

As soon as that thought entered my mind, I wanted to slap

myself. Morgana wasn't my worst fear. Losing Marcus was. And that was what I needed to focus on. I needed to get back to Marcus because the absolute fear I had seen in his eyes told me something else was wrong. He wasn't able to follow me. He wasn't coming to rescue me, and alarm bells were ringing deep inside of me.

Ignoring the pain from my skin, which I was sure had lost the top few layers, I said, "Who says I'm the foolish one?"

A look of confusion crossed her eyes. Then they went wide with realization. "No," she screamed as her abilities slipped away.

Pain shot through my head, and I fought with everything I had to ignore the unadulterated evil that came with Morgana's magic. But it was too much. I couldn't take it all. She was too strong, too evil, and I had to let go and be satisfied that I had taken more power than she would ever be able to recover from.

Morgana raced up to me, grabbed my hair, and yanked me free from the arm that was choking me. Apparently, she still had some strength.

I fell to the ground, the scorched earth once again burning my skin, but that was the least of my worries. I rolled onto my back just in time to see the man—or I should say demon with gigantic black wings—who had imprisoned me with his powerful arm.

"What have you done?" Morgana screamed in my face. She lifted her other hand, reaching toward me. I knew what was coming, and as much as I didn't know if she still had the strength in her to cast that kind of spell, I couldn't risk it. I would never let myself forget Marcus again.

With a split second to focus, I reached out to the demon and took the one thing that would ensure my escape. The ability came to me as if it had belonged to me all this time. It was as if it were my birthright.

A wicked grin spread across her face as if she were about to devour her prey. "Forget—

Before she had a chance to finish the spell, I lifted my hand to the side of me, opened a veil directly back to my world, and rolled into it, making sure I closed it behind me as quickly as I could. I knew it wouldn't hold them back for long, but I had a few seconds on them, and that was all I needed—or so I hoped.

Scrambling to my feet, I scanned the area surrounding me for Marcus, but he was nowhere to be seen. In the distance, a group of witches stood in a circle, their black robes cloaking their faces. Their heads were tipped back as they looked into the sky, chanting something in Latin over and over again as purple smoke danced in the inner circle.

I unfurled my wings, preparing to take flight when something slammed into my back and lifted me into the air.

My wings were a tangled mess as whoever was behind me carried me further and further up into the sky.

I had a crap load of magic buried inside of me that would have undoubtedly freed me from their grasp, but what I didn't have was the knowledge of how to use it. That was a completely different set of skills I had left with Morgana.

Desperate to see again, I tucked my wings into my back and prepared to fight to free myself from the grasp of whoever had a hold of me when I was momentarily paralyzed by the scene before me.

Justin and Abby appeared to be trapped inside a bubble five hundred feet up in the air. They pounded against the invisible barrier, trying to break free, but no matter how hard they tried, they remained imprisoned in the witches' spell. And Marcus... My heart stopped when I saw him in the arms of a demon, surrounded by a swirling wind of fire. But it had no effect. Demons were made of fire. Demons could also fly, and Marcus could not.

Lightning shot up from the ground, snapping me out of my state. I looked down and froze.

Morgana stood beneath Marcus, sparks of electricity swirling around her before she somehow managed to shoot it into the sky.

The bitch was aiming at my man.

Rage coursed through my veins, lighting me up in ways I never knew existed. I had power buried deep inside of me, crying to be freed. Freeing it was exactly what I needed to do.

Reaching behind me, I grabbed hold of the demon's head.

"What are you doing?" he screeched, trying to free himself from my grasp while still keeping me firmly trapped in his embrace.

I needed strength to hold on, so I took what I needed from him. We dropped a few feet as he struggled to keep holding me up.

Ignoring the demon, I focused on the electrical storm beneath me, summoning it as my own until the tingle of power coursed under every inch of my skin.

The demon convulsed under my touch as the electricity surged through his body, frying every cell and every nerve in its path.

We plunged through the sky, my body still trapped in his embrace as the electricity contracted every one of his muscles.

I let go of the demon's head, and his grip on me released as he slipped away from me.

I called on my wings then soared up into the sky just in time to see Morgana get a direct hit on Marcus.

"No," I screamed, but I couldn't hear a word of my cry. I was deafened by the blood pumping through my ears as my whole world seemed to stop. I may not have been able to die from a fall, but Marcus... We had no idea.

I charged through the sky, my eyes stinging with tears as I refused to acknowledge I wasn't going to get to him in time. The ground kept creeping closer and closer to him, and I was still too far away. It was inevitable, and there was nothing I could do.

I couldn't save him, and because of me, Marcus no longer had wings to save himself. In that moment of realization, I wished more than anything that I hadn't been selfish that day. That I hadn't trusted Morgana. That I'd been smarter. There were a million wishes running through my head but none stronger than my wish that he'd never had his wings stolen from him as his punishment for letting me live.

My stomach lurched as I continued to free-fall through the sky, plummeting to earth, and I had nothing to save me.

My wings were gone.

Justin and Abby's screams echoed through the sky, followed by one that crushed my soul.

I glanced up just in time to see Marcus shoot through the sky toward me, powered by the same plasma wings I'd just lost.

My heart soared with a mixture of disbelief and relief. Marcus was alive, but he wasn't fast enough.

Pain ripped through my body as I slammed into the ground, every inch of me consumed in the agony I was all too accustomed to.

I was broken, bloodied, and bruised, but I hadn't completed my destiny. Marcus's light burning inside of me had saved me yet again.

I tried to get up, to keep fighting, but every inch of my body cried out in pain.

The ground shook as Marcus touched down beside me. "Lu," he said, his voice trembling with fear.

Kneeling beside me, he reached for me then pulled back, afraid to hurt me any more than I already was.

"I'm okay," I said, my voice barely a whisper. My mind was foggy, and I fought desperately to remain focused. I needed to be okay. I couldn't be a liability.

A sad smile broke out across his face as he wiped my hair away from my eyes. "I thought—"

Marcus's eyes went wide, his back arching unnaturally as electricity pulsated through his body.

Morgana strode toward us, electricity dancing off her fingers and shooting into Marcus. She was killing him, and I needed to stop it.

Marcus pushed off the ground as he fought the convulsions. He turned around to face her, his back straight and shoulders square.

Mustering every last bit of energy I had, I latched my hand around Marcus's ankle and welcomed the electrical storm into my body, freeing him from Morgana's power.

Lifting his hand, Marcus reached out toward her as the wind whipped around us, sweeping the fallen leaves into a turbulent storm heading straight for her.

Thunder cracked over us, and a moment later, rain pelted down from the dark clouds above.

Morgana raised her other hand and shot another round of electricity at Marcus.

He faltered for a second before I took it away, drawing in the power as if it were mine to begin with.

Morgana's eyes went wide as she was picked up off the ground and carried by an unknown force toward Marcus, who was now glowing with the illuminating light that I'd seen only once before.

Her terrified gaze fell on me and the word, "Forget," spilled from her lips.

To my relief, her words had no effect on me. I still remembered everything.

Marcus latched his hand around her throat, choking the very life out of her as fire danced over his skin.

She thrashed under his grip, but it was no use. Even with all her magic, she'd been powerless against the two of us combined.

Absolute fear consumed her eyes as her gaze fell on me, and she gurgled, "It's true. What I promised you…"

"Marcus," I said, unsure if I'd heard her right.

He loosened his grip on her. "What are you saying?"

Fear still consumed her eyes but a sliver of hope was set free, and I wasn't sure if I'd heard her right or it was wishful thinking.

"There is a way to separate the light," she said, her voice coming out in a strangled rasp. "If you let me live, I will help you find it."

Marcus glanced at me then returned his gaze to Morgana. "I don't think so."

My mind was groggy, but I had to know if it were true. With the remainder of my energy, I took that tiny piece of her memory. Hope soared through my veins when I realized Morgana wasn't lying. There was a—

Marcus snapped her neck and the light in her eyes disappeared. *Shit!*

Realizing I had most likely lost my chance of finding out who was behind Morgana, I reached for her memories and tried against hope to find the one we were searching for.

I sucked in a sharp breath, not because I was too late, but because of the fear that was brought with the name embedded in my head. I'd done the impossible. I'd found out who we were looking for. He called himself God. I had no other name, no description. Only the word God.

Marcus threw her body to the side then kneeled down beside me, his plasma wings rustling in the wind as the storm settled, and the fire and light disappeared from his body.

He scooped me into his arms and pressed a tender kiss on my lips. "You'll be okay."

Closing my eyes, I melted into his embrace as the pain became too much, and I soon blacked out.

CHAPTER 43

I had no idea how long I was out when I heard the steady breathing of Marcus lying beside me, comforting my soul in ways that no other could.

A smile broke out across my face as I opened my eyes and saw him staring back at me. "Hey you," I said with a raspy voice.

He returned my smile, love consuming his amber eyes. "Hey, yourself."

He ever so gently caressed the side of my face. "How are you feeling?"

I tried to move, but the pain was too much. "Couldn't be better." That wasn't a lie. Even though every inch of my body was hurting, we were alive.

He chuckled. "I find that very hard to believe."

"Is she awake?" Abby's muffled voice came from somewhere behind me, making me think she wasn't in the same room as us.

I had no idea where we were, and I really didn't care. We were safe. We were both alive, and that was all that really mattered.

Marcus propped himself up on his elbow. "Yes, she's awake."

A door opened, and Abby burst into the room. "Glad you're with us again. You've scared the living hell out of us these last ten hours."

Ten hours? Crap.

I blinked in surprise then tried to get up, but the pain was still too much.

"Easy," Marcus said, guiding me back down. "You've had one hell of a fall and probably broke every bone in your body. You're going to need time to heal."

"And us," Abby added.

Marcus smiled. "And us."

I frowned, and even that hurt.

Marcus folded his hand over mine. "Let us help you heal."

"Both of us," Abby added. "That way you should be healed in no time."

"I can't. What if someone comes and—?"

"We're safe for now," Marcus said. "Take it from us."

I tried to nod, but even that was excruciating. "Thanks."

Looking between Marcus and Abby, I focused on taking what I needed. If we were going to finish this once and for all—and I had every intention of doing just that—I had to heal myself so I'd be at full strength.

Somehow they both knew their ability to heal was gone without me having to say a word.

Abby smiled. "Good. Now, I'll go make sure I've got some food here for you for when you wake up again."

"Thanks," I whispered.

"You're more than welcome." She leaned down and kissed my cheek. "Thanks for saving demon boy's life back there."

"Always."

Abby chuckled as she walked out of my sight. "'Til death do us part and all that shit."

Marcus snuggled down beside me, being careful not to hurt me but also trying to get as close to me as he could. "Get some sleep."

Closing my eyes, I did just that, wrapped in the memories of who we were, what we could become, and the nightmare that was sure to follow.

Night had fallen by the time I woke again. My bones only ached the slightest, and the rest of my pains had disappeared.

I rolled onto my side and was welcomed by the love of my life staring back at me.

"How are you feeling?" he asked.

That was the million-dollar question. At that moment, I was

perfect. But the looming knowledge of this one who called himself God was chilling my very core.

"Good," I lied. I knew I would have to tell him what I'd learned, but I wanted a few more seconds of bliss before I had to return to reality.

I ran the tips of my fingers over his shoulder then down his back. "You've got wings," I said, repeating the exact same thing he'd said to me when I'd suddenly sprouted wings of my own.

"Yeah, you gave me your wings, which I want to talk to you about but not right now." He wrapped his hand around my waist and pulled me closer to him. "Now, I just want to do this." He kissed my neck. "And this." He trailed his lips across my jaw, stopping when he reached my lips. "And this." He kissed me, almost making me forget about everything that had happened. But I couldn't forget. And as much as I wanted to get lost in this moment, I was haunted by the knowledge of what we were facing.

I gave myself a few seconds more indulgence then broke away. "As much as I want to keep going where we both know this will end up—"

"We need to talk," he said, finishing my sentence.

I nodded then pulled myself to a sitting position. I leaned forward and grabbed Marcus's hand, lacing his fingers with mine. "How's Astrid?"

"Recovering," he said. "She's still too weak to perform any spell strong enough to aid her own recovery."

"Speaking of." I returned his healing ability to him. "Where's Abby?"

"She's gone out to get you some more food because she ate the last lot she got for you."

I laughed. "Typical Abby."

"You have no idea."

"Where are Justin and Astrid?"

"They're in another room. And don't worry, Justin's taking good care of her." He chuckled. "Actually, Astrid's got Justin running around, gathering ingredients for her so she can perform a healing spell when she gets the strength."

My eyes widened when I realized how I could probably help with her recovery.

Marcus frowned. "What is it?"

"There's a lot I need to tell you and a lot I need to figure out. But the gist of it is this. When Morgana took me through to another veil, I stole her magic. Well, not all of it, considering she was still able to shoot lightning out of her hands, but I took at least half of her power."

"And you think you can help Astrid with her recovery?"

"Maybe. I don't know. But it's worth a try."

"I guess you have nothing to lose."

"The only problem is, I don't know how to use it. I can feel all this power swirling inside of me, and I don't have a clue how to access it. Magic isn't at all what I thought it would be."

"How so?"

"It takes training, dedication, and knowledge. All I've got is this untapped power, and I need to find the tap."

Marcus chuckled. "Well, I'm sure Astrid will be only too willing to show you a tap."

I shoved him. "Don't make fun of me."

He bit down on a smile. "I'm not. It's just the first time I've heard magic being referred to that way."

I shoved him again. "You're evil, you know that?"

"Come here." He wrapped his arm around me and snuggled against my side. "You know I love you."

I tilted my head back, hope for our future soaring in my heart as I looked into his eyes. "I know. And I love you, too."

Marcus released his grip on me and shuffled so we were once again facing each other. The smile had disappeared from his eyes. "You're thinking about what Morgana said, aren't you?"

I smiled. "I know what you're thinking, but it's true. She wasn't lying. There is a way for me to give back your light without me dying in the process." He opened his mouth to say something, but I quickly cut him off. "Before you say anything, I know it's real. I took that memory from her."

He sucked in a shuddered breath as he stared at me, unable to allow himself to bring his thoughts to life.

I rolled forward onto my knees and closed the little distance between us as I climbed onto his lap, facing him. "I've seen it for myself. There is a way to severe your light and return what was rightfully yours. And I know you probably don't want to risk it, but we'd be stupid not to look for the scroll because we're going to need you at your strongest for when we face God."

He screwed up his nose. "What?"

I ran my hand down my face. "Before Morgana died, I took the name of who she was working with, and that demon or angel or whatever it is calls himself God."

"It can't be God," he said.

"I know, and I don't think his name is actually God. I think that's his code name, or whatever. My point is, Morgana feared him. Like really feared him."

"And you think we need to find this scroll containing a way for you to give me back my light so that we have a chance of beating this God?"

"That's exactly what I'm saying because let's face it; you almost died back there."

"And you foolishly gave me your wings."

"If I didn't, then you would be dead. I can't die. I can hurt, but I can't die."

"Knock, knock," Abby said as she rapped her knuckles against the door.

I twisted myself off Marcus and sat beside him. "Come in."

Abby bounded in carrying a takeout bag filled with what smelled like hamburgers. "I come bearing gifts." She grinned.

"The very best kind," I said, taking the bag from her. I opened it, pulled out a hamburger, and passed the bag to Marcus. "Thank you so much, Abby."

"You're welcome." She sat on the end of the bed. "So, is someone going to tell me how the hell you managed to give away one of your appendages?"

I unpeeled the wrapper and closed my hands around the bun. "You're obsessed with those wings, aren't you?"

"I'm obsessed with figuring out how you had wings you never knew about until you were falling to your death, and then somehow you were able to give them to Marcus."

"Giving is part of my abilities."

She grabbed the bag off Marcus and picked out a burger for herself. "You see, we were talking, and something about it just doesn't sit right. How can you give one of your body parts to someone else? I mean, that's like giving Marcus your foot, or hand. How about an eyeball?"

I looked to Marcus, wondering if he felt the same way.

"I have to agree with Abby," he said.

"I was created for you. To take and give."

"See, that's the thing," Abby continued. "Justin and I have come up with a theory."

"You have?" Marcus asked.

"Yes," she repeated. "Maybe they were never Lucy's wings to begin with. I mean, think about it. That type of wings is reserved for the upper class, and Lucy... Well, Lucy isn't an angel or a demon. Marcus, you're the only one with no wings, and now suddenly you have them again. For all we know, they were yours and Lucy wasn't just created as a vessel to hold your light. Maybe she holds everything that was stolen from you."

"That's impossible," Marcus said. "They were severed."

"And how much do you remember about them actually being removed?"

Marcus remained silent.

"That's my point."

"Your theory means nothing because we can't prove..." Marcus trailed off when Abby smirked. "No way."

"No way, what?" I asked.

"Nothing," Marcus said, trying to shut Abby's idea down before I'd even heard it.

"Don't nothing me." I slapped him gently on the thigh. "We're in this together, and if there's a way to prove that they were..." My eyes widened, and a big O formed on my lips. "You want me to try giving him something else of mine, don't you?"

"Bingo." Abby took a bite out of her burger.

Marcus tossed his unopened burger onto the bed. "You are not going to try to give me one of your limbs."

"As much as the thought of having one of my limbs removed scares the hell out of me, it's worth it if we get to piece a little bit more of the puzzle together."

"You are not doing it."

"Marcus," Abby said. "It's her body. She can choose to do what she wants. And it's not as if she can't take it back. It'll be only for a second."

I zoned out as I took the opportunity to do what Marcus forbade. I changed my mind about what I was going to remove about twenty times before I decided to go with a nail. I was pretty sure that would hurt the least if it were removed.

I waited and waited. Nothing. My nail remained. Needing to know if it were just my nail that I couldn't give because it was technically a *dead* part of my body, I sucked up what little courage I had and decided to try a finger. To my relief, I failed.

Marcus shook my forearm. "Lucy."

"Huh?" I said, snapping out of my zone. "What is it?"

A smile broke out across Abby's face. "You tried, didn't you?"

Anger swirled in Marcus's eyes, turning them liquid amber.

"Calm down," I said. "It obviously didn't work."

He breathed out harshly. "You are going to be the death of me."

I grabbed him by the chin and kissed his cheek. "As I keep telling you, I'm your life."

"And those are your wings, Marcus," Abby said. "I knew it. You, my dear demon boy, are so not what we thought you were. You're an upper-class angel, and someone wants to make sure that remains a secret."

Something about what she said rang true to my soul. Marcus wasn't like them. He was special, and I was determined to find the scroll so we could figure out exactly how special he was.

In the meantime, I was going to learn everything I could about witchcraft and hone every single one of my skills to make sure that when the day came, I could safely make Marcus whole again and we would have our happily ever after.

KELLY CARRERO

USA TODAY BESTSELLING AUTHOR

SEVERED
SOULS

CHAPTER 1

*F*rustration boiled in the pit of my stomach as I sat at the foot of the bed, staring at Astrid while trying to make sense of the spell she was asking me to perform. She was still weak and needed my help to recover, and although I wanted to make her suffering magically disappear, there was one major problem standing in my way.

I may have held the power of one of the most evil witches that walked the earth, but I was clueless about how to use the magic I had stolen from Morgana.

Astrid adjusted herself against the pillows supporting her back, still too weak to get out of bed. "It's all right there in front of you." She gestured to the spell book sitting on my lap.

I ran my fingers over the old pages, trying to understand what I was supposed to do. "So, all I need to do is read this spell, and it's going to fix you?"

Astrid raised her shaking hands, clasped them together, and placed them on her chest. "Reading the spell will only do so much. You must feel it in here." She gently thumped her fist against her chest. "You must learn to connect with Morgana's magic as if it were your very own. As if you were born with it and magic is alive within your very essence."

Yeah, easier said than done. But I wasn't going to say that to her.

After everything Astrid had gone through for Marcus and me, I needed to listen to her, and somehow connect with Morgana's magic flowing through me.

"Don't look so worried, dear. Believe in yourself, and you'll see."

"You know, you sound a lot like Mava." My heart felt heavy thinking about what Morgana had done to the woman who'd given up everything for me. Morgana had killed Mava to get to me. And I owed it to Mava to not let her death be in vain.

"Contrary to what most people believed, Mava was a very wise woman," Astrid said breathlessly. "And she wouldn't want to see you blaming yourself for her death."

I raised my blurry gaze to meet Astrid's. "But I *am* responsible for her death."

"No, dear. Mava gave her life for you so you can fulfill what you were created for."

Guilt sat heavily on my heart. I was created as merely a vessel to hold and return the light to Marcus that was stolen from him. That was what I was born to do. It was the sole reason for my existence.

However, Marcus didn't want a bar of it. He didn't want to live a life without me there beside him. And if that meant never getting back the piece of him that was stolen, then he was perfectly happy— so long as I was still alive.

The memory I'd stolen from Morgana burned in my mind. There was a way for me to sever Marcus's light from my soul without me dying in the process, and I was determined to find the ancient scroll that was the key to Marcus and my happily ever after.

But first I had to learn how to connect to Morgana's magic buried deep inside of me, heal Astrid, and destroy the one responsible for everything that was wrong with Marcus and me.

I blinked back my tears. "I know, but it doesn't make it any easier. If we'd only gotten there a few hours earlier, then maybe Mava would still be alive. Maybe—"

"No, Luciana. Mava died shortly after Morgana had taken us. It was how the priestesses were able to break the spell that protected Marcus's house."

I frowned. "But I thought you..."

"You thought I was solely responsible for the protection barrier, didn't you?"

I nodded.

Astrid shook her head, memories of Mava haunting her soul, evident through her tired eyes. "I could not have conducted such a powerful spell on my own, and there was no way I could have told Marcus the truth."

The corner of my lips tipped up. "Yeah, he thought Mava was crazy."

A smile broke across her face, lighting up her soul. I wondered if I was now somehow able to read souls the way Mava had been able to. Something had changed in me, and I wasn't sure if the ability had always been there or if this was a new effect from taking Morgana's magic.

Someone knocked on the door, and I knew without looking it was Marcus. The connection between us was more powerful than ever since I'd given him back his wings. It was almost as if there was an electrical current running between us, compelling me to return the one thing Marcus didn't want.

It was so hard to ignore.

"How's it going in here?" Marcus placed his hand on my shoulder and gave it a small squeeze.

I tilted my head back so I could look up at him. My heart skipped a beat the moment our eyes locked, and the invisible current surged with new life, begging me to do the right thing.

Pushing the ever-growing urge to the back of my mind, I focused on Marcus's question. "It's not."

"Lucy just needs to believe in herself," Astrid said with that warm, frustrating smile she, Mava, and my guardians all seemed to have in common.

"And follow the instructions in this book." I tapped my fingertips over the spell.

Marcus peered over my shoulder, his gaze trained on the open book on my lap. "Seems easy enough."

I choked on a laugh. "I'd like to see you try."

"Please don't," Astrid said, her eyes going wide. "This kind of spell can cause all sorts of irreversible damage if not done correctly."

My mouth dropped open. "I thought you said all I have to do is read the spell?"

"Yes, that is all *you* must do once you connect with Morgana's magic."

"So what's the problem?" Marcus asked.

There were a million things that could go wrong, but the thing that worried me most was something Paege had said. I had somehow been marked by the two Hellhounds that were still waiting for me in a cave back in Byron Bay, and I feared what would happen to me if I connected with the power of someone as truly evil as Morgana was.

Instead of confiding in Marcus, I forced a smile. "There's no problem. I'm just trying to wrap my head around all this."

I waited for him to leave Astrid and me alone, but he had other ideas. He lowered himself onto the bed beside me and rested his hand on my thigh. "You've got this. Nothing is going to go wrong."

"Marcus is right." Astrid released a shallow breath. "All you need to do is close your eyes and concentrate on trying to connect your soul with the power that already lies within you."

Power. That was the problem. Morgana had power unlike anything I'd ever seen before, and it scared the living hell out of me. But I had to push through my fear. There was no other option.

Taking a deep breath, I followed Astrid's instructions. I could feel Morgana's magic swirling deep inside of me, itching to break free, to be connected with my very essence. But, there was also a darkness I was afraid to take in. I could feel it pressing its slick tendrils against my soul, trying to take over.

I couldn't let it take over. I needed to stay in control.

Marcus placed a kiss on my shoulder, reminding me what I was fighting for. It wasn't healing Astrid, nor was it about saving the world. The sole reason for my existence was sitting right beside me, depending on me, and I could not fail him.

I would not fail him.

With my mind made up, I slowly released the bind I had placed around Morgana's magic and allowed it to seep into my soul, taking a life of its own and connecting with my very being.

I felt alive in ways I never thought possible. I had unimaginable power running through my veins, waiting to be called upon to fulfill my every desire.

I opened my eyes, my gaze connecting with Astrid's. The smile in her eyes told me she knew the transition had been completed. Morgana's magic was now my own.

Stealing my gaze away from hers, I looked down at the spell written on the open page. My skin buzzed with electricity, reminding me of how close I'd come to losing everything when Morgana had unleashed an electrical storm aimed at Marcus.

Trying to ignore those crippling thoughts, I fought against the darkness lying under the surface of my skin and focused on the love that surrounded me.

I was ready.

Placing my hand on Astrid's shin, I read the words that would forever cement the person I was to become. "Heal the soul and forgive the wounds, and bring forth light to conceal the past."

The words themselves didn't have any significant meaning, yet somehow the magic stirring inside of me was unleashed. I watched in awe as the light in Astrid's eyes returned almost instantaneously, and her soul once again was filled with life.

"Holy crap," I whispered, barely able to comprehend what I was seeing. "I can't believe I did that."

Astrid easily pulled herself into a sitting position, away from the pillows. "Thank you." She swung her legs off the bed then stood and smoothed down her boho dress.

I twisted around to face her and caught Marcus's gaze and the underlying...fear? Something was troubling him.

He forced a smile. "See, all you need to do is have faith in yourself."

"And the knowledge of how to access the power," Astrid added. "Which, my dear, I'll be more than happy to help you connect with, but first I would like some fresh air. I've been stuck in this room for far too long."

She paused by the door. "Where's Justin?"

"He's gone out for a bit with Abby, but he should be back in about an hour," Marcus said.

Astrid gave him a curt nod then disappeared into the hallway.

I waited a few seconds then turned toward Marcus. He no longer displayed the concerns he had moments ago, but they had been there, and I wanted to know why.

CHAPTER 2

$\mathcal{M}$arcus forced a smile as he closed his hand over mine. "Hungry?"

I was hungry. I seemed to always be hungry lately. But eating would have to wait. Something was bothering Marcus, and my stomach was twisting into knots, hoping his concerns didn't have anything to do with Morgana's magic. I could still feel her power coursing through my veins, begging to be freed. What I'd just done to Astrid only teased my senses. I wanted more. I needed more.

I once again had to ignore my desires and focus on Marcus. "No secrets."

He stared at me for a few moments, an ongoing battle raging in his amber eyes.

"What is it? What's wrong with me?"

He slowly lifted his hand then brushed my hair behind my ear. "Nothing is wrong with you."

I tilted my head to the side. "Marcus…"

He sighed. "It's nothing really."

"By the look on your face, it doesn't look like nothing."

"Okay, I'm probably being paranoid, but it's just… I can sense something different inside of you, and I don't know if it's a bad thing or what."

"I can sense it, too," I said, my voice barely a whisper. I was afraid to give voice to my thoughts and fears, in case I somehow jinxed myself.

Apparently, I had the power to do that now. And it scared the hell out of me.

I bit my lip but released it as Marcus lifted his finger. "Do you think all magic is either good or evil?" I asked. "Or do you think it comes down to the witch?"

He shrugged a shoulder. "I don't know. And honestly, I think Astrid is the best person to speak to about that."

"But you think me taking a piece of somebody so evil is going to…?" I couldn't finish the sentence. I was terrified of the prospect of becoming like Morgana.

His face softened, and I knew I'd hit a nerve. Marcus was afraid just like I was. "I think it's something we need to be aware of." He caressed the side of my face with his hand. "We'll figure this out. And right now the one person who might be able to shed some insight is right outside."

"Astrid."

Marcus nodded. "Give her some time to recoup. Then I'm sure she'll be more than happy to help us figure it out."

Yeah, she was more than happy to teach me how to connect with an evil witch's magic, which could be my very undoing. No one could know exactly what dangers lay ahead because I was the first of my kind, and I would undoubtedly be the last.

So much was riding on me—on my new abilities, and I prayed it wouldn't be the death of me or, more so, Marcus.

I stood and paced over to the window then peeled back the curtain and peered outside. Black clouds blanketed the sky, casting an eerie green glow over everything in sight. I had no idea where we were, but one thing was for sure—Something was coming. I could feel it in my bones. We'd awoken a beast when Marcus killed Morgana, and everything that had happened up until that point was nothing compared to what was lying in the shadows, waiting for the perfect moment to end what it had started all those years ago.

"Is this your doing?" I asked, praying I'd gotten it all wrong and Marcus was just giving Abby and Justin coverage while they traveled during the daylight.

Marcus stood, came up behind me, and wrapped his arms around my waist as he gazed out the window. "This isn't me."

Fear twisted my stomach into knots. I'd known it the moment I first saw it, but I wanted to be wrong. "Someone's coming for us, aren't they?"

He nodded against my shoulder. "I just wish I knew who this God is."

If only Marcus hadn't killed Morgana so quickly, then maybe I could've found out. Then again, I could already feel the effects from taking what I did from her, and I wasn't sure I could've coped with too much more.

Evil brimmed within me, lapping at my soul, trying to pull me into its depths. But I couldn't give in. I had to be stronger than Morgana.

Whoever God was, we were going to need an army to take him/her down. Either that or one supreme entity that we so happened to have. "We need to find the scroll," I said, focusing on the clouds swirling in the sky.

When Marcus didn't respond, I twisted around in his arms and repeated, "We need to find the scroll."

"And how do you suppose we do that? Do you think it would be lying around, waiting for us to find?"

I glared at him.

He breathed out harshly. "Sorry. I can't…"

"You can't what?"

"I can't risk you."

I cocked my thumb behind me. "I don't think you've got a choice. Whoever has done this to you and me isn't happy. They're not going to just sit back and let us destroy them. We need to be prepared. And as cool as my ability is, somehow I don't think it's enough. I mean, it could be, but that's not a risk I'm willing to take."

Anger swirled in his eyes, but I knew it wasn't directed at me. Marcus knew we didn't have any other choice, but that didn't mean he liked it.

We needed to find the spell that would allow me to sever Marcus's light from my soul without killing me in the process. And no matter how hard it was for him, we didn't have time to sit down and figure out all the problems and the variables. A shit storm was coming our way, and we had to either stay ahead of it or run into the center and be prepared for the inevitable.

Marcus wasn't prepared for the inevitable. And truth be told, neither was I.

I wanted to live. I wanted my happily ever after.

I clutched his shirt in my fist. "We have no other choice." I'd intended for my words to come out strong, but they didn't. So much was riding on the next few days. And, in a world where knowledge was power, we could be damn sure this God person would stop at nothing to keep us in the dark.

Marcus's jaw popped as he looked out the window at the clouds churning in the sky. "We should start at Morgana's."

A smile spread across my face, which was kind of crazy considering I was excited to go back to where Mava had died and where Astrid had suffered unimaginably at the hands of Morgana and those that followed her. However, I was excited for the chance to figure out how I could fulfill what I was created to do and not destroy Marcus in the process.

"Whatever happened to the rest of Morgana's witches?" I asked.

Marcus ran his hand down my arms then entwined my fingers with his. "You mean the other priestesses?"

I nodded. "Witches. Priestesses. Whatever."

"Well, considering you're part witch now, you should probably use the correct terms."

I scowled at him. "I am not a witch."

The corner of his lips tipped up. "Technically you are. You can do magic now."

Closing my eyes, I let out a slow breath. I didn't need reminding of who I was now or the evil battle my soul was fighting against.

Marcus let go of my hand and cupped my jaw. "You can do this. You can fight this evil. It's not going to take control of you." He pressed a tender kiss on my lips. "Come on; we should probably talk to Astrid about our plans."

I nodded against his hand, wanting to believe his words but knowing I may not have a choice in the matter.

CHAPTER 3

*T*he hairs on the back of my neck stood on end as I leaned against the patio door, watching Astrid standing outside, staring up into the sky. Her raven-colored hair was blowing in the wind, and she had an air about her that told me she could sense something was off.

I furrowed my brow as I nudged Marcus's side. "What is she doing? And why is she standing on the grass with no shoes on?" It was freezing outside; nothing like the warmth of Byron Bay that Astrid was accustomed to.

Marcus gave me a small shrug. "I have absolutely no idea."

We opened the sliding door and stepped into the icy wind. I pulled my jacket tighter around me and stuck my hands into the pockets, trying to keep my fingers from freezing off. I hated to think how cold I would've been if I hadn't had the luxury of my paranormal blood.

I frowned. Even though I'd seen my blood countless times when I'd tried to kill myself, I had no idea what my genetic makeup really was. Doctors had done countless tests on me, so I must've had what was considered "normal human blood," which meant that my paranormal side had everything to do with my soul, the very essence of what made me, me.

"Something is coming," Astrid said, breaking me from my

thoughts. Her face was still tilted toward the sky, watching the eerie cloud formations swirling above us. A second later, she spun around, her gaze landing on me. "We need to prepare." She grabbed my forearm and dragged me toward the door.

"Hang on," I said. "We need to talk to you about something."

"Inside. It is not safe out here." She dragged me into the house.

Marcus followed us inside, giving me a look that told me he had absolutely no idea why she was acting so strange. Only a few minutes ago, she'd been calm and collected, and now Astrid acted as if she were on something.

I pulled back, trying to stop her from dragging me any further. "I'm not sure what Justin has told you, Astrid, but we found out from Morgana that she wasn't lying all those years ago about there being a way to separate Marcus's light from me without me dying in the process."

She spun around to face me, her hand still tightly gripping me. "How can you be so sure?"

I yanked my arm away from her. "Because I stole that memory from Morgana right before she died."

Her mouth formed the shape of an O. "Well, that changes everything."

"It doesn't have to," Marcus said under his breath.

I glared at him, wishing he'd accept it was inevitable. I would forever want to fulfill my destiny.

He held my stare for a few moments then turned away and headed for the kitchen.

Astrid placed her hand on mine and whispered, "You can't blame him for worrying. His whole life has revolved around you, your safety, and your well being since the moment you first met. It's going to take time to readjust."

"See, that's the thing. If we don't find this scroll, or spell, or whatever it is that can separate his light from my soul, I'm just going to die anyway." When she drew her brows together, I added," I can only live for one hundred years, and then I'm going to die anyway. Then Marcus is going to spend the next eighteen years waiting for me to reappear in his life, only to go through all this shit for another eighty-two years."

"I get it. I really do. But, that doesn't mean he's not afraid."

"Afraid of what?"

"If Morgana is wrong."

Crap. Even though I knew the truth of this spell and its existence as my very own memory, the reality was the memory wasn't mine. It was Morgana's. There was every possibility that this was her final payback should anything have happened to her.

She could be sitting there in the afterlife, laughing and rubbing her hands together as we played right into her trap. For all we knew, this unknown spell I'd stolen from her memory truly did exist, only it didn't do what I'd been led to believe it would.

There was still a whole heap of uncertainties, and I now understood why Marcus had his reservations.

But, fear played no part in war.

And war wasn't only brewing; we were trapped inside the kettle without any way out other than destroying the beast that was trying to contain us.

I raised my gaze to meet Astrid's. A knowing look consumed her eyes. She knew my truth without me having to say a word. She knew if it came down to it, I would make that ultimate sacrifice, whether I lived to see another second or not.

Astrid leaned closer to me. "We must not be foolish. But it doesn't mean to say Morgana wasn't telling the truth. Maybe there is a way."

I forced a smile. "I guess I have to wait and see."

Marcus walked into the room carrying a tray of ham and cheese toasted sandwiches. "We have to wait and see what?"

Thinking quickly, I said, "I was just telling Astrid we're going back to Morgana's to see if we can find out anything about the spell."

Astrid's eyes dilated, letting me know exactly how she felt about our little trip I'd sprung on her.

Marcus set the tray on the coffee table then took a seat as he grabbed one of the toasties. "We won't be able to stay there too long as we have to get back to Byron before dusk."

My eyes widened in surprise. "We're going back to Byron?"

Marcus paused as he was about to take a bite. "Of course, we have to go back. I hate to think what Ruby and Scar are getting up to, considering they haven't eaten for over twenty-four hours."

"Crap."

Astrid took a seat on the couch opposite Marcus and grabbed her sandwich. "Who are Ruby and Scar?"

I breathed out harshly. "I guess nobody's told you about my Hellhounds?"

She stilled, the color on her face draining the moment I mentioned the beasts. "Please tell me I heard that wrong."

I leaned back against the dining table behind me. "It's a long story, but basically I stole the minds of two Hellhounds that where after Justin and Abby, then focused their thirst onto a group of Soul Scrapers coming our way. Somehow, the Hellhounds changed their allegiance to me."

"You've been marked," she said under her breath.

"Wait. What does that mean?" I strode over to the couch and sat down beside her. "That's the exact same thing Paege said to me."

Astrid raised her brow. "You've been talking to Paege about this? I am not sure that was wise."

"We had no choice," Marcus said. "We needed her help to cast a location spell so we could find you."

"She helped you find me?" Astrid asked in surprise.

I nodded. "Yep. You have Paege to thank for your rescue. Justin and Abby tried casting the spell outside Morgana's castle, but it said Mava wasn't there."

She closed her eyes and slowly shook her head as the corner of her lips tipped up. Opening her eyes, she said, "You all thought that was Mava's lock of hair in the safety deposit box, didn't you?"

"Justin thought it was. We all went along with it because he seems to know so much more about us than we know about ourselves." Marcus took a bite of his cheese toastie.

"Ain't that the truth?" I said under my breath.

The smile dropped from her face. "The lock of hair was yours, Luciana—in case we needed to find you."

Marcus grabbed another sandwich. "That's what Paege said."

Astrid let out a controlled breath. "Paege knows about the spells?"

"Paege doesn't remember anything," I said. "I removed her memory of us ever being there that night right after we left, but I'm not sure it was necessary. She didn't seem to be malicious or untrustworthy. She seemed to kind of like me."

"Looks can be deceiving, my dear."

"But her memories aren't," I reminded her. "She was genuinely relieved I was the one Morgana feared."

"That's not what I meant." Astrid twisted so she was facing me. "Paege may have good intentions, and she may want to see Morgana's reign end, but she's weak. She will fold the moment someone stronger than her applies the slightest bit of pressure."

"Astrid's right," Marcus said. "Look how easily I got her to talk when we paid Paege a visit at her shop the other day."

"I would've talked, too, if someone was threatening me with fire."

"No you wouldn't have," he replied as if the thought of me caving in wasn't even a possibility. And the truth was, he was right. I wouldn't have. I was loyal to the very end—to him. After all, that was how I was created to be.

I leaned forward and grabbed a toasted sandwich before Marcus finished them all. "Anyway, what does all that have to do with the Hellhounds marking me?"

"Right," Astrid said. "It appears that whenever you take something from someone, an imprint of their essence crosses over to you, and then when you give, the same thing happens. That would be why the Hellhounds changed their allegiance to you and why you feel the evil from Morgana's magic."

"A piece of her has imprinted on me?"

She gave me a tight-lipped smile. "It seems that way."

"Great," I mumbled then took a bite of my toastie, the warm cheese spilling into my mouth.

Astrid placed her hand on my knee. "But, and there is a very big but, magic is neither good nor evil. You have the choice of how you wish to use it."

I swallowed. "Yet you said Morgana's evil imprinted on me."

"A small smudge against your soul, but you can still choose light over dark." Astrid grabbed the last sandwich. "And believe me, when you learn to control what you've taken from Morgana, you'll be unstoppable."

"Morgana was stoppable," Marcus reminded us.

Astrid grinned at him. "But Morgana didn't have you."

CHAPTER 4

*CW*hat Astrid said about Marcus was playing on my mind. Morgana and this God person had gone to such great lengths to keep us from finding out the truth.

Marcus was a supreme being—even if he didn't know it yet. Which got me thinking, if he still didn't remember, maybe it wasn't just Morgana that was the cause of Marcus's memory loss. Maybe Morgana was merely a piece in a gigantic puzzle.

"I don't think we can wait for Justin and Abby any longer," Astrid said, breaking me from my thoughts. She popped the last bite of her cheese toastie into her mouth.

"I agree." Marcus stood and picked up the platter covered in blobs of melted cheese.

I rose to my feet. "Where are Abby and Justin anyway?" I hadn't seen them since I'd woken up, and considering everything that was going on, I wouldn't have thought they'd stay away from us for too long.

"They've gone to look for something of Morgana's," Astrid said as she stood. "But it seems they didn't find it."

"Find what?" I asked, getting frustrated. I thought we were done with all the cryptic riddles and crap.

"Hasn't Marcus told you?"

I frowned as I watched him walk toward with kitchen. "Told me what?"

"Justin went looking for the medallion that allowed Morgana to manipulate the veils," Astrid explained. "She used it to get Mava and me over to her place in New Zealand, and we think that's how she's been able to keep Marcus and Justin from getting to Titus."

Shit. "We need that medallion."

"Yes, we do."

That was the understatement of the century. If that medallion was out there in someone else's hands, we were going to have one hell of a time trying to get to where we needed to go. Whoever had control of it could literally play with us for all eternity.

We couldn't let that happen.

Marcus came back into the room, a bottle of water in hand. "How are we doing this?"

"We'll need a car," Astrid said. "You can either come with me or fly overhead with Lucy."

"There's a car in the garage you can use, or I could take you and come back for Lulu."

She choked on a laugh. "No thank you. I prefer to keep my feet on the ground."

"Suit yourself, but we'll be flying." Marcus wrapped his arms around me from behind and planted a kiss just below my ear. "If that's okay with you."

I twisted my head around so I could see him. It was cold outside, and the wind was going to make it that much worse. But the look in his eyes as he talked about flying would make the freezing conditions worth it.

He'd longed to get back into the air—where he belonged, and I wasn't going to let a little thing like freezing to death get in the way. "Sounds perfect."

And it was.

Snuggling up against Marcus's chest as we flew through the air on our way to Morgana's was like a dream come true. Marcus's soul lit up his eyes as we soared through the sky, making sure we stayed close to the car Astrid was traveling in on the windy road below.

Marcus nestled me against his chest; his strong arms wrapped protectively around me, making my heart race. He was everything I'd imagined and so much more. Watching him now made me remember why I hadn't returned his light the moment we first met all those years ago. The tenderness of his heart was a stark contrast to the rage that lurked in the shadows. He still hadn't found his true self, but it was sitting there, just out of reach, waiting for him to take back what was rightfully his.

Marcus descended and landed perfectly amongst the lush green gardens out front of Morgana's castle.

Lowering me to my feet, he kept one arm wrapped tightly around my waist then pulled me against him. "You have no idea how long I've wanted to do that."

"Fly?" I asked, a little breathless. My heart was practically beating a hole through my chest, and it wasn't because my body was pressed against the man I loved. It was because the magic seemed to come to life as soon as we were within the walls of Morgana's estate. It was as if her magic knew it was home.

He nodded. "With you."

I curled my hand over the curve of his neck. "You've already done that once."

The smile in his eyes dropped. "That wasn't the same."

"I know." I pressed a kiss on his cheek then stepped back as Astrid's car pulled up to the closed iron gates at the start of Morgana's driveway.

I looked around as Marcus opened the gate with muscle power rather than electricity. I tried to ignore the unsettling nerves in my stomach that were bubbling their way up my esophagus, choking me.

Morgana was dead, but her memory was still very, very alive, and it unnerved me. And that wasn't all. The painful reminder that we'd lost Mava within these walls hung like a wet blanket, smothering what was left of me.

Doing my best to shake my thoughts away, I focused on Astrid driving the white station wagon, which Marcus had "borrowed" for her, through the gates. Once she stopped, she got out.

Rubbing her hands up and down her arms, she strode over to us. "I don't like this."

I narrowed my eyes at her. "Don't like what?" I hoped she was going to validate my own concerns, but at the same time, I wanted to know if I was overreacting because the truth of what we were about to do was very, very dangerous. We were walking into the lion's den, and we had no idea who was home.

She stared up at the castle and shook her head slowly. "Something doesn't feel right."

Marcus slipped his hand into mine. "That's a great help."

Astrid gave him a small shrug. "Don't say I didn't warn you."

"You haven't warned us about anything."

"Marcus!" I said, chastising him.

He cast me a sideways glance, a smile creeping across his lips. "Relax. I was only stating a fact."

Astrid turned her back to us. "Don't blame Marcus. He can't help it. It's who he is."

"Rude?"

Marcus scowled at me.

She chuckled, her back remaining to us. "No, Luciana."

I waited for her to explain why she thought he couldn't help it, but she didn't.

Marcus took the opportunity to change the subject. "We should probably start in Morgana's room."

Astrid nodded. "You check there, and I'll go to the library." She headed toward the castle.

Marcus and I followed a couple of yards behind. Astrid was on a mission, and I wondered if there really was something to worry about, or if she was feeling that way because of whatever happened to her and Mava when she was last here.

The only explanation I could come up with for the bad feeling was that the magic I'd stolen from Morgana was now connecting to something in her estate. What that could be was beyond me. "Do you think Astrid's right?" I asked Marcus as we headed up the garden path.

"I think she's wary, and I think she has every right to be."

I pulled him back. "Do you think you could try being a little nicer to her? She is here trying to save our asses, and she doesn't need you coming down on her."

"I wasn't coming down on her. I was stating a fact. There could be a hundred reasons why she feels that way, and without any evidence, it means nothing."

"So, you're saying my feelings mean nothing?"

His face softened as he tilted his head to the side. "I'm not saying that. What I'm saying is I need more than just feelings. I need to know what we're up against if I'm to protect you. I need to know if walking in there with you is dangerous." He pointed to the castle.

"Of course, it's dangerous," I said. "Everything about us is dangerous. And maybe all Astrid is saying is that we need to watch out." I don't know why I was so frustrated with him. What he'd said really wasn't that bad. I'd maybe even over-reacted, but I couldn't help it. Something had set my nerves on overdrive, and I wasn't just scared for myself; I was afraid for him. But mostly, I was terrified I was going to walk into that house and suddenly not be able to control the dark side of the magic simmering inside of me.

Marcus studied me for a few moments then said, "This isn't you."

"What if it is?" I asked, my voice breaking. Somehow he'd known what was on my mind without me having to say a word. I didn't know how he was able to do it, but I was relieved. I couldn't voice my fears because I was afraid they'd come true thanks to the untrained magic I now held.

Marcus ran his hands down my arms then laced his fingers with mine. "*You've* got control, not Morgana."

I nodded, even though I wasn't sure I believed it.

Marcus momentarily glanced toward the house. "We better catch up."

Crap. Astrid was almost to the front door.

We hightailed it up the winding path, easily catching up to her. I wanted to believe I'd somehow been struck with the ability to move like the Hellhounds, but I knew the reason we'd caught her before she entered the house was something very different.

Fear. I could see it in her soul.

The idea of going back inside had Astrid on edge, and now that we were two seconds away from entering, she was getting cold feet.

Of course, Marcus wasn't. He opened the door and stepped inside, then waited for us to enter.

Taking a deep breath, I squared my shoulders and followed.

The moment I crossed the threshold, a force of power rushed through me like a tsunami.

CHAPTER 5

I sucked in a sharp breath, trying to control the magical current running through my veins. I felt alive in ways I never knew possible. Power coursed through every cell in my body, craving to be used.

The darkness of Morgana's magic that I'd tried to bind began to push, begging to be free and take over my soul.

I couldn't let it. I needed to be in control.

"It's happening," Astrid said, her voice barely a whisper.

Marcus's wide eyes glanced momentarily at Astrid before returning to me, his pupils turning that shade of amber that told me he was afraid. "What's happening?"

Astrid pushed her way inside, taking me with her. "There must be an amulet somewhere in here. Morgana would've connected her life source to it to feed her power."

I gaped at her.

"But don't worry. It may not be a bad thing."

"May not?" Marcus asked.

"There's no way to be sure. It could be neutral, or it could be dark magic."

I swallowed hard, trying to ignore the buzzing going on underneath my skin. "Knowing Morgana, I'd have to go with the latter."

"You're probably right. But that doesn't mean to say you can't control it." She spun around to face me. "You are neither good nor evil. You are purely a vessel. Nothing less, nothing more."

I waited for Marcus to dispute her statement, but he remained silent. I wasn't upset by his silence. I was relieved. The sooner we accepted what I was, the easier our mission would become.

"You need to learn to control the war going on inside of you," she continued. "You need to choose light over dark."

The problem was I couldn't ignore the darkness trying to take over my soul. It was too strong. But what I could do was try to learn to use that darkness. I grabbed her hand as she turned away, stopping her. "Is evil stronger than good?"

She narrowed her eyes at me. "Why do you ask?"

I didn't respond. Neither of them would understand. I barely understood myself, and I couldn't help but think they'd take it the wrong way. If I was merely a vessel, then I could balance and take what I wanted when I wanted.

There was only one fault to that theory; evil was already inside of me. It was a part of me. Just like Marcus's light was a part of me. He was good. But then again, he said he also had a darkness he could control. And if he could control it, then so could I.

"Never mind," I finally answered her.

Marcus took a couple of steps toward me. "Whatever you're thinking, stop it right now."

I tilted my head to the side. "I wasn't thinking anything."

He raised a brow.

"I wasn't," I said under my breath as I headed to the sprawling marble staircase in the middle of the foyer. It rounded its way up to the second floor then continued to the third and fourth levels.

I dreaded searching through the castle for what we were after. There were so many spots that Morgana could've hidden information. And those were the places I could see. Even though I had a perfect memory of the blueprints of the castle, there was probably a whole heap of secret passageways and rooms we weren't even aware of.

My heart felt heavy with the reminder of what had happened that day. I couldn't afford to let my emotions about Mava get the better of me. She wouldn't have wanted me to let her death distract us from finishing what she'd started. I owed it to her. Mourning would have to wait.

Marcus and Astrid caught up, flanking my sides as we ascended the stairs.

When we got to the first floor, Astrid turned to me. "Repeat these words: "Departing presence come to light and seek out those who come to pass."

"Departing presence come to light and seek out those who come to pass. What does that—?" Before I could finish my sentence, I knew exactly what it meant. I could feel it within my soul as magic coursed through me, warming my body in the process. Two very distinct forms of energy I'd never felt before bounced off me. I didn't have to ask; I knew it was Marcus and Astrid. I could feel them.

She smiled. "Congratulations. You just cast your second spell."

"A bit of warning next time would be nice."

"Really?" Marcus said with a smile. "Because I thought it was kind of obvious."

I jabbed my elbow into his side. "Maybe to you."

He chuckled, and for a rare moment, I forgot what kind of danger we were in and got swept away in everything that was Marcus. But it didn't last long. We were in the house of one of the most evil people I'd ever known.

There was no forgetting that in a hurry. But, for those few seconds, I did. And it reminded me of everything I had to live for— to fight for. Our happily ever after was going to come true—even if I had to tear down this world and the next to find that damned scroll.

Marcus hooked his arm around my neck then turned to Astrid. "Are you sure you'll be okay to split up?" And there was my kind and caring man I loved.

She nodded. "I'll be fine. There's no one around."

"Don't be so sure," Marcus said. "Until we locate the medallion, all that can change in an instant."

Astrid nodded again. "Duly noted." She smiled and took off down the wide hall to the left of the staircase.

Marcus pulled me closer to him. "And that goes for you, too."

I tilted my head back so I could look at him. "I could say the same thing for you."

"There isn't a second that goes by that I'm not aware there's a huge possibility someone might try to take you away from me. Which is why you need to stay by my side."

Of course, he thought what I'd said referred to me. I wondered if he ever considered he might be in danger himself.

We continued up the stairs, memories of the castle's layout I'd taken from Marcus guiding the way. I knew exactly where we were going but had no idea what we'd find.

The castle was eerily quiet and was accentuated by our footsteps on the marble floor as we crossed the landing and headed down the hallway.

I'd feared there would be a spell of some sort that would keep us from entering Morgana's room, but the door opened without any fuss. The magic in my veins hummed as I followed Marcus into her room. It wasn't a bad sensation; it was actually kind of nice.

I was not expecting nice. I'd imagined I would be overtaken with evil the moment I stepped inside her quarters.

Floor-to-ceiling windows looking out onto the perfectly manicured lawns of her estate stretched across the far side of the room. A mahogany four-poster bed sat against the right wall, and there was a large seating area complete with worn leather books piled on the side table, sofa, and every other piece of flat furniture surrounding it.

"She was looking for something," I whispered more to myself than Marcus.

He strode over to the pile of books stacked on top of the side table and ran his fingers over the cover. "I think you're right."

Marcus picked up the book on top and flipped through the pages, opening to the first piece of paper wedged inside.

"What's it say?" I peered over his shoulder, trying to get a better look.

He shrugged. "I'm not sure. It looks like another spell to me."

"It has to be important; otherwise, Morgana wouldn't have marked it."

Marcus gestured to the other books piled on the table and the lounge. "They've all been bookmarked in at least one place or another."

My hopes fleeted as I scanned the old leather books. He was right. There were so many pages marked with paper, material, or anything else that appeared to be in arm's reach at the time Morgana had read through them. That was if it was even Morgana. "You know, someone could've set this up to throw us off. Make us waste our time on the trivial stuff instead of searching for the meaningful information hiding someplace else."

"Could be. But we'd be stupid not to see if there's a pattern." He took a seat on the only free spot on the couch as he continued to flip through the pages.

Sighing, I put my hands on my hips and glanced around the room. There were so many places to search, and I didn't know where to start. "Where would you hide your treasures, Morgana?"

I knew she couldn't answer me, but that didn't make me stop talking to a dead person. My needs and wants were the polar opposite. I wanted to stay as far away from Morgana's presence, but I needed to become close to her if we were going to figure this whole mess out.

Time wasn't on our side, and I had to push my doubts to the back of my mind where they belonged.

Deciding to start on her bedside tables, I rummaged through the drawers then moved onto the dresser. Every piece of furniture in the room looked to be made over a hundred years ago, and I felt bad for ripping the drawers out and dumping them on the bed as I searched for anything that would be of use to us. But I had to do it. There was no time to be careful.

Every single drawer was immaculately presented, unlike my own drawers I stuffed to the top to never be able to find anything. It was almost as if someone had already come by and made sure there was nothing for us to find. Either that or she'd had some serious OCD issues.

That wouldn't surprise me. Morgana had been a lot of things, and none of them would have been possible without precision and order.

Coming up empty, I made my way back to Marcus. "Find anything useful?"

With his eyes still peeled to the open page, he said, "Not yet." He glanced up at me. "That's not to say I'm an expert in witchcraft. You are, but you can't read Latin."

I scowled at him. "I'd hardly call myself an expert. I don't even know how to cast a friggin' spell."

"You may not have the knowledge yet, but when you do, you're going to be amazing." His eyes glistened with a fiery light as if he could see something I could not. And like all things Marcus, he didn't bother sharing what was on his mind.

He was right; I was going to be amazing. Either that or I'd done the very thing they'd wanted me to by taking a piece of Morgana. For all I knew, she'd planned it from the beginning and I'd not only stolen a portion of her magic, but I'd also taken a piece of her soul, and she was now infesting my body like a parasite.

Needing to keep moving, I headed to the door to the right of the bed. If I was correct, it would lead to her closet and bathroom.

"Don't go too far," Marcus warned as I twisted the handle.

I rolled my eyes and didn't bother answering him. He knew what was behind the door, and he also knew no one else was waiting inside to jump me.

Pushing the door open, I found exactly what I'd expected. Rows of perfectly presented clothes hung on racks and others were folded in drawers. It was like something out of a magazine, not at all like a normal person's closet stuffed to capacity and mountains of shoes taking over the floor.

Then again, Morgana had maids—and magic. Magic could do a lot of things and maybe cleaning was one of them. I could only hope.

I ran my fingers over the dark wooden drawers as I tried to figure out where the best place was to start. Where would a witch hide her doll tied to her magic or stash her most valuable prophecies and spells?

Morgana had been a lot of things, and smart was at the top of her list alongside her evilness.

Deciding to start on the left, I rummaged through drawer after drawer, sifting through every piece of clothing, socks, and shoes. I searched under the bottom and the back of every piece of furniture, hoping I'd find something—anything that would help us in our quest.

Nothing.

There wasn't a damned thing to be found.

I threw my head back and let out a strangled whimper. I was so sick of Morgana's games and the tricks she played. Even in her death, she was still playing with our lives.

"You okay?" Marcus called out.

Tilting my head back down, I said, "I'm… fine." I whispered the last word as I realized something I should've seen straight away but had been too stupid to notice.

Magic.

CHAPTER 6

*D*odging the piles of clothes strewn across the floor, I took a few steps toward the end of the closet then turned back to the door. Something was off.

"Lulu?"

"Yeah?" I said absentmindedly as I took another step forward, my mind completely consumed with what I thought I was seeing. My eyes went wide as the wall began to shimmer. "What the hell?" I said under my breath as I reached for the wall.

Marcus bounded into the closet as the tips of my fingers disappeared into the plaster. "What are you doing?" The fear in his voice reverberated off the walls, sending fear spiking through my heart.

I yanked my hand back partly because he'd scared me and partly because... well, I'd stuck my hand through a freaking wall.

I swallowed hard as I tried to wrap my head around what I'd found. "There's something behind the wall."

Marcus's gaze ran along the length of the closet. Then he furrowed his brow as he stared at the wall in front of me. "This room should be longer."

My heart skipped a beat. Finally, we were getting somewhere. "I know, right?" I turned back to the wall and reached toward it.

Marcus's hand closed around my wrist before I'd even realized he'd moved. "No."

I slowly swiveled my head so I could look him in the eye. "Please tell me you didn't just tell me no—again."

He lowered my hand by my side. "I did, and I'll say it again. No."

I barely registered what he'd said. Something inside of me was compelling me to find out what was hiding behind the wall, to dismiss all rationality and seek the unknown.

I quickly reached out with my other hand and felt a magnetic pull drawing me into what lay beyond getting stronger the closer I came to the wall.

Marcus caught my arm, wrapping his fingers around my wrist to stop me from going any further. "Don't be so foolish. It could be a trap."

I raised a brow. Frustration boiled inside of me, and no matter how much I tried to be levelheaded, I simply could not. "Foolish?"

"Yes, foolish. Something is behind there, and we can't see what it is. Don't be so quick to rush into the unknown where Mogana's concerned. Or are you forgetting what she's done to us so far?"

I closed my eyes as I tried to expel my need to jump in without giving it the consideration it deserved. Marcus was right. It could be a trap. And this freakish desire I had to dive right through the magical barrier should've been enough to alert me to the dangers of what was possibly hidden within. But that was the thing. It was almost as if something was calling to a piece of my soul, begging me to enter the unknown.

It had Morgana written all over it. Even in death, she was still trying to control me.

"I'm not forgetting." Opening my eyes, I took a step back to put some distance between the wall and me, hoping it would lessen the pull of whatever was trying to control me from within.

It worked, and I finally had a moment to think clearly, without the temptation to dive right in.

"Good." He squeezed my hand. "I'm not saying we shouldn't try to figure out what's behind the wall. It's just that I don't think we should rush in. Magic has the power to make us do things we wouldn't normally do. It's what you have to learn to pay attention to because that's when you're at the greatest risk."

Everything he said was true. I needed to fear. But I also needed to push past that fear if we had any hope for the future we both were so desperate to have.

Marcus let go of my hand and placed the tips of his fingers on the wall where mine had gone through not more than thirty seconds before. He couldn't get through.

I reached forward, expecting my fingers to touch the plaster like Marcus's had, but mine slipped through the wall as if it weren't really there and was merely a figment of my imagination. "What the hell?"

I yanked my hand back as Marcus ran his fingers over the wall. "You can't get through," I said in disbelief.

With his hand flat against the wall, he slowly turned to me, his eyes doing that molten lava thing they did when he was either upset or afraid of whatever I was trying to do. "No."

"No what?" I took a step toward him, the pull of the wall latching onto me, drawing me in with its tendrils, trapping me within its web. It felt good.

He pushed off the wall and stalked over to me. "No. You're not going through."

I folded my arms across my chest, frustrated that I couldn't let the magic pull me into its depths. "And why not?"

He raised a brow. "You seriously have to ask that? We just had this conversation."

"No. *You* had this conversation." I lowered my arms to my sides and took a step closer to him. "And I agreed with you, and I still do. But the thing is, you can't see what's behind that wall and *I* can. No matter how much you want to protect me from every single thing in this world, the truth is you can't. I need to do this for you, for me— for us. Because, God damn it, I will not let your fear ruin our chances." I stomped my foot like a pathetic tween not getting her way. "Why do we always have to do this?"

He folded his arms across his chest. "Do what?"

"This!" I gestured between him and me. "You know I need to see what's on the other side of that wall. Why can't you accept it and help me do what needs to be done?" In the back of my mind, all I could think about was whether he was protecting me or his light. I wanted to chastise myself for even considering it, but since my old memories had resurfaced, so had my doubts.

He stared at me, unwavering as his molten lava eyes swirled with fear.

I sighed, placed my hands on his biceps, and tried to ignore the pull. I needed to convince Marcus to let me through. "Look. I know this is dangerous, but so was Morgana and so is this God. If we're going to end this once and for all, we can't keep doing this. We have to take risks. You have to be okay with me taking risks because this is my fight, too. And whatever is behind that wall could be the difference between us being stuck in this loop for eternity or finally being free from the arseholes who've controlled our lives for so long."

Marcus's face softened. He lowered his arms and curled his hands around my hips. "You win. You can go through."

It wasn't about winning this argument with Marcus. I was fighting for him and me. I stood on the balls of my feet and kissed him. "Thank you."

He cupped my jaw in his hands. "But I want you to promise me you'll do this my way."

"And your way is?"

Marcus reached into the pocket of his jeans and retrieved his phone. "Take a video of what's behind before you go through."

I smiled. "Sounds like a plan."

It wasn't really much of a plan, but at least we were doing something.

I snatched his phone from him. "You won't regret this." I turned on the recorder, reached toward the wall, and paused. Marcus may have agreed to this, but he was still going out of his mind with worry.

Taking his hand, I laced my fingers through his then stuck my other hand through the wall.

Relief swept through me when the seconds ticked by and nothing grabbed me. I desperately wanted to get through, but I had to be smart about this.

Rotating the phone around, I made sure I got all angles of the scene on the other side of the wall then withdrew it and glanced up at Marcus. He seemed as relieved as I was—maybe even more. "See. Nothing happened."

I stopped the recording then pressed replay. The screen lit up with what appeared to be a small bar area. Only there weren't bottles of alcohol stored on the shelves. They were ornamental crystal canisters filled with various colored liquids and things that reminded me of Mava's kitchen. On the bench was a pewter cauldron encased with black gems around the rim, and beside it were an old parchment and a slim, leather-bound journal. "It's a potion room."

"So it seems." Marcus grabbed his phone from me and played the video again.

When it finished for the second time, he pocketed his phone. "I want you to be careful."

I blinked in surprise. "You're okay with me going in?"

He gave me a tight-lipped smile as he nodded. "You said this is your fight, so go on. Go fight."

My lips curled up. "You never cease to amaze me." I planted a kiss on the side of his cheek then headed to the wall. I stopped briefly and gave him another smile. "Wish me luck."

"I don't believe in luck."

I chuckled. "Of course not."

I drew in a deep breath and headed through the wall.

CHAPTER 7

$\mathcal{M}$y body tingled as I passed through the wall into Morgana's secret potion room.

Energy buzzed beneath the surface of my skin, trying to reconnect with Morgana's spirit. I could feel her evil energy as if she were standing right beside me.

But that was stupid. Morgana was dead, and the only part of her that remained was her magic, which I now possessed, and whatever the hell she'd connected her magic to, which I would bet my life was in this very room.

It was calling to me, but I couldn't figure out where it was coming from. I moved the items on the shelves, trying to find where it was but came up empty. Maybe it wasn't an item like Astrid had thought. Maybe it was the actual room and the magic it possessed. After all, Marcus couldn't get through, and something was telling me, neither would Astrid.

Shaking my thoughts away, I focused on what I'd gone in there for. I grabbed the parchment and the leather journal and was about to leave when I noticed a six-inch cylinder tucked behind a neatly folded black cloth on the bench.

I sucked in a sharp breath the moment my skin touched the ice-cold metal. A dark electric current surged through my fingers, running down the length of my body.

I had no idea what was inside, but one thing I knew for sure, whatever it held, was dark magic—and it brought the fear of God into me.

I almost laughed. I did fear God. Or at least the one who called himself that. I'd be stupid not to.

The road that lay ahead was going to be filled with dark, evil magic, and no matter how afraid I was, I had to remain strong and focus on the light.

Lifting my gaze, I turned in Marcus's direction. I couldn't see him, but I knew he was there. He was my constant reminder of who I was and the power I possessed.

Doing one more scan of the room to see if I missed anything else, I picked up the cylinder and did my best to block the evil presence trying to possess my soul.

Satisfied I wasn't going to find anything else, I stepped back through the wall and was met by a very relieved Marcus.

He gave me a once-over—as usual.

I handed him the journal and tapped the cylinder against my hand. "I think this is it."

"Let's open it and find out," Marcus said, making a grab for the cylinder.

I pulled it back, out of his reach. "I think we should find Astrid before we open it."

Marcus drew his brows together. "Why's that?"

I studied the intricate pattern chiseled into the metal. I wasn't sure what exactly the picture depicted, but it gave me the creeps—especially the eye with a ruby in the center of it. "This is dark. And I mean really dark."

He drew in a deep breath then released it slowly. "Let's go find Astrid."

We headed through the house and down the stairs, stopping at the first floor where we'd split from Astrid. I couldn't feel her. "She's not here, is she?"

"Nope." He tilted his head to the side and looked down the stairwell. "She's somewhere down there."

Getting used to my new ability was a little hard. I had felt Astrid's presence when I'd first done the spell, but I couldn't feel her at all now. The only reason why I knew I still had the ability was because I could feel Marcus like a beacon, calling me to him.

579

We continued down the stairs and headed to the right, where we found her in an enormous room filled with at least twenty tables with cauldrons, jars of various ingredients, and walls lined with shelves holding thousands of books. It was a sight to see.

Astrid was sitting on a stool behind a cauldron, pouring some sand-colored powder into the pot. Her hair was pulled up into a very loose bun with strands framing her face. She was completely captivated in whatever she was doing, so much so that she didn't even notice us walk into the room.

Marcus cleared his throat, but she didn't acknowledge our existence.

"Astrid," he called out.

Her gaze darted up to us, her eyes going wide the moment they locked onto the cylinder in my hand. "Where did you find that?" Her voice was sharp and, if I was being honest, a little afraid, which scared me that much more.

At the mere mention of what was in my hand, my gaze was drawn to it like a magnet. "I found it in a secret room inside Morgana's closet."

"It was hidden by magic behind what appeared to be a wall in her closet," Marcus added.

"You shouldn't have gone in there without me."

Even though neither of us had mentioned Astrid while we were discussing finding out what was behind the wall, Marcus gave me a look saying "I told you so."

Astrid swiveled off her seat and strode over to us, wiping her hands on her dress. "Let me see."

I handed her the cylinder.

She sucked in a sharp breath the moment she made contact.

"So it's not only me that feels it," I said under my breath.

"Feels what?" Marcus asked.

Astrid lifted her gaze to meet his. "This is very dark. The kind of dark I didn't think even Morgana would be part of."

CHAPTER 8

*C*hills danced over my skin, causing the hairs to stand on end as I stared at the cylinder in Astrid's hand. "What kind of dark magic are we talking about? I thought Morgana was the evilest of them all."

"Yes, Morgana was evil. But this is dark."

Jesus Christ. I wished at least one person I knew would spit out what they were trying to say instead of speaking in riddles. "Aren't dark and evil the same thing?"

She shook her head as she continued to study the cylinder. "Good and evil are the nature of the witch that holds the magic and how they choose to use it. Dark magic is the magic itself. There are very few covens that still use it today, and it's very unsettling to see Morgana was involved in such practices."

"Really? Because I kind of thought that would be exactly what Morgana was into."

She looked up at me. That smile she shared with Mava and my guardians was plastered on her face. "No, dear. You don't understand. Dark magic is ancient. No good can come from it."

"Are you saying we shouldn't look at what's inside?" Marcus asked.

"I'm saying we need to be careful and prepared because you might not like what you find."

I swallowed hard. Something about the cylinder told me I would most definitely not like what I found. But fear was for the weak, and I was determined to be strong. "Well, let's see what it says."

Astrid studied me for a few moments and then gave me a curt nod. "I agree, but here is not the place."

I frowned. "Why's that?"

"Because this place already contains enough darkness. We need light to balance dark."

I glanced at Marcus, hoping he understood what she was saying.

He shrugged. "And where do you expect to find this light?"

"Back home where the sea meets the sand."

"You mean the beach?" I asked.

"Yes, dear. And we must wait until the moons align." She held the cylinder out to Marcus.

"Well then," Marcus said, taking it from her, "we're in luck because when we're finished here, we're heading home, and if my calculations are correct, that would mean we only have to wait until tomorrow night for the moons to align."

"You are correct." She turned on her heel and scooted back to where we'd found her. "I've taken the liberty to make another batch of the potion that will hide our presence, and I'd like you, Luciana, to conduct the final spell."

"Me?" I asked in surprise.

"Yes, you." She waved me over. "For if I performed this last part, it would only last a day, maybe two, at most. But you..." She trailed off as she looked at me in awe. "You have the power to make this last for years."

Well, shit. Just another thing I had to thank Morgana for.

I rushed over to Astrid. "You mean no one will see us coming?"

She nodded. "They will not be able to feel you, but that doesn't mean you're invisible."

I furrowed my brow as it dawned on me that even though we'd already taken these concoctions, I could still feel both Marcus and Astrid's presence. "The last lot didn't work properly. How can you be so sure this one will?"

Astrid tilted her head to the side. "Why do you think the last lot didn't work?"

I rested my hands on the table. "Because I can still feel both you and Marcus, and I'm guessing that means you can feel me, too."

She smiled that infuriating smile. "And so you should be able to feel those within your coven."

I scrunched up my face in confusion. "What coven?"

Marcus strode over to us. "What are you saying?"

"This spell works to protect and shelter us from those outside of the circle."

I let out a slow breath through my teeth as I tried to calm down and not shake the answer out of her. "What circle?"

"Us." She gestured to the three of us. "As well as Abby and Justin. We may not be a conventional coven, but we are one nonetheless."

Biting down on my smile, I bumped my shoulder against Marcus's. "Bet you never thought you'd hear that." I was positive he was reeling on the inside. In the past, witches were not his favorite people, and now she was saying we were family.

Marcus twisted around to face me, leaning his hip against the bench. A smile spread across his face, not at all what I'd expected. "Told you I'd believe in the tooth fairy if it meant we'd break this curse."

"Only it's not a curse," I said, stating the obvious.

"No, it's not," he agreed. "But who knows where this will lead?" He held up the cylinder between us.

I had a feeling we were going to be in for a world of trouble. "But first, we must hide."

CHAPTER 9

*O*stared at the shot glass in my hand, wondering how such simple words had the ability to hide our presence from those outside of our circle.

Circle.

It was time to face the fact that I was a witch and not just any old witch. I was powerful beyond belief. And no matter how much I didn't want Morgana's magic, I couldn't offload it to someone else. There was too much power contained inside of me, and even though I trusted Astrid, my past decisions taught me that my judgement wasn't always right. Magic had a way of deceiving people, making them believe things that weren't real.

I couldn't afford another setback.

"So this is it?" I asked, holding up the shot glass. "I drink this, and then they can't find me for years."

"That's it." Astrid raised her glass.

We clinked our glasses together, and I forced myself not to gag as I downed the contents. When I recovered, I asked, "Why can't you make this stuff taste better?" I looked around for some water. "Surely you have the power to make it taste like candy or something."

Spotting a tap on the table located near the far wall, I darted over to it, turned it on, and rinsed out my mouth.

Astrid laughed. "I would if I could. But unfortunately, it would interrupt the purity of the spell, which is something we can not afford to do."

The water didn't do much to ease the metallic taste plastered to my mouth, but at least it diluted it a little. "Why was this one so strong?"

"Because you cast the spell."

I sauntered back over to them. "Are you telling me that by me saying—?"

Astrid's eyes went wide. "Don't say it!"

"What? Why?" I asked, scrunching up my face in confusion.

"Because you will cast another spell that will affect the one you've just done."

Crap!

I breathed out harshly, wondering what would've happened if I had let the words slip from my lips. By the look on Astrid's face, I didn't want to find out. "This whole magic thing is going to take a little getting used to."

Marcus placed his empty shot glass on the table. "Don't be so hard on yourself. It takes years for a witch to learn the magic they were born with."

"You have the power to do and control so much, but you lack the knowledge to do so," Astrid said.

Marcus turned to Astrid. "That's where you're supposed to come in."

Astrid twisted off her stool and stood. "And I will. But right now there are more pressing matters."

"Ain't that the truth," I said under my breath. "How much longer do you need here?"

"Well, we still have the rest of the castle to search through."

"That could take days," Marcus said. "We have what we need, and the sooner we get out of here, the sooner we can find out what's written on this scroll."

"We can't do that until tomorrow, so I may as well stay here while you two go back to Byron and look after your little friends."

I scoffed. "You're seriously not suggesting you stay here by yourself after everything that's happened to you and..." I couldn't bring myself to say her name. Being so close to where Mava had died was tearing at my heart. Mava never deserved to die, and I didn't understand how she could so easily have given her life for mine.

But that wasn't actually true. She had given her life for Marcus. We were all fighting to return him to his rightful place without me dying in the process, and now Astrid was continuing what Mava had begun.

Marcus spread his hand across the small of my back. "We can send Justin or Abby back here to keep an eye on Astrid."

"Justin would be of better use to me," Astrid said as she picked up the journal I'd found with the cylinder and began flipping through the pages. "He knows what we're after and will cut my work here in half."

"Justin it is." Marcus pulled out his phone and put it to his ear. "How soon can you be here?" He nodded before disconnecting the call.

"What did he say?" I asked.

"He'll be here in another couple of hours."

"Why so long?"

Marcus pocketed his phone. "Because they're still trying to locate the medallion that manipulates the veils."

"Good." Astrid closed the journal and tucked it under her arm. "That will give us some time to try to find the source of Morgana's power in here."

I frowned. "What?'

She headed toward the door. "The source of the connection you felt when you entered the castle."

Marcus and I glanced at each other and shrugged.

Catching up to her, I said, "I presumed I was feeling the dark magic cylinder because I was drawn to that like nothing I've ever felt." Except for Marcus but they didn't need reminding of that. Our connection was a given.

She spun around on her heel, and I had to pull up short so I didn't run into her. "Whoa."

Fear lit up her eyes, turning them white just like I'd seen on Mava the first time I'd met her. "That thing is calling to you?"

"Umm..." No matter how much I didn't want to be connected, the fact remained I was. The look in her eyes was telling me that was not a good thing. "Yeah. I was drawn to it."

Astrid closed her eyes and let out a slow breath. When she opened them again, they'd returned to normal. "We must make sure. We need to know if you were drawn to the cylinder because of what it contained or if you were drawn to it because it contained a piece of Morgana."

Jesus. Why do these witches continue to speak in riddles that make absolutely no sense to me?

"And how do we do that?" Marcus asked.

She spun back around and continued down the hall. "First, we must determine if it was, in fact, this cylinder that Lucy was attracted to in this house by removing it from the estate."

"Sounds easy enough."

Five minutes later, I once again stood at the front door with Astrid by my side. Marcus was flying just outside the grounds, waiting for the okay to bring it back to us.

"Do you feel anything?" Astrid asked.

I placed my hand on the door handle and waited. "I feel a connection but not like it was before."

She nodded. "Let's go inside."

I pushed the giant wooden door open and stepped over the threshold. The rush of power returned to my soul; however, I didn't feel the evil pull I'd experienced before. "It's not the same."

Astrid breathed out harshly. "As I feared."

I bit my lip, trying to calm my nerves. My heart was practically pumping a hole through my chest as I attempted to come to terms with what it meant. I didn't just have Morgana's magic; I was also connected to a darkness like no other.

She put her hand on my forearm and gave it a gentle rub. "Don't worry, dear. You are not human, and you're not angelic or demonic. You must remember you are a vessel created merely to contain."

This vessel has feelings, and I wanted to scream it at the top of my lungs. But Astrid didn't deserve my frustration, and we had no time for any outbursts.

I let out a slow breath and tried to refocus. "What exactly does this mean?"

"It means you are connected to that dark magic. We must be careful, for if it lands in the hands of another, that person will have control of a piece of you."

My heart skipped a beat. "That thing gives whoever holds it the ability to control me? Are you friggin' serious?"

"It's connected to Morgana, and thanks to you and Marcus, all that is left of her is lying inside of you. Now, if someone wanted to, they could break that connection, and from what I know, that would mean Morgana's magic would be halved."

"Why?"

"Because it's no longer able to draw from the piece of Morgana's soul that remains within the cylinder."

"And if I don't find a way to give Marcus back his light, then I need her magic to fight this God."

She nodded. "Exactly."

I tilted my head back and groaned. "Then I guess that thing better stay with me until we've found a way for me to survive without Marcus's light."

CHAPTER 10

*W*e spent the next couple of hours searching through the piles of books in Morgana's room while we waited for Justin to arrive. Well, Marcus and Astrid searched through the books. I splayed out on the floor, staring absently at the ceiling. I was of absolutely no use to them. I couldn't read Latin, and apparently, there wasn't a spell that would make me fluent or even a beginner.

My stomach was rumbling, and I desperately wanted to eat, but I wasn't going to go shopping for food in the castle. Knowing my luck, the other priestesses poisoned all the food in case we came back here and were stupid enough to trust them.

I jerked into a sitting position the moment I felt someone else close by. "Who's here?"

Marcus peered at me over the rim of the book in his lap, the corner of his lips tipping up. "Relax. It's only Justin."

"So that's what he feels like," I said more to myself than Marcus.

Justin pushed the door open and entered the room. "That's what *who* feels like?"

"You."

Astrid rested the book she was reading against her knees. "Lucy now has the ability to feel us."

"Good." Justin sat on the arm of the couch where Astrid was sitting. "What are you looking at?"

She sighed. "Spells, spells, and more spells."

"Why?"

Marcus closed the book he was reading and dropped it on to the wooden floor. "Because Morgana thought to place markers in every bloody book she owns and now we're left trying to figure out why."

Justin picked up a book and turned it over to look at the back cover. "The other witches could've done this to waste our time."

I crossed my legs. "That's what I thought."

"That may very well be true," Astrid said, "but we need to make sure we're not leaving any valuable information behind."

Justin flicked through the first couple of pages of the book. "And let me guess; you want me to help you search through all of these?"

Marcus stood. "You got it." He walked over to me and held out his hands, helping me to my feet.

"Are you sure you'll be okay while we go?" I asked.

"I'll be fine," Astrid replied. "Justin will take care of me and make sure we get to Byron before we need to perform the ritual."

Justin frowned. "What ritual?"

"Astrid can fill you in while we're gone." Marcus wrapped his arm around my shoulders. "Where's Abby?"

"She's pressing some witches for information."

I shuddered thinking about what exactly she could be doing to a bunch of hopefully not innocent witches. Marcus had more control of his anger than Abby seemed to, and he'd almost burned down Paege's shop when she wouldn't spill the beans on other witches. I would've hated to be on the receiving end of Abby's wrath.

Marcus dropped his hand to mine and laced our fingers. "Let us know if you find anything. And I mean anything."

"Yes, boss," Justin said with a smirk.

"Of course, we will," Astrid added. "And we'd appreciate it if you'd do the same."

Marcus nodded then led me to the doors leading out to the balcony.

"I guess we're flying from here."

He opened the door and held it wide for me. "It's the quickest way."

"Right." I stepped out onto the sandstone pavers, the ice-cold wind stinging my face. "Shit."

"What's wrong?" he asked.

Ignoring Marcus, I popped my head back inside. "Astrid?"

"Yeah?"

"I don't suppose there's a spell for making me feel warm?"

She chuckled then stood and strode over to me. "Not exactly. But there is something that will hold off the elements for a brief time."

"How long?"

"About an hour. But it could be longer for you."

I ran my hands up and down my arms. "Sounds good to me."

"Okay, then say these words. "Expel the elementals and protect from within."

I repeated the words and instantly felt the ice-cold wind disappear. The wind was still there, but it was no longer cold. "Wow."

She smiled. "Be careful where you use it, because feeling the elements can keep you out of danger."

"How so?"

"The magic stops you from feeling, but you can not avoid the damage the elements can do."

Marcus put his hand on my hip. "I think what Astrid is trying to say is that you can walk through fire without feeling the burn, but you will still burn."

"Exactly."

"Right," I said. "No walking through fire for me."

"I wouldn't think this one would ever let you get that close." She gestured to Marcus.

"I think you're right about that." Although, I wasn't as sure how true that statement was as I had been a few hours earlier. Marcus seemed to be warming to the idea of accepting that I had to put myself in danger. There was no other choice.

Astrid closed the door and went back to hit the books again.

"I guess we should get going."

Marcus swept me up into his arms then leaped into the air, his wings unfurling from his back as if it were second nature to him.

I stared at him in awe. He was truly a sight like no other, and I was lucky enough to be in his arms for the next hour or so.

The feeling of being lucky lasted about twenty minutes. Then came the stiffness, which turned into aches and pains. Marcus did his best to keep me comfortable, but considering we were crossing the ocean, there was nowhere to put me down so I could stretch my legs. I had to accept this was the way it had to be. I wasn't going to take anything more from Marcus.

Eventually, the land came into view and the lights twinkling in the dusky sky acted like a beacon. Marcus swept down and landed amongst the trees near the crystal mountain.

I practically jumped out of his arms and fell to the ground, my legs too stiff to stretch out quickly enough. A laugh escaped my mouth as I rolled onto my butt.

Marcus kneeled down beside me, a smile playing on his lips. "You okay?"

I nodded. "I am so sore after that flight." I stretched my arms over my head then to each side. "I don't know how you guys do it without getting any kinks."

He placed his hands on my shoulders and began massaging them. "I guess it's because we were born to fly, whereas you were not."

I let my hands fall on the ground between my legs. "Thanks for the reminder."

Marcus sat on the ground beside me and wrapped his arm around my shoulders. "I may have been born to fly, but you're the one who's special."

There was no arguing the point that *he* was the special one because I would always be special in his eyes. "Let's agree to disagree."

He planted a kiss on my temple before getting to his feet and helping me up. "We better get inside and feed those two."

"That's if they haven't already run out on us."

"Somehow I doubt that." Marcus took my hand and led me through the dense bush toward the entrance to the cave.

"How can you be so sure?" I couldn't feel them, and I was pretty sure Marcus couldn't either. That was most likely because of the crystals hiding their prints, not because the Hellhounds might not be there.

"Because you gave them an order."

"That's it?"

"That is all that matters to them."

CHAPTER 11

*R*elief washed through me as we entered the cave and my night vision kicked in. I no longer had to rely on a torch to see in the dark or depend on Marcus to keep me safe.

A soft orange glow emitted from the crystals lining the walls and ceiling of the cave as if they were guiding us through the maze. I hadn't noticed it the last time we'd been there, or maybe I just hadn't been privy to the supernatural beauty until I stole the Hellhound's vision.

My stomach was in knots as we made our way through the twists and turns until we came upon the cavern that had been home to my two new pets. I had no idea what to expect and prayed Ruby and Scarlett wouldn't attack me the first chance they got.

The Hellhounds ears pricked up and their heads snapped in our direction. A soft growl emitted from their throats, quickly increasing to a loud rumble as they rose to their feet and bounded over to me like a loyal dog would do to its human owner. But these were not dogs, and no matter how much they appeared to love me, I needed to remember how dangerous they could be.

"Hi, girls." I rubbed their faces as they smashed their heads against my shoulders.

Marcus spread his hand across my back, supporting me against the weight of the beasts. He stretched his arm around me and gave Ruby a scratch behind her ear.

She leaned into his hand, a soft growl rumbling in her throat.

I had to remind myself it was a purr and she was happy, because it sure as hell didn't sound that way.

"Relax," Marcus whispered into my ear. "They're not going to hurt you." He gave Ruby a couple of pats on the head then said, "We better get these two fed if we want it to stay that way."

"And where do you suppose we're going to get some souls for them to feed on?" I hoped to God I wasn't going to have to go out there and find some innocent human for them to feed off.

Marcus bit down on a smile. "They eat meat as well."

Scar pushed her head against me, making me take a step back as I steadied myself. "Where are we going to get some meat?"

"The shops. Where else did you think we were going to get it from?"

I glared at him. "I dunno, maybe a supernatural food chain I'm not aware of."

He chuckled. "That would make things a whole lot easier than walking into the supermarket and buying up half the meat department."

I swallowed hard. "How much do they eat?"

"A lot."

Of course, they did. "I guess we better get going then."

Scarlett lifted her giant paw, placed it on my shoulder, and pulled me toward her.

For a second, I thought she was going to try to eat me, but I was strangely pleased when her enormous tongue landed on my cheek and slid up to my hairline.

I choked on a laugh. "She's not playing with her dinner, is she?"

"Don't stress. She's just showing you some affection." Marcus pushed her off me. "I know it's weird to think Hellhounds can be like this, but they are. Only, it's usually to their demon master."

Ruby pounced on Scar, pushing her back. Then they began to rough play with each other.

I shook my head in amazement as I watched them. The beasts I'd seen when we were in the sewer tunnel in Morgana's estate hadn't behaved anything like what Scar and Ruby were now. It was hard to imagine those beasts could have a friendly, playful side. But sure enough, I was seeing it firsthand.

Marcus slipped his hand into mine and cocked his head toward the exit.

I nodded then turned my attention back to the girls. "Ruby and Scarlett, stay." I had no idea if it would work a second time, but they didn't follow us as we backed out of the cavern and made our way through the tunnels.

When we were in the open, Marcus scooped me into his arms and took off into the sky. A few minutes later, we landed amongst the trees near the shopping strip.

Marcus folded his wings into his back. "We might need to get a car to carry the food back."

I frowned. "I thought you were joking when you said half the meat department."

He shook his head as he led me through the trees toward the road. "Unfortunately not."

"How do you know so much about Hellhounds anyway?"

"It's common knowledge. They have ferocious appetites that need sustaining."

We stepped through the last of the tree coverage and into the overgrown grass the council had neglected to maintain.

Humans were walking the streets, completely oblivious to the world around them. A few stared at us for a couple of seconds before continuing on their way.

An elderly couple whispered something to each other then glared at us with disdain.

I leaned into Marcus. "I think they assume we've been fooling around in the bush."

"Better that than the truth."

Crossing the road, we headed toward the supermarket, but before we got to the other side, my stomach twisted into knots as the sound of giant paws slamming into the asphalt behind us reverberated up my spine.

CHAPTER 12

 *M*y heart pounded as I whipped my head around, prepared to come face-to-face with another demonic monster.

Marcus placed his hand on my forearm. "It's only the girls."

My mouth dropped open as I watched Ruby and Scarlett pound the pavement, coming toward us. They were twenty feet away from me, out in the open around the multitude of humans, not hiding in the shadows like I thought they would.

A car beeped its horn, breaking me out of my stupor. I snapped my head in its direction and apologised to the driver, who appeared ready to bust into an abusive tirade until he saw Marcus turn his way.

We took a couple of steps back and moved onto the sidewalk as Ruby and Scarlett slowed down to follow us, closely.

I glanced around to see if we were the only people who could see the five-hundred-pound monsters walking down one of the busiest streets in town. Sure enough, everyone remained focused on themselves, completely oblivious to the Hellhounds walking amongst them.

"What are they doing here?" I whispered loudly.

Marcus shrugged a shoulder. "It seems they missed you."

I glared at him. "Not helping."

Ruby was the first to greet me. She lifted her giant head and curled it over my shoulder as she raised her paw and swiped it over my back. Thankfully, her claws were retracted; otherwise, she probably would've cut me in half.

I stumbled back, but Marcus caught me before I hit the pavement and made an even bigger fool of myself than what I was sure I already had done. No one else could see why I was falling over my feet and probably thought I was a drunk or drug addict.

I knew I should try to pretend they weren't there so I didn't bring any unnecessary attention to myself, but they were too hard to ignore. Especially when they were intent on showing me exactly how much they cared about me.

"Abby would love to see this right now," Marcus said with a laugh.

I glared at him again. "Not helping," I managed to get out.

Wrapping his arm around my waist, he lifted me off the ground, swung me behind him, and set me on my feet.

"Easy, girls." Marcus raised his hands then placed them on their necks as they tried to duck around him and get to me. He chuckled again and said, "I think you're just going to have to get this over and done with."

I gripped onto Marcus's shirt. "Get what over and done with?"

"You're going to have to give them what they want."

"Shit." Taking one last look at all the people around me who were about to think I was a hallucinating lunatic, I resided to the fact that I was going to prove them right then made my way around Marcus.

The girls smooshed their heads against me as they'd done in the cave, only now we had spectators.

A few mothers ushered their children to the other side of them and briskly walked away from us, while others stared, unable to take their eyes off the freak.

I was used to being a freak. I just wished they'd see what I saw, because I was positive they would be looking at me in awe or fear rather than amusement.

No one would see the truth, though. And, thankfully, the girls quickly got over showing their love for me.

"What do we do now?" I glanced between the girls and the supermarket.

"We go shopping."

I jerked my head toward him, my eyes practically popping out of my head. "With them?"

"No one can see the girls but us."

"And we're just supposed to take them inside with us? They won't even be able to fit down the aisle without bumping into everyone's carts."

"I guess you could try making them stay again. Not that they listened to you last time."

Fear bubbled away in my tummy as I prayed that wasn't the first sign the Hellhounds were beginning to switch their allegiance back to the demons. "Do you think it's wearing off?"

"Not likely." When he saw the confused look on my face, he continued. "I don't think they would be as happy to see you if they were switching sides again. Maybe, they were really hungry and wanted to be fed."

"Maybe."

"Or they could sense something we're unaware of."

The hairs on the back of my neck stood on end as the words left his mouth.

Since we'd returned to Byron, we hadn't run into a single supernatural creature other than the girls. And for Byron Bay, that was saying a lot. The place was usually littered with the supernatural world. Soul Scrapers were practically part of the scenery. Come to think of it, we hadn't seen any since we killed Morgana.

Sure, the weather was weird, and there was an undeniable dark energy surrounding Morgana's estate, especially that secret room of hers, but not one single supernatural person or thing had come close to us.

"What's wrong?" Marcus asked.

I bit my lip as I tried to figure out exactly what I wanted to say to him. Marcus already thought I needed protecting, and I didn't want to give him any more reason to think I was at further risk.

Eventually, I decided to go with the truth, after all, that was what I kept asking of Marcus, and it wouldn't be fair if I didn't do the same as I expected of him. "Is it just me, or is it strange that we haven't come across any Soul Scrapers or any other creatures?"

Marcus breathed out harshly as his gaze darted to the woods and then to the girls. "Honestly, it's more than a little concerning. But if you're right about this God, then we can't assume we're not being watched."

"What do you mean? I thought you could sense others?"

"I can but not a Possession if they're only watching from a distance. Then there are hidden cameras that he can use to keep an eye on us. Or maybe he's waiting it out."

"Waiting what out?"

"For you to die."

CHAPTER 13

$\mathcal{T}$ime.

Time was on his side.

They had an endless supply.

And I had a constant reminder that my life would only go on until I turned one hundred. Then I would die, only to be reborn on this crazy merry-go-round.

I wanted off.

Panic was snaking its way through my veins, quickly taking over as the truth of Marcus's words sunk in. It made too much sense. "We can't let him wait."

"We're not going to." Marcus wrapped his hands around my hips. "I'm not going to lose you again." He raised his hand to cup my cheek then brushed his thumb across my lips. "I've already lost you too many times, and it's not going to happen again."

The pain in his eyes that I hadn't seen for weeks returned with vengeance. "I will not lose you again."

I gripped his shirt. "Then we better give him one hell of a reason to come out of hiding."

Marcus smiled, the pain in his eyes slowly lifting. "Something tells me you're going to give him every reason in the world."

Hooking my arms around his neck, I kissed him. Nothing in this world was going to get in the way of us. Marcus was never going to experience my loss again. Unless…

I shook my thoughts away and focused on what was important. Him.

While there was hope with finding this spell that would separate Marcus's light, I could not let myself consider the alternative. Marcus deserved better than that. He deserved his happily ever after as well.

Something slammed into my thighs, tearing my lips away from Marcus's. I looked to the side and saw a very hungry Scarlett staring back at me, begging to be fed.

All I wanted to do was remain in Marcus's embrace, but we had more pressing matters to deal with. I wasn't sure how much longer the girls could go without food, and I didn't want to find out.

Running my hand under her chin, I said, "How about you go inside, and I'll stay out here with them."

Marcus nodded. "I would say make sure you stay with them, but I don't think that will be an issue."

I chuckled. "I don't think I could get away from them if I tried."

He leaned down and gave me a peck before disappearing into the supermarket.

Ten minutes later, Marcus came out pushing a trolley loaded with meat.

"You really did buy up half the meat department," I said.

Ruby and Scarlett dove at the trolley, their mouths open and drool dripping from their razor sharp teeth.

Marcus whipped the trolley to the side a split second before they latched onto it. "They can't eat this here. There are too many people."

I leaped in front of the Hellhounds, praying I wasn't about to become the alternative dinner menu and raised my hands. "Wait, girls. Wait."

It took everything in me to keep eye contact with Ruby and Scarlett instead of looking at the humans who were practically boring a hole in my head as they stared at me, the crazy girl talking to her imaginary friends.

Marcus took off across the street, the trolley bouncing and smashing on the asphalt.

I glanced to the side, making sure he was across the road and heading into the scrub before letting the girls go.

Ruby and Scar darted onto the road then leaped over an oncoming car a nanosecond before they caused an unexplainable accident.

Breathing out a sigh of relief, I turned to the humans and instantly wished I hadn't. These past few months, it had been a miracle that no one looked at me as if I were the freak they'd all believed I was for my entire life. And now people were watching me the same way.

Nothing I could say or do would change it. I had to embrace who I was, and screw what everyone else thought of me. Marcus did and so could I.

I smiled at them then darted across the road and disappeared into the woods, where I found Marcus standing a good ten feet back from Scar and Ruby as they tore through not only the meat but the trolley as well.

I made my way to Marcus and slipped my arm around his waist. "Jesus, these two are vicious."

Marcus dropped his arm over my shoulders. "You don't want to see them tear into an animal."

"I don't think I will ever get used to feeding these girls." No matter how much I wanted to, I was sure I would never forget the sound of bones crunching between their teeth.

That memory would stay with me forever.

My heart stopped as a low rumble erupted from the Hellhounds' mouths, quickly growing with intensity as their ears pricked and heat rose from their skin as if it were on fire.

Something or some*one* was here.

CHAPTER 14

*W*ith my heart in my throat, I looked up at Marcus to get a gauge on the situation. Sure, we had two Hellhounds and he could practically rip anything in two, but I was still afraid.

Marcus sighed as he glanced through the bushes to the right. "It's only Abby."

Relief washed over me when she came into view and it was clear no one else was with her.

"It's only Abby?" she slurred. "That's all you can—?" She tripped over a tree root and almost face-planted into the trunk of another. "I'm okay; I'm okay."

Ruby and Scarlett stalked toward her. One going to the left and the other to the right as if they were about to circle their prey.

"You're drunk," Marcus said.

Completely ignoring the girls, she let out a drunken laugh. "You'd be drunk too if you had to do who I just did."

"*Who* I just did? Or *what* I just did?" I asked. "Never mind. Don't answer that."

Abby grinned as she sauntered over to me. "You owe me one." She spun on her heel and pointed at Marcus. "You do, too."

She tipped her head back as she planted her ass on the ground and sat cross-legged, her palms splayed out behind her, supporting her weight. Her head swayed momentarily as she looked between Marcus and me. "Aren't you going to thank me?"

Marcus folded his arms across his chest. "Thank you for what? Getting drunk?"

Abby laughed again. "No, demon boy. For this." She reached into her shirt and searched for something between her breasts. She retrieved a long silver chain with a copper circle encrypted with gems dangling on the end of it.

Marcus's eyes went wide. "Is that...?"

With pride in her eyes, her head bobbed.

"Is that what I think it is?" I asked.

"Yep." Abby threw the necklace to me. "It's your ticket to anywhere you want."

My eyes widened as I studied the medallion. I could feel the power held within, but I wasn't sure if it was good or evil magic. The lines were blurred, and I hoped it meant the user was the deciding factor. "This is what Morgana used to manipulate the veils, isn't it?"

"The one and only." She swiveled her head to the side. "Now, are you going to call off your pets?"

"Huh?"

Abby cocked her head toward Scarlett, who was still stalking around her, head low, and appeared seconds away from attacking.

"Oh, yeah. Sorry." I folded my fingers over the pendant. "Ruby. Scarlett. That's enough."

They ignored me and continued to circle Abby.

"Why aren't they doing as they're told?" I asked.

Abby tilted her head to the side and raised a brow. "And what exactly did you tell them to do?"

"I think she's saying you need to be a little more specific," Marcus said.

I breathed out harshly. "You could've just said that."

She grinned. "Then I wouldn't have had the pleasure of watching you try to figure it out."

Trying not to smile, I glared at her. "Maybe I should let them eat you."

Abby choked on a laugh. "I'd like to see them try. I'd fry their asses before they had a chance to take a bite."

Even though Abby was drunk, I was pretty sure she could do exactly that.

I clapped my hands together. "Ruby, Scarlett, come here."

Both girls snapped their heads in my direction and did as I commanded, their gigantic, muscular bodies hiding my view of Abby.

Marcus strode over to me and took the medallion from my hand. "We need to keep this safe."

For a second, I thought he was going to keep it himself, but he proceeded to fasten the medallion around my neck and tuck it under my shirt.

"I still haven't heard a thank you." Abby's face popped into view as she squeezed between the Hellhounds. "Do you realize what I had to put myself through to get that for you?"

"Thanks, Abby." I smiled.

Digging her elbows into the girl's chests, she pushed her way through.

A low rumble came from deep within Ruby and Scarlett as they glared at Abby.

Marcus chuckled. "I don't think they like drunk Abby."

"They can get in line with the rest of the female population," she said. "Except you, Lulu. You love me no matter what. Because me and him"—she screwed up her face as she pointed to Marcus—"that ain't never going to happen."

Marcus ran his hand over his face. "We need to get you some coffee."

Her eyes perked up. "And wine. I've run out already."

With everything that was going on with us, more alcohol was the last thing she needed, but I couldn't help laughing. "You don't need any more wine. Maybe a spell, but no more wine."

Abby's face slumped. "Vodka?"

Forcing myself to remain straight-faced, I shook my head. "You need to sober up."

She waved me off. "We need to celebrate; that's what we need to do. I mean, do you know how much time that thing will save us?" She pointed to my chest.

Marcus hooked his arm around Abby's neck. "We'll talk about celebrating after you have some coffee."

"And where do you plan on making me this coffee?"

"Well, your house is still standing."

She looked off in the distance. "Huh. So it is."

I raised my brows. "Please don't tell me you can see your house from here." Her home had to be at least five miles away and was obstructed by shops, trees, and a hundred or more other houses.

"No," she said as if it was just another stupid thing to come out of my mouth. "What made you think I could see through things?"

I sighed. "Never mind."

With one arm still around Abby's neck, Marcus grabbed my hand and led us deeper into the bush. "Now, I want you to follow us straight to your house. And that means no stopping at the liquor store or anywhere else for that matter."

Abby stopped in her tracks. "We're flying?"

"Yeah. How else do you think we're getting to your house?"

"Oh, I don't know. Maybe using the thing I had to screw that piece of shit to get."

Marcus grimaced. "You did what?"

"Not *what*. *Who*?"

"Who are you talking about?" I asked.

Marcus barked out a laugh. "You didn't…? Seriously?"

Abby gave him a tight-lipped smile and nodded. "Now you know why I'm drunk."

Marcus ushered us forward. "Maybe you do deserve another drink."

"Thank you!"

"Who are you guys talking about?" I asked again as the Hellhounds fell into line with us.

"No one you know," Marcus said. "Just someone Abby has a long history with."

"And it ain't a good history," she added.

"Right."

We walked another few minutes in silence then stopped.

"This should be far enough." Marcus dropped his arm off Abby's shoulders and turned to her. "Now please follow us closely."

She saluted him. "Yes, sir."

"I mean it, Abby. There's something strange going on at the moment, and I don't want you being so blasé about everything."

Abby dropped her arm, and for a second, she looked sober again. "I know what's at risk." Her gaze darted to me. "I've got you."

Marcus nodded. "See you there."

Before I realized what was going on, Marcus already had me in his arms and he flew into the clouds. He was born for those wings, and I felt stupid for ever thinking they had belonged to me.

A few moments later, he glided below the clouds until his estate came into view.

My eyes widened as I looked at the carnage below. "Holy crap," I said, my voice barely a whisper.

What was once an architectural masterpiece was now in ruins. Half the roof was missing, and what I could see of the inside was a mess. The place was uninhabitable.

Marcus lowered us into what was left of the back patio area and set me on my feet.

Chunks from the house were in the pool, and debris was scattered everywhere. The outside wall connected to the kitchen was no longer there, and fragments of glass hanging from a few of the doorframes were all that remained of the sliding doors.

I glanced up at Marcus. "I'm so sorry."

He curled his arm around my waist. "You have nothing to be sorry for."

"Uh, yeah, I think I do," I said, staring at the mess. No matter what he said, I still felt responsible since my choices were the reason we were in this mess to begin with.

"Houses can be rebuilt. You can not."

I wanted to remind him that I, too, could be reborn, but now wasn't the time to be technical.

Abby landed a few feet away from us. "Told you they destroyed the place." She walked through the back door and into the kitchen.

I leaned into Marcus. "What is she doing?"

"I have no idea."

She returned a minute later with the coffee machine in her arms. "Yours makes better coffee."

Marcus chuckled. "You do realize we have the same machine."

"You have a better machine because your coffee always tastes better." She strode toward the garden wall then leaped on top.

"Maybe it's the barista, not the machine," Marcus called after her.

Abby snorted. "Whatever, demon boy. It's my machine now."

CHAPTER 15

I don't know what I'd imagined Abby's home would be like, but I'd never guessed she would be the type of girl who opted for an exact replica of Marcus's house. Apparently, she'd felt like a change from the traditional beach house it was when she bought it many years ago but couldn't decide on the details for her remodel. She'd asked Marcus's architect and builder to surprise her and ended up with a carbon copy.

I guessed that was what you got for trusting a witch as your builder.

Abby lay stomach down on the sofa, legs crossed and feet swinging in the air behind her as she studied the cylinder in her hands. "So let me get this straight. You can feel the black magic when you hold this thing? And you can only open it on a full moon, or it will combust?"

I leaned back on the couch opposite where Abby was sprawled. "Yes, I can feel the evil magic, and no it will not combust if we open it now, but Astrid said we need to open it under a full moon."

She raised her gaze to meet mine. "Why?"

I glanced toward the bedrooms, hoping Marcus would hurry up and finish in the shower so he could answer her never-ending questions about things I barely knew anything about. "I have no idea. All I know is Astrid said we must wait until tomorrow."

"Because of the full moon?"

"Yes, because of the full moon."

She rolled the cylinder over in her hands. "And you're connected to this somehow?"

I sighed for what felt like the millionth time. "I'm connected to something. We're just not sure if it's what's inside or the cylinder itself."

"And opening it under the full moon will confirm which it is?"

"I think so."

Abby studied it a moment longer. "What if we open it tonight? It's almost a full moon. Will this thing even know the difference?" She waved the cylinder back and forth as if I was confused about the subject of our conversation.

"We're not opening it," I said, trying to keep myself from sounding as frustrated as I was feeling. "I think the magic connected to the cylinder knows the difference. And I also think you don't want to be the one to mess with what could be the only thing that can help me return Marcus's light without me dying in the process."

She huffed. "Tomorrow night it is then." Abby rolled off the couch and somehow landed on her feet. "But now, I must go get ready."

I looked at my phone. 7:58. "Is the club even going to be open this early?"

Abby snorted. "It never closes." She tossed the cylinder to me and walked away with a skip in her step, heading down the hall toward her bedroom.

Thanking God I was finally free of her never-ending questions, I curled my legs up on the couch and rested my head against the cushion as I turned the cylinder over in my hands.

The nerves under my skin hummed wherever I came in contact with the cylinder. I knew it wasn't good, but I couldn't turn my back on it. I was learning to deal with Morgana's magic, and I would learn to control whatever the cylinder was going to release.

"What are you thinking about?" Marcus asked, making me jump.

My heart skipped a beat or three when I swung around into a sitting position and saw Marcus half-naked, standing only a few feet from me. He wore a pair of jeans and nothing else as he rubbed his wet hair with a towel, completely oblivious to the effect his nakedness was having on me.

"Well?" he prompted.

It took me a couple of seconds to remember what he'd asked. "Um…" I forced myself to look away so I could focus. I had no idea why I was reacting to him that way. It wasn't the first time I'd seen him without his shirt on, and yeah, he had always taken my breath away, but seeing him this time was different. Either he'd changed, or I had, and I was hoping it was him because I was sick to death of not understanding myself.

Still holding the towel, he dropped his arm to his side. "Are you okay?"

I shook my thoughts away. "Um, yeah. I was just thinking about this." I held up the cylinder.

Marcus dropped the towel over the back of the couch, sat beside me, and took the cylinder out of my hands.

The moment I lost contact, my nerves settled down and so did my excessive appetite for Marcus. "What the…?"

He frowned. "What's wrong?"

I snatched the cylinder off him and instantly felt the return of my overly intense lust for him.

"Okay," he dragged. "You can keep it if you need to."

I glanced between Marcus and the cylinder. "This thing is doing something different to me."

"Different, how?"

"Um, it's making me have inappropriate thoughts about you."

The corner of his lips tipped up. "Inappropriate thoughts? Do tell."

I smacked the cylinder against his chest. "Be serious."

He leaned back and rested his arm across the top of the couch as he twisted around to face me. "Okay. All jokes aside, what is going on?"

Barely registering what he'd asked me, I stared unashamedly at his pecs. Then my gaze drifted down to his abs and kept going.

Marcus placed his finger under my chin and tipped my head up until I was looking into his eyes. "Focus."

I dropped the cylinder on the couch between us. "I have no idea why this is happening now, but I have serious lust issues whenever I come in contact with the cylinder and you're in my vicinity."

He grinned. "And that's a bad thing?"

I whacked his chest with my hand. "Yes, it's a bad thing when I can't control it and have absolutely no idea why it's happening. Think about it. Why would something of Morgana's that contains black magic cause me to lust after you? It doesn't make sense. And why is this only happening now? I felt nothing when we were at Morgana's home."

"I'm going to pretend you mean you felt no extra lust toward me because I kind of expect you should feel something for me after all these years that you now remember."

I glared at him. "Of course, I'm attracted to you. I'd be blind not to be. You know that, and you also know how much I love you. But this is different."

Dropping the smirk from his face, he said, "Maybe it has something to do with Byron, or the almost full moon coming out. Or maybe that thing connects to you on a deeper level the longer you're near it."

He twirled a strand of my hair around his finger. "There are a million possibilities, and right now, we don't have time to figure this out. We have to get ready to head to the Devil's Playground and see what we can find out before we traipse down whatever path we'll be thrown onto when we open the cylinder tomorrow night."

"You're right," I said. "We only have to wait for another twenty-four hours or so."

"Exactly." He placed his hand over mine and pulled me to my feet as he stood. "And now, you need to get ready so we can head out."

I looked down at the jeans and top I was wearing. "This isn't good enough?"

He leaned in closer to me and whispered, "It stinks of the girls, and I'm not sure you want everyone knowing about your new pets."

"Point taken." I couldn't smell a thing, but Marcus was a hell of a lot more sensitive than I was.

"You can borrow something of Abby's. I'm sure she won't mind."

Dread pooled in my stomach as I feared what exactly I would have to wear. Abby was a succubus, and I wasn't sure she had anything that wasn't overly sexy.

And I was right. After I had a shower, I wrapped the towel around my body and followed Abby into her closet. "Holy shit," I said, staring at the racks and racks of clothing, filled to capacity.

There were more clothes than days in the year. This girl had a major shopping addiction.

Abby grinned. "I would tell you to pick anything you want, but I think you might need a little help finding something that would appeal to your uh… style."

I frowned. "What is wrong with my style?"

She shook her head. "Nothing. It's just… not me."

"Fine," I said. "Do you have a pair of jeans or something?"

"I have something."

I raised a brow. "Are you seriously telling me you don't have one pair of jeans in this entire room?"

"That's exactly what I'm telling you." Abby darted to the side. "But I do have these cute pants that will look really hot on you." She pulled out a pair of leather pants.

"I am not wearing those."

She shrugged and put them back. "What about this?" She grabbed a red dress that looked about two sizes too small and shoved it against me.

"I am not wearing this." I peeled it off me.

Abby tilted her head to the side and looked me up and down. "You've got a good body under all those clothes. Maybe you should show it off a little."

"What else do you have for me?" I asked, ignoring her comment.

After what felt like an hour, I finally compromised on a cami and pair of dress shorts that would've come just below Abby's ass but sat lower thanks to my short legs.

I was surprised to find she did indeed own a pair of Converse, and no matter how underdressed I appeared with them on, I wasn't going to be stuck fighting against the supernatural world in a pair of heels. Abby may have been built for that, but I sure as hell wasn't.

"Finally," Marcus said when we reemerged into the living room.

Abby bounded in front of me, dressed as if she were going to work. "That's because your girlfriend didn't want to play nice."

I frowned. "I didn't want to look like a hooker if that's what you mean." Abby made anything look classy, but I didn't have that same blessing.

Grinning, she twisted around and winked at me. "Meet you there." She took off out the back door and soared up into the air, disappearing from view.

I strolled over to Marcus. "How long does it usually take her to sober up?"

He placed his hand above my ass and ushered me toward the back door. "Depends on how much she had to drink. But I'm guessing maybe another few hours."

We stepped outside and were immediately greeted by Ruby and Scarlett. "Let's hope these two stay put this time 'round."

By the look of them, they didn't plan on staying anywhere I told them to. The girls were on their feet, pacing back and forth, their focus completely trained on me.

I looked Ruby straight in the eyes and told her to stay. Then I did the same to Scarlett. "What will happen if these two show up and everyone finds out what I've done?"

Marcus shrugged a shoulder. "Who knows? Maybe there's a way the demons can turn them back and then use them against us when we least expect it."

"Right." I narrowed my eyes at the girls. "Stay. That's an order."

Marcus bit down on a smile, and I wanted to slap it off him. Either that or kiss it off his face because that was what I really wanted to do in that moment. Not fly off to a club filled with demonic creatures. I wanted him. I needed him. And I didn't care if it was the aftereffects of the cylinder or what.

I ran my hands up his chest and hooked my arms around his neck. "Don't suppose we could be a little late?"

"As much as I would love to say yes, time isn't something we have enough of." He planted a kiss on my lips, scooped me into his arms, and soared into the sky.

Two minutes later, we were standing in the parking lot across the road from the club. My lustful urges toward Marcus were still running on high, but I was thankfully able to ignore them when I focused on the Devil's Playground or, more so, the demons that were coming and going and the humans that were prepared to let them eat from them to satisfy the demon's desires.

"This place really gives me the creeps." I tucked myself under Marcus's arm.

"You'll be fine." He ushered me across the road, heading toward Abby, who was standing at the front of the line, chatting with the bouncer.

The guy may have been from the supernatural world, but she still cast a spell on him with her devilish good looks and charisma—even in her drunken state.

Music spilled from inside the club as the door opened and a human woman stumbled out, either sucked dry of her energy, soul, blood, or maybe a combination of them all.

No one gave her a second look—or a first for that matter. It was as clear as day she was a nothing to them, and it unnerved me.

"Finally," Abby said when she spotted us.

We stepped onto the footpath, and I did everything I could not to look at the humans waiting like cattle unknowingly lining up to get slaughtered.

The bouncer took one look at Marcus and me and sucked in a sharp breath, his eyes going wide and sweat breaking out on his forehead. He was afraid. What of, was beyond me.

"Marcus," he said then glanced down at me. "Do you think it's a good idea you brought her?"

Abby whacked his arm with the back of her hand. "I told you she can take care of herself now."

He swallowed hard. "That's what I'm afraid..." His eyes went wide as he stared into the distance over my right shoulder.

Following his gaze, I almost had a heart attack when I saw them.

CHAPTER 16

Scarlett's and Ruby's giant paws slammed against the asphalt as they tore up the road, heading straight for us.

"Shit," I said through gritted teeth.

The girls skidded to a stop a few feet away, lowered their heads, and stalked around me, eyeing the bouncer and every single other person in our vicinity.

"What are they doing?" the bouncer asked, back against the wall and hand sliding down to his pocket in what I assumed was him getting ready to pull a weapon out if necessary.

Abby barked out a laugh. "I guess the cat's out of the bag now."

Having absolutely no idea what Abby was referring to, the bouncer looked to Marcus, brow furrowed.

Marcus breathed out harshly. "They're protecting her." He gestured to me.

The look of confusion that crossed his face was priceless. He opened his mouth and shut it again almost a dozen times before finally saying, "How?"

Abby patted his shoulder. "Wouldn't you like to know?" She grinned at him before heading into the club with a swagger that made every guy in her vicinity tilt his head to the side and stare at her ass.

Not waiting around for any more questions, we strode after Abby.

"You can't take them in there," the bouncer called out.

I turned around to find the girls following, closely behind.

"Watch us." Marcus held the doors open for not only me but the girls as well.

If there was a way to get every single person to stop in a club that was pumping with the occupants completely mesmerized in their own circles, this was it. The moment the supernatural people caught sight of us, they froze. Their human partners had no idea what was going on and were the only voices to be heard in the club.

"Way to draw attention to ourselves," I said under my breath.

Marcus squeezed my hand and leaned into me. "No turning back now."

The people in front of us somehow managed to clear a path as we made our way through the crowd, heading for the sectioned off area where we'd previously had a run-in with Colton's men.

Chills ran down my spine as I remembered what had happened the last time I was here. It had been my first encounter with the Soul Scrapers, and I'd found out exactly what they could do. I'd also learned just how powerful Marcus was when he came to my rescue. Now, I had to remind myself I wasn't the girl I was the last time I was here. I was a freakishly powerful vessel that had the power to take and give. Plus, I had Morgana's magic to draw on if I ever needed it. Strangely, having Ruby and Scarlett there with me brought a sense of comfort to my soul.

It was clear as day they took their job of protecting me seriously. So much so that they were ignoring my commands. I wasn't sure if that was a good or a bad thing. But, standing in a club filled with demonic creatures, I was taking it as a positive.

The bouncers standing behind the ropes shifted from one foot to the other as they assessed our presence. Last time they'd tried to stop us, and I wasn't sure if they'd do the same again—especially with the beasts that followed us.

We came to a standstill a foot from the ropes and stared down the bouncers.

Scarlett dropped her head over my shoulder, careful not to put her full weight on me—otherwise, I was sure I would've been flat on my ass.

The bouncer with the black hair took one look at her and retrieved his weapon from the back of his pants.

"I wouldn't do that if I were you, Luke," Marcus warned.

Luke paused. "You think I can't take out a Hellhound?"

The other bouncer turned to Luke and whispered, "I think you should put that thing away."

"I think you should listen to your friend," Marcus said.

Luke stepped closer. "Or what?"

The other bouncer glared at him and shook his head. "Or they'll fucking kill you, you dumbass."

Luke glared at his friend.

"And I'm not talking about the hounds."

Marcus grinned. "Better listen to your boy there."

Abby slipped in between us. "I think you've got to ask yourself something, Luke." She ran her fingers down his chest. "How would someone like Lucy come to have Hellhounds as her guards?"

She glanced at the other bouncer. "Mike knows his place, and I suggest you would do well to use that little pea-sized brain of yours to ask yourself why? Why would a girl you thought was cursed have the ability to change a Hellhound's allegiance?"

"Abby," Marcus warned.

She turned around and addressed every single person in the club. "And that goes for all of you. You don't want to fuck with us. Morgana is dead, and I'm here to tell you the rumours are true."

Oh, God. I was sure we'd gone over the fact that we wanted to keep that information to ourselves, and now drunken Abby was spilling the beans. It was one thing for everyone to see the Hellhounds, and it was entirely something different for them to know we had the power to kill one of the most powerful witches that had ever existed.

Abby spun back around. "Now, are you going to play nice for us?"

Luke bobbed his head.

"That a boy." She patted his chest. "Where do you think we can find your boss?"

A deep rumbling growl came from Scarlett, and if I hadn't seen the cause of it myself, I would've thought she was asserting our power over the two demons standing in our way. But she wasn't.

A black shadow appeared out of nowhere against the wall in my peripheral vision. I jerked my head in its direction, but the shadow slinked away into the wall as if it had never been there.

If it weren't for Scar staring at the exact spot I'd thought I'd seen the shadow disappear, I would've thought I was going crazy again.

That was the thing; I'd never been crazy. We just didn't understand the truth of who I was. But now I was seeing things that shouldn't be there, and it had my nerves on edge. Especially because neither Marcus nor Abby seemed to be aware of the shadow's existence.

Marcus spread his hand across the small of my back and ushered me forward.

I wanted to tell him what I'd seen, but now wasn't the time. The bouncers had stepped to the side and were letting us through.

I wanted to ask Marcus what had been said while I was zoned out, but I knew it could paint us in a negative light, so I kept my mouth shut and went with the flow.

"The hounds are going to have to wait here," Mike called out to us.

With a scowl, I twisted around to face him.

Mike's eyes widened. "Only because they won't be able to fit through the doorway."

After seeing the shadow and knowing the girls were the only other ones who could see it, the last thing I wanted was to let Ruby and Scarlett out of my sight.

However, that wasn't realistic. We needed information, and I was pretty sure the girls would crash through the walls if I were in danger.

Fighting my urge to make the doorway large enough for them to get through, I turned to Scar and Ruby. "Stay here. We'll be back in a moment."

I followed Marcus and Abby down a hall, descended a small set of stairs, and stopped outside the only door on the level.

Abby didn't bother to knock before she pushed the door, swinging it wide open and smashing the handle into the wall behind it.

Colten was sitting on a black couch, his attention remaining on the human girl splayed out on his lap. He must've known we were coming but couldn't give us the decency of looking at us.

That would change.

I would make sure of it.

"Get out, bitch," Abby snapped.

The girl lifted her lazy gaze to meet Abby's. "Go fuck yourself."

Abby barked out a laugh. "You did not just tell me to go fuck myself, did you? Because if I heard right, then I'm going to come over there, peel every single one of your skank ass nails off, and shove them like toothpicks up your—"

"Enough." Colton pushed the girl off him as if he were wiping crumbs from his lap.

She fell to the floor in a heap. "Hey," she said with a squeal, blood rushing to her face.

Ignoring her, Colton stood and glanced between the three of us. "Something tells me you didn't come down for a social drink."

The girl got to her feet and scuttled over to Colton.

"Get out," he said, not bothering to look at her.

She sulked out of the room but not before glaring at Abby once more.

Colton sauntered over to a small bar area, picked up a bottle of rum, and poured a glass. "Can I get you a drink?"

"We're not here for small talk," Marcus said. "We want to know where we can find Titus."

"And we also want to know why you've been avoiding us," Abby added.

He lifted his glass and turned toward Abby with a smile plastered on his face. "I would never avoid you, my darling Abby." He glanced at Marcus. "You, on the other hand... I could go without having to see your ass for another century."

"I can arrange that for you if you'd like." Marcus took a few steps toward him. "But I think we could make it indefinitely."

Colton let out a nervous laugh before quickly downing his drink and refilling his glass. The guy was clearly nervous as hell, but he refused to play nice, as Abby would say.

With his glass half filled, Colton sauntered over to me. "Looks as if you've finally come into yourself."

"I would say looks can be deceiving, but I think we all know I'm not the girl you thought I was." I took a couple of steps toward him, pretending to be as confident as Marcus and Abby when really I wanted to hightail it out of there. "And something tells me you don't want to find out exactly what I'm capable of."

Colton stared at me a few moments then smiled. "Cute." He sauntered over to his desk and leaned against it. "Now, what can I help you with?"

Cute? I wanted to rip him a new one and show him just how cute I was.

"We want to know where we can find Titus," Marcus said.

He shrugged. "Your guess is as good as mine."

"Cut the crap," Marcus said. "Tell us where he is, and we'll be on our way."

Colton chuckled. "How should I know? I'm not his bitch nor his keeper."

He looked at me and winked.

He freaking winked.

I was done with his ass.

Lifting the corner of my lip, I strolled over to him. "I think you're lying."

"Oh, do you now?"

I stopped a foot in front of him. "Oh, yeah. I do. And I also think you must be dumb as hell to think you're going to get out of this one alive if you don't start talking."

Colton chuckled. "You should get this girl of yours on a leash if you know what's good for her."

"What did you just say? Because I think you called me a dog." I leaned in closer to him. "And you know dogs bite—hard."

A sadistic grin played on my lips as I watched him scream out in pain as I gave him the memory of when the Hellhound ripped its claws into my stomach. Only somehow I was able to amplify the pain, which I figured had everything to do with Morgana's magic. Or maybe it was the cylinder that was tucked safely away in Marcus's pocket. Either way, I was enjoying Colton squirming under my power.

I leaned closer to him. "Now, are you going to play nice?" I let up on the torture enough for him to answer.

Colton spat at me. "Fuck you."

"Language, language," I said, wiping his spit off my face with the back of my hand. "You really need to learn a little respect."

Abby laughed. "Boy, do you have a lot to learn about Lucy."

A stream of electricity shot into Colton, sending him into a fit of convulsions.

I twisted around to find Marcus sticking a knife into an electrical socket, while his other hand pointed at Colton. He was frying the bastard.

Marcus removed the knife from the socket and gestured for me to continue.

I turned my attention back to Colton. "Now, tell us where we can find Titus."

"I'm not telling you shit," he spat, blood dripping from his mouth.

I sighed. "You know, I was only being polite. You see, Abby forgot to mention exactly how special I am and the fact that I don't actually need you to tell me anything."

Confusion swept over his features as he stared at me.

I sighed again. "I've had enough of this." I focused on what I wanted and ripped the memory from his mind.

"See, that wasn't hard now, was it?" I said. Except it not only gave me the information we required, it also carried with it another evil smudge against my soul.

It was worth it, though.

Colton furrowed his brow, having no idea what I was talking about.

Titus's location was burned into my mind as if I had physically been there a thousand times. The problem was his hideout didn't technically exist.

That wasn't going to stop us.

Nothing would.

Just for fun, I sent Colton a portion of my memory of what it had felt like to drown on the tar-like substance as the Soul Scrapers tried to suck my soul from my body. Of course, I amplified it with magic to make it that much more memorable.

Abby slung her arm over my shoulder and watched with sick satisfaction as Colton fell to the floor, writhing for air and fighting off a Soul Scraper that wasn't there. "My dear Lulu, who would've known you were capable of this?"

The realization of what I was doing snapped me out of his head, allowing Colton to place the experience in his long-term memory.

A few moments later, Colton rose uneasily to his feet and brushed his hand through his hair, trying to gain his composure, but it was useless. He was rattled—big time. "What are you?"

Marcus strode over to me. "Someone you don't want to mess with."

That was the truth, and I was positive Colton now realized exactly how special I was.

CHAPTER 17

Special was one thing, and a freak of nature was an entirely different story. I was happy to be special, but I sensed something very different humming under the surface of my skin as we made our way out of the club and onto the street with Ruby and Scarlett following closely behind us.

I wasn't sure if it was because I now had another smudge against my soul—what I'd allowed myself to do to Colton—or if it was because of the almost full moon and the fact that my hand was inches from the cylinder safely tucked away under Marcus's protection.

It probably had more to do with the cylinder. After all, the tips of my fingers, which were inches away from the dark magic embedded in the cylinder, were humming like bees swarming their hive.

And it felt good.

It was as if the cylinder, or whatever it contained, was an extension of me, begging to be reunited and complete what was once an impenetrable bond.

"Lucy," Marcus said.

I looked up at him and realized he must've asked me a question. "Huh?"

He drew his brows together. "Where were you?"

Abby barked out a laugh. "She was standing with you, dumbass."

Ignoring Abby's drunken comment, I said, "I was thinking about the cylinder." I hadn't lied, but I also hadn't told him the truth. Part of me wanted to hide the way I felt around the cylinder, but the other part of me knew I had to tell him not only for my sake but his as well. I just wasn't going to tell him while we had company.

Marcus brushed his hand against his pocket. "It's still there. You have nothing to worry about."

I nodded. "So, what were you asking me?"

He studied me for a few moments, and I thought he was going to call me on my lie when he said, "I was asking you where Titus has been hiding?"

"Right," I said, focusing on the matter at hand. "I'm not entirely sure how to tell you where it is because it technically shouldn't exist."

"How can something not exist?" Abby asked. "That doesn't even make sense. Obviously, it exists if he's been hiding there. And it would also have to exist if Colton had visited him there."

I glared at her, wishing she would sober the hell up, so we didn't have to deal with her drunken commentary. If only I could…

My eyes went wide, and I twisted around to face her. "That's it."

"What's it?"

"Heal the soul and forgive the wounds, and bring forth light to conceal the past."

Abby's jaw dropped when she realized what I had done.

I grinned. "I think the words you're looking for are 'Thank you, Lucy.'"

"You just took it away from me, didn't you?"

I glanced at Marcus, who didn't seem at all impressed. He'd warned me about taking things from a demon when it wasn't necessary. "I didn't take anything away from her." I turned to Abby. "I healed you using the same spell I used on Astrid."

"Well, shit," she said. "Guess I should say thank you. And maybe you deserve a sorry as well."

"What for?"

"For outing you in front of everyone in the club," Marcus answered for her.

Abby shrugged. "At least they'll all know not to mess with us."

"Or it will have the complete opposite effect and will make that target on Lucy's head even bigger."

She held up her finger. "Ah, but you're forgetting it doesn't matter."

Marcus crossed his arms over his chest. "How doesn't it matter?"

"Because we'll kill them before they get a chance," she said. "Have some faith in your girl."

Marcus shot me a look telling me he most certainly did have faith in me but didn't want to let Abby off so easily.

"You know I saw that look," Abby said when Marcus opened his mouth.

"What look?"

She pointed between us. "The look you gave Lucy just then."

"I didn't give her any look."

"You saw it, right, Lucy?"

"I, uh..." I was stuck in the middle of wanting to be honest and not wanting to piss off Marcus. I held up my hands. "I'm staying out of this one."

I turned my back to them and went over to the girls, who were standing guard. "Besides, shouldn't we be discussing going after Titus?"

Marcus strode over and ran the tips of his fingers along Ruby's side. "Do you think you can get us to him?"

I nodded. "So long as we have this thing." I patted the medallion hiding under my top. "We should be able to get there and back before we collect Justin and Astrid for the ritual tomorrow night."

Abby twisted her hair up and held it in place as the wind picked up around us. "With that thing, we should be able to do all that within an hour."

"Unless..." Marcus started.

"Unless what?" I swatted away a leaf that had blown on to Ruby's chest, and then I looked up at the sky. The clouds were dark, and thunder rumbled in the distance as if someone was warning us to stay away. "That's not you, is it?"

Marcus shook his head. "Someone else is doing this."

"How many other people can control the weather?"

Abby let her hair fall down her back. "Too many for us to figure out who's responsible if that's what you're thinking."

"So you think someone might try to stop us from finding Titus?" I asked, trying to get back to what Marcus was concerned about.

"Maybe," he said. "Which is why we should go there now." Marcus slipped his finger under the chain around my neck. "We need to figure out how we can get you to give us the location."

"That's easy," Abby said. "She can give, remember?"

"Or I could take you there myself."

She screwed up her face in confusion. "But you can't…"

I grinned. "That's one thing I can do, thanks to that demon who helped Morgana take me from her estate."

"Shit." Marcus grabbed the back of his neck and paced over to a nearby car.

Abby raised her brows but didn't say anything.

I strode over to Marcus and gently tugged on the back of his shirt. "What's wrong?"

He looked up at the sky and didn't say anything for a few moments. Then he turned around to face me. "What if you get it wrong?"

I frowned. "You don't think I can get us there and back?"

Marcus exhaled softly. "That's not what I was thinking at all." He stepped closer to me. "I know you can get us there. What I'm concerned about is getting back here in time to perform the ritual."

"We have until tomorrow night."

He shook his head. "See, that's the thing. We don't know if time will work the same in that veil as it does in this one. For all we know, we could be gone for a couple of days and not know any different. Then we'd have to wait almost another month to perform the ritual."

"Crap." I sucked my lip into my mouth as I thought about what we should do. The last thing I wanted was to delay finding out what was in the cylinder, but we also needed to find Titus.

Abby sauntered over to us. "The way I see it, we can wait until tomorrow after the ritual and risk the chance of someone telling him we know his location and him being long gone by the time we get there, or we can head there now and hope for the best."

"I agree with Abby," I said, surprising myself. More than anything, I wanted to know what this crazy connection I had with the cylinder was all about, but we needed to jump on this opportunity while it was fresh. "Colton could've warned him already."

Marcus nodded. "Are you sure about this?"

In one more month, Marcus would no longer be able to stop me from feeling other people's emotions when I was in his presence, but I was no longer afraid. I would deal with anything this God person could throw at us. I had to. "As sure as I'll ever be."

"Then take us there."

I looked around. "What? Now?"

Abby rolled her eyes and cocked her head toward the trees.

"Oh," I said, my voice barely a whisper.

We followed Abby into the bush with the girls trailing us like a shadow.

When we were surrounded by trees, trees, and more trees, I contemplated making the girls stay but decided they may as well come for the trip. After all, I wasn't sure I could trust them on their own, and there were too many innocent souls around for their taking.

"Are you sure you know how to do this?" Abby asked.

"She knows," Marcus answered before I had a chance to open my mouth.

I smiled. Finally, Marcus was behind me one hundred percent. He believed in me, and it was strange that I no longer had to try to convince him I needed to take a chance. He finally got it, which made me love him even more.

Standing on the balls of my feet, I pressed a kiss on his lips. "Thank you."

He curled his arm around my waist. "You've got this."

"I hope so," Abby said more to herself than us.

Placing my hand over the medallion, I focused on opening the impossible veil. A smile spread across my face when the air rippled and grew large enough for us all to enter.

Taking no time to consider what we were getting ourselves into, we darted through the veil.

CHAPTER 18

$\mathcal{T}$he familiar tingle encompassed my body as I passed through and entered the dimension that shouldn't have existed. And I could see why.

The place was barren, and not in the way of the wasteland dimension we'd gone to after the demons got into Marcus's estate.

This world was different. There were technically no trees, dirt, or sky. This place was literally between worlds, and it was paper-thin in a way that things that weren't physically there looked as if I could touch them.

I reached out at what appeared to be a vine dangling from a tree, and my hand passed right through it. "How is this possible?"

"It shouldn't be." Marcus scanned the area, his eyes turning that molten amber color they did when he was alert to possible danger.

He had every reason to be concerned. We were in the unknown, and if my guess was correct, the rules of the other worlds didn't apply here.

How could they? We probably weren't even breathing in air because air wouldn't exist. Or maybe it did. I really had no idea, and I didn't want to give too much thought about it for fear my brain would explode. I already had too many things to worry about.

"Well, I think we're all seeing the same thing," Abby said, slicing her hand through the trunk of a nearby tree. She twisted around to face us. "This shit is real, and it's giving me the heebie-jeebies."

"Jesus Christ," I said. "If a demon's worried, I think I should be shitting myself." I left out the part in which I was in no way scared. I should be afraid of a place that supposedly didn't exist. I should be terrified of it.

I wasn't.

Marcus grabbed my hand and held onto me tightly. "We should get moving."

"Where are we going?" I asked.

"To find Titus."

I rolled my eyes but didn't say anything. He obviously didn't know what we were going to encounter or where we should start.

We walked through an apparition of a tree, followed by another and another. There was no point in dodging them; however, there was a part of me that expected I would smack into one of these trees sooner rather than later.

I frowned. I had no idea where that thought came from, but it was there, niggling away at the back of my thoughts as if it were a truth, but I had no idea what it meant.

Out of the corner of my eyes, shadows appeared to slither through the trees, keeping pace with us. As soon as I looked their way, they disappeared, unlike the Soul Scrapers. Not that those soul suckers had ever tried to hide from me.

These were different.

And I wasn't the only one to notice them.

Scarlett and Ruby were watching them, heads lowered, legs bent, ready to attack as they prowled to the side of me.

I was about to ask Abby and Marcus if they could see the shadows, but something stopped me. It was a warning bubbling away at the back of my mind, urging me to keep quiet, to play dumb and pretend I couldn't see what was right in front of me.

We were being watched.

I knew it as a truth. I also knew I had to ignore it. This God person was watching, and we weren't ready to let him/her know we were aware of their presence.

Maybe it wasn't actually this God person watching, and it was more like one of his minions, tracking our movements and secretly finding out as much information about us as they could. After all, I was pretty sure if it were God, they would've made themselves known by now. Why would they sit back and wait? Unless….

Unless Marcus was right and God was waiting until time ran out. That was a huge possibility, and if ignoring the shadows would allow us to get an advantage, that was exactly what I was going to do.

After what seemed like hours of walking endlessly through the dimension, Abby and Marcus came to a halt.

I leaned into Marcus and whispered, "What is it?"

He gave me a look that told me to stop talking.

Abby pointed slightly to the left of her then held up two fingers. I desperately wanted to know what the two fingers meant, but I wasn't stupid enough to open my mouth again.

My mind raced with possibilities. Was it two demons hiding in the shadows about to unleash their wrath on us? Or was Titus two yards away? Two Hellhounds were stalking us? Maybe Marcus and Abby had finally seen the shadows and were preparing to bust some demon asses.

My question was answered when Marcus drew his weapon and shoved me behind him. He didn't let go of me, but he was sure as hell using himself as a human shield or supernatural shield or whatever you wanted to call it.

Two seconds later, Abby took off to the right and Marcus the left, dragging me behind him. How he knew what to do from those few hand signals from Abby was beyond me, and I wanted in. I wanted to be able to know what Marcus was thinking—for him to know what I was thinking…

No.

I didn't.

I needed to be able to do things he would kill me for, and one thing in particular if the need arose and there was no other choice.

Shaking my thoughts away, I tried to keep up with Marcus as we ran straight into a mountain that seemed to go on forever before coming to an abrupt halt, the girls almost knocking into us as they pulled up behind us.

We were in an isolated cavern of the mountain, yet I could still see the sky. No tunnels led to this cave; it was just a hole in the middle of the surrounding rock.

"Shit," Marcus muttered as he ran his hand through his hair.

Taking the opportunity to see what he was pissed about, I peered over his shoulder, expecting to find we'd arrived too late and we'd missed Titus.

My heart sank as the scene before me came into view. I'd been right. We were too late. Only it wasn't in the way I'd first thought.

Slumped against the wall, his head fallen unnaturally beside his shoulders, was a man I could only assume was Titus. A stream of fresh blood dripped from his eyes, ears, and nose.

"Shit." Abby strode over to him. She kneeled down, grabbed the man by the hair, lifted his head to where it should've been, and twisted it from side to side. "Shit," she said again, letting go of his head and watching as it slumped to the side. "He's gone." Abby stood and turned to us, her hands on her hips. "Colton?"

"Maybe," Marcus said. "But I'm not sure he had the power to kill him."

"Agreed." Abby kicked at a pile of rubbish then stopped as her gaze landed on a packet of crisps that had been half eaten.

To my disgust, she picked it up and dug into the remaining contents.

Marcus let go of my hand and searched through the piles of rubbish, clothing, and a makeshift bed as Ruby and Scarlett went over to the guy and sniffed him, starting at his feet then working their way up to his head.

"I'm guessing that's Titus," I said, looking the other way as the girls proceeded to lick the blood off his face.

Abby paused as she was about to put another crisp in her mouth and said, "*Was* Titus." Then she popped the crisp into her mouth.

"I thought so," I said under my breath.

Dark shadows appeared on the walls of the cave, their forms taking on the shape of a face with black eyes that glistened like diamonds.

I shuddered as I tried to ignore them and pretend I was unnerved by the girls feasting off the blood dripping from Titus's dead body. My veins began to hum as the alien-like eyes grew wider, watching me with curiosity.

They were trying to see if I could sense them, see them, or get some kind of reaction from me.

I wasn't going to let them see crap.

Marcus stood blocking my view of the girls and giving me a

distraction that was so much more appealing than watching the blood being drained by two monsters. "We shouldn't waste any more time here."

Remembering what Marcus had said about how time could move differently in other dimensions, I prayed we hadn't missed the full moon for nothing. Not only would we have to wait another month to find out what was inside the cylinder and what I was connected to, but I would also be cursed with Marcus no longer having the ability to keep humans' emotions away from me.

Anger boiled in the pit of my stomach. We needed to find out who did this to Titus, and we needed to find out now.

A small dot formed in the air three feet in front of me and quickly grew until it split the cave in two, separating me from Marcus, Abby, and the girls.

Fear shot through Marcus's eyes as he stared at me with the same look he'd had when I'd been ripped away from him outside Morgana's estate. However, this time I wasn't afraid.

CHAPTER 19

I stared at the veil as it beckoned me to enter. I hadn't consciously opened it, and I had no idea where it would take us.

Staring into Marcus's eyes, I wanted to tell him everything was okay, but the truth was, I didn't even know if we would end up in the same place if we entered the veil from different directions.

As soon as I finished that thought, Marcus reminded me the cave we were stuck inside of didn't really exist. He disappeared from view as he entered the rocky wall, walking straight through one of the shadowed forms, and reappeared a second later on my side of the veil.

"I didn't mean to," I said, pointing at the air, shimmering in front of me.

"That was you?" he asked.

I nodded. "At least I think it was."

Abby appeared behind Marcus, followed by the girls. "Maybe you should close it then reopen another."

"She's right," Marcus said, staring into the veil. "The last thing we need is to find out there's another one of those medallions and we end up somewhere, fighting to get back to Byron."

I waved my hand toward the veil and closed it without so much as a thought. Considering how hard it was to learn how to use

Marcus's wings, it amazed me how easily I could control the veils when it hadn't been something I was born with.

"Should I open another one?" I asked.

"Not here," Marcus said. "We should get away from the mountain before we try to get back."

I hated the idea of walking blindly through the rocks and dirt, but it was a necessary evil.

Lacing my fingers with his, we left Titus and made our way back through the mountain with the girls following closely.

When we were at a safe distance, Marcus waved his hand in front of us and opened a veil. Rather than waiting for Abby to be the test dummy to find out what or rather who was on the other side, he pulled me through the veil with him, and we emerged into the familiar surroundings of Byron Bay.

The coast stretched out for miles in either direction and was completely visible thanks to the sun rising over the sea.

We were standing where the sand dunes met the shrubs leading into the nearby bush. How on earth Marcus knew precisely where to take us through the veils so we ended up somewhere inconspicuous was beyond me. I was just thankful we didn't have a bunch of people jumping on social media to upload footage of our sudden appearance for the world to see.

Ruby dived onto the sand and rolled onto her back as Scarlett sat beside me and licked the remaining blood off her paw.

I shuddered.

Marcus slid his hand over my back. "As gross as it was to see them feed off Titus, at least we know they don't need to be fed for another few days."

That was a plus.

I gazed at the surfers bobbing up and down on their boards then noticed a few people walking along the waters edge look our way as sand swirled and spat into the air thanks to Ruby twisting from side to side on her back. They obviously couldn't see her and probably thought it was a strange wind pattern, not a five-hundred-pound monster that could drink from their souls.

"Where to now?" I asked.

"I don't know about you two, but I'm going to get something to eat," Abby said.

I twisted around under Marcus's arm. "Kind of hard to do that when the girls won't leave me alone."

"Don't worry. I'll get you something," she called over her shoulder then took off across the road.

Marcus sat on the grass and tugged me down so I was sitting between his legs. He circled his arms around me and hung his head in the crook of my neck as he looked out at the sea. "Are you going to tell me what you saw in the cave?"

I froze.

CHAPTER 20

Quickly getting my shit together, I said, "You want me to describe Titus's body and the way Ruby and Scarlett played with him like a chew toy?"

He breathed out harshly. "You know what I'm talking about."

I slowly released my breath as I tried to decide what to say. Marcus knew I was hiding something from him. How he knew was anyone's guess.

Tilting my head to the side, I whispered, "Then you should know someone could be listening."

He gestured to the girls. "They're not worried, so you shouldn't be either, and from what I saw, they, too, could see what I couldn't."

Jesus, he was observant—and right.

Watching both Ruby and Scarlett at ease confirmed we were indeed alone. They were like an alarm system for the supernatural world, and for the first time, I was really glad I'd been marked.

If I was going to tell Marcus the truth, now was the time. "There are these shadow things watching us."

"Like the Soul Scrapers?"

I shook my head. "No. These things are different. They appear near walls then disappear inside when I look directly at them. I have no idea why you and Abby can't see them."

He remained silent for a few moments then asked, "Where have you seen them?"

"At the Devil's Playground and again at the cave where Titus was."

Marcus nodded against my shoulder. "Next time you see them, I want you to give me a signal."

"What? Like holding two fingers up?"

He pulled away and furrowed his brow.

"Never mind," I said. "What do you want me to say?"

His face softened. "You don't need to say anything. Just give me something. Show me where they are."

It took me a second to realize what he was asking. Marcus wanted me to give something to him—as in a memory or something else that only I could do without anyone finding out.

He was a genius.

Melting back against him, I wrapped his arms tightly around me, and for a few moments, I tried to pretend we were normal humans with nothing but time on our hands and just enjoy being with the man I loved on what appeared to be a perfect winter day.

Looks were deceiving, and no matter how much I tried to ignore what was coming, I couldn't. My thoughts were cluttered with the unknown and piecing together the things we had.

Abby returned carrying two bags filled with kebabs and a tray of coffees. "Ready to go?"

Placing my hands on Marcus's knees, I pushed up and stood, my stomach rumbling the second I smelled the food.

Marcus got to his feet and grabbed the two bags off her. "Are you sure you got enough?"

"I'm sure Justin and Astrid will be grateful we remembered to bring something for them."

My eyes widened. I'd completely forgotten about going back for them. "Are we going there now?"

"That's the plan, isn't it?"

Marcus nodded. "We have twelve hours until we can perform the ritual, so we better get moving."

I raised my hand and placed it over the pendant under my shirt. "How do we do this?"

Abby shrugged. "You're the witch. Shouldn't you know?"

"I'm not a witch per se, so no, I don't know."

"Geez. Witches can never seem to take a joke." The corner of her lips tipped up, and she winked at me.

I bit down on my smile.

"I imagine the same rules apply as going through any veil, only you can move through space," she said. "Think about where you want to go and take us there."

Sounded easy enough. Doing as instructed, I imagined opening the veil to Morgana's bedroom where we had left Astrid and Justin to the task of reading through all of those books.

A veil opened in front of us. I prayed I hadn't screwed it up and we wouldn't end up walking into a trap.

Abby didn't seem to share my concern. She grabbed a coffee from the tray and took a sip as she strolled through the veil.

Marcus held out his hand to me. "You ready?"

"As I'll ever be." I placed my hand in his. Then, with my heart in my throat, we strode through the veil.

A split second later Morgana's room came into view. Only, it was empty. Astrid and Justin were nowhere to be seen, and neither was Abby. If Astrid hadn't given me the ability to feel others' presence, I would've thought Abby might have ended up in another part of the world. But sure enough, I could feel her presence slipping away as she made her way down the hall.

"Looks like they've finished up here." Marcus gestured to the books piled on the floor in multiple stacks to the side of the lounge.

"Looks like it." I spun around to see where Ruby and Scarlett were and froze.

They were standing beside the closed door to the closet, their ears pricked and heads tilted to the side.

I nudged Marcus and cocked my head toward the girls. "Do you think they can sense the secret room?"

"Let's find out." Marcus strode over to the door and pushed it open.

The girls fought over who would go through first. Then, Ruby fell back, allowing Scarlett to push her way through the opening, ripping the frame from the plaster as if it were cardboard.

Following them into the closet, my suspicions were confirmed when the girls stopped at the end of the room and pressed their noses against the wall. They could sense something was behind there, but they could not access it themselves.

Like the previous time I was there, the darkness of the room was like sirens of the sea, beckoning me to come closer so they could pull me into their grasp and never let go.

Marcus snaked his arm around my waist as I raised my hand to the wall, the tips of my fingers slipping through as if we were once again between worlds where we'd found Titus.

Unlike last time I'd been in the closet, I had no intentions of actually stepping through the wall. The fear of those shadowed creatures waiting behind there scared the crap out of me. Marcus couldn't save me, and for all I knew, I would be sucked away to another plane, never to return to him.

I dropped my hand to my side. "Let's go find the others."

CHAPTER 21

$\mathcal{T}$rying to get the girls to follow us was useless. So, we left them in the closet, completely mesmerised by the wall, and made our way downstairs where we found Abby, Justin, and Astrid back in the potion room, standing around a table with a cauldron bubbling away with murky, green sludge.

"I hope you're not expecting us to drink that." I pointed to the cauldron.

"If you want to enhance your power under the full moon, you will," Justin replied.

Abby waived her hand under her nose and laughed. "I'm so freaking glad I don't have to drink that shit."

I glared at her. "Thanks."

As bad as the concoction smelled, I knew I'd have to suck it up and drink whatever they told me to. In the meantime, I would satisfy my hunger with a kebab and hope I didn't bring it back up when it was time to swallow the concoction.

Marcus placed the bags of kebabs down on the table where our coffees were sitting.

"About time." Abby snatched a kebab out of the bag almost as soon as it hit the table. "Do you know how hungry I am?"

Astrid barked out a laugh. "Do you know how annoying it is to listen to you harp on about food?"

"That was mild. Believe me, she gets much worse," Justin said.

Abby grabbed the kebabs and passed them around to everyone except Justin. "You can get your own."

Marcus grabbed a kebab out of the other bag and tossed it to Justin. "As much as I love you, Abby, Justin's right. You're a pain in the ass to listen to when you're hungry."

She huffed as she tore open the wrapper and dug into her kebab.

"Abby told us Titus is dead." Justin sauntered over and grabbed a coffee.

Marcus leaned his hip against the table. "Yep. And I think we have Colton to thank for that."

Justin raised a brow. "You think Colton killed him?"

"No, dumbass," Abby said with a mouthful of food. "Colton's too weak to kill him like that. It must've been an upper."

"Upper as in upper demon or angel?" I asked.

"Exactly."

Marcus and Abby proceeded to fill them in on everything that had happened since we'd headed back to Byron. Thankfully, Marcus left out the part about me seeing shadows with eyes. That secret would remain between the girls and us.

"So, did you find anything useful while we were gone?" I asked, pulling myself up onto the table beside where Marcus was standing.

"Unfortunately not," Astrid said. "But we did discover Mava's body has been removed. Who did it is anyone's guess."

"Wouldn't a Soul Collector have come for her soon after she died?"

Marcus snaked his arm around my waist. "Soul Collectors don't work with witches the way they do with humans. The supernatural world is more final. If you die, you're gone. There's no moving on to another level of existence."

"Jesus," I said, realizing how important it was for them to survive. I always thought they would end up with the humans in the afterlife Marcus had told me about.

Guilt for keeping Marcus's light already consumed me, and now I felt sick thinking about the possibility of him ceasing to exist just so I could live.

I wanted out of this merry-go-round, and I wanted out now.

"How long until that stuff's ready?" I cocked my head toward the potion bubbling away in the cauldron.

Astrid picked up a long wooden spoon, stirred the mixture, and raised the spoon, letting the green goo drip off. The stuff was thick and looked as if it would choke me on the way down.

But I was game.

I slid my hand over Marcus's shoulders. I was doing it for him.

"It should be ready in another few minutes." Astrid placed the wooden spoon on the table. "Until then, we should probably discuss preparations for tonight."

"What do we need to do?" I asked.

"Drink that shit for one." Abby gestured to the potion.

Astrid continued, "We must time it right, and we must be prepared for those who want to stop us."

"Do you think we'll be targeted?" Marcus asked.

"Yes, I do," she said matter-of-factly. "Whatever that scroll contains could be enough to end this all."

"As in kill this God person?" I asked.

"Exactly."

"And if it's not?"

"Whatever it contains is of enough importance to be hidden behind a wall that no one other than yourself can access, and I think that has everything to do with you taking a piece of Morgana. If it's not able to destroy God, it must be something Morgana never wanted anyone to find."

"Then wouldn't someone have tried to take it from us by now?" I asked. "We haven't even seen a single Soul Scraper or Possession since we killed Morgana."

Abby furrowed her brow. "Yeah, I noticed that, too."

"Plus, we also had a hell of a time trying to find that veil hopper." Justin pointed to the medallion hanging from a chain around my neck.

Abby raised a brow. "*You* had a hell of a time? You didn't have to do shit. I was the one who had to…" She shivered. "I can't even say it; that's how disgusting it is."

Justin laughed, and she punched him in the shoulder.

"And we thank you for lowering your standards to help us out," Astrid said. "But for now can we just focus on tonight?"

"Sure thing," Abby replied.

Astrid picked up a soup ladle and scooped the green sludge from the cauldron. "Pass me that cup, Justin." She pointed to a wine goblet of sorts.

He grabbed the goblet and handed it to Astrid, who then proceeded to pour the goo into it.

She scooped another spoon full and slowly tipped it into the goblet until the liquid touched the rim.

I gulped. "I'm assuming you want me to drink all of that?"

"If you want to do this right, yes."

Taking the goblet from her, I held it up to my mouth and gagged. "Holy crap this stuff smells awful."

"Hold your nose," Marcus suggested.

I didn't think that would do anything, but the moment my gaze met his, I found all the persuasion I needed. I was doing this for him —for us.

Tipping the goblet up to my lips, I spilled the mixture into my mouth. I didn't take my eyes off his for fear I would spew it back up again. It was bad. But he was worth it.

Relief washed over me when the goblet was empty and I'd somehow managed to swallow all of the contents without choking.

Marcus took the goblet from me and handed it to Astrid. The look in his eyes told me he knew exactly how I'd gotten through it, and if he could, he would've taken it for me.

He would've done anything for me.

He'd already done everything for me.

I wiped the sludge off my lips with the back of my hand. "What now?"

Astrid handed me a glass of water. "Now, we get you ready for tonight."

"I thought we'd already discussed what we needed to do."

Astrid gave me that same smile that irked the hell out of me. "No, my dear. We haven't even started."

CHAPTER 22

$\mathcal{I}$ wasn't sure whose idea it was for me to wear a black cape complete with a hood, but I was glad to have something to cover the archaic symbols Astrid had drawn in blood all over my body.

Staring at my reflection in the floor-length mirror in Morgana's bedroom, I had to admit I looked straight out of a gothic, vampire photo shoot. Only this was real. The blood was real, and even though it was my own, it still grossed the hell out of me.

We were minutes away from leaving the safety of Morgana's home and heading to Byron Bay. I'd never thought I'd call Morgana's castle safe, but thanks to the protection spell Astrid and I had placed around the castle, it was exactly that. Safe.

My stomach churned with fear of the unknown. Astrid had warned us we should be ready for anything when we arrived. This God person was unpredictable, and none of us truly knew what he was capable of.

Marcus came up behind me and wrapped his arms around my waist. "You'll be fine."

I rubbed my temples, trying to focus on what needed to be done and ignore the doubt bubbling away in my stomach. Then, I realized I was smudging the symbols Astrid had drawn on them. "Shit."

Stepping closer to the mirror, I assessed the mess I'd made. "Damn it."

Marcus lifted my hair off my shoulders and away from my face. "I don't think it'll matter if they're not perfect."

"Oh, it'll matter." I grabbed the dagger off the dresser and pressed the blade into the tip of my finger. I barely winced as it pierced my skin and blood pooled on the end of the blade. "Everything has to be perfect, and I'm not going to be the one to stuff this up."

Marcus took the knife off me. "You're not going to stuff anything up. We're going to go back to Byron, you're going to do what you need to do, and the rest of us are going to keep you safe—if you should need protection."

I leaned in closer to the mirror and smeared the blood over my temple, trying my best to repair the damage I'd done to the symbol. It looked pretty good, but knowing how particular Astrid was with everything, I'd have to check with her to be sure.

Marcus let go of my hair and neatly tucked it behind my ears so it wouldn't stick to the fresh blood. "It's fine," he said as if he could read my mind.

Astrid tapped on the open bedroom door. "It's time."

I twisted around to face her, the knots in my stomach constricting at the thought of what we were about to do. When Astrid had first mentioned the ritual, I had no idea it was going to be this complicated, let alone that I'd be covered in blood.

Now, we were minutes away from figuring out what about the cylinder I was drawn to and the possibility of God sending out his minions to stop us.

"We're ready," Marcus said. "But you might want to check the symbols are correct." He pointed to my temple.

I gave her a tight-lipped smile. "Sorry. I smudged them and I tried to fix them, but I don't know if they're right, and I know how important they are and—"

"Calm down, Luciana," Astrid said with that patronizing smile of hers.

Letting out a loud sigh, I slumped my shoulders and tried to let go of all the paranoia consuming my every thought.

It was impossible.

I wasn't built to let go of something. I needed to give it away to someone.

I had no one to give it to. So, I had to suck it up and deal.

Placing her fingers on my chin, Astrid turned my head from side to side as she inspected the markings. "You're missing something." She released her grip on me.

"See," I said to Marcus. "I told you it was wrong."

The corners of his lips tipped up. "Actually, you told me you weren't sure."

I waved him off. "Semantics."

His grin grew wider, making my mood lift. I hardly noticed Astrid pricking my finger and couldn't look away from him until she physically turned my head.

Astrid dipped her finger into the pool of blood that was trickling out and painted what felt like an eye over my temples then connected them with one in the center of my forehead. "These extra markings will not only help you connect your third eye to the magic within but also to that around you," she explained. "You'll need to draw on your power and not hold back in doing so."

I scrunched up my face in confusion. "How am I supposed to do that? I don't even know what the hell I'm doing."

"You'll know." She wiped her blood-smudged finger on her dress, leaving a small dark stain.

Raising my hand, I stared at the blood still dripping from the small wound. It looked like any other human's blood, but it was far from it. And it was time we figured out how special it was.

Shaking my thoughts away, I pressed my finger against my jeans to stop the bleeding. "Where are the others?"

"Justin is downstairs with Abby, getting a quick bite before we head off."

"That'd be right," I said. "What about Ruby and Scarlett?" After a few hours of staring at the wall in Morgana's closet, they'd decided to prowl around the house, inspecting each and every room on their way.

"They'll be coming with us," Marcus said.

"I agree." Astrid strode over to the window, peeled back the velvet curtain, and looked up into the night sky. "But just be warned that they might not walk away with you."

"You mean they'll die?" I asked in surprise.

She nodded. "You've seen how easily Marcus and the others were able to take them down. Scarlett and Ruby will be no different."

"Isn't there anything you can do for them? There must be a spell or something." I'd only had them for a couple of days, and I knew they were demons and all, but that didn't change the way I felt about them. They'd grown on me, and I wasn't sure if it was because of their allegiance to me, or if it was because I'd been marked. Either way, I wanted to protect them, as they were trying to do for me.

Turning her back to the window, she gazed off into nothing and slowly shook her head. "I'm sorry. There's nothing we can do in such a short amount of time."

"Then maybe we should leave them here."

Marcus ran his hand down my arm in a soothing motion. "They'll be fine. We'll look out for them, and they'll do the same for us—or at least for you."

"How will you even know which ones are Ruby and Scarlett if there are others around?"

He laced his fingers with mine. "Because they feel like you."

Astrid furrowed her brow at me. "Can you not sense yourself in them?"

I shook my head. "I have no idea what you guys are talking about."

"Well, we can." She strode across the room, heading for the door. "It's time to move, so there's no time to explain that which we do not know and can only guess the reasons why."

I started to follow when Marcus pulled me back.

"We'll be down in a minute," he called to Astrid, his eyes never leaving mine.

"What's wrong?" I asked when we were alone.

Marcus tugged me closer. "I want to make sure you're okay."

"Of course, I'm okay," I said a little too quickly.

Tipping his head down, he looked deep into my eyes, stripping away the facade I'd built up pretending I had this when deep down I was scared out of my mind. "You don't need to put on a brave face around me. I know this is scary, and if I'm being honest, I'm afraid as well. So, I can completely understand if you're freaking out a little—or a lot." He smiled.

"I'm not afraid of the same things you are. And I'm not afraid because we're probably going to encounter creatures out of my nightmares. I'm afraid because so many things could go wrong, so many things could go right, and it all depends on me. No one else. Just me. Our lives are weighing on my shoulders and whether I do this right."

He pulled me closer until my chest was flush against his. "You're not in this alone. This is a combined effort, and we all play our own special part in it."

I stared up into his amber eyes, knowing how true his words were, yet they did nothing to take the weight off my shoulders. He was mine to give life to, not the other way around. Yet he couldn't see it that way. I was all on my own with that one.

Knowing I wasn't going to win that conversation, I leaned my head against his chest and breathed in deeply as I tried to calm my nerves.

Closing my eyes, I remembered everything I was fighting for. Memories of the years gone by flooded my mind. All of the lies we'd been told, the pain Marcus had endured, and the torment placed on both of us raised my spirits and my determination.

Marcus folded his arms around me and kissed the top of my head. "We better not keep them waiting any longer."

Forcing a smile, I lifted my head and stared into his eyes. "I won't let you down."

He brushed my hair behind my shoulder then cupped my jaw in his hand. "You never could." Marcus placed a gentle kiss on my lips. "And as much as I'd love to show you right now just how deep your perfection goes, I can hear a very antsy witch downstairs, freaking out about missing the alignment of the moon."

I sighed. "Better not keep the witch waiting."

We made our way downstairs, where we found Abby and Justin digging into Massaman curry. The smell drove me crazy, and I wanted nothing more than to satiate my cravings for Thai, but we didn't have time.

Abby shoved one more spoonful in her mouth then hopped off the kitchen bench. "Let's get moving." She practically skipped over to me and studied my markings. "What is all that crap?"

"It is not crap," Astrid said. "Every symbol will help Lucy draw from the earth, sun, and moon—"

"You do realize it'll be night when we get there."

"Just because you can not see it, doesn't mean it is not there."

44

"No." Abby twisted around to face her. "It'll be on the other side of the world."

That patronizing smile of Astrid's spread across her face. "Who said I was talking about the sun in this dimension?"

A big O formed on Abby's lips. "Gotcha."

Astrid strode over to me. "Now, you remember what you must do?"

I nodded. "Read the spell under the moonlight then open the scroll."

"Correct."

I drew in a deep breath then released it slowly. "Let's do this."

She lifted the hood of my cape and placed it over my head. "Remember, the cylinder may not contain what you are hoping for."

"I know."

Astrid smiled before turning her back to me. "Are we all ready?"

Justin put down his bowl of curry and placed his hand on my shoulder. "We've got your back."

"Til death do us part and all that shit," Abby said with a smile.

Returning her smile, I lifted the medallion from my shirt and rubbed my thumb over it.

Without raising my hand, the air in front of me began to shimmer as the veil opened to Byron Bay.

Astrid had said not to get my hopes up, but I couldn't help it. Somehow I knew this was it. This was the moment we'd been waiting for.

Marcus grabbed my hand and squeezed it, letting me know he was there for me and he always would be.

Abby and Justin moved in front of us, and the girls immediately fell behind me as Astrid stood on my other side.

"Let's do this." Abby grabbed Justin by the neck and pushed him forward with her.

We followed them, the familiar tingling sensation flowing through my body until I materialized on the other side, standing in the middle of the sand, the ocean to my left and the woods to the right.

Relief flooded through me as I looked at my surroundings. There was no one there but us and the girls, who were rolling around in the sand.

Astrid had been worried over nothing. Part of me was relieved, but another part had me on edge because if there was no one here to stop us, there probably wasn't anything of value in the cylinder.

It was another dead end, a time waster someone had planted to further manipulate everything we did.

Head tipped down, Astrid raised her hands to her mouth and began chanting something in Latin. I was about to ask her what she was doing when she lifted her head and threw her hands up.

Balls of fire flew into the air, further lighting up the night sky. Then they landed in a perfect circle surrounding us.

She turned to Marcus. "It's time."

Marcus nodded, withdrew the cylinder from his pocket, and handed it to me.

The moment my skin touched the cool metal, the ground began to shake, swallowing the balls of fire into the sand.

I thought this was all part of the process until I saw the fear consuming Astrid's gaze.

They were here.

CHAPTER 23

*M*y heart leaped into my throat as the sand rose into the air, taking on the shape of demented creatures that looked too much like Soul Scrapers with the way their concave eye sockets stared at me.

Shrill screams erupted under the moonlight as humans flocked toward us from the shadows of the bushes, their faces contorted into evil monsters that looked straight out of a horror movie, hell-bent on using whatever weapon they'd picked up along the way after their bodies had been taken over.

The sea rose, and with it came an army of demented souls reminding me of the creatures from my tunnel experience when I'd gone to Purgatory. Their wet, slimy skin was flapping in the wind, revealing oozing puss that covered their decomposing flesh.

If I didn't know better, I would've thought I was amidst a zombie apocalypse.

A blade of fire ripped past my head, and sand sprayed my face, yanking my thoughts back to the war around me.

I snapped my head to the side in time to see Marcus come down on another sand creature, his blade slicing through the particles, having absolutely no effect on them. He may as well have been fighting a Soul Scraper in its smoke form.

Heat blasted from behind me, singeing the fabric of my cape. I whipped my head around and saw Abby in all her glory somehow turning the sand monsters into glass.

Justin came down on the freaky glass sculptures, smashing them to tiny pieces while Abby moved onto the next and the next. They were a never-ending army of monsters that were relentless in their pursuit of me.

A slick, wet, slimy substance latched around my ankle and pulled hard, tripping me over. The cylinder slipped from my hands and landed in the sand as I face-planted.

I reached out and grabbed it as the sand began to shift, swallowing the cylinder and me into its depths like quicksand.

Just before I was completely submerged, whatever had latched around my ankle snaked its way up my leg, wrapped around my waist, and dragged me back.

But I wasn't letting go of that cylinder. I knew now more than ever that whatever it contained was everything we'd been searching for.

Flipping onto my back, I assessed my surroundings, my eyes going wide when I saw the creature that had hold of me, or more accurately creatures. There were at least ten of those water-zombie monster things dragging me into the ocean, and no one was coming to help me.

My gaze darted to the side, and I realized why. Marcus was caught up in an epic battle between the sand creatures, Soul Scrapers, and trying not to harm the humans who had been taken over by the Possessions. If it weren't for the innocents, I was sure he would've turned the beach into a fiery mass of destruction, instantly illuminating the sand creatures as a threat.

I wanted to scream at him for help, but how could I value my life over theirs? These humans had families. They were mothers, fathers, and there were even kids amongst them.

Abby had her hands full as she somehow turned the majority of the sand into glass. Then Justin smashed them into tiny fragments that glistened like blood under the now blood moon sky.

I desperately searched for Astrid, but she was nowhere to be seen.

Panic rippled through me as fear of being double-crossed again crippled me.

Ice-cold water splashed onto my feet then quickly covered my body, snapping me out of my needy stupor that so wasn't necessary.

I wasn't helpless. Sure, I was afraid, but I certainly wasn't helpless.

I was a witch, and I had the ability to control things I didn't understand.

Wind swept across the ocean. A split second later, Marcus snatched me up from the water and lifted me into the sky, the slimy tendril wrapped around my ankle snapping as we flew higher and higher into the air.

Clouds quickly took on the forms of Soul Scrapers falling from the sky and spreading across the land below, turning the scene into black smoke as they attempted to dodge Justin's and Abby's attacks.

I jerked my head around to tell Marcus we needed to help them, but all air expelled from my lungs the moment I saw his molten lava eyes staring back at me. He was a god, but he wasn't complete. That part of him lay inside of me, and in that moment, I wanted to betray him more than I'd wanted to in my entire life. Everything would stop if I just fulfilled my duties. All those humans down below would be released and could go back to their families instead of facing the very real possibility that their loved ones would attend their funeral because of my selfishness.

"Don't you even think about it." He flew us higher into the sky then pulled up, his plasma wings reflecting off the blood-red moon, turning them into a magical light display as they moved back and forth as we hovered in the sky.

Gripping the cylinder in my hand, I twisted around and looked down at the war raging below. Watching our friends stand up and fight against the creatures while we stayed safely in the sky was something I couldn't allow. "We have to go back."

Marcus shook his head. "We can't—"

"We can, and we are." When he opened his mouth to argue, I added, "Have you ever seen anything like this?"

He didn't answer.

"Exactly. And you and I both know it has everything to do with what's inside this." I held up the cylinder. "We need to find out what's inside, and we need to do it now before we miss out on the chance and have to wait another month before we can try again, all the while having to look over our shoulders, knowing God is coming for it.

"This might be our only chance and—"

He placed his finger over my lips, stopping me from talking anymore. "I was going to say I need time to get things in order."

"We don't have time. Astrid said we have a small window to perform the spell and…" I trailed off as dark clouds rolled across the sky. Everything suddenly made sense. Marcus wasn't trying to stop me or leave the fight to Abby and Justin. He was trying to help in the only way he could.

"We don't have time for me to get this wrong. We need to do this right."

I nodded.

"Now, when I take you back down, I'm going to need you to forget about me and the others and concentrate on what you need to do."

Lightning ripped horizontally across the sky just above our heads, forming a spiderweb of electrical currents desperately aching to connect to the earth, but I wasn't afraid. I knew it was Marcus, and I knew he had my back. They all did—except for one person. "Astrid betrayed us…"

He shook his head. "No. She's faithful to the end."

"The end? What are you—?"

Marcus placed his finger over my lips again, and as much as I wanted to slap him one, I kept my anger under control. "Concentrate on the now."

Holding his gaze, I nodded.

Marcus stared into my eyes. "Are you ready?"

I nodded.

Pressing his lips to mine, he kissed me gently then flipped me in his arms so I was facing away from him. A moment later, he swept through the sky, heading straight for the center of the war zone.

He leaned down, whispered, "You've got this," and dropped me onto the sand.

Doing my best to ignore the electrical storm ripping down from the heavens above, I tilted my head back and looked up at the moon, praying the spell would still work now that the symbols covering me were washed away. I recited the ancient words, "Solis, luna, praesidium."

The hairs on my arms and legs stood on end as electricity hummed under my skin, quickly building with intensity until I began to shake as I lifted off the ground and was propelled into the air by an unknown force into the electrical storm that surged around us, almost blinding me.

The shrill cries of the creatures below rang through my ears, and no matter how hard I tried to block them out, I couldn't help but hear the screams of those trapped under the demons' control. They begged me to help them, to release them from their captors.

I had to ignore them. I had no other choice.

Raising the cylinder in front of me, I placed my hand on the end and twisted the top off.

I flipped it over, and a warn cloth fell from inside onto the palm of my hand.

I fumbled with it for a few seconds as I desperately tried to unfold it and see what it contained, while trying not to drop the cylinder.

Opening the parchment, my eyes widened as I stared at the words written on the cloth. "No," I said, not able to believe what I was seeing.

CHAPTER 24

$\mathcal{T}$he moment the word left my mouth everything around me fell quiet. In an instant, the sand creatures had disappeared, the zombie-like creatures had slipped back into the sea, the Soul Scrapers had slunk back into the shadows of the bush, and the humans stared blankly at their surroundings as they tried to figure out what had happened and how they had gotten onto the beach.

Dropping, my feet hit the sand, and I fell to my knees as I stared at the silent mess around me. Justin and Abby appeared to be waiting for another round of attack, but there was none coming. And Marcus couldn't take his eyes off me. Everything around him was forgotten, his focus solely on me and what I was holding in my hands.

Stealing my gaze away from his, I scanned the area to see the damage to the innocents. Panic filled the air as the humans realized they were bloody and battered and didn't have a clue how they came to be that way.

The children's cries for their parents broke my heart. I had no idea if their families had been ripped apart in an effort to stop me from opening the damn cylinder that held no value.

Marcus trudged through the sand, heading straight for me from behind. I didn't need to see him to know who it was. I could feel him. I could also feel Abby and Marcus—and Astrid.

I scrambled on my hands and knees in her direction as Marcus's words became clear. She wasn't dead, but she was close to it.

"I've got her," Justin said, rushing over to Astrid.

Tears slipping down my cheeks, I fell back and landed on my ass as Justin carried Astrid's limp body in his arms.

He kneeled down beside me and laid her on the sand. "She's still alive, but you've only got seconds to make this work."

Wiping my tears away I nodded and repeated the words that had healed her the last time.

Unlike last time, it didn't have the same magical effect on her. It didn't bring her back to the strong woman I'd grown to know her as.

Astrid's eyelids slowly rose, and she stared warmly into my eyes, thanking me without saying a word.

"Her life force is returning," Justin said, removing the chain that had wrapped itself around my heart when I'd feared yet another person was going to die because of me.

"It was all for nothing," I said more to myself than the others.

Marcus kneeled beside me. "What do you mean?"

I opened the parchment and read the same riddle that had been tormenting me since the very first time Mava handed it to me.

> "The moon rises, and
> Light and Dark eclipse.
> An ancient one will impede,
> And memories will forget.
> Time stands still until
> The light will bloom,
> And shines on the key that
> Unlocks the door to Destiny."

Abby snatched the parchment from my hands. "Is this a joke?"

I shook my head, trying to wrap my mind around how close we'd come to death—for nothing.

Screw Morgana and all of her minions. They'd played with us from the beginning of my existence, and they were still having fun with us now.

Astrid's fingers brushed over my knee. "The cylinder," she said, her voice barely a whisper.

My eyes widened as I remembered it might not have had anything to do with what was inside.

I lifted the cylinder and stared at the intricate carvings, trying to figure out if there was anything I was missing, but as much as I wanted it to, nothing jumped out—

My heart skipped a beat when I saw it. A black gemstone wedged inside the cylinder, only visible with the reflection coming from Marcus's wings.

I tried to control my reaction because I had no idea if any of God's creatures were still around, watching, waiting for me to slip up.

Sirens blasted through the air as police and ambulances made their way down to the beach to attend to the humans who'd fallen into a mass hysteria as they each came to terms with their memory loss and injuries.

Marcus grabbed my elbow. "We better go before they show up."

Nodding, I got to my feet, the cylinder firmly gripped in my hand. As much as I wanted to help the humans, I knew we had to get going.

Justin scooped Astrid into his arms and carried her toward the bush, away from the prying humans' eyes.

The rest of us followed a couple of steps behind, and it wasn't until we were amongst the trees that I remembered the girls. "Ruby and Scarlett—"

"Feeding," Marcus said.

A sigh of relief escaped my lips. They were alive, and I had no choice but to ignore their natural instincts to feed. I knew without asking that it was only the dead ones they were sucking dry. The girls were mine, and I would never give the order to bleed someone dry for the hell of it.

Marcus scooped me into his arms. "They'll follow when they're finished." He pushed off the ground and headed in the direction of Abby's home. Part of me wondered why we were flying when I had control of the veils, but the other part knew this was what Marcus and the others needed.

They craved the feel of the wind on their wings, the normalcy of those moments as they flew through the sky, releasing all the pent-up energy into the air surrounding them.

I had no such release. Everything I experienced stayed bottled up inside of me and all I could do was absorb all the turmoil, letting it become a part of me.

A few minutes later, we touched down in Abby's backyard and followed them into the house.

Justin laid Astrid on the lounge then disappeared into the kitchen and returned a few moments later with a glass of water. He propped Astrid up on the pillows and helped her drink a few sips.

I shuffled my feet, trying to work out if I should tell them about my discovery. If I did and someone was watching, I would give away my biggest clue so far.

Or maybe it was just a crystal and nothing more. Astrid was the only person who would know for sure, and I had no idea if I could ask her.

Catching Marcus watching me, I closed my hand over the top of the cylinder and pretended there was absolutely nothing of interest.

He sauntered over to me. "Not here."

How he knew what was going through my mind was beyond me, but I was grateful he'd made my decision easier nonetheless.

I sat on the couch, facing Astrid, and turned the cylinder over and over in my hands as I tried waiting for the best moment to ask her something. The problem was, we didn't have time to waste. And no matter how much I wanted to give her the space she needed to heal, I had to do this for us. "Am I right in thinking there's no protection barrier placed around this house?"

"Nope. Nada," Abby said as she strolled toward the hallway that led to the bedrooms. "But you can put one up if it makes you feel better." She disappeared from sight.

I looked between Marcus and Justin. "If I do this, will it cast out whoever might be here already? Or will they remain because they're already inside the protection barrier?"

"You'll have to wait to ask Astrid about that."

She gave me an apologetic smile that looked more like a twitch. I really hadn't helped her enough, and it was driving me crazy watching her so lifeless. I couldn't even ask her why that was the case. She wasn't strong enough to answer me.

I supposedly had the power of one of the most powerful witches in the world, and I was still helpless to fix my friend.

"It depends on how it's done," Marcus said, surprising me.

Justin raised his brows. "You know how it works?"

Marcus sat beside me. "I know how it worked when Astrid placed it around my home. I can't imagine it would be much different for Abby's. Plus, Lucy and Astrid just placed one around Morgana's. I'm sure she can do it again."

"But they got through the last one..." Justin trailed off as he realized what he was saying. Of course, they got through the last one. Mava had died, and her spell had died with her.

"Do you think you can do it on your own?" Marcus asked, breaking the silence.

I sucked in a deep breath then exhaled slowly as I tried to figure out if I could do it on my own. Sure, I had the power, but I lacked the knowledge. And without Astrid's help, I could very well cast the spell, allowing everyone to think we were safe, all the while we had creatures already inside, watching our every move.

Unfortunately, we didn't have any other options. Relatively safe was better than nothing. And right now, I was willing to try anything.

Nodding, I stood and paced to the center of the room, standing next to the fireplace that separated the living and dining rooms. The cool cylinder started to heat up until it was almost burning—in one spot. The exact spot where the gemstone was hiding inside.

Slipping my finger inside the cylinder, I was met with intense heat as the gem burned under my skin, sending electrical pulses through my body. With it came an understanding of things I shouldn't know. Things I desperately needed to know for our protection. The crystal was speaking to me, guiding me and filling me with a sense of both darkness and light.

Spinning on my heel, I faced Marcus and Justin. "I can do this spell, but I'm going to need something from you all."

"Which is?" Marcus asked.

"I'm going to need either a hair sample or better yet, blood. Yep, I want your blood."

Marcus furrowed his brow. "Astrid didn't need anything like that."

Energy buzzed under my skin, wanting to be freed. "I know. But I've got this feeling, and you're going to have to trust me."

"What kind of feeling?" Justin asked.

"The kind where I know I'm right, and you both just need to do as you're told so I can get on with my job." Staring into the guys' eyes, I knew I sounded ludicrous to them, but I didn't care. I knew what I had to do.

Slipping my finger inside the cylinder, I rubbed it across the gem, praying that it wasn't the effects of the stone controlling me in a way that would be detrimental to us all.

Like the previous time, I was met by a warm electrical current, confirming what I needed to do.

Astrid lifted her hand barely an inch off the couch and nudged it against Justin's thigh. "Trust her."

Her voice was weak, but with it came strength and authority, something I lacked.

"Whatever you say." Justin reached into his pocket, pulled out his knife, and sliced it across the palm of his hand. Black blood spilled from the gash, reminding me that his blood wasn't like mine. "Where do you want it?"

"Come here." I waved him over to me.

Standing up, the blood dripped from his hand and fell onto the wood floor. "Shit."

"Abby will get over it. Just bring your blood over here." I sat cross-legged on the floor and brushed the area in front of me, getting rid of the few particles of dust that had settled on it. "You, too, Marcus."

I grabbed Justin's wrist, pried open his hand, and shook the blood onto the floor. "That'll do."

I let go of Justin's hand. "Your turn, Marcus."

He removed his blade from his pocket and sliced it across the palm of his hand. His blood was black like Justin's, but Marcus healed faster. Almost as soon as he'd ripped the blade through his skin, it healed, and he had to start again. "How much do you need?" He shook his hand, allowing the blood to drop onto the floor.

"That'll do." I held my hand out to Marcus. "My turn."

He shook his head. "Not me."

I furrowed my brow.

"Never again." The pain in his eyes was a stark reminder of the torment he'd endured having to drive that knife through my heart in almost every single one of my lives.

I would never ask him to go through that again.

"You'll never have to." I reached up, grabbed the knife from him, and sliced it across my hand, barely feeling the sting that would normally accompany it.

My blood spilled onto the floor, a stark contrast to the surrounding black drops from Marcus and Justin. I may not have been human, but I was sure created to look like one.

"I'm going to need Astrid's and Abby's blood, too."

"I'll get Astrid's," Justin said.

"And I'm guessing you don't want to wait for Abby to finish up in the shower?" Marcus asked.

A few weeks ago, I never would've suggested Marcus be in the same room as his naked best friend. But now I couldn't care less. The longer we left it, the greater the chance that I wasn't going to be able to perform the ritual to cast all unwanted guests from the house.

Darkness was closing in on us. And although I couldn't see it, I knew without a doubt that someone was there, watching us. Waiting for another opportunity to destroy any chance we had of ending this game.

"We don't have time to wait," I said to Marcus. "Are you okay with getting it from her?"

"Can't you?" Justin asked as he sat beside Astrid.

I shook my head. "I need to stay here with this." I gestured to the splatters of blood covering the floor.

"It's not as if I've never seen her naked ass before," Marcus said, heading toward her bedroom.

"I think everyone's seen it," Justin added. "It goes with the territory."

I remembered the time Abby had confided in me that she would not have chosen that life if she'd had the choice, and it pained me to think what her punishment would be for going rogue in an effort to help Marcus and me destroy everyone who stood in our way.

A minute later, Marcus came back, his hand wrapped tightly around Abby's wrist as she held a towel around her body with the other.

"Do you really need freshly spilled blood?" she asked. "Couldn't you have poured it into a cup or something so I could finish my shower in peace?"

It probably would've been fine, but I wasn't telling her that. "Fresh is best." I grinned.

She rolled her eyes and held out her hand. "Fine. Take my blood."

Marcus turned her hand over then sliced her palm with his blade. Droplets of black blood spilled from her wound and onto the floor. "That wasn't hard now, was it?"

She waved him off then trudged toward her bedroom.

When she was out of earshot, I turned to Justin. "A cup should be fine for Astrid."

"I heard that," Abby called out.

Marcus chuckled.

Justin downed the glass of water and pierced Astrid's skin with his blade. He wasn't careless with his knife like he had been with himself. With Astrid, he'd only sliced enough to get a few drops into the cup. Then he stood and brought it over to me. "Will this be enough?"

Taking the glass from him, I nodded. "It'll do." I tipped the glass and let the red blood spill from the rim, dripping onto the floor amongst the rest of ours.

When I got as much of Astrid's blood out of the glass as I could, I handed the cup back to Justin. Then, with the tips of my fingers, I smeared our blood over the floor in an archaic symbol that revealed itself in my mind.

Unintelligible words flooded my subconsciousness, quickly growing with intensity until they were all I could think about. I had no idea where the words were coming from, but I knew they wouldn't stop until they were released.

So I did.

Closing my eyes, the words spilled from my lips. They had no meaning to me, but the moment the murmurs came to life, so did the magic that surrounded me, consuming every fiber of my being. An unexplainable force expelled from my body, spreading like an atomic bomb reaching and consuming Marcus's home in its path, extending down to the beach and water's edge, and up to the road.

Then it stopped, and silence spread as far as I could hear.

I opened my eyes, an unfamiliar sensation taking over my soul as I became one with the nature around me. "We're alone."

CHAPTER 25

"*J*s someone going to tell me what the hell just happened?" Abby stood in the hallway, dripping wet with a towel loosely wrapped around her body. Her hair was now a tangled mess and covered in dark green sludge unlike it had been a few minutes ago when Marcus had dragged her ass out of the shower. And I was positive the goo wasn't some special shampoo or hair treatment.

Marcus and Justin laughed, gaining a scolding glare from Abby who looked two seconds away from ripping the smiles off their faces.

Marcus bit down on his grin. "What happened to you?"

"Don't start with me, demon boy," Abby warned. "Now, is someone going to tell me why the water coming from the showerhead turned into a sludge-spewing, cyclonic tidal wave that splattered this green shit all over my bathroom?" Abby lifted her hair to emphasise the disgusting mess she was covered in.

As funny as it was, I couldn't laugh, for I knew the truth. "You should be safe to wash it out now."

She cocked her hip and raised a brow. "What did you...?" Abby trailed off when she noticed the symbol sprawled across her floor. "And what the hell is that?"

"That is what's keeping all the things that go bump in the night out of your home."

"We go bump, and I'm still here." She stepped closer to get a better look.

"Hence me needing your blood."

"Huh." Abby spun on her heel. "Well, I'm not stepping foot in that bathroom anytime soon." She trotted to the back door, opened it, and headed toward the stairs leading down to the beach.

"Where is she going?"

Marcus shrugged. "How far does the barrier reach?"

I stood and went into the kitchen with Marcus following. "Past what's left of your house, a good portion of the sea, and up to the road."

Justin strolled over to us, rinsed the blood-smeared glass under the tap in the sink, and put it into the dishwasher. "How did you know how to do the spell?"

I leaned my ass against the stone bench and held the cylinder tightly in my hands. "There's…"

Marcus shook his head, warning me not to say anything.

"Don't stress," I said. "The walls no longer have ears. Apart from us, there's not a single living cell within this dome."

"Are you sure about that?"

I nodded.

"How can you be certain?"

I shrugged. "I just am."

Marcus stared at me for a few moments then said, "If you say so."

"I know it sounds weird and all, but you have to trust me." I frowned as I thought about the black gem. Maybe it was a trap, and all I'd done was create an illusion of safety. That was a very real possibility. "Shit."

"What's wrong?" Marcus and Justin asked in unison.

I debated telling them my concerns for about two seconds before deciding to hell with it. "There's a stone wedged inside the cylinder that seems to be somehow connected to me. I know it seems crazy, but when I touched it, I felt heat, electrical pulses, and knowledge. I knew exactly what to do to expel any living cell from our surroundings. I know it could be a trap, but I get this feeling it's not. It's as if something or someone is helping us. Or maybe this stone was connected to Morgana's magic, and it allows me to draw on a greater power and knowledge. Whatever it is, I know it worked, and we're safe."

"If you believe, then so do I," Marcus said.

"Good enough for me." Justin grabbed another glass out of the cupboard and filled it with water.

I strode over to the kitchen sink and looked out the window. So much had happened, yet I still felt we were running around blind. Sure, I had this gem that helped me when I needed it, but I highly doubted it was going to lead us directly to God.

Just to be sure, I rubbed my finger against the gem.

Nothing.

Not even a warm, tingling sensation.

The gem was cool to touch and gave off absolutely no vibes.

Marcus came up next to me and placed his hand on the small of my back. "Are you okay?"

Still staring out the window, I nodded. "What's the plan now?"

"I have no idea."

That made two of us, and I highly doubted Justin or Abby would be keeping an epic plan from us.

Astrid, on the other hand... But she was almost dead to it, so I couldn't know for sure.

Abby bounded up the steps, all evidence of the murky sludge had disappeared, and she once again looked like the sexy goddess she was in the towel wrapped around her body.

She stepped inside and ruffled her wet hair. "I think I might do that more often."

"Do what?" I asked.

"Bathe in the sea." She plonked her ass on the stool and twisted it from side to side. "You should try it some time."

"Yeah, I don't think Lucy is up for that." Marcus said exactly what I was thinking.

She shrugged. "Her loss."

Justin sauntered back into the kitchen, pulled up the stool next to Abby, and sat. "We need to make a plan about what we're going to do next."

"I'm planning on eating," Abby said. "But you three can strategize away." She hopped off the stool and opened the fridge.

Marcus leaned his hip against the bench. "Titus is dead, Morgana's place held nothing of interest except for the cylinder, and we can't get to any of them in the afterlife, but I would like to see if Colton was the one responsible for Titus's slaying."

"That sneaky little bastard probably talked as soon as we left the club." Abby dropped a few containers on the bench. "We should've killed him when we had the chance."

Justin grabbed the closest container and dragged it toward him. "You know, I don't think Titus knew what he was doing, and maybe he didn't even realize Julius had given me the order. He was hiding for Christ's sake."

"You think he was hiding from God or us?" Marcus asked.

"Both."

My heart skipped a beat when the warmth returned to the cylinder, exactly the way it had when I learned how to cast the protection spell.

I slipped my finger inside and sucked in a sharp breath as an electrical current surged through my body, bringing with it numbers, which I knew without a doubt were coordinates to our destination. I could see the location in my mind. It was a tiny island in the Pacific Ocean, away from any civilization.

Pressing my finger harder against the gem, I said, "I know where we have to go next."

CHAPTER 26

*M*arcus furrowed his brow, his steady gaze holding mine. "Did you get another vision or something?"

I nodded. I didn't blame him for worrying about me. This whole connection to the mysterious black gem was freaking me out as well.

"Where are we going?" Justin peeled the lid off the container of food.

Abby scrunched up her face in confusion. "What the hell are you guys talking about?"

Realizing Abby hadn't been there when I told Justin and Marcus about the magical properties of the gem, I gave her a quick update and watched her confusion turn into curiosity.

Abby grabbed the cylinder from me and peered inside. "Oh, you're right. There is something inside." She poked her finger into the cylinder. "But it's not hot."

I snatched the cylinder off her and stuck my finger inside. Like the last time, heat radiated from the gem, and with it came the coordinates.

Marcus watched me with curiosity. "It must be like Astrid said; you weren't attracted to the parchment; it was the cylinder itself you felt the connection to. Or more so, what was infused to the inside of it."

He grabbed a knife from the block and held out his hand.

"What are you going to do?" I asked.

"Get the gem out. Unless you're happy to carry around the cylinder with you everywhere you go?"

Of course, I wasn't. I handed him the cylinder.

Marcus slipped the knife inside, and a moment later, there was a *pop*. He withdrew the knife and placed it back in the block. Turning back to us, he tipped the cylinder upside down, and the black gem slid onto the palm of his hand. "Here you go."

I picked up the gem and rubbed it between my fingers. The familiar warmth radiated through my body along with those coordinates on a never-ending loop in my mind. Along with the numbers, I was consumed with longing to be alone with Marcus. But now was not the time.

Raising my gaze to his, all air expelled from my lungs as an unexplainable magnetic force drew me to him.

"Do you have any wire, Abby?" Justin asked, snapping me out of my lustful thoughts.

"Do I look like the kind of girl that would have wire lying around?" Abby grabbed a handful of forks out of the drawer and dumped them on the bench.

"Point taken." Justin grabbed a fork and stabbed it into the honey chicken. "What about you, Marcus? Do you have any wire?"

"In the garage."

Justin grabbed his food, hopped off the stool, headed outside, and disappeared to the right.

"What does he want the wire for?" I asked.

Marcus shrugged.

"Right." Squeezing the gem in my hands, I quickly forgot about Justin's whereabouts as the numbers repeated. "I need a map."

"Can't help you with that one either." Abby picked up a fork and pried open a container, revealing fettuccini covered in thick, white sauce.

My stomach rumbled, but I couldn't bring myself to eat with the numbers consuming my every thought.

Marcus brushed by me as he headed out of the kitchen. "Wait here."

He returned a few moments later with a laptop and placed it on the counter. "What are the numbers?"

I shuffled closer to him to get a better view of the screen and repeated the numbers that were burned into my memory.

A few moments later, the location showed up on the screen.

"There's nothing there," Marcus said, pointing to the blue screen, depicting the ocean, void of any land in sight.

I shook my head. "It's there." When he and Abby looked at me dubiously, I added, "Don't ask me how I know; I just do."

Abby twisted the laptop around to face her. "Like the way you knew how to cast the protection spell?"

I nodded. "You guys must think I'm crazy, but I'm telling you there's an island there, and I know how to get to it."

"Trust her," Astrid's weak voice barely carried into the kitchen. I wondered why I was unable to help her get better. I had all these new abilities that seemed far more advanced than being able to perform a healing spell.

Something wasn't right.

Marcus wrapped his arms around my waist from behind, snapping me out of my thoughts and sending me once again into my lustful state. "I do trust you."

Abby stared at him for a moment then shrugged. "What's the worst that can happen? We turn up and nothing's there? Then we go home."

"Exactly," I said, but I knew without a doubt that the mysterious island was the next step in our hunt.

"So, when do we leave?" Abby dug her fork into the dish and swirled the pasta around it.

I pulled Marcus's arms around me tighter, stealing comfort from his embrace. "Now."

"What about Astrid?"

"What about Astrid?" Justin asked, returning with a thin wire in hand.

"We're going to check out the coordinates, and I think someone needs to stay here with Astrid to look after her."

"I'll be fine," her soft voice barely carried into the kitchen.

"I'll stay with Astrid," Justin offered. "We can't leave her alone when she's like this."

Astrid remained silent.

"Sounds like a plan." Abby shoved another forkful of fettuccini in her mouth.

Justin held out his hand. "Can you pass me the gem?"

I wrapped my fingers tighter around it. "Why?"

He sighed. "I was going to make it into a pendant so you can add it to your necklace rather than carrying it around in your hand all the time."

Okay, well that made perfect sense. But I wasn't sure I wanted to be connected 24/7 to the gem and the unexplainable magic it held over me. Then again, I couldn't afford to lose it. "Thanks." I handed it over.

I watched in awe as he twisted the wire around the stone as if he'd spent many hours learning the art of jewellery making. Then, he handed it to me.

I unclipped the chain from around my neck, slipped it through the wire encased around the gem, and replaced the chain around my neck. The warmth of the gem sitting against my chest was a stark reminder of everything that was crazy in my life. But looking at the man standing next to me, completely oblivious to the supreme being he was created to be, cemented my newfound knowledge deep in my heart.

We were going to end this, and our next step was this mysterious island that technically didn't exist.

But first, I needed to eat. I grabbed the last container and opened the lid. Not bothering to heat up the contents, I dug into the lasagne as if I hadn't eaten for two days.

Marcus opened the fridge, pulled out ham and cheese, and proceeded to make enough toasties for all of us.

I carried the tray with toasties and juice into the living room where Astrid was still lying on the couch, looking as if she were minutes away from death.

Performing the ritual to help unlock the mysteries of the cylinder had taken more out of her than I had realized. Too many people had suffered in their quest of restoring my memories and setting all that was wrong in the worlds, right again.

But setting things right was never going to be that simple.

God would never let it be.

Pain and suffering was sure to come, and I prayed that when we arrived back, I wouldn't find out Astrid had become yet another casualty in our war with God.

"Are you sure there's nothing else I can try to make you better?" I placed the tray on the coffee table then helped her into a sitting position.

"There's nothing you can do." She squeezed her eyes shut momentarily before feigning that she was okay. "For some reason, you're not able to reverse the damage, and I'm more worried about the reasons why."

I furrowed my brow. "What do you mean?"

She gestured for the juice.

I picked up the glass, handed it to her, and watched as she downed half the contents.

Astrid lowered the glass and rested it against her stomach. "Do you still feel Morgana's magic inside of you?"

I nodded. "Stronger than ever."

"Right. Then fighting off the demons must have taken a toll on me that not even you can fix."

There was more to her theory. I lowered myself down beside her and spoke softly enough for only her to hear me. "What are you not telling me?"

She stared at me for a few moments then let out a shallow breath. "Either that or someone wants me to stay here." Astrid looked pointedly at the gem resting against my chest.

I jerked back, my hand instantly going to the pendant. The idea of the gem controlling a part of me so much that I was unable to perform a simple healing spell wasn't out of the question. It had already connected with my mind by no more than a touch. It was a part of me, feeding me with information, and I didn't want to consider it was also a hindrance.

Severing my soul from Marcus's light was my top priority, and I didn't want anything getting in the way.

If Marcus caught on to the fact that the gem might not be everything I hoped it was, there was a good chance he would try to stop me from going where it was telling me to go. And no matter how much I knew Astrid could be right, I had no doubt in my mind that this was the exact next step we needed to take.

Astrid clenched her fingers around my wrist and whispered low enough for only me to hear. "Just because it might be controlling you, doesn't mean that you shouldn't be controlled." She released her grip on me. "I am but a pawn in the path that needs to be walked."

My heart was racing, and I needed to calm down.

She forced a smile. "Now, can you please pass me a toastie?"

With my thoughts still consumed by everything she'd said, I did as she requested and sat the tray on her lap.

I stood and was about to go back to the others when she latched her hand around my wrist. I twisted around to see her. Her eyes were steely—unwavering and consumed with a fierce determination.

"You are stronger than you think." She stared at me for a few moments before saying, "Trust yourself."

Not knowing what to say to that, I nodded and took off toward the kitchen, the possibilities of what was to come consuming my every thought.

Justin was sitting on the stool, Abby on the bench, and Marcus was rinsing off the plates in the sink. They appeared completely oblivious to my little chat with Astrid, and I prayed I was right. Otherwise, Marcus would probably lock my ass in a room and throw away the key—and the gem.

"What was all that about?" Marcus asked as he stacked the dishwasher with the plates and cutlery.

"Uh, Astrid was just giving me a pep talk, telling me to trust my instincts and all."

He stared at me for a few moments, and I could've sworn he knew the truth, but he nodded and left it at that.

I sat on the stool next to Justin. "So, are we all ready to go and check out this island?"

Marcus shut the dishwasher door then wiped his hands on the tea towel. "Let's do this."

Abby hopped off the bench. "Show us this mysterious island of yours."

My heart was still racing from my conversation with Astrid. In the back of my mind was a niggling suspicion that I was indeed being controlled, and I feared it might not be for good. But that didn't mean it wasn't the right path. Sometimes you had to go through hell to come out on top. I of all people knew that. After all, I'd had to go through my own personal hell in those tunnels to find out who I was.

Hell didn't scare me.

Failing Marcus did.

I drew in a deep breath, praying that we landed on solid ground rather than ending up in the middle of the ocean, dripping wet and without any leads.

That was not a possibility.

Unconsciously, my hand touched the stone, and I was once again reminded of the power that lay within.

With the coordinates to the hidden island still on a repeat in my mind, I lifted my hand to the medallion and opened the veil.

The air rippled in front of me, and with it came an unrelenting calling, whispering for me to follow. It was as if a rope had been lassoed around me and was pulling me into the unknown.

As much as I craved to go through first, Marcus had other ideas. And like last time, Abby went through first.

Marcus laced his fingers with mine and gave a little squeeze. "Ready?"

Unable to form any coherent words, I nodded. Then, we stepped through the veil.

I sucked in a sharp breath as I emerged on the other side and came face-to-face with a wall of tribal warriors, weapons raised and—

A sharp sting shot like fire through my chest, followed by another and another, darkness quickly taking over my soul and dragging me into its depths.

My vision was blurry, and I desperately fought the urge to close my eyes as I dragged my gaze down and saw three darts protruding from my chest.

I sucked in a strangled breath when I saw dark lines snaking their way across my chest. I tried to lift my hand so I could get the darts out, but my arms wouldn't co-operate. My head swayed to the side as another sting shot through my neck, and then I was out cold.

CHAPTER 27

Soft kisses trailed down the curve of my neck, waking me from my sleep. My eyelids fluttered open momentarily, the weight of them becoming too much for me to hold for more than a second before they closed again.

A soft groan escaped my lips as the kisses made their way across my shoulder and tentative hands caressed the curve of my hip.

Once again, I slowly lifted my lids as memories of my last moments awake flooded my mind. Adrenalin surged through my body, snapping me out of my weary state and into the reality that was far from anything I'd ever encountered before.

I was curled up on a low-lying bed amongst colored cushions scattered across the floor of a room lined with sheer curtains against what appeared to be thatch walls, which I thought was strange for a tribal hut.

"Easy there." Marcus's gentle voice broke through the hysteria I was quickly drowning in. If he was here with me, then that meant we were okay. The tribal warriors hadn't tried to kill us as I'd feared, and by the looks of it, we weren't prisoners.

I almost laughed. As if a tribe of humans could be any match for Marcus—or even Abby and Justin. And the three of them together were an unstoppable force... Except for God. We had no idea what we were up against, and I prayed this island held at least some answers as to what was install for us.

Rolling onto my back, I stared up into Marcus's amber eyes. Peace settled over my soul as he caressed the side of my face and leaned in for a kiss. A kiss that stole every single ounce of my focus away from my strange surroundings and pulled me into all that was Marcus.

I hooked my arms around his neck and fell completely into the moment as if we were the only two people in the world and nothing else mattered.

Just him and me.

Together forever.

Like the way we were—

Someone that was definitely not Marcus cleared their throat.

Marcus pulled away from me, irritation turning his eyes… almost black.

I shook my head, trying to get the drowsiness from the darts out of my system.

Yeah, that wasn't going to work.

Stealing my gaze away from Marcus, I turned my head toward the woman who—

Jerking myself into a sitting position, I sucked in a sharp breath as I stared at the goddess before me. She was everything I wasn't. Tall, dark hair, golden skin, toned body, and she wasn't afraid to show it. All that covered her was a tiny piece of sheer black material, leaving virtually nothing to the imagination.

She strode farther into the hut, a look of disdain evident in her eyes as she glared at me while somehow still able to keep her nose raised in the air. She wore an air of arrogance that only came from power. "My father asked me to come introduce myself and make sure you feel welcome. But I can see you've already made yourself quite at home." The corner of her lips tipped up into a smirk.

I'd only just met her, but I already didn't like her. Something about the woman unnerved me, and if I'd learned anything over the years, it was that I needed to trust my instincts. Then again, trusting my instincts was what had gotten us here in the first place.

Subconsciously, I lifted my hand to my chest, my heart skipping a beat or five when I didn't come into contact with either the gem or the medallion.

They were gone.

"Thank you for your welcome, Kora," Marcus said, barely hiding the irritation in his voice. He obviously wasn't fond of the girl either.

Her gaze held mine then flicked down to my chest before quickly diverting to Marcus. "Supper will be served at sundown. Don't be late."

She glided across the floor and made her way through the door, taking her air of superiority with her.

"Who is that?" I asked. "And where the hell are we?"

Marcus stood and picked up his shirt. "We are exactly where you brought us, and that is the leader's only daughter." He slipped his shirt on.

I climbed to my feet. "How long was I out?"

"A little over a day."

My eyes went wide as panic set in. We'd traveled to a place that technically didn't exist, and I'd been unconscious for over a day, completely at their mercy.

I'd hoped this place held the key to our next move, and now it seemed to have slipped through our fingers. They'd taken the gem and our ticket out of here.

Marcus held my gaze as he sauntered closer to me, a sense of peace spreading over me with every step he took until he was all that I could think about.

It was as if I still had the gem with me, amplifying the love we shared and making me forget about everything that mattered.

Marcus cupped my cheek in his hand.

I was happy to forget.

He spread his hand around my hip and pulled me closer.

I was happy to succumb to the moment.

He brushed his lips over mine.

I was happy.

But I knew it was a lie.

It was magic.

It had to be. But no matter how much I told myself I needed to get out of there, away from whatever madness had entrapped us, I couldn't help succumbing to the moment.

If he wasn't worried, then I wouldn't be either.

Hooking my arms around him, I fell into all that was Marcus, letting him consume my every thought.

Pulling away too soon, Marcus laced his hands with mine. "The sun will be down any minute now. We better not keep our hosts waiting."

The lustful fog was slowly leaving my mind, and I could finally think about something besides Marcus and the way he—

I shook my thoughts away. I needed to stay focused and couldn't let myself fall into him again. "Who are our hosts?"

A grin spread across his face. "Well, let's just say you were right. However, the natives here aren't usually welcoming to strangers."

I puffed out a laugh and rubbed my hand over my chest where the darts had covered my body. "That's the understatement of the century."

Letting go of my hand, he brushed my hair away from my face. "Once we got a chance to explain why we're here, their leader gave us permission to remain as guests on their island while we find the answers we seek."

I frowned. "That's a bit of a one-eighty, isn't it? They shot us on sight, and now they are happy to play nice? That doesn't make any sense."

"Well, that's because you weren't awake for the negotiations."

"Negotiations?"

He nodded as he slipped his hand around to the small of my back and ushered me toward the door. "Let's just say they were more than happy to take us in after they realized we were from the supernatural world." Marcus chuckled. "And they took an awful liking to Abby." He leaned in closer and whispered, "They worship those of her kind here."

A big O formed on my lips. Not only had I brought us to an island that shouldn't exist, but the people also happened to be devil worshipers.

Lucky for us, we had Abby on our side.

Marcus swept the curtain covering the doorway to the side, revealing a whole new world that made my skin crawl.

CHAPTER 28

*T*he last of the day's light cast shadows over the land as men —painted in what looked to be blood—moved around the fire in a slow rhythmic motion, contorting themselves into positions that made me cringe.

Men and women dressed in loin cloths sat in a circle around the dancers in a trance-like state, moving in time with one another as they swayed back and forth, their heads rolling in circles and their gaze never wavering from the flames that leaped into the air, swirling and dancing as if they had a life of their own.

There was no wind on the island, which meant it had to be magic at work. What kind of magic these people possessed was yet to be determined. But if I had to guess, I'd put my money on the darkest kind. The type Astrid had warned me about.

But that wasn't what had stolen my breath. Surrounding the circle of chanting humans were stakes with human skulls and decaying heads on top, plowed into the earth as if they were trophies won in a battle or taken for the killer's own sick pleasure.

A chill ran down my spine as my gaze drifted over to the limbless beast roasting on a spit when there didn't appear to be any animals around. Apart from the chanting, the land was eerily silent, and it unnerved me.

Marcus leaned over my shoulder and whispered into my ear, "Don't give them any reason to reconsider their hospitality to us."

Swallowing hard, I nodded. We needed these people—or something that was on this island, and it was going to be a great deal easier if we remained on friendly terms.

How I was going to be civil to a group of people who put people's head on stakes around their kitchen was another story.

Nevertheless, I was going to try.

Putting on my I'm-not-physically-ill-seeing-mutilated-bodies-all-around-me face, I strode with just the right amount of confidence and respect toward the fire with Marcus by my side.

We sat cross-legged on the ground, forming part of the circle surrounding the fire, and watched the entertainers with disgust as they slit the throat of the animal on the spit, and blood spilled into the bowl they held beneath.

Witchcraft was definitely at play. There was no doubt about it. The beast would've bled out a long time ago. Yet, the blood poured like water from a tap.

The tribe proceeded to pass the bowl between themselves and drink like hungry vampires feasting on the blood.

In their own sick twisted way, maybe they were.

Not vampires in the folklore sense, but from what I could see, these people worshiped those that resided in Hell.

No wonder they loved Abby.

Leaning into Marcus, I asked, "Where's your bestie?"

He furrowed his brow. "Who?"

I rolled my eyes. "Abby."

"Right." His gaze returned to the performers. "She's following up what's going to probably be another dead end lead, and I'm pretty sure Justin's still with Astrid."

"Is she feeling any better?"

"I have no idea. There's no cell reception on the island."

I frowned. Something about Marcus was off, and I wasn't sure if it was him or if it was me. Whichever it was, the uneasy feeling in the pit of my stomach was quickly growing.

"What is it, my dear?"

And there he went again. Marcus didn't speak that way, or maybe he did and I'd never noticed?

I wanted to slap myself.

Marcus was no longer a mystery to me. I remembered him throughout every life I had, and he hadn't spoken that way in years, which meant he'd either suffered trauma to his head, or something far worse was at play.

Fear bubbled its way up my throat. Something had changed since we arrived at this island, and I hoped I hadn't made the wrong decision by insisting we travel to a place no one—not even three ancient beings—knew anything about.

All the conspiracies racing through my mind was doing my head in. My life was filled with deception and unknowns, and I couldn't help but think that maybe I'd fallen into another trap.

Maybe this was God's way of keeping me off the grid until I'd run out of time in this life and we were back to square one.

I couldn't let that happen. I needed to find answers—now.

The only problem was we were surrounded by a magic I didn't understand, and no matter how much I tried, I couldn't determine who held the power.

I couldn't even feel the magic inside of me. It was as if it had been hidden, or it had been stripped away the moment we landed on the island.

We couldn't let God win.

Marcus brushed my hair away from my face. "You're doing that thing again."

I furrowed my brow. "What thing?"

His eyes turned a darker shade of amber. "Where you let your imagination run wild."

Staring into his eyes, it was as if he were but a shell of his former self. This wasn't the man I'd fallen in love with. It wasn't even the man I'd obsessed about in the hut. This man was different. And no matter how much I tried to figure out exactly what it was about him that had changed, I couldn't. It was as if a fog had been cast over my mind and I was barely staying afloat.

Forcing a smile, I said, "Sorry." I leaned in closer to him and whispered, "It's just this place kind of gives me the creeps."

He stared at me for a few seconds then flashed me that smile of his that usually melted my heart.

That didn't happen this time.

Silence fell over the land, stealing my attention away from

Marcus as Kora strode toward the center of the pit with an entourage of men trailing her like bees to their queen.

The men were tall, well defined, and carried an arsenal of weaponry along with bamboo-like sticks strapped to their hips.

These men were the ones who'd peppered my chest with darts.

A chill ran down my spine as I watched them follow her over to a chair made from reeds and give her a small bow before once again falling behind her, watching, protecting, never once conversing with one another as they protected their princess.

She leaned back in her throne, not bothering to hide how bored she was with the attention her people were showering on her.

The beast was carved only by her authority, and people ate only after she'd taken her first bite and had given her approval for them to proceed.

My stomach rumbled as I stared down at the bowl of meat placed before me. I was beyond hungry, but I couldn't bring myself to take one bite for fear I wasn't actually going to eat an animal and instead they were feeding me flesh that belonged to one of the newly deposited heads that were staked into the ground not more than a few feet away from me.

"Eat up," Marcus said as he scooped a chunk of meat into his mouth. "It's best not to offend our hosts."

Twisting around to him, I was about to confess my thoughts of what exactly he had just chewed and swallowed when I stopped in my tracks. Marcus was watching me, and I mean watching me in a way he'd never looked at me before.

My heart clenched with fear. The man sitting beside me was no longer the man I was born to save. Something was seriously wrong, and I knew in my heart I could no longer trust he wasn't once again imprisoned with a spell that was beyond my ability to break.

Stealing my gaze away from his, I gestured to the empty throne beside the one Kora was occupying. "Where's their leader?"

Marcus shrugged a shoulder. "I have no idea."

Something in my gut told me that was the biggest lie of them all.

CHAPTER 29

Surrounded by at least one hundred people, I'd never felt more alone.

The empty shell of the man I loved sat beside me, his body now overtaken by someone I didn't know, whom I wasn't connected to.

I couldn't explain how I knew, and more importantly, I didn't know how I would get him back.

Fear had spread its icy tendrils over my soul, further stealing my connection to—

My throat closed when my eyes momentarily locked with Kora's. She knew. It took all of my control not to sprint over to her, wrap my hands around her neck, and squeeze the life out of her evil temptress body until she talked.

But I didn't need to go to such drastic lengths when I could take.

Focusing all my efforts on stealing that one piece of memory away from her, I waited for her knowledge to become mine.

And I waited.

It didn't come.

Shit.

I released a shuddered breath as realization set in. I was powerless, and the man sitting beside me couldn't be trusted. The severity of the situation quickly sunk in when Marcus's eyes blazed with black swirls, taking over the amber.

Something had taken over his soul, and there wasn't a damn thing I could do about it. I was all on my own.

Snapping myself out of the hysteria I was quickly falling into, I resorted to the fact that I was stuck on an island, unable to trust anyone around me, no magic to save us, and I didn't even have wings to get us out of there.

I was at the mercy of devil worshipers that may or may not have been trying to turn me into a carnivore, and I had to hold my shit together if I wanted any chance of getting us out of there alive and in one piece.

Knowing what I had to do, I leaned over and placed a gentle kiss on Marcus's cheek then scooped up a large chunk of meat and shoved it into my mouth.

If I had to eat humans to get us out of there, that was what I was going to do.

The meat was unlike anything I'd ever tasted before. It wasn't disgusting, but there was something definitely not normal about the texture. No matter how much I wanted to spit it out, I chewed it and swallowed, all the while trying to pretend I was enjoying it.

Marcus gave me a small smile. Then he turned his attention to Kora and her merry men. Every so often, I caught Marcus watching me out of the corner of his eye. He wasn't talkative, which also wasn't like him.

He was usually the one to have a plan ready to put into action. Marcus wasn't the type to sit back and wait unless... Unless my safety was at risk.

But it wasn't that. His behavior was completely out of character. Throughout the hundreds of years I'd known him, I had never truly lost my connection to him—until now.

Thankfully, we weren't expected to stay for long after we'd finished our meal. The princess had risen and sauntered back to her home, or wherever it was that she'd crawled out from, and the rest of the people began to disperse.

Marcus stood and held out his hand for me.

My heart hammered inside my chest as I wondered, or if I were being completely truthful, feared what was going to happen next. Something wasn't right, and I was afraid what the night would bring.

These people he referred to as our hosts were complete nut jobs, and I wouldn't put it past them to chop off our heads while we slept then serve us up as their next meal.

Marcus swept the cloth door to the side and held it open for me. "Will you be okay here for a while? I have to attend to further discussions with the leader."

I shook my head. "I'm coming."

Anger momentarily swirled in his smoky amber eyes before they returned to normal. "It's nothing of any importance." He cupped my cheek in his hand. "Besides, you need your rest."

It took everything in me not to tell him the hell I wasn't introducing myself to the man who'd stolen my magic, gem, and medallion, and had undoubtedly screwed with Marcus's soul, but something inside of me was screaming to shut my mouth and do as I was told.

I needed time to figure out what was going on, and I needed to do it alone.

Playing the part of the unwitting soul mate, I leaned into his hand and closed my eyes, my lips tipping up into a tired smile.

Marcus leaned into me and placed a gentle kiss on my forehead. "I won't be long."

Watching him walk away was almost a relief. I could finally breathe again, and that scared the hell out of me.

Letting the curtain fall back into its place, I headed further into the room and stood there, not knowing what to do.

I hated doing nothing. I hated waiting. Time was running out, and the more time we let slide through our fingers, the further Marcus was slipping away from me.

With a new round of determination consuming my soul to turn over every rock on the island until I found what I was looking for, I spun on my heel and stopped dead in my tracks.

Kora was standing two feet in front of me, a look of fear in her eyes.

CHAPTER 30

*K*ora glanced back at the door then returned her gaze to me. "Don't leave this room."

I glared at her. "You don't tell me what to do."

She latched her hand around my bicep as I pushed past her. "I know you've already begun to see the truth, and if you want to wake up tomorrow remembering today, then I suggest you listen to me."

"Are you threatening me?" I'd had enough of this island and all of its inhabitants.

She let go of my arm. "I'm trying to help you." Her pupils dilated, and she once again glanced at the door. "I'll come back tonight. And whatever you do, don't tell him I was here." Kora disappeared.

As in one second she was standing in front of me and the next... *poof,* she was gone.

People didn't go poof.

Witches, angels, and demons did. But humans? No.

A second later, Marcus entered the hut, his casual smile dropping the moment he locked eyes with mine.

I held my breath as he scanned the room almost as if he knew she'd been here.

I wasn't the slightest bit tempted to tell him all about Kora's little visit and her cryptic message. I wasn't sure I believed her. Not that I had any idea what I was supposed to believe.

All she'd really said was that I needed to trust her if I wanted to keep my memories.

My mind and soul were playing tricks on me, and I had no idea what to think, what to do, or whom to believe.

One day ago, I never would've thought twice about placing my trust in Marcus, but now…

Tipping my lips up into a smile, I pretended to be oblivious to whatever was going through his mind. "Back so soon?"

"Akuji rescheduled for a little later."

Akuji. So that was the infamous leader's name.

I sauntered over to Marcus and ran my fingers down his chest. "Can't say I'm not the slightest bit happy to have you here to keep me entertained." I kissed the corner of his lips then swiveled around and headed over to the foot of the bed. "Do you know how boring this place is? There's nothing to do in here." I gestured to the naked walls, void of a TV and the lack of anything besides the pillows.

Marcus came up behind me and spread his hands over my hips, making me suck in a sharp breath. Not because he surprised me in a good way. It was because I felt a darkness within his soul.

He'd often talked about this darkness he possessed, but somehow this was different. Or maybe it wasn't, and it was exactly what he had warned me of.

My mind was going crazy with the endless explanations to what I was feeling.

One thing I knew for sure—I didn't want to sleep with the man holding me in his arms, and by the way his hands were moving over my body, it was exactly what he wanted from me.

That was so not going to happen.

Using the oldest trick in the book, I placed my hands on my stomach and slightly leaned over. "I don't think that food agreed with me."

Okay, so that wasn't the oldest trick in the book, but my stomach was disagreeing with processing what was probably a human. There were bound to be problems with that.

Pinching my eyebrows together, I twisted around to face him. "Don't suppose—" I slapped my hand over my mouth as bile rose up my throat. "Where's the bathroom?"

Marcus opened his mouth to reply, but I couldn't wait any longer.

I burst out of the hut, ran into the bushes, and almost keeled over as I vomited. When I thought there was no more that could possibly come out, another bout rose up my throat.

When it was finally over, I wiped the back of my hand across my mouth as I took in my surroundings. An eerie sensation washed over me, begging me to come forth and follow its unspoken calls, leading me into the unknown.

The last time I'd experienced such a calling was when I'd discovered that secret room of Morgana's where I found the gem, which in turn led us to this island of secrets.

I quickly looked over my shoulder to see if anyone was there. Marcus was standing right behind me, as silent as the night. "Holy shit. You scared the crap out of me."

"Sorry," he said. "I came to make sure you're okay."

I drew in a deep breath then released it slowly. "I'm okay. I may have food poisoning, but I'm okay."

"Good." He gave me a barely noticeable nod. "Now, what were you looking at before?"

I drew my eyebrows together. "When?"

"Before you saw me when you were looking into the forest."

He knew.

Any other time I would've told him exactly what I'd felt, but something deep inside my soul was telling me to keep my mouth shut if we ever wanted to find out the truth.

I scrunched up my face in confusion. "I was trying to get my breath again after spewing my guts." I crossed my arms over my chest. "Or didn't you notice?"

I prayed turning it back on him would work.

His face softened, and he brushed a strand of hair away from my face. "Of course, I noticed. I was only wondering if you'd found what we came here looking for."

"I wish," I lied. The truth was I was almost positive I'd found what we were looking for.

Something was hiding amongst the trees, and I was going to find out what. But for now, I would continue to play the ignorant guest, happy to leave our future in the hands of the man I no longer loved.

Sleep eluded me that night. My mind was racing with everything that had happened since we arrived on the island, and no matter how much I tried to make sense of what was going on, I couldn't.

Marcus had left to meet with the elder a little over ten minutes ago, leaving me all alone in the hut surrounded by freaks.

I peeked out of the curtain, trying to see if anyone was watching me. There had to be. They'd be stupid not to watch me. But I had to try to get out of the hut and find out who or what exactly was calling to me in the woods.

"I wouldn't do that if I were you."

CHAPTER 31

*A*lmost jumping out of my skin, I whipped around, my heart stopping when I saw Kora standing not more than two feet in front of me, her hair pulled back and a look of fierce determination in her black eyes.

She wore a dark cloth that barely covered her necessities, and she held something tightly in her fist. "You need to leave this place now, and I'm going to help you do it."

I stared at her with my mouth hanging open, trying to figure out what her deal was and how the hell she'd "poofed" in here.

"All will be explained soon, but you need to trust me—and before you go on about how you are not supposed to trust a stranger, I need you to forget what your brain is telling you and trust your soul, because we both know it's telling you to do exactly what I say."

I sucked in a sharp breath and nodded.

"Right." She gestured toward the door. "I will cloak you as much as I can. It will fool everyone except my father, but I've come up with a contingency plan to make sure we won't have any trouble from him."

"What about Marcus?" I asked.

The corner of her lips turned up. "You and I both know he's not the same man you came here with."

I narrowed my eyes at her, anger boiling in my soul. "What have you done to him?"

"Calm down, Luciana. All will be remembered but only if you quit asking questions and come with me—now."

I had two seconds to decide what to do. On the one hand, I didn't trust her as far as I could throw her, yet another part of me was screaming to listen to her, and I had to figure out which to trust.

Taking my chances, I gave her a nod. "Show me the truth."

She held out her fist and opened her hand, revealing the gem I'd found in the cylinder that gave me the location to the island I was now trapped on.

"Where did you get that?"

Kora grinned. "Who do you think sent it to you?"

Holy. Shit.

"There's no time to explain. We need to move now." She closed her hand around my wrist and somehow glided through the wall to the left, dragging me with her as she headed into the bush in the direction I'd experienced that freakish calling.

My feet stung as sticks and rocks cut into me, and I chastised myself for not insisting on putting on shoes before we left. Kora may have been able to walk through walls and trees and whatever else got in her way, but she wasn't able to make me walk on air.

I watched her with morbid curiosity, wondering what exactly she was. Human wasn't an option, and as far as I knew, angels and demons couldn't walk through solid objects.

This girl was different. For whatever reason, she was helping me, and I wanted to know why.

A moment later, we came to a halt in front of a majestically haunted tree that looked as if it were thousands of years old. The root system spread out over the land in every direction, and the deformed trunk spread high into the sky above the canopy of the other trees.

"What are we doing here?"

She let go of my hand. "You'll see. Kora strode to the tree, placed the gem—my gem—onto the trunk, and whispered something under her breath.

Wind rustled the leaves as a magical current swept around us and disappeared the moment she removed the gem from the trunk.

"What just happened?" I asked, a mixture of fear and wonder spreading over my soul.

"Restoring the stones ability." She sauntered over to me. "Now, we must do this right if you are to remember."

"Remember what?"

"Everything that's happened since you arrived on this island forty-five days ago."

My breath got caught in my throat. "But... I only arrived yesterday."

She raised a brow. "Are you sure about that?"

I wasn't sure about anything anymore.

When I didn't answer, she said, "Your love isn't here. He never was, and he never will be until you remember and we work together to end this ridiculous obsession my father has with you."

My eyes widened. "What does your father have to do with anything?"

Kora's grin spread across her face. "Everything."

CHAPTER 32

*M*y heart was pounding as I tried to process what Kora was saying, or not so much saying. If what she was telling me was right, I'd been manipulated since the moment I'd arrived forty-five days ago.

I'd spent over a month on an island and had no memories other than today. By the look in her eyes, this wasn't the first time we'd had this conversation. But it was going to be the last.

"What do I need to do?" I asked.

"You need to be at one with the stone. It will absorb the cloud that's covering your memories and will restore your power that has been hidden."

"Why are you helping me?"

"Because I'm more like you than you'd ever think possible." She drew in a deep breath then released it slowly. "Why do we do anything?"

Memories of Marcus and me together through the ages flooded my mind. He was everything to me, and I'd do anything for him. "For love."

She nodded.

We shared an unspoken understanding for a few precious moments before she said, "I need to make you one with the stone if either of us are going to get our happily ever after."

694

Tilting my head to the side, I nodded. "Whatever it takes."

"Good, because this is going to hurt like a bitch." She withdrew a knife she'd somehow concealed under the see-through material of her dress. "Turn around."

"What are you planning to do with that thing?" I gestured to the blade that looked similar to the one Mava had used on me.

"Turn around."

Breathing out harshly, I did as she asked. I had no idea why I trusted her, but I did.

"Hold your hair to the side."

Again, I did as I was asked. I gritted my teeth together, trying not to scream as the blade dug into my hairline where it joined my neck, feeling way too close to my spine.

A second later the pain stopped, and I thought it was over until she wedged something inside of me and my head exploded with memories of everything that had happened since I arrived on the island forty-five days ago.

Everything Kora had said to me was true. We'd tried to pull this off before and failed. We'd talked, we had become friends, I knew what she was running from, I remembered Ari, the man she'd fallen in love with, and I knew who God was. And most importantly, my love for Marcus had been restored.

The man I'd kissed only hours ago wasn't the man I loved. He was the man I despised.

He was the man I was going to kill.

"You remember," Kora said.

I nodded. "Marcus is God."

"This Marcus is God, or I should say my father is God. And right now, your Marcus is out there, trying everything he can to get through the veil and rescue you. But the veil isn't going to be splintered for long. And I'm going to have to play my part in trying to stop you from escaping."

My heart was practically pounding a hole through my chest as I tried to wrap my head around the fact that there were two of Marcus.

Kora raised her hand then dropped the medallion, catching it by the chain. "You'll need this to escape."

I snatched it from her hand and squeezed it tightly.

Kora looked up into the sky. "You'll need to move quickly." She gestured to a section of the sky to the right of us. "It's about to crack, but it won't stay open for long, and I need you to get out."

Following her gaze, I noticed a thin line crossing the sky. It was my way out.

She strode over to the tree then paused. "Promise you'll come back and finish what you started."

"How will I come back?"

Kora gestured to the back of her neck, and I knew my key was now part of me.

"I promise."

Kora smiled before lifting the knife and plunging it into the tree.

A scream echoed throughout the night as the tiny slit in the sky fractured, opening wide enough to let me through the veil of magic.

"Go now," she yelled.

I stared at her for a moment then sprinted through the forest, blood spilling from my body as razor-sharp rocks sliced through my skin.

I didn't stop.

And neither did Kora.

"Here," she yelled. For a moment, I thought she was still helping me, but I quickly realized she was playing her part when a force of burning hot air slammed into me, stealing every ounce of air away from my vicinity.

I gasped for air, but it was futile.

Kora let out a wicked laugh as the ground began to shake, and monsters began to emerge, taking on the resemblance of demonic angels, complete with wings.

Fire burned under their skin, and their bones crunched as they clicked into place.

"Now," she mouthed and glanced momentarily up at the sky.

Not needing to be told twice, I pulled out the medallion and froze when I saw Marcus in the distance, racing toward me—only I knew it wasn't him.

I needed to leave, and I needed to leave now.

Following the steps I'd taken to get here, I rubbed my hand over the medallion and flicked my hand up into the fractured sky, opening the veil.

I was finally free.

A shrill scream erupted from my throat as something plunged deep into my back.

But it was too late. I was through.

CHAPTER 33

ollapsing onto the familiar wooden floors of Abby's house, I watched, paralyzed by fear as the veil began to close, praying no one was going to follow me through since I would be powerless to stop them.

I could barely move thanks to whatever Kora had done to me, and no matter how much it hurt, I couldn't be angry with her.

She needed to do what had to be done to keep our secret. I would forever be in her debt for the risk she'd taken in helping me get free.

Relief washed over me when the veil closed, locking that world from this one as Justin came into view. His eyes widened in shock. Then he raced toward me and withdrew the knife Kora had plunged into my back.

His mouth hung ajar as he shifted his gaze from the knife back to me. "You're alive."

"You can't get rid of me that easily," I said with a small laugh, but it came out a little more strangled than I wanted to admit. The knife had dug deep into me, and even though it was no longer inside of me, it still hurt like a bitch.

And it wasn't just the pain that any knife in the human world would cause. This was different. A fire burned within every inch of my body that had surrounded the blade.

Justin collapsed to his knees beside my head and scooped me into his arms. "You have no idea how happy I am to see you, but Marcus is going to have a fit if he sees you like this."

"She's back," Astrid's voice carried over to me from somewhere in the room.

"She's hurt," Justin said as he gently laid me on the couch. He pulled his phone out of the pocket of his jeans and put it to his ear.

"I'll be fine. Just give me a few minutes," I lied. Minutes weren't going to heal my wound, but magic would. And if I was right, I had all the power in the world again.

Concentrating on healing my wound, I drew on Morgana's magic and sucked in a sharp breath when I was met with a power I hadn't possessed before.

At first, I thought it was coming from the gem, but then I realized it was also stemming from the wound on my back.

With not much more than a thought, I could feel my body melding itself back together again.

"She's back," Justin said into the phone.

My heart melted the moment I heard his voice through the phone asking Justin in no uncertain terms what exactly he was suggesting.

"Lucy's alive, and she's sitting right in front of me," Justin explained.

Twisting myself into a sitting position, I snatched the phone out of his hand and put it to my ear. "Come home."

There was a long pause before a million questions exploded from his mouth, but I could barely understand a word that he said thanks to the wind slamming against the speaker on his end.

Tears slipped from my eyes as I laughed, the first laugh in over a month, and it felt good.

I knew it wouldn't last.

Once I told them everything I'd learned, things were going to get messy, but for now... I would be happy.

Wiping my tears away, I sat on the couch and talked about everything except for where I'd been for over a month. Most of the conversation was lost to the wind, but it didn't matter.

I'd thought I'd lost my connection with Marcus, but that was far from the truth. My love for him had never wavered, and it never would. It just didn't extend to his doppelgänger.

Finally hanging up, I handed Justin his phone then cast my gaze over to Astrid.

She was still weak, but at least she was able to sit up on her own and move around a little.

"I'm sorry," I said. "I should've done this sooner." As soon as the spell crossed my mind, Astrid's eyes lit up with an energy I hadn't seen in a long time.

Closing her eyes, she tipped her head back and breathed in deeply.

Justin sat beside me, unable to take his eyes off me. "Looks like you've learned a thing or two since you've been gone."

Astrid tilted her head back down. "Thank you."

I smiled. "I'm sorry I couldn't fix you sooner."

Justin twisted in his seat so he was facing me. "Where the hell have you been?"

A strangled laugh escaped from my throat. Hell was right; only it wasn't the Hell they knew of.

"Well?" he prodded.

"There are a million things I need to fill you in on, but I'd prefer to tell you both when Marcus and Abby return, so nothing is lost."

Disappointment crossed their eyes, but they didn't object.

"Where are the girls?" I asked, changing the subject.

"We took them back to the cave while you were gone because it was the only place that they felt at peace," Justin explained.

I pretended to be a little disappointed when in reality I was relieved, considering I was planning to take everyone back to the island and I didn't want the girls to get caught up in God's claws.

The wait for Marcus and Abby to arrive was harder than I'd thought it would be. Sure I had a medallion that opened the veils, but that wasn't very useful when I had no idea where a person was, and there was nothing but sea around them. So, I had to wait like every other supernatural person.

My heart skipped a few beats when I felt him. I jumped up from the couch and raced outside just as Marcus landed. I didn't even need to look at him to know that he was my Marcus, not the shell of my man who I'd spent the last forty-five days trying to escape.

I didn't give Marcus time to put his wings away before I threw myself into his arms and wrapped my legs around him, never wanting to let go. I felt safe, loved, and connected, a stark contrast to what I'd experienced with his doppelgänger.

Marcus wrapped his arms around me and released a shuddered breath. "I can't believe you're here."

Melting into his embrace, I kissed the side of his neck then whispered, "I'm here."

He pulled back, pain consuming his eyes like when I first reconnected with him at rehab. "Are you okay?"

Unfolding my arms around his neck, I unhooked my legs and stood on the pavement, my chest flush against his. "I'm okay now."

Abby swept down from the sky and landed beside us. "I don't believe it." She drew her wings into her back as she strode toward us and wrapped her arms around us both. "Do you have any idea what you've put us through?"

She released her grip on me. "Especially this guy." Abby gestured to Marcus. "He has been a complete wreck since you disappeared. Whining all the time."

When Abby saw the look on his face, she grinned. "Kidding." She covered the side of her mouth with her hand and mouthed, "No I'm not."

I chuckled. "I've missed you, too."

Her smile dropped. "What happened to you?"

"I was with God."

CHAPTER 34

"You what?" Abby practically spat.

Marcus's arms tensed around me, trapping me within his embrace as if the mere mention of God would somehow make me disappear.

Justin leaned against the back doorframe. "Not what, *who*."

I sighed. "Let's go inside so we can talk."

I almost didn't think Marcus was going to let me out of his embrace long enough to allow me to walk inside, but he eventually did.

With Marcus's arm still wrapped tightly around my shoulders, we made our way into the living room where Astrid was waiting for us.

"You know who this God is?" Astrid asked as Marcus, Abby, and I sat on the couch opposite her, and Justin eased himself into the seat beside her.

I nodded as I looked at Marcus, an identical replica of the man we'd been searching for, the man who had tormented our lives for so long. "God isn't who we think he is."

Marcus furrowed his brow. "How so?"

Abby placed her hand on my forearm. "Please don't tell me you developed Stockholm syndrome."

I almost choked. "Uh, no. I definitely don't have any feelings for the man, that's for sure."

Drawing in a deep breath, I glanced between my friends. Then my gaze landed on Marcus, and I couldn't look away. "It's uncanny how much you look alike."

Scrunching up his face in confusion, he jerked his head back. "We look similar?"

I swallowed hard, knowing my next words were going to change everything. "Identical."

Fear rippled through his soul, evident through his eyes, which were now swirling with molten lava, unlike the black pools of God's.

"How can that be?" Astrid said more to herself than to us.

I shrugged a shoulder. "I have no idea. All I know is I was stuck on an island with a bunch of devil worshipers, a man pretending to be you, and his daughter whom I owe my escape to. Oh, and I'm pretty sure I ate a human at least a dozen times."

"You what?" Abby spat.

"I'm going to kill that bastard." Marcus rose to his feet and paced the room. I could practically see steam rising from his skin.

"That's the whole idea. But you can't just go in there and expect to walk out a victor. This guy is something else."

Abby raised a brow. "Are you saying we can't take him?"

"No. What I'm saying is God is far worse than Morgana, and he's connected to a power I don't understand.

"These people live off the land like humans did hundreds of years ago, but it's only because they choose to.

"I spent forty-five days on the island, tried to escape about a hundred times, and had my memory wiped almost daily. Sometimes twice a day. They'd taken my gem and the medallion and stripped the magic that I possessed the moment I landed on the island, and there was absolutely nothing I could do about it. Not even you guys could get through his magical veil hiding his freak world."

A shiver ran down my spine as images of the heads on stakes entered my mind. I still wasn't sure if those heads had belonged to what were once some of his people who'd disobeyed him, or if he collected humans in the outer world and brought them back as his trophies. For all I knew, they could've been witches or some other demonic creature—or maybe even angelic. I really had no idea.

Marcus stopped in his tracks. "Are you saying we should give up and let the asshole get away with everything he's done to us?"

"Hell no. I promised Kora I would come back for her and finish this once and for all."

Justin narrowed his eyes at me. "But you're saying we have no chance against him."

That grin of Astrid's spread across her face, and for once, it wasn't directed at me. "No. What Luciana is saying is that this is going to be harder than you first thought, but there is a way." She paused for a moment. "How else do you think Luciana was able to get away?"

"Exactly," I said, even though I had absolutely no idea how we were going to bring him down.

I sifted through memories of every conversation I'd had with Kora since the moment I discovered how much she despised her father and the life he expected her to live up to.

"There's a legend that the people on his island believe," I said. "They were once normal people, living their lives like any other humans until one day, it became apparent that an unwed woman in their tribe was pregnant, which was forbidden. And so she was beaten until the baby was dead, but in doing so, the mother died as well.

"They buried her in a tomb, as was customary at the time. But that night, screams could be heard echoing through their village, cries of the mother kept those who'd partaken in the killing awake that night, and they continued to occur every full moon.

"Fast forward four years and a small boy was found alone in the forest, possessing abilities that brought the fear of God into them. They believed this boy was the child that was killed in the womb, and the demons took him under their wings, raising him as if he was one of their own."

Abby snorted out a laugh. "That's absurd. Demons don't give a shit about some baby."

I shrugged a shoulder. "Nevertheless, this is what they believe, and from that day forward, they've worshiped this child who never died. Except, the child has grown into a man and has been alive for hundreds of years."

"So he's immortal?" Abby asked.

"I think we all knew he was," Marcus replied. "But if this legend is true, I don't understand what his connection to us is?"

"Neither did I," I said. "That is until I befriended his daughter. You see, Akuji technically shouldn't exist. There was no heartbeat when his mother was entombed. And don't get me started on how they think a bunch of demonic creatures helped him escape the tomb."

"Hang on," Marcus said. "That doesn't make any sense. You see, immortals can't procreate, so how on earth does he have a daughter?"

"This guy conceives at least a dozen children a month, but—and here's the sick part—he's killed every single one of them at birth except for one. Kora."

"What makes her so special?"

"Because she came into this world the same way as her father."

CHAPTER 35

I felt ill, thinking about how Kora was brought into this world, and I was once again beyond grateful that Marcus and I would never have a baby. "I asked her that question many times before she finally talked. And once she told me, I understood why. You see, it was believed that the only way for baby God to have been born was for him to claw his way out of his mother's womb and…" I swallowed hard. "Kora was the only child to have killed her mother in the same way."

"Holy shit," Abby whispered in disbelief. "These guys are freaking insane."

"Tell me about it," I said with a nervous laugh. "Have you ever heard anything about this demonic child?"

She shook her head. "Never."

Marcus returned to his spot beside me and leaned back in his seat. "I still don't get what his beef with me is. I've never heard of this guy or this supposed demonic spawn, and yet he's done everything he can to keep me from becoming who I was destined to be."

I twisted around to face him. "But you're forgetting that he is you —or another version of you. You guys are seriously carbon copies of each other, so much so I couldn't tell you weren't him at first."

"At first?"

"Every single day, God tried to make me believe he was you, but it never took me long to become suspicious."

"How so?"

I curled my hand over his. "Because he's not you."

"Come on," Abby said. "You've got to give us something a little better than that."

"Well, that's the thing. There isn't something better than that. Apart from his vernacular being a little off, the only reason I felt something wasn't right was because my feelings for you quickly disappeared. Our connection was gone, and at the time, I believed it was because God or someone on the island had cast another spell to try to separate us, but then I discovered the truth."

Justin rested his elbows on his knees. "So what you're saying is the only way we can tell Marcus and God apart is if we hold a piece of his soul within us?" He rubbed the back of his neck. "We're royally screwed."

"I think you're all focusing on the small instead of the large," Astrid said. "You see, we should be asking the question, why do they look alike? Were they created from the same mold? And why is it that God can procreate when Marcus cannot?"

I turned to him. "Have you ever tried?"

He looked away.

A grin spread across Abby's face. "He's never *not* tried."

He snapped his gaze to meet mine. "Until I met you."

"That's right," Abby said. "We all know how committed you are to your dearest Lulu."

I sighed. "I'm not naive enough to think you never slept with anyone before me." However, I wasn't surprised he didn't sleep with anyone while he was waiting for me to return. Once you met your soul mate, no one else existed. "But are you sure that no woman ever fell pregnant?"

"He never stuck around long enough to find out," Abby said before Marcus had a chance to open his mouth.

I glared at her. "Thanks, *Marcus*."

She grinned. "You're welcome."

"I'm not sure Marcus's possible love child is the main focus point," Astrid said, trying to get us back on track. "It is merely an observation that should be taken into account. After all, it doesn't appear that God's daughter lives according to the same values as her father."

"Then what are we supposed to focus on, oh wise one," Abby said, getting a little impatient.

"This." I twisted around and lifted my hair away from my neck, revealing a barely noticeable lump under my skin.

"Your hair?"

"No, Abby. The stone Kora placed under my skin has infused with my mind and soul."

"You're only telling us about this now?" she practically spat.

I let my hair fall back into place as I turned around in my seat. "Kora sent this to Morgana's knowing I and only I would find it."

Marcus drew his brows together. "Why you?"

"Because I am the key to this whole thing." My eyes widened as so many pieces of the puzzle fell into place. "What if he is the dark, you are the light, and I am merely the key that will end it all? You two are obviously created like no other. You are two of the same, and the only thing that separates you is whatever is inside of me."

Abby raised a brow. "I think there's a whole lot more that separates Marcus and God. Or are you forgetting we were powerless to break through the veil to where you disappeared, and we spent forty-five days proving so."

"Exactly," I said. "God is more powerful only because he has what Marcus doesn't."

"So what you're saying is that all you'd need to do is give back Marcus's light and then he'll be able to overpower God's dark—or at least be on par—so that Marcus can destroy him?" Justin asked.

"That's never going to happen," Marcus said, daring anyone to object.

"Anyway, back to this crystal Kora gave me. I think—" My mind flashed with images of that haunted tree and the power it possessed that allowed me to escape. "The tree," I said more to myself than to the others.

"What tree?"

I looked at Astrid. "Have you ever heard of a magical tree or plant or something living that holds a source of power?"

"I explained to you earlier that a witch can place part of themselves, or their magic if you will, in an inanimate object, which is what we'd considered when we first found the stone that's now in your neck."

"We didn't consider that," Marcus said, his eyes swirling with molten lava, revealing exactly how pissed off he was that we hadn't included him in that discussion.

Ignoring Marcus, I replied, "But what about a living thing? Because there's this tree on the island that looks scary as hell, and I think it holds some form of magic."

Astrid gave me that smile of hers. "Well, I think it's safe to say that a living thing can hold magic. You're testament to that."

"You're right. I don't just hold Morgana's magic. I was also blessed with another form when Kora put that thing in the back of my neck, plus I was created to hold a piece of Marcus's soul."

"So destroy the tree and destroy his power?" Marcus said.

I pulled my eyebrows together as I remembered what happened when I left. "Kora stabbed the tree, which opened the veil enough for me to slip through."

"Shit," Justin said. "The only way we can all get through this veil, so we can have any chance of destroying God, is if we destroy the tree on the island that's protected by the veil."

"We're screwed," Abby added.

"Not necessarily." I grinned as a tingling warmth spread across my neck. "Kora will help us."

"After she helped you escape?" Marcus said. "I doubt that asshole will let her anywhere near the tree."

"God doesn't know she helped me."

"How can you be so sure? We could be walking into another trap."

"Not likely." I grinned. "She stabbed me in front of him to make sure of that."

"She what?" Marcus spat.

"She had to."

Justin stood from the couch, strode over to the TV cabinet, and picked up the knife he'd pulled from my back. "Kora stabbed you in the back with this knife, and you trust her?"

I sighed. "Look, Kora explained that she needed to make her father believe she was trying to stop me from escaping. And really, I think a knife to the back is a small inconvenience for her helping us take down God."

Justin pressed his finger against the point of the blade. "Why exactly is she going against her father?"

"For love. What else?" When everyone looked at me with confusion written all over their face, I added, "She is expected to rule, and she is expected to do so without any regard for her people. She is to love no man. But you can guess that didn't work out too well for her when she met her soul mate."

"Jesus," Abby said. "She's one of them."

CHAPTER 36

Staring at Abby, I waited rather impatiently for her to let us know who exactly Kora was. When it became apparent she had no intention of explaining herself, I asked, "One of what?"

"Kora is a Gaizar," she said. "Think of it like a succubus, but instead of roaming Earth to find our men, she rules over a bunch of them and continues to draw from them until they eventually die. Then, she'll find a new group and continue the cycle." Abby furrowed her brow. "But Gaizar's don't possess any magic."

"Which is why they're drawing from another source," Astrid said.

"The tree."

Something still wasn't making sense. "But isn't this all pointless if she is going to destroy her soul mate anyway?"

Abby nodded. "Maybe she doesn't know."

Marcus tucked his fingers under the hem of my shirt and spread his hand across the small of my back. "Or maybe she's hoping you'll help her."

The moment his skin touched mine, I wanted to make everyone in the room magically disappear so I could show him just how much I missed him. Alas, I could not.

Actually, I could, but I had to keep myself in check and focus on the war.

Staring at the floor, I furrowed my brow. "How was it that I wasn't able to feel them?"

"Feel who?"

I lifted my gaze to meet Marcus's. "The humans on the island. I should've taken on their emotions, but I didn't."

"Because you broke Morgana's curse when you destroyed her," Astrid said as if it weren't obvious.

Maybe to her.

I prayed she was right.

Leaning into Marcus's side, I took comfort in his proximity to me and the way he was somehow able to calm every nerve in my body while at the same time sending them into a wild frenzy, aching to be connected to the man I loved.

He wrapped his arm around me, securing me in his embrace. "So, what are we supposed to do now? Wait for a signal from Kora?"

I tilted my head back to look at him. "That's exactly what we need to do."

Abby stood. "Then until Lucy's neck starts buzzing, we can eat." She strode into the kitchen.

My stomach rumbled. For the first time in over a month, I was not afraid of what I was likely to consume. I still wasn't sure if I had eaten a human, and I really didn't want to know.

"I'm going to order some pizza," Abby called from the kitchen. "Anyone want any?"

"Me," I said a little too quickly. "But I want a vegetarian." The thought of putting meat in my mouth was enough to make me gag.

"I'll have a vegetarian, too," Marcus said, surprising me.

He knew how much that one offhanded comment of mine had affected me, and I was beyond grateful that he respected me enough not to shove it in my face so soon.

Marcus kissed the top of my head and laced his hand with mine. "Want to get some fresh air?"

I nodded.

"I'll let you know when the pizza arrives," Justin said as we headed outside.

The cool evening air refreshed my soul, a stark contrast to the warmth radiating in every direction from the stone wedged inside my neck.

We made our way down to the beach in silence and sat beside each other on the sand, our legs bent at the knees.

Marcus bumped his shoulder against mine. "Are you okay?"

I breathed the salty air deep into my lungs then released it slowly. "Ask me when this is all over."

He stared at me for a few moments then asked, "He didn't hurt you, did he?"

A million different scenarios must've been racing through his mind, and I owed it to him to tell him the truth, no matter how painful it was.

I sucked in my lower lip as I tried to figure out the best way to explain how easily I'd been fooled in the beginning and how there had been many times I almost betrayed him before I figured out it wasn't him.

Marcus tapped my lip. "You've got to know by now that you can tell me anything." He placed his finger under my chin and tipped my head until I had no choice but to look into his eyes. "I'm here for you. And if you're worried that you're not able to tell me something you've done, then I want you to know I understand." He paused for a moment before continuing. "No matter what happened, nothing will change between us."

Okay, so he was thinking the worst, and I couldn't let him continue to throw around the idea that I had been forced to be with our enemy or unknowingly done so on my own accord.

I twisted around to face him and sat cross-legged. "I never slept with him, so get that idea out of your mind." I sighed. "I did kiss him, and I did want him, but it never lasted long enough for me to act on it."

I grabbed his arm and pulled it away from his knees. "He never forced me to do anything, but that's not to say he didn't try. And I think that was his way of figuring out I knew something wasn't quite right about him."

A smile broke out across my face. "When have I ever not wanted to be with you?"

The corner of his lips tipped up. "You didn't when we were at rehab, and I could list at least another few hundred times."

I gently whacked him on the shoulder. "You know that doesn't count."

He caught my hand and laced his fingers with mine. "I know.

And really, I would never have blamed you if God had deceived you into thinking he was me. I just know how much that would've torn you apart."

I lifted his hand to my lips and placed a gentle kiss on his knuckles. "Well, then I guess it's lucky we have nothing to worry about."

Marcus guided me onto his lap so I was straddling him and cupped my face in his hands. "I missed you so much."

"I missed you too," I said, my voice choking up. I may have had my memories wiped daily, sometimes twice, but once I'd regained every single one of my memories since I arrived at the island, they had compounded into a mess of fear, longing, and desperation to once again be in Marcus's arms. And now that I was, I didn't want to waste a second of it.

Closing the distance between us, I kissed him, reveling in the way our bodies connected. All my worries vanished the moment my lips met his, and I was pulled into a world void of all the drama that was our life.

It was my own little safe haven, and I never wanted to leave.

But, of course, all good things had to come to an end, and ours did when Justin came outside to tell us the pizzas had arrived.

"Damn, they make pizzas too fast these days." I placed my hands on his shoulders, pushed myself to a standing position, and stepped to the side so Marcus could get up.

He chuckled. "We have all the time in the world to pick up where we left off. Or at least until Kora tells us to get our asses over there to save her."

Something told me it wouldn't be as long as Marcus hoped. And I was right. About halfway through our meal, my neck started to tingle as another message came through.

"The war is about to begin."

CHAPTER 37

*E*veryone stopped and stared at me as if they were waiting for me to say "just kidding" so they could continue their meal, then possibly have days if not weeks before we were summoned to finish the war God had declared on us hundreds of years ago.

"Kora is ready for our return," I said, trying to get my point across.

They looked between themselves and sprung into action.

"Justin, you come with me. Marcus, you and Lucy do whatever you have to for you to connect or whatever it is you do so we can finish this," Abby barked as she headed down the hall.

Doing as he was told, Justin followed her.

I furrowed my brow as I looked up at Marcus. "I thought you were the bossy one."

"You have no idea how much that girl loves to fight to protect the ones she loves." He pushed his chair back as he stood. "But she's right. We need to come up with a plan of attack."

"Destroy the tree, destroy God's power."

"Do you know where this tree is located?" Astrid asked.

I nodded.

"Good. Then I'll help you blast that thing into a million pieces."

I shook my head. "No. You can't come with us."

Fierce determination consumed her gaze. "I can, and I will."

I shook my head again. "I can't have you die for me as well."

"It's not your choice to make."

Actually, it was. As long as Kora held the veil open on her end, I controlled who I took through with me. No matter how much Astrid wanted to help, she'd already done everything she could for us and more than I could ever thank her for.

We didn't have time to argue, so I let her believe I'd caved to her request and prayed I'd live to see the repercussions of my decision when I returned.

"I'm not letting you out of my sight," Marcus said.

"I know."

"Then we let Justin and Abby be the distraction while we find the tree."

Abby walked into the room with Justin in tail. "Offering me up for the slaughter again, I see."

"Always," Marcus said, the corner of his lips tipping up.

She threw a knife to Marcus. "I wouldn't have it any other way."

"Where's the knife Kora stabbed me with?" I asked.

"It's over here." Astrid strode into the kitchen and collected it off the bench. "I took a good look at this while you were both outside. I believe the blade holds a special power, and I'm wondering if Kora left it with you on purpose."

I took the knife from her, immediately sensing what she was talking about. "I told you we could trust her."

Astrid tilted her head to the side. "Either that or the knife could be your undoing."

I rolled my eyes. "Will everyone please stop trying to make me doubt her allegiance?"

Her face softened. "All we're trying to do is make sure you aren't wearing any blinkers. If the past has told us anything, it's that you can't always trust those who appear to help because they very well could have their own agenda that doesn't align with yours."

She was right, but that didn't mean I was going to ignore the overwhelming feeling in my soul telling me I could trust Kora.

Heat rose in my neck, along with a sense of urgency. "We have to go now."

Taking the medallion between my fingers, I said, "You all need to be touching me if we want to make sure we go through as one."

I waited until they all placed their hands on me. Then I opened the veil. Just as we were stepping through, I looked at Astrid, and a blast of wind came from within me, knocking her onto the couch with precision I hadn't possessed before.

The look of betrayal in her eyes was something I'd never forget as I closed the veil behind us, making sure there was no way for her to follow us through.

Our feet landed on solid ground, where we were met by a wide-eyed Kora with blood dripping from her ears and nose.

She glanced to the side, fear consuming her gaze. "He knows."

*a*bby stepped forward. "I'm guessing you must be Kora and you're talking about your father figuring out you helped Lulu escape."

Nodding, Kora wiped the blood that was dripping down her lip with the back of her hand, smearing it across her cheek.

"Which way is the tree?" I asked.

Kora pointed to the right.

Abby wiggled her brows, a sadistic smile spreading across her face. "Game on." She raised her arms to the side and lit up like the little demon she was, tearing through the bushes to the left.

Justin sighed as he looked at the trail of fire Abby left in her wake. "I guess that's my cue to follow."

A steady breeze swept through the trees for the first time since I'd stepped foot on the island weeks ago, and I was pretty sure it was neither Abby nor Justin who had caused it. Marcus was the only one of us that could control the weather, and I knew it wasn't him, which only left God or one of his freaky men.

"Are we right in thinking that your father's magic is tied to the tree?" I asked.

She nodded, her once perfect complexion marred by soot and blood. "All of our magic is, but I don't have time to explain." Kora turned on her heel and sprinted through the forest in the opposite direction to where Abby and Justin had fled.

Dark clouds blanketed the sky as we tried to keep up with her. Well, *I* tried to keep up. Marcus had to slow down for me to have any chance of keeping up with him.

We wove through the dense vegetation as shrill screams echoed through the forest, coming from everywhere and nowhere. Every time I thought I had the location, the screams would change direction. It was almost as if the walls of the veils were thinning and the sounds of hell were seeping through.

My lungs felt like they were on fire, and my legs were turning to lead. Kora had long disappeared, and we were on our own, searching through the trees for any sign of her or the magical tree.

Coming to a stop, I put my hands on my knees, trying to ease the pain soaring through my body.

Marcus came to a halt and jogged back to me. "Are you okay?"

I shook my head, sweat dripping down my forehead. "We should've been there by now." I drew in another deep breath. "I don't even know where Kora is anymore."

He scanned the forest, worry consuming his gaze. "Neither do I."

The fact that I didn't know wasn't that much of a concern, but Marcus? Marcus had a built-in GPS system that not only applied to the land but also worked on humans and other supernaturals.

His was natural. Mine was not. He should've been able to feel where she was.

"This isn't working." Marcus popped out his wings and stretched them to the side as if he were relieving tired muscles. "We need an aerial view."

"It's too dangerous," I said. "We'll be too vulnerable out in the open."

"As opposed to hiding in the trees where I'm pretty sure he's manipulating our surroundings or our perception of it."

Marcus was right, but I didn't think going up was—

The ground shook, stealing my thoughts as the dirt morphed into mud, and those hideous creatures emerged from below, clawing their way to the surface.

"Move," I screamed.

But I was too late. The creatures latched their hands around my ankles and dragged me down, submerging me in the mud.

Rage coursed through Marcus's eyes as he tried to grab hold of me and pull me to safety, but it was useless. It was as if he were in another veil that was paper-thin, running parallel to this one.

"Find the tree," I screamed, my words muffled by the mud seeping into my mouth as the creatures pulled me under.

He must've heard me because his eyes lit up with molten lava as he stared at me, a million promises made without saying a word. Then he took off into the air.

The creatures spread their muddy hands over my head and shoved me under, dragging me into the pitch-black depths beneath.

It wasn't the first time I'd been in a similar predicament, and if history was anything to go by, it probably wouldn't be the last. But like the previous times, I had my own weapon that could help me get free. All I needed to do was work out how I was to take from these creatures when I barely knew what they looked like.

There were always limitations to magic, and it seemed I no longer was able to pull from the magic within my soul.

God controlled this world and had the power to do everything… Except, I still controlled one thing he could not.

Fighting the beasts, I slipped my hand onto my chest, relief pouring over me when my fingers closed around the medallion I hoped would once again save my ass.

I may not have been able to use my magic, but that didn't mean that magic didn't still exist and was open to manipulation.

Seeing my plan spread out before me in my mind's eye, I focused on slipping through, opening another veil similar to the one the mud beasts had drawn me into.

It worked.

Panic seized my body as I realized that although the creatures could no longer hold me down, I was still in fact down, submerged under the ground with no way to get free. The medallion was no longer allowing me to jump distance through the veils.

I was buried alive.

CHAPTER 39

*D*irt hit the back of my throat as I desperately tried to suck in anything that remotely resembled oxygen. But with every breath I tried to draw in came more dirt, sending me into a fit of coughs.

My options were bleak, and for all I knew, there was a very real possibility that my immortality had disappeared and I was as vulnerable as any human.

God had the power. And even though he hadn't created me, I was pretty sure he was able to destroy me.

The spell surrounding my creation would bring me back to life, but we would be starting at square one with me having no idea who Marcus was.

I couldn't let that happen.

Racking my brain, trying to figure out a way up, I realized the only way out was for someone to dig me out or to use my medallion to jump veil to veil, slowly propelling myself up toward the surface with every jump.

It would take time we didn't have, but I was out of options.

It took six veil jumps before I was finally high enough to break through.

My whole body shook as I sucked in a lungful of fresh air and coughed the remainder of the dirt out. I'd come dangerously close to losing consciousness, and I didn't want to think of what could've happened if I were stuck in the earth for another ten seconds.

Pushing myself to my feet, I surveyed the landscape, making sure I was alone before I set off on my next move.

Satisfied that neither God nor none of his henchmen was around, I once again held the medallion, opened another veil, and slipped between the layers, praying God would no longer be able to touch me physically or with his magic.

Tilting my head back, I looked up into the sky in search of Marcus.

Black clouds still blanketed the sky, making it impossible to see him, and I had to keep telling myself that he was probably using the clouds as coverage and he wasn't lying dead somewhere in a pool of blood.

Abby and Justin weren't to be seen, and neither was Kora. The mud creatures had disappeared, and the land appeared to be at peace.

Appearances were deceiving.

I could feel God's eyes on me. It sent every nerve in my body crawling with fear.

Closing my eyes, I focused all my strength on clearing my mind of his torment, and pushing it back on him, creating an invisible barrier he couldn't pass.

I had no idea if it worked, but one thing was for sure: I could no longer feel his presence.

Taking the opportunity to get away, I dashed toward where I thought the tree was located and was relieved when the familiar warmth spread over my neck.

The gem was working, which either meant I was getting closer to its source of power or Kora was sending me a message.

Another few yards and I discovered it was the former.

With newfound energy, I sprinted toward my target.

My heart leaped into my throat when Marcus stepped out from behind a tree fifty yards in front of me and came to an abrupt halt, his gaze locking with mine.

We'd found each other.

Relief flooded through me. He was alive and—

He wasn't alone. Two demonic hounds were chasing him, each

with two heads, and they, too, were passing right through everything that stood in their path.

Without thinking, I opened the veil, slipped back through to the dimension they were in, and sprinted toward Marcus. If I could just get to him in time, he could grab me and whisk us up into the air, away from the hellish beasts.

My eyes went wide, fear engulfing every fiber of my being, when I realized that although I could see him, I didn't have the connection.

It wasn't Marcus. It was God.

CHAPTER 40

I skidded to a stop and made a grab for my medallion, only I was too late.

A smirk ripped across his face as his arms closed around mine, and he took off into the air, carrying me with him.

"Sleep," he whispered, his voice void of any emotion.

My mind went groggy, and my vision swayed, turning the trees below into a sea of green as he soared across the sky.

But I didn't fall asleep.

Desperately fighting against succumbing to his spell, I drew on the warmth radiating from my neck. It was no longer burning like it had all the other times when it'd helped me, but it kept me conscious. And I needed to remain that way.

Shifting me so my back was against him, God gripped my forehead, forcing me to look down. "Fine. You want to fight it? Then you can have a front row seat to your lover's demise."

A blinding light flashed in front of me, stealing my vision.

I blinked hard a few times and breathed a sigh of relief when my vision cleared, but it was short-lived.

All air escaped from my lungs the moment my gaze landed on Marcus. He was limp and tied to the tree we'd been searching for. I cried out to him as I watched his blood-covered battered body intensely, praying he'd move—he'd breathe.

He didn't.

The smell of death seeped into the air, causing bile to rise in my mouth. I tried to look away, but God had locked me in place. I couldn't blink, couldn't move. I was in suspended animation, lost in my emotions, loss, fear, and heart-wrenching heartache, wishing I had never pushed Marcus into fighting back.

He was happy to go on living with our curse, enjoying those few brief moments together before I was ripped away to start all over again.

Hell, we could've stopped when we'd killed Morgana. God hadn't come after us. We'd had our chance, and I blew it.

It was all my fault.

Losing myself in a sea of destruction, God lowered us until I was standing no more than a yard in front of Marcus.

"You really thought you could kill me?" God laughed, an evil laugh filled with no remorse. "And before you get any ideas that your other little friends will come to save you, take a look at what happened to them."

He twisted me around and shoved me a good twenty yards to the right.

I skidded across the ground, my hands and knees stinging as the rocky earth sliced through my skin like knives.

Fearing what I was about to see, I tentatively looked up through watery eyes and almost choked on the bile that shot into my mouth when I saw them.

"No." I scrambled back, needing to get away from them. "No, no, no, no."

God laughed as he grabbed me by the top of my hair and dragged me back toward them. "Look at them."

"No," I cried.

He lifted me into the air by my hair and shoved me against them.

I screamed, tears wracking my body as I stared into first Abby's lifeless eyes then Justin's—their heads staked into the ground like the ones surrounding the campfire.

God had won.

Curling up into a ball, I rolled over and stared at Marcus, a million regrets going through my mind, but none more than the death sentence I'd laid upon Marcus the moment we first met.

I shouldn't have been selfish. I should've given it back.

But that one pause... That one reckless decision was his demise. I'd killed him. I'd—

My heart stopped when I saw the smallest flashes of light come from Marcus, a mixture of fear and hope fighting over my soul. It was only quick, and I wasn't quite sure if it was another trick—a glitch in the veils—or if I was delusional. But the more I thought about it, the more it made sense.

I was alive. And if I were alive then I prayed that meant Marcus was, too and what I saw now was no more than an illusion God wanted me to see, wanted me to lose myself in.

I wanted to believe that if Marcus was dead, then I would be, too. After all, I was created for him, and if he no longer existed, then neither should I.

The answer to my question was no more than ten yards in front of me, stretching up into the sky and imprisoning a resemblance of Marcus against its trunk.

Rage coursed through me, mixed with hope, regret, and an unrelenting need to make things right. To peel away the layers of deception God had created and strip him of his magic.

But I wouldn't make it close enough to destroy that tree with God standing so close by, watching my every move with sick satisfaction.

I needed to be smart. I needed to play his game.

Pushing myself up onto my knees, I crawled on all fours over to Marcus, tears still spilling from my eyes, partly to keep up the deception, but mostly because deep down I feared I was wrong, and when I destroyed the tree, Marcus would still be dead.

God followed me as I slowly crawled over to Marcus. Then he pushed his foot against my back, slamming me into the ground.

Blood spilled from my lip as I tried to get back up, but my efforts were futile. He was too strong. And he wasn't moving his foot off me.

Squeezing my eyes shut, I whispered to myself over and over again, "This isn't real. This isn't real."

God bellowed out a laugh, sending a chill racing down my spine. "Oh, this is real." He removed his foot from my back and kicked me in the ribs, flipping me over.

I winced as pain radiated across my chest and back from where I'd been kicked.

726

"It feels real, doesn't it?" He walked over to Marcus and retrieved a knife from behind him, bringing the fear of God into me.

I glared at him, refusing to let him see how real it felt.

"Don't struggle, and this will all be over." He stalked toward me. "No more pain. No more tears."

Gritting my teeth, I lifted myself into a sitting position and scampered back, trying to distance myself from him. "This isn't real. This isn't real."

God threw his head back and laughed. "Keep telling yourself that, because I know you feel it. That helplessness? The regret? The loneliness? It only comes from one thing."

I shook my head as I continued to scamper backward.

"That's right, Luciana." He chuckled. "Luciana. Even your name is a lie. You may hold a light, but you are far from good. Yet, they think *I'm* selfish. At least I don't pretend to be something I'm not."

My back hit something hard, stopping me from going any further.

Everything he was saying was true. I was a liar. I was selfish. And everyone I loved had paid the ultimate price for it.

People I cared about had died. How many was yet to be determined.

God kneeled beside me and placed the tip of the blade on my jaw, just beside my ear.

I gritted my teeth as he dragged it across to my chin then lowered the knife and rested the bloodied tip of the blade against my chest.

My heart hammered as I stared at the only blade in existence that could end my life. I wasn't sure how God now had possession of it when Marcus hadn't brought it with him.

In the past, Marcus was the only one who had held the power to end my life, but I had no idea if that was still the case.

I didn't want to find out.

Lifting my hand to my chest, I made a grab for the pendant, hoping I could slip through the veils and get away from him.

It was gone.

A smirk spread across God's face. "Looking for this?"

He lifted a chain around his neck, revealing the medallion—*my* medallion. My only way—

Fire burned across the back of my neck, making me suck in a sharp breath as magic flowed into my soul.

God's eyes went wide, and he whipped his head toward the tree. "What have you done?" He practically flew toward the tree, his feet never once touching the ground.

A slender arm wrapped around my waist as a hand slapped across my mouth. Then someone dragged me into the tree behind me.

CHAPTER 41

J struggled in the person's arms, praying this wasn't another one of God's games and I wouldn't be stuck in the tree trunk forever.

"Shh," Kora whispered, her warm breath blowing against my ear. "It's me."

I relaxed in her arms, grateful that my fate was no longer in God's hands.

She removed her hand from my mouth. "We need to be quick. He's going to figure it out and come after me."

I nodded.

"Follow me." Kora took my hand then sprinted out of the trunk and through the forest, slipping in and out of veils faster than I could register when and where we were.

One second I could feel the earth beneath my feet, and the next we were running on air.

Coming to a halt, my stomach dropped when I saw Marcus not more than ten yards in front of me, slamming his hands against an invisible barrier, his mouth opening and closing as if he were screaming, but no sound came out.

He was upset, but he was okay, and more importantly, he was not dead, slumped against a tree as God had me believe.

"Marcus," I said, choking on his name.

He continued to slam his fists into the air, completely oblivious to me being there.

"What's he doing?"

"He's trying to get to you." When I drew my brows together, she added, "Let me show you."

Kora placed the tips of her fingers on my temples, casting me into another world. A world where I was trapped on the other side of a veil from Marcus, and he had a front-row seat to the sickening show, where he was the star and I was the costar that wouldn't live to see the end.

My hands were tied above my head with strong reeds that had cut into my skin. Blood dripped down my arms like branches of a river, joining up with the eternity symbol carved into my chest. My skin was battered, bruised, and bloody from the numerous beatings Marcus had been powerless to stop.

Ten of God's warriors stood around me, along with one man that looked way too much like a witch doctor or whatever they were called when you were talking about demon worshipers. He was chanting something as he caught the blood spilling from my body in a human skull.

His eyes were pitch-black, and he possessed an evil presence that made my skin crawl.

He passed the skull to the warrior closest to him then held out his hand. A moment later, fire erupted from his finger. He moved forward, grabbed my jaw with one hand, and shook the fake me until my eyes opened.

Panic ripped through fake me, and I begged for my life as he lit my hair. The fire spread all too quickly, and I watched myself scream in agony with no one around to save me.

The demon witch retrieved a knife from his waist, sliced off a chunk of my burning hair, and dropped it into the skull. The moment it hit my blood, the contents erupted into a black flames, soaring into the sky, morphing into demonic creatures, trying to escape.

Demon witch dipped the knife into the blood then drove the blade into my heart—

I sucked in a sharp breath as Kora let go of me, pulling me out of the vision or whatever the hell it was I'd just experienced.

"We have to get him out," I practically screamed as Marcus dropped to his knees.

She shook her head. "My father has created this impenetrable veil, which others can only access by the medallion he took from you or if the Tree of Life no longer exists"

"Then we have to destroy the tree." Having no idea where the damn tree was located, I took off in search of it, but Kora was in front of me, stopping me before I got more than two steps.

"It's pointless," she said, her eyes filled with sorrow. "We aren't strong enough to break through the tree."

"Maybe not by yourself but the two of us combined—"

She shook her head. "The life is tied to my father. He alone holds the power. He cannot be killed by any one of us, and the only man who stands a chance is locked in a world he can't escape."

"We have to try," I cried. "We can't leave him there."

"No, no, we can't," Marcus's voice said from behind us.

My heart stopped.

Whipping my head around, I sucked in a sharp breath when I saw the doppelgänger to the man I loved.

He raised his knife and pointed it at Kora. "Now, you… I'll deal with you later." He turned toward Marcus and paused. "Don't get your hopes up about leaving here, because you'll never find the tree."

Fear engulfed Kora's eyes as she stared at her father.

"You're not leaving," I said through gritted teeth.

God smirked. "And what makes you think you can stop me?"

"Because I am what you fear."

He tilted his head to the side. "What is that, my dear?"

"I have the power to take." Focusing all my energy on God, I drew in his power as I had done with Morgana, but it was too much.

My head snapped back as the evil spread through my soul, destroying everything that was good in me to make room for him. I desperately tried to hang on, but there was too much of it. God's power kept coming like a never-ending current connected to the pits of hell.

God let out a sadistic laugh then stepped through the veil, coming face-to-face with Marcus and cutting my connection to him.

I'd failed.

Marcus slowly turned to face him and opened his mouth, his

words muted by the veil that we could not pass through. But actions spoke louder than words, and Marcus was filled with wrath I hadn't seen before as he drew out his blade and stood, ready to destroy the man who had played with us for so long.

God threw his head back and laughed.

A few words were exchanged between them. Then blood spilled, and none was God's. He was the ultimate weapon, a step ahead of every strike Marcus made.

My heart was in my throat as I watched, powerless to help, powerless to stop it, powerless to save him. He was going to die, and it was all because of me.

Hope sprung when Marcus landed a blow, his blade slicing down the side of God's face, black blood oozing from the wound.

Maybe Marcus stood a chance. Maybe—

Blood splattered against the wall of the veil, obscuring my view of the fight.

God brought down his blade, driving it through Marcus's shoulder and pinning him against the tree behind him.

My eyes widened as I realized what had just happened. God could slip through the veil into this world.

God had sliced through the veil and pinned Marcus to the tree, leaving the veil open by a sliver. If something could get out, then something could get in.

My life flashed before me, every single moment I'd spent with Marcus, all the years I'd been in pain and the love we had for each other. It all could've been avoided if I had done what I was created to do.

Marcus wouldn't be staring down the face of death with only a small chance of escape. He wouldn't love me. He wouldn't miss me. He would be complete, living the life he was destined for.

But he did know me. He did love me. And he would miss me. There was no doubt in my mind that what I hoped I could do would bring utter devastation to his world.

He was already devastated. He already thought I was dead.

I would not let it end this way.

Marcus was too filled with rage for pain. He used the opportunity to drive his knife into God's ribs, only the blade didn't make it past the bone.

God laughed as he pulled the knife from his ribs and pointed the blade over Marcus's heart.

This was my chance to make things right.

I'm your key, and I'm unlocking your destiny. With tears in my eyes, I finally let go, giving back what was Marcus's all along.

CHAPTER 42

*M*arcus whipped his head toward me as God slowly slid the blade into his chest.

My heart stopped as Marcus's eyes turned molten lava, and they were staring at me.

He was staring at me—and I was still alive.

It didn't work.

I could feel him.

A million questions raced through my mind as God's eyes lit up with fear. "No," ripped from his mouth as he swung his head toward me, his voice no longer muted by the veil.

It was down.

"You're alive," Marcus murmured, mimicking my thoughts.

"This isn't possible," God screamed.

Marcus lifted his hand, wrapped his fingers around the sword, and pulled it out of his chest as if it were a splinter.

God stepped back, shock written all over his face. But it didn't last long.

Spreading his arms to the side, blue electricity soared from his hands, coming straight for me. Only it didn't hit.

Marcus stood before me, his arms and wings protectively wrapped around me and Kora, shielding us both from the electrical storm that was directed at us.

"You may be invincible now," God spat, "but that doesn't mean your loved ones are."

"We need to destroy the tree, and you're the only one who can do that," Kora said to Marcus.

He nodded. "You go find the tree while I keep him busy."

Stretching out his wings to further shield us, Marcus lowered his head and kissed me. "You shouldn't have done that."

I bit my lip. "I should've done it the moment I first saw you."

He glared at me, a mixture of love, anger, and frustration brewing in his eyes. He was mad, just as I'd imagined he'd be. But he'd get over it because we were somehow both still alive to talk about it.

I stood on the balls of my feet and kissed him one last time. Then Kora ripped me from his lips and dragged me through the forest faster than I'd ever run before.

Sparks of electricity scorched the earth around us as we darted through the trees, slipping between the veils, allowing us a direct path.

I squealed as strong arms wrapped around my waist and lifted me into the air. I'd felt these arms way too many times before to not know who they belonged to.

The black wings were also a dead giveaway.

"Abby," I whispered, my voice choked with tears.

"The one and only," she said.

Justin pulled up beside me with Kora in his arms. "You have no idea how hard you guys were to find."

I could guess. It was impossible to find someone who didn't exist in the veil they were searching.

"We need to find the tree," Kora said, her focus completely on our mission and not the fact that she was flying in the arms of a man she didn't know.

"You mean that big old thing right there?" Abby gestured over her right shoulder where the Tree of Life as Kora so often called it, stretched above the canopy of trees covering the island.

"That's it," she whispered.

Abby and Justin landed a few feet away from the tree and set us down.

"So all we need to do is destroy the tree?" Abby asked. "Sounds simple enough." Fire ripped across her skin, turning her into a demonic creature far worse than anything I'd seen before. She'd always hated that side of herself but was now embracing it with everything she had to save not just her best friend but also me.

She may have looked like a demon, but her soul was as angelic as they came.

"You can't destroy it," Kora said as Abby futilely smashed her fists into the trunk.

No matter what Abby tried, the tree remained standing, completely unharmed. It was as if the tree was flame-retardant and made out of the strongest material on Earth.

That was the thing. We weren't dealing with something from Earth.

"Marcus," I whispered into the air.

Like a moth to a flame, Marcus tore through the sky with his carbon copy in front of him, a blade through God's chest and a ball of fire encasing them.

At least I prayed it was Marcus who had God and not the other way around. My heart couldn't take any more loss.

They shot up into the air then plunged toward the ground, straight into the tree. There was a sickening thud followed by a crack, and the tree shattered into a million pieces.

A dark mass billowed from the tree, dispersing into multiple spirit forms similar to those that had passed through my body when Morgana had taken me.

Kora let out a puff of a laugh as tears streamed down her face. "They've been released."

Thousands and thousands of what I knew to be souls swarmed around us, blocking our vision of where the tree once stood.

Abby returned to her normal, perfect self, once again hiding her true identity. "Guess that brings new meaning to the Tree of Life."

With my heart practically pounding a hole through my chest, I gingerly made my way to the tree, praying I would feel him. That Marcus was still alive.

I stopped in my tracks and sucked in a sharp breath when I felt him, stronger than I'd ever felt him before.

The souls parted, revealing Marcus standing over God, who had a sword through the heart, pinned to what was left of the tree stump.

Marcus pushed the blade farther into his chest and stepped back.

I had no idea what he was doing, but it soon became clear when the first soul shot through God's body, came out the other side, and disappeared into a pinprick of light, followed by the next one, and the next. God's body convulsed as thousands of souls ripped through him, stripping him of his life until he was a casket of his former self.

Marcus leaned down and placed his hand over God's heart. A second later, light blasted from Marcus's hand.

God's chest rose into the air as the last of what remained of his soul left his body, shattering into an explosion of light.

The light disappeared, and God dropped to the ground, lifeless.

He was finally dead.

With watery eyes, I made my way over to Marcus, wrapped my arms around him, and buried my head against his chest, a million emotions wracking my body as he folded his arms around me, and I relaxed in his embrace.

We were safe. We were both alive, and the logistics of it didn't matter.

God was dead.

CHAPTER 43

$\mathcal{M}$arcus held onto me for what felt like an eternity, until my tears ran dry and I could once again face the world and the evil that existed in it.

The others had long disappeared, having gone back to reclaim our home, knowing we were safe and no longer needed protection.

Marcus was complete. What exactly that meant was still to be determined. But I felt it—I felt him. And there was a power within him that lit up the world.

Tilting my head back, I looked up into his amber eyes and was amazed to see specks of light swirling through them. His light had been returned, and it was evident in everything about him. "How...?"

He smoothed his hand over my cheek. "How are you still alive?"

I nodded.

The corner of his lips tipped up into a smile, and he cocked his head to the right.

Following his gaze, I spotted Thomas, the angel who created me. "What are you doing here?" I asked, stepping out of Marcus's embrace.

Thomas strode toward us. "Now that the tree is gone, we can once again return to the plain that ties this world to the others."

"You mean this island?"

"Yes, this island," he said with a smile on his face that rivaled the witches and my guardian, Alissya. "The tree of life bound our worlds kind of like a gateway between our dimensions that allowed us to come and go as needed to keep peace and harmony within the worlds."

"Then one day, it was disconnected," Alissya said, emerging out of thin air. "And it was controlled by your brother who used it for his own selfish desires, trapping the supernatural souls from passing on to the other side and drawing on them to further empower himself."

My jaw dropped open. No wonder God was so powerful. He didn't just hold the power of an immortal supernatural creature; he had a connection to an unlimited supply of magic.

As much as that information blew my mind, there was one thing that stood out. "You knew about this all this time?"

That smile of hers spread across her face. "Not all, but some. The rest of it became clear upon the brother's demise."

"God is Marcus's brother?"

Marcus slid his hand over my shoulders. "We were made from the same mold, except he took something from me."

"Tried to take," Thomas corrected. "That is why you were created, Luciana. We needed to find a way to make things right, but we didn't have full knowledge or even the power to stop him. All I could do was take the part of Marcus that Akuji was trying to destroy and keep it safe, which was why I created you."

"It took almost everything I had to protect Marcus's light, but it was worth it."

"How am I still alive?" I asked.

Alissya gestured to Marcus. "I think you already know the answer to that."

Screwing up my face in confusion, I whipped my head around to Marcus. "You knew?"

He shook his head. "Know, not knew."

"Right."

Marcus stared at me for a few seconds, the light in his eyes glistening with unmatched power. "Selflessness was the key. You needed to give unconditionally, putting my life above your own, knowing you weren't going to survive but giving my light back anyway."

I tilted my head to the side and looked at Alissya. "Why didn't you tell me all this before?"

"Because then it never would've been a selfless act."

Anger poured through me. "Why would you guys do something like that? Why would you put that condition on me? Making us believe I would die if I gave it back." I glared at Alissya and Thomas. "You guys are sick."

Those smiles spread across their faces infuriated me even more.

"They didn't," Marcus said, placing his hand on my hip. "That was my brother's doing. He intervened during the process of your creation and put a condition on your existence that he never believed would be met."

He pulled me closer to him. "But you did, and he was foolish to think otherwise." Marcus cupped my jaw with his other hand. "You're as selfless as they come."

I gripped his bloodied shirt in my hand. "How do you know all this?"

"Because I am the ruler of the underworld. It's my job to know the sins of every creature that walks this world and the others. And before you jump to the conclusion that I knew all of this and hid it from you, I didn't. I forgot who I was, who I was created to become. That knowledge returned when you gave me back my light."

Holy. Shit.

I always knew Marcus was special, but this was taking it to a whole other level.

He smoothed his thumb across my cheek. "I may not be destined for this world, but I think it goes without saying that you're destined for me, as I am for you. And no one can stand in our way."

Marcus closed the distance between us, drawing me into a deep, searing kiss filled with a promise of a life of unknowns, power, immortality and each other.

Together, we would rule the underworld and punish those that deserved it the most.

Starting with Akuji and Morgana.

ALSO BY KELLY CARRERO

Unearthly Paradox Series

Paradox

Addicted

Traffick

Enigma

Evolution Series

Evolution

Tormented

Deception

Vengeance

Contained

Reclaimed

Unleashed

Severed Wings Series

Severed Wings

Severed Hearts

Severed Minds

Severed Souls

CONNECT WITH KELLY CARRERO

Sign up to Kelly Carrero's VIP club to be notified of upcoming new releases and giveaways at www.kellycarrero.com

facebook.com/kellycarreroauthor
twitter.com/KellyCarrero

Made in United States
Troutdale, OR
04/02/2025

30190634R00433